Queenslanders All Over

Queenslanders All Over

To Luce & Guy

with love & best wishes

Joan .

Joan Burton-Jones

BOND
UNIVERSITY
PRESS

First published by Bond University Press
© Joan Burton-Jones 2009

Edited by Kathleen Stewart

National Library of Australia Cataloguing-in-Publication entry:

Burton-Jones, Joan Patricia.
Queenslanders all over / Joan Burton-Jones ; edited by Kathleen Stewart.
Includes index.

ISBN: 978-0-9806187-0-9 (pbk.)
        978-0-9806187-1-6 (hdbk)

1. Australian literature--Queensland--20th century
                --Collections.
2.   Australian literature--Queensland--21st century
                --Collections.

        A820.809943

Published by Bond University Press, an imprint of Bond University Limited
University Drive
Robina, Queensland, 4229
www.bond.edu.au

Printed by Watson Ferguson & Company
Salisbury, Queensland, 4107

Front cover photographs:
Indigenous child dancer courtesy of Jeremy Geia www.laurafestival.tv
Surf Life Saving courtesy of Harvie Allison www.harvpix.com
Construction Supervisor courtesy of Ian McDonald, Humes™ Cemex Australia
Elliot boys mustering courtesy of David and Judy Elliot, Belmont Station, Winton

Back cover photograph:
Flight of Budgerigars by George Chapman, Birds Queensland Photogroup

To my mother, Katherine Hamilton (née Daveney), whose strength of character, creativity and loyalty to family and friends was my inspiration for this book.

PRIME MINISTER
PARLIAMENT HOUSE
CANBERRA ACT 2600

FOREWORD TO QUEENSLANDERS ALL OVER

As you read *Queenslanders All Over*, it's easy to imagine yourself on the back verandah of a Queenslander, listening to one remarkable story after another from the men and women who have built today's Queensland.

The stories range from farming families who made Queensland home in the 19th century, to the successive wave of migrants throughout the 20th century. They are men and women; city and country; from business, sports, arts, science, education and the wider community. Each person's story is different. Yet together, they reflect many common themes – like the importance of family and local communities; the satisfaction to be found in hard work, achievement and a gritty determination; the way our rugged land has shaped us as a people. Together, these stories provide a uniquely Queensland perspective on the seasons of life.

These stories highlight vividly the diversity of past experiences and future possibilities of Queensland in the 21st century. I am confident that beyond our State's 150th celebrations in 2009, *Queenslanders All Over* will be of enduring interest to generations of Queenslanders.

I am delighted to commend this celebration of the extraordinary stories and achievements of Queenslanders who might otherwise be called 'ordinary'. It is an inspirational reminder that each of us can make a difference, in our local community and in our nation – and that as it's been said elsewhere - close up, there is no such thing as an ordinary life.

The Honourable Kevin Rudd MP
Prime Minister of Australia

Kay Faulkner: Master Weaver

The fabric of society, like the fabrics depicted here, is dependent on the strength, unique qualities and interdependence of all its threads.

The stories in this book represent a cross section of human threads making up the social and cultural fabric of Queensland.

Earth Force, (detail) hand-woven, loom-controlled shibori, cotton, fibre reactive dyes, 90x200cm. 2007.
Image courtesy of Andrea Higgins.

Transparent (detail) hand-woven, loom-controlled shibori (devoré), cotton, nylon, 50x200cm. 2006.
Image courtesy of the artist.

 Kay Faulkner: Born in Brisbane, Kay has been a professional hand weaver since 1983. She has had solo and group exhibitions in Australia, Canada and the USA, and her work is held in public and private collections both here and abroad. Kay has been invited as a lecturer/workshop tutor to many international venues. Her work has received prizes both nationally and internationally and appears in many respected publications. While her weaving practice is broad-based, she has gained significant international recognition for her woven shibori and hand-woven velvet.

Table of Contents

Preface

Like many Australians, I've travelled abroad a great deal over the years, but I'd never looked at my home town or state in quite the same way as I'd looked at other places. Now, in my third age, I've turned my traveller's eye on Queensland, partly because of my love for this place and partly as a voyage of discovery. My mother's and grandmother's generations were full of fascinating people, many of them pioneers, who, when passing away, often took their stories with them. I wanted to capture some of these stories from the people concerned or from their families. I also wanted to capture the spirit of contemporary Queensland. However I didn't want to simply write 'about' Queenslanders, as I believe a story told directly, from the storyteller to the listener, holds more intimacy and immediacy than any third party account. I chose instead to hear and record these stories verbatim, with the individual storytellers speaking directly about their work and interests, and how they came to live and work here.

I remember my son Andrew telling me about coming home by ferry in the evenings, looking at the lighted windows of offices, houses and apartments and wondering a little about who was there and what their lives were like. I've often done the same thing – and perhaps you have too. I thought this would be an interesting opportunity to meet some of these people and a chance for them to share their stories.

I wanted to find out what it is that makes Queenslanders who they are, both quintessentially Australian, yet as different from their counterparts in other parts of Australia as San Franciscans are from New Yorkers and Londoners are from Liverpudlians. Thinking about this question suggested a number of themes which are reflected in this book.

One of my key themes has been to show how Brisbane has changed from the sleepy country town of my childhood to a modern vibrant city, the fastest growing in the country – now racing towards a hugely promising future as a tourist destination and a centre of learning, as well as a safe and attractive place to live, both scenically and climatically. With the speed of change and entrepreneurial get-up-and-go character of a young, sophisticated city, there is always a risk of disconnect between people. In small towns everyone knows everyone else, but in cities this is clearly impossible. However, like the threads in Seattle's Web of Life, our interdependence is nonetheless real, as many of these stories show.

One of Brisbane's great charms is that it still retains many of the qualities of the country town; people tend to be open and friendly and clearly enjoy living here – in their view it deserves its tag of 'Australia's most liveable city'. Many of the storytellers comment on this aspect of life here – like Perry Bartlett, walking to work, remembering grey skies in Melbourne and feeling 'just a little bit guilty'. Then there's the larrikin element (so typically Australian) which runs through many of these stories – like the afterhours antics in the old Brisbane fruit and vegetable markets and the cockroach races at the Story Bridge Hotel.

Like people, cities also experience watersheds in their development – defining events that leave a mark, both on the landscape and on the way we as citizens view ourselves. In Queensland, defining moments have included the 1974 Flood, the 1982 Commonwealth Games, Expo 88 and Cyclone Larry. I wanted to capture how it felt to be a part of these events from the people who were there.

Towns and cities, like the people in them, are multifaceted. It's often said that two major forces in life are work and love. Some manage to combine these two with great success, as in Rhyl Hinwood's story, where love has been an enabling force leading to great collaborations and memorable works of art.

It's also said that people are at their happiest and most productive when pulling together for a common cause, so communities are a central theme of this book, as are those serving the community. How many of us have ever wondered what it's like to be deaf, or to be a teacher of deaf children –Trish Taylor has been both. Or to be an SES volunteer, like Mac See, who headed the Civil Defence Force when the devastating '74 flood struck – he recounts stories of that time and the beginnings of the State Emergency Service (SES) as we know it today.

Reality, of course, is another issue. As in the fireman's story – reality is often quite unlike the film depiction of it! This book looks at reality from the perspective of the people who live that reality – truth really is so often stranger than fiction.

For most of us the lion's share of our day is spent at work, in one form or another. Work for one, of course, may be the relaxation of another – the difference perhaps between the singer and audience, the sportsman and spectator. Then there's the unpaid, unsung heroes, like the housewife who helps in the school tuck-shop and uniform shop, also involving herself in her local community's affairs – but whose hobby remains a 'hidden talent' – until later when it wins her international acclaim.

These stories are about people 'giving it a go'! Whilst some succeed, others fail but try again, often succeeding against tremendous odds. Sadly, as shown in Joyce Weeks's story, life isn't played on a level playing field, making the 'fair go' more difficult for some to achieve than others.

The vexed question of perceived value also bears consideration. We are, for example, accustomed to valuing doctors and other 'professionals' in society – but what about the people in the fruit and vegetable market, or the cabbie, and others like them whom we see each day on buses and trains, or in the street (yet barely notice), who work long hard hours for little recognition, but without whom the city couldn't operate efficiently? Their stories are here, full of courage and humour. All the story tellers are given equal recognition in this book. Official titles and awards are therefore not included alongside their names in the Contents list, appearing instead in the context of their individual stories.

Whether well-paid, lowly paid or voluntary, work is effort, yet some of it makes us feel good and some of it doesn't. Apart from being valued by others, it helps if we can also see something tangible for our efforts – like the dress designer whose most prized creation was worn by Miss Australia as she was crowned Miss Universe!

It's not just the young either who are stretching their minds and indeed their bodies here, with third-agers joining the young in flocking to learning institutions and gyms. Mary Daly of U3A (the University of the Third Age) talks of 'teaching as Socrates may have done it', while Peter Dornan's story discusses the origins of Sports Medicine in Queensland and provides some interesting insights on research into health, both physical and mental, for all ages.

There are stories here of Queenslanders involved in many unusual and innovative activities from farming barramundi and crocodiles to conserving butterflies and establishing cocoa plantations. Fascinating stories of exploration and discovery are interwoven with insights of what it's like to live up north or out west, as recounted in the stories of the nascent pearling industry starting up off the tip of Cape York, Australia's largest dinosaur fossil find at Winton and opal mining in the outback.

Though young in world terms, the city of Brisbane is developing a reputation for cutting edge technological research, as evidenced in stories from the Centre for Hypersonics, the Brain Institute and the Institute for Nanotechnology at the University of Queensland. These stories also show how, through the generosity of a quiet foreigner's philanthropy, the much talked of 'brain drain' appears to be reversing, with an inflow of the best and brightest researchers being attracted to this state from all points of the compass.

When speaking to these different story tellers about what they do and how they came to be doing it, I wanted to find if there were essential differences between doing it here in Queensland rather than elsewhere. I found this quest intriguing. Sometimes the differences are obvious but other times less so. It's almost the opposite of the well-known French phrase *plus ca change plus c'est la même chose* in that the more these occupations appear the same as their counterparts elsewhere, the more one can see differences – especially perhaps amongst those who've come here from elsewhere and are 'doing it their way' here. Time and again I found those new frontier attitudes of 'giving it go' and 'nothing's impossible' – irrespective of age or circumstance.

Given the large canvas that needed to be encompassed in this book, the research for it has been conducted over a period of more than four years. Some of the people I've spoken to in that time have since passed away, while others have changed jobs, but their stories remain as part of the fabric of who we are as Queenslanders and where we've come from.

I've divided the contents of this work into two volumes each having three parts:
Volume I: Sport; Business; Community and Service.
Volume II: The Arts, Expositions and Festivals; Historic Capital Landmarks; and The Smart State.

Categorisation posed a dilemma at times in that several stories could have been placed in more than one category, however I hope readers will be able to dip into various parts of the book and find the type of stories that interest them.

In summary, every country has its own identity, but so does every regional centre – that intrinsic 'something' that defines for its people their sense of identity and their link to that particular place. Apart from family, most of us only really know the people in our own circle of work, school or other community activity in which we're involved. For this book I've drawn from a selection of people, both old friends and previous strangers, to show something of the fascinating tapestry of people that make up my home state of Queensland and its capital, Brisbane.

Australia has truly been the Lucky Country for many of those who've come here from all corners of the globe. The history of cities all around Australia is relatively short in that this country was settled by Europeans less than 250 years ago. In

Brisbane's case, considerably less than that, so the people who've settled here in Queensland have tended to make a larger impact on the modern history of this place than people in similar fields in European or American cities during the same time span. Many, as a result, have been pioneers in their field. Occasionally their stories have had to be recounted posthumously by close family members.

I've enjoyed this journey and spending time with the many wonderful people I've met over the past few years. They come from various walks of life as well as many ethnic backgrounds. Most of whom, whilst embracing their 'Australianness', have retained a pride in their roots – as Vince de Pasquale said when I spoke with him on the phone recently, 'You hear all this laughter and noise we're making? We're bottling this year's wine!'

PART ONE: Sport

'It's not the size of the dog in the fight, but the size of the fight in the dog.'
- Archie Griffin, two-time Heisman winner, USA

As children, our family is the first team of which we are members. The next team we join is school and here we learn organised team sports. Young people with an interest in sport have many options. If sufficiently talented they can go on to become professionals, either as elite sportsmen and women or as coaches. Others study human movements or sports medicine and return to their sports in any one of a number of supportive functions, such as nutritionists, personal trainers or physiotherapists. Participation in sport can change the way we look at life – for the blind, or even the shy, the courage employed in sport translates to increased self-confidence in everyday life. Even as spectators there's much to learn from a game well played – especially if being a *good sport*, not just a winner, is also part of the ethos on display.

Jaya Savige: Poet

The Day They Painted the King Blue

When Dad says *Lang Park* we suspect
he means *Suncorp Stadium*. At twenty
he tattooed
four Xs on his arm, in honour of the
brewery,

but this embarrasses him: at Christmas
when it's hot and he goes shirtless, he
sits
so that the tat is inconspicuous.
Thirty years

& six kids later, the twins have
finished
playing nippers, kicking up whorls of
sand
towards the cherished flag, negotiating
the rip

that tears into the bay, practicing for
January.
We take him on the train to Milton
station,
where the little man in the bowler hat
looms

beside the beer factory, beacon of the
city,
not far from the footprints of Oxley.
Word is someone has painted the King
blue;

some of us imagine the culprit,
not a disgruntled former player
hoping to rouse the team from its slumber,

but a cunning marketer, charged
with regaining a share of the air
from those greedy Lions at
Woolloongabba.

Dad thinks this is just cynical jabber;
the insurance ad this month said all worth
saying:
Tunza Carroll quoting *Henry V* to Darren
Lockyer,

the speech upon the eve of St. Crispin's
day,
*For he today that sheds his blood with me
Shall be my brother*. He knows we aren't
English

about to crunch the noble heads of France
(unless of course the cockroaches are
French).
But though the sacrilegious act has fired up
the team

to tackle till they've naught left in the tank,
it is something of a *fait accompli*: the
sponsors
being the first that captain Lockyer has to
thank.

Jaya Savige was born in Sydney in 1978 and moved to Queensland in 1984. His first collection of poems, *Latecomers* (2005), was completed while he was a Masters student at the University of Queensland, and was awarded the Thomas Shapcott Prize and the New South Wales Premier's Prize for Poetry. Jaya is currently a Gates Scholar at Christ's College, Cambridge University.

The Making of a Champion

Ashley Cooper – Tennis Champion

He was winner of eight tennis Grand Slams and played in two winning Australian Davis Cup teams. We sit in the boardroom at Tennis Queensland where he's a board member. Ashley still looks very much the athlete. He talks about his involvement with the new State Tennis Centre at Tennyson and laughs heartily as he shares memories about the old Queensland Lawn Tennis Centre in Milton, where he played in his heyday…

'Milton – there's a few interesting stories there! It was built on a dump. There's the incident when big Bill Edwards, who was President of Tennis Queensland at the time, went up for a smash on the centre court and came down and nearly disappeared into the court. Big Bill was about twenty stone, a big fella, the roof gave way on the old rusted tank below the surface, and in he went – up to his chest!'

I now live in Brisbane, but I'm a Victorian by birth, from Eildon, North Eastern Victoria. I was about eight years old when I started playing tennis. My father and mother were both school teachers and both played tennis, so I picked up tennis from them. They'd play Victorian country tennis, travelling from town to town, and I'd tag along and have a hit in between sets.

I didn't play any fixtures or matches at all until I was thirteen, but Dad must have thought I was a reasonable sort of a player 'cause he entered me in the Victorian fourteen and under school boys' event down in Melbourne and drove me and my younger brother Terry down to it. It was the first time we'd been to 'the Big Smoke' and we wanted to see a lot of movies and things. We stayed at the Victorian Coffee Palace, which was a fairly inexpensive hotel in Melbourne. It's still there, I think.

Dad said, 'We'll stay here as long as you're in the tournament. As soon as you're out, we're back home.' Anyway, I drew the number one seed first round! I didn't know any of the players. I only found out later he was the number one seed. It was a first to ten games set and I'm losing 9-1 because I didn't know how to play. I can still recall walking back to pick up the balls at 9-1 and Terry with his hands through the fence saying, 'Dad's gone to pack the car!' I won that match 10-9 and ended up winning the tournament. It was incredible. We moved down to Melbourne not long after that so I could have the opportunity to play more tennis and competitions, and it went from there.

I first came to Brisbane in late November or early December 1951, when I was fifteen, as part of the Victorian Junior Team, to play in the Queensland Championships. We flew up in a DC3, which took all day to get from Melbourne to Brisbane. I can remember flying in to Brisbane at night and seeing all the single tennis courts lit up all over the place. Those backyard tennis courts used to be a real feature of Brisbane. When the real estate picked up people sold them for housing, so there's very few of them left.

Looking back, tennis was very big in Australia. There was a grass court circuit that started in Brisbane and finished in Perth. The Australian Championships was on grass. They were all grass courts. I always enjoyed playing in Milton because I found Brisbane different to the other cities. It was tropical and hot and humid and I liked that sort of thing, and the colourful crowds. All those tin houses on stilts and tropical banana trees and palms, it was like coming to another world! The crowds were very knowledgeable about tennis and it was just great playing here. The outside courts at Milton were a bit bumpy, but the centre court was very good.

I can recall when we first came up to Brisbane in the fifties. We stayed at Lennon's Hotel and would catch the tram to Milton and then 'two to the Valley' and eat at Nicks or Mama Luigi's. It was 'steak and the works' for seven shillings and sixpence! At the start of the movies they'd play *God Save the King* and we all stood up. Brisbane was just a big country town in those days.

Milton tennis centre – there's a few interesting stories there! It's a flood-plain but originally it was a dump. There's the incident when big Bill Edwards, who was President of Tennis Queensland at the time, went up for a smash on the centre court and came down and nearly disappeared into the court. Big Bill was about twenty stone, a big fella. The roof gave way on the old rusted tank below the surface, and in he went– up to his chest!

Another time, Neale Fraser and I were playing a doubles semi-final at Milton against Lew Hoad and Ken Rosewall. Neale was having trouble getting his first serve from one end. I was saying, 'For Christ's sake just get your first serve in,' and Neale was saying, 'I'm trying, I'm trying.' Anyway, after the third set we were down two sets to one when Mervyn Rose, who was watching in the stands, called out that he thought that the service court at one end was a foot too short! After a lot of mucking about, the referee came out with a tape measure and it was a foot short – that's why Neale couldn't get his serve in. Lew Hoad was having the same problem – they were serving from the same end. I'd never seen such a thing before in a major tournament.

I remember the first year I won the Queensland Championships at Milton. I played the second round on an outside court against Les Flanders, who was about six foot four – I think he came from Warwick. He had a huge serve and the balls were bouncing everywhere. He was within two points of beating me in the fifth set, but he tightened up a bit and missed a volley and then served a double fault. I got through that match and ended up winning the tournament.

Tennis Queensland's done a survey which we've shown to council and government, showing the decreasing number of courts used in Brisbane for fixture play. All the single courts have practically disappeared. The survey we did showed that while Perth and Adelaide have smaller populations than us they've got 400 or so courts being used for fixture playing and Brisbane's got 150 – we're way behind. With Brisbane growing so quickly we'll need probably 250 courts in the next ten years. It has to happen or the numbers playing will continue to drop. The council's now started to realise this and hopefully in the next few years we'll see some changes.

Wheelies tennis is growing. I was doing a clinic up in Maroochydore and there was this fourteen-year-old wheelie that played really well. I said to him, 'Do you play tournaments?' and he said, 'Yes, I'm in the Australian team. I'm going to London and playing in the International Wheelchair Championships!' I asked him, 'Where do you play? Have we many tournaments in Australia?' and he said, 'Yes, they have some, but not a lot, we haven't got any in Queensland,' so I said, 'Well, I think we better have a look at getting a tournament.' There are no centres around that can cope with it now, which is probably why the wheelies here haven't got a local tournament.

Tennis was big when I was young and front-page news all the time. We were employed by sporting goods companies and part of our contracts was that when we weren't playing in the major tournaments, we were available to conduct tennis clinics and give exhibitions and sign autographs and that sort of thing. We did this right across Australia. In Queensland I can recall playing pretty much in every town and there'd be 500 to 600 people show up and watch. That's not happening now because the professional players are constantly overseas. That's one of the reasons why tennis has declined a bit here.

Pat Rafter's been a terrific role model for young Queensland kids. We really need another one like him coming up. There are quite a few good young players in the 12 to 14 age bracket, but there's a lot of water to go under the bridge for them. The group of players coming up immediately behind Lleyton Hewitt, Mark Philippoussis and Pat Rafter is struggling a bit.

A lot of children today are inclined to play team sports. The point we try to get across is that it's very difficult to play a team sport when you're 30, 40, 50 or 60 – at some point you just give up and go and watch it. Whereas with tennis it's a long- term asset; you can go on playing – all your life if you want to.

It's becoming more difficult to get the schools to promote tennis, because you can take forty kids out on an oval, where you can only fit four on a tennis court, so at Tennis Queensland we're offering to run fixtures for schools. We're picking a centre which will run school fixtures and offering it at a very cheap rate, to say four or five or six schools in an area. They have to bring the kids, but we run the coaching programs. Once they start playing fixtures, that's when kids stay with the sport. When it's just coaching and they don't get fixtures, they lose interest.

Mal Anderson is still very much involved with Tennis Queensland. Every year Mal goes out and visits a number of country centres with the top juniors in the state and gives clinics and exhibitions. He's been doing that now for fifteen years or so. He does a great job in the country areas. Evonne Goolagong had her 'Getting Started' program aimed mainly at Aboriginal girls out in the country and Pat Rafter has helped us with promoting the State Tennis Centre.

Now, in 2007, work's well advanced on the new State Tennis Centre at Tennyson, on the river, which will have a five and a half thousand seat stadium, all completely roofed. As well as the stadium court there'll be 22 additional courts –16 cushioned hard courts (the same Plexicushion surface as the stadium court and the Australian Open courts), 4 clay courts, and 2 double grass courts – a total of 23 courts and all the grand slam surfaces. It'll be one of the Tennis Australia national training centres, so we'll hopefully be producing more Pat Rafters and Rod Lavers and Roy Emersons. We also aim to be able to cater for disabled tennis and run a quality disabled tennis program.

Apart from the State Tennis Centre we've got a regional facility development program in conjunction with the state government. Tennis Queensland is making a financial contribution to both the new State Tennis Centre and the Regional Facility Program, with the state government providing the bulk of the funds. We'll have $15 million spent on upgrading regional tennis centres. There'll be probably five regional centres in Queensland with a world standard tennis facility in each one of them.

On 4 January 2009 the State Tennis Centre will host the Australian combined men's and women's hardcourt tournament. The women's hardcourt, which is at the moment being held on the Gold Coast, and the men's hardcourt, currently held in Adelaide, will both move to Tennyson and be combined as a lead-in tournament to the Australian circuit, culminating in the Australian Open.

At the moment the new centre at Tennyson is loosely called the State Tennis Centre. Traditionally we don't tend to use corporate names in tennis and we hope it will be named after a top Queensland player.

Postscript: On Friday 2 January 2009 Queensland's new 23-court tennis centre at Tennyson was opened. The main stadium's Pat Rafter Arena seats 5500 spectators.

Greg Ritchie – Cricketer for Queensland and Australia

We met in his office at the Broncos Club when he was running a travel agency there. In the 1980s he played first-class cricket for both Queensland and Australia. After retiring from cricket he became known affectionately as 'Fat Cat' for his role in a comedy act on Brisbane's Triple M Radio. That was where he met up with a sick little girl called Jamie Zellar...'

Photo courtesy of Stephen Gray,
Queensland Cricket Association

'Someone donated $45,000 in coins – they put them in an industrial bin just on the outskirts west of the city. That was Brisbane at its best; I've never been so humbled in my life!'

I grew up in Ipswich and went to Silkstone State School from 1965 until 1972, before moving to Toowoomba. In my combined family there were seven siblings with many grandchildren and we were all very close; we still have thirty for lunch at Christmas. I played soccer from the age of five with St Helen's Soccer Club in Ipswich, which is now combined with the Coalstars. Ipswich supplied seven of the eleven players in the 1956 Olympic Australian soccer side and I lived in Booval within four miles of where six of those soccer players lived. The Australian captain, Bob Lawrie, taught at my school in Ipswich, so I was very fortunate in having great coaches. I played soccer for Brisbane from age ten through to age sixteen in the Brisbane representative side, and I even came back down from Toowoomba every weekend to play sport in Brisbane.

I learnt my cricket at Ipswich under a guy called Rick Mahoney MBE, one of the few non-school teachers to be honoured in the area of junior school sport – he was a wonderful coach. I played representative cricket for Ipswich and Toowoomba. Then in

1978 I left Toowoomba to move back down to Brisbane to play for the Wynnum/Manly Cricket Club here in Brisbane. I lived at East Brisbane just down the road from the Gabba, with Mal Freeman, who was best man at my wedding and who is still my best friend in life. He was a very good cricketer and now lives at Mount Cotton.

My uncle is a gentleman called Col Duce. Duce Cars and Trucks was started up by Col's eldest brother Norm and they had four car yards in the Valley in the '60s. In those days we'd come down from Ipswich, park the car at Woolloongabba and then, with my mum and Auntie Noela Duce, we'd catch the tram to see Uncle Col down in the Valley. Children under eight were free and I loved the tram! Opposite Duce's, Ray Lindwall, a former Australian test cricketer, had his florist shop and it was there that I first met Ray and had a cricket bat signed by him.

In 1964 or 1965 my auntie brought her children and Mum brought me down to see the Queen. I was five then and I can remember her coming along Queen Street in her carriage and what a great moment that was. Later I used to come down to work with my granddad, who worked for Uncle Col, helping him clean cars. Having a day in Brisbane, working with your grandfather, was just the most wonderful thing for an eight- or ten-year-old boy.

My father and grandfather would take me to Mount Crosby weir as a young boy and we would swim at College's Crossing in the days when there was ten foot of water and you could see ten cents on the bottom. It's sad that with the pollution it's not the same now. I remember there were bloody big eels – it was terrific!

The Ekka was something you just saved up all year for and it was the talk of the town. I came from a pretty humble background and we'd start talking about the Exhibition three months away and if someone gave you five or ten cents you'd save it. I remember my grandfather used to give me twenty cents if I scored a goal in soccer at the weekend. Twenty cents would get me one ride on the dodgem cars or a sample bag, so that was big! We had wonderful times at the Ekka, both with my parents and later on taking my own children there.

When I was eighteen I moved to Brisbane to live as I wanted to be a professional cricketer. You used to have to try and go to England in the off-season to get as much cricket in as you could. So to pay for my fares to England I worked for quite a few night-clubs in Brisbane as a drinks waiter, a doorman. A whole host of jobs. I got to meet Billy J. Smith, Don Seccombe and Joy Chambers. You'd see Babette Stephens and Jim Iliffe and all of those people. It was great – I fell in love with Brisbane and I've yet to find a city in the world that I feel is as comfortable.

The first day I played cricket for Queensland was 12 November 1980. I got to the ground and put on that wonderful Queensland jumper and the Queensland cap. I looked around the dressing room and there was Jeff Thompson, Greg Chappell, Kepler Wessels, Martin Kent and Alan Border, all legends of the game, and me, a kid, two and a half years out of school. The smell of the Gabba and the smell of the dressing room – I'd always dreamed of being in that dressing room and I thought, 'This is really happening!' We won the toss and we fielded – which was good as I didn't want to bat first day. I was very nervous as a batsman. I walked out onto the ground and I looked up in the grandstand and saw both my grandparents and my mother and father and I shall never forget the looks on their faces. I could see them standing there clapping and

I was thinking to myself, 'It can't get any better than this.' I'd dreamed of this all my life! It was extraordinary – that was a very special moment.

I have a wonderful recollection of Jeff Thompson and his first Dino Ferrari. I think it probably would have been the only one of its type in Brisbane at the time, and it was awesome to see it belting around the streets. One Thursday afternoon he turned up to the Gabba for Shield practice with a police car – siren blaring – right behind him. All the policeman did was drive in the gate, watch Jeff get out of his car, and yell out, 'I don't care if you drive 100 mile an hour, Jeff, just use your indicators!' That just typified Brissie!

Happy Jack was a gentleman I had a very soft spot for. He'd walk around the Gabba ground and he'd yell out and support Queensland all day – he'd drink a hell of a lot during the day. Invariably when the game had finished and the entire crowd had gone and we'd changed and showered, you'd walk out and Happy Jack would be stumbling down the road. There were many times I drove him home to New Farm.

The first time I walked onto a ground for Australia it wasn't in Brisbane but in a place called Multan in Pakistan. It's the oldest city/town in Pakistan. I can remember that day very well, I scored 65 and it got me a place in the first Test. Still, to play at the Gabba was unique. It was wonderful to play in a golden era of cricket with people like Greg Chappell and Jeff Thompson – to play with those two men is something I'll remember and treasure for my entire life.

Talking of great cricketers, I met Sir Donald Bradman twice. Once during a Test Match in Adelaide in 1986. We were playing India and I scored 128 in the Test Match and I saw Sir Donald on my way to the lunch room. He and Lady Bradman both congratulated me. Later I met him privately and got to chat to him for 15 or 20 minutes with two other people – he was an extraordinary man!

Julia my wife and I met at a party of a mutual friend in 1979 and we dated for three months before I went to England for six months in 1980. She's a Somerville House old-girl and my three daughters, Sarah, Loren and Emily, have gone to that school too. My youngest daughter played cricket at school level and I coached her team. That was great fun!

One incident from when I was playing cricket typifies for me how Brisbane has changed in just the last twenty years. In 1980 or 1981 I was in the Sheffield Shield side and we were about to embark on the southern tour, flying to Adelaide. In those days at the old Eagle Farm airport you would walk through the old hangars straight onto the tarmac, which we did. Anyway, we got onto the aircraft and sat down and the hostess said, 'Welcome on board flight such-and-such to Sydney.' The entire Queensland team was heading to Adelaide, so we all went, 'Oh, no, no – stop!' and we got off and walked across and got onto the other plane. A lot of other people had got on the other aircraft, and everyone was laughing and joking in the middle of the tarmac! It was so innocent in those days. Now hasn't life changed? You tell Americans or people in London today that in 1980 you could still walk out onto the tarmac in Brisbane and just get on any plane you liked, and they'd say, 'You're kidding!'

The three years I did on breakfast radio in Brisbane on Triple M was great. The show was called *Fat Cat* (that was me), Marlow and the third person – well, we had quite a few third persons. In those three years I got to talk to Brisbane a hell of a lot and that was good. You get to know what a great community it is. One particular occasion really stands out. There was a little girl of four or five years of age, Jamie Zellar, who was very, very sick with a tumour behind her eye. She had lost one eye and needed urgent treatment to save her other eye and her life. There was only in one place in the world, in Canada, that could do the operation. So we started a fund-raising drive for her one morning on the radio and we raised $180,000 in three and a half hours. That's a special thing for Brisbane to have done! She went to Toronto for six months with her family and that saved her sight and probably her life. They were an extraordinary family and Jamie Zellar was a beautiful little girl. It was amazing where the donations came from, including the business community and people off the street. Someone donated $45,000 in coins – they put them in an industrial bin just on the outskirts west of the city. That was Brisbane at its best; I've never been so humbled in my life!

Trevor Vayro – Cricketer, Past President, Blind Sport Australia

He walks with confidence, using only a stick as his guide. Guide dogs for the blind were not available when the accident happened and, having learnt to manage without, he now doesn't feel the need for one. He speaks of his love of sport, particularly cricket, and how important the older players had been when he was learning, in imparting their knowledge and building up his confidence.

'The feeling of running in the open field, well that was my fear, until I got the confidence to do it. I was encouraged by the older players, the ones who were totally blind, to stretch out and not to be frightened.'

I was born in 1939, in a farming area near Toowoomba. At the age of four my father went overseas to fight in the war and the family moved to Wynnum in Brisbane, as my mother had relatives there. I went to the local primary and high schools and left at the age of fourteen, after doing the scholarship exams. In October 1953 I became an apprentice at a foundry in Wynnum and just six weeks later in December I was blinded in an industrial accident there – I lost my sight in both eyes. My father was also involved in the same accident and lost the sight of one eye.

I was hospitalised at the Royal Brisbane for seven or eight months. After that I was transferred back home before being moved into the school for the blind. There I met other young children from different parts of Queensland. This was my first meeting with children who had been born blind or blinded through various eye diseases, but none of them had had an accident like I had, so I had to make some adjustments. I was particularly impressed with the young children who had developed what we term 'shadow blindness' – sensing there's an obstacle nearby. They clap their hands quickly, which gives a vibration back off any obstacle, like a tree or wall. I was never able to develop this faculty fully, probably because I was born sighted.

At the age of sixteen, after I left the blind school, I trained in typing and English at the commercial college for twelve months and then found a position at an electrical company, where I worked for the next thirty-four years. Since I left, I've done voluntary work – I've always enjoyed that.

When I was at the school for the blind, the teacher there knew I was very keen on sport, so she mentioned my name to the secretary of the Queensland Blind Cricket Club, Ian Stewart. Ian came to visit me one lunch hour and said that they were always on the lookout for new players, and would I be interested in coming to cricket? I jumped at the opportunity. That was in November 1954. I played for a period of thirty-eight years and I'm still a member after fifty-four years, though not as a player now.

Blind Cricket is played with the mandatory eleven players in the team, seven have partial sight, (5% of full sight is partial sight), and the other four are totally blind like myself.

When the totally blind bat, they are allowed a partially sighted runner to run for them – the risk being that two totally blind players running on the pitch might collide or run into the stumps!

That first time I went out there, I met, together with the president of the team we were playing against, called the Koala Sporting Club, a team of all sighted cricketers from the western suburbs area of Brisbane. The president took me out and showed me the stumps, which are made of a light-weight metal. When the ball strikes the stumps it gives a ringing sound so that the blind players are able to hear it. The stumps are also coloured an iridescent yellow, which is the most suitable colour for partially sighted people to see.

The ball that we used at that time was a hand-woven cane ball, made by the employees of the Industrial Institution for the Blind at Dutton Park. Inside it had bottle tops and a lead weight to give it the rattling sound. The balls we use now are machine-moulded in Taiwan from hard white plastic with metal bottle tops inside as before. You bowl underarm and the ball must bounce three or four times so the blind batsman can hear the sound and gauge its position as it approaches. The partially sighted players don't require a call as they're able to see 7 to 8 metres down the pitch. The totally blind are allowed to ask the batsman 'are you ready?' The batsman answers 'yes' and the wicket keeper also gives out a distinct call and then you bowl to the voice.

I was a very good bowler, but not a good batsman – it took me four innings before I scored my first run! I was terribly depressed and asked the other senior players, 'How on earth do you hit the ball?' They explained to me that I needed to wait one or two seconds before I went into my shot, because the ball didn't come onto the bat as quickly as it did in sighted cricket. I found that when I delayed my shot by about a second I made contact and, all of a sudden, after the fifth game, I scored about ten or eleven runs in one innings. I was really exhilarated that day!

With fielding, we have a 45-metre ground, where the sighted cricketers have 80 to 85 metres in the field. The boundaries have a white chalk line or a rope that's situated on the ground. As soon as you run past the boundary you feel your foot touch the rope. That's how you know that the batsman has scored a boundary or that you're still inside the boundary.

Partially sighted players are able to take catches and there are occasions when totally blind players take catches – usually it's when the ball hits you in the chest or the body. I've made several catches like that, but it's never come straight into my hands.

The thing with blind sport is you have to have quick reflexes, and because of your blindness you have to develop your other senses – particularly your hearing. Once you switch on to the game and don't let outside noises distract you, you can focus on the sound of the bowler bowling the ball and listen to it coming from the batsman's bat. Similarly in the field – you may call out to players fielding near you, so you can judge the distance between you and them.

The feeling of running in the open field, well, that was my fear, until I got the confidence to do it. I was encouraged by the older players, the ones who were totally blind, to stretch out and not to be frightened. All this was when I was just fifteen and it gave me confidence in lots of other ways. My dad and my mum were very supportive too and also my three brothers and my sister. When I wanted to practise at home there was no shortage of brothers to practise with.

At the age of nineteen I was appointed captain of the club team and from 1957 through to 1965 I captained the club team and the Queensland Team. I was a right-arm medium fast bowler, a late order batsman and I fielded as a cover point or gulley fieldsman. At that time our national championships were held every two years. It took many years before Queensland won their first championship in 1988. I was thrilled to bits at the time and I'm pleased to say that Queensland has won another five or six championships since then. It took seventy years before Queensland's sighted cricketers won the Sheffield Shield here in Brisbane and we had to go through more or less the same struggle as they did. In '92 we played a series against various teams in New Zealand, including an Australia–New Zealand test match and in '96 we went back and played three international games.

One of the funniest off-field incidents was when we were celebrating a win by Queensland against Tasmania. We went back to our hotel and one of our supporters invited us up to his room to have a drink. In those days they were the big bottles and everyone used a glass. A player said, 'Anyone got a spare glass?' and someone said, 'Yes – there's one in the bathroom.' It had some water in it and he tipped it out the window. Then one of the players came out of a shower and said, 'Where's my glass eye? I left it in a glass of water in the bathroom' – all of a sudden there was mad panic. We ran outside – fortunately it was a ground floor room and the fully sighted manager found the glass eye for him. Then he had to clean it up, of course. Whenever we visited him again, we always remembered to take our own glass so we didn't risk getting the one the glass eye had been in!

I didn't dance until I was blind. We had classes at the Blind Society in South Brisbane, where they had a lovely dancehall. I actually met my wife, Daphne, through dancing with her at a party when I was twenty-two. We just clicked and within twelve months – though we'd never 'seen' each other – we were married. She later became a volunteer with cricket for the blind and served as a scorer for Queensland for more than twenty years and scored for Australia on both tours to New Zealand.

The first World Cup was held in Delhi, India, in 1998. I've enjoyed my two visits to India, first to Delhi and then to Chennai where the second World Cup was played in 2002. Cricket is like a religion to the people over there, and especially to the blind people. They were wonderful experiences; the people were very courteous and warm in their hospitality.

In 1961 I fortunately won the award for Queensland for the best totally blind player, and also, being captain of Queensland, I was invited up onto the stage and Sir Donald Bradman presented me with my trophy. That was a very rewarding moment for me in my career. In the mid-70s, Greg Chappell, then Queensland captain, came out with his Sheffield Shield team and I played against Greg. That was also a wonderful experience.

I served as president of the Australia Blind Sports Federation from 1998 through to 2005. That encompasses about ten sports for the blind. Originally cricket and lawn bowls were the only two sports available to the blind, but in 1980 the Federation offered sports such as tandem cycling, athletics and field events, swimming, sailing and other sports like goal-ball and swish – that's table-tennis for the blind.

I'm involved with the Queensland Narrating Service, which has rooms in West End, Brisbane. I served on their committee for seventeen years. Throughout Australia there are about eleven or twelve producers of audio books for the blind. The Queensland Narrating Service often put in a request for a particular book and if it hasn't already been taken up by one of the other producers, it's then granted and they send the book out to one of their narrators. A lot of blind people want personalised reading done and many of the blind high school and tertiary students need educational books recorded on audio. I resigned from that Committee in 2002 and I've since had life membership bestowed on me for my services.

Part of my role as delegate for Blind Cricket Australia and also as the president of Blind Sport Australia is to make sure that we have paralympian sport now for the blind. I received the Order of Australia Medal (OAM) in the Queen's Birthday Honours in June 1993 for my service to cricket. I've never known who started the process by mentioning my name, but it's very pleasing to think that somebody made the effort.

Wayne Bennett – Broncos Rugby League Coach 1988-2008

Wayne is a quietly spoken and unassuming man with a pleasant down-to-earth manner. He said he's interested in the book 'because it's about people'. His love of rugby and his dedication to those he coaches is legendary.

'I got my eye cut open in the first game and I got some stitches in it and the medical guy didn't give me any anaesthetic and that was a huge moment for me, getting through that without making out I was a coward.'

I first came to Brisbane in 1966 and I've been here on and off ever since. The longest period I've been away was three years. I came as a police cadet and I was based in the old police barracks at Petrie Terrace. I lived for three years in the barracks and it was a great learning period of my life. Learning about myself and learning about discipline and being part of quite a large group. Paddington and Petrie Terrace then weren't very well developed. Paddington was a bit better than Petrie Terrace, but all the restaurants we see there now, they certainly weren't like that. The Windmill Café was there, Howie's came a bit later on, it came about '68, and the trams used to go past. Then they made the one-way system in the late '60s. We often used to stand on the verandah there and see cars going the wrong way! They weren't used to it.

I suppose the other memorable thing for me was the parade ground at the actual barracks itself, where we lived and ate. It looked down over the city and was where we had all our ceremonies and that. It was a very hallowed piece of turf. You'd get into trouble if you even walked on it. To see it today – it's a car-park! I suppose the other thing that stuck out in my mind is when they replaced policemen on point duty with traffic lights. In that three-year period I remember that all changing.

And the Vietnam War – there was a huge demonstration in Roma Street. Some of our instructors had to go to the demonstration and there were thousands. From where the Roma Street Fire Station is now, (it wasn't there in those days) right back down Roma Street to about where the railway is, the street was absolutely packed with demonstrators. A huge battle took place there that day and the police locked a lot of people up. It was a pretty horrific scene. We were in civilian clothes, we weren't in uniform in those days, and I got in a bit of a vantage point and watched it all.

I spent three years in Toowoomba as a policeman when I was young, from when I was twenty to twenty-two. I'd gone to Toowoomba to play football. They'd approached me and they got me transferred there. Then, when it was time to leave, I left the police force actually for six months and went overseas and I played in England. That was good. I didn't play all that well, but I enjoyed the experience. I came back to Brisbane to play football and joined the police in Brisbane and they stationed me in Brisbane. I spend nearly twenty years in the police. I left in 1985.

I played for brothers when I came back to Brisbane. I left Toowoomba in 1972 and came back to Brisbane in 1973, '74 and '75. I didn't play in '76. I went to Souths in '77. I coached at Souths from '77 to '79.

It was a huge change from playing to coaching. As a player, all you've got to worry about is yourself. As a coach, you've got the whole team and the responsibility that goes with it, and a lot of other things as well – it was a huge change! I left Souths in 1979, then I coached at Brothers from 1980 to 1982. It wasn't as much fun being a coach as being a player. They weren't going to offer me another year, so I left and I never coached in '83. I had a year out and I came back to coach Souths in '84 and '85.

The standout memory is that we played in the Grand Final in '79 at Souths, which was a great effort. At the time they hadn't been in a Grand Final for something like twenty-five years, so that was a pretty big occasion. Then in 1985 we won the Grand Final at Souths – so that was pretty big too!

There were a lot of low times and that. I first coached at Souths in 1977 and we finished second-last, I think, and that wasn't a very nice experience, and in '78 we did better and then '79 we played in the Grand Final.

In Brothers we struggled a fair bit too, and we only made one semi-final. I think we finished last on one occasion. It was a difficult time for me. It was tough – it's still tough, but it was very tough then. Young coach trying to make his way – it probably made me what I am.

I arrived at Lang Park about 1962. I think my uncle came down with a side from Warwick and I came down as a young boy on the bus with all the players. I remember being there as a twelve- or thirteen-year-old and thinking I'd like to come there and play one day. I vaguely remember being there on the day and the team playing and how excited I was to be there and how excited I was going home on the bus. I remember promising myself on numerous occasions that one day I'd play there. It was the end of the season in 1970 when I played my first game there.

I remember playing for Queensland at Lang Park. That was in 1971. I'd been a police cadet and I'd looked out from the barracks on so many occasions at Lang Park and wanted to play there and play for my state. I'd got selected and we came down in the bus and I'll never forget, as we came down the hill, you could see all the people, and the atmosphere of the night, and I was just so nervous, and I was questioning myself, 'Why am I doing this to myself?' I got on the field and scored in the first three minutes of the game. I don't even remember catching the ball; I just remember putting the ball in over the try-line. I can't remember much else about it. I felt very proud of myself to have made it that far.

I played for Australia that year as well. We did a short tour of New Zealand and I went on that tour with the Australian team. It was very exciting that first time and again I was just twenty-one years of age. I was young and the day I put on my Australian jersey – I felt it was a pretty special moment for me, you know, to have come from my background and to have achieved that. It meant a fair bit to me. That had always been a goal of mine, a dream of mine, to do that.

I think we lost the test match. I got my eye cut open in the first game and I got some stitches in it and the medical guy didn't give me any anaesthetic and that was a huge moment for me, getting through that without making out I was a coward. All the other players were saying, 'You'll be right, Wayne,' so I assumed it was normal not to have anaesthetic and I got stitched without it! When I came home my eye was swollen and infected, quite a mess actually. The fellow who had stitched it was Australian, but he wasn't a doctor, he was a sports trainer. He was pretty incompetent, but I survived the ordeal – and it probably made me a bit tougher. I wasn't feeling tough, but I had to be tough that day. I had no alternative.

By 1977, I was coaching Brisbane Souths and I've been coaching pretty much ever since. I've managed to make a career out of it. I never thought I'd be a coach. It wasn't something that interested me, but an opportunity came along to coach the kids in 1974. I was still playing then, but I thought, 'Oh well, I might be able to give something back since the game has been very good to me.' They asked me would I coach them and I said, 'OK, I'll coach you.' I was only twenty-four. I started to coach them and it all went from there for me. At no stage did I ever sit down and think, 'I'll be a career coach' or 'I'll coach this team or that team'. I just got busy and did the best I could and all of a sudden people started asking if I wanted to do another job, and eventually I became coach of the Broncos and coach of Australia.

Rugby League's had a huge influence on my life, but it's not the game so much but the people in it. My father played, my uncle played and when I was young all my role models were footballers or ex-footballers. My role models have been men that have gone on after football and done things with their lives, so I've modelled myself on them. I'd never want to do anything to disgrace the game, because I feel I owe it so much and I'd had so many great moments. It's given me such a great experience to be involved with young people, and hopefully make a little difference in their lives. I'm a coach trying to make a little difference, that's all.

The 1985 Premiership at Souths was a great moment for me personally. It was probably the catalyst to go the next level that I've been at now for a number of years. It was just a real breakthrough for me and the club and it got rid of all the doubters and the knockers – there're always plenty of them. Then I got to coach Queensland State of Origin '86, that was the first time I ever coached Queensland at State of Origin level. We won the series in '87. That was a really wonderful series and it was a great highlight for me. The Broncos' five Premierships were something special. We won five Premierships. I coached State of Origin in the '80s, in the '90s and in the 2000s, so over a twenty-year period I've been able to remain at the cutting edge of the sport. That's one of the things I've enjoyed: knowing that over the twenty-year period I've been able to maintain that edge.

I hope I've spent a lifetime helping people – that's what coaching's about to me. It's about helping people achieve their goals and their dreams and realise how much they can be.

John Eales – Australian Rugby Union Captain 1996–2001

Being a team player is something you learn early and his first team was 'family'. He and his elder sister chat happily about growing up with siblings, parents and grandparents all under one roof, memories of Nonna's homemade bread wafting across the conversation…

In conversation here with his sister Bernadette Byrne and pictured above with their grandmother.

> *'As far as I was concerned, growing up with our grandmother in our home added an extra dimension to our growing up; for me as a kid that was a really important relationship.'*

John: Mum and Nonna, my grandmother, were interned here because of the war and as Italians they probably copped a bit of grief as they went through life. They tried not to move away from the Italian heritage, but at the same time not impose it on us. Australia is now much more accepting of all nationalities than it was in the 1940s and 1950s, when Mum was growing up, and even more accepting than before that. Nonna came to Australia in 1924 and quickly learned to love the country and embrace it as her adopted home. At home we also embraced our Italian heritage, but we children didn't speak the language. Mum and Nonna spoke to each other in Italian, but not to us – I just picked up a few words here and there.

Because Lara (my wife), who is Chinese, has never spoken anything other than English and I've never spoken anything other than English, our children haven't learnt the other languages in our family, but they've certainly got a rich heritage. We call them Chitalo-Australians (Chinese, Italian, Australians)!

When we were children, we were spoiled with great homemade Italian cuisine – not the typical restaurant fare. Almost every day Nonna would bake her own bread. I'd look forward to her baking the bread and going and getting fresh bread out of the oven. There's nothing like it. We had Italian biscuits and things like that. I remember kneading the bread dough with her sometimes and occasionally she'd let us make our own shapes.

One day, in 1991 after we won the World Cup, I went back to Nonna's village, San Giorgio in Italy, and spent a couple of weeks staying with my relatives. I heard all the old stories of Nonna and had lunch in the house that she was born in, which was like a little farmhouse, *Casina Cerina*. It was wonderful. First we went to church, at the church that she went to. I actually drove along the road that she used to have to walk all the time as a kid going to school, and it must have been a bloody long walk. There're a lot of hills! Nonna used to talk about walking in the snow sometimes. She left school in Grade 3, I think.

Bernadette: Yes, but she always lamented that, didn't she? She'd like to have continued to study and become a teacher.

John: She became quite big as a speaker in the Italian community in Cairns. She was asked to speak at just about everyone's funeral, apparently, and she took it upon herself to do it and do it well. She was a wonderful lady, very close to all of us and certainly I got a lot out of our relationship – it was fantastic.

Bernadette: John, do you remember the holiday we had up to Cairns to see Nonna's friends and where Mum had grown up? Nonna had been living in Brisbane with us since I was a baby and she'd always dreamed of taking us all back up north to meet all their friends and remember we drove up in the four wheel drive?

John: That was in 1981.

Bernadette: Yes, and we went from one Italian feast to another. We'd sit down at a table at 11:30 in the morning and there'd just be one course after another until the evening. There might be a short break for some play in the afternoon and then they'd have pasta dishes and *crostoli* and fruit. It was like Christmas every day. Those people were her best friends; some of them would have been interned with Nonna, Mum and her brother Alf in Melbourne during the war.

When we were children we were always involved in the process of making spaghetti. Mum and Nonna would do it together and we would all join in. We used to have to knead and roll the dough, and help cut it into strips.

John: Yes, that's the meal I always ask Mum to make when I come home to Brisbane.

As far as I was concerned, growing up with our grandmother in our home just added an extra dimension to our growing up; for me as a kid that was a really important relationship. I know our kids now have very close relationships with their grandparents, as a lot of other kids do.

I think it was about eleven months after Mum and Dad got married that Nonna and Nonno (Mum's parents) moved in.

Bernadette: ... and they were there always. Dad was excellent with that. He and Nonna didn't talk a lot to each other, but they had a nice comfortable relationship and they both respected each other very much. Nonno was very sick most of the time I knew him. Mum basically looked after six kids and nursed her invalid father. In fact she nursed both of her parents very tenderly as they were aging.

John: Mum could play the piano and she had all her qualifications to be able to teach the piano too and she passed at a very high standard there, three sets of letters actually, but none of us took it up. There was a lot of music in the house, and we'd listen to a lot of Dad's music, things like Joan Baez and Johnny Cash.

Bernadette: Burl Ives, the Seekers.

John: ... and Dolly Parton!

Bernadette: There were a few attempts to get us to learn the piano, but we didn't really take off with that, unfortunately. We didn't learn dancing either, though Dad actually pulled off a ballroom dancing championship at one stage.

I remember, John, when you phoned us from overseas before the 1999 World Cup, and said, 'If Australia gets into the final, I want you all to come across,' and you'd organise it for us. That involved Tony and I, Rosaleen and Damian and Tara and Mum and Dad. Our sister Antoinette and her husband Rob were already in London. So the rest of us were all here back in Brisbane, waiting on the outcome of this game. It was South Africa versus Australia and it was the longest match of our lives!

It went into extra time and finally we won – Australia 27, South Africa 21. We were jumping up and down and phoning each other and saying, 'We're going, we're going!' Two days later Damian and Tara, Tony and I flew off together to London, where we were being met by my sister Antoinette and Robert (who's now her husband).

John: Gabrielle, Bernadette's middle child, she was the youngest at that stage. How old would she have been then, Bern?

Bernadette: She was four months old and I was wondering if we could get this little baby across there? But of course they're quite portable when they're very young and we bundled her up and had her in a sleeping bag on the top deck of the London buses and in a pram in the subways, and it was great. After some sightseeing in London we travelled together to Wales and had a wonderful reunion. The whole family was there.

I remember the atmosphere there being electric, walking to the game and seeing all the different nationalities that had assembled in Cardiff and the incredible excitement and that good-natured feeling that was around, in the pubs – and having a little baby guarantees you extra attention.

John: I remember after the final when we'd won and we were doing the lap of honour at the end, actually running into Dad, who was with Lara. I gave Lara a hug and a kiss and then shook Dad's hand and gave him a hug as well. That was something very memorable.

Bernadette: I remember that was a special hug, because Dad was a very loving man, a beautiful man, but probably not overly demonstrative when we were growing up. He became so, though, during the period when he was very sick, before he passed away in June 2005.

That match was the most extraordinary event that a family could have shared together. It was very special and we've got the photos that capture that magic.

We always seemed to have one of our three children as a little baby at the different matches we went to see over that time, John. They were tremendous years, and then, if you were overseas, you'd always manage to telephone us in the middle of the night and tell us the good news. You'd put on various Wallabies and All Blacks, too, to talk to us, after we'd been asleep for hours and we'd be trying to think up something coherent. That went on for years – it was a tremendous time!

John: Nonna died the following year. She could never have made such a long trip. In all her time in Australia she made one trip back to Italy and that was in 1954.

Bernadette: Nonna would watch everything on TV.

John: I'd always wanted to get Nonna into the Wallaby gear. She always used to go to 9:30 Mass in the morning and I thought, 'If ever I'm going to get her it's going to be coming back from morning Mass, because she'll be in a good mood,' and I finally convinced her to get into my jersey and shorts and socks and we got a few photos and they looked great. It was just that once that she did it and we got these great photos that I've got hanging on the wall at home. That would have been about 1993, when she was about ninety.

As for my life post-rugby, I love it. The move to Sydney's been good, because it's probably given our family more independence; we desperately miss our parents, but they still get down here a fair bit. It was a decision I had to make as well, because if I didn't make that move, then I would have been on planes more often than I am.

It's definitely broadened a lot of my professional horizons and also socially as well. My brother and sister live down here, so it's not as if we're separated from family totally – and it's just one hour's flight to Brisbane.

Bernadette: Yes, and the distance really makes you appreciate one another.

John: My son Elijah started playing rugby in 2005, but from our point of view it's not important whether he does or doesn't – it's whatever suits him, as long as he enjoys it.

Bernadette: I agree – give them the chance to do something they enjoy.

John: I was always very keen to do public speaking. Storytelling is a really important part of life. People communicate in stories, and legends are passed down through stories. I've been very fortunate to have had the rich experiences that I've had in life and that I now can tell people about them.

Players nowadays have to manage more commitments than I had when I was running around. I've been lucky to have my manager Chris White, a great mate, a guy I went to school with. I believe the key is to just live your life as an ordinary person – ordinary in the very positive sense of the word. If you do that, that's where you'll be able to influence most people. Everyone is part of a community and that's where you can have most effect, just through living a normal life.

Paul Biddulph – Queensland Deaf Rugby

2005 Players' Representative and

Team Captain for Australian Deaf Rugby Union

He's a member of 'Jeeps', he tells me, explaining that the origins of the Ashgrove-based GPS (Jeeps) Rugby Club goes back to the late 1880s (even before the Australian Rugby Union was registered). This makes it one of Australia's oldest rugby clubs. It has a proud history, having produced both representative and professional players along with 29 Wallabies.

'Chris and I learnt our first words in sign language (most of them swear words, just for a laugh). That night opened my eyes towards deaf people and how they are a team in their own right. Not just a football team, but a team of men and women communicating in their own way.'

I was born six weeks premature and got badly jaundiced, which is why I have a hearing impairment. Deaf Rugby players have different levels of hearing impairment. Some are genetic; some were born with some disorder or got sick when they were less than six to twelve months old, for example, meningitis, rubella, even mumps. Some of the players have a hearing loss due to industrial noise or accidents. To play Deaf Rugby, you need an average hearing loss of 25 decibels in both ears. Someone who is totally deaf in one ear is counted as 50 decibel (or db) loss. I have an average loss of around about 46 db, 36 in my right and 57 in my left, (to contend in the Deaf Olympics, you need to have a loss of 50 db in your good ear).

I grew up in Roma in south-west Queensland. All through school I wore hearing aids. Because of this I copped a bit of teasing and bullying. After I left school, because of working in noisy environments, I stopped wearing them. Over the years I have learnt to concentrate more and listen harder in conversations. If I miss something in a conversation, I can usually tell what is being said by body language and facial expressions. A lot of the profoundly (totally) deaf players can tell who a person really is by this. People can lie or bend the truth a little. A deaf person can't hear the lies, but they can pick up on the body language, because they have had to read sign language all of their life. My speech has improved over the years, even though there are a lot of words I still can't pronounce, because I will say them as I hear them, but I bypass these words and use words with a similar meaning. If there is a lot of background noise, I can't hear or understand anything anybody is saying!

I first played Rugby Union when I was sixteen. When I was twenty-three I moved to Brisbane and two years later started playing senior Rugby Union. I joined GPS or 'Jeeps', as they are known at Ashgrove. The GPS rugby club has been very helpful for the deaf players from Queensland. In 1994 at the age of twenty-seven going on twenty-eight I retired from playing for my club after playing 207 games. Every deaf player must still play for a Rugby Union club/team and be registered with the ARU (Australian Rugby Union). The Australian Deaf Rugby team has the same format as the Wallabies, Queensland Reds, All Blacks et cetera, and, like them, is a representative side. Players are picked on their ability to play the game regardless of their hearing level. Some profoundly deaf players are better than players with full hearing. The players must also be Australian citizens or permanent residents.

In the late 1960s, a man by the name of Keith Blesimo played one test match with the Wallabies. He was totally deaf in both ears, but with the ability to lip read and with help from his team mates he could play the game at a top level. Another well-known Wallaby can only hear out of one ear. His name is Daniel Herbert – also a GPS player. Maybe there are other top level players with hearing problems that we aren't aware of. Maybe some don't even realise that they have a hearing problem. One of my team mates from GPS didn't know he had industrial deafness until a hearing test was performed on him, and now he is part of the Deaf Rugby squad. It was when I first started playing for GPS that I noticed one of the young players in Colts (under 19) wore hearing aids. His father Trevor was coaching one of the Colts's teams. I asked the boy's father, 'How does he know what the lineout calls are?' He told me that the halfback (or it could be any team member within view) puts his hands on certain parts of his body, for example, head, to let Graham (his son) know where the ball is going – very similar to what we are doing in deaf rugby now. It was through him that I found out about deaf rugby when it first started. Graham first started playing rugby when he was nine. That's how his father got involved with coaching rugby. Graham is now a qualified carpenter. For the latter part of his school life, playing rugby helped him get an education at a normal school. People, including school kids, teachers and coaches, realised that, because you're deaf, doesn't mean you can't do normal things in life.

The rules of deaf rugby are exactly the same as normal rugby, except we have a few unwritten codes. The most important part of playing deaf rugby is not only teamwork with your own team, but also with the other team – meaning that, when the whistle is blown, people from both teams let those that didn't hear it know. One way of doing this is to stop moving and raise both arms in the air. A person from either team could cheat using this method by stopping someone running when the whistle hasn't blown, but in practice this doesn't happen. One thing about being deaf and playing sport is that noise such as yelling from the crowd, or sledging from the other team, doesn't distract you. On the other hand you have to be a lot quicker with your eyes and also learn how to read the play of the game. Another thing deaf players need to rely on a lot is instinct; some have more than others, mainly due to different levels of experience in the game.

When I went to Sydney with Graham for the first ever deaf rugby training camp, I wasn't sure what I was in for. Graham had flown down the night before, to catch up with some friends. I was told that someone named Craig would pick me up from the airport, and he would be wearing a Manly football jersey. After finding Craig, who is totally deaf and can't talk, we hopped in his car to go to the sports ground. Another deaf player, who also can't hear or talk, was riding with us too. I can tell you, it is not easy sitting in a car with someone trying to sign to another person and drive at the same time! During training that day, I met another boy named Chris (whose hearing was just a little worse than mine.) Chris was about the same age as me and also didn't know how to sign, so we stuck together. I'm glad I met Chris that day, because if I hadn't, I don't think I would have continued on with deaf rugby. When I first got to the field, all the players were standing around signing to each other. I didn't know how to sign at that stage, although I have picked a little up over the last few years.

That night after training, we all went to the local RSL (Returned and Services League). It was here where Chris and I learnt our first words in sign language (most of them swear words, just for a laugh). That night opened my eyes towards deaf people and how they are a team in their own right. Not just a football team, but a team of men and women communicating in their own way. Some deaf people can lip read very well and have also learnt to talk. There was music at the RSL club, and some of the boys and girls got up and danced. Chris and I asked one of the girls how she could dance if she couldn't hear the music. She replied that she could feel the vibrations on the floor. After the music stopped, she was still dancing. I went up and said to her, 'I thought you said you could feel the vibrations in the floor. The music has stopped.' She told me she knew, but she just liked dancing!

At one training run, the coach was giving everyone a blast for whatever reason, and says, 'Geesh, why won't you blokes just listen!' and I walked past and whispered to him, 'It's because they're deaf.' The coach, being a serious sort of bloke, had to turn away so no one could see the smile he was trying to hold back. After playing a lot of top grade football, in both codes, I couldn't believe how quiet it is on a deaf rugby field. In regular games there is a lot of talking and yelling. In a deaf game, it's all sign language – even though you get a couple of grunts and moans every now and then. In the first test against New Zealand Deaf in our first year, after five minutes into the game, we were packing a scrum and I said to the ref, 'I bet this will be the quietest game you have reffed.' He looked puzzled, but I bet after he thought about it he knew what I was talking about.

There have been some times when a couple of us have been talking to people, in various places, about how we play Deaf Rugby and what it's about. Some people ask us if we have a bell in the ball. I think they get confused about Blind Cricket and Deaf Rugby. We explain that a bell wouldn't help much as we couldn't hear it!

The 1982 Commonwealth Games

Glynis Nunn Cearns – Heptathlete

Olympian and Commonwealth Games Gold Medallist

Glynis was an international athlete for twenty-five years and has an abiding love of athletics. She has been appointed to several major sporting positions, including National Education Manager of AUSTAR Communications (Switched on Schools) and National Selector for Athletics Australia. Now a mother of two, Glynis particularly enjoys her coaching positions, where she's been able to directly affect the lives and career paths of upcoming athletes.

> '... you get a certain amount of points for how well you do in each event, so even though you are competing against others in the event, you are really competing against yourself and the score book.'

I was born and grew up in Toowoomba. My parents moved around a little – living in the town and then out on a farm and then back in the town. Basically I was brought up in the country on a farm. I left Toowoomba in 1978 when I went to Brisbane to attend Kelvin Grove Teachers' College to study Physical Education teaching. I lived there for the three years of my study and then for a further year when I started working at St Rita's, Clayfield. My first impressions of Brisbane were not good, as I was not used to the traffic and the hectic lifestyle. I got used to it though, and really, home is where you make it. It became my home until 1982, when I left to go to Adelaide. I couldn't get any financial support; in Queensland you really needed to be based in a water sport to get any funding then. I couldn't get coaching here either, so I moved to be with my coach down there.

I started doing athletics when I was nine – my first state title was in the 800 cross country as a ten-year-old. I started doing all events from an early age, because I just enjoyed competing and doing the various events. Again, I did these in Toowoomba and the surrounding areas, but mainly competed in interclub competition at Downey Park in Brisbane. My favourite events were the hurdles and the long jump – mainly because these were my best events, and when you get a bit of success it goes a long way.

To be a heptathlete you have to be the best all-round athlete in the competition. You are the most versatile of the athletes. To me it meant an awful lot. We had to do the most in training, as we had to work on our weaknesses in the events that were not our best, as well as maintaining our standard in our strong events. Heptathlon is about competing against a score book, as you get a certain amount of points for how well you do in each event, so even though you are competing against others in the event, you are really competing against yourself and the score book. Heptathlon was only introduced in 1982 as it used to be the Pentathlon – a five-event competition. They changed it to the Heptathlon because they thought that the five events were too suited to the speed/power athlete, so they introduced the 800 and the javelin. I did my first 'multi-event' in 1973, though, as a twelve-year-old. I competed in the national under-15 competition as a thirteen-year-old and got second, so I suppose this was the start of my career. This event was held at Lang Park on the grass, before it became a major football venue.

I competed in Brisbane for all state titles, all school competitions and, in some instances, the Australian championships. I was a young country kid coming to the 'big smoke' to compete and I found the atmosphere terrific.

To have the Commonwealth Games in Brisbane was really something special – nearly my home town – certainly a home crowd and we, as athletes, didn't have to travel for hours and days to compete overseas in a major event. Instead, they had to travel to us. We also put on such a good show! One of the major pluses was that my parents could watch me and be there – this was a really big thing for me.

My memories of that time are basically only of the track and the Games, as we spent most of our time at the residences at Griffith University. I do remember that Brisbane put on some lovely weather and that the Games were enjoyed by everyone. I competed throughout the entire Games, as I was in the heptathlon, the 100-metre hurdles and the long jump. I didn't have too much spare time.

When competing, or when I used to have contact with children in my sport, it was always great when they would come up and ask for autographs – it meant that someone, whether it was the children or their parents, recognised your performances as being significant. There's one story that I'll share – it was when I was teaching at a school on the Sunshine Coast – I brought the cross-country team down to a competition and some of the Brisbane kids came and asked me for my autograph – some of the kids in my school team quickly asked, 'Why do they want Mrs Cearn's autograph?' I just smiled, because the kids at my school just saw me as their teacher and not as an athlete. One of the other kids from my school finally piped up and said, 'Mrs Cearns is Glynis Nunn, you dill!'

The site of the Commonwealth Games will always bring great memories – the winking of the eye of Matilda the kangaroo – the visit by the Queen and my first major victory. The site has changed a lot since that time in 1982, so inevitably some of the magic has disappeared.

The popularity of the heptathlon won't increase unless we get more athletes competing in it – at the moment it's a very difficult event to compete in and this won't change because there are more sports that offer more to their competitors – including money for playing. There isn't too much that will change this.

The imprint that I would like to leave on my sport in Queensland and in Australia is that 'I cared not only for the sport, but for the athletes'. I work tirelessly coaching and building the pride of the participants and the status of the sport, and while I don't ask for recognition, it's nice if this time and dedication are noticed by the ones that really count – the people that you work with. This happens, though, because my athletes always thank me and I have a very special training squad – the squad is called 'Nunn-Better'. I suppose the other thing that I'd like to be remembered for is for participating in a worldwide sport and to be remembered for having performed and achieved drug-free on an international stage.

Lisa Curry Kenny – Swimmer

Olympian and Commonwealth Games Gold Medallist

*Born in Brisbane, Lisa now
lives on the north coast with
her husband Grant, Surf Life
Saving's Ironman gold
medallist from 1980 to 1983,
and their children. She has a
busy business career and
derives obvious enjoyment
from her contribution to
women's health and fitness
issues.*

*'When I carried the Olympic torch, I stopped and let a little kid hold the
torch, and you know the organisers told me off and told me I was holding
up proceedings and to hurry up, but I thought, "You know, that little kid
might one day hold the torch themselves; you don't know what it means to
them."'*

I remember the heat in Brisbane when I was growing up; it's one of the reasons why I
started swimming. I used to do jazz, ballet and piano lessons and it was terribly hot one
day, so my mum took me down to the local pool and that's where I started swimming.
From the age of thirteen I was very involved in my swimming career. It probably
stopped me from doing a lot of other things that normal kids did, although my dad used
to drive us to the Gold Coast every weekend and we spent that time swimming in the
surf and he'd take us out fishing. I think over the years I was so involved in my sport
that the city may have passed me by a little bit. I actually started swimming at Hibiscus
Gardens, which is still there in Mount Gravatt. Then, after Hibiscus Gardens, I moved
to Langlands Park Pool, which is at Stones Corner, and in the winter time we used to

go into the Valley Pool to train, because Langlands Park wasn't heated. I remember the bitter cold mornings at the Valley Pool and my coach rugged up in his jacket, walking along the side of the pool. I've very strong memories of the Valley Pool and Langlands Park, in particular. Of cold, of extreme heat, of the lanes being so crowded. The fact that we were all there trying to achieve the same thing, the camaraderie amongst everybody, trying to fit in our schoolwork as well, and then being picked in overseas teams and going away. It was all very exciting and it really was some of the best years of my life. My coach, Mr King, was one of the most successful swim coaches in Australia. He often had eight or ten swimmers from his squad in the same team, so there was a lot of competition at training. There was also a bit of cat-fighting, which you always remember, but at the end of the day they're all really exciting memories.

Some of the swimmers I still see, but the people that I'm with at the Coast now are probably my closer friends. I've lived now half my life in Brisbane and half my life on the Sunshine Coast. Some time ago I went to my 25th school reunion in Brisbane and all the girls looked absolutely fantastic. I don't think we looked our age at all, though we're all over forty now! We had a really good time – it was great.

In 1980 I went off to my first Olympic Games in Moscow and during our training camp for that they took the swim team out to Chandler pool when it was being built. I intended retiring after Moscow. I'd been offered a couple of scholarships to universities in America, so I was going to retire from Australian swimming and go over there. But once we saw the pool being built at Chandler and they explained to us how the Commonwealth Games were going to be here, I said, 'I'm not going to give up swimming now. I'm going to keep swimming and I'm going to swim in this pool one day!' It was a fabulous pool and the Brisbane Commonwealth Games were a real turning point for Brisbane. It was very exciting for a lot of people; it really show-cased Brisbane. There were a lot of tourists here, of course; a lot of national and international coverage, and it showed that Brisbane had a lot to offer. Since then Brisbane has grown considerably.

I've had many good times and some funny ones too. Once, and it probably wasn't funny at the time, but this was swimming and talking about the cold and the Valley Pool – we used to put the lane ropes in each morning, and we were taking them out after training. I was still in the pool and my coach, who was quite elderly and all wrapped up in his jacket, tugged on the lane rope to try and pull me in from the other end. Just being funny, I thought, 'I'll teach him,' and I tugged on the lane rope and accidentally pulled him in. It was then that his whole squad realised that he actually couldn't swim! He was one of THE most successful coaches in the world and he was scrambling to the side of the pool. Apart from that, he was freezing cold! One of the other boys had to go home that morning just in his togs, because he'd given him all his clothes. It was funny for us at the time, but it wasn't funny for him!

Grant and I actually met at the Commonwealth Games, on the last night. I was sitting on the edge of the pool with a photographer, and he was being escorted past me to meet the Queen and, as he passed me, the photographer stopped and introduced us and I thought, 'Gee, he's a bit of a spunk!' and then I met him again later on that night – it was actually five o'clock in the morning, at a bar. He was just leaving to go back to the Coast to train and when he left I said to my friend, 'I'm going to marry him one day.' That was twenty-two years ago! Our meeting was just by accident – maybe it was meant to happen.

I only retired from swimming in 1996. My last Olympic Games was in '92, but I swam again in '96. Regardless of when I made comebacks and swam, I think one of the most satisfying things for me was the fact that I could pass on all my experiences from my swimming career and things that I had learnt. A lot of them were from Mr King, and I was able to pass on what I'd learnt to many other people and help them to be inspired and realise that they could actually do whatever they put their mind to. This is what I'm continuing to do today through my coaching, my speaking, through my work with Fernwood Women's Health Clubs (which is all females), and just whoever I come in contact with, so they're able to be the best that they can be, just through understanding what it takes. Sometimes I think, 'Why was I put on this earth? It probably wasn't to swim but to learn all the things that I have so that I could help others.' I get a lot of satisfaction out of doing that.

I have a variety of jobs, of which three are voluntary. I've done some work for World Vision and travelled to Romania to do a documentary on the orphanages and AIDS hospital over there – that was really exciting for me. I'm also chairman of the National Australia Day Council where our main role is to choose the Australian of the Year. That's a voluntary position that was given to me by the Prime Minister. I've also been coaching voluntarily for the past twelve years. I do it because I love it and it helps me develop as a person and it lets me pass on what I know to other people as well.

There was a little girl in Broken Hill that I met and she was a beautiful little girl and her name was Jaimi. I always remember her. There was another beautiful little girl. She was six when I was swimming and I was a teenager at the time, and she was my little right-hand man. She'd follow me around everywhere and she'd sit on my lap and she'd hug me all the time – I was kind of her favourite, but unfortunately she was killed in a car accident. A drunk driver hit their car. It's things that happen to you like that, that affect little ones that are around you, that make you think about life – so you go on a bit of a crusade about drinking and driving.

I've met lots of little kids over the years that are really special in their own way – even when I carried the Olympic torch, I stopped and let a little kid hold the torch, and you know the organisers told me off and told me I was holding up proceedings and to hurry up, but I thought, 'You know, that little kid might one day hold the torch themselves; you don't know what it means to them.' I always take time to speak to children and encourage them and to listen to them – because when I was ten I was inspired by Shane Gould. I didn't speak to her, I just saw her on the TV, so I know, as sports people, we're role models and that we can actually inspire people to do things they never thought possible. It disappoints me these days to see sports people who won't sign autographs or don't have time to have their photo taken with kids, because it means a lot to them. The Sunshine Coast has retained its sort of 'little beachside area' quaintness about it. We do get our tourists, but not like the Gold Coast, so I'm really happy to live up here. I think it's the best place on earth. People come up to South East Queensland for the warmth, for the sun and for the lifestyle. People from down south, New South Wales and particularly Victoria, are moving up here – our secret is out!

The Goodwill Games – Brisbane 1991

Francis and Portia Rigby – Ice Skaters

Ice Dance competitors representing Australia

We meet in a coffee shop. Francis talks of the enjoyment he and his wife Portia derived from ice dancing and the friends they've made. Though they've now retired from competition, the memories are still fresh and his face lights up when recounting special moments.

'The penny dropped in relation to what was different about skating in Brisbane; we felt like we were skating in front of family.'

I started skating when I was nineteen. I played basketball prior to that. I was up in Townsville and one day I took my little brother ice-skating – an unusual thing to do in the tropics. I had good natural balance and, after we finished and I was taking my skates off, I was approached by a Polish chap, Wojtek Bankowski, one of the ice-skating coaches at the rink, and he said to me, 'Would you like to be a champion?' I decided right then, 'Well, if I'm going to do it, I'm going to do it properly,' and I started training 40 to 50 hours a week on ice. This was while I was doing my degree in economics at the James Cook University, and working full time in an art gallery and picture framers – the missing ingredient, of course, was sleep.

They had what we call an Aussie Skate program that normally takes about two years and I did it in two weeks. I started private lessons for an hour a day with the coach, but the most important thing was time on the ice practising what I'd learnt. After I'd been skating about two weeks I started dancing with a partner called Kristel. I was nineteen and she would have been fourteen at the time. Twelve months later we went to the Queensland Championships and then in the second year of my skating we went to the Australian Championships. We ended up coming second in a novice division. The levels basically go from primary to novice and junior, then senior. I loved competing, but, after that, Kristel and I decided to go our separate ways.

Portia had started roller skating in Townsville at eight or nine years old and took up ice skating as soon as there was a rink there. The Polish coach went to Townsville and suggested she take up ice dancing. He got her a partner and within two years they had got to the Junior World Championships, where they did exceptionally well. After that her partner found the pressure too much. He was at uni at the time and he basically stopped skating, so she was without a partner and was left to do singles again for about five or six years, until I came along. My coach had actually had me training with Portia just to improve my level. Because she didn't have a partner at the time, Portia wasn't competing, but she was judging. At the time she had finished her Bachelor of Engineering and was halfway through a PhD in Civil Engineering, which she's now finished. She did some lecturing at QUT (Queensland University of Technology) and now she's at Pine Rivers Shire Council.

Anyway, I approached her and asked would she like to take up competitive skating again – obviously there was still a bit of work for me to do to catch up to her level, but she jumped at the opportunity. We got married probably twelve months from when we started skating together. The day we got married we left for the UK, where we trained in Nottingham where Torvill and Dean were based. We had a coach called Tony Beresford and spent twelve months there. Then we decided to come back for the Australian Championships in 1998 in Melbourne. We did our Senior International test together and passed that before competing in the Australian Championships, where we ended up coming second. My parents had just moved down to Brisbane with my younger brother, who was studying violin at the Conservatorium of Music, so Portia and I decided to base ourselves in Brisbane and stay with my mum and dad for a bit.

At that time there was a Canadian ice-dance couple in Brisbane and a lady with them called Ma Hui, who was the Chinese National ice-dance coach. We started training with her and then we had the opportunity to go to the Four Continents Figure Skating Championships in Halifax Nova Scotia. Then we came back and trained in Australia in Brisbane for the next twelve months under Ma Hui, or Helen, as we call her now, and Svetlana Latina choreographed our routines.

Next we went to the Australia Championships in Adelaide and we won the Australian Championships in 1999. From there we went to the World Championships in Nice.

During 2000 we agreed to do an ice-show at Dreamworld. We'd started doing what we call 'Adagio', which is a mixture of pairs and ice dance, so you do overhead lifts and throws and things like that and this was like a small ice tank, probably no bigger than half a tennis court. It was in a tent with no air-conditioning and it was summer time. The temperatures hit 45 degrees outside and in the tent it was maybe 46 or 47.

The ice was melting, so we were virtually skating on slush. They had to put coloured cordial in the cracks so we could see them while we skated – because the show's got to go on! I've never dropped Portia in a competition, but we did a lift and my foot just stuck in the soft ice and I half-dropped Portia face-first on the ice. Fortunately it wasn't a complete drop, so she wasn't hurt, but when I picked her up she was absolutely drenched – and we had almost a minute of the program still to dance. It was not something you forget.

We did the 2000 World Championships in Vancouver and ended up 32nd in the world. At that point we knew we weren't going to get too much further in relation to world championships. I thought I'd love to skate for Australia, but to continue to compete at the World Championships and maybe qualify for the Olympics, we'd have probably needed another eight years of training.

We thought that we would probably just hold out until the Goodwill Games, as we'd heard a whisper about them coming to Brisbane and that we were more than likely going to get an invitation to skate, as it's invitation only. So we decided to start our professions but keep training until the Goodwill Games, which were planned for September 2001. I started working as a financial advisor at that time and I've been doing that ever since.

Shortly after returning to Brisbane in March 2001 we received a phone call from Ice-Skating Australia, informing us of our invitation to skate at the Goodwill Games in September. Wow, what a way to finish our sporting careers! This was going to be our last competition before we hung up our skates from the competition circuit. For the next six months we continued our training regime of 4 to 6 hours a day with coach Ma Hui, as well as working full time.

With a new competition comes new programs – music has to be chosen and cut, programs developed, which involved flights to our choreographer Svetlana Lapina in Sydney. It also involved time spent in the early hours of the morning at Ice World Acacia Ridge, practising and perfecting the new routine. New costumes had to be designed and made, and all this had to be done and perfected in the six-month time frame (rather than the usual nine to twelve months).

Part of the journey for us was sharing our home city with fellow athletes and friends from all over the world, including Elvis Stojko, the four-time Olympian and world champion, who had fallen in love with Brisbane when he visited us the previous year and was looking forward to spending more time here.

With the start of the competition came all the press releases and registration, all a part of what we love about competing, and then the first look at the ice floor at Boondall, with the Goodwill Games logo under the ice; it looked amazing.

Then it was day one at the Brisbane Entertainment Centre and time to show off our dance in front of our family from Brisbane and Townsville. There was a capacity crowd and the sound of support really lifts your performance. To top it off the Olympic cheer squad from the 2000 Sydney Olympics was there, antics and all. We felt like we had already won the competition, even though we were ranked 32nd in the world and competing against the top- ranked couples in the world.

A day in between to rest and prepare for day three, the one we both had been waiting for, to unveil the new free-dance program and perform it for the first and only time. Our families were in the crowd and we skated not for the judges but for the crowd. The penny dropped in relation to what was different about skating in Brisbane; we felt like we were skating in front of 'family'.

In the dressing room, taking off our skates for the last time at an international event, we were approached by the Goodwill Games organisation to skate one last time in the Parade of Champions on the following Sunday. The problem, however, was that we were told that we could not perform any of the programs we had performed during the competition. They wanted us to skate an exhibition program. This was the first time it had been mentioned to us and we had no exhibition program ready. There was no question we would skate, but we just didn't know what program we would perform!

A quick hello to family and off home to do what normally takes nine months in one night – choose music, cut the required length of music and choreograph the program. The advantage of being married and having skated together for six years: you know how each other think and move. So we spent until 3am the following morning choreographing the new program for the Parade of Champions, scheduled for early Sunday evening.

On Sunday morning there was time for our allotted five-minute practice with music to mark out the program and ensure everything fitted and flowed and then straight into the practice for the closing ceremony. No time now to go home and freshen up. It was time to touch up make-up and hair and start warming up. This included practising lifts that had never been used in a program before!

Once again skating in front of a Brisbane crowd helped our performance and, even though the program was not as polished as we would have liked, there were no errors. After the performance fellow skaters and people that watch us train came up to us and said that the program and performance was fantastic.

The Goodwill Games also provided us with a great start in our life outside of skating. The prize money went towards the purchase of land on the outskirts of Brisbane and what we always wanted – our own home!

Olympics and Paralympics

Sydney 2000, Athens 2004, and Beijing 2008

Mark Knowles – Hockey Player

The Kookaburras won gold in the Athens Olympics and bronze in Beijing. We met in March 2007 as Mark and the team were contemplating a busy year ahead leading up to the Beijing Olympics. Hockey, he told me, is still only played semi-professionally in Australia. He and other members of the Kookaburras also play professionally in Europe.

'I suppose my most treasured and fun memories were winning and the celebrations we had as a team ... I think we were one of the most successful sporting teams in the history of the Olympic Games. It was the first Olympic Men's Hockey gold medal we'd ever won ...'

My father's family are from Rockhampton and my mother's family are all from Tasmania. My mother moved to Queensland in her mid-twenties, because she wanted a change of life and a change of weather. My grandparents and family still live in Rockhampton, including my older brother Brent and older sister Karen and their children, and we're all still playing hockey. Mum and Dad are Australian veterans' players and played a high level for Queensland and Tasmania at senior level. Mum's now playing for Queensland. My younger sister Camille is also still playing hockey.

I started playing hockey when I was four; at that stage Mum and Dad were very high up in Rockhampton hockey. Dad was president of my hockey club, Southside United, for six or seven years and Mum was the president of Rockhampton Hockey Association for five or six years as well. So there was no chance of me getting out of hockey!

Queensland had eight players from the Olympic Team in 2004, and we are the only eight male hockey Olympic gold medallists from Queensland ever! I think the most interesting thing about all the guys is there's only one guy out of those eight who's a Brisbane-based player. Everyone else is from country Queensland.

We all started in junior hockey. I played for Rockhampton against all of my best mates from the Sunshine Coast, Brisbane, Ipswich and Toowoomba, and all around Queensland in the under-13s. We've played right through since then, up the age groups to the under-18s and under-21s. That's when I first started to play with all of the guys who I play with now in the Queensland Blades and also for the Kookaburras in the Australian team. The first time we all played together was in 2002 in the Queensland Blades and we came second in the National Hockey League. In 2003 and 2004, we won! We're playing together for six weeks a year, but we train together day in and day out. A lot of us are based in Brisbane now, with a few boys still living in Perth at the Australian Institute of Sport.

Since the AIS is based in Perth, all eight Queenslanders in the Olympic team had to live in Perth for six months before the 2004 Olympics. As Queenslanders and country boys, we developed great friendships. A few of my good Queensland mates are Liam Young, Robbie Hammond and Nathan Eglington. Mateship and building friendships are two of the great advantages of team sport.

In Athens before the opening ceremony we had a welcome for the Australian teams and Delta Goodrem, a great Australian singer, was there and sang for us. Two days later we played a joke on Jamie Dwyer, a best mate of mine from Rockhampton. We told him that Delta wanted to have a date with him, so he dressed up in his full suit and tie and everything. I think he had a bit of an idea, but he played it well. We got Delta to have a photo with him and everyone got quite jealous. In the end it was a good omen because Jamie was the highest goal scorer for the tournament. He won us the Olympic Games in extra time with his goal. He had an unbelievable tournament. We need to get Delta to every major tournament from now. Whether it's Jamie or someone else, we don't mind, but we should have her there. That was definitely a high point for all of us!

I suppose my most treasured and fun memories were winning and the celebrations we had as a team. I think we were one of the most successful sporting teams in the history of the Olympic Games. It was the first Olympic Men's Hockey gold medal we'd ever won and everyone used all the clichés about getting the monkey off our backs. It was a relief, but it was also a lot of hard work, which made a lot of difference to the game, in that we did a lot on the mental side of 'why hadn't we won and what can we do to win?' They were the interesting things for me as a young guy – I was only twenty and the youngest ever male hockey Olympic gold medallist from Australia.

Hockey is very much a March to September sport for most people in Australia. In Europe they play from October to February/March. The problem is that our strongest competitors, the Dutch, the Germans and the Spaniards, are all·playing their best hockey then. They want to always play us in our off season, so very rarely do we ever get a season off. During the European winter we play both as the Australian team and for European clubs. I play in Rotterdam in the Netherlands at the moment. I'm signed on a professional contract over there. In my contract I have a clause that, any time a national commitment for Australia comes up, I have to make myself available. For example, I started in September last year and we had a camp for Australia in February, so I had to come home, just for two weeks. We maybe play just four or five games at home in the year, but we play forty internationals overseas a year, so, in a hockey sense, we're better known overseas than we are here.

In Rotterdam the coach is Dutch, but it's good, because we have five international players: two Pakistanis, two New Zealanders and one Australian, so our common language is English. The coaching is done in English, the team meetings are done in English, and we speak in English on the field. In some ways it's hard for me, because I'm trying to learn Dutch to make myself fit in. I ask for a sandwich at a café and the waitress will say, 'OK, that's fine – there's your sandwich and your change,' straight back to me in English. At least I won't starve!

Hockey has definitely changed in terms of professionalism. My Rotterdam Hockey Club bought me for around AU$35,000 to play over there. It's still only semi-professional in Australia, so everyone in the Kookaburras National Men's Team still works or studies. I'm studying personal training; I'm not sure what I'll do later, possibly coaching or nutrition or personal training.

We had the World Cup in September in Germany last year and that still ranks as one of my best and also worst memories. We were playing well and we should have won the final in front of 13,000 screaming Germans, but we actually ended up losing – so that's a career high and a career low for me! The eight of us Queenslanders were in that team as well.

One of my worst times was in 2003. I'd played very well for Queensland in the National Hockey League and we won our first National Title since 1991. I made the Australian National Team for the first time, but ten minutes before the end, I was chasing a striker for Western Australian in the final in Perth and he changed direction towards me and I stood on his foot and broke my ankle severely – two bones. I had it in a cast for ten weeks, and then had seven weeks of rehab. I was nineteen, stuck in Perth and missed my international debut and the whole hockey season. I started training again in the middle of September and, two minutes before the end of the first day's training, I broke the same ankle again, so I was straight back in the cast for another eight weeks! I couldn't work; I was living on $180 a week from the Australian Institute of Sport scholarship and paying rent at a friend's house of $60 a week. Luckily I was given an opportunity in January 2004 to train for the Olympics. Even now, four years later, I still strap both my ankles for training.

We're professional in the way we train. Typically we'd train Monday to Friday from 6 am to 8 am, then I'd go to work from 8:30 am until 4 pm and back to training from 4 pm until 7 pm. Despite the training, I've never missed out on a party and having a good time. We know our limits and know what we can and can't do.

Before the World Cup last year I had an unbelievable opportunity to play in Rockhampton, my home town, for the Kookaburras Australian Men's Team. The problem was that I had severe bone damage in my toe from the Champions Trophy in July in Spain and had it in a boot for four weeks, so I missed that opportunity to play in front of friends and family. That was a tough moment, since we very rarely play in Australia. We played two games against Korea, who are number five in the world. It was a fantastic event in Rockhampton – in front of a very large and partisan crowd. Even though I wasn't playing, it would still rate as one of the highlights for me, to see my family and people in a country town, who actually love hockey, just go ballistic. Jamie Dwyer, another Rockhampton boy, a great mate and good family friend, and Mum, being the president of Rockhampton Hockey, organised it very well for us, so it was a great day for country sport in general.

Now we're leading up to Beijing. We're ranked number two in the world to Germany. They beat us in the World Cup Final. We were ranked number one in the world for three years: 2004, 2005, 2006. We've lost that crown now, and I can tell you from the twenty-four guys in the national squad now, we're putting in a big effort, because we want that back! Very rarely does any sporting team win back-to-back events. We really want to win back-to-back Olympic gold medals. The Dutch did it in 1996 and 2000 and now it's our turn. We go to Beijing to the Olympic venue in August 2007 and the Olympic qualifier against New Zealand in September and the Champions Trophy in December in Pakistan and then in February 2008 we have a centralised training program where we all have to move to Perth. Everyone has to leave their jobs and move out there. It's a very intense and concentrated training program. We have to be there 'til the Olympics and I think we finish there in the last week in August, hopefully with the gold medal!

PS: I contacted Mark early in September '08 to congratulate him and the team on achieving their bronze medal in Beijing and to ask if he'd like to add a postscript to his story – to which he replied... 'It wasn't quite what we had hoped; however, it's four years of hard work and this bronze medal is still very special to me. Bring on London 2012, that's all I can say now.'

Brooke Stockham – Paralympian Swimmer

She has a sunny disposition and her positive attitude to life is obvious. You can feel her enthusiasm and determination as she describes how she longs to help other athletes with disabilities – she explains that this is because she wants to give back as much to disabled sport as she's been given.

'I remember someone telling me that they took their children to watch the Paralympic Games in Sydney because they couldn't afford to go to the Olympic Games, and they saw this man in a wheelchair from one of the other countries playing basketball a day or two before – and when they saw this guy in the wheelchair again they were saying, "Look, that's the basketball player we saw yesterday," and their mum was saying she thought it was great. They'd identified him as an athlete, as a basketball player ... That's the attitude we need to get across – not just to look at someone and think, "They've only got one arm or they're in a wheelchair," but to see their abilities.'

I grew up in Giru, which is a small sugar cane town about 60 kilometres south of Townsville. My parents live on a farm there, where we grow and harvest sugar cane. I was born in 1982 and Mum took me for swimming lessons when I was a couple of months old, so I've been involved with swimming all my life. I started swimming training from the age of eleven. I joined a swimming club in Ayr, our closest town, and started swimming training there a few afternoons a week after school.

I was born with one arm; my other arm is like a little arm with little fingers on the end. Because I learnt to swim at such a young age, I think I learnt to compensate in everything I did. A lot of people say to me, 'How do you swim straight – with one arm you'd go around in circles,' and I say to myself, 'What's it like to swim with two arms? I wouldn't know.' I've only ever had one arm all my life, so I've just learnt to do things and compensate with one arm.

A lot of people assume it was thalidomide, but it wasn't, and nobody's really given us an answer to why it happened. The only thing we think it could be, and no doctor has ever really said that's the cause, is that Mum had X-rays very early in the pregnancy, when she didn't know she was pregnant with me. We think that could have caused it, but we don't really know.

When I got to around fifteen, I started getting serious about swimming. In 1996 I saw the Games on TV in Atlanta and thought, 'Wow! This is great – maybe I could do that!' I'd been swimming for a couple of years and I'd made State and I'd made the Open Nationals. I was going to Brisbane a couple of times a year for training camps and competitions, and I felt that if I really wanted to give it my best shot, I'd have to move there, so in 1998 I moved to Brisbane and went to boarding school at St Peters Lutheran College in Indooroopilly for Years 11 and 12. I didn't have any relatives in Brisbane and I only got to see my family a couple of times a year, so that was a really hard time for me.

The club that I joined was St Peters Western and Paul Sansby was my coach. The 100 metres breast stroke, the 200 metres individual medley and the 100 metres butterfly were my three main events. Late in 1998 I got selected for the World Championships team and competed in Christchurch, New Zealand, where I won a silver medal in the 200 individual medley. It was around then that I thought, 'I think I could make the 2000 Paralympics team – that's what I'm going to be training for now!' I started doing gym and swimming ten 4 to 5 kilometre sessions a week. When we had the trials in 2000, I made the team and I was just over the moon – I was so excited! I hadn't seen Mum and Dad for probably a couple of months and the family was saying, 'Yes, we're coming to see you at the Paralympic Games!'

We had a training camp in Canberra before we went to Sydney, where we went into the athletes' village. Because all the Australians are in the one section, we got to meet the athletics team and the cycling team and so on. I can remember the first time I walked into the food hall at the athletes' village. You've never seen a tent as big as this! It's just massive and its open twenty-four hours a day. It took me about half an hour to walk around all the different food sections – they even had McDonalds! McDonalds was a major sponsor and I thought – how tempting is that, to have to walk past McDonalds every day 'til I've finished competition.

Then there was the opening ceremony. I hadn't seen Mum and Dad for a long time and I knew they were going to go to be there, but I didn't know if I'd be able to see them in the crowd. Being the 'home country', we had to wait in the tunnel for all the other countries to come out first. I remember waiting in the tunnel and the feeling we had – excitement mixed with anticipation. Then they announced 'Australia!' We marched out from the tunnel into the stadium and the whole crowd was just cheering for us. Oh, I just cried! I looked at my friend Judith and she was bawling too! We couldn't say anything. We marched around the whole oval and it felt like it went on forever and we were dancing around and carrying on like idiots – we were so excited.

Then it was time for us to sit down. They had seats for us on the oval and we sat down and the announcer's trying to quiet the crowd and for some reason I just turned around and there, about ten seats back, was my mum and dad and all my family. I just couldn't believe it! This is in Stadium Australian, which holds 80,000 or so people, and my parents were just behind me! I got up from my chair and ran up to see them and everyone was looking at me. Then my parents got up from their seats and Mum and Dad were both crying and giving me a hug – yeah, there was a lot of emotion! I'd never seen my dad cry before. My older brother Ashley would have loved to have come, but Mum and Dad and Ashley, we run a business here (in Giru) and that was the main crushing season, so he had to stay home and look after the business while Dad was away, but he was watching it at home on TV.

I was eighteen at the Sydney 2000 and one of the rookies of the team. I had a bit of a naïve attitude; I was thinking, 'Yep, I'm going to win!' That was all I really focused on. My first race was the 200 individual medley. I remember when I finished the race and I looked up at the scoreboard and it's '3' and it was – well, I was excited, but there was a bit of disappointment too; I'd been so determined to win. But then I looked up in the crowd and saw my mum and dad just going crazy with excitement, so I was happy, and I got my medal and everything.

That was my first race and the following day I had my 100 butterfly. On paper I was ranked 2nd in the world, so I was hoping that I'd be able to get another medal, but in the heat swim in the morning before the finals that night, I swam five seconds slower than my personal best. I looked up at the scoreboard and thought, 'Oh my God, I've come 8th; there's no way I'm going to qualify for the finals.' I remember getting out of the pool, saying to myself, 'I can't cry. If they see me cry, they'll think I'm weak, and I can't let them think that.' I remember picking up my clothes from my basket and walking down to the warm-down pool at the other end of the pool and all the time I'm holding back my tears. I saw my coach and he didn't even say anything to me. Then I just cried my eyes out. I was very, very upset.

I had two days where I was not competing and then one more individual race to go, the 100 breaststroke – another one of my pet events. I was thinking, 'I'm not going to stuff this one up.' I went into the 100 breaststroke giving it everything I'd got and ended up getting a third. That was probably when I really started to appreciate the magnitude of what I'd done. I was just ecstatic after winning a bronze medal in that race. So yeah, Sydney 2000 was – phew, a bit of a roller-coaster – up and down, up and down. The closing ceremony didn't have the emotion of the opening, but there was a hell of a good party after it in the athletes' village, that's for sure!

Later, when I made the team for Athens, I thought, 'Wow, I'm so lucky. Of the Paralympic Games that I could have been to, the two I went to were the best. Being able to be at home in my home country with my home crowd and then be able to go back to Athens where it all started. I've been so lucky!'

In January 2005 I retired from competitive swimming and began focusing on my studies at uni (James Cook University) studying Secondary Education, where I specialised in PE and also did SOSE (Study of Society and Environment).

I completed my teaching degree in 2006 and am now working at Scots PGC, a private school in Warwick, and loving it! I'm teaching PE and SOSE in middle and senior school. I'm hoping to bring a few of my experiences into the classroom and hopefully inspire other children – especially children with disabilities, to be able to excel and achieve their dreams, whether it's sport or music or whatever.

I'm involved with the Sporting Wheelies and Disabled Association. They're a Queensland sport and recreation association that helps athletes with disabilities and I'm on the committee here in Townsville. I really want to give back as much into disabled sport as they've given to me. I hope that with what I can put in, and with the help of others, maybe we can get more exposure for people with disabilities. We're not any different from able-bodied people. We have the same dreams and we work just as hard in training – yet we still don't get that recognition. It's very disappointing sometimes, but I think the attitude of the public is slowly changing. I remember someone telling me that they took their children to watch the 2000 Paralympic Games in Sydney because they couldn't afford to go to the Olympic Games, and they saw this man in a wheelchair from one of the other countries, playing basketball a day or two before – and when they saw this guy in the wheelchair again, they were saying, 'Look, that's the basketball player we saw yesterday,' and their mum was saying she thought it was great. They'd identified him as an athlete, as a basketball player instead of saying, 'Look at that man in the wheelchair, Mum.' That's the attitude we need to get across – not just to look at someone and think, 'They've only got one arm or they're in a wheelchair,' but to see their abilities.

Being involved in disabled sport, I've seen some really severe disabilities where I've thought, 'Holy cow, I'm so lucky to have one arm, compared to seeing this person who's got no arms and only half a leg.' I've seen this chap and he's swimming and competing. He'll kick with that stump and touch the wall with his head. I see people like that and I think, 'Geez, I'm lucky!'

Ashley Adams – Paralympian Shooter

It's a great accomplishment to represent your country at the elite level in any competition. Ashley has represented Australia at the Paralympics in Athens and also in Beijing. The strength of the man shines through in his steady gaze. For a fit young man to become a paraplegic is about as tough as it gets, but as the old adage goes 'life is what you make of it' and Ashley's smile lines show that he's enjoyed many triumphs.

'...when we got up these stairs the bloke in there says, "You shouldn't be here; you don't belong here!" This was at the New South Wales Championships and Margaret was with me and she said, "Ashley's here to shoot!" and that's what we did and I did well.'

My great-grandfather started a mail run out here in Western Queensland way before the 1900s. Afterwards, he ran the local hotel at Yalleroi – it's a ghost town there now. They then moved to a property called Henley Park. At sixteen my grandfather moved onto a property of his own and he started from there; that was *Sydenham* and we still own that property. At *Darracourt*, where we live now, it's an additional area to it. We then bought another property next door called *Rellim*. We used to run sheep, but we run cattle now. The nearest town is Blackall.

I went to college, then came back home to work on the property. I was twenty-six years of age when I had a motor cycle accident, racing in a competition near the local town. I broke my back at T5 (thoracic T5) with a complete fracture, which left me a total para. In hospital I saw a lot of other people that were damaged, but I considered them lazy. I took an attitude that I wanted to get home as soon as I could, so I worked and worked in the gymnasium. I went into the hospital in May and by my birthday in October I was out of the hospital, with a full broken back recovered, and I had a car and I was driving. There were people there in the hospital that had their accidents before I got in there and they were still there when I left.

When I came back home I just wanted to do things. One of the first major things I did was drive a 'dozer. I learnt I could climb a rope by my hands and that used to be how I'd get in the 'dozer. Since then I've done about 5,000 hours 'dozer work, mostly scrub-breaking and building dams, because I can get in and be there all day by myself. I've had some fires and things like that, but that's all right. I was able to control them and put the fires out with extinguishers on the 'dozer. We don't have mobile phones out here, but we have two-way radio – it's safe like that.

Then I met Margaret. It was strange, I suppose, just one of those things that happens. She was working in the local town and we met at parties and things. She was a bit different. She's not one of those people who just wanted to look after me in the sense of nursing; she's not that type of person. We got along like normal people do. We went to places having fun and the usual B&S balls and all those things and we got married.

I enjoyed a bit of shooting while I was at school. I'm a bit of a perfectionist – that's probably how I'm dealing with shooting now. Margaret said to me back in 1992 or something like that, she said, 'Ashley, why don't you shoot for the disabled and go to a competition?' That started everything. In '92 I went to the first competition in Adelaide. They gave me a rifle and I shot very well, but the people that were running the organisation thought it was a fluke. I could have gone to the Barcelona Olympics, but they didn't think I was good enough or responsible enough, so they kept me out of that.

Then I bought my own rifle and it just bloomed from there. I started shooting with the able-bodied, because I could lie on the ground and shoot in the 'open prone' events. One thing I'll always remember is when I went to a competition in Sydney and my wife Margaret was there with me and when we got up these stairs the bloke in there says, 'You shouldn't be here; you don't belong here!' This was at the New South Wales Championships and Margaret says, 'Ashley's here to shoot!' and that's what we did and I did well. That was one of the encouraging things that I've done and I'll never forget when that bloke said that. It stirred Margaret and me up so much inside – I didn't even think of being disabled. I've never thought of myself as being a disabled person – I was never born disabled. I've had two lives: I've had an ordinary life and a disabled life, so I can think like an ordinary person can, but I've also got to get the best out of myself – the person I'm working with all the time.

I can't do everything, so I let other people do the things I can't do and I try to make it easy for the other person to do the job that I can't do. I can open a gate single-handed; I've invented a gate latch like that. Most of the gates on this property can be opened single-handed. I've designed them that way, because I need my other hand free to hang on so I don't fall off the four-wheel bike. That's been the other highlight – these four-wheel motor bikes; I use them all the time. I've been out on the property here for the last hour and a half and probably did 20 miles among cows and calves and waters (watering points) with a pistol beside me in case I find anything that's got to be done; that's how I manage. You have to make things easy for yourself. Like cattle mustering: we use lanes (two fence lines with about 30 metres width between them). On these two properties I've probably got 20 kilometres of lanes. I've got regular watering points too. I've designed everything that way, so it's easier for everyone who works here, and they like working on the property when it's easy like that.

The other highlight of my career was winning my first Olympic bronze medal in Athens. The other competitors didn't even consider me to win a medal, but I just had this in-depth feeling that if I worked at it, it was possible, and I'd be pushing for it. I nearly got a higher medal than that too, in the air-rifle event. Then I won a silver medal in the .22 rifle event – well that just put the icing on the cake!

The other thing is the family's working behind me the whole time. If they weren't looking after me … they're the other part of the team. They back me up in different ways. Then, when I go away, my whole motto is that when I'm out of Australia, the people from Australia paid for me to go away, so it's my job to do as best I can for them. That's why I devote everything I can to the shooting. It's not a holiday for me; I'm out there to do my best, and I don't let any of the coaches or anyone down, if I can help it.

At the Athens Olympics we were going out to the range and there were three of us in the bus: me and two shooters from Israel. One of them was the open shooter and also a coach. This was the day the Queen of Sweden was visiting the range and there was high security and our bus went the wrong way into the range and we were pulled up with machine guns. The Israeli coach, he's an officer in the army, he thought we were being hi-jacked and it became fairly heated in that bus. In that split second it was nearly one of those major incidents, but we cooled it down. Then, later, we met the Queen of Sweden at the range. Recently, when they were visiting Australia, the King and Queen of Sweden invited Margaret and me down to dinner in Sydney with them. That was certainly a highlight.

Margaret and I have had a son, Iain. He was born in 1991. He'll more than likely become a grazier. He likes being out here and he's been at the International with the shooting and been to the Olympic Games and he's seen a lot of different people. We've had a number of international visitors at our property here and that opens everyone's minds up.

On the property, we're breeding Santa Gertrudis cattle and I've been following a process that Genetic Solutions, a company in Brisbane, has developed, called 'GeneSTAR'. They've developed a technique where they use the DNA from a hair follicle in the animal's tail. We take a hair sample from the tail and they analyse it. Some animals have the enzymes which cause meat to tenderise after the animal is killed but before rigor mortis sets in. It saves the people cryovacing meat for 21 days at zero degrees to tenderise it. The meat is ready to eat in the first few hours. Being a sort of scientific person and interested in new things all the time, I've been following it and have become heavily involved with it. It's very interesting and not controversial, as it's scientifically proven. Last year it won the award for the most innovative thing for the beef industry.

The people at Genetic Solutions like helping an athlete, I suppose. Like a family of people working for you, whether it's in shooting or friends. It's good for the future of the beef industry and I've been helping them and they've been helping me with what to do and how to go about it in the planning of our cattle herd.

If people say something like 'you can't do that', well that inspires me to do it! That's full on. The other thing with the shooting: there're a number of people that didn't think Australia should be represented in the open event, which is designed for able-bodied shooters, by a person who's disabled. Well, I've shown them; not only have I done that, but I've got to the top of Australia in the Olympic event – 'open able-bodied prone' shooting with a .22 rifle for the English match. In this event I shot as Australia's number one at the Oceania's at Belmont in November 2005. That was something I never dreamed of – and I've done it!

Postscript: Margaret, Ashley's wife, told me that he won the 'Beef Producer of the Year Award for 2008' at the Brisbane Royal Agricultural Show.

Representing Australia at the Beijing Paralympics, Ashley attained 4th place in the Mixed R6-50M Free Rifle Prone SH1 final – just 0.8 of a point behind the Chinese bronze medal winner.

Racing

Pam O'Neill – Australia's First Woman Jockey

She greets me warmly at the door of her north Brisbane home. She looks very fit and younger than her years. I follow her through to a large, comfortable living room, passing her Pink Jockey shirt and a framed painting of her favourite horse 'SuperSnack' among other riding memorabilia.

'I think my first day of riding was a special moment. I rode three winners on that day, and that was a world record, because no male or female had ever ridden three winners on their first day.'

Before I became a jockey, I used to lead horses up to Eagle Farm racetrack, but I had to hand them over to a male there, because the rule said women couldn't handle a horse on the racetrack. That would have been in the late '50s, when I was about fourteen. Anyhow, later on I became a strapper and I was the first female trackwork rider at Eagle Farm.

I always loved horses. I grew up in Kent Street and when I was about seven, Bart Sinclair senior used to be a trainer down the end of our street. Round Ascot in those days, there were 32 racing stables and my dad used to love racing. He was a fruiterer and I used to love getting up early with him and we'd be in about four o'clock in the morning at the markets there at Roma Street, buying the fruit and vegetables for the shop. He was a hobby-trainer and we'd go to the horse sales together. My mum would say, 'If you two get another horse, you'll be sleeping on the street!' We'd come home with another horse, but we never finished out on the street!

I joined pony club when I was about thirteen. I was one of the first in the Hendra Pony Club after it was formed and we won the first 'teams of four' ever held at the Royal Exhibition. I remember old Bill Edwards, a great man and a wonderful person, was in charge of the exhibition then. When I became a jockey, an attraction they used to hold at the Royal Exhibition was draught horse races and the jockeys used to go in there and ride the draught horses. The next day I couldn't walk because they were so wide, we'd ride them bareback!

We used to stage a ladies race, one race in the meeting, and they staged one at Eagle Farm called the Dame Merlyn Myers Race. It was an international race and they invited girls from all over the world and I won it. It was a big success, but I still wanted to ride against the men.

Then I met Anna Kohler and I told her about my plight, that I wanted to race against the men and there was a rule against it. This was when discrimination against women was in, and she was a friend of Al Grazeby, a Member of Parliament, and he fought with us to get the rule changed so that women could ride against the men! She died of cancer and I dearly miss her.

It took us sixteen years to get the rule changed – that was in 1979 in Queensland and I became the first Australian woman jockey. How it got changed was that Linda Jones wanted to come over from New Zealand to ride in the ladies race at Eagle Farm and next to ride against the men. There was no rule in New Zealand to say that women couldn't ride and she'd been made an apprentice jockey there. They let her come and they half-amended the rule so she could ride in the Doomben Cup, which had always been a men's only race. I'd been riding in a lot of ladies races at the time and I'd won all over Australia, but there was still no female licence in Australia when Linda Jones came over. I lent her my saddle because we were good friends, and she won the Doomben Cup! About a couple of weeks after that I got my licence; they never made me an apprentice, I had to go in as a full-fledged jockey against all the top male jockeys.

My first day was down the Gold Coast where I rode three winners, so it was like the end of a fairytale that I'd been fighting for so long. I found the boys congratulating me as I was pulling up. They were terrific. It was a special moment – no male or female had ever ridden three winners in their first day. Everybody was there, and photographers and everything. The only thing I regretted: my dad died at the age of fifty-four and he never saw any of this happen, and he was all for it. Then the next week I went back and rode another three winners! Those were six different horses and they weren't horses that were set up for me to win on or anything like that. Three of them never won another race. I think I had Lady Luck sitting with me – I think maybe I had my dad there! About a month later they let me come to town and I think I rode for a couple of weeks, but didn't ride a winner. Then I came to Doomben and I won my first race there – I'll never forget it. They presented me with a cheque to make the day special and I told them I wasn't going to frame the cheque, I was going to spend it! That was my first winner in town.

It's surprising with jockeys how hard they've got to waste – that's to lose weight. I remember one time I lost three and a half kilos in one week – it's a lot of weight to lose, but it's a job you love doing and if you didn't like doing it you wouldn't do it, because there isn't much night life. You're always watching your weight; you're up early in the morning.

I can understand a lot of the jockeys not going to the track. There's so much racing going on now in Australia, they're riding about four or five days a week. Sometimes jockeys don't even ride the horses before they race on them. I think it's the horsemanship really with the jockey. When I was teaching down at Deagon I tried to make a horseman out of them before teaching them to ride – you've got to understand your horses a bit. I still hold the record in Queensland for winning the most races on the one horse, and that was *Super-Snack*. I can do anything with him. Everybody that's ridden him he's thrown – he's thrown me a few times too, but he's a horse that you had to get to know a bit.

I left school at fourteen. I didn't like school. Later, when I was standing in front of a blackboard teaching the students at Deagon, I'd think, 'Geez, here I am teaching – I never thought I'd be writing on a blackboard!' I left school at fourteen and worked in a dress salon in the Valley called Peggy Hunt's. I used to love the atmosphere in the Valley. I always remember the shop windows at Christmas and I took my children in there too and showed them the windows. You'd get the tram into the Valley and walk up to the Exhibition Grounds to go to the exhibition.

I went to Ascot State School; three generations of my family have gone there now. You look at it today and it's more like a private school than a state school. I went up for sports day the other day, for my grandchildren, and they said to me, 'Did you have your sports up here when you went to the school?' and I said, 'No, we used to go down to Crosby Park to have our sports.' I thoroughly enjoyed going there, but it's totally changed now.

I remember Ascot when the races were on. If the cars were parked down in our street, they had a big crowd, and Saturday you'd see people going in the tram and they'd be hanging off the sides, getting to the races, the trams were that packed. People would be walking down Racecourse Road and the women wore hats and gloves, and they went to town too. My grandmother used to do that all the time. When I knew Mum was going to town I wanted to go with her, but then I wanted to come home quick! I sort of miss those days. I miss Ascot the way it was. I can still see those big old houses in Racecourse Road and Mrs Banks's shop on the corner of the street. I remember, even going back ten years ago, I could walk around Ascot and you'd know everybody – now you wouldn't know anyone. I always used to say that if you felt depressed you could walk up the street, there'd always be somebody to talk to that you knew. I think a lot of that's gone. I've found it here, being a little bit further out, that we get on well with our neighbours and we all talk and that, but I think a lot of the city's changed. That's just my view of it.

My son Gavin was born in 1963 and he used to be a jockey. He got too heavy, but he and I rode in a race together and all he wanted to do was beat Mum! He run second and Mum come nowhere, but he should have won the race, so his trainer went mad at him. My daughter Cherie, she was born in 1962 and works with the horses. I bought my granddaughters a pony and I taught them riding. Taylor was born in 1997 and

Celine was born in 1996. One will make an equestrian rider and the other will make a jockey, for sure – she's got more go and more cheek in her than I've ever seen – she's telling me how to do it now!

I have always tried to hold on to my femininity. I used to always try and dress nice after I finished, but when I was out there, I was very competitive with the men. I'm now Secretary and Treasurer of the Jockeys' Association in Queensland and on the board of the Australian Jockeys' Association, and I've been there for a long time, so I think I've also got the respect of the men. I think in all my years of riding I only had two arguments with two jockeys and at the end of the day we were the best of mates. I've had a lot of fun in racing. It's really an industry I love. I've got a passion for it and I hate anything going wrong in it.

I've just got a nice recognition, because the BTC, the Brisbane Turf Club, wanted to make me an honorary member of their club for the contribution I've made to racing. I thought that was nice. There was a big night at the Hilton Hotel and all the legends from around Australia, George Moore and Mel Schumacher and all the top jockeys in Australia, were there and I was invited as one of them. I felt very humble and proud to be standing up with people like them – it was really lovely!

What's next for Pam O'Neill? I don't know, I've always loved a challenge, so if one comes up I'd love to take it on. I've always said to my family: when I die I want to be cremated and I want to be thrown over a racetrack – so I can trip somebody I mightn't like. I believe people are put on this world for something and I reckon I was put on to buck the system and be the first woman jockey in Australia.

Trevor Jones – Camel Racing in Boulia

He's the Lord Mayor of Boulia, proprietor of the local pub, and also a grazier. He's in the pub when we speak, with people coming and going and greeting him as they pass. The races have been part of the town's calendar since 1997 and have attracted a huge following – swelling the population during that brief period each year from a few hundred to several thousand.

'People start coming in 8 to10 days beforehand now, to pick out the best site. We've only got 30 accommodation rooms in town, so basically everyone has to come out and camp. They pitch tents or bring their caravans, or just roll their swag out.'

The Boulia Desert Sands camel races kicked off in 1997 as an idea that was floated around a few western shires by Paddy McHugh. Boulia jumped on board and offered to assist in running them. We have good facilities here and on the 19 and 20 July 1997 we had the first camel races here. I wasn't involved then but I worked on it after the second year, and I took over the presidency in 2002.

At the inaugural camel races they just went and caught a mob of camels out of the wild, brought them into town about five weeks before the races and trained – or tried to train – them to run around a track. We had wild camels racing down the track with lots of spectators each side and no one knew where the camels were going to go, or what they were going to do. Some bucked and some turned around and ran the other way when they saw and heard the crowd – so it was very exciting. There were a few bruises from some of the jockeys when they got bucked off and a few irate punters, I suppose, when camels turned around and ran the wrong way!

Nowadays the camel races attract a crowd of about 2,500 to 3,000 annually to Boulia – and this is a township of 300 people, so it just swells our population no end. It's a huge economic boost to the community. It brings about a quarter of a million dollars into the township, because people start coming in 8 to10 days beforehand now, to pick out the best site. We've only got 30 accommodation rooms in town, so basically everyone has to come out and camp. They pitch tents or bring their caravans, or just roll their swag out.

Boulia itself is situated in the middle of a cattle area. There're 61,000 square kilometres in the shire. Predominantly it was sheep in the 1950s and 1960s, but more people went into cattle through the late '80s and '90s when the wool crashed. It's also a council town – where council's probably the major employer outside the cattle industry. I'm the mayor of Boulia and I'm also the publican.

We have a lot of old characters around that come into the hotel. Old Davo: he comes in and tells stories about his crocodile hunting days. His father used to own whaling ships down at Eden in New South Wales, but then he came out here putting up windmills on the properties. Davo's retired now, but he can recount stories of min-min lights and the early days. The min-min lights have intrigued travellers here for years, because it's similar to a light but will follow travellers at a distance for miles and then all of a sudden it'll be in front of them. I've seen them myself. We used to see them all the time, on our way in to town to the movies – like a pale headlight, but without the glare.

In the early days we also had the wild camel catching competition. They used to catch the camels – two people had to get a rope on a camel and get it on the ground in the shortest possible time. We had complaints from people, so we've stopped running that event, though it had been hugely popular with the crowd, which was the unfortunate part about it. Camels are very noisy animals and they're very vocal – they're well known for spitting and racing down the track and then all of a sudden turning around and going the other way!

Some people say it's not as much fun to watch the races these days as it was in the early days, because it's become very professional. There's $20,000 prize money for the weekend, so people start training three months out! We have camels come from all over Australia. The biggest number of nominations we had was 69 camels; last year I think we had 41.

People get into the theme of the events for the weekend. Some come dressed up as Arabs and last year we actually had a 'desert garb' competition. We used to have belly-dancers, too, but we don't have them any more – I think it might have been the wives stopped that!

When they're trying to book accommodation, I say, 'We have no rooms left available, but we've got 61,000 square kilometres out there that you can camp in!' We've good facilities set up at the racecourse/rodeo grounds, where the camel races are held, so there's two big shower and toilet blocks there and people just set up camp all along the river. The accommodation overflows into the town itself – some people have up to 8 and 10 tents in their backyards, with friends staying. The town copes very well and most visitors are understanding and quite willing to camp.

We have bookies on-track. It's fully legal to bet at the camel races and has been since the first year. It's not the same as horseracing where you can see a bit of history on the horse – people just go out and pick which camel they like, or see them walking past and say, 'He looks OK – we'll put our money on him.'

We've really turned the camel races into a carnival type atmosphere. We have a lot of activities over the weekend. We've got children's entertainment running all weekend, with children's performers on site. We bring in entertainers from as far south as Sydney and we have concerts on the Friday and Saturday nights and fireworks. Then we have tug-o-wars and tow-the-Toyota competitors, wool-bale rolling and kicking the football – to see who can kick the football the furthest. We have a country music concert with two acts on the Friday and Saturday nights and the bar closes at 1am on the Friday.

The camel races start on Saturday morning at ten o'clock with 10 heats that day – 5 for the 400-metre race and 5 heats for the one-kilometre race. On the Saturday night there's the kid's show with fireworks and then another concert. The fireworks don't seem to worry the camels, but we've had a problem now and again with dogs going astray – they don't like it at all, and horses get terrified with fireworks, but not the camels. Then, on the Sunday, there's half a day's racing again with 5 novelty races for the camels that haven't won during the weekend. Then we have the two big finals – the 400-metre final at ten o'clock and the 1500 metres at twelve o'clock with the presentations at about 12:30 and then it winds up with everyone having a drink on the Sunday afternoon ready for the big clean-up on the Monday!

We've been fortunate: we've never run out of beer and, being the publican, we've always got good access to get some more. Running out of beer would be my worst nightmare!

There's three months of organising that goes into it beforehand and a lot of food vending stalls come in. There's a food canteen that does hamburgers and hot-dogs and chips, the potato man and the German sausage man and the cappuccino man and ice-creams and fairy-floss and all that sort of stuff, and they set up market stalls in the horse stable as well. There's no shortage of food and there's a good variety.

Sometimes though it gets very cold, because it's in the middle of July – it can get down to about one degree Celsius in the early hours of the morning. A lot of people are out sleeping under the stars, but if they have enough to drink they sleep through it – we seem to sell a lot more rum when it's cold!

Sailing

Richard Crooke – The Queensland Royal Yacht Squadron

His wife Susie is a well-known artist specialising in paintings of sailing scenes from the Moreton Bay area. Richard has been sailing almost all his life and speaks with warmth of sailing and people in the sailing fraternity.

' ... the old adage used to be that the mullet run in May ... but the old Aboriginal story was that if you had a really good lot of parrots around the end of April or early May you were going to get a very good mullet run!'

There are various sailing clubs in Brisbane, but the one that I'm a member of, Royal Queensland Yacht Squadron, was originally called the Royal Queensland Yacht Club. In 1951 the club acquired the leasehold on some premises at Bulimba on the river opposite Hamilton. In hindsight, the club was particularly fortunate in that they attracted a large group of young fellows who weren't necessarily all that wealthy or good at sailing, but were very progressive. I was about the youngest in 1952 when I started sailing. The river sailing progressed and we had various classes. In 1956 the club mounted a serious challenge for representation in the Australian Olympic yachting team in Melbourne. Despite coming a close second in a number of challenge events, we actually didn't make the team that year. But in every Olympics from 1960 onwards we've had a member of the club represented in the Australian Yachting team, either as a competitor or involved in the team management. I don't know that any other little club around the world has been able to achieve that.

In 1964 the club moved its premises down to Manly and by then we had changed our name to the Royal Queensland Yacht Squadron. The open water sailing did a lot for us. It turned us into a very competent group of open water sailors, still in the dinghies, but we had many Olympic classes. Probably the next major step we took as a yacht club was to build our marina, which started in about 1980. Now we're probably in the forefront of marinas in Queensland. We've got 500 berths down there and that's a fairly tidy little marina by any standards.

In the '80s an increasing number of our young members started competing abroad. As a result of them going offshore we became quite an international yachting venue. In 1991 we hosted the Olympic Class International 470 Series and had 120 boats from 23 nations sailing out of Manly.

Nearly all the recognised world championships have been sailed at Manly at some stage or other over the last 20 years. We call the old place 'regatta city' for that reason. There was a substantial growth in the Squadron's international vision at that time and I think it's paid off handsomely for our young sailors – they've done very well as a result of that. It's a bit like the swimmers – it's no use swimming and competing in Australia all the time. If you want to know how you're going, you've got to get out there with the rest of the world.

We have two main types of competitive sailing vessels at Manly: one is what we call dinghies (they're basically 30-footers down to about 10-footers), and then we have racing yachts. Manly is inside Moreton Bay and it's probably 4 to 5 hours sailing to get out into the ocean. We run some offshore events, mainly for our own club members, but usually in company with other clubs from around the Moreton Bay area. We put on an overnight race to Double Island Point, close to a 200-mile race, and some of the other yachting clubs around the Bay join us, and we join with them in theirs.

The club has many activities apart from sailing, including a major power boating and fishing division. We had a very prominent commodore at one time called Jock Robinson. Jock was a great fisherman and loved to go outside over the bar at South Passage. He had a very well-known boat called *Flood Tide* built in about 1947 and he used to take any of the young fellas, and the old fellas too, from round the club. They called it 'Jock and his Indians' and they'd go outside fishing nearly every weekend in the winter when the sailing wasn't on.

He'd say, 'Come on, we're going down the Bay, so get yourself down to the boat on Friday afternoon after work.' We'd go across the Bay and invariably have a few drinks on the way and then we'd pull up inside the bar and the next morning at dawn we'd be out over the bar fishing. On the Saturday night he'd cook up a roast and after the roast was done he'd put these long fatty loin chops in the pan and roast them while you were eating the meal and then they'd sit in the pan overnight. The next morning, he'd pull one of these fatty cooked lamb chops out of the pan and say, 'Here's your breakfast. Get that down your throat,' and you'd hardly finish swallowing it when he'd take you back out over the bar and it was usually in pretty uncomfortable conditions. If you could keep your breakfast down you were allowed to come again!

The dear old fellow met his end out there. They were coming in round Cape Moreton late one afternoon and when they got to where they were going, the rest of the crew suddenly realised that Jock was missing. They went back, but they never found him. He had been in poor health and the suggestion was he'd had a heart attack and had just fallen over the side. Anyhow, he ended up where he'd love to be, in his favourite spot – so that was it.

There are some famous fishing stories involving sharks. In the mid fifties there was a well-known radio identity called Bob Dyer. Bob and his wife Dolly used to go over to Tangalooma in his fishing boat called *Tennessee Three*, when the whaling station was still going there, and they got some world records shark fishing. The story goes that they'd get a half-dozen major sharks around the back of the boat, just off the whaling station, where, of course, they loved to be, because of all the blood and guts from the whales. Dolly would have a very large Queensland blue pumpkin in boiling water on the stove in the boat. A crew member would pick the shark which looked the largest and they'd whack the shark-hook through this boiling pumpkin, rush out the back, hold the pumpkin up near the biggest shark and down the neck it would go. The shark didn't like having a red hot pumpkin in its stomach and so didn't fight for long after that – so the story goes!

There've been a couple of very unfortunate incidents in Moreton Bay. One particularly unfortunate story involved a friend of ours called Vic Beaver. I had lunch with him one Friday afternoon at the yacht club. After I'd left him, about five o'clock, he and his son-in-law and a friend at the yacht club suddenly decided to go on a fishing weekend. They told their wives, but they didn't tell the club and they weren't on the register as having put their names down, so the club wasn't looking out for them. Anyhow, this was Friday night. On Sunday morning someone suddenly realised that Vic and his crew hadn't been sighted, so the search went out and everyone gathered round and tried to find them. What had happened: they were only a little boat and it was an unpleasant night with scuds and rain showers and poor visibility and, as they'd been going out across the bay, this big inbound container ship had hit them. They hadn't seen it and it hadn't seen them. The three fellows actually got off the boat with the icebox off the back deck. That was about nine o'clock on the Friday night. The three of them floated around Moreton Bay for all of Saturday and they'd take it in turns, one of them would get in the ice box and the other two would hang on outside. Anyhow, by Saturday night the tiger sharks had found out where they were and proceeded to pick them off in the water one by one. The second man was taken early on Sunday morning. After the mad search on Sunday morning they found the third one still alive on the icebox, but Vic and his son-in-law had both perished during the night, taken by the sharks. It gave us a good shakeup and made us all aware of putting our names on the list when we were going somewhere with the clubs. The sharks are still there in the bay, but when you go to Peel Bay on a summer's day people swim all over the bay – I can't believe it; we'll pay the price one day.

The old adage used to be that the mullet run in May – and you can see them sometimes just as a black swarm from the beach, that's what the professional fishermen go after in May. The old Aboriginal story was that if you had a really good lot of parrots around the end of April or early May you were going to get a very good mullet run! What the association is I can't tell you and I don't know that anyone can, but, anyhow, that was the Aboriginal gossip at the time. Certainly we parked our car under some trees in April and when we came back to get it the parrots had been doing their bit and it was on our car. Anyhow we saw the mullet-bloke, the fisherman, on the beach a couple of weeks later and I said, 'Having a good run this year?' and he said, 'Oh yes, a wonderful run this year!' I don't know if that proves the story or if it's just an interesting coincidence.

Game fishing has quite a keen amateur following in Moreton Bay. They have a Tangalooma Tournament in February each year. We don't catch the giant marlin that they get up in North Queensland, but we do catch some quite sizeable fish: 300 and 400 pounders – they're black and blue marlin and another very popular one we call bill fish, which is the larger of the pelagic species of sailfish. You might inadvertently kill a fish, but, generally speaking, it's a 'tag and release' situation. For those sport fishing cups they'll go both inside and outside the bay, and the really hot time for them is February and March, because that's when the northern blue fin tuna come and I think a lot of the bill fish follow the northern blue fin tuna.

We're supposed have a school of some 300 to 400 dugong in Moreton Bay, but having been going down to the bay for over 50 years I can only recall one or two occasions when I've actually seen them in close company. The dugong is a very timid species. The noise the jet skis make would normally mean that the dugong would go to the bottom. There're a lot of turtles in Moreton Bay and I don't think they get hurt much by vessels. They also are pretty timid. They're more inclined, I think, to have problems through getting caught in pots or nets. I've never heard of a dugong getting caught in a fish trap or a net. I guess it can happen, but I've never heard of it.

The council has put traps on the drains and that has made a significant improvement to the water purity, specifically in Manly Boat Harbour. Porpoises are now being seen up towards Story Bridge, where they haven't been seen for years. When you get tides averaging two metres flushing Moreton Bay twice a day in and out, you're moving a tremendous volume of water in and out and that water is pristine. That's a major factor enabling Moreton Bay to maintain its condition. Fifty years ago when you went down Moreton Bay, you never brought any rubbish home at all; it all just went over the side. Today I don't know anyone who doesn't bring all their rubbish home – if it's biodegradable it still goes over the side, but, generally speaking, bottles and plastic and all those non-degradable substances, they all come home these days for dumping.

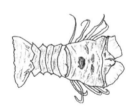

PART TWO: Business

'We will either find a way, or make one.'
- Hannibal

Business, or more particularly, work, is something we all do, if only for the income it enables us to spend on food and clothing, a roof over our heads and other necessities of life for our families and the lifestyle we enjoy. Some of us are fortunate enough to also enjoy the work we do. Many of those who do are entrepreneurs who have started their own business and have a deep interest in its success. Many of these businesses are small and very 'hands on', while others have grown to be large enterprises. Irrespective of their size, however, the individuals who started these businesses invariably remember their origins with pride, including the hard times, the humour, and the love and support of people who helped them to their early successes.

Ross Clark: Poet

The Social Life of Plants

They're weeds, of course, and not native at all,
you remark to my pointing out a stand of bamboo
I have long enjoyed, its childhood's airy castling,
its wind-chimes and flutes yet to be harvested.
I can recall enough botany to know that *weed* is
a social category, not a Linnean one. Like *pest*
in the animal kingdom, its transplanted creatures
rampaging too successfully in new habitats, or
iconic native species thriving against the purposes
we have colonised their environment for, trying
to create a mirror hemisphere here in this Terra
Australis still too Incognita.

Lunch is a cornucopia of tropical fruits and
exotic salads and local wines, now *proudly*
holding their own in the world market, though
I'm a beer man myself. Then the afternoon sky's
prayer-gong moon and squabbling lorikeets
and the swish and rattle of the bamboo grove. . .
We are growing to this land.

Ross Clark: After one career as a state secondary school teacher, Ross now teaches part time at two Brisbane universities while writing poetry, haiku, short fiction, and works for teenagers. His most recent poetry volume is *Salt Flung into the Sky* (2007). He is the recipient of a Centenary of Federation Medal, and a Johnno Award, and some of his words may be found on plaques in the streets of Brisbane. www.crowsongs.com

Gwyn Hanssen Pigott: Potter

Still Life with Two Cups, 2005. Translucent porcelain. Photographer: Brian Hand

Photographer:
Sonia Payes

Gwyn Hanssen Pigott trained with master potters in Australia and the UK. She established studios in London and France before returning to Australia in 1972. Since 1981 she has been based in Queensland, presently near Brisbane. Her work is regularly exhibited internationally and is part of many overseas collections in Europe, USA, Japan and the UK, including the Victoria and Albert Museum in London. It is in the collections of all Australian state galleries; Parliament House, Canberra; and many regional galleries. In 2002 Gwyn was awarded an OAM. She is represented in Australia by Philip Bacon Galleries, Brisbane; Rex Irwin Art Dealer in Sydney; and Sophie Gannon Gallery in Melbourne.

Food and Wine

Katherine Hamilton – A Chocolate Factory in the Family

This is the story of my mother, Katherine Mona Hamilton nee Daveney (affectionately known as Kitty) and her factory, known as K.M. Daveney, which I'm told was Queensland's first chocolate factory.

'There were soft centres and hard, including caramels, fruit jellies, ginger and nougats, mint creams and truffles, fruit fondants and honeycomb, rose and violet creams. Skilled girls dipped the finished centres in bowls of liquid dark or milk chocolate and set them on thin metal trays to cool and set. Many of these chocolates would be "topped" by other girls, using walnuts, blanched almonds or even crystallised violets, depending on the centres. Specialty lines were also made: ornately decorated Easter eggs, and, at Christmas, chocolate-coated brandied cherries and beautifully detailed marzipan fruit.'

Born in Sydney in February 1901, Kitty was the fifth daughter in her family. Her father, an English lawyer, was none too pleased when first told he had another daughter, as he'd been hoping for a son. Those were the days when women kept having children until they succeeded in providing their husbands with a 'son and heir'. Harold, the much longed for son, was their sixth child and was forever known by the rest of the family as 'Boy'.

The family lived on the banks of Sydney Harbour, in a house called *Little Vendale*. They had a bountiful apple tree, a lawn tennis court and a jetty with a much loved little rowing boat. It was a wonderful environment for six active children; however, when they lost their father, the family found themselves in straightened circumstances. At that time an elderly French confectioner and *chocolatier* visited their mother, explaining that her husband had been his lawyer, but due to cash flow problems, he was unable to repay his debt – he wondered if he might be allowed to repay in kind. He proposed teaching all he knew of the confectioner's art to one of the family's daughters, who in turn could instruct the family if they so desired. The offer was accepted and Marjorie, the eldest child, became an eager student in the art of making chocolates.

From this humble beginning a tradition was born – the family's chocolates soon gaining a reputation as among Sydney's finest. In the late 1920s the Queensland company of Finney Isles (later taken over by the Sydney firm of David Jones) approached the family and offered to sponsor the move to Queensland, if one of the girls would set up a factory to supply them in Brisbane. Kitty had recently lost her fiancé, so she volunteered to head north. The factory, known as K.M. Daveney, began in Brisbane on the upper floor of Finney Isles' Queens Street store, but as it grew in size, Kitty moved the factory to new and larger premises of her own in Fortitude Valley.

In the Valley the chocolate factory covered the third floor of S.A. Best's building in Gipps Street, close to the Story Bridge and, in its heyday, twenty-five people worked there, mostly girls, in full white aprons with white caps to cover their hair. They worked in different areas, some preparing delicious centres which were then poured into moulds in the starch room. There were soft centres and hard, including caramels, fruit jellies, ginger and nougats, mint creams and truffles, fruit fondants and honeycomb, rose and violet creams. Chocolate was melted in large copper pots suspended over boiling water. Skilled girls dipped the finished centres in bowls of liquid dark or milk chocolate and set them on thin metal trays to cool and set. Many of these chocolates would be 'topped' by other girls, using walnuts, blanched almonds or even crystallised violets, depending on the centres. Specialty lines were also made: ornately decorated Easter eggs, and, at Christmas, chocolate-coated brandied cherries and beautifully detailed marzipan fruit.

The trays of chocolates were put briefly into large ice-chests (this was before modern refrigeration). When they'd set, these trays of chocolates were then stored on larger wooden trays which were stacked above each other for ventilation, until they were packed. Some of these chocolates were destined to be hand-wrapped in patterned gold or silver foil, and all would be placed in fluted paper cups, and packed into elegant silver or gold foil boxes, edged with delicate paper lace. The boxes, in turn, would be tied with wide white satin ribbon then wrapped in cellophane, before being stacked for collection by the customers.

The factory sold wholesale to the four largest retail stores in Brisbane of that time: Allen & Stark, T.C. Beirne, Finney Isles and McWhirters and the confectionery was all handmade to their orders. None of these firms exist today, however, as all were later taken over by two larger southern firms, David Jones and Myers.

Kitty was a beautiful woman with long black hair, fair skin and large brown eyes, but she was shy and lonely away from her large close-knit family, so it wasn't long before she agreed to marry a handsome and attentive young Scotsman, Ian Hamilton, who'd followed her from Sydney. They were married in St John's Cathedral in Ann Street.

Their first home was in Hamilton and over the next six years two children, Donald Anthony and Joan Patricia, were born at Clayfield's Turrawan Hospital (now part of Clayfield College) and baptised. In 1940, the Lady Gowrie Child Centre was opened, and by the end of that year 57 children were enrolled – one of whom was Kitty's son, my brother Don. The chocolate factory, redolent with warm, exotic aromas, was within easy walking distance and Eunice, who helped my mother to care for him, used to take Don there in the mornings to meet and play with other children.

In 1946 we moved to Japan to join our father, who'd been seconded to the occupying American forces. Gordon Horn, the factory manager, was left in charge of the day-to-day running of the factory during this time and it was nearly five years before the family returned to Australia. Back in Australia, both Don and I attended boarding school. Mother would see us off from the old Roma Street station – me to Glennie in Toowoomba and Don to Scotts College in Warwick. These were the days of steam and the different schools had their own designated carriages. The platforms were crowded with parents and children, the latter with luggage for three months at school – then tears of farewell amidst smoke and soot as the train pulled noisily away from the platform. The sight of a steam locomotive still evokes memories – often more sooty than romantic for children of the '50s!

Like many other families during and after the war, my mother lost her husband and Don and I our father. Mother buried herself in work and family responsibilities and her much loved elderly mother came to live with us, as was common in those days. Her mother's company and companionship during this time was a great comfort. Mother was a thoroughly modern woman, successfully running her own business while putting her children through private schools and maintaining her own home and garden. Life for women on their own was difficult in those days, but Mother spoke little of the problems she encountered – her ready smile and sense of humour endearing her to many.

Like most women of that era, Mother would generally phone her grocery orders through to local shopkeepers, who would later deliver to our home, but every now and then she'd visit them personally, particularly when visitors were coming and she wanted to 'see' what was on offer. If I was home from school I'd accompany her on these expeditions and the local butcher shop remains a memory from this time. The floor was covered in sawdust and a sign on the wall reminded people 'It is an offence to expectorate!' This I was told meant the customers were not to spit! The shop was full of conservatively dressed housewives waiting their turn to be served, all wearing neat hats and gloves with straight seams in their stockings, their hems well below their knees and wearing sensible shoes. Surely the butcher didn't expect any of them to spit? That sign was to remain one of the mysteries of my childhood – now both the sign and the shop have disappeared in the mists of time!

Running a factory during the week made Kitty's garden a refuge. Full of fragrant flowers that attracted native birds and butterflies, it was a constant joy to her. There she also grew the violets destined to be crystallised for topping on her chocolates. When we were young she kept chickens and a flourishing herb and vegetable garden. This was in Bardon, just six kilometres from the Brisbane CBD, yet in those days early each morning you'd hear the neighbourhood roosters crowing over their respective territories.

Mother corresponded with all her family and felt enormous pride in their achievements. Her brother Boy (Harold Daveney) became a respected engineer, the youngest employed to work on the construction of the Sydney Harbour Bridge. Her sister Mabel Lemaire's beautiful wood carvings became collectors' items. Mother's niece, Rose Campbell, the eldest daughter of her sister Muriel, wrote the life story of our grandmother, Catherine Margaret Daveney, entitled *Gold Dust and Violets*. As a child, my grandmother had been a student at the Fort Street Model School (Sydney's first school). It was my cousin Rose's book, along with interviews subsequently conducted with Mother herself, that resulted in my great-grandmother's story being inducted into the Australian Stockman's Hall of Fame in Longreach (USH-No00048 in the name of Catherine Richmond), an event which gave my mother enormous pleasure.

After leaving school my brother Don joined the Australian Estates, one of Australia's big five pastoral companies. During this time he met and married Lorne Ruhle, a pretty country girl he met in Pittsworth. They built a home in Brisbane and soon Mother's life was blessed with two little grandchildren, Lee-Anne and Tony.

From the early sixties I travelled extensively, eventually meeting and marrying Alan, an Englishman then working in the West Indies, whose address I'd been given by a friend of my brother's as 'someone I should meet if I visited the Caribbean'. On our return to London I met Roald Dahl, at the South Kensington home of Helen Alexandrou, a mutual friend, and we enjoyed an interesting evening discussing memories of the chocolate factories in our respective childhoods. Those same childhood memories were reflected in his book, *Charlie and the Chocolate Factory*.

In the 1970s, Mother delighted in visiting us in London and travelling to Europe with our children – Katherine, her namesake, and Andrew. She was thrilled to be invited one year to a garden party at Buckingham Palace, but the other visits which gave her particular pleasure were to the premises of Fortnum & Mason and Floris Chocolates near Piccadilly Circus. Their chocolates, too, were handmade and a favourite, we'd been told, of Sir Winston Churchill, among others. Mother spent several happy hours with their managers, discussing different recipes and techniques.

In Australia during the '60s and the early '70s, handmade chocolates became an expensive luxury when compared with their machine-made competition. After her four largest clients were taken over and two were subsequently closed, her business came under increasing pressure; labour intensive specialty lines had to be cut and finally she decided to close her factory.

When I returned with my family to Brisbane, Mother came to live with us in Anstead. She was now eighty. Her mind was as alert as ever, but with age she became physically frail. Over the years her brother and sisters and all her close friends had passed away and she missed them dreadfully, so I encouraged her to attend coffee mornings at the local church. Mother had always been shy and meeting new people at this late stage of her life wasn't easy, but she soon found herself looking forward to these outings. She was no longer solely dependent on her children or grandchildren for news. She had her own news to share with them and it gave her a new source of pride and independence. Her birthday parties grew and became a source of joy, not just for family, but for many of her friends who lived locally.

As her eyesight deteriorated she preferred to stay home when we went on brief holidays, so the owner of the local supermarket kindly delivered perishables while we were away. One day he arrived at her cottage and knocked, but no one answered. He called out, but still no answer. Now worried, he went inside and found Mother lying on her bed and thought she must have died. To his amazement, one leg slowly lifted and went down again and then the other. Now in her nineties, Mother was concentrating on her exercises and simply hadn't heard him. He left the groceries on her kitchen table and returned to the store, highly amused and much relieved!

Mother always wore fine lace collars and was, as our son Andrew described her, 'a pretty amazing lady'. I remember her delight when in the early nineties Cadbury's flew a staff reporter up from Melbourne to interview her for an article about her chocolate factory and her long association with their firm.

Mother had a strong sense of family and delighted in her grandchildren's achievements. Lee-Anne became a successful model, while Katherine (her namesake) became a successful interior designer with an international company in London. Her grandson Tony obtained a position in the banking industry, while Andrew gained his doctorate in the USA and accepted a position in Vancouver at the University of British Columbia. Kitty and her chocolate factory had beneficially touched all their lives. Her beloved son, my brother Don, passed away in 1996 from an aneurism and was sorely missed. Mother herself passed away two years later, at the age of 97.

(A close friend comforted me by saying, 'No one truly dies, as long as they are remembered.' Kitty, my mother, was much loved and lives on in the memory of family and friends – as does the memory of her company's French chocolates, as I'm often reminded by those who were fortunate enough to taste them.)

Murray Livingstone and Arch Martin – Fruit and Vegetable Markets

(Owners of Mister Fresh & Associates)

It's a charming street of neat houses and gardens in leafy Sherwood. A flower-edged garden path leads to the door where I am welcomed by Beryl, Murray's wife, who shows the way to the living room. Beryl sits quietly on the sofa, while Murray and Arch sit opposite each other with their guest in the middle. Arch looks rather reserved, but Murray's eyes are twinkling. He obviously intends this to be fun – and it is!

'The cool stores that the products were kept in were sealed and bolted into the concrete floor, but the air pressure inside them was building up and during the flood they used to go off like rockets – right through the roof of the market! After the flood went down, the water that had built up underneath the tarmac came up like Mount Vesuvius and spewed into the air!'

Murray: My father and my grandfather were marketers and growers. Arch's business and our business in the Turbot Street market were next door to each other and we were highly competitive. Yet we had a sort of camaraderie that isn't found today – or am I wrong, Arch?

Arch: I suppose you could say that, Murray. The further you move away from the action the less you have that camaraderie. Certainly it's a different atmosphere in the new wide open market that we have now, than when the market was in those old buildings in town.

There was a big market in Roma Street and the Board of the Brisbane Fruit and Produce Exchange, as it was known, which was in Turbot Street. Most of the action was inside that building. There were about 8 or 10 businesses that had frontages in Turbot Street, and we had one of them, but our main business was inside the Exchange.

It was all very restricted, and closed in. But in those days all the trucks were little. Most of the fruiterers had only 1 to 3 tonners, so they all fitted in. This was one of the reasons why the markets eventually had to move out to Rocklea. The trucks and the transportation system had grown to such an extent there was no room for the semi-trailers to get in or out.

We had to pick up rail deliveries, consignments from 'Roma Street Goods Yards', as they were known then, and from South Brisbane Interstate Goods Yards too. We did a lot of pickups from the wharves, because we had regular ships that came from Tasmania.

Murray: Archie and I used to wait for those boats to come in.

Archie: They'd come in every fortnight.

Murray: Just like a train!

Arch: As soon as they heard that the boat was coming, the wharf would ring up and say, 'The boat's docked!' Then every truck around the place went straight to the wharf. Some of the fellows got up to a few pranks. One bloke used to go around putting grease on the steering wheels of the other competitors' trucks so that when they got in to try and drive them they couldn't! If you got to the wharf late you were in BIG trouble!

The Turbot Street market was also known as the 'bottom' market and from there we handled the majority of that stuff from Tasmania, and in fact sold a lot of it to the merchants in the Roma Street market.

Murray: That's how the Roma Street market really got going, from a relatively overgrown farmers' market, into a traders' market. They used to buy product in Turbot Street that they didn't have access to, like Tasmanian apples, and sell them in Roma Street.

Murray: It made the facilities able to cope for longer for the amount of trade that was being done. Otherwise we would have had to move from town to the sticks long before. Still, looking back, there were lots of funny incidents in those days…

Arch: Yes, the shop fronts had grills and people would throw fruit at each other and at the grills! One bloke specialised in potatoes, but most of them were soft fruit – as soft as possible!

Murray: When they hit, they would explode and it would go all over everybody! And we all had a pretty good idea who threw what!

The people in the markets in those days were from a generation that started work in the Depression. It was like the railways, the same people following the same trade, generation after generation. They were always considered 'below' most other people in the community – and that's not true, not true at all, but people at large would believe that and even today would look down on people who work in the markets.

Arch: Very definitely. It still applies, but it was more so forty years ago.

Murray: Yes, because everybody was scrounging for a living. Nothing moved in the market if you didn't have it on your shoulder or in your arms or on a two-wheel wheelbarrow.

Arch: There were no forklifts before the market moved from Roma Street – there might have been one, but we didn't use pallets in those days. They started here at Rocklea.

Murray: My grandfather was a local grower in Queensland, mostly vegetables, but types of fruit too. The next generation there were only two boys, one that was ill at the time. They carried on the business, exactly the same.

Arch: Yes, our grandfathers. Well, they built it, you see. They had a shop in George Street, opposite McKenzie's – you remember McKenzie's shoe shop? It was on the corner of George and Herschel, around where the old National Bank used to be.

Murray: Yes, McKenzie's was well known! It was run by a father and son and they had a very strong connection with the market people. It was their business and they were so faithful to their customers that if they saw you walking down George Street at any time, they'd rush out and give your shoes a polish. When the market moved to Rocklea they followed, but in the 1974 flood their business was completely destroyed.

Archie: Dad was on the board of the Fruit and Produce Exchange. He used to wear a waistcoat, always.

Murray: So did mine.

Arch: Yes, yours did too. They didn't wear a three-piece suit, though. It was too hot.

Murray: He always wore a hat and a waistcoat!

Arch: By the time the move to the new markets in Rocklea came, we were just so pleased to get out from Turbot Street. Murray and I, some days we'd get a call at midnight to come in to unload the semi-trailers, because you couldn't cope with them otherwise and a couple of times I worked all night and the next day. We were working at least from two o'clock in the morning 'til four in the afternoon in those days, so we were just…

Murray: Killing ourselves!

Arch: Yes, it was terrible. We were in our prime then – in our thirties, but it was tough, really tough. In the end we were just pleased to get out – it didn't matter where. Anything was going to be better. In Roma Street and Turbot Street buyers could walk in at two in the morning, demanding to be served, and you couldn't do anything about it. So when we went to Rocklea, the first thing we did was build a fence around it. The retailers all said, 'We're not going to put up with this. We'll push a truck straight through that gate on the first morning,' but then they realised they could sleep in longer. That changed everything.

Murray: Within a month or so it all settled down. That was in 1964.

Murray: In the early morning of the Saturday of the long weekend of January 1974, I got a ring here at home from a bloke in the market who said, 'You'd better get across to the market. It's flooding!' When we got to the back gate, it was under water and this fellow was coming along with a boat. We got into that and sailed over the top of the market fence, into the market proper. There were all the vehicles, fork-lifts, trucks and everything else, and people's businesses, their records, their stock, all under water.

Arch: Yes, twelve-foot under water!

Murray: I believe it can happen again! But those are the sorts of things that people forget. The city didn't have any fresh fruit for the best part of a week and we began to see some profiteering starting. So the market people got together and said, 'Right-ho, let's use Moolabin railyards,' which were above flood level. Everybody pooled their supplies, and it worked perfectly. It filled a whole week of supply to Brisbane, and cut out all the shenanigans that were going on.

Arch: There was a pallet sitting on top of one of those telephone poles in Sherwood Road after the flood went down – that's how high it was. When you go down Sherwood Road past the motors on the left and you cross the bridge, as you come along, the first telephone pole had a pallet on the top of it for ages!

Murray: Yes, for ages, and there was a live pig on the awning of the commercial centre out the front after the flood went down. We saw things that we never imagined could happen and there are people outside who haven't got the slightest idea that it could happen again. The cool stores that the products were kept in were sealed and bolted into the concrete floor, but the air-pressure inside them was building up and during the flood they used to go off like rockets – right through the roof of the market! After the flood went down, the water that had built up underneath the tarmac came up like Mount Vesuvius and spewed into the air!

Arch: There was no power into the market, but everybody had a phone. The PMG, as it then was, hooked up one line into each business.

Murray: Most people couldn't get into the market when the flood was on, so they came back after and one fellow walked in and his whole office had been tipped outside on the floor, and all his stock was gone. He walked around for a minute and put his hand to his head and said, 'Only one good thing that's happened about this is all our records for the last forty years have been washed away!'

Arch: He saw the funny side of that all right, didn't he?

Murray: He made use of it too!

Murray: Thinking back to the old markets again, some of the best characters were the barrowmen. We had three barrowmen on Turbot Street and George Street corners. The barrowmen used to come to the market to see what was plentiful for the day. It might be say, beans, so they'd buy enough beans to fill the barrow and sell them all before tea time. They could short-change you and you wouldn't know anything about it. The only way to do it was when they counted the change back into your hand, you'd tip it back into their hand and say, 'Now count it back to me!'

Arch: I remember, in those days, on the trams – it was only tuppence to the Valley. One section for tuppence and four pence to town!

Murray: That's right, and five pence from Moorooka to the other terminus on the other side of town.

Arch: I didn't go to Cloudland. Did you?

Murray: I did, but I didn't meet my wife there – we met in the National Bank in Queen Street. Actually, what happened was that I knew Beryl before the war and I went away overseas and I met her cousin in the same air crew in Ceylon and when I was coming home he said to me, 'Say g'day to my cousin Beryl' – so when I came back I said, 'G'day,' and from then on it just grew! *(a smile is exchanged between he and Beryl)*

Arch: (laughing) She put the handcuffs on him!
   Actually I met my wife Betty at the Presbyterian Church in Toowong.

Murray: (with his eyes twinkling) Now look at us: broken down, old-fashioned.

Arch: (to laughter all round) Rubbish – absolute rubbish!

Vince De Pasquale – Nanda Pasta
'The Australian company that sells spaghetti to Italy'

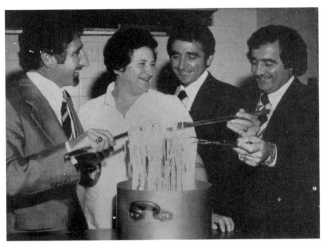

There's a neat rose garden in front of the Spring Hill office where we meet. The walls and desk of his office display photos of family and business achievements and Vince speaks about both with obvious pride. It's clear that although he enjoys being, as he says, 'an Italo-Australian', he also enjoys the old Italian traditions.

De Pasquale brothers: Ralph, Vince and Victor, with the cook

'You hear this noise and laughter we're making? We're bottling this year's wine!'

The company was founded round about 1947 or 1948. Dad was born in Sicily and I and my two brothers were born in Sydney. Dad was approached by three or four of his friends about the possibility of starting a pasta factory. Dad was always a believer that if you're ever going to do anything you should get the right ingredients. The principal ingredient of pasta is semolina, which is the crushed heart of the wheat, so he put the factory in Brisbane, because it's not too far from Toowoomba on the Darling Downs, which is where the hardest grain wheat in the world comes from.

Dad came out to Australia in 1927. He told his father, my grandfather, 'I'm going to go to Australia.' His dad said, 'Oh yeah, that's good,' because he misunderstood it. He'd never heard of Australia. He thought that Dad was saying Austria, which was just up the road! Dad's father in Sicily was a merchant, (they used to sell tomatoes and olive oil and so forth) and Dad thought, 'Well, maybe there's a market for those things here in Australia,' so he brought some tinned tomatoes and olive oil out here with him. In those days olive oil in Australia was only available in the chemists, because it was treated more as a medicine. He also brought out with him nearly one ton of spaghetti! It took him twelve months to sell that in Australia – pasta wasn't a very well known product in Australia in those days – people used to put just canned spaghetti on toast.

There were five partners originally in Nanda Pasta and they came to Queensland and established the factory at Northgate, Brisbane. Northgate is near the suburb of Nundah, but Northgate was small then and not as well known as Nundah, so they'd agreed that seeing it was near Nundah they would call it 'Nundah Macaroni Products'. When Dad went to register the company and the business name, they gave Dad a form to fill out. Dad's English was limited, so he said to the official, 'Well look, you fill out the form.' The official started filling out the form and said, 'All right, Mr De Pasquale, what do you want to call it?' Dad said, 'We'll call it Nundah Macaroni Products.' She said, 'How do you spell Nundah?' If you say the name of the suburb Nundah with normal Australian pronunciation, but then spell it in Italian it becomes Nanda – so out of a very innocent phonetic spelling mistake, the name of our company was born as 'Nanda Macaroni Products'! We started from there and eventually the De Pasquale family bought out the other partners.

Anyway, getting back to the story, there was a great migration round about 1950/51 of migrants from Italy into Australia. Most settled in Victoria and New South Wales – Queensland is the least populated Italian migrant state. So obviously there were a lot of continental delicatessens down south and we went direct, selling our pasta to them. We used to send semi-trailer loads to Sydney and Melbourne and the business grew and grew with the Italian community, but other Australians still did not buy it. It was the same in New Zealand. I remember when we went over there one time, seeing the spaghetti in the shop kept near the dog food! There had to be a real education for the pasta.

It used to be same with calamari here – in the old days it was used for bait! The same we used to say 'cannelloni' and 'fettuccine' to people and they'd probably think we were talking about some Italian grand opera or the name of an Italian composer, but now eating pasta is very trendy and calamari too. Sure, I think the migrant population has made a big difference to the Australian way of life and our eating habits. In my own lifetime – I was born in 1937 – and I've seen a tremendous change in our eating habits. It's been great.

Mama Luigi was here in Brisbane during the '50s, but the Americans had actually made her famous during the war. She was a real Italian mama that brought to the table for the public real Italian cuisine. Spaghetti was always there; it would either be spaghetti and chicken or spaghetti and schnitzels, put on the table there in the real old-fashioned way of cooking. It was as though you were eating at home in her kitchen. She became very famous. She would have to be credited with giving the real taste of pasta to a lot of people who had never eaten pasta before.

The company grew and our production with it. We were manufacturing 300 to 400 tons per week, working twenty-four hours a day, seven days a week. All the family was involved. My father was the managing director, then there was my older brother Ralph, myself and my younger brother Victor. There's three years and ten months between the three of us, so we all worked very, very closely together. In the early 1960s Dad went into semi-retirement. Me and my brothers, we carried on the business and grew it. We had offices and warehouses all throughout Australia and New Zealand. We exported to 36 countries throughout the world.

We exported our pasta to Italy. A lot of people, they think that's just a story, but in fact it's a true story. We did export our products to Italy. I remember my elder brother

Ralph and me in 1968 or 1969, we went to Milano and we brought samples of our products there to a wholesaler who took us to a restaurant called *Restaurante de Riccone*. We showed them our pasta and said, 'We'll have this pasta,' and they said, 'Will it take four or five minutes to cook?' and we said, 'No, you'll have to cook it for twelve to fifteen minutes.' They said, 'No pasta cooks for twelve or fifteen minutes.' I said, 'Well, this one does.' The chef came in and said, 'This is pasta that we've never ever seen before in our lives.' It was great and it all started from there!

We won worldwide acclaim for our quality. We won fairs in East Germany in Cologne for two or three years in a row. There came the great saying in our advertising, 'The Australian company that sells spaghetti to Italy.' I think we've still got the bills of lading, the name of the ships and everything. It was very interesting and it was a very, very proud moment for us to be able to say, 'Well, you can go to Italy and eat pasta – and you can go to Australia and still eat the best pasta in the world.'

The pasta business was very kind to us. Finally in 1999 we sold to Nestle – but I don't want to go into that story, because what happened to it afterwards was too disappointing.

Most Australian capital cities, like Melbourne and Sydney, had great Italian communities and they were building their own clubs. The consul here approached us and spoke to my brother Ralph and said, 'Look, we'd really like to have an Italian club here in Brisbane.' The first approach, I think, was made in 1968 or 1969. My brother said OK and he was elected the first president. We did it a little bit different, because we said, 'We don't want to call it the Italian Club, because, after all, we're not Italians. We're proud to be of Italian origin, but we are Italo-Australians and we would like to call it the Italo–Australian Club, not the Italian Club. We are Australians and we want Australians to enjoy the benefits of the Italian community – so they agreed and it was called the Italo–Australian Centre. It was finally built in 1970. It's a very successful club. Actually, one time I think it was the most successful and popular club in Brisbane. I can remember when we first built it. Our company Nanda donated the bar and it was called 'the Nanda Bar' – you couldn't eat spaghetti at the bar, but you could drink a lot of Italian wines!

It's an Italian tradition to make your own wines, and bottle your own tomatoes for your own tomato sauce, do your own pickling, whether it's chillies or capsicums or eggplants. A lot of the traditions of Italo-Australians are preserved more here in Australia than they are in Italy. We're still making our wine now in our generation! I've just recently had cousins that come out from Italy and they just could not get over it. They said, 'Oh, I think I can remember my grandfather used to make his own wine.' I'm sure that happens not only with the Italians. I'm sure it also happens with all the other ethnic communities and their traditions.

We normally make Shiraz. We use the Shiraz grape and we make a blend of Shiraz Cabernet, a Grenache Cabernet – always red wines because we believe wine should be red! It's very interesting, there's a club called the Abruzzo Club, which is another club in Brisbane. (Abruzzo is an area in Italy. It's on the coast south-east of Rome.) Anyway, the Abruzzo Club has competitions in the wines we've made. One of the guys is with us and we make our own wine, so we enter our own wine and I think the last three or four years our wine has been the top wine. We're expecting a phone call from Mr Penfold any day!

Dad, he was a proud man and was very proud to have us in the organisation working, and in the latter years he used to come in to the factory in the morning and have a cup of coffee with us about ten o'clock and then go home, and then he'd come in, in the afternoon at three o'clock and have a cup of tea with us and go home again. We had roses in the front of our offices and no one was allowed to touch those roses except him. Dad always used to have the front office, regardless of whether he was there or he wasn't there. Everyone always respected him as the elder and so forth. He was in the garden one day, pruning, with his hat and his work clothes, and a guy from some company came in and he says, 'Listen, I want to speak to the boss. Where do I go and speak to the boss?' Dad says to him, 'What boss do you want to speak to?' 'Well,' he says, 'I want to speak to the big boss; the real boss,' and Dad says, 'OK. Well, you go in the reception and you sit down and wait. He'll come out and see you.' So Dad finished off his job cleaning the roses, went round the back, changed and came up to this man and says, 'Well, how can I help you?' This fellow nearly fell over!

We met our wives here in Australia. My wife is of Italian origin, like me. Italo-Australian and we met here in Brisbane and were married in 1962. I met my wife at an Italian Christmas function dance, and we started dancing and danced the night away together. That was the 24 December 1961. My dad and mum were married on 29 January 1936. I came back from New Zealand and it was my dad and mum's 25th wedding anniversary and we'd organised a big function. I'd asked my wife Ann to come. She wasn't my wife then, and we were married on 28 January the following year.

We have three sons, Franco, Marco and Gino. Franco's my eldest son. He's a lawyer, and my other two boys have Bachelor of Business degrees. Franco is now managing director of a company that we've got called National Childcare, so he's running that. My other two boys are in the advertising business, De Pasquale Advertising. Even with my elder brother, the three of us are still in business together. We've always been in business together, for as long as I can remember. My eldest brother's son Tony looks after the operations section of our childcare centre with my son Franco. So we've got him here in the business too. Another of Ralph's sons, Sandro, works out of the Sydney office. So all the families, we still work in together.

Cos Zantiotis – Samios Wholesale & Retail Delicatessen

Samios must have one of the busiest little car parks in Brisbane, with private cars and shop vans all trying to get in and out at once. The buzz of conversation inside the shop alternates between English and Greek. An abundance of large cheeses and salamis are

displayed behind the counter, along with huge containers of olives. Other shelves are packed with bottles and tins from every corner of the globe. As well as supplying locals, they wholesale to other delicatessens and also export. Cos's mother is in the front office and shows the way to Cos's office. He took over management of the business after his father died, but this is a family concern and his mother and brothers, Theo and Tony, are all involved.

'... they can smell the smells of Europe, the cheeses and the other deli lines ... Every day, the mums and dads, they walk through the door and take a big breath and they say, "This just smells fantastic!" Then the kids come in after them and go, "Phew, it stinks in here, Mum!" Ten years later, those same kids are bringing their own children in here and the same thing is happening to them.'

The Samios deli business was started by my father's uncle, the late Peter Samios, who came out to Australia from Greece in the early 1920s. They came from the island of Kythira, where our family originated. We think he started the business around 1924, but it's been a registered business since 1934. He sponsored my father to come out here to live in Australia.

My mum and my brother Tony are in the business with me and my sister worked in it for a time, doing the books when we were in Charlotte Street, and my other two brothers, Spiro and Theo, also worked here.

My dad's uncle passed away in the early 1970s and left the business to my dad and his brother. Then Dad's brother Peter passed away around 1982 and Dad ran the business from that point on himself. I came into the business around 1987 or 1988. I'd moved to the Gold Coast and I did my own thing for twenty-odd years, before I came into this business. Dad was very happy to have me come back here. Sometimes ethnic families are a bit stern and you can grow a bit apart because you hate being told what to do all the time.

Originally the business was in Charlotte Street in the cellar underneath the old Greek Club, which was behind the Greek Orthodox Church of St George in the city. The Greek Club and the church have just celebrated their 75th birthday. We're involved with the Greek Festival in Brisbane occasionally and we're very involved with the Greek Festival on the Gold Coast – that's where I live now. We're getting hassled to open a Samios on the Gold Coast and I'm very keen to do that.

In those early days just before the war, migrants were really only Italians and Greeks. Out on the cane farms in North Queensland and Northern New South Wales, basically in a lot of those ethnic communities, they were running traditional cafes, not delis as such. They were selling the malted milkshakes and the steak and eggs and three veggies. At that time Samios were supplying those people with their necessities, which included some of the Greek wines. We were the only ones who could get them; you couldn't buy them in Australia. Times progressed and those people grew older and their children started growing up. The parents worked hard and put their kids through the best boarding schools and sent them off to the best unis and those kids became lawyers and doctors. They weren't interested in cooking steak and eggs in the family café. So a lot of those cafés in Ingham and those sorts of places slowly started to disappear and, as a result, so did our business up there. So we centralised back into Brisbane, catering for the Greeks who had come here to live and work in the city.

Once the Greek Club and the church decided to sell in the city and move to West End, we moved out here to Woolloongabba – that was about thirty-five years ago now, just after the Brisbane floods in 1974, because the cellar where we were in the city went under during that time.

Over the years we've added about an extra 3,000 lines. When people can't find something anywhere else they know that nine times out of ten they'll get it here. Basically our business is split into three parts: one third retail; another third wholesale, supplying other delis and restaurants and cafés; the other third is export. We export fish eggs to Japan. These are from the mullet, or, as they call it in Japan, *karasumi*, which we dry and smoke. I like to think it's a way of repaying for some of the imported stuff we sell – it balances it up a bit!

People's tastes have changed over the years and so has our business. It's not just ethnic customers anymore; we're attracting more and more Australians. People are buying their focaccias and trying the sun-dried tomatoes with a few olives, and their *melanzane* (eggplant) and haloumi, which they fry on the barbecues with their eggplants and stuff. What we've been selling for seventy years has now become trendy. Five or ten years ago we sold hardly any haloumi cheese and now it's very popular with everybody – and that's a very specialised Greek Cypriot kind of line. It's a fried cheese, basically. Our deli trade is getting busier as our Mediterranean-style foods become more popular. People are eating more and more legumes because they realise it's good for their cholesterol. There's less dairy in what we sell because they don't have cows in Greece. It's mainly sheep's and goats' products. Basically we buy in bulk and package everything down so we can offer value for money. We also sell quite a few religious items in here which you wouldn't think you'd sell in a deli, but dealing with the Greeks, they're looking for their little icons. My dad used to tell me it wasn't how we sold, but how we bought, and that's a pretty good adage for most people in business. It's how we buy products where we make our money. We've got a good list of people we've dealt with, some for over thirty, forty or even fifty years.

Two of the ladies have been here since we moved to Woolloongabba, so that's thirty-five years each. They treat the business as their own and I like to think we look after them like they're our own family too. We all laugh together and we all cry together. They know the product, too, so if someone comes in off the street and wants to ask about this or that, nine times out of ten they can tell people what they want to know. They're a fantastic asset for our business.

As a business we're over seventy years old now – we're probably the oldest deli that's running in Australia at the moment under one family, and probably under one roof, for that matter. We can say we're old, but we can also say Samios is about the smell – they can smell the smells of Europe, the cheeses and the other deli lines, not just disinfectant on the floor that you get in other stores. Having said that, it's very clean in here, our ladies treat it like their own house. Every day, the mums and dads, they walk through the door and take a big breath and they say, 'This just smells fantastic!' Then the kids come in after them and go, 'Phew, it stinks in here, Mum'! Ten years later, those same kids are bringing their own children in here and the same thing is happening to them. I always find that quite amusing.

Things are changing again now. Organics are becoming very popular. Not necessarily with the Greeks or Italians, they're set on what they like to eat, but with Australians generally. Greek farmers don't use a lot of chemicals anyway. Some of the bigger olive plantations on the mainland would be looked after that way, but the stuff from the islands is very traditional, grown on terraces. Even in our own family with the property we have on the island, it's specified in our inheritance that there are four olive trees on this block of land. It's very important to the Greeks that they own four olive trees. Fifty years ago, that was their supply of olives and oil for the year.

With our own island, Kythira, before the war, there were up to 30,000 people living on that island. Now, seventy years later, there are less than 5,000 permanent residents there. Most of those people either went to the United States or Australia. Now, when we go there, most of the old villages are deserted, the houses are collapsing, the rock walls are falling over. Because of the Greek way of inheritance, it's cheaper for the families to accept an inheritance as a family rather than an individual. What happens is that the owner passes away and they leave their inheritance to their family, so instead of one block being left to you, for instance, it can be left to seventy people. That in itself is creating a problem in Greece at the moment. You try and get seventy people to agree on something! I think that will change. They're talking about bringing in a rates structure and, if rates aren't paid, then they'll take the property back and sell it to someone who is going to do something with it. That should make a difference.

There are other differences between our lucky country in Australia and what's going on in Greece. The Greeks in Greece reckon we're the best Greeks, because we keep the culture, whereas the Greeks over there are very blasé and couldn't care less about their heritage. The Greeks that live here really care about their place over there, and the dreams they have about the Greek Islands and stuff. Although I have strong connections to Greece, I don't speak Greek, which is probably one of my only regrets.

My mum's Australian and she speaks a bit of Greek, but we never spoke any Greek in our house. My wife is Scottish ancestry. We're like a story out of the *My Big Fat Greek Wedding*. My kids are going to Greek school and hate it, but I keep telling them they need to go there to learn. This year I took my son Ziggy to Greece for the first time – I told him he'd got to speak some Greek while he was over there and play with the other kids. My daughter Madeline's done that the last couple of years and has had an absolute riot. I was sitting on the balcony there, watching them play with the kids in the street and, when they came up, I asked if they were speaking Greek and Madeline told me Ziggy was teaching them to swear in English – they had mates for the whole holiday! But they learned a lot and had an absolute ball.

Since going to the Coast I've had a heavy involvement with touch football. I started a club and I'm lucky enough to have football fields named after me down there. My dad did a lot of that kind of thing with soccer. I guess I followed what he was doing without consciously going out to do it. For me there's more to life than just work. We work hard and we work fairly long hours, but I like to think that when I get in my car to go home, that's the end of work for me until I get here the next day. I never take my work home. I've got other interests there, my children and my family, and I still put in time with my football club – that's my other love in life.

John Robinson – Robinson's Family Wines

He's a multi-talented individual, having combined business as a successful vintner with his work as a solicitor in a busy legal practice. He's had a rich and varied life, he tells me, his smile reflecting fondness and pride as he points to family members' photographs. He talks of their vineyard near the town of Ballandean...

Heather and John Robinson being given an award at the Queensland Wine Press Club 2005

'... my son Craig has researched the Granite Belt climate of Ballandean and has found that during the ripening months of January, February and March, it is climatically the same as Margaret River in Western Australia and – this may surprise you – it's the same as in Bordeaux in France during the ripening months of July, August and September in the northern hemisphere.'

I developed a passion for wine during my stay in France in 1964 and 1965 when I tasted the perfumed *Fleurie* of Beaujolais and the soft, seductive Pinot Noir red wines from Beaune in Burgundy. After my return to Toowoomba, I practised law and rekindled my interest in wine by joining the Toowoomba Beefsteak and Burgundy Club, where I learned about the wines of Australia in blind tastings with a small group of friends.

I met my wife to be, Heather Salter, at the St Vincent's hospital rodeo ball in Toowoomba. She told me that her family had previously owned Saltrams Winery in the Barossa Valley in South Australia. Saltrams was founded in 1859 and had a great reputation for its wine. I told her about my stay at Lyon in France when I taught English during the week and on weekends spent time skiing in the French Alps and visiting vineyards in Beaujolais. One thing led to another and we were married in 1968. At our wedding reception the only wines served were Saltrams wines – Saltrams Vintage Brut Champagne, Saltrams Chardonnay, Saltrams Mamre Brook Shiraz and Cabernet Sauvignon. It was the wedding feast of Cana all over again – a great wedding – the best I've ever attended. Our honeymoon was one big wine crawl from the Hunter Valley in New South Wales to Rutherglen and Milawa in Victoria.

The idea to grow grapes and make wine, as a hobby, grew over the next year and I looked at land to buy in Toowoomba, at Warwick and at Ballandean on the Granite Belt of Queensland. The Granite Belt is an extension of the New England Tableland into Queensland. It's a cool region and snow occasionally falls there in winter. On the advice of Dick De Luca, I bought land at Ballandean from Jack McMeniman. Dick told me that Ballandean had a climate that was generally unaffected by cyclonic weather and was a cool region well suited to quality grape production.

After I bought our Ballandean property at Lyra, I realised I had a major problem, for though the best vineyards on the Granite Belt were situated at Ballandean, they were planted with table grapes, not wine grapes. Where was I going to source my vines and what varieties was I going to plant?

Dick solved that problem for me when he provided me with Shiraz cuttings from a small plot of vines he had growing on his property. This was in 1969. A noted wine authority from Victoria told us later on that these Shiraz vines were some of the best Shiraz virus-free vine material in Australia. More important to me was that the fruit flavour of the grapes from these vines was absolutely magnificent.

Establishing the vineyard was not easy. It wasn't just a case of clearing the land of trees, ploughing the ground, planting the vines, establishing the trellising and spraying the vines with the right fungicides. You also had to keep the rabbits, kangaroos and wild pigs out of the vineyard. This meant you had to build a six foot high fence around the land to be planted.

Heather helped as best she could, but she was somewhat restricted as she had given birth to Ken. Brett was born in 1970, to be followed not long after by Craig. Heather gives credit to the exercise she had in digging the rabbit netting fence along our property boundary as the reason she never had any difficulty in labour when giving birth to our son Brett!

In 1971 I spent a week with Max Lake at his Lakes Folly winery in the Hunter Valley where I gained some insight into what was involved in winemaking. John Beeston, the noted wine writer, was there as well and Len Evans was a frequent caller, and at the end of the week we tasted Max's Chardonnay and Cabernet Sauvignon wines.

I realised then that expertise was needed to make good wine, so I enrolled as a student at the Riverina College of Advanced Education at Wagga Wagga – later to become Charles Sturt University – under Brian Croser of Petaluma fame, and Tony Jordan, who went on to run Domaine Chandon in Victoria's Yarra Valley.

In 1974 I made my first wine out of Shiraz, which I labelled *The Family*. I thought this was fitting as Heather and our children were all there when it was made and bottled. As there were little or no Cabernet Sauvignon, Pinot Noir or Chardonnay vines in Queensland, we had to make representations to the Queensland Primary Industries Quarantine Department to introduce them into Queensland. With grapes produced from these introduced varieties, I was finally able to make wine from all the best wine varieties.

In 1975 I blended Shiraz, Cabernet Sauvignon and Pinot Noir grapes together and made a wine which I entered in the Brisbane Royal National Wine Show. Surprisingly, it won a gold medal. I was as stunned as were the interstate wine judges. It contained more Shiraz than Cabernet or Pinot. It had a minty character with a fleshy Pinot mid palate and a long finish from the Cabernet Sauvignon. It was really a lovely wine.

Again in 1976, I put what I learnt at Riverina College, now Charles Sturt University, to good use at the Stanthorpe Wine Show by barrel fermenting a Chardonnay, and won a gold medal. What gave me a lot of satisfaction about winning this award was that Doug Seabrook, the noted wine judge and wine merchant from Seabrooks in Melbourne, told me he was surprised by its quality.

Winning these awards gave me a lot of pleasure, as it proved to me that the Granite Belt could make wine equal to the best wines that could be made in South Australia, Victoria, New South Wales and Western Australia.

In 1979 we built the winery as it now stands. The locals called it the Taj Mahal. I am told that the building is a visible landmark for the RAAF on flights from Queensland into New South Wales. It has magnificent views of the Ballandean valley and township and the mountains to the east. The winery contains a lot of ideas I developed from my visits to wineries in Australia and overseas. We have refrigeration to most of the tanks and one third of the building is insulated and used for barrel storage. A stainless steel crusher/destemmer and a semi-automatic Wilmes airbag press enabled us to produce quality free-run juice. Though we can crush up to 80 tons of grapes, our crush has never exceeded 40 tons. We are, what you would call, a boutique winery.

We made some very good red wine between 1980 and 1986. In 1981 *The Australian* newspaper judged our Shiraz Cabernet as one of the eleven best Shiraz Cabernets in Australia. We did well with our 1980, 1982 and 1983 vintages, getting gold medals and trophies in wine shows in most of those years.

In the 1980s, Heather and I made the decision to devote more time to our family and to participate in their activities: rugby union, soccer, basketball and swimming. We had what we called a 'Hoon Van' and Heather seemed to be the bus driver for the boys and all their mates to all their sporting activities. Anne was just one of the boys and had to learn how to play touch football and to stand up to her brothers on the basketball court. Craig captained Queensland in one of the age groups in basketball while Anne represented the state as a breaststroke swimmer. Brett, at Downlands College, and Ken, at Marist College, Ashgrove, faced each other in the front row of their first-fifteen sides. Brett tackled Ken, and then helped Ken to his feet. There was no dirty play in that game. It was probably one of the cleanest games of rugby I've seen.

Heather and I had travelled overseas in 1975 and visited all the major European vineyard regions. It was a great holiday and it turned out to be a catalyst· for our making sparkling wine in 1988.

Rather than have the wines suffer from lack of attention, we employed·Rod Macpherson and Phillipa Hambledon as winemakers. I had long discussions with Rod and Phillipa as to how the base wine should be made and in particular the need to use little or no sulphur in it before secondary fermentation took place in the bottle.

The 1988 vintage brut sparkling wine, made using traditional French *methode champenoise* technology, was a real success. We won the trophy for the best sparkling wine at Griffith in New South Wales against all other wineries in Australia and since then have had continuing success with our vintage brut at the Royal National Show in Brisbane.

Robinsons Family Wines are now being made by my son Craig. Craig has researched the Granite Belt climate of Ballandean and has found that during the ripening months of January, February and March, it is climatically the same as Margaret River in Western Australia and – this may surprise you – it's the same as in Bordeaux in France during the ripening months of July, August and September in the northern hemisphere.

Craig studied oenology at Charles Sturt University and was able to find employment at Houghton's Wines in Western Australia, where he gained valuable white wine experience. He followed this by working for Hardy's in South Australia at Padtheway and Reynella. BRL Hardy red wines are regarded as some of the best red wines made in Australia and the knowledge that Craig gained from working with Hardy's red and white winemakers has been invaluable to Robinsons. He has an excellent wine palate and has been an assistant wine judge at many wine shows. Craig lives and breathes winemaking and I believe him to be one of Australia's best winemakers.

My daughter Anne has completed a course in viticulture and generally handles marketing and promotion for the winery. She was winemaker in 1999 with Craig telling her what to do by telephone. They obviously combined well together as the1999 Cabernet was regarded as one of the best Granite Belt wines made in Queensland that year.

Recently we have had the *Courier-Mail* include Robinsons Family Chardonnay 2005 Vintage in the list of Queensland's Top 20 Wines in the 2008 *Queensland Food and Wine Guide.* James Halliday, the noted wine writer, in his 2007 and 2008 *Australian Wine Compendium*, rated our winery fourth out of five, and in 2005 John and Heather Robinson received the award from the Queensland Wine Press Club for the most significant contribution by an individual to the wine industry in Queensland.

Heather and I get a lot of satisfaction from having Craig and Anne carrying on doing what we both started. They work well together at the winery, because it is what they both want to do and they take pride in it.

Ken, Brett and Mark are all now working in other fields. Ken is a software engineer with a degree in Information Technology and Law. Mark has a degree in Human Movements and has just graduated as a doctor. Brett has a PhD in Clinical Surgery from Oxford, has captained the ACT Brumbies and played rugby for Australia. He is presently the Queensland manager for one of Australia's largest insurance companies. Ken and Brett also have six healthy children between them.

My wife Heather has always been at my side supporting me and our family and encouraging me in all my endeavours. Even though we've made some nice wine, I really think that having the children we have is the high point in both our lives. Our family is close-knit and, I am pleased to say, caring of each other. Perhaps working together at the winery was a factor in this happening.

Farming with a Difference

David Elliott – Grazier and Dinosaur Hunter

He and his wife Judy were flying down to Brisbane with their children for an award ceremony at the Queensland Museum, so we agreed to meet over dinner that evening. My first impression of David was of an open, sunny smile and the firm handshake of a countryman – I noticed too the small insignia of a dinosaur on the pocket of his denim shirt...

'I was watching these blokes when they came in to see what their reaction was when they first saw it. I remember they walked in there and they just stood there and Alex Cook's jaw nearly hit the floor and Joanne Wilkinson was there and she just stood there, her eyes like saucers and she said, "Wow!" No one else said a word. Then they all started talking at once, they got so excited. So that was it – it was the biggest dinosaur ... found in Australia.'

My ancestors, the Elliotts, came to Australia in 1838 from the United Kingdom. My great grandfather was the first Elliott to come to Queensland. He was a bullocky and he moved up to Queensland in the late 1800s carting materials for the railway that was being built west of Rockhampton, and he followed the railway out. My grandfather was actually born under one of the bullock wagons on the way out to Winton, and my father was born in Winton, and, though I was born in Brisbane, my family's been living in Winton for over a hundred years.

Dad was always picking stuff up. He was interested in everything to do with nature and geology and stuff like that. There'd be rocks in the shed, there'd be rocks in the bathroom and Mum used to find them all the time in the washing machine and she was always going crook 'cause there'd be another rock jammed up in one of the washing machine hoses.

As kids we grew up like Dad: we liked to look at things and pick them up. If you didn't know what it was, you had to go and find out. I was only seventeen years old when Dad died. He'd only been crook for a couple of months before he died and losing Dad was probably the biggest blow I've ever had in my life. I'd just left school and come back onto the property to work with him and was really getting to know him as an adult. My uncle Harry came and stayed for two years and helped us run the property and got me started 'til my brother got through pastoral college and then we were on our own. They were the two most important men in my life, Dad and Uncle Harry, and I named both my sons after them, Bob and Harry.

Ten years later, in 1984, we bought Belmont and I came to live here on my own. My brother Ian – he was always called Joe – he stayed on the family property. In 1985 Judy first came on the scene. Our next door neighbours had a couple of little kids and she came to teach them. Judy was a governess. Near the end of '85 we got a bit of a friendship going. We used to get on the radio and we had a radio courtship. The whole neighbourhood used to come in on the UHF radio to listen to us. Everyone used to tune in to us mucking around. She had me singing songs and playing guitars on it and she was just the same. We had a tremendous amount in common. Judy's an absolute ratbag, that's what I love about her, I guess. You know, she's just one of those people that make you smile when she walks past. That, and the fact that she never wears shoes! When she was pregnant with our first kid they used to say she was bare foot and pregnant, and she was. We got married down at Koraleigh in 1986.

The first ten or fifteen years we didn't have much to do with the fossil side of things. I was always picking up stuff, a bit like Dad, coming home with pockets full of rocks. We focused more on family. We had four kids: Bobby, Irene, Harry and then Koraleigh, who was named after where Judy came from. We built the place up and put in sheds and fences and dams and spent every cent we made on the place. It was hard, but we've got a nice place out of it.

It wasn't until the mid '90s that I really started finding fossils. The first thing of note I found was when I was fire-ploughing once. I saw a rock shaped like a footprint, so I put it in my lunch-box and took it home. Over the next few months Judy and I came back several times to this place and we found more of these little footprints and little bits of bones and tiny little sharp pointed teeth. We thought they must have been from ancient lizards and were pretty keen to show somebody, so we talked to Dr Mary Wade, who was at the Richmond Museum at the time. She said she'd call in and see us one day, which she did. We plonked this big plate full of lizards' feet and teeth in front of her and her eyes widened and we thought, 'We've got something here,' and she said, 'Ooh, look at all the lovely lung-fish tooth plates.' What we thought were lizard's feet turned out to be lung-fish tooth plates. The sharp pointy teeth had belonged to sharks. They'd swum around in the inland sea here about 100 million years ago.

It wasn't 'til about 12 to 18 months after that, that I found a dinosaur bone. In early 1988 I was out mustering early in the morning. I had a fairly big mob of sheep and I was walking them along towards home, when I looked off to the side, and I thought I saw what looked to be a piece of dinosaur bone. I'd always reckoned that one day I might find a dinosaur bone and this looked right, so I swung round and went straight back and jumped off and grabbed this thing. It turned out to be a big hunk of white petrified wood and I was just getting back on the motorbike, when, across the other side of the bike, I noticed a big grey rock. I had a quick look at it and it was a big chunk of dinosaur bone!

I remember coming back for lunch that day and dumping this big piece of dinosaur bone on the table. After I identified the type of rock it was preserved in, I knew where to look and so I started finding more stuff. In December 1999 I found the Elliot dinosaur bone. I'd found six other sites by then. Elliot was number seven and it was found in exactly the same circumstances as that first bone I found. I was mustering a mob of sheep that had only just been shorn 3 to 4 weeks earlier, and I was going flat out on the bike trying to hold this mob together on my own, when I had to dodge a bunch of rocks. As soon as I dodged them I knew what they were. I came back the next day and had a good look around. It turned out there were about five patches of bones there – several dinosaurs spread out all over the place!

We were busy at the time and didn't go back until late in 2000. We went and collected them then and started putting them together and you could see one was the knuckle end of a big leg bone. It sat on our table for six or eight months and it just got that way, 'What are we going to do with this bone?' That's when we contacted Mary Wade the palaeontologist again and told her we had something else we'd like her to have a look at. Mary called in on her way to Brisbane and said, 'Ooh, it looks like it might be one of the biggest ones we've seen.' She told the Queensland Museum and a month or six weeks later Alex Cook from the Queensland Museum and Scotty Hocknull, who became Young Australian of the Year in 2002, and a few other paleontologists called in on their way out to Richmond for the opening of the second stage of *Kronosaurus Korner*, the marine fossil museum out there.

I was watching these blokes when they came in to see what their reaction was when they first saw it. I remember they walked in and they just stood there and Alex's jaw nearly hit the floor and Joanne Wilkinson was there and she just stood there, her eyes like saucers, and she said, 'Wow!' No one else said a word. Then they all started talking at once, they got so excited. So that was it – it was the biggest dinosaur that had ever been found in Australia!

They went out and had a look at the site and we agreed that they'd all come back in September and have a dig. They turned up in September and dug for days, but they were really getting nowhere. It was on the second last day and they were pretty dejected that they'd found nothing and moved very little dirt. Alex was alone and I said to him, 'Would you like me to bring the tractor down?' He said, 'Oh yeah, that'd be great if you'd do that!' I brought the tractor down straightaway that afternoon and we did a bit of digging until it got dark.

Early the next morning, the day before they were due to leave, they went off to look at another site. While they were up at the other site, Judy and I went back to the tractor and started digging. A couple of hours later, Judy starts throwing her hands up and carrying on, so I jumped off the tractor and out of the bucket had rolled the top of this femur – it was all in one piece, about the size of a big basketball. I said, 'What's that?' and she said, 'It's a bone,' and I said, 'No it's not!' and she tipped it over and you could see where it broke off the shaft; you could see it was bone! We kept digging for another twenty minutes or so and then pulled up for smoko. Judy made a cup of tea and we decided we'd get the head of this femur we'd found and dress it up like a little man.

Alex had left his hat down at the site the day before, so we stuck his hat on this rock and sat it up on this little table they had there while we had smoko.

Finally they turned up. I called them all and said, 'I'd like you all to meet Elliot!' and pointed to the little figure all dressed up on the table with Alex's hat on it. They all gave a bit of a chuckle and Alex grabbed his hat and was starting to walk away, and then he said, 'What's that?' and I said, 'What do you think?' He grabbed the rock and tipped it over and then they were all laughing and clapping us on the back and shaking our hands and carrying on! It was just one of those amazing things – one of those real highs. The news about this big femur was released to the media and everything went berserk. We had media chasing us everywhere and ringing people in town trying to find out where it came from.

We realised there were probably many more dinosaur bones here, so we formed a non-profit organisation, Australian Age of Dinosaurs Inc., and in about December 2002 we had the inaugural meeting. We set up a committee and started building a museum display in town, so people would have something to see.

A couple of years ago we started preparing bones out here. That means getting the rock off them, so you can see exactly what the bone looks like. Most of the fossils in this area are from the age of dinosaurs, round about 95 million years old. There're beautiful plant fossils, conifer leaves and little conifer cones and big round angiosperm leaves. You can see every little vein in the leaf – they're absolutely beautiful, some of them. They're the plants that the dinosaurs were eating. We've found fossils all the way down to fairly recent times – less than 2 million years old. We built a dam here in 1996, on a big clay pan and at about 22 feet we got the jaw bone of a diprotodon, a 2-ton marsupial very similar to a wombat. It's the largest marsupial ever known. At the other end of the dam we found the pelvic bones of a giant tree-eating kangaroo. I think they grew close to half a ton. It's amazing how much there is to find in this district. Lark Quarry, where the stampeding dinosaur footprints were found, is on the other side of town. It's the best set of running dinosaur tracks in the world.

Last year, Australian Age of Dinosaurs was given a 3,600-acre mesa just outside of Winton. It belonged to the Britton Family in Winton and they donated it. It's the most incredible place, with deep ravines and cliff faces. You can see for miles up there and Judy's and my dream is to build a world class dinosaur museum there, something that people will want to come to from overseas and all the school kids from Australia will want to come and see. We're working really hard to do that now. That's our dream!

Postscript: When I spoke to David recently, he said he had great news to share: 'There are so many people and organisations helping us today and, to top it all off, we have been allocated $1 million through the Queensland Government's Q150 Legacy Infrastructure funding program. Now we can build a dinosaur fossil preparation lab on the mesa with caretakers' cottages and walking trails, and the Winton Shire Council has built a beautiful winding road all the way up to the top. We are so proud to be a part of it all. What a fantastic legacy for Queensland and what a wonderful way to celebrate Queensland's 150th birthday!'

Serena Sanders-Drummond – 'Pearl Girl'
Founder of the Queensland South Sea Pearl Company

The pearl farm is on Turtle Head Island offshore from Escape River, around 20 kilometres from the tip of Cape York Peninsula, so we'd agreed to meet on her next visit to Brisbane. She brought her computer with photos of her island home, and the pearl farm there. She was wearing a pearl pendant, the size and lustre of which spoke volumes about the quality of pearls that can be produced in Queensland waters. As she talked, we looked through photos on the computer of her island and the cottage there – the pictures looked like paradise, complete with the serpent – in this case a four-metre croc. Living with nature took on a whole new perspective ...

'... the sea snakes all come ashore for one or two nights every year and mate on land and this happened to be the first two nights of our honeymoon ... They were everywhere and we had to step over them walking home from dinner – it was like a scene out of Raiders of the Lost Ark.*'*

When I was twelve years old I saw a Jacques Cousteau movie and decided I wanted to be a marine biologist. I lived in Victoria and fortunately I was quite good at school, so I put my mind to it and I applied to James Cook University in Townsville, where I did my undergraduate in marine biology, majoring in marine biology and marine botany. Then I studied the feeding habits of abalone for my honours degree at Melbourne University, because I wanted to be near my family. After that I lived with my sister there for a year and we decided we'd go to Western Australia together, where I got my first job with WA Fisheries in 1983.

My first job with WA Fisheries was looking at ways to breed pearl oysters, scallops and abalone. I was very fortunate. I had some of the big gurus of Tasmania, the bacteriologists and the aquaculture people, come over to Western Australia to train me up, and I became the algal culturalist for the project. The following year, 1984, we set up a pearl hatchery in Broome. The first thing I did up there was to go out on one of the last remaining pearling luggers, the *DMcD,* to try to get brood stock. The sea was rough and there were all these men and I remember walking around the deck thinking, 'Oh God, I can't walk, there's no rail' – I thought I was going to fall over the side! That was my first experience in Broome and I've been going there ever since. After that I went overseas for a couple of years, before coming back and working for the government again for a while. Then I got offered a job in Darwin to develop a pearl oyster hatchery with the person I'd first trained with – so I went to Darwin and we set up a hatchery there.

While I was at the hatchery I got offered a job to set up a pearling museum, which was sponsored by Paspaley (the biggest pearl producer in Australia) and the Port Authority in the old Powerhouse area. The idea was that within twelve months I had to get the exhibition up to a standard to hand it over to the Northern Territory Museums and Art Galleries – and that happened, but by that stage I was totally sick of Darwin. I'd got Ross River fever and I felt like I was going spongy in the brain, so I went back to James Cook Uni for a year, on a pearl oyster feeding project again, and that's where I had the idea, (that was in 1994) that there was all this wealth of opportunity in Queensland just waiting to happen!

I got tempted back to Western Australia to work for Arrow Pearl Company as R&D division manager, later becoming general manager. One day I said to Steve Arrow, who owned it, 'Steve, I really want to do something in Queensland.' He said, 'Well, Serena, if you're going to do that, I'll be part of it too!' I went to a few other friends and they said, 'OK, we're in, let's chuck in $1000 each and you go and do a feasibility study,' so that's how it started.

In 1999 we came over to Queensland and had a look at all the existing pearl farms and the possibilities of new sites. My friend Spence (one of the group) and I stayed in Escape River doing a study there, taking water samples. It was terrible: the buildings were nearly falling down and we'd got sick after two days. We were about to jump in the water to do a bottom sample when I said to Spence, 'What's that?' and he goes, 'It's a croc!' I said, 'That's it! Stuff it – let's get out of here!' The owners were desperate to sell, but we said, 'No, we're not interested.' It wasn't until we got back and analysed all the water samples for pearl oyster food that I realised the Escape River site was the best site for growing pearls – crocs or no crocs. It wasn't good for people, but it was great for pearls! We had to go back with our tails between our legs to the Japanese owners of the site and say, 'Sorry, but we actually are interested after all.' In November 2000 we brought a boat and a bunch of diver-tradesmen from Broome and came down to the site and got it liveable. I came over in March 2001 and was up at the farm by August. I was supposed to go up there temporarily, but four years later I was still there.

In October 2001 we got the lease and licence in our name. We had to do it all by hatchery shell, because there weren't enough wild stock. We can't bring the animals in or out, so it's completely Queensland based. We don't do much diving at the farm, because we see a lot of crocodiles there, including a sixteen-footer – we've had Steve Irwin's mob up there to catch one that ate two of our dogs. They didn't get the big one, but they got one that they considered to be a rogue; one that had a funny eye and a deformed back, and they said that he was opportunistic and preying on dogs – he was quite dangerous. They trapped him and took him away to a zoo somewhere. We've still got the sixteen-footer and he's seen occasionally on the beach here and there.

I never imagined I would end up here. Over the years I've done everything, from being a biologist to a pearl-diver. I was one of the only women divers to start with. When I first worked for Fisheries, women weren't allowed on the pearling boats, because they went overnight. I'll never forget the first time I came back and saw the boss at the marine research laboratories. I'd just spent ten days at sea on a boat with a bunch of boisterous, wild pearl-divers and he said, 'We haven't seen you for ten days, where have you been?' and I said, 'At sea!' He said, 'But women who work here aren't allowed to go to sea,' and I said, 'Well, it's too late now – I'm back, aren't I!' After that it became a joke. They used to say to women who were employed there, 'Women aren't allowed on the fishing boats – oh, except Serena!'

Years later I dated one of those boisterous pearl divers from that first trip at sea. That lasted on and off for nearly ten years, but it's difficult keeping a relationship when one or both of you is always at sea. We were still together when I moved from Broome to Queensland to set up the pearl farm, but the distance was just too far this time. I got to the farm in September and he'd already decided he was going to go off travelling overseas for six months from Christmas. I thought, 'He's going off to America. I'm fed up with men – that's it! I'm just going to be single and get on with this farm.' I caught a charter plane up to Horn Island airport to fly back to Victoria to be with my family for Christmas. I was sitting at the airport and happened to bend down to pick up something I'd dropped and I looked across about three seats up and there was this gorgeous pair of boating shoes and matching leather briefcase. Being a boatie myself, I thought, 'Who belongs to that?' We ended up sitting one row behind each other on the plane. It's a funny story, but he told me a long time later, that, as he walked behind me up the gangplank, he had this feeling, 'This is the woman I'm going to be with for the rest of my life.' We hadn't even spoken at that stage and he was in a long-term relationship with someone else. As we got off the plane and walked across the tarmac, we started to talk and exchanged cards. His name was Mark and he lived on an island near New Guinea, and I lived on my island off Cape York.

Mark and I got married eighteen months later. We had a sunset wedding on the beach at Stradbroke Island with the whales and dolphins in the background and carpet pythons on the rocks and a full moon – it's just an amazing place. He teaches plumbing and gas fitting to Torres Strait Islanders. We've been together for over three years now. My friends used to say to me, 'How can you meet the man of your dreams on a deserted island?' There was just me and two others on my island and at times I was on my own. I think on a good day he can do the trip in three hours in his boat and on a bad day once it took him seven hours. Mark used to come down whenever he could. That's why he bought a boat, so he could come more often, and occasionally I'd go up to his island, which is very 'islander' – women in big flowery dresses, happy and dancing. It's a great culture.

Mark wanted us to get married, but, as we wouldn't see each other that often, we couldn't face living in the camp at the pearl farm, so he said, 'I'll build us a beach love shack.' We picked our spot and we built it on the sand dune looking out over the pearl farm. He keeps his boat there and, whenever he's there, we spend our Sundays in the boat, diving off the nearby islands or exploring the rainforest, the termite mounds that remind me of Broome, or the pandanus country and saltbushes. It's truly remote and magnificent. There's no television or newspapers and so we've become sunset and moonrise watchers and love exploring and collecting flotsam and jetsam. We've got heaps of collectibles for our future house on the mainland somewhere when we finally get to live together as a normal married couple.

For me, the love of this work was the ocean and the oyster. I've not had any children, but I've had millions of baby oysters! Apart from the pearls, for me now the love of it is really the culture of the people and the lives of the people who've been brought into this industry. There's such a multi-cultural influence in it.

I have some great memories. One time I was being dragged around the sea bed by my dive line from the boom of the fishing vessel looking for pearl shell, when I met a banded sea snake that thought I was its mate! It must have been my blue and yellow wetsuit – the snake wrapped itself around my head, mask and arm. I thought it had bitten me and that I was about to go into convulsions, when I heard the three bangs on the hull to tell all divers to come up. At the surface, the diver on the line next to me said, 'What happened to you? You never picked up a single shell for the last ten minutes.' I said, 'I was too busy playing with an amorous sea snake and trying to figure out if he had bitten me or not!'

It's weird, but snakes have played a significant role in my life, even on my honeymoon. Sea snakes all come ashore for one or two nights every year and mate on land and this happened to be the first night of our honeymoon. The snakes slithered up from the ocean, as the hut was right on the beach. At dinner, we were eating and the waiter casually leaned down and picked up a sea snake from under our table and threw it back in the ocean and kept on going like nothing had happened. They were everywhere and we had to step over them walking home from dinner – it was like a scene out of *Raiders of the Lost Ark*.

I've spent four years at the farm and have achieved my mission to get a farm, set it up and produce a large quantity of hatchery-reared shell that are seeded. We're now in commercial production, so we're not far from the money now. I'm not sure what my next project will be, or even if there will be another one. I'm getting older now and have to think of slowing down and enjoying married life. I could be tempted to do another museum, though. The *DMcD* ended up in the Pearl Luggers museum in Broome, and I was lucky to be involved with this project as well as the Darwin Pearling Exhibition. I'd love to do something on the Torres Straits. I've become very attached to the Aboriginal and Torres Strait Island people. I might try to learn how to make jewellery and do some designs of my own – pearl shell or pearls – who knows? The world is my oyster!

PS: September 2008, Serena now owns and manages Sirene Pearls in Proserpine www.sireneseapearls.com.au

Mark Nucifora – Surviving after Cyclone Larry

As president of the Innisfail Banana Growers Association, Mark has been intimately involved with the industry's recovery since Cyclone Larry hit the area on 20 March 2006 with Category 5 intensity. He remarked on the camaraderie and sense of cohesion the crisis had evoked in the town…

'People were giving free pizzas away… There were a lot of people trying to help each other out during those times. There were people housing other people for weeks, because their houses had been destroyed… All those types of things were important and everybody was trying to cheer each other up. There were signs on the highway, 'Get a life, Larry!' or 'Larry, go find a wife'… People've got a lot invested in the place, not just financially but emotionally.'

My grandfather emigrated from Italy in the last century and when he came over he cut cane with the gangs of cane cutters until he could get his own plot of land where he started his own little farm. My father took over from him. We got into bananas about eight or nine years ago. We're still in sugar cane, but now we grow bananas as well. I was an engineer down south and I came back to the farm when sugar was not in a good financial state, so we made a decision to go into bananas. We have taken land for the bananas that was sugar-cane land and we grow both bananas and sugar on the same farm. When Cyclone Larry hit on 20 March 2006, everything got absolutely smashed! The cyclone came through and it damaged the sugar cane and the bananas and the entire infrastructure and sheds and the house where we used to live. All were damaged.

On the Wednesday before the storm we heard the first reports that it was building out in the Coral Sea. It had been five or six years since we'd had a cyclone cross the coast and they'd only been Category 1 or 2. I guess there was a feeling that Larry was so far out it would go somewhere else and not hit us. As the week progressed it kept getting closer and closer but even on the Saturday night I went down to watch the football in Townsville, because we couldn't believe the cyclone was going to hit us. I think a lot of people felt like that. There was actually a local feast the *Taste of the Senses* that happens in Innisfail every year and there were still people at the feast on Sunday when the mayor came in and said, 'Guys, you better go home and prepare – the cyclone's coming towards us!'

There was a mad scramble when we realised there was a real probability that Larry was going to hit us. We were going around all the houses and sheds picking up as many things as possible that could turn into flying missiles and trying to fasten things down as much as we could. On the Sunday afternoon we went out with two or three employees and picked some fruit ahead of the cyclone, as much as we could basically put in the shed; that was all we could do before night. On Monday morning, at 4:30 or 5 am I woke up and the wind was howling and we realised it was coming straight as a die, at us! That's when we lost the power; it was three weeks after that before we got it back on.

In the middle of the storm I guess everyone was mainly worried for their own personal safety. The phone lines were still connected at that stage and, because the power was out, we listened to the ABC radio, using batteries. That was very good, as they kept up the warning reports and people were ringing in saying what was happening. We've got brothers and sisters in Cairns and Sydney and places like that, so we had a lot of people ringing up to see what was going on and if we were OK. We were luckier than many because we were in a solid, newly built house. Some were in older houses that got severely damaged. You hear stories about people who lost their roofs and walls and had to get out of their house, because it was disintegrating around them, and get across to a neighbour's place – that would have been absolutely frightening!

After the cyclone the cane recovered quicker than bananas, so we managed to harvest a crop off that in July, whereas we weren't really able to harvest anything from the bananas until the following January. Obviously the amount of sugar we harvested was reduced because of the damage from the cyclone breaking the sticks. It was very, very wet. From the day of the cyclone in March, right through 'til early August, it drizzled and we never had too many fine days. That meant the recovery of all those crops was much more difficult. The ABGC (the Australian Banana Growers Council) visited the area with various politicians and they really lobbied the government hard to help us out. From talking with other farmers I could see that we were all in the same boat in terms of damage. It was horrendous. We'd lost our entire crop; all the money we'd spent over the last six months basically had gone down the drain. We had a massive clean-up operation ahead of us to get the farms back into a workable situation and it was obviously going to cost money, fixing up irrigation et cetera – it was tough! People were just stunned for maybe a month or so and a lot of people got out of the industry. We had two or three meetings about what we were going to do to try and get our industry back on track. I wasn't involved with the local chamber of commerce, but I'm sure they would have been helping local businesses in town and lobbying governments.

I think we got two grants from government to tide businesses over between when Larry hit and when they could start getting money back through their insurers. The initial figure was around an initial $1000 cash per person straight after the storm, and $10,000 per business and we got that pretty quickly. The federal and state governments did a marvellous job in helping us out and we owe them a debt of gratitude for everything they tried to do for the Innisfail community in terms of initial grants. People were giving free pizzas away. The army was up here giving away ration packs and fresh water. There were a lot of people trying to help each other out during those times. There were people housing other people for weeks, because their houses had been destroyed. I had a mate of mine, Marty Wilshire, come from Townsville to work on the farm for a weekend. He didn't have to do that, but he was a friend and he did that for me. We had friends ringing from interstate and even backpackers from overseas that had worked on the farm when they were in Innisfail emailed us to find out how things were going.

For the local people the biggest thing was trying to be patient, because obviously it was very difficult. We had problems with everything. We had trouble with the phone, because there was no electricity to operate the power at the various stations. Not only were you trying to do your own thing, and help other people out, but you had to put up with not having the things that you'd normally have. There was a big ecumenical service with all the big religions in town at the local shire hall and that was another good event. The ABC radio was helpful, giving out information all the time and having live broadcasts out of the Innisfail area. All those types of things were important and everybody was trying to cheer each other up. There were signs on the highway, 'Get a life, Larry!' or 'Larry, go find a wife!' I can remember listening to one guy on radio talking to Pat Morrish, and she said, 'How did you fare?' He said, 'Well, I lost my roof,' and she said, 'Oh, I'm sorry to hear that,' and he said, 'That's all right; I found it later a kilometre down the road!' A frequent saying was, 'It's not too bad; there are people worse off than us.' I think everybody had that sort of attitude, coupled, of course, with a bit of impatience due to the time it was taking for work to get completed. That wasn't necessarily anyone's fault; it was just the enormity of the damage that was done and getting the people to come here to fix it. The fact that it continued raining so much also made life very difficult. It was a very difficult time, especially those first four or five months. There were still some people in July 2007 who hadn't had their insurance work completed.

We had to get on with our lives – that's what you've got to do – but I think it's mentally scarred everybody. When you hear the wind getting up, or you hear reports of a cyclone, you remember Larry and hope it won't be something like that again. Having said that, we're all getting on with our lives and the industry's coming back strong. Like after a bushfire, everything's burnt out, but then it re-grows. We're slowly getting back on track. To get back to the pre-cyclone production, it will take about two or two and a half years. Since August 2006 I've been president of the Banana Association, so I'm close to all that's going on. The town has got a lot of new buildings, because a lot of the old ones were damaged, and that's brought a new lease of life to the town. I think, for all those people who were here before Cyclone Larry and came through it and have stayed on, there's a sense of having survived. Because of the severity of the storm, relationships have been built – either people have helped you or you've helped them. There's been more activity between people like that due to Larry and it's brought people closer. When you go through hard times like that together, you learn lessons from it.

Justin Goc – Farming Barramundi

Hinchinbrook Island is one of Australia's largest National Park islands and is divided from the mainland by the Hinchinbrook Passage, a veritable maze of mangrove-lined creeks, generally only frequented by fishermen who know where to go for great catches of barramundi and Mangrove Jack. This is the workplace of Justin Goc, who explains that people are not the only customers for the fish he farms ...

'We look at sharks as our farm policemen, because if we see sharks jumping we know there are some barramundi that have escaped somewhere – then we have to try and find where the problem is.'

When I was twenty-one years old I was living in Tasmania, which is where I had grown up. I decided I needed a change, so I packed my bags and headed to Far North Queensland to try my hand at barramundi farming. I expected it to last only about a year, if that, but a year turned into ten years and then into a career.

For the first four years, I was working at our hatchery in Mourilyan Harbour near Innisfail. Then I went back to Launceston in Tasmania, where I did a year's course at the University of Tasmania, and after that I became the farm manager here at Con Creek in the Hinchinbrook Channel.

Mostly the fish in the hatchery get chosen from different places, either from the wild or other farms, to ensure that there's no genetic overlap. It's a closed circuit where we have all large fish – we spawn from them. The fish are kept in a temperature and light controlled room that emulates summer conditions, which are the normal environment for the fish in which to spawn. A female fish is injected with hormones to induce spawning. It releases eggs after forty-eight hours. The male fish sense the hormones released by the females and release their sperm to fertilise the eggs – this happens within fifteen minutes to ensure the success of the spawn. The eggs are then collected and transferred to the hatchery for hatching and distribution in the hatchery facility.

After they've spawned, we rear them into fingerlings and then the fingerlings get shifted down on specially made live-fish transporters to our farm site here at Con Creek. We can ship about 80,000 to 90,000 down in one trip. They're only approximately one and a half grams each at that stage. We put them onto our barge and take them out to sea and put them into the nets and then their life at the sea farm starts.

The farm is in a channel between Hinchinbrook Island and the mainland and everything is floating – everything that comes on or off the farm has to come via a boat. We don't have any land access other than back at Port Hinchinbrook, which is approximately thirty minutes away by boat.

When I was working at the hatchery, we used to get stories about how bad the farm was in respect to its equipment and its ability to fend off sharks, crocodiles and all the natural predators that you get in the ocean. When I eventually made it down to the farm and was in a position to make some decisions, we tried a lot of different things to address these problems. We started with predator nets, which are cloth nets of large mesh. It was thought they would stop crocodiles and sharks and different things from getting in, but that didn't work. They ended up biting through the nets and causing all manner of problems for us! Then we looked to another solution – that was steel mesh and that worked well for approximately a year, but once it started rusting, crocodiles and sharks were able to work their way into the cage and get our stocks, so we went back to the drawing board again!

Finally we came across a product made in Japan. It's a totally plastic net woven into a useable mesh size. We've had that in there for the last year and a half and so far have had no losses. We've also worked on weighting systems that minimise the effects of tidal pressures causing movement of the nets. It's a two-pronged attack: you don't put too many fish in there or it'll cause a problem, and you have enough weights in there to counteract the tide to some extent.

After they've been on the farm for about a year, I'd have about 6,000 fish in one of these nets. We give them a diet that's been specifically formulated for barramundi mostly derived from fish meal and various vitamins and minerals that the fish require.

Initially we started off with just plate-size fish, but it proved incredibly difficult to keep to that very narrow size range. Over summer when the fish are growing wonderfully, you can keep sustaining the same amount of fish of a given size, but over winter, once they stop growing, it's very difficult when people want a particular size – say 500 grams. We eventually decided to move totally away from plates and now we just harvest when they are three kilos and up (approximately 60 to 65 centimetres in length and about two to two and a half years old). At the moment our market is all Australia, but that can change with the currency. Two or three years ago, when the currency was 50 cents to the US dollar, we were putting a lot of fish through America. I think some of our barra went to some of the White House meetings and those big conventions and they were paying something like US$80 to US$100 for a small portion of barramundi! We obviously didn't get that; it went mostly to the middlemen. But as soon as our dollar went up over 70 cents, it all evaporated and currently, of course, they're not interested.

In my experience barramundi would have to be one of the best fish to grow because right from the larval stage they'll either eat easily produced food or a manufactured diet. You can feed them a type of small animal that's easily cultivated, called a 'rotifer' and there's other food sources that we can feed them on as well, called artemia, which we get out of tins – you might have heard of 'sea monkeys' that kids play with? You can buy them in little tins and add water to them and after a couple of days they hatch and turn into little animals. When they hatch you can feed them to the fish and the barra derive enough nutrition from them for a while. After seventeen days, you're able to feed them a formulated diet and they stay on that diet for the rest of their life.

We have resident crocodiles and plenty of sharks. We look at sharks as our farm policemen, because if we see sharks jumping we know there are some barramundi that have escaped somewhere – then we have to try and find where the problem is. Touch wood, we haven't seen any sharks jumping, so that's good! We have dolphins, sting rays and crocodiles – barramundi is the crocodile's number one food source. I've never had a close call with crocs, but there was one that still remains in my mind. He was a good four to five metres long and I was feeding the fish at the time and he just sat there and watched me – he wouldn't move and I climbed out of the boat and climbed onto the cage and walked towards him on the cage and he just stayed there. Then all of a sudden he just sank down and I didn't see him again – that particular crocodile did worry me.

About five years ago, after I finished studying at university in Tasmania, I met my future wife Lisa and we took control of the farm from the previous management team. The place wasn't in a state that was conducive to growing fish, so we had a lot of work to do. To make it worse, we were contending with enormous tides – we call them 'king tides'. They're notorious during the summer months (January to April) and they cause massive stress on all our moorings. At that time of year the tides can drop three metres in six hours, so it's an enormous tidal run, up to nearly four knots in speed. We were there one day and there was a line of cages in front of our main body of cages. The ropes broke on the one in front and all of the cages broke free and basically smashed through our whole farm. Everything was being held pretty much by one rope – we were in a very precarious position. All our cages could have been swept away!

It was chaotic sorting it out. We worked continuously day after day – it was an incredibly stressful period, but we managed to get everything in a semblance of order. I'll never forget it because my father's the managing director of the company and I was talking continuously to him about it and the problems we'd had and he said, 'Well, either way, no matter what happens, you've got to look at this as a learning experience.' It was good advice. Now, after going through that experience and learning the lessons it taught me, I'm much more able to deal with things that happen on the farm.

There are crocodiles in Port Hinchinbrook – it always amuses me, the people moving about in small boats, while there are crocs on the banks of the river. One incident I'll never forget – there was a family of people in a boat and the father, for some unknown reason, was transporting the family over to the other side of the bank to have lunch, and the tide was rising. I was shaking my head and saying to myself, 'What the hell are you thinking about?' The tide comes in that fast and there's crocodiles there and he's trying to scramble all the kids off the bank back into the boat to get back to the other side – it was an absolute nightmare! They were OK – I just couldn't believe he'd done it! Tourists just don't understand the environment sometimes.

My son Ethan is eight years old now and I've also got a baby daughter called Indyanna, whose four years old, and she's already got me wrapped around her finger. Every day when I come home from work, Ethan says, 'Did you catch any barramundi today, Daddy – did you see any crocodiles? Did you see any dolphins?' He's very inquisitive. He's still a bit young, but I occasionally take him down to show him all the different things, from the fingerlings feeding – where you throw in a bucket of food and the fish just go berserk on the top of the water – to the fish-feeding of the big fish. We have fish that are albinos – perfectly white; I think it's a genetic throwback. Out of 100,000 fish you might get 50 that are white or white and black – even rarer, and I've only seen this once, a pure gold barra.

In South East Asia, they grow barramundi (they call it Sea Bass there) and they have enormous farms over there, but I consider their product's inferior to what we produce here in Australia. We always get enquiries to put samples into Europe, either into London or Germany or France, but the problem with Europe is that they want large quantities. For example, I had a phone call from a guy who asked, 'Could you fill a forty-foot container with barramundi?' I said, 'I guess I could, but after that I wouldn't have any left to fill the next one!' The problem with most overseas markets is they require huge amounts and we're only a small farm. When they ask for hundred-ton allotments, it's currently beyond our scope. I'd love to go that next step, but we are in this World Heritage area, so what we have now, that's it – and there are good arguments for that. We have good access from here to all the markets, airports, facilities and infrastructure. We're pretty happy with where we are and what we're doing.

Barry Kitchen – Growing a Cocoa Industry

He retired after seventeen years on the board of Cadbury Schweppes and together with some friends has established a new venture, a cocoa business in Mossman, Far North Queensland, where they're working with the local mill and farmers. Mossman's been a sugar town for years, but sugar isn't doing as well as it used to. Born a Queenslander, Barry's enthusiasm is obvious as he speaks of the potential for a coca industry here and his enjoyment in helping it develop.

'... the beans will be further processed into cocoa liquor, cocoa butter and cocoa powder, and later, with the addition of sugar from the mill, chocolate ... What's evolved is a very strong partnership... with the whole community.'

I was born in Brisbane and I'm still a very passionate Queenslander, despite now living in Melbourne. Back in the early 1900s, my family, through my mother's side, were involved in the dairy industry in Rocklea, now a suburb of Brisbane. I can always remember, as a child, being taken to my great-uncle's farm and seeing the cows milked by hand, seeing the billy of milk on the kitchen table when everyone was having their afternoon tea, and people scooping up cream off the top of the milk, so I feel I've had a long association with the dairy industry.

I grew up in Queensland and went through university, where I studied science. I was interested in the food industry and when I was offered the job as a researcher in the Department of Primary Industries Dairy Research Laboratory, I felt I'd really come back to my grass roots. I spent about eighteen years in that job. I met a lot of incredible people while researching the diseases of the cows and composition of the milk. I wasn't just a laboratory guy; I was out there talking and working with those salt-of-the-earth dairy farmers. Along the way I completed two more degrees, a Masters and a PhD, and built up a fairly good research reputation both locally and internationally through publishing articles and chapters in books.

After reaching a fairly senior position in the Queensland DPI Dairy Research Laboratory, I was offered a job in Victoria to run the Victorian government's Food Research Institute in Werribee on the western side of Melbourne. Two years later a head-hunter came along and asked me if I wanted to have an interview and it turned out to be Cadburys. I knew nothing about the way chocolate was made, so I was a bit hesitant – but then I remembered two things from my childhood. When I was very young my mother, to treat herself, used to go down to the shop and she'd buy a quarter-pound block of Cadbury chocolate and come home and sit down with me and eat it. In doing so, she used to tear the silver paper off the outside of the chocolate, roll it up into little balls and then put the silver balls in her hand and ask me to guess how many silver balls there were. It was a game I loved playing with her and she'd do this regularly. As a result I had always remembered this purple wrapper. I thought it was funny, this memory from my childhood, and here I am being offered a very senior position in the company that made the product. The main selling point of Cadbury's, of course, was that 'glass and a half of milk' – that to me said 'dairy industry'!

That was in 1985 and I was placed on the Cadbury Schweppes board of management straight away. We moved house to the other side of Melbourne and I got involved in all the issues that big corporates have. I ran their total science program and their R&D and I began to learn about the chocolate industry and how powerful it is, not just in Australia but around the world. Sitting behind it was some incredible science and technologies, so there was ample opportunity to get a scientific buzz whilst still running a big department and being a member of the board. I learned an enormous amount about cocoa growing, about cocoa processing and about the whole industry, right from the farm to making chocolate.

In 1997 there was the Asian economic crisis and the price of cocoa beans and a lot of commodities fell. Our main sources of supply at the time were countries in Asia. Because of the economic crisis, there was a lot of political unrest and upheavals and we were not getting the quality of the beans we wanted – it was effectively putting at risk our ability to make chocolate. We managed to do it, but it was a very tough time.

The Asian crisis made me start thinking. If this got worse rather than better, what sort of a legacy would I be leaving for whoever came on board after me? I said, 'I think we should try and start something in Australia in terms of cocoa growing.' The idea was a long-term project that would reduce the amount of money the country was spending overseas and would give Australian farmers and growers an opportunity for an alternative crop with reasonable money in it. It had to be seen as a long-term thing, but if Australia applied its scientific knowledge to growing a crop that was usually grown in very basic agricultural conditions in third-world countries, I felt we should be able to do it – that was my theory, anyhow!

I realised up-front that one of the big issues would be the cost of labour here. The labour cost in harvesting cocoa in other places around the world is very low. We had to demonstrate that this crop could be grown effectively and efficiently in Australia and with good yield. We had to show that local diseases wouldn't kill it or knock it around like in other parts of the world. We knew that if we could prove that scientifically it would provide encouragement to farmers to commercialise it.

I was able to get into the offices of the top people in government and in the end we were able to put together a program and a project that was funded by Western Australia, Northern Territory and Queensland. Cadburys put money in and we attracted some funding from the federal government, through the Rural Industries Research and

Development Corporation (RIRDC) a federally funded body which do unusual crops and research. It was about 1999 or 2000 that we got that up and running.

That project finished in June 2005, after five years of funding. There were trial plantations placed in the Ord River region of Western Australia and another one outside of Broome. There was one east of Darwin and then two in Queensland, one up in Mossman and one at Innisfail. These trial plots were about a hectare each and each of the researchers had a job to do in terms of monitoring all the issues with pests and diseases and pruning. They measured growth rates and eventually the yields they were getting off all these plantations. We wanted to prove that the hybrids we used would grow and flourish and produce high yields – and in doing that to learn about all the problems of plant husbandry.

Some of those trial plantations failed, but that's good in science, because you learn. The trial plantation in Darwin was OK, but you get so many very hot days without any cloud cover there that the plants struggled a bit. The two in Western Australia were not good. The two Queensland plantations have really been the champions. They had the right position with the rainfall and temperature and all the things that give you the right mix to make the crops flourish. We were getting yields that were four to five times greater than any other commercial operation around the world, which offset some of the costs in relation to labour.

It's still very marginal, though, because in Australia you've got to pay people about $15 an hour to pick the fruit. You can't pay $2 an hour like in some of these other countries. We had to figure out if this was still viable while complying with Australian local labour rates.

In 2002 I decided I'd had enough of corporate life, so I retired and was able to sit back and look at what I wanted to do with the rest of my life, and what else I wanted to achieve. I'd been involved with this amazing project, which I'd really taken the leadership in and made sure it happened and it was something I was passionate about, so I said, 'I know about cocoa and the international issues and trade and I know how to make chocolate, why not for the first time do something for my own benefit?'

There were a few other mates of mine who'd retired from Cadburys around the same time and I had a good network of professional people who'd had enough of corporate life and were looking for what they could do themselves. We didn't believe that Cadbury's would want to commercialise cocoa growing, because Cadbury's are not cocoa growers. They were more concerned with helping Australia develop a new industry and, long-term, ensuring their own line of supply. Chatting over a few cups of coffee, we said, 'Well, we know all this stuff and could probably do it as well as anyone – why don't we have a crack at it?' So we did. We put some money in and started up a chocolate company.

Long term, we knew we'd be cloning and grafting, but short term, to get us going, we went out and sourced seed from Malaysia and Papua New Guinea. We've set up our own business now in North Queensland, where we import seeds regularly. My wife Barbara is a horticulturalist and involved in the business as well, and she and I went around interviewing a number of nurseries in North Queensland before choosing Yuruga Nursery on the Atherton Tableland as our supply chain partner. They propagate the seeds and look after the seedlings for 3 to 4 months and at that age we sell them to growers in the region or plant them ourselves in our own plantation.

Our plantation is only about two hectares and we intend to only have about 10–20 hectares ourselves. We put in 1,200 trees per hectare and we're expecting, when the trees mature, to get about 40 tons of pods per hectare, which is very high compared to anywhere else in the world. They return the first pods within three years of planting and usually mature around about 7 to 8 years and they live for about 100 years. So you've got a tree, which, if you look after it, will continue to give you a good return.

Turning up as 'southerners' in North Queensland to start preaching the gospel of cocoa – the first reaction from the locals naturally was going to be, 'Who are these people?' We had to build our credibility and get the community behind us. The first port of call was the Mossman sugar mill, which is the heart of the township of Mossman. It'd been there since 1894 and a lot of the characters in Mossman, their families, go back to when they first settled the area to grow sugar.

Today the people who are running the mill are the great-great-grandsons of these initial pioneers in the region. They're very proud people and we went to the mill because we thought there were possibly some very good synergies in working with an established agricultural industry like sugar, with the way we'd want to collect and process the cocoa pods.

At the time we went up there the sugar industry was on its knees. The cane growers at that time were getting poor returns and the world prices were low. If cane collapsed, it would be an absolute disaster for the township and the whole region. So we came at a time when the mill directors and farmers were willing to listen to our proposal. We talked to the Douglas Shire Council, the mayor and all the people we believed were important to get this high-level message across of what cocoa could mean. We had to work hard at that, but over time, we've developed some really good relationships and friendships as they realised we were sincere and were there to set up a business for the long term – one that would obviously make a profit for us, but also improve the lot of the whole community. We now have two full-time employees stationed in Mossman to support the cocoa growing and processing project.

We've now set up our own plantation and we've also sold seedlings to a number of cane growers around the region who've committed to develop small plots of cocoa and they've already got plants in the ground as well. Our model is to encourage a lot of small growers around the total region. Rather than having one whopping great plantation which could get knocked out by a cyclone or by some unknown pest or disease, we want 1 to 2 hectare plots scattered all around the region.

If we can get about 300 hectares planted in the next five years, we've got an industry that can stand on its own two feet. We sell them the seedlings, we give them the necessary expertise and we've set up an extension and training partner in Mossman who'll be responsible, with our help and involvement, for training the growers how to grow and look after the cocoa. Any new technologies that we develop we'll provide that information free of charge to the growers. For doing all that they have a guaranteed supply contract that we will buy their pods at a certain price – and they've got that now. They know what they're going to get based upon today's world prices in dollar returns from their land, providing they look after the crop properly and get the right yields.

We have built the first stage of our central processing operation close to the mill, so all the pods can come into the one point and we'll process them by fermenting and drying them to produce dry cocoa beans. From there the beans will be further processed into cocoa liquor, cocoa butter and cocoa powder and later, with the addition of sugar from the mill, chocolate will be manufactured. What's evolved is a very strong partnership with the mill and with the whole community. The land we've used to put our plantation on initially is owned by the mill and they've leased that to us, so we've got the infrastructure now and we can just continue to build that up.

Linda Jaques – A North Queensland Coffee Plantation

Her voice is clear and bright, with an accent tracing her heritage back to the UK and Africa. Their plantation is set in Mareeba, an agricultural township in the mountains behind Cairns. This is very much a family concern and they were justifiably delighted recently to learn that their coffee has been short listed for use in Parliament House.

'... we found that coffee had in fact been grown up in North Queensland between 1890 and 1920. It had even won prizes for best quality on the London and Marseilles markets.'

Ian Hewitson, of *Huey's Cooking Adventures*, was up here on our coffee plantation with his TV production team recently and did his cooking show using Jaques Coffee Liqueur in a crème caramel and a tiramisu. When his show went to air we had 10,000 hits on our website and were sending coffee and liqueur all over Australia. We have opened our coffee plantation for coffee and microlight tours and have a café and landscaped gardens for visitors to enjoy our beautiful coffee.

I was born in Zanzibar, grew up in Kenya and did some of my schooling in England. I completed my Registered Nurse's training in London and then went back to Africa and married Nat Jaques, a handsome young coffee farmer in Tanzania. My parents, Andy and Pam Bell, were in the tea industry in the Highlands of Kenya. So I was brought up with tea and married coffee!

The Jaques family coffee plantation boasted 180 acres of coffee on the slopes of Mount Kilimanjaro, which was very romantic, right on a crater lake. But the economic and political situation got too much in Tanzania. We had barbed wire fences and guard dogs and loaded guns beside the bed, so we decided that life's too short to have to put up with things like that. We immigrated to Australia and came in on my nurse's qualifications, because they didn't need farmers at the time. Leaving Tanzania, they only allowed us to take $2,000 minus the value of our personal possessions. This was to start a new life and the rest of the money they placed in a frozen bank account and were to send us $1000 a year but to this day we have never seen a penny.

My sister Jeanette was already living in Perth and she had just had her first child there and my parents had gone out from Kenya to be with her. My mother had fallen over and when she got to Perth she was complaining that her breast was very sore and they found she actually had breast cancer. We arrived in Perth at about four o'clock in the morning and I saw my father's face through the glass at the airport and I thought, 'The baby's died.' I could just see that something awful had happened. He told me, 'Your mother's going in for a radical mastectomy this morning.' We stayed and looked after her and then my mother and father went back to Kenya. We bought a ute and a campervan that sat on top of it, one of those piggyback campers, and we headed across the Nullabor, looking for places to grow coffee.

We travelled right the way down to Adelaide, Melbourne and up into the mountains to Kosciusko and then got to Brisbane and found some East African friends who happened to have a coffee tree in their back yard. We thought that was interesting, so we went to the Department of Primary Industries and they said, 'I guess you could look through the archives of old Queensland agricultural journals,' which we did, and we found that coffee had in fact been grown up in North Queensland between 1890 and 1920. It had even won prizes for best quality on the London and Marseilles markets. We thought, 'Great, this is going to work!' We then headed up to this area but found that land prices were very, very expensive, so we then came back to Brisbane and I got a job at the Wesley Hospital and worked there and my husband worked as a real estate agent.

Nat continue to look for suitable land and we found there was a priority special lease on land up here in Mareeba, North Queensland, so we packed our bags and came up here and cleared the land and planted. We set up a nursery with five different varieties of coffee: one from New Guinea; one variety was Arusha, which is the place where we lived in Tanzania; Bourbon; a Blue Mountain one; and a South American one. When they sent the seeds in, Customs fumigated them with methyl bromide that effectively kills! Fortunately it was only a mild dose, but we had an anxious six weeks waiting to see if they'd germinate.

By this time we were actually living in a garden shed with the little campervan as kitchen beside the irrigation channel. We lived like that for about six months. There was no TV and of course I got pregnant. The bath was the old Tanganyika boiler – I think they call them donkeys here – a forty-four-gallon drum filled with cold water and you had to light the fire underneath it to heat the water. We hung a bit of hessian round the bathtub to give us a bit of privacy while we had our bath under the stars – it was real pioneering! Meanwhile we were getting a house built – well, Nat was actually building it with Ernie, a brickie and a real old character. He would disappear for days getting drunk and we would haul him back. We're about fifteen kilometres from the nearest town. It's not too far, but there was no road into the property. There was an access road and the neighbouring farmer had planted his tobacco on it, so we had to go in by a very long route over anthills, until they finally put a road in for us. The electricity couldn't be brought in unless there was a road. We didn't have a phone either and I was very, very pregnant by this stage.

I remember going in to the electricity board and jumping up and down and saying, 'You're going to kill my baby,' and eventually the power was connected. From all the digging and house building I developed pre-eclampsia and ended up in hospital for a rest. Young Jason was born on 11 June, a very large boy, via Caesarean section. Then Nat's brother Dick and his wife came up from Sydney to join us in the project and we planted 120,000 trees. They were all seedlings from the seeds we'd grown the year before. We'd put all the earth into pots in the nursery and had cleared all the land and put in an irrigation scheme. That was a huge undertaking.

We decided we'd have to do something about harvesting, because, in East Africa, we used to employ 300 to 400 people during harvest and we thought there was no way we could do that here. So, as my husband's very clever with machines, he started designing a harvester. We got hold of a berry picker from New Zealand and had it modified, but it just fell to pieces; it wasn't strong enough. So then we got a development grant and had Australia's first coffee harvester actually made here in Cairns at QEA Shipbuilding, based on my husband's design. Meanwhile another big bouncing boy, Robert, came into the world.

Then along came Mr Keating with 'the recession we had to have'! We had 100 tons of coffee sitting on the trees; it was our first big harvest and we were going to try out the Coffee Shuttle One harvester machine. But the banks wouldn't let the harvest proceed. They said, 'No, that's it.' We'd borrowed quite a lot of money and with 22% interest rates they wouldn't let us harvest to pay back the debt, so we walked away with nothing! We lost the houses, the factories, the farm and our dream, and went into liquidation.

I went back to nursing full time and we decided we really should have another go. We borrowed more money and got this present block of land and had to clear it all from scratch again. We planted 50,000 trees this time. I was working and bringing in an income and my husband was out here on the farm and contract harvesting and selling coffee on the show circuit. It takes five years for coffee to give a commercial crop, so the fifth year we had a beautiful flowering and thought, 'This is great; everything's going well.' Then the Department of Primary Industries came along and said, 'There's a papaya fruit fly in the area,' and we said, 'But this is coffee,' and they said, 'This is a national emergency – we've got to spray to try and kill it.' We said to them, 'No one's ever found a papaya fruit fly in coffee.' We didn't use any insecticide or fungicides on the coffee ourselves and had no spraying equipment, so they came in with four-wheeler motorbikes and mist-sprayed the entire plantation with ten consecutive sprays, using a cocktail of chemicals. They'd done no research on the effect those chemicals would have on coffee and effectively killed 50,000 trees. All this took place in October 1996 and we are still fighting for compensation. This is the largest civil case to be heard in the Supreme Court in Cairns.

So, for the third time, we thought, 'The Jaques motto is "never say die", let's have another go!' Third time lucky, call it perseverance or madness, of which I might say there is a very fine line! Of all the coffee farms in the area that were sprayed we're the only ones that have planted on new ground with clean stock. We're now in full production and we have harvested our coffee, and are producing over a ton per acre, which is a world-class coffee. In October 2006 we won gold, silver and bronze in Sydney against 240 national roasters and it was blind tasted by international and national judges. In November 2006 we won the Business Enterprise Award for Queensland, so the future is looking good.

The growing of coffee is an art and a science and we have been able to use quality control through each stage of growing, irrigating, fertilising, harvesting, wet and dry processing, right through to the roasting and packaging. As if that isn't enough, we decided to try a bit of agro-tourism and have had visitors from all over the world fascinated by the involved process of getting the coffee from tree to the cup. In 2006 we recorded 65,000 visitors and it's continued to grow. In 2007 I was awarded runner-up for Queensland Rural Woman of the Year for my project for caffeine-free coffee. As demand for our coffee is outstripping supply, we have planted another 50,000 coffee seedlings. With increased planting, new state-of-the-art processing equipment has recently been installed.

Our plantation tour includes a ten-minute movie in our twenty-five-seat air-conditioned movie theatre, a guided tour of the world's first coffee harvester, a taste of the coffee cherry (a natural fruit) and then a safari in the 'Bean Machine' around the plantation. Back at the plantation café, a choice of espresso coffees and a taste of Australia's first coffee liqueur are included. Jaques coffee liqueur is made from all natural ingredients using our coffee concentrate made on the plantation. We like to support local industries and have our liqueur made at Mount Uncle Distillery, fifteen minutes down the road. The rock candy is made in Kuranda Candy Kitchen and the gold and silver coffee bean jewellery in Yungaburra at the Gem Gallery.

Our eldest son Jason has joined us in the business and with his skills as a Microsoft Systems Engineer he has computerised the irrigation and fertigation of the coffee. He created our website www.jaquescoffee.com and the Internet online shop. With his skills he has also made a movie, which is shown as part of the coffee tour, and has put together the audio system on the 'Bean Machine', which takes the visitors on their safari around the plantation. If anything breaks down, he fixes it. We are so lucky to have two wonderful sons.

Our youngest son Robert joined the business in January 2007. He has his private pilot's licence and is a microlight instructor, and with Nat, my husband, they run a flying school and take visitors on flights, T.I.F (Trial Instructional Flights), around the area and over the coffee plantation.

Our coffee, which is insecticide and fungicide free, is distributed through Coles and Woolworths from Townsville north, and also in IGA stores, cafes and restaurants in Sydney. With the online Internet shop, www.jaquescoffee.com, we send coffee out all over the world. Coffee is in our blood, and our vision is to have Australians drinking Aussie coffee in the not too distant future!

Peter Fisher – Crocodile Farming and Conservation

I first spoke with Peter in 2005. He and his family have farmed crocodiles in Mareeba since 1992. He told me that crocodile skins are often sourced from wild crocodiles  *through poaching or approved ranching programs, but that wild crocodiles taken in by his farm are not killed. They're kept to form a living genetic material bank. Farming crocodiles in this way he sees as a sustainable use. Peter has been elected as a board member of the Crocodile Management Advisory Committee to assist in formulating a long-term view on crocodile management within Queensland.*

'... *I used to weld up these road tankers for the fuel companies, BP, Shell and the like, and when you get inside them to weld them up, you feel like you're gonna have a good day or a bad day – every day's been a good day so far because we've got back out of them. It's the same with crocodiles; you can have a good day or a bad day ...*'

We got into crocodile farming accidentally. I was working on a property up North and we were supplying meat to a big crocodile farm next door, the Edward River Crocodile Farm. We thought, 'If they can make a go of it there like that, we should be able to do it ourselves.' It was another seven years 'til we worked out how we were going to do it. We got a licence in 1992.

I like to think of this as a pretty joint effort. It's not only myself, it's the family, the wife, the kids, the whole lot. Everything we do here is a 'we' – without the family it wouldn't be much of a farm.

I was the one that was supplying meat to this other big farm up North on my own and that was a real blast. It was good money and I liked the job – no boss, out in the bush all day, living out of the swag, basically. We were shooting wild pigs and got paid for it– that was the best part! Wild pigs are the nemesis of crocodiles. They're the worst things God ever made in Australia. They destroy the crocodile nesting habitat so quickly, and they're a real pest. I feel real passionate about crocodiles. Poor buggers, they need a hand.

Crocodile farming is something totally different, because you're dealing with something that all it knows how to do is kill – there's no ifs and no buts – if these blokes get a hold of you they'll tear you limb from limb.

In 2005 we looked at about six farms all up in Queensland and thought, 'How can we make it easier and safer on us and more hospitable for the crocodile?' So we built them some very animal-friendly pens – it's like they live in the mansion, while we live in the dog box! Our breeder pens are a heavy steel mesh pen with a concrete pond inside. Our biggest croc's about fifteen feet (over 4.5 metres). They've got ample water, ample sunshine and ample shade, everything a crocodile needs. In the next life I'm gonna come back as a big male crocodile – four females and you just lie in the sun and wait for a chicken to fly over the fence – not hard to take!

Crocodiles hate the world, they hate each other, hate people, just hate everything. The big male's in control. If he doesn't like the female, he'll kill her. If she doesn't like him, she'll try and tear him apart. Females don't like each other. Males don't like each other. So we isolate all the big stuff. With our single pens, we've got about forty all up and they become very labour intensive in that you've got to go out and feed and clean 'em individually.

The other part of the job – and how we put money into the place – is that I used to weld up these road tankers for the fuel companies, BP, Shell and the like, and when you get inside them to weld them up, you feel like you're gonna have a good day or a bad day – every day's been a good day so far, because we've got back out of them. It's the same with crocodiles; you can have a good day or a bad day.

We put the males in with the females in September. We'll give the male two weeks with her, then back to his pen and into the next one. Two weeks at a time, pretty hard life to take – four females and, if you don't like her, kill her. We lost one female to a male. She was in his pen and all the business was over and done with and she took a swipe at him, bit him around the nose, and he just said, 'Well, cop this, you silly bugger,' and just beat her to death. It took five hours, but there's nothing we could do. It's a really brutal life being a crocodile.

We lost a big male that we got from Weipa. He was picking up all the rubbish in the harbour, and when we got him back here he lasted about three months, he was chock-o-block full of these plastic Coles bags – he just couldn't pass 'em. When he rolled over you felt you sort of let him down; you feel really terrible about it. Besides Mum dying, that's probably the saddest point I ever felt in life. A really big animal that just died on us and we couldn't do anything about it.

Nesting season is usually January, with thunder and rain triggering the female to begin building her nest. They lay about January here and they're the best mothers God ever made; they protect that nest with their life. We've got a set of gates that just drop down and lock her in the water. She becomes super-aggressive then and so does the male, because something's going on. You've got a three-quarter-ton animal pulling at the gate and he's trying to tear everything down. They can climb too – they can get two thirds of their body off the ground. Something that's fifteen foot long, if he comes up eight feet, now that's a pretty daunting sight climbing up a fence ten feet away from you. And it's a good feeling. I do the welding work on those pens, so if there's anyone to blame, it's me – I'm a boiler maker, fitter, welder, by trade and I make sure that gate there is going to stop where I put it.

You can kill the egg by shaking it or turning it over. You've got to get the egg as quick as you can and mark the top, being as gentle and as careful as possible so you don't tear the embryo away from the egg itself, get it back, clean it, get it into the incubator and get it away, all while the female's trying to get in and kill you – and the male too.

The sex of the animal is set by the temperature on the eggs in the nest, so you can make females or males, whichever you want. It gives you a God-like feeling. We try for males; we set our incubator for that, more for the speed of production. We've got to get them as big as possible as quick as possible, because demand for this stuff is just absolutely astronomical.

We pick the eggs up on day one and we mark on our calendar exactly 80 days. As sure as God made little green apples, on the 80-day mark you open the door and here they are, all waiting for you! Once they start to hatch, the whole nest will hatch together. One'll bust out and he'll let the whole nest know it's time to go. When they're opening they've still got rather weak jawbones. But this little animal, his one idea is to kill you – and he's only 10 inches long.

From the incubator we take them into our nursery building, which has full environmental control. We start 'em on a red meat blended diet. They get into it quite quickly, and if you keep them at the optimum temperature of thirty-two, their immune system's 100%. They can digest food within a day or two. We get a very high survival rate. I'm a bit pedantic about the conditions we give 'em; I make it as clean and hygienic as possible, more like a hospital.

We've got about 11,000 crocs on the farm. There's a lot of growing size animals, up to five feet, and up to 500 per pen. When you've got to go amongst 'em and grade 'em – you've got to walk through 'em all, and they're all trying to kill you. You've gotta have eyes in the back of your head. We wear gum boots so we don't get our feet wet. You learn about crocs; they become very predictable – or the majority is! My gumboots leak a lot now – they've been bitten a few times! We use those plastic rakes to hold 'em back and keep 'em at bay. Getting life insurance is pretty hard!

Crocs are just like normal people, they get to that teenager stage where they start to fight and show off how smart they are, in crocs that's about the seven-foot mark. That takes about three years for us. After they reach seven foot, you've got to process them or keep them away from each other, because when they become territorial they just tear each other apart.

What we do then, we'll actually stun the animal so it's knocked out for about five minutes. If the skin is of a suitable quality to be processed, we'll then process the animal. I don't like using the word 'kill'. If the skin isn't suitable, we put them back into another holding pen. You can normally grow out the marks. We're looking for advanced animals. We're trying to modify and push the genetics a bit. The Holy Grail for us is 40 scale rows from the neck to the back leg, basically, and there are very, very few crocodiles that have got that scale count.

The stunner – that was a real ton of fun when we first got it! We were trying it on all size animals and we stunned a ten-footer. There were two of us and we thought, 'This is great; he's knocked out!' So we brought him out of the pen and we were dragging him along, when we realised we hadn't stunned him enough. He'd become alive again and was really cranky. The stunner's about twenty feet away and we're sitting out in the middle of the flat with him and he's trying to beat us all to death. The other bloke had a roll of insulation tape in his pocket and we eventually got the croc's head tied up and his legs up behind him, but he gave us a whale of a time for probably 10 to 15 minutes. It was all fun – but if someone had let go, someone would've died! The other fella was just a young bloke wanting a bit of work experience – he said, 'I'm not coming back here!' But you know, we had to learn with the technology. No one had ever tried it before on big animals. I wouldn't want to work for anyone after doing this.

There are 23 or 24 species of crocodile and alligator worldwide, but the salty is the absolute elite – its scientific name is *crocodylus porosus*. With crocodile, all the skins are exported. With companies like Hermes, Gucci and Versace, they like to tan their own – it's like KFC. It's all their own secret herbs and spices, know what I mean? As for the meat, crocodile meat takes up the taste of what you feed them. It's a white, bland meat, but it takes up a marinade very well. You can do wonders with it. It's expensive, but people don't realise how much goes into feeding crocodile, compared to beef.

We've got two girls born in 1995 and they love the crocs. I've a boy who was born in 1990. He recently won an International Air Force Cadet Exchange (IACE) to Canada and hopes to go on to officer training in the Air Force or Army. I've got a Thai wife, Thasanee. She's been in Australia for twenty-odd years, but she's still a Buddhist and she keeps telling me you don't kill animals unless you absolutely have to or you won't be reincarnated as a human. She keeps saying I'm going to be reborn a rat! I can't argue with it. She knows, though, that if we don't farm and kill it, this will become like other Asian countries, where the species is completely depleted – wiped out. She loves the big animals and really cares for them – probably more than what I do. It balances out your life to have a good partner like that.

We get a few tourists through here and we get school groups come out. We're not that far out of town, just 10 miles north of Mareeba. We bring anyone out that will take notice and hope they go back and think, 'What the hell are we doing to Nature?' The wild population of *porosus* has been nearly shot out worldwide – this is the last stronghold, Australia and New Guinea. We see ourselves as a sort of bank of crocodiles for the rest of the world.

We sold the farm in September 2007 and for the time being I'm still managing the farm under contract for the company that bought it. I've started another business, Crocodile Consultancy International, where I'm supplying advice and knowledge to anyone who requires it. I moved a large croc from Magnetic Island to Sydney for Taronga Zoo recently. We've kept another portion of land where we're farming goats and pumpkins. It's a bit different than farming crocs. The goats get into more trouble than Flash Gordon. I think the crocs might be a bit smarter – I know they're easier to work with!

Fashion Then and Now

Antoinette Ogilvie – My Husband Patrick, Milliner Par Excellence

I first met Toni and her husband Patrick when I was just sixteen. Those were the days when ladies, even young ladies, never went to town without hats, gloves and stockings. A Pat Ogilvie hat was the epitome of style and, after my début, I was given one of these beautiful creations as a birthday present by a much loved aunt. Years later, Cecilia McNally (affectionately known as the Duchess of Spring Hill) told me she was planning to hold a fashion parade for charity featuring the Ogilvie hats, as she knew so many people who'd kept them. She said the idea was popular, but sadly Cecilia passed away before it happened.

'Everyone loved him. I think that's because he could make the ordinary extraordinary. When he walked into the room, you knew you'd have fun.'

Patrick developed his millinery business out of his lunchtime hobby. He worked for the state government, in the Treasury from 1942 to 1950, having studied accountancy. But in his lunch hours, he'd make hats and headpieces for the girls who worked in his office and hid them under the stairs of the Treasury Building to dry! Eventually, he decided to give up his day job and follow his passion and become a full-time milliner – this was a pretty brave decision in a conservative town like Brisbane in 1950. He went to Sydney to study millinery and there he met Freddie Fox. Years later, whenever we travelled to Europe, Patrick would always go to London to see Freddie, who had then become the Queen's milliner.

When Patrick got back from Sydney in the early fifties, he worked with his aunt Kitty in the basement of Greddans. They had a very successful business in Chanel-style classic linen, embroidered suits and frocks, and Patrick started to make hats and handbags to enhance the outfits. From there he set up his own business in Rowes Building, and his sister Maxine worked there with him. She worked with him for the rest of his life, as did Lorraine Wotley, who did all the cutting and sewing of his designs. Things quickly took off – everyone wore hats then, with every outfit, as well as gloves, handbag, shoes and seamed stockings. He built an impressive local and country clientele. His prices were always in guineas: twenty guineas was a lot for a hat in those days, but it was all the rage to have an Ogilvie hat and lots of different women wore them. Shop girls would save up for an 'Ogilvie Creation'. Our youngest child, Sarah, grew up in the 1970s, when hats had really gone out of fashion, but she remembers going over to see friends and their mothers would take their Ogilvie hats out of the cupboard to show her and at the time she thought they were a bit 'tragic' and couldn't understand what all the fuss was about. But now she's an adult she says that she realises these mothers were showing her more than just a dusty old hat; they were remembering Patrick's care, attention and service, which ensured that the hat was just what they wanted. When they put those hats on, especially created for them, they were transported beyond the everyday and felt so good about themselves.

I met Patrick when I was eighteen and on holiday in Surfers Paradise. It was February and it was raining and raining, and I didn't know what to do, so I phoned my grandmother (I was brought up by her) and she suggested I go to visit an aunt in Toowong. So I went there and my aunt was worried, because she didn't know any young people, but her daughter did, and the person she knew was Patrick! So we all went to dinner at Lennons, including Patrick – Lennons was the place to go in those days. The next day was Sunday and Patrick collected us and we went down the coast for the day, then I went home on the Monday and he followed me to Sydney. He was the most charming, beautiful man. We were married later that year, on 1 June 1956.

During the fifties, Patrick worked with Gwen Gillam in Brisbane. They 'dressed' all the key women in town. He'd laugh about the times when he'd have the wife of a well-known business man in one chair, and the same man's mistress in another chair across the room. He was a great diplomat, so everything would go smoothly. I remember the first day he got his hat boxes to pack his new creations in. They were very glamorous – black and shiny, with a big pink bow – and the first person who came and bought three hats that day was the Madam who ran the brothel down in Edward Street, and out she marched with her three Ogilvie hats in their shiny hat boxes, and he just couldn't believe it! But he always saw the funny side of things. That's what all our children remember about him. He could make you laugh about anything; take you out of a bad mood or a blue mood in seconds and make you laugh. He could make anyone feel like the most important person in the room, and he genuinely cared about people. This was partly why everyone wanted to buy his hats, I think.

When the graziers' wives came to town to celebrate Show Week, they all wanted to buy Patrick's hats. They would buy three or four hats, different hats and outfits for each race meeting, and they'd buy 'fascinators' for the cocktail parties at the Queensland Club and Moreton Club. If you went to Lennons during Show Week, all the graziers would be calling Patrick a 'Ned Kelly', because they thought their wives had spent a lot of money on his hats, even though they had spent just as much or more on their akubras! But they were still proud that their wives were wearing the latest and best hats.

Pretty soon, Patrick was getting very well known for his hats. He also came to public notice through charity parades, like the Miss Australia Quest, and he was invited down to Melbourne several times to sit on the committees to judge the Miss Australia Quests. He continued those parades throughout his career. He also visited country areas like Toowoomba, doing parades there for charitable causes.

Sometimes people wanted the prestige of an Ogilvie hat, but didn't want to pay for it! I remember one time there was a particular citizen, quite well known, who went to the races in a hat which Patrick had made especially for her. It was beautifully stitched – just exactly what she'd asked for. She came into the shop on the Monday afterwards and said her husband didn't like it and she wasn't going to take it. She hadn't paid for it, of course, and she said she'd never worn it, but, unfortunately for her, the girl who had stitched the hat had been sitting two seats behind her at the races and told Patrick. That sort of thing did happen. Patrick was really an artist, and such a kind man, not a business man, so he would be too generous-hearted about credit, and sometimes he'd never get paid.

Really, Patrick would do anything for anyone. Our daughter Dominique says that he looked for opportunities to help people and be kind, to make people's lives easier. He would do the shopping for people who were sick. Dominique remembers the time she asked her father if he would make the uniforms for her softball team at Stuartholme School. The teachers kept asking her to get a quote – but by that time Patrick had put everything else in his workshop on hold, designed the uniforms, had them made up by his seamstresses, and given them to the school for free. They were the only softball team to have couture uniforms with hand-finished hems!

There's a story about some nuns and that'll give you a sense of Patrick. He was walking down Edward Street in Brisbane one rainy day when he saw some nuns getting out of a taxi, so he went up to the driver's window and paid the fare, and then raced back to his shop in Rowes Arcade. But the nuns wanted to know who the mystery man was, who had paid their taxi fare. So they went into the arcade, but he had disappeared. They went into the cake shop and told the shop assistant what had happened and she said, 'Oh, that has to be Patrick Ogilvie!' and she sent them up to his showroom. The nuns became great friends of ours, and every year Mother Bernadette would bring a group of four nuns to stay with us. The nuns would vie with each other to come, because they always had a great time. It was in the days when nuns didn't get out much and couldn't drink. Patrick would have sing-a-longs round the piano with them, and would get them all drinking sherry.

Patrick loved a party and he could make any occasion fun. He was a great dancer – a regular Fred Astaire. In fact, when he was young the local newspaper dubbed him the 'Young Fred Astaire' – I think I've got still got that newspaper clipping somewhere. He and his sister Maxine used to do a little 'soft shoe shuffle' routine, and he would tap dance with my cousin Pauline. He had all sorts of little phrases which could make you laugh and our son Brent has collected all those. Patrick also adored champagne. It was his drink. He and our friend Bernadette O'Shea would do weddings together. He'd do the bridal veil and the bridesmaids' headdresses and she'd do the flowers, and at the end of a busy day of weddings, they would relax with a bottle of champagne – now Bernadette is a champagne expert. Our daughter Sarah says that the 'style' and bubbles of champagne sum up her dad's personality. Patrick also loved to play the piano, especially all the old songs. There was the time when we were burgled; we heard a noise in the middle of the night and Patrick went down to investigate. He didn't see anything, so he sat down to play the piano for a while and then came back to bed. In the morning, we saw all my credit cards lined up under the piano and we realised that

Patrick had given the thief a bit of a concert – obviously the thief had hidden under the baby grand piano when Patrick had come downstairs!

Patrick came through two crises and this was caused mostly by his large clientele in the West. The West suffered great drought and during that he suffered. Debts were never paid. Sales were always 'on account' and in those days no one pressured anybody to pay, there was no 'payment in thirty days'. There was no such thing. So you could wait up to three months or nine months – and then sometimes it didn't happen at all.

Then, of course, when the bouffant hairstyle came into style, hats went out of style. Those were hard times financially for us. Patrick went into ladies' fashion then, but his heart was really in millinery. He still had a faithful following, and he made the wedding veils for his clients' daughters and granddaughters. Our son Mitchell says that people still come into his shop and say things like, 'Ah! Your father! I was the Wool Princess in 1952 and he made my hat!' – that sort of thing – and Mitchell rolls his eyes and thinks, 'Gosh, Dad, you must have been so old!' But it's lovely, really, because he gets to hear such nice things about his father; women come in and say, 'Your father was wonderful, and he made my wedding veil.' With Patrick it was always a friendship as well as a client relationship.

Patrick gave us the most wonderful years. He was really a family man. He got on well with everyone and was always concerned for people, but his overriding concern was his family. I think the high points of his life were probably when his children were born. He was so proud of everything they did, never judgmental, always ready to listen to them and talk through problems with them. They've all inherited his creativity in some way or another, though I have to say they have all got a better business sense than he had! Two of them, Mitchell and Dominique, have followed in his footsteps, working in fashion. He would be so proud of all our four children today, and would have loved watching our seven grandchildren growing up.

When Patrick became sick, we received about five hundred letters from people, from the governor of the state to the checkout woman at Woolies where he would go to buy our groceries. Everyone loved him. I think that's because he could make the ordinary extraordinary. When he walked into the room, you knew you'd have fun.

Vale: Patrick Joseph Ogilvie, 13 May 1925 – 29 April 1997

Bora Hwa Sook Lee – Bora Couture

Her fashion studio is nestled in a quiet square in Newstead and the room we're in there is elegantly furnished. One of her most famous creations is a fabulous gold dress worn in 2004 when Jennifer Hawkins won the title of Miss Universe. This dress attracted many admirers keen to purchase it, but Bora wouldn't sell…

'… when I made that dress I cry, I feel glad, I bleed – my blood is in it, my skill's in it, my sweat's in it! It's very meaningful for me.'

I was born in Seoul, Korea, and since childhood I've always been interested in the creative arts. I also loved using my hands and I loved art (painting and drawing) and ever since primary school I've been fascinated with fashion. My family was involved in the fashion industry and I was always interested, but I never expected it would become my career. When the time arrived, though, it was so natural for me. I realised I was at a stage in my life to focus on a career, so I started fashion.

At the age of twenty-two, I was living in San Francisco studying business. I was there four years and it was there I met my husband Jimmy. We were both studying in the same college. After we married we moved to the Solomon Islands to live before moving to Indonesia for seven years. It was after that we decided to move to Brisbane. Language has never been a problem for me. In San Francisco I learnt English, then, after my time in Indonesia, I now speak fluent Indonesian. Fortunately I have always had the ability to learn languages with ease. I remember when I first arrived in Brisbane in 1996, I was intrigued that there weren't as many cars and high-rise buildings around – so different to the busy cities I had got used to living in. I studied fashion at the TAFE in Brisbane for four years.

The first parade I had was the RAQ (the fashion awards).There was a 'student' category and at this stage I didn't know what RAQ was, all I knew that it was an event that all the students in my class were preparing for. This was my first competition and my garment was in the final and was shown around Australia on TV. I was very excited and then thought to myself, 'Next time I will make it better.' That's how I built my ambition.

After my years at TAFE, I relocated to Italy for a further year of studying fashion design in Milan. I really wanted to prove myself in the fashion industry. I was thirty-five and already had my son, but I realised how important formal training in the industry was for my career. I wanted to prove to myself that I could succeed. I returned to Brisbane and had an exhibition in Sydney Fashion Week. At that time, representatives from the Singapore Fashion Week Organisation visited the Sydney Fashion Week and were impressed with my collection and invited me to showcase at the 2000 Singapore Fashion Week. My designs were featured in the international forecasting fashion magazine, *Collezione*. I was very proud and extremely happy.

Upon return from Italy, I joined the RAQ Open Category Professional Competition and I won Supreme. I won the evening category and I also won the bridal category. The following year I really wanted to win Supreme again and that was how I created the gold dress. I worked on it about six months; whenever I was free I would be working on it. It was made of Chantilly lace and was fully beaded. It took me about 2000 hours to make it, spread over a period of about six months. The base was constructed by machine and the outer layer was a fully beaded gown in which I beaded on top of it again. It was unique in texture and beading. It was also very heavy, weighing eight kilograms. I constructed the garment to have an unusual vintage gold finish. The Chantilly lace was based on top of tulle. Without the beading it was quite sheer, but due to the weight of the beading, I put an extra layer of heavy tulle underneath. This was hand-stitched every five centimetre apart to make the dress strong.

After the gown was completed, I was very happy with the result. I joined the RAQ again and got into the final, but I didn't win anything! I was so disappointed, because when I made that dress I cry, I feel glad, I bleed – my blood is in it, my skill's in it, my sweat's in it! It's very meaningful for me. The next day in the *Courier-Mail*, one of the judges was talking about the show, saying, 'This is not about money; it's supposed to be about fashion.' Because a lot of beading was involved, he thought it was a lot of money I put in. Everybody, they have a different way to look at it – but at the time I was so hurt, because it was really my work and I had created it!

I was invited to enter the New South Wales competition, so I sent the gown, because it was sitting there and I'd spent so much time making it, and it won the Supreme in New South Wales. That was two years in a row I won the Supreme and they inducted me into the Hall of Fame. I was so appreciative.

The dress was in New South Wales when it was spotted by Jennifer Hawkins (who was Miss Australia then). Jennifer asked me if she could model the gown for Miss Universe 2004. The dress suited her perfectly; it was as if my direct intention was to make the gown for her. I realised what an amazing opportunity it was for me to represent Australian fashion with such an elegant and beautiful woman wearing it. I was incredibly proud when she was crowned Miss Universe wearing my couture evening gown. I received congratulatory emails from all over the globe. It was such an amazing feeling. There were many purchase inquiries about the gown, but in my heart I had no intention of selling it. I didn't wear it, but I still wanted to keep it. That dress had a lot of meaning to me; money could not make me part with it.

The fashion industry is very exciting. Fashion parades are so full of energy and creativity. Backstage is incredibly frantic and if a parade is not organised and planned properly the audience can feel it. The day after a show, I feel satisfied if I'm approached personally, or at my boutiques, by women who are interested in my designs. Parades also have unpredictable incidents, either on the catwalk or behind the scenes. I remember when Jennifer Hawkins stepped on the hem of a wrap skirt I had designed for her, causing it to fall off her, baring her beautiful bottom to an eager global audience! It was extremely embarrassing for both Jennifer and me.

I live and work in Brisbane as my husband and I know it is a wonderful place to live and raise our son. I regularly travel overseas and interstate to Sydney and Melbourne for additional inspiration, then I return to Brisbane to focus and apply myself. I am always interested in the parades in Europe, as I love haute couture. As I am involved in the Asian market, it's also important for me to know the trends and designers within Hong Kong Fashion Week. Brisbane possesses such a unique cultural identity and is expressing it more in fashion, the urban environment and lifestyle, which is all really exciting. The creative arts scene in Brisbane is exploding.

I design for a lot of celebrities, for award nights such as the Logies. I also design for a lot of brides and mother of brides and school formals. We have cocktail wear they can buy off the rack, but the haute couture, those are the one-off creations designed specifically for my customers. For that I have to know the occasion, which month (the climate, whether it's going to be indoor or outdoor), their body shape, their character, whether they like to show off or they are quite a conservative person. In five minutes talking to them I can tell what sort of person my client is, especially the way they dress, the way they talk and move, I can tell. This is instinct, but also experience; I have been consulting with clients for almost a decade now.

I thrive on the opportunity to dress Australian celebrities. A great example was an Oscar's party held in Australia. There was Courtney Act and Ricki-Lee Coulter from *Australian Idol*; the journalist, Frances Whiting; and Miss World Australia winner, Sarah Davies. The Australian Volleyball athlete, Nicole Sanderson, and Natalie Blair from *Neighbours*, were there too. So there were six girls. I dressed them and we all walked down the red carpet individually and were interviewed. I have very good people surrounding me, especially all my staff. Fernando, my Sydney stylist, granted me the opportunity to dress Gretel Killeen for *Big Brother*, Delta Goodrem for a music video shoot and Kerri-Anne Kennerley for a Logies award night. I also designed and constructed the wedding dress for Kathleen de Leon-Jones. I am extremely grateful for the word of mouth recommendations from my celebrity clientele.

Another fantastic career highlight for me was Australia Week in Los Angeles in January 2005. This gave me the opportunity to showcase my designs and meet famous Australians, such as Olivia Newton-John, Keith Urban and Delta Goodrem. The Queensland government is a major sponsor and when Her Excellency, Quentin Bryce (the Governor), went up to the stage and give out the prize to Mel Gibson and Nicole Kidman. She made such a beautiful speech and I thought, 'Ah, she's wearing my dress – I dressed her!' I was so happy! Then Jennifer Hawkins went on stage and it was the same thing. She's such a down to earth person; she possesses such a friendly, down to earth personality. Having two of the most beautiful representatives from Australia on the stage in LA had me thinking to myself, 'My God, these stars are wearing my gowns in Hollywood!' It was like a dream.

A strong understanding of culture is important for me when designing for different markets. In Korea they have a 5,000-year history and these things for me are all combined – not intentionally, but in my mind, so when I create it's not actually European or Asian or some part of a specific culture – that's the difference that I have. It is very advantageous for me and I really appreciate that I had that opportunity. Australian designers who export fashion have their own distinct style. It is most important we increase recognition from the global market that Australian fashion is just as inspiring as European and New York fashion.

The styles I sell in Shanghai differ slightly from those I sell here. I usually keep design silhouettes similar while mixing up colours and details to suit the trends and culture within each. Asian culture, fashion-wise, is more conservative. The market is for funky fashionable but quite conservative in the colour, style and cut. It is uncommon to show cleavage, arms much and don't tend to wear those thin spaghetti straps. In Korea, especially, parties at night and, like, awards nights are becoming increasingly popular. The women dress quite sexy, like backless dresses with cleavage showing, but this is more for the formal celebrity events.

Right now I'm concentrating on retailing my label in the Bora Stores in Sydney and Brisbane, as well as with exclusive boutique stockists nationally. I have recently appointed an agent into the United Kingdom market and then I'd like to expand into the Middle East and the United States. I'm already expanding in Asia and my Home Shopping label in Korea is really popular. It's all very exciting.

Many people ask me: what is in fashion? What are the current trends? I don't really go round with the trends. For me the important thing is that the dress is for a woman – to make her look and feel wonderful! One day, if I have a chance, my ambition is to have a design college where I can pass on my skills. I'll have my exhibition room which the students can come and visit to view construction and appliqué techniques. I would love to exhibit my prize-winning dresses for the students to see. All my winning dresses I intend to keep together for this ambition.

Gordon Merchant – Billabong

In the early days the banks 'just laughed' at his requests for an overdraft to grow – but, despite this, his business survived and prospered. The pleasure and the camaraderie he enjoyed with his workers in those early times is unmistakable in his voice ...

'Looking back, it was exciting when we moved into our first factory in Miami ... There were only about fifteen of us then ... There were lots of funny things that happened, lots of positive experiences ... I think everybody that worked there really enjoyed it, and we had very little staff turnover; it's still the same today. At times it would get so hot and humid in the summer and someone would start a water fight and it would be on for young and old.'

I first came to Queensland in Christmas 1960, with my parents and my younger brother, for the school holidays. We towed a caravan all the way up from Sydney, which was quite an ordeal in those days. That was my first experience of Queensland. I think there were three shops in Griffith Street at that time and the steam train still ran through the middle of town. There was very little at Broadbeach, just the hotel and nothing much else around it.

I'd come from Maroubra in Sydney, which was a city beach, and to me the Gold Coast with all its beautiful point breaks was just like heaven. The ocean and weather were so warm and the landscape and scenery was so beautiful, everything Maroubra wasn't at the time. I think we only stayed about a week and I hated leaving and always wanted to come back. Later – it seems crazy now – I used to drive up for weekends just to get back there.

In October 1968 I travelled overseas and caught a boat to South Africa and was away for about two years. When I returned, I came back and lived on the Gold Coast and I've never left. I was building surfboards at the time, but before I left to go overseas, I helped a friend, Tom Moses, start a clothing business. There was nothing like surf clothing around that you could buy in those days and I figured Tom could make a real go of it. Most of the people that were attempting to make board shorts didn't have a clue. They didn't surf and had no idea what surfers wanted. Tom thought it was a good idea and called the brand Kream Clothing. I helped Tom design the first range and then I went off travelling to South Africa. When I came back in 1970 Tom had built up quite a successful and thriving little business.

A couple of years passed and I was getting frustrated with building surfboards. The chemicals were starting to affect my health. I was looking for something else to do and that's when I meet up with my partner, Rena. Rena was making the odd board shorts and crocheting a few bikinis as a sideline to try and make a little extra money. I thought I'd have a go at this and try to make some board shorts and bikinis with her. That was in 1973.

We were actually living in a tiny little home unit or annex, actually, on the headland at Miami at the time. We had three little girls: Elyza, Lee and Astra, so there were five of us living there and trying to run a business out of there as well. We had all our fabric underneath our bed because there was just no room to put it anywhere else! It was so claustrophobic in there, but somehow we managed. We used to pull the fabric out, put it on top of the bed and then cut the things out on the kitchen table. We had this little kitchen table and I used to cut them out by hand. I had big calluses on my fingers from using these huge scissors. Rena would sit there with a little Singer hand sewing machine and sew them. We were making about twenty pairs a week and I'd take them down every Friday afternoon and sell them to the local surf shop. It cost us $2 for the material. The surf shop paid us $4 a pair and sold them for $6. They were really bad; something like your mother would make you! I think we still have a few pairs in the Billabong museum. But that was how we got started.

Back then, we were living at Miami on the top of the headland overlooking the beach facing back up to Burleigh Heads. We used to go down to Burleigh and I'd surf while Rena sat, sewed and sun baked; it was idyllic.

It took a while to grow, because we had no money; we were just living from week to week. We'd go down to the local haberdashery to buy the fabric, so it was costing us a fair bit for our material. We then started buying the same fabric from Target, which at the time was cheaper than going to the local wholesalers up in Brisbane. We'd buy about thirty rolls of fabric at a time. They'd ring it up a yard or a metre at a time. The people stuck in the queue behind us at Target must have been so frustrated!

We later moved into a bigger unit on the same property that had a large room that we used for our stock and as a cutting room. At the time we had about a dozen different machinists working out of their homes. I'd travel from Kingscliff up past Southport to pick up the shorts as they sewed them. I wasn't happy with the overall quality that we were getting and I figured we needed to get it all under the one roof to achieve a more uniform look. So we moved into a small factory just down the road at 8 Hibiscus Haven, Miami. It was about half way through 1975 when we made that move.

The factory was only 1,000 square feet, but it seemed huge to me after the confined spaces we were used to. I thought, 'Oh, my goodness, I'm never going to fill this; it's always going to look half empty!' but within twelve months it was full, with racks hanging off the ceiling. I remember the ceiling was starting to bow because of the weight of the fabric!

By then we had enough volume to buy our fabric from Paterson, Reid and Bruce; and Caesar Fabrics, the fabric wholesalers in Brisbane. This made a big difference to our production cost, plus we could get a better quality fabric in the colours we wanted. We were using a cotton gabardine twill and lightweight poly cotton poplin to make the board shorts. They had a buttoned fly and we were able to buy the buttons, fabric and thread all from wholesalers.

It took some time before we were able to develop a market for other garments to widen our range. We'd started with bikinis and board shorts, but I was desperately trying to get something going for winter. We'd shut the factory down for three months over winter, then we'd reopen again and try and get all the workers back for summer production! It took a little while to get past this stop-start situation. I started developing a corduroy walk short and decided to make a jacket out of the same corduroy. It sold really well. Then we started trying to expand our winter range for girls, but things would take off and then suddenly stop as the fashion changed. We had no continuity and were just stumbling along. All the profit we made through summer we'd lose through winter because of our fixed overheads and not being able to generate enough income. Once we continued making summer clothing well after the Christmas period and ended up with all stock and no money! We had to work really hard to pay back all our debtors and survive.

Prior to starting, I hadn't done any study on clothing manufacturing at all. My mother worked as a machinist for a while at Anthony Squires in Sydney and after school I'd peek into the factory to see what went on and then listen to Mum talk about work and what it was like there. But when I started myself I still didn't know the fundamentals of doing business. The only experience I'd had was watching my father as a boy selling eggs, cream and poultry from the farm in Paddy's Markets in Sydney on a Friday afternoon. I'd watch the traders there and realised that the more effort and thought you put into it and the harder you worked the more likely you were to succeed. One thing that did help me in those early years was that I was a participant in a sport I was designing for and got a lot of feedback from the guys. It gave me an inside running on what to design, what had worked and what hadn't and how to approach advertising.

I believed our biggest opportunity was to do something internationally, but for a long time that was just a dream, as we were still struggling to survive in the Australian market. Our export business started when Ed Ogawa approached me from Dropout Surfboards, Japan, with an order for board shorts. Later, I was approached by Bob Hurley, a small surfboard manufacturer in the US who wanted to try manufacturing Billabong over there. I liked the guy and we started manufacturing board shorts in Australia for him and exporting them. A few years later I helped set up manufacturing Billabong garments in the US.

Our winter range came about from the jackets that we had initially started and then getting requests from people that snowboarded or skied. With their feedback we had an idea what was needed. It's a very technical area, but we succeeded, because our approach was to not try to make something really technical. We made something that worked for skiing but that was also 'street clothing' that could be worn as a normal garment. We've come a long way since those days and now have the technical expertise as well.

Looking back, it was exciting when we moved into our first factory in Miami. There were only about fifteen of us then. It was difficult on the Gold Coast to find quality machinists. There were just a few quality people that had children and had chosen to stay at home. As a result, we had flexible hours, so if they needed to be home early, they started early and vice-versa.

I think everybody that worked there really enjoyed it. We had very little staff turnover; it's still the same today. At times it would get so hot and humid in the summer and someone would start a water fight and it would be on for young and old. I remember one day when two buyers from Myers came into our factory. I was fixing a sewing machine and they walked right up to me and asked if they could speak to the manager. I turned to the girls and said, 'Who'd like to be the manager today?' and they all put their hands up! Everyone really pulled together and we were proud of the product we made.

Highpoints – apart from moving into our first factory – were being able to export, especially to the US. I think the main reason we were successful was the fabrics that we used were more suitable for surfing and the designs and the colour range were different and interesting. It was a different look to what they were used to in the US. Another major highpoint for Billabong was actually floating the company on the Australian Stock Exchange and seeing the public response that made it so successful.

In the early days the clothing business used to have a bad reputation for a lot of fly-by-nighters. People would just come in, get credit, build up a ton of debt and then declare bankruptcy. I remember when I first approach banks for a small overdraft to try to build up stock they'd just laugh at me. Later, when we didn't need the money, they all raced in wanting to lend us money! It's been an amazing story, really, from such a small humble beginning to see the business as it is today.

Bikes and Boards

Russell Tucker – Riding and Retailing Bicycles

Russell Tucker (centre), Winner of the World Points Score Championships, Sydney, 2007

The name of Tucker has become synonymous with cycling in Rockhampton. Like his father before him, Russell's sport has become a way of life. He still rides competitively and his business attracts both the elite and social sport enthusiasts. He's also enjoyed competing internationally and in October 2007 won the UCI Track Cycling Masters in Sydney.

'I was out training in Brisbane one day and a guy comes up to me and says, "Hey, man, you want to come to America with me and race?" Well, I tell you, I was like the petrol – first on the plane!'

We were born in Rockhampton. My mother and father grew up there, and so did we. I was in Brisbane after that and that's where I suppose I got the idea with my bike shop career. I got a job with friends working as a process server and they also owned a bike shop. After a while I got sick of Brisbane, so I moved back to Rocky for the 'quiet life'.

When I got back to Rocky I worked for a while with a friend in a Mobil service station just helping out and that's where I learnt how to handle cash. I had a background as a motor mechanic – I'd done a trade as a motor mechanic and then, with the help of my friend in Brisbane, I decided I'd do a bike shop. I found a little shop and I went down to Brisbane and they helped me getting stock. It was funny setting it up, because me and a friend put paper up at the windows (to stop anyone looking in) built the bikes up and put some stock on the walls, then opened the doors. I didn't have a clue what was going to happen. I think I took $37 that day and I was wrapped – now here I am eighteen years later still going!

I've two brothers, Byron and Kenrick, who are both older than me. The whole family races. My father Ken, or Reggie, as he's affectionately known, has raced all his life and we used to follow him around a lot, obviously watching him racing when we were little. He wouldn't allow us to race 'til we were twelve years old, and we still race today, which is great – I'm forty-five and I've been racing all that time and still do. Dad got into racing through his family. When we all started racing he used to train us (and still does) and he and Mum used to drive us all around the country. It used to be nice when we'd win all the Queensland titles we raced in. I think that was probably the best memories I have of us all out there together. The nice thing is that my brother Byron and I raced in October 2007 at the world masters track championship and Dad was there with us! The championships were always held in Manchester, but they've come to Sydney for three years. I won the World 20-kilometre points race and Byron finished fourth in his.

My brother Kenrick went to the Olympic Games in 1980 and 1984 and won the Commonwealth Games in Brisbane in 1982. He doesn't include himself in cycling so much anymore; he's stepped away from it a little bit. He still rides his bike, but he's not competitive.

I sponsor a lot of the cycling events here and also the Rydges Triathlon. It's one of the main triathlons on the Australian calendar and I also sponsor the local Tri Club. We have training rides three and four times a week and then we race. I race the local races and I sponsor the riders. I'm always out there heavily involved – in the shop with the bikes and equipment, positioning them and helping to make people the best they can be, and helping them out with training programs as well. Rocky is and always has been a great place to cycle. We have up to 100 people all ages and sexes turn up some weekends for local club racing and Triathlons. We have also had a lot of world champs come from here. That's what I love about it all. It's great to see the kids come through and do so well and also to still be able to race and train with them.

Representing Australia was really nice to do, racing in Europe. We first went over in 1982 and then back in 1984 and 1985 and I was fortunate enough to get a trip to America in 1996. It was neat how that happened. I was out training in Brisbane one day and a guy comes up to me and says, 'Hey, man, you want to come to America with me and race?' Well, I tell you, I was like the petrol – first on the plane! It's really good to go away and just become a professional cyclist for a while again. That was a great time. You're being paid to ride a bike and do what you love doing. I tell all the young fellas to go over.

I don't get involved with training the young yet, because I'm still training myself. I'm on the bike every morning. I'm up at four o'clock and riding between 60 and 80 kilometres a day during the week. At weekends, if we're not racing, we do a100-kilometre-plus ride – we go looking for mountains and things like that. I've got a trainer here in the garage and I train on that and I also put other people on that and help them train as well.

My dad's still heavily involved with cycling. He still trains riders at the velodrome here and takes them away to state and Australian titles. He trained Anna Meares and her sister Kerry, a couple of world champions, and he trained Miles Olman. Dad's seventy-three and he's still at the track training a new junior, Philippa Hindmarsh, who competed in the World Championships in Mexico in 2007 and will hopefully follow in the footsteps of the Meares sisters.

My wife Tina rides but just socially and we have a little boy Jayden, who's five and he races BMX, and he gets a lot of fun from it – that's what it's about at his age too. I maintain that I still race because I've enjoyed the years I've been doing it. I've never been made to do it; I've always wanted to do it. You can't put pressure on kids to make them do it; they've got to want to do it. I want to see him enjoy riding right through his career like I have.

My brother Byron has two boys. They're fifteen and seventeen now and they're still racing and very competitive, but they live in Townsville. Byron is two years older than me and he raced in the Worlds with me as well and Dad came down with us as well so that was nice.

A few years back I spent two years on the board of Cycling Queensland. As one of the executives there I'd fly down once a month to Brisbane for meetings.

We carry probably over half a million dollars worth of stock here in the shop, from bikes to bits and pieces, so it's a large concern. We cater for the whole family, from the children through to athletes and elite athletes. We also cater to the general public who just want to get fit. We always try to help them out and generally get them out on training rides, so they can do riding in the mornings or whatever they want to get fit. With the kids it's important to make sure they're comfortable – if they're not comfortable on the bike before they leave the shop, they're not going to ride it. We want to see more bums on bikes. We've spoken at schools, but, unfortunately, with litigation the way it is, they don't push riding anymore because of the safety aspects of riding on roads. We still have a very strong triathlon comp which I sponsor and we race Sunday mornings at the beach. The Rydges resort are good, as we use their complex to run them out of, and the local surf club come up and do the water safety.

Yeppoon is about 40 kilometres from here. It's a nice little area and they run about a dozen events a year there and we have one major one which I help at. We have 400 to 500 competitors come there from around Australia to compete and I look after the bike maintenance and take a mobile shop down for the weekend. It's a busy weekend, but it's great to do, because it's all about the bike and that's what I love!

Gail Austen – Retailing to Surf and Skate Enthusiasts

The shop is physically and visually busy with a K1 Kayak suspended from the ceiling and kite surfing kites and other gear to tempt the aficionados of surf who come here for the latest and greatest. Work in the shop continues around us as we speak, with young people discussing the pros and cons of various offerings. Gail is quick to laugh at her adventures and misadventures

'Surfing – it's a way of life. It's a free-form, raw-energy sport, an explosion of nature and the person.'

I was born in Australia in Botany in Sydney and in 1966, when I was twenty-one, I went to England and I was there till Christmas '72, when I came home. I've been in business all my life in Australia – lots of different businesses. I had a box business and a bottle business; in the modern idiom you would have called me a recycling business. We drove past the pubs and saw they used to burn the beer cartons, so I made an arrangement with all these hotels from Brisbane to Ipswich to collect the boxes once a week. I stored them at relatives' and friends' houses and sold them to firms like McWhirters, who needed them to sell things in. I was doing that from when I was about fourteen and did it for years

One time I found a dealer in Breakfast Creek, called Bowman's, who wanted to move a huge aluminium shipment to Italy and he didn't have any containers. So I talked a chemical company into letting me take all the caustic soda drums that they had for free – I found out from a chemist that caustic soda doesn't affect aluminium. Then I sold the dealer all the drums to ship his stuff to Italy.

I was about seven when I started making a living. That came about because my grandfather was a wheeler dealer – an entrepreneur. He was the first man to sell ice-cream on the streets of Sydney. When they brought in electricity he bought up all the gas lights in Sydney and sold them for scrap. When Queensland Railways changed the line, he bought all the railway lines in Queensland and sold them for scrap – that was the sort of character he was. He died when I was very young, but as I grew up I used to work in the business that he'd created. I'd be in the factory as a little tiny kid sorting out nuts and bolts, learning what was copper and what was brass and how to separate them. Today the business is run by my uncle's sons and it's one of the biggest in the country. It's a machinery merchant's business called Hare & Forbes.

I had a car accident here when I was eighteen and broke my spine and that changed my life. Opportunities for women to get into business were very limited in Australia at the time. I couldn't get a loan; I couldn't get even get a business licence without a man signing the documents. I'd read about Europe and London and I felt there was more opportunity for a woman there – so in July 1966 I went to England.

I was only in London two weeks when I started a business – by accident. I was walking down Portobello Road, where they have the market, and I saw two ladies standing arguing. Apparently one of them was the owner of the Georgian house they were standing outside and the other wanted to set up a stall outside it. The lady with the Georgian house had a very modern looking garage down beside it and so I said to her, 'Why don't you rent her that garage and you could make a quid and she could sell her clothes?' The lady from the Georgian house said, 'Who are you?' I said, 'I'm here from Australia,' and she said, 'So what's this got to do with you?' I said, 'It's none of my business; I just felt you could do something that would help you both.' The lady – Annie her name was – said, 'I'll rent it to you and you can help her, but I won't rent it to her!' I looked at the girl and said, 'Do you want a partner?' And that was it; we started in business. We rented the garage for 30 shillings each Saturday. She designed and made clothes and I sold them. It began a whole new era for me. It was a wonderful period. Carnaby Street had just begun and we were the first people to sell fashion – as it was then – in Portobello Road.

Time passed and I had a decision to make. 'Do I want to buy a house here or go home?' But the decision was made for me. My mother wrote to me saying she was concerned about my brother and sister in Australia. My sister was working for my brother, who was making surfboards. She was making clothes and they were selling them in a little business he'd started. My mum thought it was a good idea, but was concerned that they weren't concentrating and she thought that maybe I could come home and help them.

I arrived back in Australia on Christmas Eve and on Boxing Day I was round at the factory where my brother was making the surfboards. I had a good look at everything, and it took me only half an hour to work out what was wrong. If you run a business you've got to have a factory that's organised and you don't go surfing every day! I sat down with my brother and I said, 'Look, I can help you if you want help, but you'll have to get organised. You'll have to open a shop in Brisbane and you'll have to have someone like Mum working in the shop every day. Alternatively, if you want to cruise along having a good time and then go broke, just keep doing what you're doing!' My brother decided to go along with the idea. I said I'd only help for a while, no more than three months – and I'm still here running the business, which we called Goodtime!

The reason for my interest and my brother's interest in surfing dates back to our early years. We were born in Redfern in Sydney and were surfing when we were little babies at Bondi and Maroubra; we just grew up with it. My brother and sister both had wonderful talents in making things. She was always a seamstress and is still making clothes today. My brother started making surfboards when he was in Sydney for a company called Jackson Surfboards. Then he worked for Joe Larkin in Brisbane, then

Ray Woosley on the Gold Coast. Later he decided to start up on his own and shape his own surfboards and that was what he was doing when I came back from London. I discovered then that surfing was changing the way people dressed, the way they did their hair – turning the Australian male into a whole different person. I could see an opportunity to be part of that development and it was exciting.

After I'd looked at the business we opened in Brisbane, and then in January there was a women's surf contest on the coast. I went to the presentation and Ma Bendall, who was over fifty at the time, ran third. I walked up to her and I said, 'How come you've come third in Australia when you're over fifty?' She said, 'Well, they don't compete!' and I said, 'Why not?' and she said, 'Go and have a look and you'll see why.'

I went to the competitions and I saw the women being thrown into competitions where there was no surf and they had put their little kids in to judge them. I thought, 'This is ridiculous!' When I left Australia, Phyllis O'Donnell had won the World Championship and I couldn't believe that between 1964 and 1972 not a single woman in Australia had done anything else. American women were doing it all. I said to Gordon Phillipson, who was then running the Surfing Association, 'Look, do you want women surfers to become world champions?' He said, 'That would be wonderful, Gail,' and I said, 'Well, the way you're doing it, that'll never happen. If you want something to happen I could do something about that.' God knows why I said that! Anyway, he said, 'What are you going to do?' I said, 'Well, I want to form an association and develop the Australian women surf riders into a group of women who will win world championships and, when they do, I'll retire from it!'

That was another challenge that I took on and I did exactly what I said I'd do. I developed the organisation and got them in the water. I didn't train them, but I gave them the vehicle on which they could develop their skills and that went Australia wide. I'd met Pamela Burridge when she was a teenager and she eventually won the world title after being bridesmaid at least three times. The day they rang me to say she had won the title was the day I retired.

So here I was in Australia in 1973, saying I'm only staying for so long, but within three months I'd founded the Australian Women's Surf Riding. Next I started the Queensland Skateboarding Association, which became an Australian association, and then later on I founded the Brisbane Boardriders Association. I was involved in women's rights in surfing and the rights of kids in Brisbane in skateboarding – skateboarding was totally taboo then! All these activities were connected to the business.

Surfing – it's a way of life. It's a free-form, raw-energy sport, an explosion of nature and the person. People who come in here won't water-ski or fish, and they won't snow-ski, but they'll ride snowboards. Wakeboarding has only come into the store in the latter years because of kite surfing. I even sold hang-gliders at one stage.

My brother died when he was forty-nine, after a long battle with cancer. Brian had nurtured people like Peter Townend and Robert (Rabbit) Bartholomew and Michael Peterson, who all became legends in their surfing career. As boys, they all worked in the factory. You'll see Goodtime boards from that era, like the PT Bonzer, the MP Pin Tail and so on. Right from the start my idea was to always encourage new ideas. We still manufacture, but I no longer own the factory. I've got three factories in Australia that work with me now, and people overseas as well. I design what I want. We have five or six brands and I have people shaping different models.

I was introduced to the Cerebral Palsy League many years ago by a friend, Jan Crane, and I've done a lot of work since then for people with the disease. It's awful to have a wonderful mind and a body that won't respond. I thought to myself, 'I wouldn't like that,' so I went to help those kids and adults. I ran and competed in a canoe event called the Goodtime Brisbane Valley 100 for twenty-one years and raised over half a million dollars over that time. I helped a young lass who needed a voice machine. I got some of the money she needed for that.

I've been involved with Active Aging at various times. I've been involved in the Masters Sports, both as a canoeist and in other fields. There was a guy called Mike Nugent years ago who used to make wheelchairs and used to participate in the canoe races I ran. I actually bet him that he couldn't paddle to Moreton Island – it cost me $500! He was a very famous paralympian who still makes wheelchairs.

In 1997 I won the Australian Telstra Award. It's all about working for women's rights, better conditions for families in business and the working poor – the same things I've worked for all my life. I'm the only small business owner who's ever won it. There's nothing wrong with organisations making a profit, but you have to have a social bottom line as well.

From the start the principle in this business has been to draw on the talent of new and upcoming young people. That way you've always got fresh ideas – you're the one being copied rather than the copier. Young people don't just come here to work; they come to be trained. They could be studying to be a doctor or a lawyer or any young person with a sense of commitment. I tell them it's no good coming here unless you've got some sort of commitment. If you haven't got one and I can't help you find one then you'll have to go and do something else – commitment is what this business is all about.

Houses – Designing, Building and Moving

Lindsay and Kerry Clare – Architects of GoMA

We'd arranged to meet for coffee at the Gallery of Modern Art (GoMA). This beautiful building was a project they won against competition from around the world. Lindsey explained that he and Kerry had started their practice doing residential and small alteration projects in the Sunshine Coast region and quickly became involved in community and small public projects. One of these was the Cotton Tree social housing project, which has since been the subject of national and international research studies and exhibitions.

'*The Ten Shades of Green Exhibition was organised by the Architectural League of New York and travelled from there throughout the USA for five years. The Cotton Tree was the only project from the southern hemisphere and was selected because of its architectural excellence and environmental sensitivity.*'

Lindsay: I was born in Queensland and grew up in the northern suburbs of Brisbane. My father was a wood turner and he ran his own business from home. I grew up in what people would describe as a 'Queenslander'. It was a very small house and I lived out on the verandah, which had roll-down blinds, timber shutters and no windows. The timber louvres could be retracted or pivoted to suit the climate. Later, when I did architecture, I realised I had learned to understand weather patterns and climatic issues because of having to deal with them living on this balcony all my younger life.

Kerry: … and he had the north-east corner.

Lindsay: My grandmother lived on Bribie Island and she had what was basically a Nissen hut, a very simple and fundamental dwelling.

Kerry: She actually lived in a Queenslander but she had the Nissen hut as extra accommodation for grandchildren, when they came for a holiday.

Lindsay: We used to stay in this little hut on Bribie with the shower under the water tank. Again there were no windows, just plywood shutters that she used to prop out. We spent holidays close to the water. It was what you might call a genuine Queensland experience. At school I did a lot of art work. I had a very good teacher, Rex Backhaus-Smith, who is now a highly acclaimed Australian water-colourist; he taught us a lot about light and landscape. It was the late '60s when I finished school. I didn't know what I wanted to do and I ended up working in Brisbane doing quantity surveying for four years, but I didn't do a lot of measurement and estimating work. I actually spent most of my time on a building site. When I was twenty I decided to do architecture and got a job with Gabriel Poole in Mooloolaba and a year later Kerry came to join the office.

Kerry: I grew up in Sydney. Later my parents moved to the Northern Territory and we lived in a standard Northern Territory issue house in Darwin. It was a house with louvres like Lindsay's, which suited the tropical environment. At high school in Darwin I started becoming interested in the idea of designing houses that would work with the weather and with particular sites and things like that. When I finished school I headed back to New South Wales for a year, but then transferred to Queensland, because my parents ended up buying a farm on the Sunshine Coast. I'd seen an article about this architect, Gabriel Poole, who had done some very innovative houses, so I decided to front up and see if I could get a job there, which I did – and that's how Lindsay and I met.

Lindsay: In those days we were studying part time at QUT (or QIT as it was called then) so we had to drive to Brisbane two or three times a week. It was on the old road which used to go through Caboolture and it was quite a journey.

Kerry: We had a job during the day and then had to travel 600 kilometres a week to go to uni at night and then do all the assignments at the weekend.

Lindsay: It was very interesting working for Gabriel Poole. He was born and bred in Queensland and was originally a jackaroo before he became an architect. He subsequently became a gold medallist for the Institute of Architects.

Kerry: And a Queensland boxing champion.

Lindsay: He was quite a character and still is. He was trained at the University of Queensland, but he had a natural talent for making do – he was also very inventive, and we learned a lot from him. I was there for almost five years and it was a great apprenticeship.

Kerry: Gabriel had to move to Noosa, so we started working with another firm. We'd just finished six years of architecture and we were still very new to the field. People started coming along saying they'd like us to do a small house for them, so we'd take them to the firm that we were working with, but they said, 'No, we really don't want to get involved with houses.' So we thought we might just as well start our own practice. Our boss at the time, Kerry O'Rourke, gave us some drawing boards to set up our business. It was very good of him to do that, because he'd wanted us to get more involved in his practice. Anyway, we set up our own little business in a rented house down on the river.

Lindsay: We painted and edge-stripped some doors, which we used as desks, and started business with the two borrowed drawing boards. We had no cheque account, so we had to earn the money in cash and then go round and pay all our suppliers. We had a very old car and no telephone. We made appointments to see clients on the public telephone up the street.

Kerry: Plus we had a baby crawling around the office.

Lindsay: But we did have three or four incredibly good clients who helped us through this period and within a year I think we had about four or five people working with us. The buildings we were doing then were basically houses and small apartment buildings. After a few years we gradually moved into small community buildings and small public and education buildings. These days you learn to start a business with a business plan – that's not the way we did it! Being aged twenty-seven and twenty-two, respectively, I think clients were quite apprehensive when they came to our office. We looked like the office juniors and they wanted to see someone who looked like an experienced architect!

Kerry: We certainly had a credibility gap for a while.

Lindsay: Still, we've managed to work together now for close on thirty years. The Sunshine Coast period was tough and there were times when we paid wages on Bankcard and sold cars and things like that to keep the business going. It's an incredible commitment to run a business and particularly one that is to some extent an artistic pursuit, but we've found that if you're working with a good client and a good builder then it's very enjoyable.

Kerry: Along the way we had five children. So getting going in business was intermingled with babies and nappies and kids coming into the office after school to raid the biscuit jar – a really 'holistic' experience.

Lindsay: Our children have grown up visiting building sites and having other architects and clients visit us regularly. Kerry and I talk about aspects of buildings and design at all sorts of odd moments. There's nothing more we enjoy than going away together, just the two of us, and then we generally look at architecture. Environment, culture and architecture are all intermingled in our minds.

Kerry: We took the children for a big camping trip across Europe and Scandinavia – the eldest was ten at the time and the youngest four. There's a famous Finnish architect called Alvar Aalto, and we really do enjoy his work, so we decided to visit a number of his buildings. We'd be walking up the steps to a public building and they'd go, 'Oh no, not another Aalto building.' We didn't even have to tell them it was one of his.

Lindsay: Travelling with five young children leads you to experience buildings in different ways than you had imagined. They don't go up the stairs; they climb up the walls! Still, it was a good way for us to experience and test lots of well-known architecture.

Kerry: Most of our children have wisely decided that architecture is very hard work and they've gone into other careers, but one daughter is an interior designer and we do work with her at times. I enjoy that because she knows where we're coming from and there's a very good working rapport.

Lindsay: We were in Buderim and Mooloolaba for twenty years and in that time we maintained a fairly constant staff level of say six to eight people. We did a number of houses, public buildings, apartment buildings and some small commercial buildings. It was very rewarding and we got a lot of recognition in terms of awards and publications and invitations to speak overseas.

Kerry: But the problem was, no matter how hard we tried, we just couldn't push into the larger work. One reason for that was the way Quality Assurance was introduced into architectural practice. Suddenly an office that had been running successfully and doing quality work was required to get QA so that the quality of the process could be 'measured'. It was very expensive to get certification; it would have cost us about $50,000, the cost of a house in those days. So we didn't have QA, which in turn meant we couldn't get any more of the education sector jobs that we had been doing very satisfactorily before QA came in. Fortunately, in 1998 we were invited by the New South Wales government architect's office to go to Sydney and assist with public projects for two years. We had access to QA then, because we were working with a government body and they had certification. That was what drew us away from Queensland.

Lindsay: As design directors for the New South Wales government architect we were able to do projects like the National Environment Centre in Albury, the Number 1 Fire Station in Castlereagh Street in the city, the Water Police Headquarters and upgrading the Circular Quay ferry wharves. It exposed us to a lot of high profile public projects. We were thinking of coming back up to Queensland, but then we were asked to do quite a large school in New South Wales, so we stayed to do that. Then the Queensland Gallery Competition was announced and we entered for that.

Kerry: Being an anonymous competition, the judges had no idea who had done the architectural drawings and there were one hundred and seventy-four entries from around the world. Anyway, I think they short-listed twelve and then opened up the envelopes to find out who the firms were. We'd changed our name from Clare Design to Architectus and when they opened up our envelope they said, 'Who's Architectus?' When they found out that we were Queenslanders I think they were amazed. They had short-listed somebody from their own backyard!

Lindsay: When it got down to the final five we all knew who we were and who we were competing against …

Kerry: … there was an Italian designer, an English firm, another from Sydney and one from Melbourne.

Lindsay: … all very highly regarded architects. Anyway, we managed to win the competition and that was obviously a highlight for our team here at Architectus. Afterwards Kerry and I took charge of the project. It's one thing to win a competition but to see the project through and have it completed and seeing it work so well after all these years has been very rewarding. The Queensland Art Gallery was also very supportive and good to work with.

Kerry: We enjoy combining the artistic design with the functionality needed and the gallery client understood that. We're very pleased, because we feel it is a truly Queensland building. It's contemporary and yet it's still a statement that says this is Brisbane, this is Queensland, and this building belongs to where it is.

Lindsay: We felt that it was important for the building to respond to its site on the bend of the river, its place in the city and to the Asia–Pacific region. The building's prime purpose is to connect people with art and the building does this physically and culturally. The architecture is about light and lightness.

Kerry: We were able to bring these qualities to the interior spaces and this seems to have been an aspect of the work that people who visit GoMA enjoy. The artworks have to be protected from the strong natural light and yet people respond to varying levels of light – morning, afternoon, summer, winter. We have tried to make the people-spaces connect to the light, the river and the city.

Lindsay: We were pleased that the curators from the gallery have been so supportive of our approach. Fourteen gallery spaces have been created, each with its own character and function, differing in scale, material and the use of light – our approach has been to provide a serviceable, flexible frame for the art – more about the potential for art than the creation of a building as an object. It's a great privilege to go back now and see people enjoying the spaces.

Andrew Kennedy – Master Builder

Moorooka is a quiet suburban area and the house where we meet is approached from the side by a long drive. He's modernised it himself over time. The table in his office is strewn with plans for buildings he's currently working on.

Photo courtesy of Anne Kennedy-Levesque

'Bricklaying's a four-year apprenticeship covering many aspects of the trade ... there is still work to do adding to and restoring old buildings ... I like to think the craftsman's skill is still very much alive and well in Queensland.'

I can thank Wally and Sam for getting me into building. Wally Neale was my sister's boyfriend and an apprentice bricklayer while I was at school and he'd extolled the merits of bricklaying to me. Sam Heyburn was a bricklaying contractor that I left school to go to work for, but for some reason that didn't come together. Sam and Wally have both passed on now. I went on looking and found another employer offering a bricklaying apprenticeship, just down the road from my folks' house in Wynnum North.

Bricklaying's a four-year apprenticeship covering many aspects of the trade including some of those skills that would be lost if they didn't have apprenticeships to retain that body of knowledge. For example, there're different bonds in brickwork, they're not just all staggered. There's English bond and Flemish bond and that's just two. Then there are different styles of arches. There're flat arches and Gothic arches, among others. I've had to use these skills at times, but sadly it's become very much a rarity, because we've knocked down most of our heritage buildings in Queensland. Still, there is work to do adding to and restoring old buildings, so those skills are still valuable. I like to think the craftsman's skill is still very much alive and well in Queensland.

Later on, after doing my apprenticeship and having worked as a bricklayer, I studied the carpentry trade and got trade recognition for that as well, so I can claim two trades. But the trade that you begin with and learn as a young person is the one that I think is ingrained. You see yourself as 'one of them' for the rest of your life. It's a particular asset, though, to have learnt and understood the mechanics of another trade, because it's much harder for the practitioners of that other trade to later snow you about things, for example, about the quality or the speed that they can do things. So all the experience I've gained in other trades is a good thing. Also, when looking at other buildings I think it helps you pick up where things are built in an amateurish way, and you can see the different eras in which things have been built.

Some of the things about 'the good old days' weren't so good; people thought things then were built very strongly and in some cases they were, but some of the heavy timbers were used in the wrong places. Consequently, if you walk under a house that's sixty years old you're likely to see significant bows in the bearers where they've sagged down over time. Even though in many cases things are done with much lighter construction these days, it's more likely that the depth of timber will be used in more appropriate spots. This kind of knowledge helps you to understand building from the point of view of valuing or knowing which houses can be extended easily and that type of thing.

There was always that bit of uncertainty involved in the building industry and there still is because people are often afraid about whether they're going to get paid or not. There's loads of money passing through, but most of the operators don't get to keep that money. They're getting money for services and they're passing it on to the various employees, sub-contractors and suppliers.

I remember when the metric system came in. It was 1966 and I was fifteen years old. Weights and measures changed a couple of years later. It impacted enormously, not so much on what we were studying but on our mental capacity to do the things we did. For example, when setting out brickwork, we had memorised by rote the inches and fractions that each course would go, but when it became metric that was all mucked up! I've been with metric long enough now, though, to embrace it.

In the early days my boss would end up each afternoon either in the Waterloo Bay Hotel or in the Manly Hotel where he made a lot of probably dubious contacts, but he did get himself involved in all sorts of work. Restumping and raising houses was one of the things we did, so at a very tender age I was charged with the responsibility of jacking up people's houses and pulling stumps out, usually with help, but sometimes with a fair bit of responsibility on my young shoulders. Those sorts of things taught me to have the attitude of tackling anything, which helped me later when I became a contractor myself.

I remember the toughness of the trade before we had much mechanisation. One time we were to build a house over at the Gap, a sultry place behind Mount Coot-tha, protected from all kinds of cool breezes. We unloaded the picks and shovels from the back of the Holden ute and set out in this shale and clay to dig a foundation. We bent up the steel and tied it together and then mixed the concrete by hand. There was no backhoe to dig the foundations, no Readymix truck to come and no concrete pump to pump it in, so it took probably about two weeks to do the foundations, work that can be done in a day or two now and it was terribly hard. Those experiences were probably good for my development.

The world of bricklaying in Brisbane at that time included a lot of Poms! I think one of the reasons for this was that, up until the time I did my apprenticeship, bricklaying was a rarity. We didn't build many brick homes here; they were mostly wood. Brick homes grew in popularity here from the 1960s, when the brick veneer idea took off. There was a big increase in demand, but there weren't many trained people around, so Englishmen were getting jobs here and they were generally respected as good tradesmen. They'd learnt to work quite fast in their cold climate and it was a matter of great respect when a brickie was fast, if he was neat as well.

Clerks of Works were the bane of our lives as bricklayers, because they'd come round and ask for things that were generally difficult to do. For example, they'd request we keep the bricks well wet before laying. We'd wet the bricks, but the moisture disappears off them in the heat and the Clerk of Works would turn up and complain, 'Those bricks aren't wet!' Traditionally, you'd have a bucket of water and a dipper and you had to perpetually be damping the bricks down – you won't see it happening these days. Some bricks are now silicone coated, so they're not as thirsty, and that helps.

I worked for about seven years in Rockhampton and Mackay then returned to Brisbane around 1976. At that stage I was mostly working for myself, because I'd become a registered builder and a contractor when I was in Mackay. There was a time when I was going backwards and forwards, still catering for some cane farmer clients up in Mackay. I enjoyed going back there for the hang-gliding! I've been doing it a long time now, so I've become somewhat used to the risks and it's good to look down and watch people going about their work.

When I returned to Brisbane, I lived in the Redlands. I tried to make a name for myself as a quality builder and built some landmark homes round the area. In 1986 I became a member of the Master Builders and at that time I went to QUT and did a diploma course in Building Project Management to enhance my management skills in dealing with subcontractors. A fellow I met invited me to be on the Master Builders Housing Committee and it went on from there. I've been the training delegate representing Master Builders at CTQ (Construction Training Queensland) and for the last four or five years I was Treasurer of both those organisations. I've now stepped down from those positions, but I'm still involved in the State Council of Master Builders and I'm still the Master Builders Representative to CTQ. This is a name that doesn't mean a lot to many people, but it's the advice-giver to government on training and the need for training. It also dispenses grants to encourage the continuance of the apprenticeship system, to encourage people to properly train young people for the future.

I became a contractor at about the time the government was bringing in the Act to require builders to be registered. There was a lot of shonky building going on and they wanted to control who could be a practitioner and who couldn't. Some of the carpenters who had been a long time in the industry were very resentful that mere bricklayers were being registered as builders. There are quite a number of bricklayers that I've known who've become registered builders and very good ones too, but there has always been a sense of competition and animosity between other builders who felt they had more of a right to be a 'builder', because they were carpenters. It's interesting that in Australia we have a tradition of building wooden houses and they tell me that in England the bricklayer is more likely to be the master contractor, because the buildings are predominantly brick – carpentry there is considered more a finishing trade.

On a building site you've typically got a head contractor who's just dealing with one person from each trade: bricklayer, carpenter, electrician and plumber, and there might be some socialising and mateship within that team, but it doesn't usually extend to the head contractor. I've been mates with the people who worked with me and I've included some of my trusted employees as friends and we've occasionally gone away together and things like that. A friend of mine made this type of rapport a subject of his uni thesis and referred to it as 'strategic alliances'. He tried to draw the industry's attention to the fact that building a rapport with a firm's practitioner was worth spending time on and developing and valuing. Otherwise you've got to educate somebody else on your special needs every time from scratch. That wider team exists for me at the moment; our electrician is a fellow who's worked for us over a long period, the same with our plastering contractor, and the same with our plumber.

It was an honour to be presented with an award by the Lord Mayor for excellence in building in 1994. We've been fortunate enough to win some awards for homes that architects have designed and I've built. We won House of the Year for Brisbane in 1997 and in 1999 we won Best Project Home for the whole of Australia.

Shane Naumann – A1 House Removers

He's moved houses for over twenty years. Experience counts in this job. His wife takes the calls and makes the appointments and he takes it from there.

'I move the houses and if I've cut them in half I put them back together and put them on stumps, put the roof back on and that's the end of my job.'

I started in this business in 1981; Dad was going for probably twenty years before that. Dad's name is John Naumann and he worked all round Brisbane. The biggest change in our business over the years would be the trucks. Dad had old ex-Army Studebaker trucks that only went thirty miles an hour flat out down a hill! Today we've got trucks carrying houses along the highway at eighty kilometres per hour.

As a teenager I worked with Dad for about a year, but when you're a teenager, you and your father don't always get on, so I left and got another job. In 1979, Dad sold his business to someone else who continued to employ him. I left my job and came and worked with Dad but under the new owner the business only lasted about twelve months before he went bankrupt and we all lost our jobs. Dad and I said to each other, 'Well, what we know best is shifting houses,' so in 1981 I came in as a partner with Dad and we started up a whole new business. Dad had sold all he had in the previous business so I drew $1000 out of my Bankcard and Dad sold a little boat for $1300 and that was our 'kitty'– then over the next few years we built the business back up. In 1986, when he turned fifty, Dad stepped out of the business and I took it over completely.

Mum and Dad's property is at Deception Bay, which is where we have our business. My wife was working in a garage just up the road from us, with her brother and mother and father. I met her in the garage one day and we went from there. Our business has always been moving residential houses, mostly in and around Brisbane. Moving a house involves several steps. For a start, you've got to get all the council approvals, just the same as you would do if you were building a new house. The building approvals and plans have to be submitted to council then when the house is ready to move I come along and if it's an average-sized house I'll cut it in half with small electrical saws. I take the roof right down to a flat ceiling because otherwise you're too high to travel out on the road. We get the house on the back of the trailers and transport them in the middle of the night – always after midnight. They like you to be off the road by about 6 am.

Before we do a move, we go out and check all the roads we're going to travel on so we know what obstacles are going to be in front of us and that we can fit through. Sometimes the traffic lights might be in your way, so we apply to the local or state government and they send someone out in the middle of the night and watch us undo the bolts, lay the traffic light down and then stand it back up again after the house goes through. It takes more time when they have to be re-cemented in.

The power lines get in your way at times and some of them have to be lifted. For many years we lifted them ourselves. We just made up a timber stick and you'd stand there and lift it up and let the house go underneath it. A few years ago they stopped us from doing that. Now we have to get Energex to come out and do it.

It takes a crew of 3 or 4 men to move a house. I got my first hydraulic trailer in 1989 and they'd probably been on the scene for a couple of years before that. I got my second one in '91 – they were about $100,000 each in those days, but they're nearly twice as much now. It's made our industry a lot easier and safer.

Over the years we've had houses we've cut in half and when we've moved them to the new site people have said, 'Don't put the two halves back together. The house is a bit small and we'd like to make it bigger.' So we leave the two halves 3 or 4 metres or something apart and people then come and build in between them with their builders. Other times I've taken little workers' cottage-style houses and people have already had a house on their property, but they wanted it bigger, so they've joined another house onto it and made one big house out of two.

When you move a house you can either put it down low set, 600 millimetres off the ground, or you can have it high set. Eighty per cent or more are high set since people can build underneath it if they want more space.

We've taken a few houses over to Russell Island and Macleay Island. We take up the whole ferry, so there's no room for anyone else. Around six or seven o'clock in the morning the ferry comes in and we drive on and he takes us across to the island. It's always a bit more difficult working on the islands, as you've got to get vehicles, materials and men all over there to get the work done.

I've never lost a house, so I've been lucky that way. I've had a couple of close calls over the years, though, where things like the hydraulic rams on the trailer have blown just at the wrong time. I remember one time we were coming up from the coast in the middle of the night and we had the customer following us on the road watching his house getting moved. It had been wet and one of the wheels of the trailer got a bit too close to the dirt shoulder and, being wet, it slid down the edge a bit over a little slope. Then, with the weight of the load, the back wheels started sliding down and you couldn't stop it. The whole lot fell over on its side, with the house still on the trailer. One side hit the ground and the other side was right up in the air – you could walk right underneath it. This happened with the customer right behind us, watching!

I wasn't there personally, but I got the phone call in the early hours of the morning to say what had happened. Anyway, the guys flagged down a passing tow truck and hooked on the winch rope of the tow truck to one side of the trailer, which was right up in the air, so as to put some weight on it and hold it there. Then my fellas went down the other side of the house, which was on the ground. They dug underneath the outside wall and set some jacks up and started jacking it back up again. By six o'clock that morning they got it right back up again and had parked it on a flat area that was beside the road. I got down there early to meet up with the customer. He'd been up all night, he'd had no sleep, he was very tired and he'd seen his house fall over – what do you say to him? But he was fine. We repaired any damage we'd done and next night we got it to where it was going.

I just stick to my line of business. I move the houses and if I've cut them in half I put them back together and put them on stumps, then put the roof back on and that's the end of my job. The customer afterwards comes along with his plumber and his electrician and his builder to do all the refitting of the services and any further renovations he's going to do.

Moving Moreton Bay Girls College was the biggest job we've ever done. It was a three-storey building. The first storey, with brick walls, all got demolished. The second storey, being the main house, we cut into seven pieces, and the third storey was the attic in the roof. It was done in 1986 and we moved it to Airley Road in Pullenvale. Most other house removers weren't interested, it was just too big, so in the end we came along and did the job. From memory it probably took about three months. Back in those days it was about $60,000 a move. It'd be more expensive today. Jobs like Moreton are once in a lifetime; we'll never shift anything as big as that again, because a house that size just would not become available for removal in the first place.

We try to separate the costs of any removal, the whole job, preparing the house, cutting it up, taking the roof off, and at the other end putting it all back together on stumps. That'd be more expensive than the part in the middle, which is moving on the road. That does come into the expense. Naturally it's less if you've got to move the house 50 kilometres around Brisbane than if you have to take it 500 kilometres out into the country. We've got to have police escorts when we move on the road. Everyone's getting paid double time on the road in the middle of the night. It depends on the size of the house as to how many police we have to get. If it's a reasonable size of a house, say anything over 6.1 metres, it's generally two police and one pilot vehicle.

A piece of a house can measure from about 4 metres wide to 8.5 metres wide. Say you have a worker's cottage-style house – they're often 8.5 metres wide. You'd need three lanes of road for it to fit through. If the road only has two lanes then your house overhangs both sides of the road. That's one reason you need police escorts.

The boom years in this industry were in the '80s and early '90s. Back then you'd have two crews with four men in each crew, plus a full-time mechanic and you were shifting 70 to 80 houses a year. The country people were even doing it. Every second job was right out in the country. The furthest north we've been was a little place called Calliope near Gladstone. Out West, the furthest was the other side of Mount Isa, between Mount Isa and Camowheel, just before the border. They come across this little house in Albion and we picked it up and moved it right out to their property. It took us three days and two nights to get there. Once you get the other side of Dalby, you're allowed to travel on the road during the daytime. That trip was about 2000 kilometres – a once in a lifetime job!

Tourism and Conservation

Terri Irwin – Australia Zoo

Terri had just returned from overseas and was heading up north when we spoke. Her dedication to her husband's memory and the business they built together is a driving strength, as is her sense of family.

'When I was a little girl growing up I was very lucky because my parents always included me in everything and growing up with a business that was run out of our home I was very comfortable and familiar with the family enterprise and spending quality time together as a family. I've grown up and continued that with my children, living and working at Australia Zoo.'

It was in 1991 that I came to Queensland as a tourist and I happened upon a little wildlife park called the Queensland Reptile and Fauna Park near the town of Beerwah. I went there because I was mad keen on wildlife and the day I went there was a man doing a demonstration about crocodiles.

He was speaking about crocodiles with such respect and love and passion, saying how they're wonderful mothers and quite kind and gentle to each other and talking about attributes of these animals that I'd never considered before. It really caught my attention and after the show I went up and talked to him and just found him to be the most amazing man I'd ever spoken to in my life, and of course he turned out to be Steve Irwin.

Our chance meeting; in one afternoon we hit it off and it just seemed like destiny. What I couldn't possibly imagine was that, within the next few months, not only would we fall in love and get married, but I'd be doing this incredible work with some of the largest and most venomous reptiles on the face of the earth. I'm quite proud to say that I fell in love with Australia even before I met the man, and Queensland has always been my favourite place.

I think Steve was able to bring up a lot of issues that I hadn't really considered before and I appreciated his approach to conservation. He always said it was important to protect habitat. He said you had to consider and protect the species, but he also said you must never lose sight of individual animals and that consideration for each individual animal is also important. That brought us to dedicating all of the money we earned from filming the documentaries and movie, merchandise sales and anything that was involved with the *Crocodile Hunter* series to conservation; 100% of the money went back into our conservation projects. Initially there wasn't much money, but Steve's ethics never changed and throughout our life together that money enabled us to purchase tens of thousands of acres of land for habitat preservation, to work through Australia Zoo to protect endangered species and then, also, to establish the Australian Wildlife Hospital and consider the individual animal's needs. It also enabled us to do important research on the wildlife that we love, both to protect wildlife and wild places, as well as humans.

Through it all I was never far away from the true spirit of adventure, no matter where I went in Australia. We have some of the most unique and amazing wildlife on the face of the earth, from the eleven most venomous snakes in the world, to the largest reptile, which is the salt water crocodile. We've got strange egg-laying mammals like platypus and echidna, and almost everything in this country has a pouch. Koalas, of course, are so special, because they don't compete with us agriculturally and they don't kill and eat us, so there's very little reason not to love a koala! Steve always said, 'If we can't save koalas, what hope can we have for other wildlife?' He had a true appreciation and love for all animals. He said that vultures are as important as eagles, and crocodiles should be considered equally with other animals.

I was so thankful that Steve brought this new awareness to me and I was so glad when we would do wildlife rescue work or help rehabilitate something back to the wild. I also felt like a Wildlife Warrior, because we always were fighting the wildlife bad guys. There are people who farm wildlife for their skins, and some of the heinous and cruel things that happen, from tiger farms to bear bile industries, are just horrific. There were times when, together, we would just sit down and shed a tear or two, because it was often so overwhelming. But, through it all, we agreed we would stand shoulder to shoulder and fight the good fight, and remain Wildlife Warriors. And that's the feeling that I still have today: that it's important work.

I so admired Steve. He dedicated his life to doing what he believed in. I think he was probably the best dad in the whole world. He was a very wonderful family man who included us in everything. He lived and died for the wildlife that he loved and I think he set such a tremendous example for any of us to strive to make the world a better place. For me, personally, while I am drawing breath I'm going to do the same thing – to be the best mother I can, teach my children the importance of conservation and caring for the planet, and hopefully I'll be able to leave the world a little bit better as well.

When I was a little girl growing up I was very lucky because my parents always included me in everything and growing up with a business that was run out of our home I was very comfortable and familiar with the family enterprise and spending quality time together as a family.

I've grown up and continued that with my children, living and working at Australia Zoo. I've found that with your extended family, particularly grandparents, it's a two-way street and that, if you want your grandparents involved, and your grandkids, you need to extend invitations for spending time together. With Steve's dad it means including him in research projects, and with my parents it might be something like simply scheduling time to sit in the garden together. It is very important to work on keeping the family together and involved and particularly with elderly family, there is a wealth of information and wisdom and every older person is like a living library and we need to cherish our time with them.

Historically, there are wildlife concerns, the environment, and then the humanitarian issues. We're learning more and more that we truly are all interconnected, that when we lose a species on the planet it's like taking a brick out of the house, it may not seem significant, but if we keep doing that long enough, the house falls down. It's important to approach life not saying, 'Gee, whether an orangutan survives in the future or not, how is that going to affect me personally?' We need to appreciate that at some point this interconnectedness *will* affect all of us. We're seeing it more and more with the issues of clean water and global warming and trying to survive in an ever-shrinking world. Steve saw that very early on, long before Al Gore with his good work. Steve was looking down the same track and I appreciated his foresight and hope that I can continue to educate people through our wildlife documentaries and locally in our communities. We work a lot with schools, particularly in the Cape York Peninsular with the wonderful local people, with people who may be working in the mines, and in the Aboriginal communities. Just working to continue this education, both locally and globally, is so important.

I've a book that's coming out. In Australia it's called *My Steve* and in America it's very closely titled *Steve and Me*. I was determined with this book that it would not be a story about the Crocodile Hunter that people might have seen on television, but the story about the real-life action hero that I knew – the legend that was also human and had good days and bad days like the rest of us.

With Steve, if his kids came into a room and he was in the middle of a meeting, he would always stop what he was doing to take time with his children. That's something that a lot of us give lip service to – actually practising it just takes a little bit of effort.

We're instigating a wonderful event called Steve Irwin Day, which we will be celebrating every 15 November. From Queensland, right around the world, we will be celebrating Steve's ability to prioritise his family and the wildlife that he loved, and the passion that he had to 'do it now'. We hope to encourage people every year to stop and think about doing something with their family, something that may involve wildlife, and reflect back on what was so important to Steve and our family, and hope that that will help humanity and our environment as well.

Paul Wright – The Australian Butterfly Sanctuary

Kuranda is a popular tourist destination in the mountains behind Cairns and the Butterfly Sanctuary there enjoys a steady stream of visitors. Paul has done all sorts of jobs from opal mining to writing copy for ad agencies but says his childhood love of butterflies has provided him most happiness and success.

'One day we got a phone call from America. A very nice young man told us he'd been to Australia and had seen the Butterfly Sanctuary ... He then put a proposition to us. If he brought his girlfriend out to Australia, could we clear the aviary of the public while he proposed to her ... A month later, our young American couple appeared ... They entered the aviary to be alone with the butterflies after 3 pm when the other visitors had gone. Our staff all sat out in the staff room, waiting. An hour passed and they didn't reappear. Someone suggested that perhaps she'd said "no"! One of our staff members couldn't take it any longer...'

My life with butterflies began when I was about fifteen years old, while I was at Timbertop, the country campus of Geelong Grammar School in the mountains near Mansfield in Victoria. The idea of the country campus was to toughen us up and help us to learn how to survive in the bush. I spent a year there as a student in 1958. Every weekend, irrespective of the weather, we had to camp in the forests up in the mountains. We had a year to study whatever we liked so long as it had to do with the natural world. It was an all-boys school in my day, and some boys studied plant life, some studied birds, others reptiles or mammals and some pursued geology as an interest. One boy decided to make a study of ants – he later became an internationally renowned entomologist.

Butterflies weren't my first choice of study – I chose wasps! Some weeks into collecting my specimens a rather large and angry wasp decided that he didn't enjoy my enthusiasm for getting up close and personal. Later, while recovering in the school's sanitarium, with my swollen hand and arm throbbing from the encounter, I gazed out the window and watched as a butterfly fluttered about some bushes outside. 'That's it,' I thought, 'butterflies!' So I began to collect them. My interest in butterflies quickly deepened and it never left me and, like the boy who studied ants, it one day became my livelihood, and through me the livelihood of many others.

After eleven years in boarding school (having started when I was six), I didn't relish the idea of several more years of incarceration at university, so for the next three years, I worked my way around the world. I eventually returned to Australia and my then home town of Melbourne, where I was given a job as a writer for a public relations firm. Two years later I was taken on as a copy writer for Cathay Advertising, then Singapore's largest ad agency. In 1973 I became a creative director of Marklin, another major Asian agency. During those years I made many sojourns into the central highlands of the Malay Peninsula to collect butterflies. It was a passion that kept persisting.

In 1974, I moved to Malaysia and took up living on the edge of the jungle, on the outskirts of the town of Johor Bahru. I had begun to feel tired of the incessant deadlines demanded by commercial writing and the empty trendiness of the advertising world. One day in my garden, I watched as a Rajah Brooke's Birdwing – a particularly large and spectacular Malaysian butterfly – glided slowly down through the trees, finally settling on a nearby flower. As I stared at my new and incredibly colourful companion, an idea slowly formed in my mind of building a huge, live butterfly exhibit in a garden enclosure of such size that neither the butterflies nor the people that came to visit would realise that they were actually confined. It would be a sanctuary – for both the butterflies and the people who came to visit it. I knew there'd be problems, but I bided my time researching, planning and formulating ideas.

In the early 1980s I resigned my job and returned to Australia, taking up residence on the Gold Coast, where I met Sue, my future wife. I told her about Asia and the butterflies and I suggested that we should go for a holiday back to Asia, to see my brother, who was living in Kuala Lumpur. Secretly, I was looking for something that might set me on the path to what I wanted to do with butterflies.

After some months in Kuala Lumpur I was becoming a little discouraged. Then Sue saw an advertisement in a KL newspaper. It turned out to be a fellow selling specimens of dead butterflies and exporting them around the world. The butterflies were being taken from the wild up in the Cameron Highlands. In talking to the man, I said that I wanted to breed butterflies – to farm them for live display. He shook his head. 'Impossible,' he said. 'You'll never beat the virus.' I'd heard before that it was extremely difficult to breed butterflies successfully as a business, because eventually the virus and other pathogens would get in and decimate your stock, but I just saw this as a challenge!

We returned to Australia and I started to import butterflies in display boxes from our Kuala Lumpur source and sell them through souvenir stores and other outlets, but it was none too successful. I continued to dream of my live exhibit and progressively a concrete plan developed in my mind.

I decided that the best location for the butterfly sanctuary would be Kuranda in the mountains of Far North Queensland. There were two reasons for this. One was that the most colourful and spectacular butterflies in Australia breed naturally in the Cairns area and in the surrounding tropical rainforests. The second was that the Kuranda train is primarily a tourist train, funnelling people into the Kuranda village. The train would bring visitors to the sanctuary.

Sue and I packed up the house on the Gold Coast and moved to Kuranda. We found a large uncleared parcel of land close to the village centre. I hired an Aboriginal neighbour and he and I spent months clearing the fence line with chain saws, leaving as much as possible of the forest for aesthetic reasons.

The centrepiece of the sanctuary was to be the huge 'flight aviary'. This became a truly cavernous building – enough for epic butterfly flights. It took three years to build and landscape. It became the largest single-span aluminium building in Australia, its massive RSJs spanning 60 feet without ground support. The building – or aviary, as we now call it – is a massive glass house, 120 feet long, 35 feet high to its apex and enclosing some 3,336 cubic metres of space. Inside are fully grown rainforest trees, ponds and waterfalls. Air vents in the roof automatically open and close to sustain an equable climate, as butterflies only fly within given temperature extremes. Being in the middle of a cyclone zone, the building also had to be designed to withstand cyclones.

I next had to find out how to feed thousands of butterflies each day, all year round. Butterflies feed on nectar from flowers and flowers only produce nectar once a day. So if you've got a thousand butterflies, you need thousands of flowers, blooming all year through, and that's a very hard ask. It took me a year to develop the answer. I found it by studying butterfly vision and finding how they see in ultra-violet light. I found that while flowers are colourful to us, they are even more so to butterflies, as they radiate very strongly in the ultra-violet end of the light spectrum. This is how they attract butterflies – who in turn serve the flowers by pollinating them. Once I understood this, I was able to design specially coloured artificial feeders to attract the butterflies. The next thing was to find an artificial nectar mix to place in the feeders. The results were spectacular. There was no need to worry about the flowers any longer. The feeders worked so well, even nectar- eating birds used them.

Feeding butterflies costs the princely sum of around $40 per year! The caterpillars, from which the butterflies come, however, cost a fortune to breed and maintain. Each species of butterfly eats a specific type of food plant, and acres and acres of these must be grown to sustain a large caterpillar population. Extreme care must be exercised; you'll kill the caterpillars if you give them food plant that has been sprayed and chemically contaminated. We learnt through trial and error and our success rate improved over time. Today it's a staggering 95%. But we're ever vigilant, for nature has a way of coming up with new and deadly pathogens when least expected.

The construction of the butterfly sanctuary was totally consuming. At one time during the three-year construction phase I worked straight through for 421 days without one day off. Then one day we got close to our grand opening. Sue became active in the administration, setting up the kiosk, administering to the sales staff and to our tour guides. I trained the guides in their tours. These tours were designed to be both entertaining and informative. The guides explain all about our butterflies, their life cycle, their quirks and habits.

It was just prior to opening that my financial backers became nervous. They talked of pulling out. I didn't need this. We were now so close. But they saw that $1.5 million and three years had gone into the project and there were still no guarantees it would work. I managed to convince them to keep the faith and hang in. Finally we had the grand opening in July 1987, officiated by Lady Flo Bjelke-Petersen. Within weeks the Guinness Book of Records confirmed that we were, at that time, the world's largest butterfly farm.

Our trials and tribulations, unfortunately, were far from over. In our first year we got hit by Cyclone Joy. I went into the big flight aviary at the height of the storm and looked up as the building heaved and groaned and watched as the glass roof began to break up. I thought, 'Please, not now, not after all these years and all this effort.' The eye of the cyclone was still 150 kilometres off the coast of Cairns, but even so, the winds that battered us were reaching 150 kilometres per hour. She was a Category 4 cyclone – of Darwinian proportions. She hovered and teased us for a full day and then, ever so slowly, she began to withdraw to the south. It took us three months to clean up the debris of broken trees, smashed fences, glass and other building materials.

Next we had the pilots' dispute. With 75% of all tourist arrivals in Cairns flying in, you take out the air component and it's devastating. Our visitor numbers went down, but we held the fort, largely thanks to a sympathetic bank manager.

I tried various unusual approaches in promoting the sanctuary. One I particularly remember still brings a smile to my face. It involved President George Bush Senior (the father of George W Bush) who was coming out to tour Australia, including North Queensland. I thought, 'Good, I'm going to send an invitation to him at the White House, to come and see the butterflies while he's here.' I knew full well he wouldn't come, because he'd have such a full schedule, but I also knew that the Americans are gracious people and would answer my letter. I got a reply back on the White House letterhead. 'On behalf of the President, we regret that, as much as he would like to come and see your facility, he does not have time on this trip.' I then phoned the *Cairns Post* newspaper and asked if they could find a suitable file photo of President Bush looking sad. They said, 'Yes,' and I said, 'Well, here's the story,' and it got printed in the *Cairns Post* with George Bush looking suitably sorrowful and a story saying he regretted he couldn't come to see the Australian Butterfly Sanctuary. It was terrific publicity – particularly for an event that was never going to take place!

One day we got a phone call from America. A very nice young man told us he'd been to Australia and had seen the Butterfly Sanctuary. He told us he had a girlfriend, and that she adored butterflies. He then put a proposition to us. If he brought his girlfriend out to Australia, could we clear the aviary of the public while he proposed to her. It was all to be a big surprise for her. We agreed and waived any charges. A month later, our young American couple appeared. He was extremely nervous. They entered the aviary to be alone with the butterflies after 3 pm when the other visitors had gone. Our staff all sat out in the staff room, waiting. An hour passed and they didn't reappear. Someone suggested that perhaps she'd said 'no'! One of our staff members couldn't take it any longer and took a peek. She returned, beaming. Our love birds were locked in a passionate embrace. There was a collective sigh of relief in the staff room. Later, we saw the ring. It was a magnificent cluster of diamonds in the shape of a butterfly.

In mid-2004, after twenty years developing the sanctuary, we took on, as a 50% partner, another iconic North Queensland tourism entity, Rainforestation/Tropic Wings, the region's largest inbound tour operator. With this union, the future of the Australian Butterfly Sanctuary is most certainly assured.

Trevor Long – Sea World

He's been in this business one way or another since 1970 and in Sea World since 1973. He's now their Director of Marine Sciences and is heavily involved in their conservation program.

'We rescue many animals ... Back in 1992 we got a humpback whale on Peregian Beach. There were 7,000 people there and we were able to undertake the first large baleen whale rescue ever to be successful here in Australia ... Sea World's had many firsts ... We were the first people in the world to ever hand raise a young neonate dugong.'

I started coming to Queensland in 1968 or 1969, because I was in love with the ocean. I used to do a lot of surfing and diving in Sydney, where I came from, and I'd come up here at weekends to surf. The surfing was a lot better and the diving much warmer than what we'd get in Sydney.

I eventually moved here in 1970 and I was able to get employment at the Aquarium Restaurant on the Isle of Capri at Surfers Paradise. The owner, Jack Taylor, an older man, was an inventor. He actually invented the snap-freeze and he used to have Taylor Cold Fridges – not many people today would remember that. Jack became a bit of a father figure to me. He helped me to meet up with professors of marine biology in UQ and the ichthyologist at Queensland Museum and he was able to send me over to San Francisco to Steinhart's Aquarium on a work experience program that really advanced me.

In 1973 Keith Williams had just started Sea World here on the Spit and he asked me to help collect fish and build his Oceanarium and progress Sea World. At that stage I was diving with guys at Marineland of the Pacific, a large Marine Park on the Gold Coast. Keith's idea was all very embryonic, but I agreed to help him to collect the fish. We did a trip up to the Barrier Reef on his big 72-foot motor cruiser called *Odyssey* and collected specimens for the Oceanarium.

Keith continued to ask me to come and work for him and eventually I moved over here in August 1973 and have been here ever since. I started here as a diver and also worked with a lot of animal rescues. I was involved in my first rescue of a humpbacked whale in a shark net in 1974 off the beach here at Southport Surf Club.

In my time at Sea World I've grown and changed positions and gone through many learning processes. I've travelled overseas on many occasions, researching and investigating animal exhibits and relevant husbandry needs. Now I'm the Marine Sciences Director of Sea World and responsible for all of the exhibits, animals and their welfare, the veterinary side, the education and their husbandry. We design and build all the exhibits here at Sea World and I'm heavily involved with the design process and have become a bit of a specialist in water treatment. Here at Sea World we're filtering over 100 million litres of water from our exhibits like Dolphin Cove with up to 30 million litres of water turning over every five hours.

In the early days, back in the '70s, all the animals were caught in the wild. You couldn't do that today, but all of those techniques that we developed then we use for animal rescue now. For example, back then when we were collecting animals like dolphins, we learned that stress was a huge issue. We'd swim out to the dolphins as early as we could and we'd talk to the animals and try to settle them right down. They are very social and, with somebody beside them, talking to them slowly and quietly, we learned that they'd settle down.

It takes a long time when you get any animal back here, whether it's a shark, a groper or a dolphin, to get them used to their new environment. These animals are used to feeding on live fish and we've got to get them used to feeding on dead fish, which takes quite a lot of time. A lot of animals have what's called a 'learned helplessness', which makes the process even slower, but if we can show these animals that we're not going to harm them, we can get very positive responses from them.

At Sea World we have many, many species, including sharks and dolphins. Certainly our flagship species are our dolphins. Sea World has 30-odd dolphins and they come from a variety of places. Some come from the wild and were caught by us and some have been caught in the wild by other aquariums. As these aquariums closed down, we've taken on their animals. We've got animals from Sydney, Adelaide, Port Macquarie – from all over the place.

We're very fortunate that we've got a very good breeding program. All the animals are DNA tested. We understand the parentage of these animals and we're managing them in such a way that it will aid conservation. We're keeping them very true in relation to the genetics. At the moment 60% to 65% of our animals are born in captivity. As part of our program, we're working with other parks around the world on artificial insemination for marine mammals, which is a fairly new thing.

The numbers of seals are building right around Australia. This year in Queensland, I think we've had three New Zealand fur seals. We've got two little ones here now going through quarantine at our Vet Centre. They're not well as they've been bitten by sharks. In fact, we've currently got seven animals that have come into Sea World like this.

Sea World has got the only marine mammal quarantine facility in Australia and we take in a lot of stranded animals. We get a lot of dolphins and whales that have been caught in nets or had fishing line around them and we've been able to put these animals through our Vet Centre. A lot of the animals released are tagged. All the whales are released, but no seal can be released back to the wild, because if it takes a pathogen or bacteria that it's picked up from being in a captive environment, it could infect the whole colony of animals in the wild. If a seal comes into Sea World in a debilitated state, say with shark bites, then if they are also right out of their natural distribution, they remain here as 'ambassadors'.

Because of the range of injuries marine mammals receive, our vets get opportunities no one else gets. One of our veterinary doctors would be one of the leading marine mammal specialists in this country.

Back in 1992 we got a humpback whale on Peregian Beach. There were 7,000 people there and we were able to undertake the first large baleen whale rescue ever to be successful here in Australia. Since that time we've done another one up at Coolum Beach. Back in '94 we built a pontoon that would lift up to 60 ton and used it to free a whale that was trapped in a river for 110 days down in the Manning River at Taree. The equipment that was established for that animal has now gone on to save a number of whales caught up rivers and estuaries and bays within Queensland and New South Wales.

Sea World's had many firsts. I've been here for 34 years and I'm very proud of some of the work we've done. We've worked on dugong research with Dr Janet Lanyon at University of Queensland. We were the first people in the world to ever hand raise a young neonate dugong. Every year between November and February in Queensland the dugong mothers give birth to their young. For whatever reason, it could be storm activity, predation by sharks or other issues, mothers and calves often get separated. Over the years we'd received numbers of these babies each Christmas. People would phone us and Parks and Wildlife would phone us, saying, 'What can you do?' So we were taking these day-old or two-day-old animals in, but the problem was that secondary infections kept killing them.

Anyway, one day about eight years ago, we received a day-old dugong with the umbilicus still attached to him. The little dugong, affectionately called Pig, came from Ayr near Townsville and was flown here by Qantas. Pig became a bit of an icon for a lot of people in Queensland at the time, especially around the Brisbane area.

At this stage we'd had three and lost three at various stages: 4 weeks, 6 weeks and 8 weeks. Pig had to be bottle fed every two hours, and one of our vets, Dr Wendy Blanshard, slept with it for something like four months! It was an intense operation.

Our aim was to release it back to the wild, because dugong numbers in Queensland have probably declined about 60% over the last two decades, so we released Pig when he was three. He was released first in a pool on the southern end of Moreton Island that had sea grass and he was left there for three months. We had a satellite tracking device on him that he was towing around the pool. Wendy would go to that pool every day and we had accommodation for her on the island. We eventually took him out of the pool about 3 to 4 months later and released him, but, three days after we released him, he lost his satellite tracker. A shark had probably grabbed onto the tracker. So Pig was out there without the tracking device and we didn't know where he was. We could only hope that he was going well!

Eight months later we got a call to say there's a sick dugong in Moreton Bay. We went there but couldn't find it. We got another call and still couldn't find it and this went on until eventually we located this animal and it turned out to be Pig. Eight months after he was released, he was brought back to Sea World. When he was released into Moreton Bay he was 202 kilograms, but he lost a third of that body weight in those eight months and was in a very poor state. He was malnourished and had been beaten up by the dugongs in Moreton Bay. We'd tried to socialise him before the release, to try and educate him to what a dugong was. We'd put mirrors in his pool, so he knew what a dugong looked like. We were able to familiarise him with stingrays, with dolphins and even small sharks, trying to get him prepared for the things he would meet once we released him, but we still couldn't give him all those life skills that are learned from Mum.

He continued to go downhill to the point where I actually said to Wendy that I thought we'd have to euthanase him, but she convinced me to hold out for one or two more days and it turned out to be a thiamine deficiency. She then started to treat it and he improved! He's still with us now and on display today. We also got another young female three years ago from Rockhampton, during a big storm when she got separated from her mother – these were two very successful dugong rescues.

We've built a mini-science centre where we try and educate people about the plight of dugong and their declining numbers, which has a lot to do with human impact, and what we've got to do if we want to turn the situation around. We still continue to conduct dugong research in Moreton Bay and Hervey Bay with Queensland University. We haven't bred any dugong in captivity yet. Our lone female is a long way from sexual maturity; she'll be ten before that.

We've now established the Sea World Research and Rescue Foundation. We put in a lot of money (about five hundred to six hundred thousand dollars a year) and invite expressions of interest from researchers and universities. We advertise in *The Australian* every February that we've got monies available for research for marine vertebrate biology, physiology and ecology and we get people applying from all over Australia. We have an independent scientific advisory committee that's headed up by Dr Michael Brydon that assesses what we're going to fund. Since 1990 we've funded over 100 different marine research projects from Antarctica right through to the Barrier Reef. We're very proud of that. We've also got a 20-metre research vessel, which I'm the master of, so we use that vessel and our other 8-metre vessel and we make these available to researchers. They normally wouldn't be able to afford to charter such vessels, so it makes things a lot easier for them.

Taxis on Land and Sea

Bill Parker and Don Rainbow – Yellow Cabs

Bill's office, where we meet, is in the 'admin building', the nerve centre of the organisation with its state of the art satellite monitoring, computing and radio control. This backs onto the workshop where Don presides, ensuring the cabbies that come in and out all day get fast and reliable repairs, so they're off the road for as short a time as possible.

Left to Right – Don Rainbow, Operations Manager, and Bill Parker, General Manager, outside Yellow Cabs Workshop

'I said, "Where are we going?"and he said, "I'm going to the doctor's at Moorooka. You head that way and I'll tell you where to go." So we're driving along towards Moorooka and my passenger seemed to have dozed off. I got to the Moorooka shops and found the bloke had died!'

Bill: Yellow Cabs started off in America with John Hertz from Hertz Rent-a-Car fame. He was a car salesman. This was in the 1920s and he was getting all these trade-ins on the cars he sold, and he didn't know what to do with them, so he decided to put them on as cabs in Chicago. He later built a manufacturing plant to produce a purpose-built cab. He'd read that the most prominent colour in people's mind is between yellow and orange. So they painted all these cabs a sort of yellow-orange and called the manufacturing plant the Yellow Cab Company. General Motors later bought it out.

In 1926 the first fleet of Yellow Cabs started in Brisbane. We've still got one of these cars, and the boys here maintain it. In 1952 a fellow from Ampol, an Australian-owned fledgling oil company, flew into Brisbane and found the only Yellow Cab left in Brisbane that was still operational and he bought the colour rights and trade name. Ampol eventually sold their rights in Yellow Cabs to two private family trusts which split the company into two. They had the Workshops and Company Cars Division and then they had the Call Centre Division. I took over as the manager of the workshop division and the company cars. That was in the early 80s.

Don: I left high school in December 1969 and in September 1970, when I was sixteen, I started in the Yellow Cabs Service Station here on Logan Road as a driveway attendant.

Bill: The structure of the cab industry's quite interesting. The person who owns the cab licence is self employed. It's like a franchise; they pay to participate in the system, to access the colour rights, the radio room communication and the account base. So they have a certain amount of freedom and when they're out there driving their own cab they're their own boss. We certainly have a code of conduct, a code for the presentation of cars, and we like the good old-fashioned values of courtesy.

Many types of people drive cabs. We have solicitors, barristers, pilots, theologians, electrical engineers, computer software people – you name the profession and they're driving a cab.

The work we do here at the head office is geared to keeping cabs on the road. We've a series of workshops, panel shops, mechanical workshops, tyre bays and spare parts. Unless the cabby's out working, he can't earn any money, so time's of the essence. Everything that's done is designed around getting the vehicle back on the road as quickly as possible.

When I joined the company people were talking about 361 and 489 and 124 and the model of their cars being XY Falcon, et cetera, and I used to think, 'This is a language that's totally foreign to me!' But I soon learned that cabbies don't know other cabbies names, so they refer to them by their cab numbers. They say, 'There goes 168 down the road there. You know 168, he's got that AU3 Model Falcon – it keeps blowing the right-hand headlight!' Another fellow will say, 'Yeah, well that guy that owns 382, he's had the same problem but on the other side.'

We restore all our own cabs. We've got a whole fleet of antique and other old vehicles that have borne the mark of Yellow Cabs, from 1924, 1937 and 1955. We've also got a New York cab that they've restored. A good mechanic is someone who can diagnose the fault with the vehicle and that's truly an art in itself.

Today LPG plays a dramatic role in this industry and there's a lot of safety issues with LPG, so for someone to be proficient in that area and be awarded the recognition of his peers is a big thing. I think for Donnie, personally, to rise from putting fuel in the cars to becoming a very good mechanic and then become a very good LPG diagnostic person and fitter is a credit to him. The company recognises his ability.

Don: One of the early wheelchair access vehicles, we called it the Pope-Mobile. It was a Falcon station wagon, but it had been modified. The floor at the back had been dropped down and the roof had a dome setup and the person in the wheelchair would sit up overlooking the roof of the cab as they were driving along. There were only a couple of them – they didn't really take off. At the moment we're trying some new vans, the Mercedes vans, also the new Toyota van's been upgraded and it's looking quite nice.

Bill: Back in the early '80s we had this Chinese Papuan New Guinean called Fred who came here for an interview. He'd been apprenticed in the Coca Cola bottling factory in PNG and had looked after the fleet of vehicles that ran out of the plant, so he was a mechanic, a fitter and turner, and a host of other things. He migrated to Australia but had found it difficult getting a job, so we gave him a go. One day this cab owner came in and said to the foreman, 'Peter, my car's not running too well, can you get someone to get it running properly on gas?' Peter says, 'Yes. Freddie, give this car a tune-up, will you?' Freddie did the tune-up and the bloke hops into his car and drives out of the yard and ten minutes later he's back. The foreman thought, 'Hello, what's happened here?' The cabbie says to Peter, 'You know, I had my doubts when you gave the job to that fellow there to tune up my car, but I had to come back and tell you it's never run better!' Freddie's still with us and he's now the foreman and very well respected and liked by every taxi owner in this fleet because of his skill.

Don: We are near a creek and I remember years ago we used to have a tow truck to try and drag cars out when it flooded. With some of them it was too late – they were locked up or whatever else and the water would be up to their bonnets, so Fred used to go duck diving down into this mucky water to find something to put the hooks on, to pull the bloody things out. You couldn't believe how he could even find where he was going, but he said he used to do a lot of swimming up in New Guinea.

Bill: We don't have as many floods any more since they straightened up the creek. But in those days we had to ask the staff to come in at three o'clock on a cold winter's morning to lift everything up to save it from going under and cab owners would come down and help as well. So, to reward and recognise those people, I formed the Deshon Creek Sailing Squadron. We printed special T-shirts and little badges and gave them all wet-weather jackets. Anyway, some of these guys used to go up to proper yacht clubs and I remember one particular guy went up to Cairns and he was wearing one of these shirts and the bloke said to him, 'The Deshon Creek Sailing Squadron? I've never heard of that. Are they affiliated with us?' and he said, 'Yep,' and it was, 'Oh, well, you can come in then!'

There was an occasion when a particular driver was late in for his change of shift. He had to be back at the depot by four o'clock. At five o'clock he turns up and the shift manager says to him, 'Where have you been?' and the driver says, 'Well, I went out to an address at Moorooka and I picked up this elderly gentleman this afternoon and he got into the front seat and I said, 'Where are we going?' and he said, "I'm going to the doctors at Moorooka. You head that way and I'll tell you where to go." So we're driving along towards Moorooka and my passenger seemed to have dozed off. I got to the Moorooka shops and found the bloke had died! I drove around to every doctors' surgery in Moorooka and eventually found a doctors' surgery that recognised him as being a patient of theirs and they took the body.' The manager of the shift said, 'Well, when you first realised he was dead, why didn't you call the police?' and the cabbie said, 'No way I was gonna do that – they would have reckoned I did him in!'

On another occasion a cab owner had two sisters in his cab, one in the front seat and one in the back. As they were driving along the lady in the front seat passed away! The lady in the back seat went into hysterics and the cabbie had to tell her, 'Be quiet, love, and I'll try to do something!' Eventually he drove into a hospital and got out of his cab, leaving the deceased in the front seat and her sister still in hysterics in the back. He went into the hospital, but they said they wouldn't do anything! So he said, 'Well, if you won't, I will,' and he grabbed a trolley and started wheeling it out of the hospital to load the deceased onto it. The hospital staff eventually came and took the deceased lady. He said he wanted to let us know that he never charged the remaining passenger, but it was the worst cab fare he's ever had!

Don: I came in here one Monday morning and I found a car here with a lady in it with a couple of children and a couple of dogs. I think she was a member of RACQ and her car had been picked up, broken down, by a tow truck. I asked her who'd pay for the repairs and she got all funny and started carrying on about the people who 'were out to get me' and I asked her, 'Who's out to get you?' And she said, 'The aliens!' Then she jumped back into the car, locked the doors and wound up the windows and wouldn't talk to us. Bill turned up for work and tried to talk to her, but she didn't want to know, so in the end we called the police.

When the police came they eventually got her out of the car and she said all she wanted was to get the car fixed. They asked us what it would cost and we gave a quote. The police said, 'We'll take her to her bank and get the money and bring her back.' We sent someone up to the shops to get some food and drinks for the kids and we fixed the car and tested it. When the police brought her back I chopped a bit off the bill and she paid over the money. Unfortunately, after all this, she somehow took a liking to us and instead of leaving she hung around beside the park near here, sleeping in the car with the kids and dogs. She kept dropping in and I'd think, 'Strueth, here she comes again.' She used to say to me, 'You know there're aliens around here; they're always chasing us!' This went on for a couple of days and in the end she came back and said, 'They nearly got us last night, but we seen 'em coming and we all hid under blankets,' so this time I said to her, 'Look, I'm sorry, but the aliens have already got me – it's too late for me, but if you take the kids and get out of here, I'll hold them back.' She went and we've never seen her again!

Bob Francis - Stradbroke Ferries

Taking People, Cars and Houses on Moreton Bay

Bob's been involved with boats all his life. He and his family have lived in Queensland since 1970 and he's worked with ferries of one kind or another ever since. In the days before the Air Sea Rescue, the ferrymen often went to the aid of boaties in distress ...

'... I saw one of our Stradbroke Ferry speedboats, a small one called the Spirit of Stradbroke *stop off Goat Island... I saw the deckhand reach out of the door and pull something out of the water and it looked to me as though it was a person. Anyway, being a bit of a sticky beak, I went over to the jetty where the speedboat comes in and, when it pulled in, standing on the deck of the speedboat, there's a kangaroo, standing in the middle of all the people, quite unconcerned, as though he didn't see what all the fuss was about!'*

I grew up in Jersey in the Channel Islands. I'd always loved the sea and I had my own boat there. When I left school I joined the pilot boat in Jersey as an apprentice pilot. The pilots there at that time were all around their forties and they could stay as pilots 'til about seventy. At sixteen years old the age of forty seemed a million years away – so I decided to go into the British Merchant Navy.

My wife Anne and I came to Brisbane in 1970. I'd been out to Australia before, when I was in the Merchant Navy, but then I'd gone back to England and got married and had some children. When we first decided to come to Australia we originally planned to go to West Australia but at that time the quota for WA had been filled, so they said, 'You must go to Sydney,' and we said, 'No thank you, we wouldn't like to go there. How about going to Brisbane?' and that's basically how we got here. Our three children were still young then. Our youngest daughter Maria was three and a half years old, and Sally was about five and a half, and our son Robert was a year older. They've all grown up here and Robert is now also a skipper for Stradbroke Ferries.

When I first came out here in August 1970, Brisbane was a lovely little country town. Then high-rises started to develop everywhere and before we knew it there was the new Captain Cook Bridge going over the river, followed by the rail bridge. It was very busy on the river too. Bishop Island at the mouth of the river was actually a pumped-up island. It was the first island 'made in Australia'. They dredged the bar-cutting and the spoil from the bar-cutting became Bishop Island. They continued filling what used to be Bishop Island and now it's the new Port of Brisbane where all the ships come in and the containers.

I joined Riverside Coal, as it was then, one of about five groups of companies they had, and I started going up the river just a little below Ipswich, carrying coal. We used to bring the coal down for the power stations in Brisbane. Funnily enough, my first trip with Riverside was on a little ferry we had then at Redland Bay, called the *Tom Welsby*, to pick up vehicles for one of the sand mines. We went from the southern end of North Stradbroke Island to the northern end of South Stradbroke, which was only about two hundred yards, and then we came back to Redland Bay.

A lot of people will know the Redland Bay pub. It was actually built for the sea-planes which used to go to Lord Howe Island. If there was fog at Lord Howe and the sea-planes couldn't land there, they had to have another place to come to. They had two landing strips laid out with buoys in the water for the aircraft to land and there was a boat to ferry the passengers to shore to the pub for the night. Then next day, if the fog lifted, they'd take off for Lord Howe.

Riverside decided, in 1973, that they were going to start a ferry run from Redland Bay across to Dunwich on North Stradbroke Island, so we moved down as a family to Thornlands to be near to Redland Bay. Going on the ferry meant that I got every night at home, so that was nice. The ferry ran from Redland Bay across to Stradbroke for the next thirteen and a half years. I actually did the first ever trip on it, that was 17 October 1973.

We mainly ran just from Redland Bay to Dunwich, but occasionally we used to do extra jobs around the bay islands and one of those was running gravel across to Russell, Lamb, Macleay and Karragarra Islands for the construction of roads. In those days they didn't have any water on tap, everything was rainwater and tanks and they didn't have any mains power. It was your own generators at night if you wanted electricity. The *Venture* used to arrive at Russell Island at two o'clock in the morning and eleven trucks used to come off full of gravel. From being dead quiet, apart from the crickets at night, all of a sudden the place would be filled with the sound of eleven screaming trucks going up the road, so it was not real popular! In those days there was a lot of talk about putting a bridge across from the mainland to Stradbroke Island via Russell Island. It didn't happen in the end but if the bridge had gone ahead the noise and traffic would have been even worse.

When I was running from Redland Bay to Dunwich we also used to carry sand from Canaipa and Dunwich to Holywell. We used to go down through the Canaipa Passage, as it was then. We had to get the flood tide with us, because we used to go down with a barge drawing six feet of water and it's very shallow going through there. At low tide you've only got about three and a half feet of water. We had to time our journey through there to catch the flood tide down through the Canaipa Channel past Russell Island and Jumpinpin 'til we could see the ocean and then go through the inside of South Stradbroke Island down to Holywell just a mile north of the Gold Coast, where we took our sand. The beacons we had in those days didn't have any reflective tape on them or any lights, so at night time it was a case of using the spotlights all the time to pick out the beacons ahead so that we knew where to go. One person used to be spotting the beacons and the other person would be driving the tug that was pushing the barge. The old barge was 150 feet long and used to weigh about 1,000 tons, so you had quite a large thing going down through the inside channels like that.

In those days you used to be able to buy a block of land on Russell Island for $585 and you got one free – the only thing is you had to come back at low tide to see it because otherwise it was under water! Those times have changed. Nowadays it costs an absolute fortune to buy a proper waterfront block.

Over the years we've taken a lot of houses across to the islands, mostly to Russell and Macleay and a few have gone to Lamb. In the old days you took the house over in bits and pieces and rebuilt it over there on the island, because they basically only had passenger ferries. With the new barges we've got now at Stradbroke Ferries we can usually put the whole house on. These are timber houses, they cut the house in half and they put them on two separate trucks and the trucks come down to the ferry during the night-time when the roads are quiet. We put them on the ferry at night and take them down to whichever island they have to go to and they're reassembled there.

In the old days we used to take a couple of buses of school kids every morning from the islands and come back in the afternoon. Now the school over on Stradbroke Island is much better, but I think it only takes them up to Grade 10. Anyone over Grade 10 still has to go across to the mainland to a school in Cleveland.

The sand mine over there is the main source of industry, so there are lots of workers who come backwards and forwards in the morning and afternoon and we've got sand-trucks that do a regular two trips per day with sand.

Being out on the bay occasionally, we used to come across boats which had broken down and in those days they really didn't have any coast guard or air-sea rescue to speak of. When we saw people on boats in distress we'd pick them up and tow the boat back to wherever we were going. That was normally back to Redland Bay. Now if we come across somebody, normally we get onto the Coast Guard or the Air-Sea Rescue and tell them.

We occasionally get whales down there and we get lots of dolphins and turtles and, depending on where you are in the bay, there are quite a few dugongs. We occasionally come across a turtle that's got a crab pot rope around its neck and basically the poor old turtle can't dive properly, towing the crab pot. When we've seen a turtle in distress like that we've lowered the front door of the ferry down into the water and the deckhand with the boathook has managed to get hold of the rope that's round the turtle's neck and pulled the turtle towards the door of the ferry where the vehicles drive on and off. Then I've lifted the door out of the water with the turtle on it and the deckhand, usually helped by a couple of passengers, has managed to actually disentangle the rope off the turtle. One time I think it was a pair of them, because the mate was sort of standing by the turtle that had got caught and when we released the turtle, they both went off together, so that was a happy ending.

Another time we were over at Dunwich on the ferry and I saw one of our Stradbroke Ferry speedboats, a small one called the *Spirit of Stradbroke* stop off Goat Island. I wondered what was going on and I put the glasses on it and I saw the deckhand reach out of the door and pull something out of the water and it looked to me as though it was a person. Anyway, being a bit of a sticky beak, I went over to the jetty where the speedboat comes in and, when it pulled in, standing on the deck of the speedboat, there's a kangaroo, standing in the middle of all the people, quite unconcerned, as though he didn't see what all the fuss was about!

Jimmy Muir, he was the deckhand, said he'd spotted the kangaroo swimming across. They'd stopped the speedboat and Jimmy had leant out and grabbed hold of the kangaroo's front paw, big yank and it went into the speedboat to Dunwich. We managed to wrap the kangaroo up in a long strap of sacking so he couldn't fight and put him in the back of the car and Jack took him up to somewhere up in the bush and let him go again. We'd thought the kangaroo might have been drowning, but apparently they swim between the islands.

When Kath Walker, the Aboriginal poetess (Oodgeroo Noonuccal was her native name) died, we took her over on the ferry, the *Venture*, to Stradbroke Island. As we were about halfway across the bay, we came across two humpback whales. A little while afterwards we heard from some Aborigines that their interpretation of this was that the whales had come to pay their last respects to Oodgeroo Noonuccal. Could be right, could be wrong, who can say?

Medical

Elizabeth Teeland – Medical Retrievals

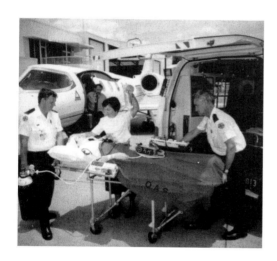

We sit sipping tea on her wide verandah overlooking the river, the view framed by tall eucalypts. She's almost always on call, ready to fly off with little notice to wherever needed, from luxury resorts to disaster sites, to recover people who are miles from home and in need of medical assistance.

'There've been lots of funny stories. We had another man who was found by the highway patrol outside New York with just a towel around his middle and a plastic bag on each foot, and no sign of identification ...'

My interest in medical assistance came about through meeting a friend, Dr Tom Biggs, on the ski-fields in Perisher Valley in New South Wales. He had set up the first company in Australia to provide medical assistance to travellers, company representatives, and people going for family reunions abroad. I'd come from a background of emergency nursing, intensive care and infection control, and my post-graduate experience at that stage was a mixture. I'd been to the College of Nursing in Sydney and done infection control and microbiology at UTS and then worked in hospitals. This friend asked me if I'd repatriate a patient who was in Los Angeles and I thought it sounded interesting, so I did that. I was forty-one and living in Brisbane when I started this work.

I was born in Adelaide and came to Brisbane as a child, and then, when I graduated as a nurse, I went abroad. I went to England and stayed there for a year, hitch-hiking around the UK and Europe. I was a nurse for a number of British aristocrats, so I lived in castles, enjoyed the company of some accomplished, interesting people and the opportunity to explore the countryside. In '69 I travelled to New York and on to San

Francisco, where I met my husband, Walter, who was working there at the time. He was an accountant and when he finished university at the University of Washington in Seattle he'd come to Australia looking for a job, but he'd found it difficult, because people didn't think he'd stay. That was in 1968 and there wasn't such a movement of young professionals around the world at that stage. Walter and I were married in San Francisco and then went to live in Alaska for three years, before coming to Brisbane.

I came back to Australia at the end of '71; Walter still had work to do in Alaska, so he followed me in '72. We were here then for a number of years, during which I worked in hospitals, but it was really just that chance meeting with a friend on the ski-fields at Perisher that led to me getting involved in medical assistance. The first retrieval was an Australian lady in Los Angeles. She'd had a serious illness and I quite liked the idea of staying in the Beverly Wiltshire and shopping on Rodeo Road as well as the new experience as an aero-medical escort. When I came back I was offered a part-time job in the office. At that stage I had two young children and was happy to work part time.

I've been employed in medical assistance now for seventeen years. Medical assistance started off when the automobile clubs in the UK would be called on to pay bail bonds for British tourists on motoring holidays. The tourists would have run over a chicken or something on a road in Spain and they'd be put in the watch-house or detained, so Automobile Clubs began providing this type of assistance. It gradually grew from motorists' assistance to legal and eventually medical assistance. Across Europe people are on the move all summer and air ambulances do 'milk-runs', picking up the not so fit patients from various countries and bringing them back home on the plane. If the patient is seriously ill and needs to be on a stretcher, there are nine seats occupying the back of the aircraft near the rear door. The backs of these seats are folded down and there's a metal framing system that is locked in over the top of them. The stretcher with curtaining around it stays there and the escort and family sit in the seats nearest. In really serious cases, they can block off one of the toilets in the area for our exclusive use. The ambulance brings the patient onto the tarmac beside the aircraft and the patient goes up on the stretcher on a high lift, is brought to the level of the aircraft door and then wheeled in. Usually we've got a portable stretcher underneath them and they're lifted on that stretcher onto the other stretcher in the back of the aircraft and then they're secured in with a series of harnesses. It's quite claustrophobic for people, because their head isn't that far from the cabin ceiling, but that's the only way of doing it. Now, with the recliner-bed, they can be made very much more comfortable.

Sometimes there is one medical assistant, sometimes two. Usually if there are two we both have to stay awake, since the person is often acutely ill. If someone from Australia has been in the Czech Republic, for instance, or Russia, they are usually flown first to London. There could then be another transfer from London to Singapore, with a couple of hour's stopover there, then they might be going to Hobart, or it could be to Auckland, so it's often thirty hours or more from hospital to hospital.

Retrievals may be covered by an individual's travel insurance. All the retrievals I've done this year have been elderly people, usually in their seventies, going to family reunions in former Communist countries. Such reunions can be quite stressful, typically involving family issues and emotional situations with relatives. As a result people may have a stroke or brain haemorrhage that can be quite debilitating.

We had a patient, a back-packer who was walking down a road in Africa, when a thief on a motorbike tried to steal his backpack. The assailant pulled him along the road for some distance before leaving him, whereupon he was run over by a truck! The call came to us from a doctor who happened to be nearby. He had him on the verandah of his house and wanted to know what we'd do about it. He said the patient had compound fractures of both legs, so we arranged for an air ambulance to come from Paris. A team took him back to Paris, where he had some surgical intervention and then, when he was stable, another team brought him back on a stretcher to Australia. Mainly its 'swooping and scooping' like this and taking someone to a tertiary centre that isn't too far away and where they can then be stabilised. Incidentally, the airlines don't mind so much if you die on the flight, but they get very upset if you nearly die, because that means a diversion, which is extremely costly in terms of time and money and inconvenience for fellow travellers!

I've been to the seven continents. I accompanied a ninety-seven-year-old to Antarctica, because she'd flown over it the year before and she had decided she wanted to take a closer look. The only way she could go was to have medical support, so we flew to Buenos Aires and then down to Ushuaia and onto a boat, which took us along the Antarctic Peninsula for eleven days.

Our company also works with governments, so, for example, we repatriated all the bodies from the Swiss canyon tragedy and when there was civil unrest in Indonesia a few years ago, several corporations, from as far afield as Britain and Mexico, contracted us to get their employees out, so we chartered aircraft and took them to Singapore.

There have been cases of mental illness, where people's behaviour attracts attention, and we've been contacted by the police who've found them. In such cases their families have to pay the costs. We had one notable case in Africa involving schizophrenia. There was an overland group from London going through to Africa and one young man had been psychotic for three weeks of the journey; he hadn't slept and everyone was taking turns and staying up with him. One of our medical team flew to Kenya and met them there. The young man hadn't bathed for three weeks, so the doctor was able to buy some clothes at a second-hand place and he said it took about three fillings of the bathtub to get him clean, but then when he got him out, the young man wouldn't put any clothes on. They had to stay in their room for three days till they could get a flight out and all meals had to be sent to the room. Unfortunately, my colleague became extremely tired one night and fell asleep at the end of the meal and this young man took off and ran naked through the hotel lobby! My friend was called post haste to remove him. Then on the flight coming home, after he'd been dressed and just as they were coming in to land at Sydney, he suddenly took off down the aisle – it took three stewards to restrain him. His home was in Melbourne and my friend didn't think he'd be allowed on the Melbourne leg, but they did let him on after some more medication.

There've been lots of funny stories. We had another man who was found by the highway patrol outside New York with just a towel around his middle and a plastic bag on each foot, and no sign of identification. He was taken to a hospital and there it was decided that he was suffering from dementia. He was put in a nursing home and had been there for some weeks, when one morning at breakfast he said, 'We don't have this for breakfast in New Zealand!' so they got on to the New Zealand High Commission and found that he had been reported as a missing person. He also had family in up-state New York, so they were called and he went up with them. I went over to get him and bring him back to New Zealand. He had long hair; the original eighty-year-old hippy. We had adjoining rooms at the Hilton in New York, where we stayed. He had an in-dwelling catheter in his bladder, so I had to get a shopping bag so we could carry this around New York, because we had things to do for three days, including getting him a passport!

While waiting for the passport, I took him to Saks Fifth Avenue and he sat on a chair while I tried on clothes, and I took him to the Museum of Modern Art, and right by the front counter was Van Gogh's *Starry Night*. He said, 'We've got that picture at home,' and I thought, 'Unlikely,' but then just forgot about it. When we got him home to New Zealand and walked up the front steps and opened the door, there was a print of Van Gogh's *Starry Night* on the wall. It had been quite a saga. I'd taken him shopping and to the art gallery, everywhere, and he had loved it. Actually, he was quite a congenial companion.

There are three main international companies involved in medical assistance in Australia, one each in Brisbane, Sydney and Melbourne, plus some other smaller groups. Our current company started out as a Brisbane owned and run organisation two years ago. It was bought out by a company in Paris and now we're part of an international network – a very much bigger organisation.

I've maintained my British registration and have even thought of working in England occasionally. Two weeks ago I was in Dublin; it was beautiful in the autumn. The place is so vibrant now, with all the autumn trees and the street sculpture in Dublin is just marvellous. It's a lovely Georgian city and so easy to get around – full of young people! A month ago I was in the Czech Republic and it's interesting to see how the Czech cities have survived unscathed, not having been bombed in the war – it's really a living museum.

The interesting thing about travel medicine, I think, is that it's become a new specialty over the last ten years and grown enormously. This is partly because people are going to places, taking their own diseases with them. We find Australians going to Canada and Alaska, leaving here in winter with colds and flu and then infecting the non-immune people, who join these tourist boats coming from their northern summer. As a result we get great epidemics of flu going through these boats – another whole new area of concern for travellers. Another factor is the growth of guest-workers in countries. All this adds up to huge movements of people across the world. Also, of course, now that pharmaceutical companies aren't finding it cost effective to develop new antibiotics, vaccines are becoming the major thing for combating infection – it's a very interesting period.

John Sullivan and Nicholas Nicolaides – Pathologists

Photo Courtesy of Sam Simpson

John meets me at the front of their headquarters. He's sprightly and has a firm handshake. He shows me into the boardroom and he and Nick sit opposite each other at the long table with their guest between them at the end of the table. Nick is frail now and very softly spoken, with a gentle sincerity about him. There's an obvious camaraderie between these two elderly doctors who've spent a lifetime building their business – as it turns out, against all odds.

'I remember preparing to transfuse a poor old man from out West, putting up the saline drip which is always used before the blood is put in place. As I was starting up the drip he looked at me and said, 'Gee, Doc, if my sheep had blood like that I'd be out drenching them right away!'

Nick: I was born in Brisbane, on Christmas Eve, 1928, at 238 Montague Road, West End. My parents were refugees from Asia-Minor during the Holocaust, the burning of Smyrna (Izmir) in 1922. They were lucky to escape. My father was lined up to be shot by the Turks and someone in authority who recognised him from his business, said to him, 'What are you doing here, John, off you go!' And his life was saved.

A good percentage of the family on my mother's side was shot in Crete by the Germans during the last war, because they were school teachers and they were hiding the Australian soldiers in the local school. My grandfather went off to get food and the Germans followed him back with the food and shot everyone, including my grandfather, my aunt and her fiancé.

In 1924, when my father came out to Australia, a lot of the people ended up in Melbourne, but he got on another boat and came to Brisbane. He worked very hard and established himself as a pastry cook and baker. He set up a business in Montague Road next door to our home and built an oven, which is in the National Trust now, because it was the first wood-fired oven in Queensland. He brought my mother and their two girls out in 1928; I was born nine months later. My mother didn't speak English when she came here, so I learned Greek. I used to help my father make the cream-puff shells on a Sunday morning in the bakehouse when I was in third and fourth year medicine. He was sixty-one when he died from a heart attack in 1955.

My wife Rene's mother also came from Smyrna (Izmir). They had left Smyrna in a similar way to my family. Her grandfather had been captured by the Turks and was to be shot, but a General who knew him in business spared him. Her father was Christy Freeleagus, Consul General for Greece. Rene and I married in 1952 and have two children, Jan and John.

John: I was born in Southport, 29 August 1925. Following various rural misfortunes, the family property at Christmas Creek in the Beaudesert district had been sold in 1922 and my father had purchased a sports and home furnishing store in Southport. My mother, Catherine (Kitty) Cahill was said to have been a talented pianist, violinist and artist. She and my father married in 1919 and had four children, but in 1930 she died after a long illness. At the same time, due largely to the economic climate during the Great Depression, the business failed. My father moved to Brisbane to try to make a living, and we children were taken in by various relatives in the Christmas Creek area. I was then four years old.

My father, Michael Sullivan, couldn't find permanent employment in Brisbane at that time, but took a casual position managing a bridge club; bridge at that time was becoming popular. Soon he was publishing articles in newspapers and bridge magazines, giving broadcasts, winning numerous national events and on his way to becoming a world figure in contract bridge. A detailed story of his achievements in the bridge world is told in Colin Masters's book *Mind Games*. In later years his efforts were successful in having Australia recognised on the international bridge scene. In 1974 he was made the first honorary life member of the Australian Bridge Federation. He spent the last fourteen years of his life in our family home in Toowong in the loving company of my wife, myself and three grandchildren. He died in 1974 aged eighty.

As for me, when I was four I went to live with the Waters family who had a farm at Tabooba, outside Beaudesert. Mrs Waters was my grandmother's sister. I had an idyllic childhood and attended Tabooba State School, passing the scholarship examination in 1937 and 1938. The teacher who lived at our house felt that I had some talent and it would be a shame not to get further educated. Also in the house was a retired nun. This kind lady, Eileen O'Reilly, knowing my yearning to obtain a secondary education, suggested I say a certain prayer she gave me, asking for the chance to do so. The next day, when I finished saying it, I noticed the teacher driving out from the house and going up the road to Christmas Creek. That night, after we finished milking, the teacher came out to me with a member of the family and said, 'John, I've got news for you, you're going to Nudgee!' He had gone to see various relatives and suggested that ten of them put in five pounds each to send me to Nudgee for a year. Eileen O'Reilly had doubtless been a benign double agent in all of this.

Anyway, in 1939 I found myself in the St Joseph's College, Nudgee, and was desperate to do well in the exams at the end of that first year (1939). Fortunately I came first in the state and won a scholarship for a further year. Later I won an open scholarship to the University of Queensland, where I decided to join friends in doing medicine, and I graduated in 1948. I accepted the offer of a job for one year in the Path Department, not realising that I was thereby settling my career choice for life.

I met my wife Nell at the university. I was in fifth year when she came to the university to study Arts and we met at a Newman Society social. Nell and I were married in 1954. We have had three children – two girls and a boy.

Nick and I both did College of Physicians' exams. I wanted to be a physician at one stage but got side-tracked into Pathology and was quite happy to stay there. Nick deliberately wanted to do Pathology, I think, more than me, and this was a way of becoming registered as a specialist, by doing a local exam, because there were no Pathology exams. After a brief residency at Ipswich Hospital (1952 to 1953), Nick applied for a position in the Path Department of the Brisbane Hospital. I was Senior Registrar then and Nick joined as Junior Registrar, and that was how we met. In 1956 I started private pathology practice, taking over a small laboratory previously run by the Brisbane Clinic.

Nick: I joined the Red Cross as a specialist pathologist doing blood transfusion work and from then on I served on the Red Cross Committee, later becoming chairman of the Queensland division. I felt honoured when, after thirty-seven years, they awarded me a Distinguished Service Order and honorary life membership.

In 1958 John invited me to join him and the partnership of Sullivan and Nicolaides was born. I'd already done a locum for John in December 1957, when he was taken ill.

John: Our wives have been a great help to us over the years, combining looking after young families with helping Nick and I, particularly during those difficult early years of the practice.

Nick: They were left with the phone when we were out doing tours of the hospitals. They had to find us and leave a message for us to ring about putting another drip in or something. This was before mobile phones!

John: This was at all hours of the day and night. There was a lot of tension, too, because we might be in between hospitals and someone might ring in with an emergency, talk to our wives, and they were stuck with the problem of how to contact a technician. Nell and Rene never complained about this workload.

It was a heroic time all right, for both our families. We had technicians on at night after a while, but in the very early days you had to do everything yourself.

I remember preparing to transfuse a poor old man from out West, putting up the saline drip which is always used before the blood is put in place. As I was starting up the drip he looked at me and said, 'Gee, Doc, if my sheep had blood like that, I'd be out drenching them right away!' He thought the saline drip was the blood I was giving him.

One of the most difficult aspects for me in establishing the laboratory came from lack of the substantial financial resources normally required for such a venture. I was extremely fortunate in having the support of the Brisbane Clinic in providing an accountancy service and in helping to pay staff salaries and laboratory expenses. The major trouble was personal finance. After a few months business was booming and there were book debts of several hundred pounds, but I had run out of personal cash, so I went to the bank to get a loan. They said that they would lend me money only if someone would act as guarantor for me and there was no one to do this, so I came away with nothing. Nell was pregnant at the time and so I sent her in to plead with the manager for some relief. He relented and she was given one hundred pounds to buy food and that got us over the hump until the book debts were realised.

I couldn't afford an autoclave for sterilising things, so I bought a little pressure cooker. It was quite efficient really. I was on the founding committee of the Australian Society of Haematology and we had to run the international meeting in Sydney in 1966.

In the early days it was unthinkable for doctors to charge doctors for medical services. The only compensation was at Christmas time when it rained thank-you cards and innumerable bottles of whisky. These were the days before Medicare and medical benefit funds.

Nick: We became very busy because of our strong referral practice. I became particularly busy in the affairs of the College of Pathologists, which later led to my becoming college treasurer and college president. I was the founding chairman of the Research and Education Committee as well as chairman of the Pathology Services Advisory Committee, a committee responsible for liaising with federal government.

John: When I first started the laboratory, with minimal equipment and a heavy resuscitation workload, I was concerned that I could be fathering something that might be profitable but would always be critically limited in scope. It gives me great satisfaction to see the laboratory now supporting a considerable number of top quality specialists in many different departments. It was also most rewarding for me in my final years in the practice to be able to take up dermatopathology as a special interest and to be elected president of the Australian Society of Dermatopathology in 1983. Of course, I could never have anticipated that a pathologist in our group would become the author of what is generally regarded as the world's best textbook of Dermatopathology, but this is just what our David Weedon has done.

Nick: Yes, John, we've certainly attracted superb pathologists to our practice, pathologists such as John Musgrave, Tom Gaffney, Harry McKenna, Ron Morahan, Fred Hunt, and so many others, all splendid colleagues as well as superb technical staff, all of whom I am terribly proud to be associated with. I must admit that it's been with the support of the laboratory staff we've been fortunate to employ that we've been able to develop into a world-class practice.

Peter Dornan – Co-founder of Sports Medicine in Queensland

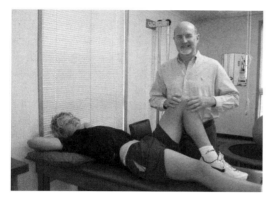

Peter Dornan treating athlete Liam Greinke

His practice is tucked behind a popular shopping complex in Toowong in a quiet and attractive setting. The reception and treatment rooms are decorated with sculptures he's created himself. He's a lean, fit individual with a steady gaze, a quick mind and a conviction that people should be more health conscious.

'We consume roughly 300 to 400 calories more than we need. No matter what form it's in, if you don't use it up in energy, that daily 300 calories is going to stay there and accumulate.'

I was raised on a farm and my expectations were that I would become a farmer. My father sent me to boarding school at Brisbane Boys College but in the last few months of my boarding school he sold the farm! Suddenly I had to consider changing the life I'd envisioned and perhaps getting a job that wasn't farming oriented. So I went to university and studied physiotherapy. I got very involved with Sports Medicine – in fact, I and a doctor friend, Kevin Hobbs, were the co-founders of Sports Medicine in Queensland – and I focused on that for about ten years. In that time I was the first official physio for many sporting teams, including the Brisbane Reds, the Queensland Team, the Wallabies and the Kangaroos.

However, after some years I wanted to see what else life had to offer, so I took my wife and kids with me in a van through Europe for about six weeks. The kids were nine and seven years old only. We went to all the museums and art galleries and looked at a different philosophy of life. By the time we got back I'd changed many things, including working out a holistic lifestyle where my whole life wouldn't revolve around my work.

I wrote a book about it at the time called *Stress and Lifestyle*. My plan was to divide my life up into six basic dimensions: professional, financial, social, creative, cultural, and personal. I devoted a certain amount of time to each, so that I had a chance of doing something with my life besides being what I still remain, a devoted physio. You haven't just got to go to work, just go to an institution and that's where you'll begin and end your days. I've called it dynamic success. It doesn't always sit well with some people, because it allows no absolute limits – it's up to the individual to formulate his or her own limits, standards and values.

Of the six important aspects I talked about, 'Professional' success means performing efficiently, with integrity and earning the respect of peers. To keep interested in what you do you've got to invest 5% of that time to continuing education and updating courses – if you don't look forward to coming into work every day you should change your work, even if that means a retraining program of up to five years.

'Financial' relates to your money and material goods and all the things that give you a feeling of security and satisfaction. One important aspect I've found was to put aside 10% of your income.

'Social' means relationships and activities you share with others, family, friends and work colleagues. It's absolutely important to belong to clubs, to organisations that extend your interests, and make sure you go to plenty of parties and theatres and picnics.

'Cultural' means things that you do for rewarding educational purposes. Self-broadening activities such as travelling, reading, studying a foreign language or taking courses, anything for the sake of learning and reading and expanding your whole vision.

'Creative' – these are the activities which express your personality and through which you grow and enjoy being a person. That means hobbies, artwork, crafts, gardening, whatever you like. It means any avenue for enjoying yourself by expressing your uniqueness. I learnt to write and I've written five books now. There are many ways to fulfil yourself through creativity. If you suppress your artistic side I think it just leads to unhappiness.

The final one was 'Personal' and success in this area means being in sound health, both mental and physical. It means reserving a certain amount of time every day to exercise, and in my case that means about forty-five minutes. I consider myself to be an industrial athlete, so I train for my job and for my life. It means you get 7 to 8 hours sleep a night. It means you look at your diet for control over your weight and your life and your energy requirements.

In this new age of freedom, everyone questions everything! It's a much more liberal attitude and it has opened up the eyes of medicine, because when patients weren't getting what they needed from their medical practitioners, they sought out alternative and complementary medicines. When you look at the statistics across the population, households now tend to go the same number of times to alternative practitioners as they do to their own doctors.

I don't think for a minute you should ever be negative about them but in future I do believe the alternative medicines are going to have to smarten up their act. Eventually they're going to be sued if they prescribe things that aren't going to help people, and particularly if they miss things like cancers. But I also believe that medical professionals are going to have to be prepared to include natural-type therapies into their own programs. Established medicine is clearly not enough; otherwise people wouldn't be going to these other therapists.

There are two big changes that have happened in the last 20 to 30 years while I've been involved with sports medicine. First kids used to have to spend a certain amount of time in physical education in their schools, and if they didn't exercise at school they certainly did at home. Then TV and computers came in, and they've dramatically changed the way children spend their leisure time. In my opinion anyone who does more than two hours of TV or computing after school is heading for trouble – even that two hours is almost too much. You'll be brain-dead and it's not good for your body.

The second big change has been the effect of fast foods. If you go into any take-away food shop, even any restaurant, the amount of food on your plate is at least twice, sometimes three times what it was twenty years ago, and we don't need that much. In short, we both do less exercise than we should and we have more to eat than we need, it's that simple! In terms of losing weight, it is simply a matter of eating fewer calories. The US government is said to recommend 1,600 calories a day for the average sedentary woman and 2,200 for men. In the year 2000, the reported daily calorific consumption was 1,877 for women and 2,618 for men – roughly 300 to 400 calories more than we need. No matter what form it's in, if you don't use it up in energy, that daily 300 calories is going to stay there and accumulate. The reason that's not very well known is it doesn't sell books – it's got to be a special diet to sell books!

There's no doubt that with any structure in your body, if you don't use it, you'll lose it very quickly. Lack of mental exercise will do the same for your brain. That's why exercises like maths, bridge, cryptic-crosswords and language are useful. There's a very big benchmark study which has been done in the States now of an order of nuns who devoted themselves to medicine. They very carefully document their lifestyle, including what they're doing mentally, as well as physically. Then, when they die, they allow the researchers to study their brains. They've been studying them for, I'd say, twenty years now – it was reported in the *National Geographic* magazine November 1997. They found that even though a lot of brains had signs of Alzheimer's, the nuns who'd stayed and kept challenged to the end, they didn't lose this capacity anywhere near as much – it was a very significant finding.

Personally, the minute I retire I'll be using my brain more and more. I won't let it ever stop! The longer you keep on studying the better. I've got friends, and I'm sure you've got friends, who are doing Masters Degrees and PhDs in their sixties, seventies and eighties. Inevitably, because you're a certain age, you'll have a certain amount of degeneration in the matrix of your brain, but you'll find that if you've made every one of those pathways work maximally your brain will still be better than someone who's forty and done little brainwork.

Forty years ago my wife Dimity became the first speech therapist here in Queensland. When she got through there were very few pathways open to teach deaf children, except through signing and maybe lip reading. If they weren't profoundly deaf they'd get hearing aids. Dimity got involved and developed a special technique to be able to use the parent as the first teacher then to use available hearing through cochlear implants or powerful hearing aids to teach babies how to speak. She got a Churchill Fellowship in 1992. Now she's started up her own charity, called the Hear and Say Centre and she can get a baby of any age and have them starting school in Grade One, completely integrated, as well as their hearing peers. Her research is assisted by neo-natal screening. She challenged the then Premier, Peter Beattie, and in 2003 he said he'd put $22 million towards a state neo-natal screening program. The minute the baby's born they can give it a special little test. The baby goes to sleep and they put little electrodes on it and you can tell if the baby is profoundly deaf or not. If that's the case she can suggest that they have the cochlear implant and with special training and coaching the baby can be completely integrated into the community by Grade One. There'll be no need to sign because signing is a very limited language, as you can only talk in a signing community. In 2003, Dimity was Queensland's Australian of the Year.

One thing I'm happy about relates to one of my books, called *The Silent Men*, about the Kokoda Trail battle, the Battle of Isurava. It highlighted the significance of that four-day battle where the Australians held on, although virtually completely surrounded and outnumbered six to one. The only Victoria Cross winner, Bruce Kingsbury, led a charge which gave them a bit more time and he was awarded his VC for this. They were eventually outflanked, but they did what's called a strategic withdrawal over three weeks back to Port Moresby.

This battle's known as the battle that saved Australia, because, had they been routed, Moresby would have been taken and it would have been a completely different prospect for Australia, and the whole Pacific Region.

I became involved and wrote a book about it, because I'd been asked to do a sculpture for the 50th anniversary of the Kokoda Trail campaign and I had selected to sculpt Bruce Kingsbury as one of the 605 men that didn't come back. He'd died up there, but I found his mate who had been beside him when he was killed. I found he'd retired down to Redcliffe and asked him if he'd help me put together a sculpture of Bruce and he did.

I presented it to the battalion and that stimulated a lot of men to come around and say, 'I was there when he was killed,' and all of a sudden these men started telling me stories that I'd never heard of before. It turned out it was the battle of Isurava and the people in it just didn't talk about it, which is why I called the book *The Silent Men*. I took their oral histories and wrote it in such a way that the reader feels they are on the front line – that opened up a great deal of interest in the battle. A lot of books have been written since then, but many people attribute the interest in the subject to my book.

I've also sculpted statues of Australia's first Victoria Cross winner, Sir Neville Howse. He was in the Boer War and when one of his troopers was shot in battle he rushed in on his horse to pick him up. The horse was shot from beneath him, so he then continued on foot, picked the man up on his shoulders and took him out of the battle, dressed his wounds and saved him.

Another thing that I'm pleased about in retrospect is the legacy I developed after being diagnosed some years ago with prostate cancer. I had a prostatectomy and that led to my being rather seriously incontinent, to the point where I was very depressed and didn't know what to do about it. There was no one I could talk to about it. Men didn't talk about those things! So I put an ad in the paper and had about seventy men turn up. From that moment on we started what was called the Brisbane Prostate Cancer Support Group and it's now the largest support group in Australia of any sort. We now have 12 groups through Queensland called the Queensland Chapter, affiliated nationally with 60 groups in Australia that formed the Prostate Cancer Foundation. We raise about a million dollars a year for funding, advocacy and support. We meet once a month and about 100 men and their partners come in and we talk about all sorts of physio-social issues, all the problems with treatment side effects, diagnosis and the horrendous decisions that go through a man's brain when he receives the diagnosis. I'm very happy about that – you could say it was one of my achievements.

Opal Mining

Paul Burton – Opal Mining in Outback Queensland

The Australian Opal Industry had its birthplace in Quilpie, the first mine being registered there in the early 1870s. Paul's father Des helped to revolutionise the industry through the introduction of open cut mining techniques. His father died in 1989, so Paul now spends his time between the mine in Quilpie and the retail side of the business based in Brisbane.

'You can be whoever you want to be out there and people accept you for who you are. There are all sorts of social misfits and people out there for reasons other than finding opal; sometimes it's just a lifestyle that suits them ... You've got 'Black Drago' and 'Red Drago' and 'Handlebar Moustache Joe' and 'No Socks Joe' and 'By-pass Bob'...'

Quilpie Opals is a family business, started by my father in 1968. At that stage we all lived in Quilpie in Western Queensland. My dad was the only pharmacist in town at the time and he got into opals as a hobby. It gradually grew and finally it took over his whole life.

From 1968 through until around 1980, Dad mined opals round Quilpie, then he decided to move down to Brisbane and open a retail store. I'd finished school in 1975 and had been back mining opals in Quilpie from about 1978 through until 1980, so when Dad moved to Brisbane I took over the mining. I'm actually a diesel fitter by trade, so I had a mechanical background, which helped with the mining process, because it's highly mechanised.

We're Queensland boulder opal miners. Boulder opal is quite separate and unique from Lightning Ridge black opal and the white opals from South Australia. Basically it's found within boulders, as the name suggests, and the opal is between virtually the top of the ground down to about 35 or 40 feet. In those days we used to open cut everything with large D8 and D9 bulldozers and the like. We just used to make this huge hole in the ground, check through everything and then fill it back in later.

Mining techniques in the last ten years have changed the industry a bit. Now it's mostly done with excavators, because excavators can get down much faster than a bulldozer, so they've become a more economical open-cut mining tool.

The southern mines are all underground. Lightning Ridge is the home of the black opal, probably the most famous opal in Australia, but it's all underground, down in shafts, and you drive off the underground shafts. The white opal in South Australia is the same; it's all shaft mined.

The sixty-four thousand dollar question is which boulder has the opal. In its simplest form, mining is simply a matter of digging a hole in the ground and when you come across a boulder that looks likely, you give it a crack with a hammer and you have a look what's inside! If I had to make a guess, I think maybe half of one per cent of all boulders may contain some form of opal and of that half percent that do contain opal, quite a small percentage will have opal that's of commercial value – there's an awful lot of dead boulder along with the amount of opal that's found.

Let's say we were going to start a new mine. What we'd do is take a look around on top of the ground and convince ourselves that there was some probability of opal being underground. The way we do that is to look for what's called 'floaters'. Floaters are pieces of weathered out boulder opal that have been sitting in the sun through the natural erosion and weathering process that all country goes through. Over a hundred years or so, the boulders crack and break open and the opal is exposed, so someone walking across the ground can actually see it. What you do is identify an area that has some floaters with some colour in them. If you like the ground you then stake a mining claim or a mining lease over that area – you obviously can't begin to mine until you've got your lease granted. You've also got to have a negotiated settlement with the Aborigines in the area, if there are any, and have an arrangement with the land holder if it's a grazing property, which most of these properties are – and, of course, pay some rent to Queensland Mines Department. There are lots of protocols and procedures that you've got to go through. High risk and maybe no return!

You then take a thirty- or forty-ton excavator and begin to dig a hole in the ground. You see if you can find where the opal that was on the surface actually tilted and the level started to descend into the ground and you follow that level down and check all the boulders on the way to see if there's any opal in them. In geological terms, in this square hundred metres there might be some good conditions to form opal but another 50 metres away the conditions may not be right. What commonly happens is when you begin to get onto some opal then in all likelihood you'll probably find another piece next door. Opal comes in what you call 'pockets'. That pocket might begin by having poor quality opal and then it leads in and in the middle you get a good quality pocket of opal and as you continue to dig it then fades back out to poor quality opal and then to nothing.

I've been in it now for about twenty-five years. My dad died in 1989 and when he died I virtually took over the retail side of the business. At that stage we had a store on the Gold Coast and fairly soon after I opened a store in Cairns, so we wound up with three stores retailing opal. From September 11 in 2001 on through the Bali bombing and SARS, all those events had a negative impact on tourism into Australia and tourism businesses like ours suffered accordingly. We've currently rationalised our operation back to a single store in Queen Street Mall.

There's plenty of excitement when you crack a boulder at the mine and find there's some opal there. Then you have to take the broken up pieces of boulder into town and arrange to have them cut and the opal separated from the raw rock and then turned into cut and polished gem stones. We had five or six cutters in train twenty years ago and we used to process a lot of our own material, but these days we employ a couple of cutters in Quilpie and mostly sub-contract the work out.

Acquiring, cutting and polishing the opal is one entire process and is quite separate from the design of the metal that goes around it. You get to the point where you've got loose opals and you've got to decide what you're going to do with them. Maybe it's going to be a ring or a pendant or a brooch or a bracelet. The highest grade of opal you can cut and polish into a gemstone that's going to go into a piece of made up jewellery, either in gold or silver or platinum. Lower grades of opal or opal that may be cracked and unsuitable for jewellery can be made into specimens – or you could polish one and make it into a paperweight or cut one in two and make it a pair of bookends. There's any number of decorative and nice things you can do with boulder opals apart from making jewellery.

My wife Melita and I work together in the business. We're not jewellers, so we contract all the jewellery manufacturing out, but we've had a lot of input into the design of particular pieces of jewellery to suit particular stones. Basically, when you've got a nice, expensive piece of opal, it's something that's quite unique. The colour works a certain way and the shape of the stone works a certain way. Opals are often a free-form shape and the colour shows and displays nicer in one direction than another, so you need to consider all sorts of aspects when you design a setting to go around a piece of opal. In all three types of opals available in Australia, red is the most valuable colour. There's red opal in boulder, there's red opal in Lightning Ridge black and there's red opal in white opals from South Australia. Opals are like paintings, they're all individual, and no two opals are the same. In our retail store here in Brisbane we sell all types of Australian opal and a full range of jewellery and specimens – basically anything that's related to opal.

The thing that I like about opal mining is knowing that you can go down at the beginning of the day and mine some opal out of the ground – it's the best feeling in the world! I suppose it's like having a chance to win the casket every day and it gets into you. Most days you don't find anything at all; parcels or pockets of opal are quite infrequent, so when you find one and you know you're onto something, it's quite a kick. It's one of those things that keep you coming back!

There're lots of characters in the opal industry. If you're a bit of a wild boy and a bit of an independent spirit, then you can be an opal miner and you know that society will accept you as such. It's very, very isolated, there's no power, no water. You need to be totally self sufficient out in the middle of nowhere. There's no catching the bus to work! People bring their own water, they generate their own power or they have kerosene lights and one thing or another. They live in tents, or caravans or humpies – like a casually made lean-to iron shed. That's the beauty of it, it doesn't really matter what you want to do, people will accept you and your story. It's very much a free, rugged, independent kind of lifestyle.

The pubs are a couple of hundred kilometres away from the opal fields, so if you want to get into town and put in a bit of time at the pub, then you've got to drive in. Of course, lots of people take alcohol out to the fields and it's a bit of a party atmosphere at times.

The lasting impression I have of the opal fields is they're just one of the last frontiers in Australia. People accept you for who you are. There are all sorts of social misfits and people who are out there for reasons other than finding opal; sometimes it's just a lifestyle that suits them. There's a big Yugoslav community – a big Serb and Croat community –and there's lots of different nationalities that blend together to make up the opal community. A lot of Italians, a lot of Greeks – some countries just naturally tend to gravitate to those sorts of occupations.

There're lots of characters out there – and they're there for a variety of reasons. You've got 'Black Drago' and 'Red Drago' and 'Handlebar Moustache Joe' and 'No Socks Joe' and 'By-pass Bob' – he was a fellow that had a by-pass heart operation twenty years ago when they were still a bit new. There're all these characters and I suppose they just become part of the place.

PART THREE: Community and Service

'The greatest virtues are those which are most useful to other persons.'
                                                                    - Aristotle

Working together for the common good is a rewarding experience for all concerned, the hardships and joys of success mutually shared.

There are, of course, many forms of community, and here we explore communities of culture and faith and communities of shared interest and service. Queensland is proudly multi-cultural and its ethnic communities provide opportunities for their members to celebrate both their roots in the 'old country' and their new home in Australia. In exploring some of Queensland's many diverse communities of interest and service we meet members of communities serving city-dwellers, others representing the country and representatives of communities that provide access to learning for the elderly, sport for teenaged youth, support for the isolated and music for all ages, from classical to jazz.

Service, like community, is multi-faceted; it can be direct, like the firemen and SES workers on whom we depend in emergencies, or indirect, as with people who work to preserve and improve the environment on which we all ultimately depend. Many community members, whose stories you will read in these pages, are unsung heroes, people who spend countless hours helping others and providing an invaluable contribution to the quality of life we enjoy.

Mark Svendsen: Poet

Travellers At Evening

Particles of night-time take their places in the sky;
Evening draws her grey shawl down on rooftop and on hill.
Quietly we're waiting with verandah tables set
For the travellers to come home and with our yellow laughter fill . . .

I am hungry, I am sore, I am weary at the core,
I need laughter, I need friends, I need food to make amends.

We will share our bread together at the table we have set
And our company tell stories understanding beyond sense
That we all are fellow travellers although some have never left
Our verandah where we sit and share the evening's deep benevolence.

Who is hungry, who is sore, who is weary at the core?
Who needs laughter, who needs friends, who needs food to make amends?

Those who came here from afar, those who've died and those who've gone.
We will sit beneath the stars, and tell their stories every one:
Tell their stories till we've done.

© Mark Svendsen 2001

Mark Svendsen was raised in the small coastal town of Emu Park and later educated at University of Queensland. In 2001 he was commissioned by Lyndon Terracini, Artistic Director of the Queensland Biennial Festival of Music to write the lyrics for a choral symphony the Rockhampton Gardens Symphony, based on the culture of Rockhampton. The composer for this work was Elena Kats-Chernin and it was performed by the combined forces of the local musical community. Mark says that this turned out to be a life-changing opportunity. He is a writer, principally for children and young adults.
(www.marksvendsen.com)

Helen Sanderson: Artist's Books in Miniature

Photographed by Jon Linkins, Brisbane

Helen Sanderson is a Brisbane artist who has held fourteen solo exhibitions. Three of these exhibitions have toured regional Queensland. Her work has been included in many selected group exhibitions, and references her upbringing in rural Australia, with a strong landscape and storytelling bias. She paints, does printmaking and creates artist's books. Drawing forms the basis of her arts practice. Her work has twice been selected for the Australian Libris awards, the Australian artists' book prize. Recently she has worked as an independent curator. Her current project is an international exchange exhibition *In Your Dreams,* showing in Canada, Germany and Australia.

Communities of Culture and Faith

Bico Athanasas – Greek Orthodox Community of St George

Here in the West End you find many businesses, from delicatessens to barber shops owned and run by Australian-Greek families, and it's here that the Community of St George and the Greek Club are based. Here too is the annual Paniyiri Festival – a celebration of all things Greek. Bico is administrator of the Greek Orthodox Community of St George. He has a firm handshake and ready smile. He shows me to a large quiet room where we can talk and describes the dual allegiances he says are felt by Australian Greeks.

'I love Greece, but on all my trips to Greece I'm always looking forward to coming home – this is home, to all of us. We love our mother country, we love it dearly, but this is home.'

We call ourselves Australian-born Greeks and we're proud of our heritage and our culture and proud to be living in such a fantastic country as Australia. I was born here, but I was brought up never to forget my ancestral culture and all the traditions that come with being Greek.

The church is the centre point within the Greek community, so you grow up near the church and you marry in the church. You have your children and you come back to the church. I've been back to Greece many times, I love Greece, but on all my trips to Greece I'm always looking forward to coming home – this is home, to all of us. We love our mother country, we love it dearly, but this is home.

I was selected as a volunteer to go back for the Olympics in Athens, but the family needed me here and I thought I'd probably enjoy it more here and also enjoy the festivities happening in the Greek community. We had a large program here for the Olympics, starting off with the opening ceremony at a Greek taverna in the Greek Club and then we had screens in the club showing the events all throughout the Games. There were parties and competitions – every day there was something on!

What started the fun was soccer. Winning Euro 2004 was spectacular – the euphoria was wonderful. We had over 1200 people in the Greek Club that morning and it was really good to see the young Greek kids waving their flags and painted and everything. We were all so proud.

Our Childcare Centre has won awards. I would say that 75% are Greek children, and there are those too from other cultures, but they learn Greek and you should see those little kids when they celebrate the Greek National Day. It's wonderful to see Vietnamese, Chinese and Aboriginal children all dressed up in Greek costumes and singing Greek songs. We've got an excellent director, and the staff, they all love the kids. We're hoping to open a day school for those kids to move into.

Our Greek school here is held on Monday afternoons and Saturday mornings. They learn the Greek language, grammar, geography and history. We are in the process of discussing with the education department about establishing a day school. It would be a private school, but it would be open for everybody, not just for Greeks. The lessons would be taught in English, but Greek will be a language that is taught from age seven, as well as the religion and history of Greece.

There are adult classes for non-Greek-speaking people to learn Greek and there's also a class within the Greek community, in our '60 and better' program that teaches older Greeks the English language – so they can communicate with the doctor, or when they're shopping or reading signs and that sort of thing.

The first Greek Orthodox Church in Brisbane was built in 1929 in Charlotte Street. In 1959 we built the church here in West End, and then, as surrounding property became available, we purchased it and that's how this complex was built. We have three programs running out of here. In the Greek Respite Centre, with the government's support, we have a couple of programs. We have the Community Options Program that involves helping people in their home with, for example, domestic assistance. So if someone is elderly (after assessment) we send in a cleaning person that goes in once or twice a week to clean for them. They pay a fee of about $3 and we clean the house for them and give them a bit of social support – this is done by someone who speaks Greek. The community employs these carers and they are Greek-speaking.

Then we have our day respite. We run three programs: we've got one here at South Brisbane, one at Taigum and one on the Gold Coast, all run out of the South Brisbane centre. We've three buses and they go out and collect our elderly and bring them in to have morning tea, lunch and afternoon tea. We also have lectures on health and games for them. We have outings for them and movies and so on. It's a respite program, so they can leave the house, come and be cared for and chat with friends. They play cards and do a little handicraft work. That runs five days a week.

We are now starting another respite program, a dementia program, and we'll be caring for those with dementia on a Saturday. Where a family has someone suffering dementia, they bring them in and we look after them for the day while they have a bit of a break. If we were to put them out in the mainstream they wouldn't go, because of the language problem.

Our next program is the Welfare. It has a few umbrellas. It looks after a playgroup which is for the kids that are not at the day-care in our Childcare Centre. There's a playgroup every Wednesday where mothers come with their children and spend the morning. They're all friends and they do outings and I think it's almost more of a social for the mothers than the kids!

We have a senior citizens' program which meets every Thursday in the Greek Club and they get together and sing songs and tell stories of the old country. How we Greeks see it, just because someone is elderly doesn't mean they're no longer useful or cared about. Our '60 and better' program is a state government initiated program of the Department of Health and our motto is, 'It is a clock – we can't turn back the hands of time, but we can keep the clock working!'

Our Welfare Centre started in 1976 and it's always provided welfare assistance for everybody, not only Greek people. We have a lot of people who are unfortunate and down on their luck in the South Brisbane area. They're sent to us from St Vinnies and other agencies and we'll give them big bags of food, jams, long-life milk, spaghetti, tinned fruit, and other necessities until their next cheque comes. There are people who need medication. They bring their scrip to us and we send them to a Greek pharmacy in West End and we tell them, 'Fill this prescription and send us the account.' There are a lot of drug dependent people, but we have taken precautions to look after our staff.

Our Welfare Centre also runs marriage counselling and preparation classes in conjunction with the priest. It also runs drug awareness programs. We target that within the Greek community, and also homeless children. Until I started working here, I didn't believe there were any homeless Greek children – but there are – and drugs are a big problem, as in other communities. Our priests, being young, are fantastic, and they can relate to the kids, which is really good.

Our church is involved in youth ministry. We have three priests. Father Gregory has been with us since 1958 and then we have the two younger ones, Father Dimitri and Father Anastasios. There're youth groups, youth activities and walkathons, social outings and a lot of things to help young people keep together. Most of the marriages are mixed marriages now, but they're getting married in the Greek Church and they're having their children baptised here – that's what's important.

We have a very good youth program. The church service that you would hear on a Sunday is done all in English on Saturday evenings and the young priests encourage families to come then. Any Saturday evening you would find 400 to 500 people, young families – not elderly. It's my generation and younger who will come and bring their children. The service is in English and they all understand what's going on. The priests orient everything towards the youth, because it's the youth that are going to continue our culture and our traditions and our heritage. Even our marriages and baptisms, they're all done in English now, although a lot of them want it half and half because of respect for the parents.

Another program that we have is our Community Care Package (CCP), the assistance given before a nursing home is required. We also have a Greek nursing home, because, as people age, they become forgetful and revert back to the mother language. The CCP program that we run here is government funded. A package is 6 hours a week of social domestic care and now we provide that for 37 packages. We look after people in their home. We'll clean for them and we'll bathe them. We'll cook a meal for them. Our carers will take them out on a social or say 'let's go for a coffee' or 'let's go to the park'. It's brilliant, because all the packages are filled. If we had another 10 to 20 we could fill them. Our nursing home has got 42 beds, and our hostel has more than 10.

People who live in the hostel can't live in their homes on their own any longer, but don't want to be a burden on their children. What they want is to go somewhere where they can look after themselves. All their meals are catered for them and there's a full-time nurse there. The St Nicholas Hostel is just here on Hampstead Road in the West End. We have cameras in the church and every Sunday they have a hook-up and they watch the church service in the nursing home and in the hostel. If there is a funeral or a wedding and they want to watch it, they can turn the TV on and watch it as if they were there. There's also a mini bus to bring them down to the church if they wish to come.

The present Greek Club was built in 1974. They needed somewhere like a church hall and they were looking at the business aspect of it as well. The Greek Club is a business. It holds conventions, conferences and wedding receptions – it's a function centre. When the Greek community needs to hold anything, it just books into the Greek Club, like anybody else! It provides a members' bar, and it provides activities for everyone – just like any other club.

The Hellenic House is our 'Boys Club' – it has fantastic food. It's open to anybody that wants to go for lunch, but Greek women don't go because they say, 'Well it's the boys, you know, going there.' They go and play their cards, backgammon and snooker.

Some ladies do great cooking and give lessons for the young Greek girls or for anybody, really, and that's done through the Greek community. The cooking classes are done downstairs and it's also done at one of the other parishes as well.

The Hellenic Dancers are the official dance group of the Greek Club. They teach the dances to the younger people and again the younger people join the group. The Hellenic Dancers have been going now for about 25 to 26 years and they perform throughout Queensland.

The Paniyiri Festival is well known in Brisbane. It's now in its 31st year and it has a great atmosphere. It is a festival of everything Greek – food, drink, wine, dancing, artwork, cooking – just everything Greek. It's very busy and very popular. Last year 50,000 people went through the turnstiles!

Our hopes for the immediate future are to establish a day school. We also want to provide more and more services, and build on the nursing home – those are our major aims at the moment.

Fausto Zanda – Italo–Australian Centre

He was president of the Italo–Australian Centre when we first spoke. The centre is a modern building with a large meeting room on the ground floor. There's plenty of laughter and greeting going on around us, with people calling in to meet up with friends. Some stop by our table and join in the conversation, while others shout a greeting and move on to join others. The food here is excellent and inexpensive, so the dining room is always full.

'We make traditional Italian regional cuisine that's cooked by volunteers, like a "casalinga" – this means a meal prepared the old traditional way.'

The Italo–Australian Centre is a combination of Italians and Australians. The club started in 1968. Originally the land belonged to another Italian club and they donated it so this facility could be built. Most people come to the club round eleven o'clock each day. They meet friends and maybe play cards; other groups come and play bowls. We've got a very large group of retired people and we organise bus trips to other clubs and trips for them up to the north coast and dinners here or lunch. We make traditional Italian regional cuisine that's cooked by volunteers, like a 'casalinga' – this means a meal prepared the old traditional way. We do this on Sundays here every two or three weeks. It's always packed then, because people love to try the different regional things.

Before the 2000 Olympics we had a delegation of visiting politicians from Italy and we organised a dinner for them, a sort of welcome. We have full-time chefs, so we try to provide the best Italian food we can. People come here because this is the centre of the Italian community – all the regions of Italy are represented here.

We have about 10,000 members. At the top we've got the Ambassador and the Italian Consul and then we've got the COM.IT.ES (Committees for the Italians

Abroad). They are the elected representative of our Italian community. In collaboration with the consular authorities, agencies, associations and committees operating in the jurisdiction, they promote social, cultural, educational and recreational initiatives. COM.IT.ES. cooperate with the consular authorities to look after the protection of rights and interests of the Italian emigrated citizens.

Downstairs we've got CO.AS.IT (Comitato Assistenza Italiani) which assists elderly Italians, and people from there go to visit our sick people. CO.AS.IT also does a pre-school in Italian.

Downstairs, we've also got the Dante Alighieri Society, which teaches Italian all year round. They've got about 500 to 600 students and members. The Dante Alighieri organises trips from Brisbane to Venice, Florence and other major cities in Italy. Then we've got another group which recently organised a trip, not just to Italy this time, but to Spain and France and Italy. These trips are every year, more or less – possibly two or three trips, it all depends if people want to travel.

At the back of the club we've got fields where they play soccer – that's the Brisbane City Soccer Club, which is also part of this club.

We normally have a festival the first week in June to celebrate our Italian Republic Day on 2 June. The festival is a mix of traditional costumes from every region in Italy. There are about 22 regions and every region has a different costume. I come from Sardinia and I am also the president of the Sardinia Culture Club. In Sardinia we've got a different language altogether from Italy, different cuisine, different costumes and many other things, but, because we're part of Italy, we're first Italians and then Sardinians.

With all the costumes from the different regions the festival is a beautiful display of colours – different dances, different singing and everyone with their own cuisine. One year we got a group of young girls and gentlemen dressed up as Romans and they escorted our State Premier from the entrance of the club to the stage.

A few years ago we did an exhibition of photos of 100 years of Italian immigrants and most of the photos were from here in Queensland. The first ship came in 1880. In those days it took six months for them to travel here from Italy. People worked picking tobacco, cutting cane and everything. In those days it was very hard for the new arrivals, but today, look how we've evolved as a community!

One of the major migrations from Italy to here was in 1955. Most people arrived in Sydney or Melbourne, but a large percentage moved to Queensland to work in the cane fields. The only problem was that Italians worked with Italians and that's why today the older generation still doesn't speak English well.

I remember some of our older members telling me about the old days. When they wanted to send letters from the post office they didn't know how to ask for an airmail stamp. Letters sent by sea could take six months to arrive in Italy, so they would hold up the envelope and make like a plane – with their arms out and saying, 'Brmm, brmm, Italy, Italy!'

Other people found food shopping difficult. When they went to buy eggs, of course, they don't know the word in English, so they used to make the noise of a chicken. The shopkeeper would usually come out with a full bird and they had to say, 'No, no – uovo.' Today we smile about these things, but at that time it was very hard for people.

When I arrived in the airport in Sydney 1970, I was surprised to find there was nobody speaking another language. Being an international airport, I thought there should be an information centre in which they spoke foreign languages. At that time I'd just finished school and we'd learned French there. I could make myself understood in Spanish, French or Italian, but none of those languages was available at the airport. I was young and very hungry and frightened, because I couldn't make myself understood. I went to the counter to buy food and there were all these beautiful girls there. I'd come dressed in the latest European fashion and all the girls kept looking at me and that worried me. I was wondering, 'Maybe my shoes are broken or something else is wrong.' Every time I went to the bar there were lovely sandwiches and milk, which I wanted to buy, but I didn't know the words. I tried French. '*Parlez vous Francais?*' 'No, no, no,' and then I tried '*Habla Espagnol?*' They said, 'Do you speak English?' but I had to say, 'Me? No, no English.' I had to wait there until the afternoon, when finally an Italian lady came around. She was an airport cleaner and she asked me if I needed something. I explained that I didn't know what you called things, so she came with me and helped me buy food and told me when the next plane was going to Brisbane. She was very helpful and so I was happy.

My sister was in Brisbane, so I stayed fifteen days with them and then I started working. At that time work was not really a problem; there was plenty of choice and a lot of Italian companies. I stayed in Brisbane six months, then I went up to Mount Isa and stayed there for seven years, because I was working building bridges. I travelled around wherever the job was, from Mareeba to Longreach and to Emerald.

There were six children in my family. My sister returned to Italy, but my mama came out here twice: when I got married and when we had our first child. She is eighty-five now and no longer strong enough to come such a long journey. During the last seven years I visited Italy three or four times a year, because I was advisor for the Sardinia region. Now my term is finished, but I'm still going every year or two. My daughter was there last year and loved it.

We started a company called Internationale Constructione, with four of us from Italy and one Spanish guy and an engineer who was Australian. We went to Charlie, the big boss of Stilcon, a company which grew out of EPT up in Mount Isa, and said, 'We want to start on our own,' and they provided a guarantee for us and we started building bridges for Main Roads. Stilcon gave us all the machinery, cranes and excavators and everything. When everybody's single they're willing to work and travel around, anywhere in Queensland. Then when we're married we find the wife is sad alone and we stop going around. I pulled out of the company quite a few years back and I came down to Brisbane and opened up another company by myself called GEO Civil Constructions. I did a few bridges here in Brisbane for Brisbane City Council and a lot of storm-water drainage and curb and channel and all those things, and I'm still working.

In 1960 the Olympics were in Rome and we carried the torch here in Australia. Our community is not getting any younger, because unfortunately immigration from Europe was reduced in 1971 – that's why I'm the last generation of Italians immigrating to Australia.

Italians worked hard in this country to get to the position they are now in and we're proud of that. Franco Belgiorno-Nettis came here in 1951 and later started the company Transfield. They started with nothing. Today they build ships and submarines. They also built the Gateway Bridge and many things.

We've got big Italian builders like Pradella and Iezzi Construction. Gino Serafini came to Australia in 1956 with no money and no English. He worked for a chain company in Brisbane, but that company closed down here, so he opened his own chain company. He worked hard and now his company is the biggest chain maker in Australia.

Nanda Pasta started to make a bit of pasta, because we Italians can't live without pasta. They were the only factory in Australia making pasta, before they sold to Nestle. Then there's Angelo's doing gnocchi and ravioli and *capellini*. They started under the house and from there they got bigger and bigger. Gambaros', same thing. They start with nothing and now they are one of the biggest seafood resellers. Serena Russo is Italian, too, of course.

Another Italian family, Peter Vidili, started producing and selling goats' milk, which now is everywhere – before there was no goats' milk in the shops. Angelo Puglisi owns the Ballandean Estate winery, his family started a farm in Stanthorpe to grow the grapes and now it's one of the biggest wineries around.

There's a lot of Italians here that make their own wine. I prefer to drink a glass of wine made from pure grape juice without any preservatives in it. Many times I get a headache from the preservatives they put in – so that's the reason I make my own wine. Of course, I also buy shop wine and when I've got people coming I prefer to give my guests the bought wine – but when they find out what I'm drinking they want the same as me!

Eddie Liu – The Chinese Club and Brisbane's Chinatown

The Chinese Club is situated in the heart of the Valley and this morning it's characteristically busy, with people sitting chatting at various tables or standing over by the pokies hoping for luck. I'm shown to 'Eddy's table' and told he's expecting me but is on the phone. Green tea for two is brought and I'm told he won't be long. He comes across the room, smiling, as though welcoming a guest to 'his place'. He's affectionately known as the father of Chinatown and the Chinese Club is clearly like a second home to him. He's elderly now, but in the Chinese community age is synonymous with wisdom and Eddy remains one of the most respected voices for his people in this city.

'When Australia entered the war I was called up. The Manpower people sent me to Brisbane in 1942. General Douglas McArthur was headquartered in Brisbane then. I became chief clerk in the small ships division at Bulimba. The Bulimba Project, that's what they called it. It was an American project and 2000 Chinese workmen were brought in to build landing barges for the war effort.'

I was born in Hong Kong and in school we spoke English – but out of school we led a typical Chinese lifestyle and we spoke Cantonese. I came to Australia when I was fourteen years old to go to secondary school at the Christian Brothers College and to join my father, a herbalist who was living in Australia. I only went home to Hong Kong for school holidays. In 1939 World War II started in Europe. After my holiday in Hong Kong that year I was the last passenger to board the *Taiping*. The Sino–Japanese War had just started and the *Taiping* was the last ship to come to Australia from Hong Kong before the war. I was happy at school here but outside of school it could be difficult, as some Australians wouldn't sit next to Asians on trams or in other public places.

When Australia entered the war I was called up. The Manpower people sent me to Brisbane in 1942. General Douglas McArthur was headquartered in Brisbane then. I became chief clerk in the small ships division at Bulimba. The Bulimba Project, that's what they called it. It was an American project and 2000 Chinese workmen were brought in to build landing barges for the war effort. China was on the side of the

Allies, so the Chinese workers were issued with Alien Certificates for work and residence. They formed their own seamen's union and they asked me to be secretary. I wasn't a seaman, but I could talk to the men and help them when they needed it and I raised funds for wartime refugees. After the war most of them went home, but six stayed and I did too. I opened a business as a fruit and vegetable supplier and became more involved in the community.

I helped people by raising funds for the Mater Hospital and the Royal Brisbane Children's Hospital and I also helped raise money for four children from Hong Kong to have liver transplants in Brisbane – doing something for the community is the best thing you can do.

When the flood came to Brisbane in January 1974, the Chinese Club had already been here in Brisbane for over 50 years. It used to be in Auchenflower. We purchased land in Dixon Street for $4000 and with voluntary labour we built the clubhouse in 1957. The building was badly damaged in the flood and we knew it would cost too much to fix, so we decided it would be better to sell and start again somewhere else.

I went to see the then Premier, Joh Bjelke-Petersen, for assistance, and he told me the only land available at that time was a block of five acres at Deagan costing $100,000. We had no other alternative, so we agreed to purchase the land. We built a new clubhouse on half the land and we decided to sell the other half. I went to Hong Kong, because I thought I might find a buyer there, a developer who might be interested. We hoped that a Chinese Temple, or maybe an aged home or Chinese garden could be erected on the land next door to the clubhouse.

The Ching Chung Taoist Association in Hong Kong bought the land and spent around $3.5 million on their project there. Members of the Chinese Club, though, were still not happy being so far from the city centre, so I approached the Ching Chung Taoist Association again and they bought the two and a half acres of land where the clubhouse was and we moved the Chinese Club here to the Valley.

There is an old Taoist temple at Breakfast Creek. In 1886, when it was built, there used to be a big Chinese community living in the area. The building was in the care of three trustees and when the trustees died it went into disrepair and vandals caused a lot of damage.

After we moved the Chinese Club to the Valley they asked me to see if we could reopen the temple. One day I got a phone call from the Town Clerk saying that the temple was going to be sold by the Brisbane City Council at a public auction. They expected the building would be demolished and the land used for other purposes – possibly a car park. We then founded the Chinese Temple Society and I went to see the Premier. I explained to him the importance of the temple to the Chinese Community and the problems about ownership. In 1963 a Private Members' Bill was introduced in Parliament 'returning the land and tenure of the temple to the Chinese Temple Society'.

We raised money from the community here and others all over the country, for the total restoration of the temple. We even raised money by charging a parking fee to weekend race-goers who wanted to park their cars on the temple grounds while they went to the Albion racecourse. In 1966 the temple was officially reopened. In 1986 we had a big three-day celebration to mark the temple's centenary. This is the only

Chinese temple in Australia that was built by Chinese builders and decorated inside and outside with Chinese architecture.

In November 1983, Russ Hinze, who was then Minister for Local Government, said that Brisbane should have its own Chinatown. They made a committee to look into the plan for a Chinatown here in the Valley. I was the secretary and director of the Chinese Club of Queensland then and chairman of the Chinatown Advancement Committee. The Brisbane City Council provided half the money, $1.6 million dollars, and the state government of Sir Joh Bjelke Petersen provided the other half. The Valley was a perfect choice, because there were already a lot of well-established Chinese businesses here in this area.

I went to China and hired people with the necessary skills. In April 1984, at the invitation of the Chinese Club, six architects and engineers including B.Z. Mo, who was the chief architect of the Guangzhou Planning Administration, came to Brisbane to design the Tang Dynasty-styled pagodas and arches for Brisbane's Chinatown. The Brisbane City Council appointed the Brisbane architect William Douglas to travel to China and Hong Kong to discuss details of the plan. The People's Republic of China presented the two stone lions guarding the entrance to the Chinatown Mall as a gift.

By Chinese New Year (29 January) in 1987, our dream of Brisbane's own Chinatown was a reality – it coincided with the Lunar New Year and we had very big celebrations that year!

In 1980 I was awarded an Officer of the British Empire (OBE) for community service and in 1987 I was appointed Honorary Ambassador for the City of Brisbane and in 2001 I was awarded the Order of Australia (OAM). Since 2001 I've been director of the Valley District Chamber of Commerce and I'm still the honorary secretary of the Chinese Club.

My wife Elizabeth was Irish and we met at table tennis. We had four daughters and two sons and they gave us thirteen grandchildren – already we have seven great-grandchildren.

I like to be involved with the community and I've helped people support good causes like the Leukemia Foundation and Guide Dogs for the Blind. I've also worked at many things, from supplying fruit and vegetables, to being a herbalist and a property developer and running a public relations consultancy. I still serve on several boards and often revisit China and Hong Kong. I would like to see a Chinese retirement village established here and also for there to be on-street parking in Chinatown, as these things would be helpful to the community.

Uri Themal – Jewish and Interfaith Communities

In this photograph you see Uri Themal (far right) with Chief Justice, Paul de Jersey; Imam, Imraan Hussain; and Anglican Bishop, Ron William;, at the official launch of 'Project Abraham – a quest for harmony in troubled times', which took place in Nerang in November 2006. Uri has now returned to Tel Aviv but at the time of our conversation he was the Rabbi at Temple Shalom on the Gold Coast. Deeply religious in his own faith he also respects the rights of others to follow their faiths.

'I recognised that people had neglected to deal with religion. Religion was not very strongly considered in the context of multiculturalism and yet, very often, religion was much more a source of conflict than differences based purely on ethnicity. So, in 1992 I created an organisation which was called the Interfaith Multicultural Forum, where I tried to bring together the idea of managing not just our cultural diversity, but also our cultural and religious diversity.'

My parents and I survived the Holocaust in Germany with the help of the German 'underground', who provided us with false papers and false names. These were non-Jewish German people who were in the Resistance against the Nazis and they helped us to survive. I was born in 1940, so all this happened between the time I was a baby and five years old. After the war, in 1949, we went to Israel and I grew up there, but my mother was very ill as a result of the Holocaust and because of this my parents had to return to Germany. I later joined them and finished my schooling there. I took a degree in political science and became a radio reporter.

In Judaism there are different streams. The Orthodox group (which has many different streams within itself) is strongly tied to the fulfilment of Jewish rituals and is essentially conservative in its approach to Judaism. The Reform or Progressive Judaism stream is more liberal in its interpretation of Jewish rituals and Jewish practices, and tries to come to terms with modern times and how Judaism and Jewish life can fit into modern times – that's the basic difference between them.

In 1964 I went to England to study for the Rabbinate and was ordained in 1968. The process of *how* I became a Rabbi is interesting. When I was studying in Berlin, we had a Rabbi in the community who was not very open to working with young people. I was the leader of a Jewish youth group in Berlin at the time and when the Jewish holidays came and we needed to commemorate those and learn about them, I went to the Rabbi and asked him to come to a meeting of the youth group and talk to us. His response was, 'Well, when you attend synagogue and go to religious services, then I'll talk to you.' Of course, that really put us off! Nevertheless I felt that my youth group needed to know those things, so, together with some other colleagues, I sat down and we studied a particular festival and what it was all about and we made a presentation about it to the youth group. It was interesting to me how my knowledge of my own religion, Judaism, increased through that activity. At the time I also entered the Jewish Youth of Berlin into a world movement called the World Union for Progressive Judaism and I used to attend their conferences with delegates from the youth group. The first time I did so we were quite taken aback when we were shunned by the representatives from other countries. You have to remember this was the late '50s and these other representatives felt at the time that, after all that had happened, there shouldn't be a Jewish community in Germany again and Germany should be boycotted. On one occasion at a conference this came to a head and I tried to explain that, whether they believed it was right or wrong, there was a Jewish community in Germany, and that community had a right to participate in Jewish endeavours and not to be boycotted. I then took it upon myself, without consultation with the president of the Jewish community in Germany, to invite the next conference to Berlin! Luckily for me the community agreed that they would host the conference and it took place and ended up with reconciliation between the former critics of the German Jewish community and the local German members, especially in Berlin, where the conference took place.

Following the conference, some leaders, young Rabbis who were part of the conference, went and talked to the president and said, 'What you need here is good leadership,' and they agreed with the community that they would establish two scholarships to send young Rabbinic students to England to the Leo Baeck College to study for the Rabbinate – and, without talking to me, they decided that I would be one of them! After some serious soul searching, I agreed. So that's how I became a Rabbi. It was due, on the one hand, to a bad Rabbi in Berlin and on the other to a need to show leadership for the acceptance of the Jewish community in Germany within the international body of progressive Judaism in the world.

In 1973 they head-hunted me to come to Perth and I was a Rabbi there until 1978. I left the Rabbinate after that and went to Canberra, where I became an officer in the Department of Immigration and Ethnic Affairs (as it was then called). I began to work there on the policy of multiculturalism. Later, in 1984, the head of the Equal Opportunities Bureau of the Public Service Board suggested that I apply to join the Bureau and there I worked on the implementation of the Equal Opportunity Legislation.

In 1986 I received my OAM for services to multicultural broadcasting and education. I was one of the people who created the community access model for ethnic broadcasting whilst the SBS was being created. We recognised very early on that a government-funded broadcasting system would initially be mainly in Melbourne and

Sydney. I was still in Perth. We had no hope of getting this fast. So we sought access to a community-run radio station which was run by volunteers out of the university and began to provide radio programs produced by volunteers in ethnic communities. This began to spread and finally happened in all major centres across the country. Variations of the model were created in some places, like Brisbane, for example, where the ethnic communities developed their own exclusive station; this is Radio 4EB.

When I was in Canberra, ethnic broadcasters had access to a community radio station. I developed a concept for a multicultural magazine which was broadcast in English with input from ethnic broadcasters and my own team, who presented original material. The program was called *Accent* (because we all had one) and I presented it live on air for two hours each Sunday for five years until I left Canberra. It was a very successful program, often used by politicians to sound out reactions to ideas they had about community relations, new policies and initiatives they thought of introducing. The program had a sufficiently high profile to warrant the National Press Club giving me question rights at their press club luncheons and media conferences.

In 1990 I came to Brisbane as a director of what was then called the Bureau of Ethnic Affairs in the state government to set up the state government's policy on multiculturalism. I worked until 2002 as the executive director of Multicultural Affairs Queensland in the Premier's Department, further developing and implementing multiculturalism for the state of Queensland.   In 2002 I took an early retirement package and went back to working as a part-time Rabbi, which is the position I'm holding now, as the Rabbi of Temple Shalom on the Gold Coast. I am incidentally the only 'Progressive Rabbi' in Queensland. My wife's name is Geraldine and we met here on the Gold Coast. She was working as a volunteer teacher in the religion school of Temple Shalom. She comes originally from New Zealand. She's involved with the community here, but she's not so much involved in the work that I do in the refugee area. But, of course, she's very supportive of it. She's just not an activist like me!

I became strongly involved with interfaith work during my time in Multicultural Affairs Queensland. At the time multiculturalism was perceived as solely relating to non-English speaking migrants, rather than as a philosophy that embraces all cultures and helps us to manage diversity – not just ethnic diversity, but many other aspects of diversity in society. Thinking about that from a philosophical perspective, I recognised that people had neglected to deal with religion. Religion was not very strongly considered in the context of multiculturalism and yet, very often, religion was much more a source of conflict than differences based purely on ethnicity. So, in 1992 I created an organisation which was called the Interfaith Multicultural Forum, where I tried to bring together the idea of managing not just our cultural diversity, but also our cultural and religious diversity. This forum still exists today and it still meets. At its inception it represented 19 different religions.

Later, Griffith University decided that they wanted to take this a step further and they asked me to chair a committee which would establish a multifaith centre and that centre was opened in 2002 and is now a very strong focal point for multifaith activities in Queensland. It was something that needed to be done.

My work for human rights began much earlier, before I even came to Australia. When I was in England I was very strongly involved in the Soviet Jewry movement, as it was called. At the time in the Soviet Union, and in the countries under Soviet influence, Jews were discriminated against and, as a result, there came a time when the Jews began to request that they be allowed to leave, on the grounds that, 'If you don't like us, let us leave and we'll go to Israel.' The Soviets refused to do this, because they considered themselves the paradise of all workers and why would you want to leave Paradise – even if you are persecuted!? There was a movement, certainly among the Jewish community in the Western World, but also others joined in, to campaign for the freedom of Soviet Jewry and I was one of the leaders of that movement. Eventually, of course, the Soviet Jews were allowed to leave and not long after that the Soviet Union collapsed, anyway.

When I came to Australia I continued this activity here, as well as participating in the fight for rights of other groups – I was among those who protested against the apartheid regime in South Africa, for instance. At the end of the '70s, when the Vietnam War ended, there were a lot of refugees coming out of Indo-China, not just out of Vietnam, but Cambodia and Laos and many of them came in boats to so-called countries of first asylum: Malaysia, Philippines, Indonesia, and some of them even made it here. When they came here, they were put in Absorption Centres. These weren't Detention Centres, but Absorption Centres, which were supposed to process people and help them settle. In about 1980, the countries of first asylum, first Malaysia and then the Philippines, said they couldn't take any more of these boats landing on their shores. They couldn't physically accommodate so many refugees and our Absorption Centres were full.

I, together with a couple of people in Canberra, sat down and tried to think of what we could do. I put forward the idea that, given that our Absorption Centres were full, we might suggest to the government the possibility of accepting those people directly into the community, where community groups would take care of them, whilst they were being processed and settled. This way, we could help both the countries of first asylum and those who arrived on our shores directly by boat. Initially the department, not surprisingly, said it couldn't be done, but at the end of these discussions they said, 'OK, within three weeks we'll bring in 20 families and you try to settle them and, if you can't, it's not such a large number that we can't cope with them.' So we went out that day and called a media conference and explained that we had this plan of putting people directly into the community. Now, at the time, this is 1980, this was an absolutely sensational concept and the media played this up tremendously and we had great publicity. Within 48 hours we had many, many more offers than we actually needed, so we settled that first batch. It was called 'Operation Camplift'; the *Canberra Times* even made a special logo and kept reporting about it. There was clearly much goodwill, including offerings from church groups and even individual families, and so after a couple of such batches came in, the government decided to make it a national policy. This policy became known as the Community Refugee Settlement Scheme – it was eventually disbanded by the Howard government, but it lasted that long! We settled thousands and thousands of Indo-Chinese refugees directly into the community and look what a wonderful success that has been.

We were not able to do anything with the Howard government, because it has a completely different attitude. What I've been describing to you now happened under the Fraser Government and the attitude then was that refugees were welcome and no matter how refugees arrived here we had a humanitarian duty to try and settle them.

Under the Howard Government the attitude was that we pick and choose whom we wanted to let in under our orderly refugee program from countries of first asylum and from refugee camps around the world that are administered by the United Nations. People who come here under their own steam were basically put in detention centres, which I think is a horrendous change in attitude and played on a completely artificial fear, because Australia has settled waves and waves of refugees since the Second World War and all refugees that were welcomed have successfully settled. There is no indication that Australia has suffered anything because of its settlement of refugees. On the contrary, it has created goodwill in the world and many of the refugees who have settled here have made very strong contributions to this country.

Janette Hashemi – Islamic and Interfaith Communities

She was born and bred an Aussie Christian, converting to Islam as an adult in the '80s, not because she had friends from that community (that came later), but because the religion itself appealed to her...

'Right at the beginning of our interfaith, when new people were coming along, a Rabbi here on the Sunshine Coast said to me, "As salamu alaikum, cousin" (Arabic for "peace be upon you") and I said, "Shalom, cousin,' (Hebrew for "peace"), because he's educated in Judaism and he knows that we're from the same family, going back to Abraham. It's very refreshing, Muslims and Jews, historically, have lived peacefully together for centuries. It's only lately, since the Palestine issue, that there've been problems.'

My first experience of Islamic beauty came to me while I was visiting the Blue Mosque in Turkey. I adored the decorative calligraphy, exquisitely painted walls; I loved the chandeliers and the spacious interior. Leaning against the pillars or sitting on the floor, devout Muslims were quietly reading their holy scriptures. To me, this was a profound experience. I hadn't seen anything like that in Australia and it sparked my interest in Islam. I was on one of those Top-deck bus tours, you know 'do all the countries in Europe in three months' sort of thing, for the under-thirty-fives! Well, when we went into the Mosque, our Australian tour guide said, and I'll never forget his words, 'There's no difference between Islam and Christianity, except that Muslims believe Jesus is a prophet and not God incarnate.' Those words, spoken off the cuff by an Aussie surfer turned tour guide, struck deep into my soul.

Years went by and I was working as a sales rep when one day, driving through Lakemba, there was a sign 'Islamic Mosque' and I thought, 'Wow!' so I boldly walked up the front stairs and in the front door. When you think this was twenty years ago and the Islamic community was small, Australia didn't really know anything about Muslims or Islam and probably for the men in the mosque to see an Aussie girl walk in and say 'Hi' was probably quite astounding, a bit of a shock for them! But, anyway, they were most gracious and they gave me a copy of the Qur'an to read.

This was at the time when there was a war between Iran and Iraq – Iraq had invaded Iran. From the Qur'an I found the true Islam very different to the Islam portrayed in the media. The Qur'an speaks of the efforts of Muhammad, who entreated the idol-worshipping Arabs to believe in the One who created them and, like the Bible tells of the trials of Jesus, the Qur'an tells of the trials of Muhammad, and, like with Jesus, the people fought against him and wanted him dead. But, unlike Jesus, Muhammad survived, and his prophethood and leadership lasted twenty-three years.

I read the Abdullah Yusuf Ali translation of the Qur'an and I was very fortunate. There are other translations which you really wouldn't want to read. But his is the most highly respected and accurate translation and the only accurate interpretation which captures the beauty of the original Quraish Arabic as it was spoken 1400 years ago by the Quraish tribe.

After I read the Qur'an I went back to the mosque and they said there's a women's centre down the road, so I went down there and I walked in. I must say, I was a little bit taken aback with women wearing their full hijab – you know, not a face covering, but the full head covering and I thought, 'Whoa, a bit scary!' But anyway, I met Abla there, she's an Egyptian lady and very knowledgeable in Islam, and I learnt a lot from her. That was twenty years ago and we're still friends. I also met Jameela, who was another convert, and we had a great time; we had Muslim parties every weekend. A Muslim party entails lovely food, praying together, talking about Islam and, of course, having a happy time, as people do – but without alcohol or anything like that. Then I met Ibtissam and she said, 'Come to my home after work and I'll give you some tuition on Islam,' so every Friday night I'd go to her home and the kids would be sitting around and we'd all have dinner and then she'd give me some Islamic instruction.

I was very lucky to meet some highly educated Muslim women, and their children have grown up to be highly educated as well, going through university in such diverse disciplines as law, orthodontics and nanotechnology, among other things. Really, with all the misconceptions of Islam that are going around now, I'm very pleased that I met some of the best people I could have met and learned from. I became active in the Muslim community. Then I met Aziza Abdul Halim. She's in the Government Reference Group and she organised for me to study Islam in Malaysia. I graduated there in 1989. Through Aziza, I met Jamila Hussain, another convert, who lectures in Common Law and Islamic Law at the University of Technology in Sydney. I suppose I wouldn't be where I am now, talking to groups of people about Islam, if I hadn't met these particular people who taught me, guided me and befriended me.

It's Muslims like all those I have mentioned who continually have to condemn all these terrorists and criminal acts that some misguided and deluded Muslims commit.

You can only describe such acts as criminal and un-Islamic! I've never even met the sort of Muslims you sometimes see on current affairs programs. Such programs show Muslims that have completely lost the spirit of Islam and give Islam a really bad name, but such people really are the minority. There are so many intelligent, good Muslims, but you never see them on television, because perhaps the media believes we won't give very good ratings! Peaceful Muslims don't have the 'shock and awe factor'.

September 11, 2001 was a tragedy in every respect and especially for harmonious relations for Muslims. However, since September 11, there's been a boom in Muslims and Christians and Jews and Buddhists and other religions all getting together to participate in interfaith. I got together with a group in 2002 and formed the Sunshine Coast Interfaith Network. The whole idea of interfaith is not for converting people, it's purely aimed at dialogue between religions and building bridges of understanding to respect the differences in the hope of promoting peace, harmony and knowledge.

Interfaith and multifaith symposiums and conferences are happening in every capital city of Australia. Griffith University has built an entire building devoted to multifaith to promote dialogue and harmony and understanding between religions. In our interfaith forums I always talk on Islam and each religion's representatives talk on topics from their religious perspective. It's all well organised; we have meetings where our core management group meets. We consult and discuss and come to a consensus on what we want to do. Other groups I have spoken to are Sea of Faith, a cultural forum at Mapleton State School, Multicultural Festivals, and the University of the Third Age. I network with Sydney and Brisbane Islamic groups, who are constantly involved with interfaith activities. There's a lot of Muslims working really hard, desperately hard, trying to build harmonious relations for a peaceful society.

Interfaith is my main activity and I am very involved with the Sunshine Coast Interfaith Network; I do the coordinating and planning for it. We always have our symposiums at the University of the Sunshine Coast. The other group that I belong to is a Refugee Action Group in Caboolture; they've been going for a couple of years and now they are starting to form an interfaith group as well.

Interfaith forums and meetings are about breaking down the barriers of ignorance and hate and fear of the unknown. For example, there was an Iraqi refugee lady, who, after years of persecution in Iraq, came to Australia as a refugee and she was abused on the railway station twice here simply because she was wearing the traditional Arab Muslim clothes. She was punched and spat on in the face. It was just dreadful and purely because of the clothes she wore. It was a case of 'You look different, I've seen people like you on TV and I'm going to punch you' – that's how some people think and it's frightening.

I remember when I first converted to Islam. I wore a scarf and someone shouted out of their car, 'Go back to your own country!' Actually, after September 11, I had a dreadful time. I had to leave my home, because I had the Islamic Society of the Sunshine Coast in the telephone book with my home telephone number. After September 11, there were too many abusive calls – mind you, it was mostly older women who left the most horrible messages of 'Go back to your own country; we don't want you here.' One man left a message on the phone, threatening that he was going to track me down and 'do the same' to me. I was really frightened, so I took my young daughter and went and stayed in a motel in Caloundra for about a week. I knew

I couldn't live in a motel forever, so I came back home and I slept with buckets of water at every window, ready to put out fires in case somebody threw a Molotov cocktail into my home. They were very frightening times. I got so many calls full of hate from people on the Sunshine Coast. They wanted revenge, they wanted my blood, because I was Muslim – but I'm a born and bred Aussie and I was equally appalled and disgusted with the attacks in America!

Every night there are terrible things about Muslims on television, which makes it really hard for the majority of us who are trying to overcome prejudices. It's a misconception, for example, that Muslim women don't work – they work the same as other Australian women. A lot of them discard their scarves to get jobs. If a Muslim woman is highly qualified, there doesn't seem to be so much prejudice against her – doctors and lecturers in universities can wear a hijab or head covering without a problem.

There are many misconceptions about Islam. In 2004 the women in Morocco had to march in the street with banners waving, using their sheer numbers, supported by the evidence in the Qur'an, to gain their Islamic women's rights. The new laws are in concordance with the Qur'an and were advanced under the umbrella of Islamic law. Moroccan women would be allowed to divorce freely, marriage age would be lifted, alimony and new property rights rules would be enacted, polygamy would be restricted and women would be allowed to choose their own marriage partners. Another misconception is about circumcision for women, or genital mutilation (because it is a mutilation). That has nothing to do with Islam, or any religion. It's purely a cultural practice in some African countries and some Asian countries.

Talking about misconceptions, I remember when a Christian pastor came to our interfaith meeting for the first time and he said, 'You think we're all infidels, don't you? The Qur'an is full of talking about us as infidels,' and I said, 'No way, when the Qur'an says "unbelievers", it's referring to the idol-worshiping Arabs of that time, 1400 years ago. In the Qur'an, Jews, Christians and Muslims are all considered "believers", because they believe in one God. Jews, Christians and Muslims share the same family history through Abraham.'

Right at the beginning of our interfaith, when new people were coming along, a Rabbi here on the Sunshine Coast said to me, '*As salamu alaikum*, cousin' (Arabic for 'peace be upon you') and I said, '*Shalom*, cousin,' (Hebrew for 'peace'), because he's educated in Judaism and he knows that we're from the same family, going back to Abraham. It's very refreshing, Muslims and Jews, historically, have lived peacefully together for centuries. It's only lately, since the Palestine issue, that there've been problems.

History is so important. Everybody at school studies the Egyptian, Greek and Roman civilisations, but most people wouldn't even know that the Islamic civilisation lasted for a thousand years, from the 7th century to the 17th century. While Christianity was suffering through the Dark Ages, burning witches at the stake and things like that, Muslims were in their zenith. It's known as the 'Golden Age of Islam'. The Islamic scholars excelled in astronomy, medicine, philosophy and mathematics. Algebra, of course, is an Arabic word, and a lot of the sciences came from the Arabs, because they were the intellectual ones at that time. Architecture is a wonderful view into Islamic beauty – from the magnificent Dome of the Rock Mosque, built in Jerusalem in 691

AD, to the Taj Mahal in Agra, India, built in 1647 AD. As the Europeans came out of the Dark Ages, they actually took a lot of the Muslim writings and translated them into their own language and used them – most historians attribute the Renaissance in Europe to the writings of the Muslims. The world's oldest university is the Al-Azhar, built in 970 AD, in Cairo. I saw a picture of Muslim women attending Shari'ah lectures in the Al-Azhar, nursing their babies in the lecture theatre – how's that for progressive!

I think I can safely say that Muslims are in their dark ages now, and it is academic and intellectual Muslims, educated in the West, or in prosperous countries like Malaysia and Dubai, UAE, where our modern 'renaissance' may grow and enlighten the rest of the Muslim world.

When a professor of Islamic studies writes an essay it gets transmitted around the world by Muslim email groups and e-newsletters. Personally, I get e-newsletters with the latest essays from US-educated Muslim academics. These professors in Islamic studies are busily writing books and disseminating the latest in Islamic thought. These people are changing the Muslim world – they are progressive and moderate in their views – bringing Muslims from the darkness of ignorance to the light of knowledge. It will be some time before this light of knowledge reaches the poor and uneducated in places like Pakistan, Afghanistan and the like.

Several community support groups have started up in Queensland over the last few years. One group, called Crescents of Brisbane, are promoting a healthy active lifestyle and they have an annual 'Cres-Walk' where all the Muslim families walk around the shores of the Brisbane River. There's another group that organises Islamic camps for all the kids and there's also male and female soccer teams that play soccer on Saturday mornings.

Many Muslims who have come from other countries adopt Australian ways and their kids go to the local state schools. A lot of Muslims have pools in their backyard, play football, enjoy barbecues and just blend into the Australian way. We are just ordinary fun-loving, law-abiding citizens who want to live peacefully, educate our kids, and work for all the nice things in life – just like everybody else.

Brian Moore – 40 years with St Vincent de Paul

St Vincent de Paul is not so much a religious community as an example of faith in action. 'Vinnies', as it's affectionately known, has been assisting needy Queenslanders since 1894.

'Someone might come to you and they might need help with a power bill or they might want some furniture, or some food or a bed for the night. We might refer them on to a hostel, motel or hotel and give them the money to pay for it until we can sort them out. Some people are very lonely; they just want to talk to someone.'

In talking about St Vincent de Paul I'll have to go right back to when I was five years old – that was in 1941 during the Second World War. We lived at Kelvin Grove in Brisbane. It was a very hard time for my mum and dad, trying to provide a roof over a family of seven children and put enough food on our plates. At that time my father was employed as an insurance salesman for the M L C Insurance Company.

In those days, the only money an insurance salesman got was a commission on what policies he sold, and not many people were keen on buying insurance during the war years. With Dad not earning a regular wage it was very difficult for the family to make ends meet. There certainly were no social service benefits to write home about, and our family had to exist on whatever Dad could earn, which wasn't much, I can tell you.

To supplement his income, he had a horse and cart and he'd cut down branches of trees and make them into clothes props, which he used to sell for two bob each to people to prop up their clothes lines. This was before Hills Hoists were invented. Myself and my twin brother Les used to go out in the cart with him and we'd be shouting out as loud as we could, 'Props, two bob each – props, two bob each!' We were amazed at the number of people who purchased them.

My mother was a seamstress, a good tailoress, but in those days married women didn't work; they stayed at home and looked after their family. The men from the local St Vincent de Paul used to come to our house to help Mum and the family out with some of life's necessities and they'd supply her with material to make our school uniforms and uniforms for other needy families that went to the convent. We weren't Catholics at that time, but because St Vincent de Paul and the nuns were so good to Mum and the family, she had us all baptised Catholics, except Pop – until about six months before his death at the age of eighty-two!

After finishing school at St Laurence's Christian Brothers College, I went to work for a couple of years, and at eighteen I became an honorary bearer with the Queensland Ambulance Transport Brigade in Brisbane. I then met Beverley at the Alderley Theatre and we married in 1955. We married young and have never regretted it.

I was an ambulance officer in Brisbane in those times and I had to go to the morgue and identify my twin brother, who was killed in a motor accident when he was twenty-eight. My mother was critically injured in the same accident and to see Mum with broken legs and fractured skull was a very, very low point in my life. My mother was a wonderful role model for me, a beautiful, caring person.

After eleven years with the QATB in Brisbane I was promoted to superintendent of the Dirranbandi Centre in SW Queensland. In those days, not only were you the superintendent, you were the ambulance officer, you were the secretary, you were the funds raiser, you were everything! That was in January 1966. My career in the Ambulance Service lasted 38 years of which 26 years were spent as a serving superintendent.

The parish priest, Father John Bennett, came round to me one night soon after our arrival at Dirranbandi and he said, 'Brian, you should join the local St Vincent de Paul Conference.' Becoming a conference member means that you still have your own job, but to be a Vincentian in those days, you had to be a conference member for three months on trial and after three months you were inducted into the society. What that meant was that you were on call to help someone with assistance. Someone might come to you and they might need help with a power bill or they might want some furniture, or some food or a bed for the night. We might refer them on to a hostel, motel or hotel and give them the money to pay for it until we can sort them out. Some people are very lonely; they just want to talk to someone. That's when my involvement with Vinnies began – over 40 years ago.

My wife Beverley became involved with the society at Dirranbandi in 1970. She's an active conference member and shop co-coordinator after a period of 37 years. She's been a wonderful friend and has been very supportive of my work in both the QATB and Vinnies. We're still together after all these years, caring for each other's needs.

In Vinnies and QATB I saw suffering from two quite different aspects and I feel blessed to have been able to help those in need. I saw people suffering from severe trauma, abuse and life-threatening medical and surgical conditions, as well as people suffering from poverty. I came to the conclusion that poverty isn't a blissful, carefree life; it's a painful state of insufficient resources. Those years of caring have taught me to be more compassionate and mindful of others' needs and have increased my spirituality.

As a Vincentian you get some very sad requests for assistance, but you also get some humorous ones. One that comes to mind: a fellow once wrote us a letter saying he had a problem and could we come out and visit him. I was at Beaudesert then and we went out to see him at his house some thirty kilometres away. He invited us into the lounge room. He was a very spic and span fellow and the house very tidy and the old vehicle he had in his yard was all polished. We sat down and he insisted we had a cup of tea with the thickest slices of bread you could get your mouth around and he said, 'Well, while we're enjoying our cuppa, I'll tell you why I want you here.' He said, 'I'm a very lonely man and St Vincent de Paul has a very good name and you say you can always help people, no matter what their circumstances. Well, I need a nice woman to love me and look after me.' He says, 'Look how clean the place is. With a good woman here I wouldn't be lonely any more – I can cook and, if she can cook too, we'd have a really wonderful life together!'

I said to him, 'That's a job for you to do! We're not an agency for finding partners, but I tell you what, here's a deal. We're always looking for volunteers. We have a big sorting centre at Beaudesert and you could come over on a regular basis and help us to do various chores like shifting bales of clothing and carrying bits of furniture here and there. You might be able to put a coat of paint on some furniture or a few other odd jobs around the place. There are quite a number of unattached ladies who visit the centre and you'd be meeting them all. You might find someone nice that you like and at the same time you'd be helping Vinnies.'

He said, 'Yes, I'd be in that.' Anyway, he didn't turn up, so we called back and he said, 'Oh, I'm too embarrassed to introduce myself to ladies; I'd rather you introduce me.' I said to him, 'We can't say to some woman she should come out and meet you – that wouldn't be right, but if you come in and do some work and have a cup of tea, you never know who'll cotton on to you or who you'll cotton on to.' He still didn't come!

We've had some wonderful successes. We've seen people get up on their feet financially for the first time, which is very rewarding. We've done budgeting with them and it's been wonderful to see them getting back to helping themselves again. When I was superintendent at Beaudesert, a woman came in. She said to the administrative assistant at the counter, 'I'd like to see Brian Moore; he belongs to St Vincent de Paul.' Her face was bruised and she had her arm in plaster and she had two little children with her.

We arranged for her to go to a safe house, we had her counselled and we had specialist people assist and look after her. It appears she had left her partner and could no longer live in a domestic violence situation. She was pregnant and she wanted no more contact with him. Finally, with Vinnies' assistance, she'd got on her feet and she sent me a beautiful letter. She said she was really happy and couldn't thank St Vincent de Paul enough.

I've been with Vinnies now for forty years and I've filled many roles, from conference member to diocesan president. What stands out for me in all that time is the fellowship of my Vincentian brothers and sisters; that's really a beautiful thing. Vinnies is really a beautiful family – a family of people caring for each other and for people in need.

Communities of Interest and Service

Mary Daly – U3A (The University of the Third Age)

Mary is president of the U3A in Brisbane. We arrange to meet at her home, where, among the many paintings on the wall, is a one of her father, who fought at Gallipoli during the First World War. This was their family home and she and her sister still live here. Lifelong learning is an obvious delight. 'I'm still a student,' she tells me happily.

'It's teaching as Socrates might have done it – under trees or wherever, asking questions and being a facilitator and a group leader, rather than a lecturer.'

In U3A there are no entrance fees, no examinations or diploma. It's just an interest group. There's nothing academic or structured about it. It's teaching as Socrates might have done it – under trees or wherever, asking questions and being a facilitator – a group leader, rather than a lecturer. A lot of our tutors have been teachers or lecturers, or involved in education in some way and they all say how different it is, teaching people who are learning because they're motivated and are coming because this is something they want to do. Our motto is 'learning for pleasure'!

U3A stands for University of the Third Age and it began in the early 1970s in France. There they use university lecturers to teach older age groups and it's very academic, except that there are no examinations – there never have been examinations in U3A, as far as I know.

When U3A went to England it underwent a 'sea-change' and became a movement of self-help among groups, sometimes associated with a centre of learning, but not necessarily. When it came out to Australia we had exactly the same idea. We don't have teachers or lecturers, as such, in U3A here. All you have to do in order to be a tutor is to have knowledge and interest in a subject and be prepared to share. We advertise that in our newsletters. If nobody's interested, it doesn't go ahead. Alternatively, you might get thirty people, and, if so, you have to split it into two classes.

Dr Jack McDonnell began U3A in Australia, in Melbourne. Dr Rick Swindell, a lecturer at Griffith University, met him and thought it would be a good thing to start it here. In 1986 they established U3A Brisbane and we've been associated with Griffith University ever since. For many years Griffith gave us free accommodation, and the use of equipment. We've moved away from Griffith now and have our own centre in Brisbane, but the university remains very supportive.

Our members can sit in on certain classes at Griffith University (not all of them) at no charge. The lecturers allow them to sit at the back and listen to the classes with the paying students. We can't sit for exams and we can't talk in the classes. Some of the other universities or centres for learning are associated with other U3As and they often give them the same privilege.

Brisbane U3A has over 2500 members. There are two U3As on the north coast and two on the south coast, plus another eighteen to twenty U3As throughout Queensland. It's very big now and has grown and spread quickly over its 23 years here. A lot of our classes are given in people's homes, anywhere where we can get free accommodation. U3A has always been for learning and for pleasure, but it also fulfils a social need. We're herd animals, we need people, and while that is not U3A's main focus, it is an important secondary focus, as people share common interests.

It's interesting how people come to join U3A. I had to retire early, because I have very severe rheumatoid arthritis and I couldn't work anymore. I was miserable because I was sick and in pain. Then my sister Tricia found out about U3A from a physiotherapist friend, when she was in the park walking the dog, of all things, and she said, 'Why don't you join?' At first I thought, 'I've been to a real university, I don't need this old people's group!' but eventually I joined and studied psychology and Latin.

There are so many of these people who have given time and knowledge freely. None of the tutors are paid, but they prepare their classes and get very devoted to them. It's interesting and humbling that people are so involved in something that is voluntary – no one is paid, including the office-workers.

An example of how U3A works was when my sister did a calligraphy class with me one year. We did it for our dog group at the park and she included photos of the dogs. Everyone loved it so much that we had to make them all a copy and they paid for the duplicating. We called it 'Yeronga Park in the Morning – a Dog's Eye-view!' The next year everyone up at the park with their dogs said, 'Where's "Yeronga Park in the Morning" for this year?' So we're starting early on doing next year's one. This is something that's now spread beyond U3A to another group.

For me it led to so much more. I started to work in the office and then they said, 'Would you come on the committee?' and I agreed. Then the president, Nick Bricknel, got an appointment in China and went off, leaving me as president! It was interesting and I felt I was giving something back. A lot of our generation feel grateful for what we've got and want to give something back.

Some of the most interesting classes, I think, are the games classes. We have a mahjong class and chess and strategic scrabble. Members of our computer class think that's the best class. They say it's changed their lives. It's no good our age-group learning computers from young people, they go too fast for you. Here in U3A you're learning from tutors of your age who can explain it slowly enough for you to understand. That's very important – we go from 'computer kindy' up to the most involved level. Every year the computer class produces a beautiful calendar that we sell to raise money for new computers.

I was born in Brisbane, but I'm Irish. My father, Geoffrey Dunsandle Daly, was in World War I; he was at Gallipoli. Often on Anzac Day they have a picture (in the newspaper) of a sniper shooting over a parapet and that's my dad! He was at Gallipoli and afterwards in the desert in Egypt. He was in the Fifth Light Horse and he was at Beersheba, where they charged a Turkish row of guns and overcame them. Later he met Lawrence of Arabia in the desert. My mother came from Charters Towers. Her maiden name was Campbell. Soon after they married this house was built. That was seventy years ago. Dad worked for the Department of Primary Industries (the DPI).

After school I studied medicine. The Royal Brisbane Hospital was short of residents doing anaesthetics, so I applied for two positions and the anaesthetic one was the one that I slotted into, so I just went on doing it. I went abroad to study in England and Canada, and then came back to the Children's Hospital, which I loved. I specialised in paediatrics and loved working with kids; it can be very sad and stressful, but very rewarding. I was there for a couple of years before becoming Acting Director for the Royal Brisbane Hospital.

One nice thing about my gaining the deputy directorship at RBH back in 1970 was that it was one of the few places at the time where a woman was treated as an equal. When I first came back I applied for a credit card, but they said I had to get a male guarantor as referee. I explained that the only men in my life were my father, who was a pensioner, and my brother, who was a university student, and they said, 'Either will do.' Eventually, the supervisor came in and said, 'Look, that's obviously being unreasonable,' so I did get the card from Allan and Stark, but that was the attitude at that time towards women. You had to have male guarantors. The RBH in the Department of Health was one of the few places where women got equal pay to men.

One time we were getting anaesthetic technicians and this gentleman from Malaya applied. He was Islamic and they said that he was the best applicant. I wasn't on the selection committee, but they asked if I would check him. I said to him, 'Now look, you're going to be working with women, I'm your boss and the head of Intensive Care is also a female, do you think you'll be able to take orders from females?' and he looked at me and said, 'Doctor Daly, I am married!' He turned out to be one of our best technicians and he was delightful.

I was appointed director at the Royal Brisbane Hospital and was there for twenty years, until I got rheumatoid arthritis. We brought up a whole generation of anaesthetists throughout Queensland. Even in other states there are people whom I helped train. I started retrievals before they had care flights. We used to go out West and up north and bring back patients whom the hospitals couldn't handle, because they were too detailed or too difficult. I retired when my rheumatologist said, 'If you don't retire from this stressful job, you'll be in a wheelchair within six months.' That was nineteen years ago.

A university doesn't teach crafts, but U3A is different. Crafts require intelligence too. Think of finger-painting, Arthur Boyd has done very well out of finger-painting. Think of things like the basket-weaving in the National University, made by the Aboriginal women, it shows their sacred places and their beliefs. Crafts can be just as important as academic learning in keeping you mentally fit. Unfortunately, we don't have any indigenous Australian members in Brisbane U3A and I don't know why. I'd like to see it happen.

In 1996 I got an AM (Australia Medal) for my work with older people. I was chair of Seniors' Week Committee for some years, I've been on the Premier's Awards committee and I give a lot of what is called 'inspirational' or 'motivational' talks to older people's groups who want guest speakers.

I collect sayings for my calligraphy and I saw a beautiful one the other day. It says 'aging is a privilege, not a predicament' and I think this is something we've got to teach everyone. Older people say that age has brought them freedom to be themselves. There was a hundred-and-three-year-old lady on television recently and they said to her, 'What's the best thing about being a hundred and three?' and she said, 'Not much peer pressure!'

Hughie Williams – Police-Citizens Youth Club

Our conversation is to be about community and more particularly his involvement with the Police-Citizens Youth Club (PCYC). He's more widely known now as the federal president of the Transport Workers' Union and it's at his office there that we've agreed to meet. Life was hard for Hughie as a young man, but he's a fighter and survivor.

'I was charged once, when I was ten or eleven years old, for stealing fruit and vegetables. I was charged before the Children's Court in New South Wales... We pinched fruit off orange trees and fish out of fish traps. We pinched fishing lines because there were fish in Lake Macquarie and we could catch fish out of the lake – and we existed on that. I was a Legacy War Orphan then and you'd do it all over again if you had to. But I was brought up before the court and found guilty on all those charges. Of course I was guilty; I didn't ever say anything else. We were hungry kids from hungry families...'

I was born in Cessnock in New South Wales in the Hunter Valley, in 1933, at the height of the Depression. I was the second youngest out of eight. At the time my father was unemployed, except for relief work, so we had no money. We were able to eat, because my parents would catch rabbits in the bush; there was nothing better than baked rabbit. We'd grow our own potatoes. If someone gave us a cow to milk we'd find ourselves with butter. We'd pick the blackberries and have blackberries and cream from the cow on a Sunday, so we managed, but it was a real struggle.

I was only about nine when my father died of injuries he'd sustained in the First World War. We were absolutely destitute then and my biggest problem was going to school in rag-tag clothing. My father had fought in the landing at Gallipoli and in France, but when he was lying in hospital for nearly two years, he couldn't get a pension or any money and nor could we. They wouldn't give us a pension until he died! Then we got a pittance of a pension and went through poverty for many, many years. I remember my days of poverty and I think it makes you a very strong person.

When I was young and still living in New South Wales I got very much involved in the Newcastle Police Boys Club and enjoyed the sport of wrestling. I was living in a little place called Neath, three kilometres outside of Cessnock. My first job was as a coalminer. I was fifteen years of age and a big young boy and I saw no object in continuing school. I had difficulty getting enough clothes together to wear, so I went out to the rubbish dump and I found something that fitted me and I wore a pair of odd boots down the mine. You had to work for three weeks in the mine before you got paid. At the end of three weeks I got two weeks pay and that day the fellow said to me, 'Listen, kid, you better get up there and pay your stump!' I didn't know what stump meant, but I went up to the shed where he'd told me to pay it and they told me, 'Yes, mate, it's going to cost you six bob!' (that was six shillings). I wasn't sure what it was for, but I thought I better do what I was told. It turned out that was union fees, so that was how I became a member of the Coal Miners' Federation.

Neath was a very small mine, with only about 12 to 14 people working there. As a fifteen-year-old, I had to work with a pick and shovel right down inside the mine. It was dark and scary work, down in the bowels of the earth, for a fifteen-year-old kid who'd just left the classroom – it was terrible, that coal mine. It was unsafe, and when the big rats would scurry past me, it used to scare the daylights out of me. In those days we used to have a special tin called a crib can for our lunch. I said to them, 'Why do we have to have a crib can?' and they said, 'Well, if you don't have a crib can, the rats will eat your lunch before you do!'

The old men, as I called the other miners, were only thirty-five-year-olds, but were already starting to get a big stoop in their spines, and their lungs were a big mess. I thought, 'Well, if I want to be a champion in sport, I've got to get out of this place.' I decided I should look around for a job, but there were no easy jobs and someone said to me one day, 'Why don't you get a job with the PMG?' They did all the telephone wires above the ground. A bloke said to me, 'Listen, kid, you won't get the job, because you've got to be twenty-one years old.' I was seventeen and a big, pretty muscly young bloke, so when I went down to the PMG and the fellow said, 'How old are you?' I said, 'Twenty-one,' and he said, 'OK, you start work tomorrow.' I was earning a man's wage, around about eight pounds a week, which was pretty damn good money. All that time I was a member of the union. I don't remember which one it was, but I joined it – everybody joined the union.

All eighteen-year-olds were called up to do their National Service, so I had no choice. When I come out of my three and a half months National Service, I looked around for a job, and the only job that was available around the Maitland area, where I was living at that time, was in a saw mill. I got a job there and joined the Timber Workers' Union. It was all physical hard work there and we weren't given a morning or afternoon break. The union must have spoken to the boss, because I always remember the day, when the big steam whistle blew, and we were enjoying our cup of tea, and the boss came out and said to us, 'Yes, you are entitled to ten minutes break, but it doesn't say that you can sit down – now stand up and have your cup of tea!' All these old fellows who'd given their lives and their work to the company all those years stood up like children.

I left there and got an easier job in a brickyard and joined the Brick Manufacturers Workers' Union. I stayed there for some years and that's when I decided, if I was going to get anywhere in life, I had to move – that's when I decided to go to Brisbane. One Saturday morning I went down into the shopping centre and bought myself two large suitcases, much to the astonishment of everybody. Some of my friends said, 'What are they for?' and I said, 'I'm leaving town!' They said, 'Where are you going to?' and I said, 'I don't know, but I'm leaving town.'

I went down to the railway station and bought a ticket to Brisbane – it took twenty-three hours on the train in those days to get to Brisbane! Within twenty-four hours of arriving I met up with some old friends of mine. They told me they were training at the Lang Park Police-Citizens Youth Club, as it was then called, so I went out there. I remember my first visit, it was 14 October 1955; I was twenty-one years old. That's where I continued with my sport of wrestling. Within two years I'd become a volunteer instructor and my wrestling career went ahead by leaps and bounds. I was the first member of that club to represent Australia.

I was then picked as a reserve in the Australian team for the Melbourne Olympics in the light heavyweight division. There was an organisation in Queensland called the Queensland Amateur Boxing and Wrestling Association. It was my ambition to separate those organisations and, after a lot of lobbying and work, I called the inaugural meeting of the Queensland Amateur Wrestling Association back in 1959 and it's still there today. But, because I'd been involved in the politics of sporting administration, I probably made some bad friends and that cost me two Olympics – the Rome Olympics and the Mexico Olympics. I'd won the trials for the Rome Olympics and I'd won the Australian Championship, but people in positions as selectors for the Games, they picked the person I beat, a fellow by the name of Ron Hunt from Victoria.

Anyway, I enjoyed my time at the club. I'd become their wrestling instructor and started coaching at a lot of schools. I coached at the Anglican Church Grammar School, Kelvin Grove State High School, the St Peters Lutheran Boys College and some others too. This was all voluntary work carried out in my spare time.

I attained my greatest ambition when I represented Australia at the Olympics. One of the greatest thrills is when you get up on the podium and you're introduced by people as representing Australia. It's an even greater feeling when you win and they say, 'The winner is Hughie Williams of Australia!' I couldn't really get much more pride than that.

I was approached one time by the Wilston Boys Hostel, where all the young criminals used to be. They used to put them in jail then when they were twelve- or thirteen-year-old kids. They said they'd asked the kids what sport they wanted to be coached in and the kids said, 'Wrestling'! I coached them for about two years, every Saturday afternoon. Some of the best parts were when the wrestling was over and I'd sit with the kids having scones with strawberry jam and coffee, and talk. Some of those kids used to confide in me – some were treated very cruelly and strapped unnecessarily. I couldn't imagine how they had ended up in these circumstances. I said to a warder, 'This young bloke over there, he's a happy young bloke about thirteen years old, he's full of joy, he's well mannered to me, he's physically in good shape,'

236

and the warder said, 'Yes, he's got about thirteen charges of house-breaking and one of assault ... that's the kid you're talking about.' A lot of those kids used to keep in close contact with me when they got out of there. They'd ring me and I'd get Christmas cards for quite a number of years. They grew up, some of them leading very respectable lives, and a lot of them attributed the fact that they were able to move along to our friendship.

I was charged once, when I was ten or eleven years old, for stealing fruit and vegetables. I was charged before the Children's Court in New South Wales, and I probably would have done it again for stealing food in those times. We pinched fruit off orange trees and fish out of fish traps. We pinched fishing lines because there were fish in Lake Macquarie and we could catch fish out of the lake – and we existed on that. I was a Legacy War Orphan then and you'd do it all over again if you had to. But I was brought up before the court and found guilty on all those charges. Of course I was guilty; I didn't ever say anything else. We were hungry kids from hungry families – we pinched eggs out of poultry farms, and these were a must for us. We were put on a bond of some kind. I was lucky, because I could have continued on with that way of life, but I got into the Police Boys Club and I wanted to be a champion sportsman. Because of that ambition I directed all my energies there.

The sort of work I'm involved in now, in this union, is altogether different to what many people would think. Widows come to see me when their husbands have been killed and sometimes we even arrange funerals. I've helped them get their pensions fixed up and things like that. We find employment for young people and assist all kinds of people, not only members of the union. We've got lawyers to help people like those widows whose husbands have been killed.

A couple of things I've lived by, I suppose, are common sense and determination. If you apply common sense and treat other people a bit decently, it helps, but you've got to be determined in life! In sport and life generally, you've got to be a pretty determined person to achieve anything worthwhile. In my life, believe me, it never came easy, I had to put in every bit of effort that I could think of.

Lyn Kelman – The Country Women's Association of Queensland

We met in the cosy, beautifully furnished little sitting room of the QCWA Head Office where she was then President. She has the pleasant open manner and fine lined sun-tanned face of a typical Australian country woman. She explains that the sense of community is very strong in country women – shared experiences of drought and flood, but also of laughter.

'... you'd ring your order through to the shop in the morning and the shopkeeper would get it ready. Then you'd go to town ... and when you were ready to go home you'd go to his shop and if he was closing before you got there, he just left all the groceries in boxes out in front of his little grocery store with your name on it and you'd go and pick up your box. Everybody knew everyone.'

My married life started in a small country town. Our property was approximately 50 kilometres out of Emerald, 800 kilometres north-west of Brisbane. Gindie is a little community made up of the school, tennis courts and the CWA Hall. The hall became the focus for our community in that all the local communities met there, not just the CWA. Church services were held there on the weekend, the grain growers met there and the graziers, it just seemed to be a focal point.

When I married I moved from Moree, where power, automatic telephone and bitumen roads were taken for granted, to a fairly isolated property near Gindie, where our only communication was by 'party line' telephone, which wasn't always reliable. Not being used to a party line was rather frightening, because you'd pick up the phone to make a call and you'd find somebody else talking. We all had our own Morse code rings and I soon learnt to recognise our call.

You tend to rely on your neighbours when you have a party line. They might be 10 to 15 miles away, but they're your closest contact and they'll come over and give you a hand if there are problems – which there were at times.

Moving to Gindie, I found we didn't have rural power – we had a lighting plant. As a new bride, if I wanted to turn the light on, I had to remember to make sure the engine was going first. I remember when my husband would go off with the men mustering and he'd say, 'Do you want the engine today?' and I'd say, 'No, it'll be right,' and then, after he'd gone, I'd think, 'Well, the house is tidy, so I'll do some cooking, or I'll do some sewing,' but you can't do anything without power, so I soon learnt how to crank this very big Southern Cross engine to get power. Those are probably some of the negative things. I think the pluses are that country people tend to network well together. If you have a problem you only need to speak to other ladies in a similar situation and you suddenly find that it's not quite the mountain that you felt it was – you can get through things.

I was married in 1964 and during those first 4 or 5 years we'd been trying to have children and I had three miscarriages. I guess the hardest part when you're isolated is in an emergency, trying to get help, whether it's medical or whatever. I lost a child due to wet roads and not being able to get out – getting bogged and having to walk home and get a tractor to tow us out, and by the time we got into Emerald it was too late. That was probably just a minor thing, because I was not the only one that has experienced a miscarriage due to impassable roads. I had to go away to Rockhampton for a month prior to having both my children. Once again this means you don't have that extended support from your husband to be with you right up until you give delivery. My mother came up from Moree and stayed with me in Rockhampton, but to a newlywed, having your first child, I think you need to have your husband. Circumstances prevent that, because your husband has to stay at home. You can't just go away from your property for a month and expect everything to keep going – even if you've got men working for you. That was probably the hardest part for me when we were having our children.

The primary school our children went to was at Gindie, a little two-teacher school with only 25 children in the school. We had to walk out of the house in time to meet the bus, which then drove the children into Gindie – the same bus went on into Emerald for the high school students. Some of those children were sitting on buses for an hour and a half in the morning and the same in the afternoon. If it rained that became a problem, because you didn't have a phone to ring the neighbours. You'd start off in the car and I just had a tiny little Mini Minor and it didn't have very much clearance. It would only take about 50 points of rain and that'd be the end of it. I'd be hopelessly bogged and you'd have a six-year-old and a tiny baby and you'd have to walk home anywhere from one kilometre to nine kilometres. Hopefully your husband would be there when you got home, otherwise you'd get the Toyota and try to plough your way back, or come back with your husband and the tractor!

In the country, you have to make a choice fairly early on whether you send your children to boarding school or not. It's lovely if you can keep them at home, because once they go to boarding school I think you lose them; they usually go on to university and then get married – they never really come back home, because they inevitably marry someone away from your area. But if you don't send them away, they're disadvantaged, because you don't have the extended curriculum things in your own home and you can't be going into town to the library all the time. It broadens their outlook, too, by going to boarding school and they tend to become very independent at a young age.

My first contact with the Country Women's Association was when my children first went to school. In a little community like Gindie, everybody belongs to everything. I was in my late twenties and I felt that CWA was for older people, not me, but I was talked into joining by a very dear friend, who'd become a member. That was in '79 and in all those years there hasn't been a year when I haven't held a position. Three months after joining I was persuaded to become 'International Officer', which I thoroughly enjoyed and three years later I became Secretary.

With CWA at Gindie the women came together once a month for regular meetings, but we also had other fun times and we'd have guest speakers come out to our little hall to talk about gardening in dry times. Our branch had about 25 members and our ages went from late twenties through to eighties. The branch at Gindie was not unusual; it was more like a family, where children were welcome to come. Nowadays people say they don't want children at meetings and I think that's sad, because the Country Women's Association first came into being for women and children to come together, where women could talk over their problems – it was a support system for women who didn't have their extended family, and I was one. My parents lived in Moree and John's mother lived in Brisbane. Unless it was a crisis at home and we asked for help, basically we got on and looked after ourselves.

If there was a dinner party at someone's place, it was just accepted that children came too; you couldn't get baby-sitters, so the children ate before we went and you put them in the back seat of the car in their jamies with the mosquito net over them and hoped they went to sleep. At dinner parties, every now and then somebody disappeared to go out and check their kids and they'd come back and say, 'Your kids are playing up,' so the other mother or father would go out. We didn't see anything wrong with that and our children survived – now you wouldn't be allowed to do it. The friends you visited might have asked three or four couples, but there might be ten kids – well, there wouldn't be ten beds, so where do you put the kids? My husband made a little platform and we used to put a mattress on the back seat, so that's how they went. There were no seatbelts and when they got tired they'd lie down – except if they knew someone. Then they'd swap cars and you'd come back and find three kids in the back seat instead of two!

When the CWA was formed it was for the friendship and support to women in isolated areas. Quite frankly, I think it's still as relevant now as what it was then. There is still isolation. When I first went to Gindie, isolation was a problem, whereas now there's rural power and there're pretty much all-weather roads everywhere. We also have automatic telephones, the Internet, and fax and things like that have really made a difference to people in the country. Years ago, many families had to rely on pedal radio for the Royal Flying Doctor (RFDS); people would have been lost without the RFDS.

The CWA had various fund-raising events. A family may have lost their home in a fire, so you'd have an appeal – a CWA luncheon or something like that. With the international appeal, the children get very involved. Each year we study a different country. It's chosen two years ahead. At Gindie we used to get the whole 25 to 30 children involved; every child entered. We always had a lunch with recipes pertaining to the country and then the children would receive their prizes, watch a video or listen to a guest speaker.

In CWA we cater for weddings and wakes and all sorts of things. Catering is probably our biggest money spinner; home recipes are often passed down. We have books that people have put their recipes into and we sell those to make money. Then we have barbecues – I'd say they're the most typically Australian catering we do, beef and lamb and maybe a bit of pork. Most people have lemon and mango trees, chooks and a house cow, so we have cream, eggs and lemons, and the by-products of those are lemon-butter, you make lots of lemon butter, and mango chutneys and jams and pickles. We made our own wine and our own mead and that was very delicious and we also made prickly pear wine – it was a beautiful red colour, but it tasted revolting!

Living on a property has its disadvantages; you can't just go shopping down the street when you run out of something. Consequently, the basic staples like sugar, flour, et cetera, are purchased in large quantities to last at least 4 months. Most farm wives keep a vegetable garden and I enjoyed being able to pick our own vegetables fresh for dinner. We slaughtered our own animals for meat and, once we had rural power, we were able to install a cool room, which was a godsend. We also made our own sausages, which were much nicer than the town butcher's. We always had chooks which supplied us with eggs daily, and also a cow, which we milked. Despite all the adversities of living in the bush, I wouldn't swap it for city life.

I remember one year it rained continually and we couldn't get to town for six weeks. We had two creeks flooded and you couldn't cross them. We also didn't have a phone because when the creeks came up the telephone line sagged in the water. Over this period of six weeks we couldn't move from the property and I had three men to cook for plus John and I and our two children. We ran out of meat and flour. We had a cow, so we had milk, but we lived pretty much on eggs – I wasn't game to kill the chooks 'cause I needed the eggs! I think I know every recipe you can make out of eggs! Toward the end we got a food-drop.

People knew that the Kelmans got cut off in the wet, so they'd fly over and drop a tin with a message in it: 'Wave your arms if you're OK, or do this if you want food.' They knew the basic was bread and a bit of fruit and stuff for the kids. That's how you communicated when you didn't have a phone.

Back then you had very little theft or any of those things. People left their keys in their cars and you could stop to have a couple of drinks before going home and that's where you met your friends. You'd probably all go to town on a Friday, and you'd ring your order through to the shop in the morning and the shopkeeper would get it ready. Then you'd go to town and do all the other jobs you had to do and when you were ready to go home you'd go to his shop and if he was closing before you got there, he just left all the groceries in boxes out in front of his little grocery store with your name on it and you'd go and pick up your box. Everybody knew everyone.

I'd like to think the Country Women's Association will still be here in another hundred years, doing the things we do – though we'll be doing them differently. This is my personal opinion, but I believe we'll need to change with the times. I don't think we'll ever lose our concern for our fellow man, but I think it's going to be in a different context. We have younger women now going back into the workforce and their children are going into day care – you don't have the mum at home now with the children. Nowadays women are looking for different things. The CWA is all voluntary, that's the thing – even my position as state president is voluntary and it's a three-year term.

Bruce Dawe: Poet

Country Lamplight *for David*

Lamplight in the country

falls anxiously on the pale grass.
How often we have seen it
leaning out of doors or
falling, broken, from windows! Always it seems
as though it had been specially lit
for a sick child, and the husband
driven off down the dim road
to get help while the mother bathes
the slick forehead, saying There... There... It won't be long, now...
The younger ones listen to the darkness
and grow very still as a sound
comes softly over the tussocks where the dew
creeps like an insect on the bent stems. Each child
strains to be first to hear the returning
ute grunting over the ruts, the tail-gate banging.

And a shadow crosses the light from the lonely doorway.
Crosses, and re-crosses.

From *Sometimes Gladness: Collected Poems, 1954-2006,* Pearson Education, 2006, and reproduced here by kind permission of the author.

Bruce Dawe has published 13 books of poetry, one book of short stories, one book of essays, five children's books (Penguin) and has edited two other books. His collected edition *Sometimes Gladness*, was named by the National Book Council as one of the 10 best books published in Australia in the previous ten years. A German language edition *Hier und Anderswo (Here and Elsewhere),* was published in 2003. He was awarded the Order of Australia in 1992 for his contribution to Australian Literature.

Service

Caring for the Environment

Craig Walker – Working as a Wildlife Officer

He looks after a wide territory, larger than some countries. Wildlife corridors with waterholes need to be established and protected. Australia is a fragile environment where, particularly in heavily populated areas like south-east Queensland, the wildlife is generally expected to make way for man. It's his job to protect wildlife while putting systems in place to encourage the community to be a part of the conservation effort.

'We have a huge army of people who give their time every day and, sometimes, every night of the week, to look after wildlife that's been sick, injured or orphaned as a consequence of human impact.'

My family moved to the Darling Downs at the turn of the century from a place called Greta in Victoria. They were graziers and they staked a claim on a selection at Bell, just north of Dalby, under the Bunya Mountains.

Through TAFE, I took a certificate course in horticulture, which involved subjects on the ecology, the environment and climate. This transformed my thinking. I realised we needed to be more responsive to the environment. I then started working for a while as a co-coordinator on youth programs. A job came up with Queensland Parks and Wildlife, doing environmental projects in National Parks with long-term unemployed youth. This was a challenge in itself, but also gave me an opportunity to use the horticultural skills I'd gained. We moved to Rockhampton and I took a position up there as a senior ranger, managing the wildlife across the district. I did that for nearly five years and then, in about 2002, was offered a position in Brisbane and that's the job I'm currently in.

This job is even more expansive; it involves threatened species' recovery, looking at issues about tree clearing, negotiating nature refuges, which is private ownership of protected areas, and all the wildlife issues that occur within that urban context. Domestic animal ownership is a big issue for us, not so much within an urban context, although it's a problem there, too, but particularly in western areas of Queensland, where we have huge threats to wildlife species, such as Julia Creek dunnarts, bilbies and koalas. The greatest threat to those particular species is feral cats and foxes.

A lot of the problems we see now are due to the animals and birds that have been introduced. One we're currently dealing with is the Indian Myna bird. It's increased rapidly to become a significant problem in the Brisbane area. The number of native birds, like great honey-eaters and all sorts of other nectar-feeding birds that have decreased commensurate with the increase in Indian Mynas, has been horrific. We're looking at a pilot project with Ipswich City Council, to monitor, trap and euthanase these animals and to assess the effects of that project in terms of its influence upon both the native and non-native species. If we don't do anything, we'll lose the native species. The Mynas don't just replace habitat and food; they actually move the young out of the nests and remove or smash eggs in the nests, so they're destroying a whole generation of wildlife.

If we look at animals like the bridled nail-tail wallaby, it's a prolific breeder and in captivity will breed like a rabbit, but unfortunately it's a victim of a number of things. One is the removal of brigalow vegetation that extended from Charters Towers to Wagga, and another, the introduction of the fox and the feral cat. First it lost its place to live and then we had these other animals appear and drive the last nail in its coffin. Its long-term prognosis is poor, but we keep trying, because we believe that's our job. We often have some very difficult decisions and dilemmas to try and overcome.

The Brisbane Forest Park is a unique area. It's National Park estate and is held in perpetuity. The EPA has done assessments over the last few years and determined important areas. Even if all else was lost, providing we maintain these particular areas (we call them 'biodiversity corridors') then we could maintain most of the biodiversity that we currently enjoy. Brisbane Forest Park, the Mount Glorious area and the D'Aguilar Ranges are within one of those important bio-diversity corridors.

Part of my role is to encourage people with reasonably large parcels of land to set those areas aside for nature refuges. What we're doing is linking current biodiversity corridors, so there's intrinsic links and wildlife corridors between important parcels of agency estate, where ordinarily it might have been lost to development or given over to pasture or whatever.

We have a really good network of wildlife carers, who are licensed under our Licensing and Permit system. The Moggill Koala Hospital here is open seven days a week and has been going for around 20 years. We have 1,500 koalas come in here every year – and a whole bunch of other animals too. We've released a koala conservation plan, which isn't going to solve all our problems, but it'll certainly make people sit up and listen and take notice of the things that are important if they want to see koalas surviving in Brisbane over the next few years. People obviously need a place to live, but they've got to balance that with the desire to see native wildlife passing through their backyards.

We have a huge army of people who give their time to look after wildlife that's been sick, injured or orphaned as a consequence of human impact. These people come in and nurture the animals for hours on end. They're required to feed them every three hours around the clock for a period of 15 to 20 weeks, until their feeding slows. These people would be permanently sleep deprived, because, once one animal is able to be fed a little less, they'll then take on another one. We get pretty cautious here about loading people up with too many animals, because we're aware of sleep deprivation issues. One lady, for example, cares for koalas and macropods and birds and would have up to fifteen or twenty animals in her care at any one time.

There're a lot of myths and misunderstandings about wildlife. I remember, in Rockhampton, a lady rang me once and she said, 'I've just killed a red-bellied black snake,' and I said to her, 'You'll have more browns and taipans round your house now.' 'Why's that?' she asked and I said, 'Well red-bellied black snakes have been known to consume browns and taipans and you'll very rarely ever see another venomous snake around if you have a red-bellied black. The red-bellied black is a relatively quiet snake. It won't bite a human unless it's really confronted – you'd nearly have to walk on it before you'd get bitten by a red-bellied black snake.' She'd thought she was defending herself, but the reverse was true.

The issues we confront on a daily basis are that people have this 'pioneer' belief, that they can conquer all and then recreate. They believe they don't need to learn to live *with* the environment that they live in. We have a population of indigenous Australians who've lived here for countless millions of years, very successfully hunting and gathering and using the foods available to them. Yet the first thing we did as colonisers of this country was to try to reshape it and recreate here what we had left back in the countries we came from, rather than learning from the native inhabitants.

I believe, in order to learn to live better in this country, we would need to have a greater understanding of both the land on which we live and the indigenous people we share this land with. If they've survived here that long, they must have done something right. In our short history here, we've gone from living in a very sustainable environment to living in a much less sustainable environment. Just look at what we're doing to our rivers and our water supply.

As an agency, we're involved in a broad range of development applications, such as the Obi Obi Creek issue at Maleny. We're actually supervising the remediation process of that. My area here goes from the border of New South Wales to Turkey Beach (about 20 kilometres north of 1770 in central Queensland) and out to the Simpson Desert, which includes Windorah, Cunnamulla, Charleville and those areas out there. It's quite a large area, with a huge diversity of land-use types and wildlife as well.

I guess I'm most proud of having changed the way we do our business in the job that I'm in now. We used to work at the species level, which means we used to address a lot of minor issues, which added up to a collective of things that weren't really focused on nature conservation. We were benefiting the community, of course, but the community also expects us to achieve some things for the environment. So we moved from a single species level to a landscape level, where we now have people out there, not necessarily telling people how to manage magpies or peewees, but going onto properties and saying, 'This is how you should manage your land for conservation, and here's some incentives for you to sign your land up to become a nature refuge.' That's what we're trying to achieve. If wildlife has a safe place to live, it'll get on with what it's been doing for the last million years.

Lee Allen – A Zoologist Working With Dingos

He has a love of the outdoors and a deep knowledge of Australian fauna. Finding the balance between the needs of man and animal in a harsh environment are critical aspects of his job.

Lee attaching a satellite collar to a dingo

'... we happened to be just a few yards away from this dog when he came across his first feral goat ... this goat looked up and saw this dingo peering at him from 20 or 30 metres away and it bleated and just started to run. Immediately, it was just like the penny dropped for this dingo ... The goat wouldn't have gone 10 metres before it was attacked and killed.'

I was born on a farm in New South Wales and grew up in the country. I always had a love for the outdoors and wildlife. My intention was to stay on the farm but at the time my wise parents told me, like my brother before me, 'You can stay on the farm, that's fine, but go away and get a trade or some profession first.' My brother became a plant pathologist and I became a zoologist. I never went back to the farm to work, but because of the work I do, I'm always on farms. One of the great aspects of this job is the wonderful characters and down to earth people you get to meet in the field! One Christmas I happened to be in Brisbane and, as I was getting towards the end of my Masters Degree in Wildlife Management, I rang up what was then the Public Service Board and asked what the departments were doing in wildlife research and wildlife management. One of the people I spoke to at the Department of Lands said, 'Come on in and we'll tell you.' Just a few days before Christmas I went and spent a couple of hours with them, talking about how they went about controlling feral pigs and wild dogs, along with a whole string of pests they had at the time.

I was fascinated by the whole organisation and then they showed me a position they'd advertised a few weeks before and said they weren't very happy with the applicants that had come in and were thinking of re-advertising. I read the ad and said, 'Yes, I could do that!' I was invited to put in a late application and a few weeks later I was offered the job. That was back in 1982 and, although the nature of my role has changed from time to time, I'm still with that organisation and still enjoying it. Initially I was involved in coordinating the pest animal control programs, principally feral pig and wild dog management. In the last twelve years I've got into full-time research, mostly centred on wild dog management. It's an enormous issue for Queensland and also for the rest of the country.

One of the constant challenges is to try and find efficient control methods that are humane, that are target specific, that only take out the problem dogs in the area where you're working. We're looking for different control methods for those areas where their impact is greatest. We've also got a project to see whether you can identify, with reasonable accuracy, a pure dingo from a hybrid, so that in National Parks and in conservation areas they can destroy the hybrids and feral dogs. We're also looking at a different toxin that basically just makes them go to sleep and fall into a coma and pass away. We then try and conserve just the pure dingo. I'm also involved, in a supervisory way, in a project looking at the management of wild dogs on Fraser Island.

The dingo's an absolutely fascinating animal; it's remarkably resilient and able to survive in all sorts of situations. For instance, back in 1993 I was involved as a researcher, monitoring the experimental release of dingos on a military island off the central Queensland coast, where there was an estimated two to three thousand feral goats. It had been part of a bombing range and the aim was for the dingos to control the spread of these feral goats and then try and reverse the really serious erosion they were having on this beautiful island. My hope was that within 4 to 5 years the dingos would be in sufficient numbers to control the breeding rate of the goats. To my absolute surprise, in two and a half years, these dozen dingos had virtually annihilated the goats – there were only four goats left, surviving on an almost vertical cliff! You can appreciate, from situations like that, just how vulnerable domestic sheep and goats are to wild dogs.

A colleague and I happened to be very close to one of these dingos that was released. They were animals that had been reared in captivity and had never hunted for themselves in their lives and, the day that they were released, we happened to be just a few yards away from this dog when he came across his first feral goat. He walked forward with his ears up and a look of curiosity on his face as if to say, 'What's that?' and then this goat looked up and saw this dingo peering at him from 20 or 30 metres away and it bleated and just started to run. Immediately, it was just like the penny dropped for this dingo! He started to go down on his haunches and down on his shoulders, his head dropped and the whole expression changed to one of a threatening predator and as soon as the goat started to flee this dog just took off and ran in. The goat wouldn't have gone 10 metres before it was attacked and killed. What we were seeing was completely innate behaviour. Something that was imprinted into the dingo's genes – something it had never seen and never done itself, ever, in its life before. Yet within seconds this whole thing just exploded in front of us – it was absolutely amazing to see.

Other than feral goats and sugar gliders, there were very few terrestrial mammals left on this island, so after the dingos had completely wiped out the goats, they started digging up crabs and eating fruit off trees and native passion fruit that used to grow there – even fruit off cacti. Later on, when the powers that be decided that they wanted to get rid of the dingos on the island, we found that the dingos weren't interested in meat baits. They'd lived and propagated – surviving mostly on a vegetarian diet! They'd just adapted to their changed circumstances. Another thing that really astounds me with dingos is their threshold for pain. When we've been tagging and releasing dingos we sometimes use a cattle ear tag, which has a big spike that goes through the ear and leaves a tag, and they don't even give any indication that it hurts – they don't even flinch. You see sometimes they inflict tremendous injuries on each other and they act like they don't even feel it – they're a tremendously well adapted and well built animal for what they do.

The dingo has a completely different strategy to the kangaroo in coping with adverse climatic conditions when breeding, but one that's just as effective and this is one of the difficulties we have with controlling them. In a dingo pack there'll be several females that will breed and, unless it's extremely good conditions, all the subordinate females' pups will be killed by the alpha female. She'll actually go and chomp them up. There's no fight. She just goes in and kills the pups of the subordinate females and then those females help to suckle the alpha female's pups. The physiological burden of lactation and fending for and feeding the young pups is shared between three or four females. The result is that, if the alpha female gets killed or wounded, there's always another one or two that are going to be able to lactate and rear the pups, so they don't have a great deal of mortality during dry periods. Unlike domestic dogs that have two seasons a year and rear two litters, dingos only have one litter of 4 to 6 pups; which is probably another adaptation to harsh environments. They sometimes have more pups inside them, but they absorb some of those youngsters before they're born, so usually they'll rear 4 to 6 pups. Their breeding season is basically the same, right across the country – it's very synchronised to the weather, probably based on day length and temperature and so forth.

Dingos work quite differently to most other predators. They have some similarities, but there are also some specific differences. A dingo pack is flexible, in that, if there's small prey that they can catch quite easily on their own, they'll be just as likely to hunt singly and not as a pack. As you slip into harsher conditions, those small to medium prey become less available and the dingos switch to hunting increasingly as a pack. When they hunt large kangaroos, they'll quite comfortably hunt as a pack of several animals. They'll either relay-chase them – one will chase it for a while, until they tucker out, and then another one will take it on and they'll keep going until they just wear the kangaroo into exhaustion, or they'll use ambush, or use other strategies to get their prey. Either way, they'll still be a pack and will keep and defend their territory.

Every year those four to six pups have either got to find themselves a position within the pack, or, what mostly happens, they get forcibly kicked out. On the basis of research to date, if they don't manage to find vacant territory or get themselves into a pack within a couple of home ranges, they're either killed by neighbouring dogs or starve trying to defend themselves.

This is a subject I'm working on fairly intensively. If you control dingos on a property and you basically empty it out of all the dingos that are there, you end up with those dispersers, which may be wild dogs or other dingos immediately coming in and finding that vacant territory and recolonising it very quickly. Some of those dispersal movements can be long, long distances. From what we've seen on a couple of occasions on Fraser Island, some of these dispersers that have been tagged at one end of the island travel the length of the island. The consequences, in terms of trying to control dingos on sheep properties, for instance, is that it means you need to extend the control of dingos to much further away from just the sheep property itself, because otherwise it'll just end up as a dispersal sink. Male dingos leave the pack when they're under three years of age and usually females leave in the first twelve months of age – in really dry seasons they'll be forcibly removed at about six months of age, or once they get through to the next breeding season. They often appear to leave of their own volition, but I suspect they're encouraged by the older animals in the pack. A dingo can live up to 10 years plus – though most dingos die in the first 2 to 3 years of their lives. It's tough being a dingo – it's a fight to the death for some of them. It's sad to have to put dingos down, but they're incompatible with sheep or goats. Some of them give the impression they've got lovely natures and they just look like a pet dog at times – those are some of the harder times.

You see other things camping out and working on dingos. I was working in the Fassifern Valley south-west of Brisbane a number of years ago, camped in this little place. I'd been working all day and I was really hungry and I happened to have some frankfurter sausages with me. I'd been boiling them up, but I was too hungry to wait, so I cut a little piece off one end of the sausage and I sat it on this table in this old run-down, disused cabin where I was camping. Anyway, then I went and got some other things while I waited for this thing to cool down so I could eat it – I walked back in and it was gone! I sat there scratching my head and thinking, 'Now what did I do with that? I know I cut it off.' I couldn't find it anywhere, so I cut another little piece and brought it back and sat it on the table and went back a few yards distance and, as I was sitting there, thinking, out behind the tomato sauce bottle came this little pointy nose and these great big black eyes. It was a little carnivorous marsupial mouse. He was so cute in his mannerisms. You could just see him looking at me and then looking at this bit of frankfurter at the end of the table and thinking, 'Now, how fast are you and how fast do you think I am?' and then he just took off and ran to the edge of the table, picked up this bit of frankfurter like a football, and off across the table. I was after him and he was up a post, along a rafter and gone in seconds! It just made me chuckle, the expression on this little mouse's face as it eyed off this second piece of frankfurter and backed itself against me catching it! It was one of those times, at the end of a day when I was really tired and hungry – one of those magic little moments, it was fabulous to see!

Another time, I was helping a fellow with radio tracking yellow-footed rock-wallabies in the Flinders Ranges and it was a 24-hour stint. I'd got the graveyard shift, which was midnight to four thirty or five in the morning, so when I finished my four or five hours up in this radio tower, I walked to the edge of this east-facing cliff face to watch the dawn. You could just see the light, and the sun was just on its way up. I sat there with my feet hanging over this precipice, watching the sun coming up and then suddenly this wedge-tail eagle came and hovered right in front of me. He would have been no more than about 10 or 15 feet away and dead level with me, though he was over probably 100 or 200 feet up in the air. He was moving at a snail's pace, probably looking for rabbits or things down the bottom of this cliff. Every now and then he'd look up and look at me and I could look straight into his eyes! Then he'd look down and concentrate again. We had probably the best part of a minute when he was within only a few metres of me. I could even see the primaries on his wing-tips moving ever so slightly to maintain his balance and his perfect stillness as he moved along, right in front of me. It was another one of the many absolutely magic moments I've had working in this job.

Ross McKinnon – The Brisbane Botanic Gardens

We've been family friends for many years. He's overseen great changes during his time at the helm of the Botanic Gardens – from flooding to huge wind storms and severe drought. The gardens are a constant source of enjoyment to many but are also a library of living plants and, as such, a great source for learning – not just about how plants survive in different conditions, but also, among other things, the curative properties of different plants ...

'We have about 14,000 students go through our "lesson in the gardens" programs, from pre-schoolers right through to university students, every year. This is a unique program; there is nothing quite like it elsewhere in the world.'

I grew up in Adelaide, but I had many holidays at family properties and stations all over South Australia and had a tremendous love of the outdoors. I could see, though, that life on the land was hard and I decided instead to study in the Adelaide Botanic Garden and at the University of South Australia. My first position was as officer in charge of the Whyalla Parks Department, where, at twenty-one years of age, I had a staff of 150. I wanted to study post-graduate landscape architecture and Brisbane was the only place in Australia with a graduate landscape program at the time. Fortunately, an opportunity arose for the position of 2 IC in the City Botanic Gardens, so I applied, and with it came the most incredible letter, which said that Brisbane City council wanted me to remain in the position for 10 years when the present incumbent, curator Harold Caulfield, would retire and Council wanted to be assured that I would then take his position. What an offer! There I was, at the age of thirty-two, with my dream come true. I was in charge of my own botanic gardens and it's a dream I've lived for the last twenty-five years.

Before I left Adelaide I was engaged to Susan Brennan, who at the time was studying teaching at the Flinders University in South Australia. I returned to Adelaide and married Sue in the Pulteney Grammar Chapel. Our honeymoon was spent driving from Adelaide to our new life in Brisbane. Three months after our wedding, Sue's father was transferred from Adelaide back to Brisbane, as Queensland manager for the CSR sugar company, so their whole family moved back to Queensland, where they had all grown up – much to the delight of Sue's paternal grandmother, who lived here. I had actually bought a house, sight unseen by Sue, in what was then the semi-rural suburb of the Gap, and there we raised our two sons, Stuart and Rory. We moved subsequently, but still live in the Gap, now on a half acre.

The new botanic gardens on the eastern slopes of Mount Coot-tha were started at about the same time that I started in the City Botanic Gardens. I was involved in some of the original design work for the new gardens and this is where my graduate landscape architecture came to the fore. Fortunately, being able to study was a tremendous asset with the new job. We had a full-time landscape architect in the early years who did all of the original designs under supervision. I came to the new Brisbane Botanic Gardens at Mount Coot-tha in 1983 to take over as curator and I've been doing that ever since. The gardens have grown to 52 hectares today. We've gone from a dry sclerophyll or open eucalypt forest paddock to the internationally renowned botanic gardens that you see today. I was one of the youngest curators and now I'm certainly the longest serving curator of a capital city botanic garden in Australia. Developing the gardens at Mount Coot-tha is rather like working on a giant jigsaw puzzle: we fill in the pieces as we go. We've now reached the full extent of the 52-hectare site, which, by the way, is 150 acres, so it's a huge botanic garden by international standards. Eventually we'll take over the adjacent Brisbane City Council quarry and develop that as stage three of our gardens – but that's a long way down the track. Once we do that it will certainly be one of the largest inner-city botanic gardens in the world, so it's a tremendous asset to the people of Brisbane, Queensland and Australia.

A botanic garden is primarily a learning institution and, unlike a public park, it sets out to educate and meet the information needs of the community at every level. For instance, we have about 14,000 students go through our 'lesson in the gardens' programs, from pre-schoolers right through to university students, every year. This is a unique program; there's nothing quite like it elsewhere in the world. It's a user-pays program and we employ 6 school teachers through that program at no cost to the rate-payers or the city of Brisbane, either, and I'm particularly proud of that. We have 100 volunteer guides and they do general and specialist walks of both the Brisbane Botanic Gardens at Mount Coot-tha and also the City Botanic Gardens. There's a Shakespeare Walk which consists of the plants used and talked about in Shakespeare's works. We also have one on indigenous plant use, all sorts of specialist walks. The volunteer guides probably cater for another 8,000 visitors annually.

We are actually the city's second largest tourist attraction after the combined attractions of Southbank, that's Southbank parklands, the art gallery, museum, and library. We're 8 kilometres from the centre of the city, so people don't just come upon us by accident. It's interesting that about 40% of our visitors are intrastate, interstate or overseas visitors, so there is a huge national and international botanic gardens viewing movement. When people are on holidays, they don't just want the plastic tourist experience. They want to see things of cultural significance, particularly the endemic plants of a region, the birds and the animals that come out of the adjacent 13,000-hectare National Park – people want to see them in a fairly natural environment. Our bird species 'counts' have doubled since the botanic gardens' inception. We have the occasional koala, the ubiquitous scrub turkey (probably a population of about 50 of them). Of course, possums and the most wonderful Eastern Water Dragon lizards, known by the local indigenous people as 'Moggills', hence the name of the suburb. These lizards are of tremendous interest, particularly to the Asian visitors, and when they chase visitors for food, there are screams all over the gardens, but they're quite harmless, of course.

Looking back, an early high point for me was in 1982, when, besides my work in charge of the Botanic Gardens, I was also appointed the venue manager for the Commonwealth Games, in charge of the archery venue at Murarrie. Another personal high point was the awarding of an Order of Australia (AM) in 1999 'for services to horticulture'. The people who work with me are another very important part of my life; I would hope they regard me as a colleague and a friend. Most of them have worked with me for my professional life and I take that as a compliment. I've been to many of their christenings, staff weddings and, unfortunately, a few funerals. In a collegial way, I think we all realise that we're building something worthwhile, and to be given this unique opportunity in your lifetime is very special. I'd far rather be physically gardening myself, I must admit, than sitting behind a desk; my greatest delight is talking with staff and discussing their plans and aspirations out there in the gardens.

Our Botanic Garden is actually a series of gardens and the most popular is the Japanese Garden. That came about by a fortuitous set of circumstances. I was at Expo 88 with my family, viewing the garden surrounding the Japan Pavilion, and the Lord Mayor at the time, Sallyanne Atkinson, just happened to be passing and I introduced my family. Sallyanne turned to me and said something like: 'Isn't it a pity that at the end of Expo this is all going to be demolished. Do you have a site for it in your botanic gardens?' I said, 'Too right!' and she said, 'Well, I'm on my way to have lunch with the Japanese Ambassador to Australia, how about I put the hard word on him?' We went 50-50 with the Japanese government in the transport costs and, as a result, we now have that garden.

On 11 November 1996 we had the official opening of the National Freedom wall in the Botanic Gardens, celebrating 50 years of the end of the Second World War. It's a national monument and council placed an advertisement in the paper inviting anybody that wanted to come along. We thought 500 or 1000, mainly ex-service people, might turn up, but we had over 3,000 people attend the opening celebrations.

I've certainly had some low points. One when I was still in the City Botanic Gardens. It was in January 1974 and I'd just started with the Brisbane City Council when we had the floods on the Australia Day long weekend. It resulted in about 7 centimetres of chemically charged mud being washed all over the City Botanic Gardens, the lower end of the city of Brisbane and about one third of the suburbs as well.

Many people will remember the appalling consequences of that. It took us 10 weeks to reopen the City Botanic Gardens but compounding this, of course, was the fact that many of the staff had suffered dreadful personal hardship, so we all helped out whenever we could. It was an awful time for everybody concerned. In the gardens, of course, we lost many extremely valuable collections and this reinforced our desire for a flood-free site for a new Botanic Gardens, and a larger site as well. It was through the foresight of the then Lord Mayor, Clem Jones, that our city's new botanic gardens came into being. I came from a traditional botanic gardens background in Adelaide and Brisbane City Botanic Gardens, both of which are now over 150 years old, so I was steeped in their histories. Here at Mount Coot-tha we had a clean sheet of paper to design our own view of what a new botanic garden should be. We aimed to create the most modern interpretation of a botanic garden that we could, and I think we've succeeded.

Today we have the world's largest collection of Australian native rainforest trees. I'm particularly proud of this, as it includes many rare and endangered plants. We designed the 25-hectare Australian Native Plant Communities Garden in geographical regions, so all the plants of the southern rainforests of Queensland are in one area; all those plants from the hot tropical forests are in another area and so on. These rainforests are a learning tool for school children, particularly valuable for the older classes, because we can give them the feeling of actually walking in a rainforest. Many urban-based kids have never been outside the centre of the city, let alone into a rainforest. They've never experienced actually plunging their hands into the cool damp mulch on the rainforest floor or smelt the smells that come with the rainforest, or indeed even experienced some of the animals that live in a forest environment, as they do naturally here in our botanic gardens.

Just about every day we hear from scientists from around the world, wanting pieces of plants for all sorts of medical and taxonomy research. Some absolutely stunning medical discoveries have come out of not only our botanic garden, but also other botanic gardens in Australia. When you realise that, within a 200-kilometre radius from the GPO in the centre of the city of Brisbane, there are 3,600 species of plants, you realise how incredibly diverse our part of the world is. If we don't represent these plants in botanic gardens, when they're gone from their native environment, and many will because we are the fastest growing region in Australia, they may be lost to science for all sorts of investigation. We've got a hugely important role to play in preserving this diversity of plant species, with botanic gardens often the last refuge for many native and even exotic plants.

I can't pretend the drought has been anything but very, very difficult. When you're charged with managing a collection of probably 14,000 plants, to see them dying, to have staff that are very upset and to see the public upset as well, is extremely hard to take personally, because there's nothing that I can do about it. There's nothing our staff can do about it. The fact is that, right at the beginning of water restrictions, I very deliberately said that we should not have any less restrictions than home gardeners. Our water resources are precious and we may be reduced to relying solely on them for drinking water. Taking a longer view, I don't think people realise just how critical our present water situation is. Whether the drought breaks soon or not, I think we have all learned some very sobering lessons.

The main lesson for our botanic gardens is that we are going completely off mains water to water our plant collections, relying wholly and solely on captured rain water. We've got plans for a huge new water storage facility. We're currently using recycled water, which I want to get away from, because I believe it's not sustainable. We are currently also using bore water, which we are desalinating because of its saltiness, with a solar-powered, wind-driven system and, once again, I don't believe ground water is sustainable, so we've got to harvest water. One of the roles of the botanic gardens is to show people the way to sustainable gardening.

Chris McKelvey – The Fight for Kangaroo Point Cliffs

He's a keen mountaineer and practising lawyer. We meet in his Toowong office, where the waiting room has pictures of famous mountains from around the world – many of which he's climbed. There's a fraternity of climbers here in the city who enjoy meeting to climb the Kangaroo Point cliffs, usually in the cool of evening when the crowds have left. He tells me the rock-climbing community was committed to the fight to save these cliffs from development, but, because of his knowledge of the law, he became spokesman for the cause.

'The area beneath the cliffs, where we now have picnic areas and open space, was to be asphalt car parking, a movement away from the use of natural space for recreation to something totally artificial, where plainly people would have to pay to enter.'

Compared to the way it used to be, the Kangaroo Point cliffs and surrounding area are being loved to death. As a climber I have the occasional selfish bit of longing for the 'old days' when there might have been a total of 40 or so people regularly using the cliffs for climbing and you knew most of them. You shared the area with few others: some lovers in their cars, a few walkers and boaties, the occasional hoon and some of Brisbane's desperate homeless people. Dereliction, neglect and a road which led nowhere kept most of Brisbane away.

Back in the 1980s it was an amazing recreational resource and parkland, sitting right in the centre of the city and just going to waste. Now it's completely different. Climbing has exploded as an activity and at some times of the day and early evening, it's very difficult to find a space on the cliffs. Myself and some of the older people I climb with, if we climb at Kangaroo Point, we arrive at nine o'clock at night, when everyone is packing up and going home. We have the cliffs to ourselves. The cliffs are floodlit, so they can be used at night. It's a beautiful time to be there, but many who now take the cliffs' area for granted don't realise how it might have been a very different story.

In the late 1980s climbers became aware that there was a proposal to develop the Kangaroo Point cliffs area for a commercial use. The cliffs' area at the time was not in the best condition. The area beneath the cliffs wasn't at all developed or maintained; although it was public park land, the area was run down. Many would not appreciate it was a park. It looked like a waste land – not an unfamiliar story.

The development proposal, which we understood had the support of the Brisbane City Council, was based on the old naval stores that gave the development its name. It involved the construction of a number of different tourist facilities, similar to a Gold Coast theme park. There was to be an aviary and a 'noctarium', a fauna park, a children's museum, an old naval dock, a nineteenth century fishing village, an artist's colony and even an 'opal mine', presumably let into the cliffs in some way. There was also to be a range of eateries to include a steak house, conservatory restaurant, food court, river deck and tavern. A couple of artificial waterfalls were also planned. The area beneath the cliffs, where we now have picnic areas and open space, was to be asphalt car parking, a movement away from the use of natural space for recreation to something totally artificial, where plainly people would have to pay to enter.

We came to hear about it because the cliffs area was zoned as Open Space. The land would have to be rezoned to Commercial Development and notices were put up advertising the proposed rezoning. Once we became aware of the rezoning application, a trip to the Brisbane City Council and examination of the development proposal made us quickly aware what was going on. The development proposal indicated that climbing would still be allowed to some extent, but the offering of some continued limited opportunity to climb wasn't fooling any of us, so we set about mobilising people against the development.

The main forces driving the public campaign were the Brisbane Rockclimbing Club, with, I suppose, me as the primary player and the Kangaroo Point Association, where the primary player was Joy Lamb. We worked together to alert the public to what was going on. One Sunday morning, in June 1989, if I remember right, we organised a major rally down at the cliffs. I can't remember people numbers now, but it was many more than we expected, drawn from right across Brisbane. We had one anxious time at this meeting. We wanted to unfurl three large banners down the cliffs, made up of large black polythene sheets with white painting saying 'save our cliffs'. We'd managed to hang them ready to unfurl below the top of the cliffs, but there was a howling westerly wind, about 40 knots. A couple of the television stations were there, as well as the crowd, so, despite the wind, we decided to go ahead with our plan, which meant a number of people abseiling down the cliffs, unfurling the banners and attaching them at ground level. The banners were quickly destroyed by the wind, flapping paint like snow over Kangaroo Point! But the media were able to get their television shots and we were able to get our message out.

The intense period of the campaign was from around early 1989 until the end of 1990, about 18 months or so. For some of us, it consumed our lives for a time, but happily so, as we were determined that something had to be done about the development and raising the public consciousness. We organised a petition to the state government, opposing the development. From memory, we collected about 6,500 signatures, from recreational users of the area, local residents and from people in the Gardens and riverside markets on the opposite side of the river. We encouraged people to lodge formal objections to the rezoning of the cliffs area. To assist, we prepared a pro forma of all the possible grounds of objection that people might want to consider in relation to the development. I understand that the council received between 1200 and 1400 formal objections to the development.

What ultimately saved the cliffs from development was a change in government with the election of the Goss Labor Government and the Sorley Council, and with it a different view of the appropriate development of the Kangaroo Point cliffs area. This strategy advocated the commercial redevelopment of the Expo site and development of public open space along the edge of the river and the cliffs. A *Courier-Mail* article of 5 October 1991 announced the Goss Government and Sorley Council Plan for the River Walkway, referring to it as 'effectively killing' the previous development proposal. A grander vision of what should be done with land along the water's edge had fortunately saved the cliffs, and a lot more besides, for the Brisbane public.

There was no celebration as such when the cliffs area was saved from commercial development. The whole exercise just left everyone with a heightened consciousness of the continued risk of commercial development in the area. And for as long as the area was run down and did not look like a park, developers still remained interested. It's only when the infrastructure of public walkways, the barbeques and other facilities went in that we knew that the commitment to preserve the area had really been acted upon.

One of the real positives that came out of it all was that it reinforced belief that the public really *can* make a difference. If there is sufficient passion and belief in something by members of a local community and those beliefs are grounded in reality, then, in a democratic society, those beliefs and their voice should win through, and in this case they did win through.

Serving our Indigenous Community

Heather Bonner – Our First Indigenous Senator, Neville Bonner

Neville and Heather Bonner with a young friend. Photo courtesy of Shay Ryan

We spoke in the early days of my research for this book. Known as Aunty Heather to many, she spoke with love of her husband's people who, in return, took her to their hearts. Shortly before she passed away, Heather wrote me a note enclosing a poem she'd earlier asked me to include at the end of her story. This poem had been read by Neville in the Australian Federal Parliament, Canberra, as recorded in Hansard 11 March 1982. In her note, Heather added the comment below.

'I love this. Nan gave it as a present to Neville and with all its rights. I had 2000 printed and included in Order of Service for my beloved's State Funeral.'

Neville's mother was staying at Ukerebagh Island, in the Tweed River down in New South Wales, visiting what we would call, back then, a 'blacks' camp, and Neville was born there on a government blanket, under a lowering palm tree in 1922. In those days Aboriginal people had to be out of town before sunset and his mother wasn't allowed to go to hospital to have her baby, so that's where he was born. He grew up there for about five years, and then he went to live with his grandparents. He said he was always cold and hungry. Later, he'd say he felt cold at the very first sniff of winter; he was cold psychologically before he became cold physically.

His mother died when he was about ten and his grandmother took him over. He was an extraordinary man. He had one year of formal education at a state school here in Queensland. Aboriginal children weren't allowed to go to normal schools, but his grandmother persuaded the local teacher to teach him for one year. He would say in speeches, 'Abraham Lincoln said, "Everything I am I owe to my angel mother," but I'm saying that everything I am, I owe to my angel grandmother!' He became a wonderful stockman, yet he spoke like an English don.

His grandmother spoke beautiful English and if he made a mistake she'd say, 'Excuse me, Neville, repeat that word again – right, that's better,' and she insisted on his learning to read and write. When he was about sixteen she died and he was heartbroken, so he decided to pack a swag and go and 'jump the rattler' to find some work. Back in those days, of course, there were an awful lot of people jumping the rattler (jumping on a goods train and riding for free). Wherever he went he'd find other Aborigines and he'd join them for a feed. Many of them slept under bridges and there, too, he'd find other Aborigines or Murris, as they called themselves, so he learned then a lot about the plight of his people.

He became a stick-picker, which meant that, after a tree had been ring-barked and branches would fall down, they'd pick them up. He also worked as a ring-barker, dray-hand and fencer. He became the head stockman. As a stockman on cattle stations you ate your meals at the woodheap, so when he became head stockman, he said, 'Well, this is it, fellas, I'm here to tell you, everyone's eating in the food hall. No more eating at the woodheap and if you don't like it, walk. I can get plenty of other stockmen,' and that was that!

Neville married a girl called Mona in Hughenden, while he was working on a cattle station there, and when their eldest son Patrick became ill, Mona wanted to go back to where she was born on Palm Island, so he accompanied her back to Palm Island. He stayed there for about fifteen years and became the deputy head of a workforce of 250 people. While he was there he used to take cane-cutting gangs over to the cane fields – that was another occupation he had.

I grew up in Ipswich, but later went to America and my children were born there. I had worked there amongst the American Indians. When I decided to come back to Australia with my three children, friends drove up from Washington State, where they lived, to Vancouver, Canada, where I was then, to see that I and my children got on the ship safely. I thank God for the lovely attention and care that family gave to me and my children. It was then that I made a vow to God that, when I got home to Australia, I would do what I could for my own indigenous people.

There was an organisation here in Ipswich, at that stage called the Coloured Welfare Council. It later became Opal (One People of Australia League) and there'd be meetings, but I wouldn't bother going. Then I'd remember my vow, but still I didn't go, and I had this argument with God off and on for about five months. At one of the monthly meetings I did attend I saw Mr Bonner. I thought I knew everything and I was talking about assimilation and he flew across the table, his eyes really blazing, because he was talking about *integration*, not *assimilation* and, of course, he was quite right – but because I was white I had thought I knew best.

At that time Neville and his wife Mona and their children had come down from Palm Island where his wife and their five sons were born. Neville had joined Opal, because it helped his people with education, housing and welfare. He'd returned from Palm Island when he'd got a call from his two grandfathers, who were elders, to come back home. They'd said to him, 'You've been mixing with the Migaloo and it's time you came back to your tribal area.' (Migaloo is Aboriginal for white fella.) They sent for Neville and he came down to Ipswich, which is pretty well in the centre of his tribal area that's called Jagera, (or Yuggera) and he took up managing a dairy farm. The

Jagera tribal area goes from the mouth of the Brisbane River to the foot of the Great Dividing Range.

I and my family developed a lovely friendship with Neville and his family. I became the honorary social welfare officer for the Ipswich Mob, as we call ourselves, and that was a wonderful, wonderful time. I was learning so much from the Aboriginal women.

At this time, I and my children were in a great big rambling house on a hill overlooking the city of Ipswich. Mona was worried that something might happen to me while I was there alone with my children. She was not getting on with her eldest son Patrick, so she asked if Patrick could move in with me to protect me and my children. He became the big brother to my children. My eldest one is Robyn and she was six months older than Patrick and she bossed him around, then there was a ten-year drop to Shay and a two-year drop to Rory. Robyn married and moved to her own home, and Patrick really did assist me to protect and raise Shay and Rory and they absolutely worshipped him. In due course Mona couldn't take it here and I don't blame her, so she went back. She went to Hughenden, but she had a massive heart attack and died there.

Opal owned this huge, beautiful place in Eight Mile Plains. Neville and I were subsequently married in the lovely garden there in 1972. I went to my daddy and said, 'Father, Mr Bonner and I are going to get married,' and he said, 'You can't.' I thought, 'Here we go.' I said, 'Is it because he's black?' He said, 'No, it's because he's Catholic!' I said, 'Father, I can assure you we're being married by a Presbyterian minister.' 'Well,' he said, 'that's all right then!' Wasn't that just lovely?

Every evening while he lived in Ipswich, or Mount Crosby, Neville would say he had had a call from the elders who had gone on before. He would go out to the Deebing Creek area, just outside of Ipswich, where there had been an Aboriginal mission where his grandparents lived, and he would light a little fire just at dusk and wait for those older people to come and he would commune with them. This went on right up until he died. Deebing Creek eventually became built out, so he had to go further and further out.

The referendum in 1967 meant that Aborigines were given the vote and allowed to be counted in the census, so Neville decided to go into politics. He was elected to the Senate in 1971. When he became a senator he had $5 in his pocket to go to Canberra. My son used to say, 'You borrowed that $5 off me, old fella!' And my husband would laugh and said, 'Yes, and I've paid you back thousands of times!' That, of course, was true. People in Canberra absolutely loved Neville. He had the first suit he'd ever owned and the first pair of proper shoes too. He was very particular about his boots. When he became a senator, he had his secretary write to R.M. Williams in South Australia, and yes, they still had his size and everything, so he ordered a couple of pairs. He never wore anything else. He'd keep lovely shiny black ones for after five or for dinner wear and the brown ones for everything else. In old photos of him you'll always see the boots.

All during my childhood I'd heard about politics, because my grandfather was the Federal Liberal politician for this area – they were called Conservatives in those days. There were two things I hated as a child, politics and the 'Order of the Eastern Star', which was something my mother belonged to.

When we became engaged he said he'd tried politics and lost and I thought, 'Great!' but when a by-election came up he said, 'That position's mine,' and, of course, he got it. I wasn't happy, but I thought, 'Well, if this is what my man wants, this is it.' Neville believed, if a law was bad, you shouldn't break it, you should change it and that was why he went into politics. He was Australia's first Aboriginal senator and he was there for twelve years.

One day he decided we would tour the state of Queensland and, since he was now a senator, we'd go in the car. He'd notify the shire clerk, or whoever, that he was arriving, and one shire we came to was actually called Banana Shire. The chairman walked in and said, 'Good morning, sir,' and Neville said, 'Don't be so bloody stupid, Alf, you used to be my boss on the dairy farm and weren't you a nigger driver. Don't call me sir!' That was the lovely thing about him; he could put people at their ease. Poor Alf said, 'No, Neville, I couldn't do that. I know you've earned your position.'

It made news, all over the nation and internationally, when it was announced that Neville was dying from lung cancer. It was so sad for the family when they all heard that their father was dying. The sons came home and, of course, Patrick came home. Tragically, Patrick hadn't been home long, just six weeks, when he himself died of cancer, and that absolutely broke Neville's heart. To see my darling husband at the funeral, oh, it was terrible, terrible, knowing that he himself was dying, but his beloved Patrick had died before him. After Neville died, I found a little diary in his office that said, 'Today I gave my beloved son into the arms of Jesus,' and I thought that was lovely. Neville was raised to believe in the old-fashioned Christianity, a very, very old Baptist.

I know for a fact, if I'd not been abroad for 13 or 14 years, I would not have noticed the plight of the Aborigines. The things I have learned by marrying into the Aboriginal community have been absolutely incredible. It was, of course, the women that taught me. All this business of walking over a bridge holding hands – it's not enough. These are beautiful people and we just took everything from them. It wasn't just that we cut off their food areas; we cut through their sacred sites. It was terrible what we did.

Neville's grand-daughter Marissa has just done six years as an assistant nurse at a big aged persons' place here. Where she comes from in Port Augusta, she and her mother and family speak their own language and I'm thrilled to death about that – that there are some living languages. It's very important.

The past ten years, perhaps, there's been this interest in the young people dancing, doing the corroboree. My husband wasn't particularly interested in that, because there was so much else that held his interest. I have a grandson who is a barrister. My daughter, she taught at a high school and her nephew became a barrister – he was the one who did the eulogy at Neville's state funeral. He said, 'Who was this man who could walk with kings nor lose the common touch.' It reflected the story of Neville's life and the love he had for us. He always found time for every one of us; nothing was too much trouble.

There isn't an Aboriginal home in the greater Ipswich area, possibly including Brisbane, too, where I could not get a feed, because that's their culture – they're very sharing people. We always stayed in a small early Queenslander home. He didn't ever want to go into a home that might be considered above the people of his race. Some of them caught up and bypassed him and he thought that was wonderful. He truly was a very special man.

Watching him on television, as soon as we saw the eyes begin to twinkle, we'd think, 'He's got ya – whoever you are – he's got ya!' I could not accept that Neville was going to die. I still think of him as though he is there. We both carried in our wallets a little bit of Sanskrit:

'My body's life and strength alone thou art,
My heart and soul are thou O soul and heart!
Thou art my being.'

(I think it came from *Original Poems Together with Translations from the Sanskrit* by Arthur Wm Ryder, Univ. of California Press, Berkeley, California, 1939 – Editorial note GR Noyes.)

The last interview he gave for the *Archive* – it was absolutely brilliant! The group came here about ten o'clock in the morning and they were going to be taping all day. They asked what the noise was, and he said, 'Cicadas.' There's no way you can cut out the top note of cicadas when you're recording. They had to go away and come again at night when the cicadas had stopped.

There were 2,500 people at his state funeral. Malcolm Fraser rang and said, 'Heather, I'm coming up.' I said, 'There's no need,' and he interrupted and said, 'Heather! Any man who'd walk across the floor against me 14 times, I'm coming to his funeral!'

No matter which Prime Minister it was, Neville would always let them know, 'I'm walking across the floor and voting with the Opposition on that one!' There were some things that were cultural that he just could not vote for.

Vale: Heather Bonner, 3 September 1923 to 21 October 2004.

A Curlew Cries
(For Senator Neville Bonner)
In Homage – Nan Ingleton, December 1980

'Our decades drift, as dust, across the void
On alien gusts, the Dreamtime tatters fly:
While dying campfires hold the dark at bay,
Through halls of power … one haunting spirit-cry:
I am your ghost, Australia, mourning still,
The trespassed shore, the broken tribes … I stand
Translating tears, for men unversed in grief
That mine may summon justice … in my land!'

Henrietta Marrie – First Indigenous Australian in the UN

I was put in touch with Henrietta by Professor Roger Leakey at James Cook University. We met when she visited Brisbane on business and she proved to be an interesting conversationalist with an engaging manner ...

Henrietta (on left) with colleagues at the Secretariat of the Convention on Biological Diversity

'It was June '97 when we left Australia and went to live in Montreal, where I started work with the Secretariat of the Convention on Biological Diversity ... the job was interesting and challenging and took me to many places ... that was another experience ... being an Aboriginal person ... in a huge bureaucracy ...(working) on a global scale.'

I was born in 1954 and raised in Yarrabah, an Aboriginal reserve south-east of Cairns. That's where I learnt a lot about my mother's people, the Kungandji and also the cultural knowledge and history of my father's people, the Yidinji, whose country is the Cairns-Edmonton-Gordonvale-Babinda region. I belong to the Gimuy Waluburra clan of the Yidinji people, my father's clan, but I grew up more in Yarrabah, in my great-grandmother's territory on my mother's side. I'm the great-grand-daughter of Ye-i-nie, who was the leader of our clan when the Cairns region was first settled by Europeans. The authorities gave him a 'King plate' in 1905, designating him as the 'King of Cairns'. His portrait photo hangs in the Cairns City Library. My traditional country is the land on which Cairns and Edmonton are now situated. The main camping ground was at Woree. They used to call it the Fourmile Camp as it was four miles from the Cairns Post Office. That's where my family got our name – from the Fourmile Camp.

I grew up knowing a lot about my culture, extended families, knowledge about bush foods and medicines, and how to survive. That was in the sixties and I also learnt a lot about the politics of Queensland at that time. My father had a job as one of the first Aboriginal liaison officers recruited through the Queensland government in the 1960s. We were transferred to Palm Island, just off Townsville, and stayed there for about three years. Dad sent both my older brother and I to St Patrick's College, a Catholic boarding school in Townsville, because the school on Palm Island wasn't up to standard, and there were separate schools for Aboriginal kids and for those of the white staff, which my father didn't like. However, St Pat's provided me with a really good education and my introduction to living in two cultures at the same time.

Palm Island had a system of apartheid that we weren't used to. When we were first there, we being with the staff and also being Aboriginal, added particular complications. Palm Island was segregated where white staff lived within a particular boundary, away from the Aboriginal people. The creek was the dividing line. The staff were on one side and the reserve on the other. When they built the house for our family it was pretty close to that creek, about 100 metres away from the non-indigenous staff houses. Over the years my father made sure that he broke down that system of segregation on the island, but it's still strong in my memory today, as if it was yesterday.

In 1971 I spent a year at Business College in Cairns. At that time the government was trying to recruit Aboriginal people into the workforce in Canberra. At age seventeen I was chosen to go down and work for the Department of Interior. Later I decided to go to university, so did a bridging course and enrolled for a Diploma of Teaching at James Cook University in Townsville and completed it at the South Australian College of Advanced Education. That was in 1984 and that's where my whole career really started.

Many things happened for me while I was in Adelaide. I met my husband Adrian and we got married in 1985. I went on to complete a Graduate Diploma in Aboriginal Studies and published my first papers. While doing my graduate diploma I approached the South Australian Museum about the cultural materials (shields with traditional rainforest designs, photos, genealogies, and so on) they had, which all belonged to my people. That's when I became involved in the repatriation issue and decided to do something for my own people. That led me to find a lot of our cultural property in other museums in Victoria, New South Wales, Canberra and Queensland.

I did a lot of research at the South Australian Museum and compiled my own inventory of our cultural property. At the museum in 1985 I met with Dr Norman Tindale. He allowed me to record our conversation, and he showed me all the genealogies he had recorded and photographs he had taken in Yarrabah and other reserves during the Harvard–Adelaide Universities Expedition during 1938 and 1939. His research laid the foundation for the government's assimilation policy. He had recorded all my family's history in this big green book and he had photographs of my grandparents, aunts and uncles. Finding these materials was a real joy; it was actually connecting me again with my own culture and my people. But my concern then was, 'Why are these things in a museum here? Why can't they be taken back home, so my people can be re-united with these aspects of our cultural heritage?' My mum and dad didn't have any photos of their parents, but the museum did. It really hurt me that white academics and students could access all this material and we couldn't. They could become experts in parts of my culture which couldn't be passed on during the mission days. We weren't allowed to learn about our culture then.

I began questioning the policies of museums and government laws and policies on Aboriginal cultural heritage and intellectual property rights. That led me to publish widely and make presentations at seminars and conferences around Australia. I became involved in issues concerning the pharmaceutical and bush food industries and the misappropriation of our knowledge concerning traditional medicines and foods. I completed a Masters at Macquarie University in Environmental and Local Government Law and attended a lot of the international meetings regarding bio-diversity and indigenous peoples during the '90s. That's how I ended up in Montreal.

I had no idea I would be going out of the country to work; in the beginning I had no idea I would even go to South Australia! The journey and the pathway seemed so long and it was a journey I never knew would lead me from one thing to another like that. Of course, when I think about those years growing up, I think about the words my father used, 'That I could do as well as anybody else and the colour of my skin didn't matter. I could do whatever it was I wanted to do and achieve' – and I did that. They were always inspiring words for me.

I applied for the position of Programme Officer with the Secretariat of the Convention on Biological Diversity (CBD) in the United Nations Environment Program thinking, 'I've got nothing to lose, I'll just try my luck.' I had a video-conference interview and it was on Christmas Eve in 1996 when the phone rang and I answered it and they told me I'd got the job! Then there was a big decision to make. I had to sit down with my husband and my son (who was seven years old at the time and recovering from a bad road accident), and we had to make a big decision to move from Australia to Canada. It was a drastic time. We had all sorts of mixed feelings, but we made that decision together. In June 1997 I became the first indigenous Australian to obtain a professional position within the United Nations.

The job was interesting and took me to many places. I was in Montreal for just two weeks when I had to go on a mission down to Santiago in Chile. The work was almost overwhelming, being an Aboriginal person, living in another country. Working in a huge bureaucracy was part of it, but I also had to work on a global scale.

My role was to assist the implementation of a number of articles of the CBD concerning indigenous and local communities and to ensure the information given was well researched and written to ensure such communities also benefited from the decisions made. The convention addressed many issues concerning indigenous peoples, including regulating access to and application of their traditional knowledge, intellectual property protection, maintaining customary uses of biological diversity, and the issue of access to genetic resources, prior informed consent and benefit sharing. When we are talking about the indigenous and local communities referred to in Article 8(j) of the CBD, we are talking about 2 billion people, a third of the world's population, who have little political power, and I had to represent their interests. It was a huge responsibility, and a privilege.

The first meeting I was totally responsible for was in November 1997, in Madrid. The meeting went well and many indigenous people from around the world came. The report from that meeting had to be deliberated by the Conference of the Parties (COP) in Bratislava, in Slovakia, in May 1998. Coincidentally, that was also when my first grandchild was born. That was a very successful meeting, because the parties established an institutional body, the Ad Hoc Working Group, which effectively gave indigenous peoples a voice in the implementation of the convention. My primary responsibility was to prepare documents for meetings of the Working Group, as well as other meetings held under the CBD, ensuring that governments were well informed to make decisions about implementation of the convention on the domestic front. The Ad Hoc Working Group still operates today and that for me was the highlight.

I also had to draft sets of guidelines for acceptance by the COP to assist governments to implement various aspects of the convention. One of my major successes was drafting the 'Akwe Kon Guidelines for the Conduct of Cultural, Environmental and Social Impact Assessments regarding Developments Proposed to Take Place on Sacred Sites and Lands and Waters Traditionally Occupied or Used by Indigenous and Local Communities'. The guidelines were my final achievement with the CBD, and I felt very proud that they were accepted by the COP as the international standard.

It was the high point of my life, being there in Montreal, working with people from many other countries and with other UN bodies, especially the other environmental conventions and treaties, and agencies such as the World Intellectual Property Organisation, the World Health Organisation, UNESCO, and the Permanent Forum on Indigenous Issues. I also travelled a lot – New York, Bolivia, Spain, Nairobi, Bonn – I used to joke about Geneva being 'my second home away from home'. It was quite an experience to be able to negotiate with parties and to represent the Secretariat at all these various meetings. In UN circles I was often referred to as 'Miss Article 8(j)'.

I worked with the UN Secretariat for six years, and that led to my current job with The Christensen Fund (TCF), a philanthropic body based in Palo Alto, California. I was 'head-hunted' for the position of program manager for Northern Australia and Melanesia, which I accepted in September 2003. I travel back to California three times a year, but most of the time I spend here.

Working with TCF is a privilege. We grant-make globally. Besides Northern Australia and Melanesia, we focus on Ethiopia, the southwest US and northern Mexico, and Central Asia. The job allows me to work with Aboriginal people on the ground as well as with other institutions, government, and the private sector. It's an interesting area to work in – very different to the UN, although it still enables me to keep in touch with the CBD. I meet so many different and interesting people and it's great to be involved with very successful projects. Since working with TCF, I have supported grants totalling around $20 million across northern Australia. My big goal is to see a United Nations University Institute for Traditional Knowledge established here in Australia.

I guess you can say my journey following the path paved for me by my ancestors has been challenging and interesting. I learnt a lot and am still learning. TCF allows me to continue to work internationally, but the most important thing for me is to work with my people in Australia, particularly the Yidinji people of Cairns.

Margaret Iselin – Indigenous Elder, Minjerribah

It's a sunny August morning and the car ferry from Cleveland to Stradbroke Island is crowded. The elders have a meeting house next to the Dunwich pre-school. Aunty Margaret greets us warmly and invites us in to join her and her husband Pat for a cup of tea and traditional 'Johnny cakes' while we talk. Soon a policeman arrives and later a doctor, both visiting the island and calling in to pay their respects. Everyone calls her Aunty Margaret and she greets them warmly, as old friends. She has been president of the Aboriginal Elders for the Minjerribah Moorgumpin Council, (covering both Stradbroke and Moreton Islands) for many years and is highly respected.

'There's close to 3,000 people live here on the island and that swells in the holidays up to 30,000. We have a lot of overseas visitors as well and they're interested in our culture. I believe education is the best path towards reconciliation and I regularly do cultural talks for school children here and others who visit.'

We've been married fifty-six years, Pat and I, and we have five children – five in four years, because we had twins. Four of them live here on the island, but the other one has a transport business over there on the mainland. We have fifteen grandchildren and thirteen great-grandchildren.

I was born in Brisbane, but I've lived my whole life here on the island. We're proud of our heritage; our people have lived here for many thousands of years. I'm now the President of the Aboriginal Elders, the organisation which is called Minjerribah/Moorgumpin Elders. Minjerribah is the Aboriginal name for Stradbroke Island. It means 'island in the sun'. Moorgumpin is the Aboriginal name for Moreton Island and it means 'large sand hill'. Our role as Elders is to be involved in everything to do with helping our community, from awareness of our cultural heritage to attending to social and justice programs and many other things.

This is a sand island, so there's no rock of any significance – just a little at Point Lookout. There are caves; there's no Aboriginal rock art that we know of from previous generations, but there are other signs of our people all around us. There are middens here that are thousands of years old – the one in front of the Marine Biology

Station is about 4,000 years old and there's another one at the Life Savers that's over 20,000 thousand years old. There are trees still alive here today that canoes were taken from. Our people prised the bark off the trees without killing them.

There's always been plenty of water and sources of food here. Our people understood their environment and they cared for it. They found food from the land like bungwal fern; the rhizome root was peeled, and then ground into flour. They also used to travel north, so they could visit the Bunya Mountains where they'd gather the fruit and bring it back to the island. Everyone had their own territories and each tribe knew their boundaries. If they wanted to go and move into another tribe's territory, they had to have a message stick to say that they were coming into that territory. If they weren't allowed, then they weren't able to go through. They always sent one person ahead with the message stick. If he was allowed in, he would then beckon for the elders to come. The message stick had symbols on it that everybody understood – a bit like an early form of writing and only the tribes knew the symbols.

They used to eat fish and shellfish, turtles, oysters and crabs. The crabs were only captured in season and the females were never eaten. The Aboriginal people sang out in their language, clacking their sticks or spears over the water. When the dolphins heard the sound, they would herd the fish into the nets. The Aboriginal people would take their share and give the rest to the dolphins. The clacking sticks were the rib bones of the dugong. The same is done in Africa. Our people made their own string from the inner bark of the cottonwood tree – that's what they made their fishing nets from. On the lakes they would catch wild ducks. The people would disguise themselves and swim underneath and catch the ducks by their legs. The people used to get 'jubbum' (witchetty grubs) hooking them out of the trees with twigs – they were then eaten raw or roasted.

Honey was used as an ointment with sheets of the inner bark of the ti-tree paper ('oogee') as bandages. The royal jelly was also given to the elderly and the honeycomb was shared. Honey was only taken in spring when the flowers were plentiful and enough was always left for the bees to rebuild on it.

Apart from the didgeridoo and the clacking sticks, they also had a drum made from kangaroo skins and would make music blowing through a leaf. There's a group of young Aboriginal people, descendants of the Noonuckle tribe on this island, who have formed the Yulu-Burri-Ba dance troupe. They've provided cultural education and entertainment here and overseas. Years ago, our people collected their red body paint at Coochiemudlo Island (meaning red stone) – the yellow and white body paint was plentiful on Stradbroke.

Brown Lake has been a tranquil place since water skiing has been stopped and our wild life: ducks, tortoises and swans, are back. The animals are back drinking of an afternoon. We work well with the Redlands Shire. We've had an agreement signed for a block of bushland they purchased with environmental money. We wrote to council to ask if we could do our cultural talks on that land. We're going to work with them and have signs showing which plants are our bush tucker plants and I'll be doing cultural talks there to school children. Anyone can go in and have a look around – bird-watchers or people who are interested in nature, and it will be a place where people can learn about our culture.

There's close to 3,000 people live here on the island and that swells in the holidays up to 30,000. We have a lot of overseas visitors as well and they're interested in our culture. I believe education is the best path towards reconciliation and I regularly do cultural talks for school children here and others who visit.

The school has purchased the building across the road. To get our young folk interested, we have an Art teacher to teach them. They are getting very involved and are selling their paintings. We started with 6 students, we now have 13, and they have since had a showing at the Redlands Gallery. We have a breakfast program where some students are given breakfast before class. This helps them to concentrate with their studies. One morning we tried boiled eggs on the menu. We didn't have enough egg cups, but since then we've been donated two dozen.

Our role here as the Minjerribah Moorgumpin Elders is to be here for our community, for our young students, for our street children and for whoever comes here. It all comes through the elders. We handle all our social problems from school through into our community. I work here in the community with them. The children who want to continue school after Grade 10 have to go across to the mainland.

We work with the police, the schools, the Justice Department, Domestic Violence and anyone we can work with. For example, we sit in with the Justice people and try to see what we can do for these young people that are called before the court. We work with the police on community issues, like graffiti and breaking and entering. I was on the panel to select our liaison officer for the community – something we'd been looking for in our community, as we hadn't had one for about twelve months.

I'm called to all the meetings we have here. I attend the meetings of the high school with our students and at the end of the year I do a talk for those who are looking to go their separate ways. Together we work out what jobs could be available for them and things like that. If there are jobs coming up for Aboriginal students, the departments in Brisbane and Redlands send us the brochures and we distribute these to our high school or to the CDEP (Commonwealth Department of Employment Program), an organisation that helps those who have left school and are looking for jobs.

There are many different organisations on the island that work for our community, one is the Housing Co-op – they have programs there where they provide housing for Aboriginal people in need. We also have a health centre here on the island which caters for the non-indigenous and indigenous people in our community. We have a nursing home and a respite centre for the terminally ill; they provide wonderful care for our elderly. The elders keep in touch with everything in the community and we try to help our people as much as possible.

Samarra Toby – Working Towards a New Dreaming

As I write this, Samarra has just turned twenty-seven. She is a graduate of the University of Queensland and Griffith University, with degrees in Science and Medicine. She's working as a doctor now in South East Queensland, but aims to return soon to Rockhampton to help the people of her traditional country.

'There was an excursion to an indigenous community called Woorabinda ... The teachers thought it would be an opportunity to promote reconciliation ... but afterwards, in the playground, I heard some comments ... They thought the indigenous children we'd seen 'spoke funny' and they thought it was a bit of a joke that they couldn't hear properly. That hurt me quite a bit, because, with the indigenous population, our children have problems with otitis media ... they have hearing health problems ... It made me decide to become a health professional ... so that I could come back one day and actually do something to address the health problems that we have.'

I was born and raised in Rockhampton, but my background and heritage on my father's side is Aboriginal, so, when I was two weeks old, Dad introduced me to our traditional country. The Gangulu people from the Callide and Dawson Valleys in Central Queensland are my people and our traditional country is bounded by Mount Morgan to the north, the Calliope range to the east, Cattle Creek to the south, and the Dawson River to the west. Our families have always lived in our traditional country, so we are able to learn about and practise our culture, visit our sacred sites, go out with our Elders, listen to stories about the Dreamtime and go to places of cultural and spiritual significance.

My grandmother is Native American and our people over there are the Northern Cheyenne. My great-grandfather was posted to Australia and fought in Papua New Guinea in World War II. He met my great-grandma, Helene, near Rockhampton. Our family has maintained very close ties to my Native American heritage and family on the reservation in Lame Deer, Montana. We go over and visit them once a year and this allows us to learn about our Northern Cheyenne culture, and practise things, such as traditional beadwork, and dancing in pow-wow.

On my mother's side, we also have South Sea Islander heritage. Back when Queensland was first being developed up north, they had a lot of sugar cane fields and the cane farmers up there would put in orders for what they used to call 'Kanakas'. That meant that white people would take boats over to the Pacific Islands and kidnap people to bring back to Australia to cut cane. My great-great-grandmother was kidnapped from Vanuatu for this reason. She was brought back in a boat, made to live in atrocious conditions and sent up north to cut sugar cane for no wage. She had to settle near Rockhampton eventually. That's pretty much my background.

I grew up in Rockhampton, which is a major regional centre, but it's actually just a big country town. It's the beef capital of Australia. I had a really great childhood growing up in a place like that – I think it keeps you grounded and it keeps you focused on the bigger picture in terms of what it's like for working class people.

My mother's a teacher. She teaches in the public school system and my father has actually worked for government his whole life. They've both been to university and have had a tertiary education, so I've had great role models.

I was in high school in about Year 8 or 9, around thirteen years old, when I had an experience that changed my life. There was a school excursion to an indigenous community called Woorabinda, about three hours inland from Rockhampton. The teachers thought it would be an opportunity to promote reconciliation between indigenous and non-indigenous people. I had relatives and friends there, so it was pretty exciting for me. We went out on that trip and a lot of students got a lot out of it, but afterwards, in the playground, I heard some comments being made by some students, who at the time were probably quite young and didn't understand the impact the comments would have on me. They thought the indigenous children we'd seen 'spoke funny' and they thought it was a bit of a joke that they couldn't hear properly. That hurt me quite a bit, because, with the indigenous population, our children have problems with otitis media, so they have hearing health problems. I think that event impacted on me the most in terms of deciding what sort of career I would want to have. It made me decide to become a health professional, to go away to university and study in the Health Sciences field, so that I could come back one day and actually do something to address the health problems that we have.

After I finished school I came down to Brisbane and did a science degree, majoring in Bio-medical Science. That was three years at UQ. I intended to use the science degree as a platform to launch me into an allied health profession or into becoming a doctor. I did that degree, but then I detoured and went to work in Canberra for the Federal Health Department. I worked doing various things, but among them there was Indigenous Health Policy and that led me to coming back to Queensland, where I worked as senior policy officer in the Aboriginal and Torres Strait Islander Health Unit, again doing Health Policy and implementing the National Strategies and Frameworks that were developed to address Aboriginal and Torres Strait Islander Health.

Then I got asked to go across to the Aboriginal community-controlled health sector. This sector is responsible for the Aboriginal medical services that indigenous people can access. It is partially supported by the commonwealth government, but also involves state health government initiatives. The aim is to provide culturally competent, holistic and responsive health care and work to increase access now, so as to alleviate the burden in the future and achieve positive health outcomes. I went across there and worked with the services and communities in terms of general practice. I was looking at things like recruiting and training doctors, mentoring students and trying to attract Australian-trained doctors into the services.

After that, I got into medicine. Graduate medicine is a four-year course. Ever since I was a child, I've always wanted to do something to help my people and I think medicine was always in the back of my mind. I think being a doctor means being a really important part of society, but particularly for my people, given our health problems, it's more important than ever. I believe we need more Aboriginal and Torres Strait Islander doctors, so we, as a community, can do things for ourselves.

I'm a big supporter of the principle that you have to want to do things for yourself and to help yourself out. I support developing our community capacity and transferring skills and education to indigenous communities and my people, so that our young people can come back and work towards a better future. If they do that, they're more likely to stay in the community, instead of having other people come in and teach and try and do things. I think, also, if you're an indigenous doctor, you tend to understand the community better or in a different way than if you're non-indigenous. You try and help in that environment and you usually know most of the families in the community. You understand the impact of historical and contemporary issues and this influences how you treat individual people, the family and the community as a whole.

The way our people approach health is holistically. It's important that doctors appreciate the overall spiritual, physical, mental, social and emotional wellbeing that you want to try and achieve when dealing with health. I have met some fabulous people here, great medical practitioners that are really good mentors and supportive of Aboriginal and Torres Strait Islander peoples and communities. They're non-indigenous, but have shown me different ways of working with various types of people.

I try and promote the Science Centre at the Queensland Museum when I can. Back in 2004 they were picking out people with a science background and I got chosen, one of, I think, twelve people, known as 'science heroes', who were chosen to tell their story. The new Science Centre is a fantastic place for people of all ages to go and get a physical appreciation of what science is. Having all different sorts of scientists up there is really good for kids. There are so many different fields and the opportunities that science can provide, and the work you can do now is just fantastic. In particular I wanted to pitch to indigenous youth that science is a great field to get into and it can lead to many different things. If just one Aboriginal or Torres Strait Islander child walks through the museum and sees me and thinks 'I can do that', then that project is a success for me.

My mother and father gave me a very solid and stable upbringing, but they also taught me the principles of dedication, commitment, sacrifice, and that sometimes things happen in life that are quite traumatic or disturbing, things like genocide and massacres – the things that happened to our people. They taught me how to cope with different types of stress and to work towards a better future, so the past is not repeated.

They provided support, not only financial, but emotional support. Without them I would not be where I am today; they are at the centre of my world.

My family has established a family company that's called the Toby Gangulu of the Callide and Dawson Valleys Native Title and Cultural Heritage Custodians Inc. My dad and mum, with the support of my aunts, uncles, cousins and, most importantly, my grand-dad, who is one of the last Gangulu elders left, set that up. The work we do was a vision my dad had from when he was in his teens, to set up a structure that would provide not only employment and educational opportunities for our young ones, but also integrate culture. The organisation does things related to native title, cultural heritage and monitoring of our traditional country. We do a lot of work with companies involved in developing industry in Central Queensland, when they develop land which is part of our traditional country and that is very sacred and important to us. We'll go through and look at things such as sacred sites, and make sure areas don't get damaged or destroyed. We're currently working on a number of major economic enterprises and making connections with the community in Central Queensland and trying to build up a solid base, so that, in future generations, there'll be some sort of support there that's linked to culture, and that will ensure the future success of our family.

The Toby family has had a long working history in the Dawson and Callide Valleys, beginning with my great-grandfather, William Toby, my grandfather, Robert Toby, and now my father, Robert Toby Junior. These connections have followed our family through to today and we have managed to maintain a positive relationship with the older white families. I think that factor is really important, as we want to foster a great relationship with people out there and work with them and give something back to the community out West as well.

Now that I've graduated as a doctor, I aim to fulfil my dream of helping my people. This includes helping them to have better health, social, emotional and physical wellbeing, both as individuals and as a community. We don't see ourselves just as individuals, but as part of a larger family who are all linked.

Judicial and Government Services

James Douglas – A Tradition of Law in the Family

Sir Gerard Brennan had suggested I speak with James because of his family's long connection with the law in Queensland. His office in the Supreme Court building is lined with books and every surface covered with papers. We sit at a small round table to talk...

'*My great-grandfather ... was a member of parliament, initially in New South Wales, where he was involved in discussions on the proposal to create the new colony of Queensland out of what was then the colony of New South Wales.*'

My great-grandfather, John Douglas, was Premier of Queensland and was the first member of my family to come here. He landed here from Scotland in about 1871, before separation. He came out with one of his brothers and took up land on the Darling Downs as graziers at a place called Talgai.

He was a member of parliament, initially in New South Wales, where he was involved in discussions on the proposal to create the new colony of Queensland out of what was then the colony of New South Wales. Later, after separation and the creation of Queensland, he held a seat in Queensland Parliament for the Darling Downs, eventually becoming Premier here for a couple of years, after which he was replaced by Sir Samuel Griffith.

He was a very early and consistent supporter of an Australian federation and, in 1859, when standing for election to the New South Wales parliament, called for a 'United Australia.' The idea of federation was not widely discussed in Queensland until 1899, when Queensland, along with the other colonies, took part in a referendum on federation. For John Douglas, the success of this referendum, and the inauguration of the Commonwealth of Australia on 1 January 1901, were the culmination of a life-long goal and one in which he played a significant, though largely unrecognised, role.

There have been a lot of people involved in public life in the family, either as judges or as ministers of the Crown. One of John Douglas's sons, Henry, was a minister in the 1915 Queensland government, as well, and another great-grandson is Dr Alexander Douglas, who was elected recently to the Queensland parliament at the Gaven by-election. He's a second cousin of mine.

My grandfather, Robert, was a judge. He was John Douglas's youngest son. He had an older brother called Edward Douglas, who was admitted as a barrister in 1901 and who later became a judge too. He had been Sir Samuel Griffith's associate. He decided to go to the bar in Townsville, because he thought there were opportunities there. There he met my grandmother, who was called Alice Ball. My grandfather was the judge in Townsville for 30 years between 1923 and 1953.

My grandfather was admitted as a barrister on 4 September 1906, his older brother Edward having been admitted on 2 December 1901. The interest out of that is that, from the time of my grandfather and his brother until now, there has been a Douglas of my direct line, either a barrister or a judge, in Queensland continuously for more than a century.

My father, also James, served in the Second World War. When he came back, he finished his bar exams and practised as a barrister in Brisbane in 1947. He, too, became a judge in 1965.

I was born in 1950 in Brisbane and grew up here. We were never pushed into the law; it was never held out to us as something that was a great family tradition to which we should aspire. I think that what we probably had as a background was more a familiarity with the individuals and personalities involved in the law.

My father used not to talk about the law at home at all until my older brothers, Bob and Francis, were in their later years as law students and they would debate issues with him. Bob later became a judge, but died, sadly and prematurely, in 2002. Francis is a prominent silk in Sydney.

When I started university, I was more interested in the arts than the sciences and thought I should combine it with a law degree, because at that stage I had no clear idea of what I wanted to do in the future. It probably became clearer to me when I worked as Sir Harry Gibbs's associate that I really did like the law.

I think my liking for the law grew from seeing the nature of the cases argued in the High Court, the issues that they gave rise to, how they were dealt with by good judges and how satisfying it was, both intellectually and, in a way, morally, because you are dealing with important issues, affecting people's lives or affecting the running of the commonwealth or of a state, and in a way where intellectual integrity is demanded of those engaged in the exercise. You really had to think hard about what you were doing, and about the reasoning processes involved and do your best to arrive at a correct decision.

One of my low points, shortly after I started at the bar, which was when these things hurt you most, was when I lost a personal injuries action for an old lady who had been injured when a car hit her on the street. She was a pedestrian and it was a difficult case to win because the car driver did not have much of a chance to see her before she stepped into its path. I thought we had a reasonable chance to win, but the judge found against her completely. I think I was only in my first year at the bar and it would have been one of my first Supreme Court trials. Similar things happened later, but they don't affect you as badly as when you are young and starting off. You think, well, is there something else I could have done for her? In retrospect, I'm sure I did everything I could for her, but of course you wanted her to win some money or get some damages.

I thought about high points, too – this is quite a contrast, in a way, towards the end of my career rather than the beginning. I was briefed in a case for a German manufacturing company against a small Australian company which claimed to have confidential information in the design of a particular type of ironing board and accused the German company for which I acted of misappropriating that information. It gave rise to some interesting points of law which were argued before the Supreme Court in a trial over a couple of weeks and decided against the German company for which I acted. We took it on appeal to the Court of Appeal here and won the appeal three nil. The other side, the small Australian company, sought what they call 'special leave' from the High Court, which is an application to the High Court to see if that court will entertain an appeal, and they won the special leave application, which meant the High Court was interested in the case sufficiently to hear a full appeal, and then, when I argued the full appeal, we eventually won three two. Now that's really a lawyer's high point. From the emotional point of view, you might hope that the small Australian company would win against the big German company, but, I suppose, by that stage of my career, the joy I got out of the case was in arguing a difficult case and achieving what I thought of as the proper legal result in the highest tribunal in the country.

Other occasions, such as becoming President of the Bar, as my father and brother Bob had been, were obviously also significant, as I've always had a great affection for the bar as a profession.

I've had an interest in comparative law since I was a student. Comparative law looks at, for example, if a legal problem arises in France, how would the French deal with it, compared to how the English deal with it, or how the Australians deal with it. So you look at a different legal system and see how they deal with the problem and you may learn something from it. We learnt something from the French recently in respect of copyright, where authors can assert moral rights to works in which they have copyright. That's an idea that developed from French law. The French – which a lot of people don't realise – use the jury system for criminal trials for the most serious offences, like murder, which Napoleon adapted from the English jury system in about 1810. Most people think of the French criminal justice system as relying solely upon examining magistrates and being an inquisitorial system. There are some interesting areas of overlap and difference. It's quite a different legal system. You realise that there are more ways to skin a cat than the ones you are brought up on.

I was President of the Bar between 1999 and 2001 and I was appointed to the Bench at the end of 2003. The Attorney-General approaches somebody and says, 'Would you like to be a judge of a particular court?' The Commonwealth Attorney-General appoints people to the Family Court and the Federal Court. The State Attorney-General appoints people to the Queensland Supreme Court or the District Court. It has to be approved by the Governor in Council too. So becoming a judge was also a notable high point of my career.

I've only been a judge for a little over three years, so it's probably a bit early for me to draw too many conclusions about the job. The work is constant and serious in its effects on the people who come to the court. I find criminal sentencing sometimes harrowing, especially with some of the young offenders either caught up in the drug scene or guilty of a violent crime causing death, sometimes because they were drinking too much. One of the worst so far, and not associated with drugs or alcohol, was when I had to sentence a young man, only eighteen, who had killed his best friend accidentally when he was fooling around with a loaded shotgun. You don't always know very far in advance the nature of the crimes you are sentencing people for and to face a case like that, almost out of the blue, with the families of the victim and the offender all lined up in the back of the courtroom waiting on your decision, is very sobering.

Some of the work is mundane, but there is a lot of variety and a reasonable number of cases arising out of interesting facts or raising difficult legal issues that I enjoy deciding. Depending on the nature of the work you are doing, you may not know in detail what cases will come before you. More importantly, most of the time you are not in a performing role. When you are presiding with a jury it is important to be in control of what is happening and to be very clear in the directions you give to the jury. That can require a significant degree of preparation, but most of the time you are there to listen and decide, giving proper reasons for your decision. The difficulty that can arise is if you have trouble making up your mind or are slow in writing the more difficult decisions – what we call 'reserved' judgments – when you need to go away and consider the facts and the law with more care to ensure you reach the right result.

Many litigants act for themselves, because they cannot afford a lawyer – that is a perennial problem and is not really surprising. There are, however, some litigants who act for themselves because they believe, if they appointed lawyers to act for them, they might receive advice they do not want to hear! Psychiatrists call some people in this category 'querulant litigants' and they can take up a very large amount of the time of the court, sometimes pushing completely untenable arguments. What you have to be careful with as a judge in cases like that, and in other cases where people act for themselves, is to make sure that the bad arguments are not obscuring other arguments that are much stronger. It's then that you wish the party had a good barrister!

Something I do know from my background is that the work I now do as a judge is necessary, important, particularly to the parties involved and sometimes to society as a whole, and satisfying personally – if you do it as well as you can.

Mac See – The 1974 Floods and Origins of the SES

I was surprised when he asked if we could meet at the casino in Queen Street. On my arrival, a gentleman in a neat suit and hat stepped forward with hand outstretched to introduce himself as Mac See. Mac said he'd worked here when it was the government Treasury building and still enjoys visiting. The SES (State Emergency Service) is still voluntary and heavily relied on in times of crisis, yet just 35 years ago it didn't exist. The 1974 flood was a defining moment in Brisbane's history and Mac See played a major role during the crisis and the subsequent birth of the SES.

'All the boats were private and provided by people in the community. They'd get their boats into the water around the flooded suburbs and our chaps would join in and help them. Often you could only get to a certain point then you had to walk the rest of the way. Our fellows would go into the houses and physically carry people out on their backs.'

I first came to Brisbane in 1939. I came down to Teachers' Training College and I had my interview here in this building where we are talking. It wasn't the Treasury Casino then. At that time it was known as the Department of Public Instruction. I was transferred to the Cavendish Road High School in 1953. They trained army and navy and air force cadets and they were looking for ex-servicemen teachers who could look after the cadets and take charge of them. I was an ex-serviceman, so I was appointed officer in charge. Then, in 1958, they asked me if I'd go on a course down to Macedon in Victoria. I asked, 'What's it about?' They said, 'Well, you're an ex-serviceman and you're interested in services, and this is that sort of thing; it's in case war comes to Australia!' Anyhow, I discovered that the commonwealth government had started a Civil Defence School at Mount Macedon in 1956. They used to bring in about 25 people every week to lecture them about the possibility of nuclear war. Basically, it was about Russia, because, previous to that, there'd been the Cuban Missile Crisis, which Kennedy had prevented.

The commonwealth government funded this Civil Defence School and I had to train as what they called 'Rescue Instructor'. It was similar to how 'Dad's Army' was established in London during World War II – it was called the Civil Defence Service there as well. It was people who weren't at the front, mostly older people in the community, who couldn't serve in any of the services. They did it in their own time and on a voluntary basis.

In 1962 the Queensland government decided they would fund a small group and establish a headquarters in an old school down in the Valley, where people would disseminate information to the community. We trained people in rescue and first-aid and signals work– all relevant to civil defence and all voluntary work. There was no SES in those days. This went on until 1975.

Barney Fogg was Administration Officer, but he retired in early 1974. Alf Martens was the Operations Officer and he went back to Police Headquarters, so that left me to 'carry the can'. I had a store man, Al Butler, and a typist and myself – plus all the volunteers who'd been trained for civil defence work in the case of a nuclear emergency.

The big emergency for us turned out to be not nuclear but the Brisbane Flood! It started on Australia Day weekend, January 1974; a Friday night, and by the Saturday afternoon all the low-lying country was inundated. It was raining on the Friday afternoon, initially just general rain, and then it became heavier and it was getting serious at round about eight o'clock at night. I stayed at the office, as there were areas in Brisbane that were starting to flood. People wouldn't have known that there was a flood coming down the river at that stage. They mostly found out only when the water started coming into their homes.

We couldn't take any part until we were officially asked by the police to do so. The chap who had been with us, Alf Martens, who was now the Assistant Commissioner of Police, decided that he would ask for assistance. This was the day after the flood started. Alf knew what equipment we had, which was simply what the commonwealth had supplied – the state had supplied nothing. Alf rang me up and said, 'Do you think you can distribute it to the volunteers?' So then I started. We had 3 big trucks, 3 utilities and we had stretchers and blankets, overalls, boots and helmets and that sort of stuff. But we had no boats and no tents. It had been assumed that if people wanted shelter in an emergency they would go to outlying buildings, so tents hadn't been considered.

The volunteers started to pour in. People that we'd never ever met, or seen, or knew anything about. They started to arrive in dozens and I had about 23 or 30 guys that I'd trained over the years, so I took 10 or 12 volunteers, equipped them with overalls, boots and helmets – all we had – and then sent them out to help.

All the boats were private and provided by people in the community. They'd get their boats into the water around the flooded suburbs and our chaps would join in and help them. Often you could only get to a certain point, then you had to walk the rest of the way. Our fellows would go into the houses and physically carry people out on their backs. I know elderly people were carried out of Tennyson, because our chaps were unable to cross the river into the Tennyson area – Oxley Creek was fairly heavily flooded, and they carried those people onto higher ground.

The council was working out what the water levels would get to – it started with the police. Alf Martens would have orchestrated a lot of it from there. Then the council and later the army. The army had the 'Army Ducks', the ones that used to run on land and water, and barges, but they didn't start operating until Sunday and they were operating mostly around Jindalee, well up the river. By then most of the people around Brisbane had moved out to higher ground and established themselves under other people's houses or wherever they could.

We established a welfare centre in a church hall on the corner of Sherwood and Oxley roads. We took over the hall, and two or three of our welfare ladies went out there and were in charge of it. We started supplying them with food. We knew we could get there, usually by roundabout routes. We had three utilities that we used to carry food. A lot of people slept there and we brought stretchers and blankets for them.

There were some amusing incidents. One of our men, who'd been trained by us in rescue work down at headquarters, was isolated on an island with quite a number of people, up near Jindalee. The water had flooded all the low country and they were stranded on this 'island'. A cow was washed ashore on it; they had a butcher amongst them, who had been evacuated, so he butchered it on the spot. Our chap said it was the best barbecue he'd ever had!

Of course, there was also tragedy. A number of people drowned – I think there were 13. One fellow who drowned was at West End when it was flooded. He decided he wanted some beer, so he dived over the balcony to swim to the nearest hotel, but never made it.

Some of the nursing homes had to evacuate people, but we couldn't evacuate them. Local people had to help – it was a 'Johnny on the spot' thing, really. We only had 40-odd specialist rescue people, but there were other people who'd been trained, too – about a couple of hundred came out and helped. The police would call and say, 'There's work to do in St Lucia. Can you get somebody there?' We had to get our rescue people out to wherever they were needed in the best way we could. Mostly they went in their own vehicles. It was worse as we went upriver, particularly around Oxley and Oxley Creek and up around Tennyson and St Lucia. The university was all flooded. South Brisbane, right across West End as far as Woolloongabba, was flooded. Chelmer and Indooroopilly and Taringa, all up along the river, that low-lying land, was all covered. Some of the houses there went completely under. Auchenflower, Toowong and Milton, down along the river there, were all badly affected. Of course, the City Botanical Gardens were covered.

All the guys went out and helped. They all did a pretty marvellous job. A few were mentioned in the press at the time, but everybody living in a low-lying area had a pretty dreadful experience and I don't think they tried to single anybody out, because many were involved – it was a general life-saving job.

There was a ship that was being built at a shipyard beside the Story Bridge at Kangaroo Point – it was about 10,000 or 12,000 tons, and they'd just finished it when the flood waters hit. It broke its moorings and swung around into midstream and they had to get a tug to hold it against the current. It took some considerable time, because they couldn't get an anchor down. The tug held it for about two days and they said that, if it had got away from the tug, it would have broached and jammed the river.

I don't think there was a problem with looting at that time – there may have been isolated incidents, but we never heard of any. You heard a few stories, like one where a chap went to the store at XXXX Brewery and got his tinny full of stubbies – little things like that, nothing really much that I can remember. We were too darned busy to bother with that sort of thing.

We had one lady down at our headquarters that sat on the phone and took names and addresses of people who were prepared to take in the homeless. But those in need of assistance generally would not take it, even though there were a couple of hundred people offering to house and feed them. They'd say, 'No, we don't want it; we'll be all right!' That happened a lot. Some of them, of course, had relatives and friends, and some of them went to neighbours.

The Brisbane City Council organised a relief fund and had quite a lot of money collected from people who donated after the flood waters were going down. They realised people had lost everything and they paid people out, so they could buy a new fridge, a new stove, or new bedding to get them back into their homes again. I thought they did a pretty marvellous job. I had an uncle and aunt who were evacuated. They had four feet of water in their house – it covered the fridge, stove, beds, toilets, the lot; they lost everything. They were given about $3,000 to get established again and I had a bit of extra furniture that I didn't need, so we cleaned their house out and got them back living there again. It was a terrible thing to have happen to you. Anywhere down along the river where it's low-lying, you can bet your sweet life that there was 15 or 20 feet of water over it – for the people concerned, it was absolutely terrifying. The rain went on during Sunday, and then continued on through Monday and Tuesday, right through to about Thursday. By that time the waters had started to go down and people were going back into their houses to clean up.

After the flood, the Bjelke-Petersen state government decided to fund the Civil Defence Force here in Queensland. They said, 'We'll give you equipment that you can use in situations like this.' They appointed a Director of Civil Defence. His name was Kevin Whiting and he was a Brigadier in the Army Reserve (or the Weekend Army, as it's commonly known), and he was an employee of the Forestry Department – a big wheel in the Public Service. I became his deputy and we worked on trying to re-establish and clean things up a bit. We were still headquartered in the same building and we still only had phones as a means of communication. This was from February 1974 right through until August, and it was still all voluntary at this stage. Anyhow, in August 1974, the new director got legislation through Parliament to get the name changed from Civil Defence to State Emergency Service (SES, as we now know it).

When the director got the legislation through, they decided to buy about $1 million of equipment that would handle civilian disasters like cyclones and floods. We allocated this equipment to branches of the SES established by the council – boats and trailers and anything we thought could be useful to them. It takes a long time to get equipment supplied, so it wasn't until around mid '75 that we had anything worthwhile in Queensland to meet natural disasters. They continue to do an excellent job for the whole community and it's great to see. It's a good feeling to have been in at the beginning.

Kevin Foster – Queensland Fire and Rescue Service

When we first talked, Kevin was manager of the Operational Policy Unit. He's retired now, after working for the service for 40 years. He spoke about the big changes he'd witnessed during those years, and of the camaraderie and courage of his colleagues in the service.

Metropolitan Fire Truck used in 1960s. Photo courtesy of W.A. Nixon, Fire Brigade Historical Society.

'In real life, fire fighting isn't as glamorous as people think, although it's often exciting and even frightening. Movies like Backdraft *and* Towering Inferno *are pure fantasy. Most of what fire-fighters see in burning buildings is just blackness, as the fire is shrouded in heavy smoke. If what they do during the fire fight is courageous or outstanding, only the individual or at best a couple of the team will know, because there are no television cameras inside in the intense heat and smoke to record the event.'*

I was born in Sydney in April 1945 and came to Queensland in 1951. I attended art school in Brisbane in 1961, with the intention of becoming a painter. Unfortunately, I couldn't survive on my income as an artist and part-time shop assistant, as it was just eight pounds a week. A friend I'd worked with told me I could get nineteen pounds ($38) a week as a fire-fighter and I thought this might be a more exciting activity. So, in February 1964 I joined the Metropolitan Fire Brigade (MFB), Brisbane, and was based at the Headquarters Fire Station in Ann Street in the city.

Training and discipline were rigorous and tough back in those days. Most of the older fire-fighters had seen military service and were generally very strong, both physically and in terms of their character. Toughness and native intelligence under extreme conditions at the fire front were praised and admired by all. The MFB was well organised and known for its aggressive combat of all types of fires, including aboard ships at sea. Ships which were on fire were often diverted from far out in the Pacific Ocean to Brisbane, where the fire fight was willingly carried out in dangerous areas below decks – we had a high record of saves here of both ships and cargoes.

It was an all-male fraternity then, as fire fighting was considered too tough and dangerous for women. The facilities at fire stations were pretty basic, even primitive, and any real comforts were only provided through a voluntary recreation fund organised by the fire-fighters. Still we managed to enjoy ourselves; entertainment at HQ included dances, which were held once a month, and boxing exhibitions, tournaments and billiards competitions, all of which the public were invited to attend.

The old heart of the Brisbane CBD contained many buildings that constituted a high fire risk. Very few had installed automatic fire protection, so we commonly had a least one serious fire in every tour of duty.

The fire engines of the day were large Mack 200 series war-time lend-lease models, as well as post-war Mack Thermodines, which carried wheeled, fifty-foot ladders and a five-crew and one officer complement. The appliances had hand operated bells for warning devices, but these were later replaced by electrically operated types. The original harnesses for the horses that once pulled the old horse-drawn fire engines still hung from the ceiling of the engine room, but the horses were long gone. The dispatch centre was called a watch room. It was located as an 'island' within the engine room. We all had duty turns in the watch room and all calls, including emergency calls, were received by the dispatcher on a PABX telephone board. Automatic fire alarms in buildings were of the open circuit type and were connected to receiving boards mounted on the watch room walls.

We all wore brass helmets until 1970, when they were replaced by polycarbonate types. The brass helmets looked great, but they were very uncomfortable to wear and we were forever cleaning them. Those of us who had worn the brass helmet were issued with one as a souvenir. Unfortunately, the one they gave me wasn't mine and didn't fit. It sits on a shelf in the rumpus room at home – a great conversation piece!

The first fire I attended was a very serious incident at the Arts Theatre on Petrie Terrace. The superheated smoke inside the building was extremely dense and acrid, so the wearing of breathing apparatus was necessary, and I experienced the benefits of fire-fighting alongside more experienced fire-fighters. A fire fight inside a building is very demanding physically, mainly due to the heat that saps the strength in your muscles. We had to feel our way with the backs of our hands; we couldn't see anything but blackness, until we discovered the main fire internally. The emotional stress this caused could only be overcome by stout resolve to continue. Eventually we subdued the fire. We were all elated at our success and this mood continued for days after, as each one of the new recruits related the particular experiences he'd had while fighting the fire.

Camaraderie was always very high and, given the toughness of the all-round working environment, it was really what kept us going. We were strongly unified in those days. Disputes and fights amongst the crew were rare and easily settled, either by consensus, or, in extreme cases, by a little boxing match. This was usually followed by all involved having a few drinks at the pub, as if nothing had happened. Most of the fire-fighters and officers (commonly referred to as 'snotties') had backgrounds in tough jobs, such as truck driving or the military. I was the odd one out, having come from a very different background in the arts. I was lucky that the 'firies' were worldly enough that this was of no concern and they readily adopted me into their fraternity. I was even luckier when a very experienced fire-fighter took a liking to me and started to mentor me into the fold. Bill or 'Webby', as he was called, had driven semi-trailers, had military service and had a wealth of life experience and natural wisdom from which I was able to learn and benefit. Whilst all of the drivers of fire engines in those days were quick and very good, Webby could do magic with a ten-ton fire truck that none of the other drivers could match. One of Webby's most famous exploits was to drive us to a small fire in three minutes, with flashing lights and bell, and return to the station even faster in two minutes 'because me cup o' tea is getting cold'!

We had many great characters, but Tom McAlister was the most revered of all of the station officers of those days. He was tough and witty with a large floppy moustache and a striking resemblance to Yosemite Sam of the Warner Bros. cartoons. He always seemed larger than life and his wartime exploits were legendary. He served at El Alamein and Tobruk, and was probably Queensland's most highly decorated soldier. He was one of the best front line fire-fighters I ever worked with. My first encounter with Tom's sense of humour was when we were damping down at the Arts Theatre fire on Petrie Terrace. Our efforts had saved the wardrobe and props section behind the stage. To our amazement, Tom emerged, dressed in tights, cloak and verandah hat, complete with feather, a stuffed parrot on his shoulder and brandishing a cutlass as he shouted, 'Avast, ye swabs!' Tom always had this talent of seizing the moment and making us laugh. At a higher level we were led by Chief Officer George Healy, affectionately known as 'the Silver Fox' or 'the Great White Father'. I had become his fire ground aide and driver, which was a much sought after position. He was a courageous leader at the fire front and greatly admired.

I went on to become the fire ground aide/driver to Viv Dowling, affectionately known as 'Limpy'. He had been severely injured at a theatre fire when he and several others fell through the roof as it collapsed. Viv Dowling was a great leader and very courageous. On one occasion, we had penetrated deep inside the burning second floor of a three-storey building on the corner of Ann and Bowen Streets, only to find that the fire had spread to the ground floor and we were on the verge of being trapped. We weren't wearing breathing apparatus, so we made our way back down through the intense smoke and heat, dragging the semi-conscious body of a fire-fighter, who had collapsed. When we were back in the street, exhausted and sick from heat and smoke, Viv quietly said to me, 'Let's get some breathing apparatus and go back and finish the job.' That was the kind of character he was. Whilst I had several other near death experiences in major internal fire fights alongside Viv, I always found that my trust in his judgment was well placed.

When officers were promoted, it was the custom for the Chief Officer to give the newcomer an introductory pep talk. When I became an officer, I arrived in Viv Dowling's office and he just looked up and said: 'Kevin, congratulations, you already know what I expect, so don't hang around here, go see about finding somebody to fill your shoes as my fire ground aide' – so much for the pep talk!

I fought fires in a number of ships, usually as the Chief Officer's aide. Some of the biggest were the *MV Mercury Bay* (bulk cargo refrigerated products), *MV Chawangi* (passenger/cargo, wool, grain and machinery) and the *SS Kos II* (ice-breaker, whaling). These fires were usually fought below decks in conditions of extreme heat and smoke, where visibility was nil.

On another occasion I was the officer in charge of the internal fire fighting at the Leuteneggers building in Charlotte Street in Brisbane's centre. This was a major fire in an old four-storey building with timber floors and a very high fire load of haberdashery and general clothing materials. My crew and I suffered from extreme heat stress at this fire and it was one of the pivotal incidents called up in the Livesley Commission of Review into the fire service that led to modernisation and the creation of a single state fire service.

I think the proudest memory I have from my days on active duty with the Fire Service was leading the fire fight at the fifteen-storey Globex grain elevators at the Port of Brisbane. A massive explosion there had blown away the 12-ton concrete lid of the number one silo, which, as a result, was left perched at right angles, like a giant biscuit on top of the debris, some 35 metres above the ground. The explosion had also wrecked the heavy steel transporter system and fire mains and spread the fire to the number two silo. There were a total of 13 silos under imminent threat of explosion. I encouraged the crews by leading the attack on the fire inside the elevators. I knew there was danger of the entire complex being destroyed and us with it, but I felt confident that the new fire fighting medium I'd developed using wetting agent in water would save the day. Eventually the fire was put out and the premises and grain were saved.

The MFB was greatly stretched during the '74 floods, in terms of capability to service its customer catchment area, which was completely dislocated by flooding. This meant that many fires either went unanswered or were attended too late to be effective. On one occasion, fire-fighters from Roma Street Fire Station were forced to stand on high ground on the William Jolly Bridge and helplessly watch a flood-bound three-storey industrial building burn to the waterline.

There was an enormous amount of silt and debris brought into Brisbane by the flood. The MFB was kept busy with the dirty, smelly work of pumping out basements and cleaning walls with fire hoses in flood-affected areas. Health officials ordered that all foodstuffs that had been in the flood had to be destroyed. This led to a decision to crush the entire stock of wines, beers and spirits of the firm of Montague Vintners – some of the veteran fire-fighters who had to hose away the alcohol were reportedly close to tears!

There have been changes and improvements in the fire service over the years. Fire trucks are now enclosed so that crews are no longer subjected to the elements as they were in the open cab fire engines. Nowadays there is more focus on accreditation in training. In the past a trained fire-fighter's qualifications had no portability. There is a wider cross section of people in today's fire service, with women as well as men becoming fire-fighters.

From the early days of volunteer brigades in Brisbane to the MFB and now the QFRS, the fire service of the day has always been provided with the best technology available at the time. Having said that, the prevalence of effective automatic fire alarms and suppression systems has meant a lessening in the number of major fires, but the sheer complexity, scale and changing profile of the built environment has meant that there are more fires, for example, where high-rise office and apartment buildings, housing possibly several thousand persons, have replaced older buildings which housed a hundred or so persons.

Today, the culture has changed from a robust male-only culture to one that's more reflective of the external community. The QFRS is now responsible for rescue as well as fire fighting. Over a third of the response activity is in providing a very high level of expertise and capability in road accident rescue, high angle and trench rescue and swift water rescue. This effectively means that the emergency work of fire-fighters is more visible and more people are reached by the greater scope of the service.

The QFRS invariably receives good press. In real life, fire fighting isn't as glamorous as people think, although it's often exciting and even frightening. Movies like *Backdraft* and *Towering Inferno* are pure fantasy. Most of what fire-fighters see in burning buildings is just blackness, as the fire is shrouded in heavy smoke. If what they do during the fire fight is courageous or outstanding, only the individual or at best a couple of the team will know, because there are no television cameras inside in the intense heat and smoke to record the event. What they feel is extreme heat and not a little fear of the unknown. This all means that fire-fighters have to believe in themselves and in the integrity of their units, to be able to function in an unpredictable and hostile working environment. It also means that, whilst being held in high esteem by the public is nice, the ability to recover for the next event is theirs alone to maintain. This is one reason why fire-fighters are a very close-knit fraternity.

Joy Arnold – Burketown Postmistress

The Post Office in Burketown was built in 1866 and is still a centre of local activity, handling postal, banking and other needs of the community.

'We get the "morning glory cloud" up here. It's a big roll cloud that varies in size, depending on the atmospheric conditions – it can go the whole length of the sky and is quite deep. The best way to describe this cloud is that it's like surf, but rolling the opposite way ... we get the people with their hang-gliders come in at that time of the year to ride the clouds like surf-riding. You have to know what you're doing, though, as they can be really vicious ... If you get on the wrong angle, it can throw you up and over!'

I arrived in Australia from England in February 1968 and went to work at the Lorne Hotel in Victoria for a few months. There was another girl there, Lauretta Kuiper, who was a bit younger than me. We got friendly and one day I happened to say that I was going to go north and travel up the coast to Queensland. We decided to get a car and take off together around Easter time. Her parents were very good and her father helped us out a lot by collecting jerry cans for petrol and things like that. We bought a four-year-old Holden station wagon and left the Easter weekend of 1968. We drove up the coast to Townsville, then inland to Mount Isa, back to Cloncurry and up to Burketown, along 1500 kilometres of dirt roads.

We finally arrived in Burketown from Geelong on the May weekend in 1968. For a few months we worked at the local hotel before doing stock work on various properties. Lauretta and I both rode horses. Horses were my profession prior to leaving England. I used to be a groom, working with racehorses and show jumpers, and exercising them, of course. Burketown was a country area and we both enjoyed the cattle and station work.

My now partner, Terry, was one of the part-owners of the hotel and also had a small property out of town; Lauretta went on the road, droving, and I stayed and worked with Terry on the property and various other stations and it just snowballed from there.

The land around Burketown is mainly savannah. In the summer we've got a lot of greenery with grass, trees and shrubs growing up with the rain, but, because of the heat, the country soon dries out again. We've got a lot of wetlands out here and we get a lot of migratory wetland birds that come in during summer and a lot of the regular birds that are here during the winter. They all go south, away from the heavy weather. Burketown's right on the banks of a salt-water river that floods. Back in late '70s and '80s, when we had floods, we sometimes used to see crocodiles coming up the street, but you'd rarely see a croc up this end of town.

When I first came to Burketown, lighting was either carbide or kerosene lamps. Fridges were gas or kerosene and wringer washing machines had petrol motors. Electricity (if you were lucky) was privately generated, until the power station was built in around 1979. Water was pumped into high tanks from a lake a mile or so out of town. The muddy water was then siphoned through the township. For washing clothes, we filled 44-gallon drums, using Epsom Salts to settle the mud; it made the water almost clear. It wasn't 'til 1983 that we finally got fresh water, pumped from the Nicholson River about 16 kilometres out of town. In 1980, the townspeople collected money to introduce TV.

I was appointed as non-official Post Mistress on 16 April 1981, also taking over the operations of the local telephone exchange. In 1985, my description changed to Postal Agent and during that year my partner and I built a new air-conditioned residence and Post Office – the first privately owned residence/business here for almost 100 years. We opened up, with no interruption to the telephone exchange, on 7 December 1985. We sold the old Post Office building to the Burke Shire Council in 1986. It's now the museum and Tourist Information Centre.

The telephones were automated in 1988. In 1993, Post Office 'Agents' became Post Office 'Licencees', which meant they could also operate a variety of retail businesses of their own choosing, to supplement incomes. Being a small township of approximately 150 permanent people, we couldn't infringe on other businesses. The township fluctuates during the dry season, with station workers, tourists et cetera. Finally, we decided to go into the stationery side of things, which has worked very well. With the General Store closing down last November, the way was left clear for me to go into the grocery industry, while still stocking the same stationery items, so I now have a modern convenience store.

My partner Terry has lived in or around Burketown since 1948, working stock. We're content and have no wish to move to any other part of Australia. Our youngest daughter, Shea-Maree, lives here in Burketown with her partner and three sons. She's helped me here in the shop for the best part of ten years and, without her help, I wouldn't have been able to go as far as I have. Our eldest daughter Gayl lives in Cairns and she does my larger orders and processes them into our system. When she was little, she was very interested in the Post Office and she learnt everything that went on just by standing beside me after school and watching what I did. When she became fifteen, I said she could give us a bit of a hand and I just couldn't believe it, how much she'd taken in. She knew exactly what to do. It was a great help. Then we allowed her to do the telephone exchange, and she did that like it was just second-nature too; she knew exactly how to speak with people. It was great.

Our youngest son, Justin, lives in Melbourne with his wife and daughter, while our eldest son Terry lives in Ireland with his wife. All four of our children received their primary education at Burketown, going to boarding schools for Grades 8 to 12. Generally, children in town have no fear about boarding schools. They all grow up with the knowledge that this is the norm after finalising Grade 7. Some also go on to university.

Looking back, when we had the telephone exchange, we were the only telephone access for 16,000 square miles. This was the old plug-and-wire type of switchboard. When I first came, we only had one line into town and there were 10 subscribers around town. We had the 'party line' system, where we had two other subscribers on the line. They were both cattle stations. Our line went from us to Normanton. In the early '80s, we managed to get Telecom, as it was called then, to put in some more lines. I think we ended up with 4 lines into Burketown for between 20 or 30 subscribers. Of course, if they had a late-night accident or emergency, we had to be on deck to take the calls and put them through to Mount Isa, where the RFDS was. We lived on the premises, so we could hear the phone whatever time it rang.

At that time we were also the Commonwealth Bank. It was only passbooks and people used to come in and do their banking and pick up wages and things like that. We were the only bank in Burketown then. Nowadays our convenience store is more or less the only general store in town. The garage has a small mini-mart where travellers can pick up bread and milk and everyday commodities, things like that, but we have more general grocery lines. At this time of year, with the wet season, the roads are closed and we can't bring anything in. The council helps to maintain supply of essential commodities.

Terry used to work on the council and he'd come home and help me with the evening exchange and maybe do weekends, or something like that. Other times I did it alone. We never really had time to ourselves. I'd get away every couple of years, but it didn't worry me; I'm not interested in going down town particularly.

I've seen my own children and other people's children grow from birth to adults, then move away for a more varied lifestyle, and later return with children of their own, continuing the family cycle. There's no cinema or dances here, not any more. When I ran the P&C, we used to get movies in on a Friday night – that was before TV, of course. I think, if some people got off their bottoms and got dances and things going again, it would be well received. The problem is, none of the young ones want to get involved in that type of thing anymore.

We get the 'morning glory cloud' up here. It's a big roll cloud that varies in size, depending on the atmospheric conditions – it can go the whole length of the sky and is quite deep. The best way to describe this cloud is that it's like surf, but rolling the opposite way. As it rolls in, the temperature drops dramatically and the wind gets very high. It's amazing to watch, the way it rolls past on a north-east to south-west line, travelling west. It can be very low, perhaps 1,000 metres, and mainly grey in colour. When the cloud comes in, you see a lot of the tourists packing up and leaving, because they think it's going to storm and they know, if the dirt roads get muddy, they'll get caught – but this isn't rain cloud. We get the people with their hang-gliders come in at that time of the year to ride the clouds like surf-riding. You have to know what you're doing, though, as they can be really vicious – they can throw you. If you get on the wrong angle, it can throw you up and over!

One time, my youngest son Justin, who was only seven at the time, was staying with friends on a cattle station across the border in the Northern Territory. They were out mustering cattle and he went along with the manager in the helicopter. The manager didn't realise the pilot of the chopper had never seen a morning glory and thought he would fly them up above it, but the pilot hit the edge of the cloud and it actually threw the helicopter about 300 metres. They were all strapped in, so they were all right, but they were lucky to survive. These clouds come across the Gulf and have been tracked as far away as Tennant Creek. I've seen them when I've been down in Mount Isa, coming home on the way to Cloncurry. They are big; I've seen the tail of one over 500 kilometres away from here.

There's a garage here with an A-grade mechanic and roads around town are largely bituminised now. We've got air services four times a week to Mount Isa or Cairns. We've a reasonably modern health centre. There's satellite TV, microwave telephones, mobile phones, computers and broadband Internet access.

Every couple of years I make a return trip to the bedlam of England to see my family, but I'm always pleased to come back. We're a small, close-knit community here in Burketown, a bit behind the rest of Australia, but still reasonably modern and happy with our lot. Who could want for more!

Queensland Icons – In the Surf and in the Air

Maurie Webb – Sixty Years of Surf Life Saving

I remember back in the '50s, when on Saturday mornings young men would stand by the roadside wearing their life-saving club jackets, so passing cars would stop and give them a lift to their surf life saving clubs on the coast. Membership of the SLSA was something that young men aspired to and young women admired. It was a totally voluntary organisation. Maurie is one of their founder members. He is seventy-eight years old when we meet and still looks a powerfully built man despite a recent illness. He is greeted warmly by all who pass us in the Palm Beach clubhouse, where we meet to remember old times.

'We used to have picture shows on the beach here in the late '40s and early '50s ... we'd make sure that we got several very tall saplings, they were the uprights, and a sheet or a piece of canvas was the screen. It was all silent movies then ...'

In the beginning, the Royal Life Saving Society was London based. Later, there was an Australian branch, headquartered in Sydney – same as everything else! With statehood in Queensland and the development of Queensland as a completely separate and a jealously independent area, the Royal Life Saving Society decided to form a Queensland branch.

As surf swimming became popular, there were some 'Royal' clubs established along the coast who decided they wanted to be part of a separate organisation. The two groups desperately wanted to guard their own turf. In 1930, the argument came to a head when the most volatile of the individual surf clubs in the Point Danger area said, 'No, we want to form a Queensland Surf Life Saving Centre.' The surfers who had dug in with the Royal eventually gave in and said, 'Yes, we can see that,' so they established a Queensland Life Saving Centre. It wasn't long before the 'Royal' virtually dropped out of the surf scene completely and Surf Life Saving became its own boss in Queensland, with its headquarters in Brisbane, which is where they still are today.

The association is still all voluntary in its service side. We've got some professional athletes who compete for very big money for the Iron Man series et cetera, but the kids that sit on the beach here every weekend in the summer don't get paid. The biggest change in the past 50 years has been in the culture of the movement. Up until the '60s, or a little bit beyond, surf clubs were a home away from home for the weekend. In the club house here, we had a kitchen, a dining room of sorts, a bunk room, gear room, first-aid room and things like that – so we were able to cater for about 30 or more. I think there were 11 banks of 3 high bunks made of galvanised frames and K-wire.

The 'living in' part of it started to drop off in the late '50s and early '60s and eventually, with the ease of transport in the late '70s and '80s, the need for it declined. The sense of cohesion and group camaraderie also, unfortunately, declined with it, but back in those early years, the '30s, '40s and '50s, it was fantastic. The camaraderie was heightened by the fact that there was very little accessible entertainment on the coast during those years. You went down, you knew your mates, you ate side by side with them at meals and you even helped the cook preparing the food. Cook was the boss. If you didn't wash up your own plates, it was almost punishable by death!

There were two groups among us: the industrial workers who had a five-day working week, and the clerical staff who worked Saturday mornings. I was one of the clerical staff. I worked shift-work at the GPO and I knocked off generally at midday on Saturday and then I headed for the train. When you got down to the coast on Friday night, it was too dark to swim, so you had a sausage roll and a cup of tea or something at the railway refreshment rooms at Bethania and then you'd catch one of the very late buses and go into Coolangatta, where there were pie shops and other places open. There was a picture show there and a couple of dance halls.

We used to have picture shows on the beach here in the late '40s and early '50s. We were almost 100 metres from the surf then, with a couple of dips between the dunes and a lot of dune grass. We used to cut down ti-trees from the swamp out the back here and we'd make sure that we got several very tall saplings. They were the uprights, and a sheet or a piece of canvas was the screen. It was all silent movies then, the old Charlie Chaplin's and things like that, shown from the club house onto the screen. We'd take the box around at half-time interval and we'd sometimes get 10 shillings in the box.

The films on the beach were very popular – so much so that the owners of the nearby Avalon Theatre complained to the film censor! I was club secretary at the time and I got a letter from the director of the Film Censorship Board saying that we needed to 'show cause' why we shouldn't be dealt with under the Act for showing pictures illegally and also because it was disturbing the profits of one of the registered theatre owners.

I couldn't ring him up, because there was no STD in those days, so I wrote him a letter, saying '…we're quite happy for you to see our situation.' He came and looked at the place and said, 'OK, where's the screen?' I said, 'Well, on that little sand dune over there, we put two posts up, with a canvas sheet between them.' He said, 'Well, what about your projection room?' and I pointed to the shark tower where the bottom half of it was sheeted in Masonite with a pop-up window in it. He wanted to see the projector, but I said, 'No, we borrow one that falls off the back of a truck every Easter and Christmas,' and he said, 'What films do you show?' and I said, 'Charlie Chaplin, Laurel and Hardy, and they're all silents.' He said, 'What about seating?' I told him, 'People bring their own, if they don't want to sit on the sand,' and he said, 'Do you charge admission?' and I said, 'No, we take the box around at interval and we sometimes get as much as ten shillings.' He said, 'I feel like going and telling the people down at Avalon that I'm ready to charge them with a frivolous complaint!'

In the '60s, the Nippers were started. A lot of people feel they'd like to take credit for it, but, as far back as the '30s and '40s, there'd been groups of kids involved who were either friends or children of members. Our club president, Andy Frizzell, who was continuous from '41 to about '63, started the Nippers here – we were probably the first club in Queensland to start a Nippers Club.

The girls got included, because the parents were reluctant to say to their daughters, 'No, you're not going down to the beach, but Bobby can; he's a Nipper.' The Nippers made a big difference to the place. Most of the clubs saw it as a recruiting ground. They started off coming at four or five years old, but the association put its foot down and said, 'No, we don't want them under the age of seven or nine.' That didn't stop the little ones coming, so almost every club had what we now call the 'Mickey Mouses'. Whereas the official Nippers have their club cap blue and white, the Mickey Mouses have a little pale green cap. They'll be down there playing all sorts of beach games and going for a wade under the strict supervision of surf safety officers, while the other ones are up here doing resuscitation or out swimming, paddle boarding or things like that.

The wheel took another turn in the mid '70s when the zealots, those females who dearly wanted to be part of the association in both awards and competition, had lots of meetings and talks and they wanted to be part of the Surf Life Saving. They said to me, 'Look, Maurie, all we want is to be allowed to go for our bronze medallion, to become lifesavers and do patrols,' and I said, 'What about competition?' and they said, 'We're quite happy to line up in a surf race with the men.'

We talked about it at the national council meetings. Some of the diehards were against it, thinking the girls wouldn't handle the rigours of surf work, but I said, 'I think they can.' Anyway, they agreed to it, and the girls did make a difference and, in the main, were accepted as part of the club. Now the girls can be in every event if they wish.

We've had a few shark attacks over the years. There was a chap that I went through my bronze examination here with in 1945. A shark attacked him at Burleigh and I knew him well and I also knew Gavin, his rescuer, who was about four or five years younger than me. Gavin dragged Leo in and he was revived, albeit he'd had a big chunk bitten out of his bum and still shows all the scars from it, but Gavin got his silver award from the association for meritorious service.

I was a Brisbane boy. I lived from 1930 in Brisbane and a friend of my brother's was a member of the club here and said, 'Do you want to join a Surf Club?' and Jack, my brother, said to me, 'Do you want to come down, too?' and I said, 'Yeah, I'll be in that!' The only way to come down then was you put your name down on the weekend before and you'd go over to the ticket office in South Brisbane and pay your four shillings and nine pence, or whatever it was, get your ticket and that was it. The other way to the coast was hitch-hiking. I had a Gladstone bag that I used to take to work with my lunch and everything else in it, and I'd painted the bottom of it 'Palm Beach Surf Club' and I'd just stick that facing the traffic. One time it was the club championships and I couldn't come down on the Saturday night, so I thought, 'I'll come down first thing Sunday morning.' I was living at Mitchelton and walked up onto the main Samford road and hitch-hiked. The first car that came past was a police car, which took me right into Roma Street near the Grey Street Bridge. I walked across the bridge and got a ride from there to Holland Park and waited there for another ten minutes when three or four jokers in a Yellow Cab, who were going to Byron Bay fishing, brought me right to the Palm Beach Surf Club.

In common with all of the people who have stayed with the surfing movement over the years, it's been about feeling part of a service, and that anything you do is not only for yourself, but for someone around you. In the main, the surf clubs are part of the community. At Palm Beach, we're the third oldest established organisation in the area. The only two who were here when we started was a general store, which included the post office and the pub! We were the third organisation here and we haven't changed hands in all that time – it's been the Palm Beach Surf Club, whereas the Post Office became official, so was taken away from the general store, and the pub's changed hands many times.

Vale: Maurie Webb, 16 June 1926 to 16 December 2005.

David Vickers – My Father, Allan Vickers of the RFDS

We were friends in our teenage years, when David was studying medicine. I remember his mother as a kind and beautiful woman. I always enjoyed my visits to his home, as both she and her husband were unfailingly kind and hospitable to their sons' friends. We sit now in David's office on Wickham Terrace, surrounded by other doctors' rooms. He's recently retired, so there's time to reminisce.

'There'd be emergency calls and he'd just be gone and we wouldn't know where he'd gone or when he'd be back. That was a bit of a worry for Mum, but they always found their way back. The maps weren't much good, but they followed railway lines and rivers.'

Dad was one of six children and he came from a pretty poor family. He had a fairly dour Presbyterian father, but a wonderful mother, who managed to look after all the kids on a shoestring budget.

Dad was able to attend university to do medicine, because he won a scholarship, but he had very bad asthma, and that plagued him all his life. His doctor told him before his final year, 'If you don't leave Sydney, you'll die before you finish this course. You should take a year off.' So he took a year off to recover his health and to earn some money to see him through the final year. He was the only one of the family that had a tertiary education, and he was the eldest. His younger brothers contributed to his university expenses after they began working.

After graduation, he went to Queanbeyan and worked as a GP for a couple of years. He used to send most of his money back to his mother to keep the family. He applied at that time to be the first flying doctor, but they said he didn't have enough experience, so they appointed Dr Kenyon St Vincent Welch. Several years later, however, in 1931, and in the middle of the Depression, he was passing through Sydney en route to England to do a surgical degree and he thought he'd drop in on Reverend John Flynn, founder of the Aerial Medical Service, as it was then known, to see how things were going. He found they weren't going well. In fact, they were in considerable debt and the whole thing was at the point of failure. John Flynn was a wonderful and very persuasive man, a bit like my father, and he talked Dad into going to Cloncurry for a couple of months, before he went to the UK, to see what he could do about keeping the thing alive. One of the sweeteners John Flynn mentioned was that the local chemist, a man named Whitman, had two lovely daughters – ultimately Dad married one of them. Her name was Lilias and she was the 'Belle of Cloncurry'.

Lilias came from a posh family, the Whitmans, who had a very strong connection with Claridges Hotel in London. Her grandfather, William Whitman, was born in Claridges Hotel in 1843. It had been owned by his maternal grandfather and was named after him. Any of the sterling silver and good things in our household are Whitman heirlooms, not Vickers!

The Cloncurry days were tough. Dad spent a lot of time trying to raise money to keep the service going, including a national lecture tour and a speech to federal parliament, which was very successful in raising money. He also took a cut in salary and, during his three years there, the balance changed from two thousand pounds in debt to two thousand pounds in credit.

The Flying Doctor Service was always a triad of medicine, aviation and radio. All of them had to rise above a totally unacceptable starting point. Initially in Cloncurry, there was no radio, just telephones and word of mouth. With radio, it was initially only possible to transmit Morse code and people on the land didn't have adequate batteries, so they had to develop a generator with bicycle pedals. Alf Traeger was the radio technician, and he developed the pedal generator and many devices, including a machine like a typewriter, which, if they typed the letters, would send Morse code. He also developed a transceiver radio, small enough to be transportable, which they could take on an aircraft. It made a transmission from air to ground, which is reputed to be the first time in the world that this had been done.

The Flying Doctor Service got to the stage where they wanted to open a second base, which was to be in Port Hedland, so, in 1934, when he was thirty-three years old and recently married, Dad took his new bride off to Western Australia. They had to build a Port Hedland base and that was taking time, so the West Australian government asked if he'd be the medical officer in Broome during the construction phase. He enjoyed his time there; he was the local magistrate, and protector of Aborigines, Mining Warden, Inspector of Fisheries and just about any other official position you could think of. Subsequently, in 1937, he went to Perth, where during the war he was Commanding Officer of the Perth Military Hospital, where I was born. Due to asthma, the army discharged Dad as medically unfit in 1943.

We all moved to Charleville, and it was wartime or just after, so, when it was birthdays or Christmas or whatever, you couldn't buy anything there. He always made our presents out of cotton reels and bits of strings and nails and things. We always lusted after something out of the shop – of course, we didn't realise then that what he was making was a much more valuable item than what you'd buy in the shop. Afterwards, Dad supervised the opening of a number of other bases. He avoided night flying, as it was too risky, and he asked people to put names on roof-tops, because the navigation in those days was very basic. All the medicines in the medicine chest were numbered, so that on crackly radios people could have some certainty they were taking the right thing. The landing strips were all dirt, often black soil, which is great in dry weather, but terrible in wet!

Dad was very caring. That's why he devoted his life to the Flying Doctor Service. He didn't make any money out of it and it was a virtual missionary situation. He received a salary and owned his own house, so that if he was killed in a crash the family would have a home, but it didn't bother him if he didn't have personal comforts, and that went for the family as well. He did all this so people in the outback wouldn't die alone for want of medical attention – yet that is what finally happened to him. In 1967, he was ship's surgeon on a ship coming back from my brother's wedding in England and, just off the west coast of South Africa, he developed cardiac failure, I think from his asthma – asthma medications were pretty dangerous things in those days, these days they're much, much better. The asthma drugs had a bad effect on the heart and he went into cardiac failure and was trying to give himself an intravenous injection and couldn't do it. It was a passenger- cargo ship and he was the doctor. The First Mate allegedly takes over if there's no doctor and he just said he couldn't do anything. So Dad died for want of medical attention.

He had a lot of respect for religion, but he didn't regularly attend church. I think he thought his religion was in deeds, not building churches. As kids we were fairly disciplined and Dad was away from home a lot. There'd be emergency calls and he'd just be gone and we wouldn't know where he'd gone or when he'd be back. That was a bit of a worry for Mum, but they always found their way back. The maps weren't much good, but they followed railway lines and rivers – landmarks were few and far between. If the weather was bad, or it was getting late, the pilot would often fly over our house before landing to let Mum know they were safe.

It was not easy to get locums, so Dad only took holidays every second year. To be on call continuously for two years in the extreme heat and dust was a long time, particularly for someone aged over fifty, and sick enough with asthma to be discharged from the army ten years before. His holiday was invariably a trip to the Snowy Mountains, trout fishing with his brothers – they had a very strong bond.

They say necessity is the mother of invention, but I think need is the mother of enterprise, which is what these men did. I mean, they did impossible things and made them work – 'have a go', I guess, was their motto! During a particular medical evacuation in a flood situation, the patient was a huge man who would have been difficult to carry and had a very painful injury of one foot. They got him into a dinghy to cross a flooded creek, but then there was a couple of hundred metres of dry land, before another flooded creek that they had to cross, so they left him in the dinghy, hooked it up behind the vehicle and towed it across the dry land, with him sitting in the back holding his leg up. When they reached the water on the other side, they put the boat back in the water and took him across the second flooded stream.

The Flying Doctor Service treated everybody, it didn't matter what creed or colour, and charged them nothing, but they did depend on donations. Sometimes people couldn't donate something, so they'd give you something else. When he went on trips around the outback, which he did a lot, the station owners very frequently gave him a sugar bag of oranges or meat or something. He hardly ever came home empty handed, because they were so grateful for the service.

In 1954 we left Charleville, because he was offered a Nuffield Foundation scholarship and went to the UK for twelve months; he put us in boarding school in Warwick, Slade, for a whole year. For a thirteen-year-old, spending a whole year in boarding school was a bit tough, but a lot of Aussie kids do. My mum went to boarding school when she was six, I think, because her mother died. She was just put into boarding school in Toowoomba, at Glennie, while her father remained in Cloncurry.

Dad lectured a lot in Britain, on the BBC, and he also helped the British Government start up a Flying Doctor Service in Nigeria. They wanted to learn how to do it from him, because by then the Flying Doctor Service in Australia had been going from 1928 to 1954, so had a pretty considerable experience. The one in Australia had been the first in the world and others have since been modelled on that.

I'd describe Dad as persistent, persuasive and quietly spoken. He was tireless in his promotion of the Flying Doctor Service, as donations depended upon its reputation and acknowledgement. Dad and Mum were both of the highest personal integrity and values. Dad was scrupulously honest and thrifty, but generous, as are people of Scottish heritage. He had an old-fashioned sense of chivalry to respect and protect women, and be kind to little children, even the dirty ones. He didn't like my mother to wear slacks – always a dress.

He'd never have more than a couple of drinks. He was never drunk in his lifetime and he didn't swear, and, despite a fine sense of humour, he didn't tell jokes much. I think he thought they were mostly demeaning of other people, so he wouldn't do that and he expected the same of us – but we could never match him. If we failed in some way, he was remarkably tolerant – once. We were never game to try him twice. He expected a very high standard of behaviour. As we grew older, he didn't forbid anything – he would just say, 'I will be very disappointed in you if you do that' – it was sufficient.

Dad was constantly recognised for what he did. He was awarded a CMG (Order of St Michael and St George), an OBE (Order of the British Empire) and C St J (Venerable Order of Saint John). He was an enthusiastic supporter of the Bush Children's Health Scheme. He would choose the appropriate children and organise their transport to the rail station for their first visit to the seaside and some metropolitan health care. For this, and other contributions to children's health, he was chosen as the 1963 Queensland Father of the Year. He was very conservative on the one hand and yet so radical in constantly attempting to do impossible things.

Unfortunately, when I did the things he would have been most proud of, he was already dead. My brother Robert is four years older than I am and both he and I followed Dad into medicine. I went to England, like my dad, to obtain a post-graduate degree, but he died while I was there, so I flew from Edinburgh to Cape Town and took over his job as ship's surgeon. Subsequently, I found myself back in Australia with no degree and no money to start again, so I worked at the university as a lecturer for two years and entered the hospital system again. There I did my training to become an orthopaedic surgeon, then became Director of Orthopaedics, then went into private practice and finally finished up being a professor in the Department of Orthopaedics.

The innovative trait in me came out because the equipment, particularly in the early days of micro-surgery, was poor, so I wanted to develop my own. I developed surgical equipment which is now still manufactured under my own name. With surgery, particularly with children's work, starting with the micro-surgery replanting amputated limbs, we ran into problems and I had to deal with those and help develop techniques for doing certain surgical procedures that hadn't been done before. In 1994, I was invited to be guest professor at the Mayo Clinic.

I published numerous chapters in text books on these subjects. I guess I inherited the surgical innovation from my dad. If you haven't got a tool, you make one, and if you're doing something that doesn't seem right, do it another way and see if it's better.

PART FOUR: Expositions, Festivals and the Arts

'A work of art which did not begin in emotion is not art.'
- Paul Cezanne (1839–1906)

Australia, and Queensland in the '50s, was often described as something of a cultural desert, but whether true or not then, no one could think that now, given the wealth of talented individuals we have providing world-class art and music for an increasingly art-loving public. While food and water keep the body alive, art and music, along with thought provoking literature, feed the heart and mind – transporting us from the every day and affecting us in ways that other things cannot.

Queenslanders today can experience myriad forms of entertainment, from classical and pop concerts to festivals of all kinds. Even fireworks have progressed from the backyard Guy Fawkes or birthday celebrations of the '50s to large-scale, computer-controlled sound and lightshows for the wider community. One of Brisbane's and Queensland's best known exhibitions, the Brisbane Exhibition, better known as the 'Ekka', originated in the late 19th century and since then has become an annual event for Queenslanders of all ages to attend and enjoy. Over 800,000 people attended the Ekka in 1988; the year that Expo 88 showcased Brisbane to the world and played a major part in the city's 'coming of age'.

Rhyl Hinwood: Sculptor

The Musician (bronze) 500mm x 250mm x 200mm
Memorial to Hazel Gray: student, teacher, acting principal at Somerville House, Brisbane.
Digital realisation, Rachel Park, Somerville House

Rhyl Hinwood Since 1970, Rhyl has designed and produced 354 commissions in carved stone and 154 in cast bronze and other materials, including the ceramic Australian Coat of Arms in the House of Representatives in Parliament House, Canberra, and the bronze *Man from Snowy River*, which is 120% life-size.

The most significant body of her work consists of hundreds of on-site carvings in the Great Court of the University of Queensland. These artworks represent the largest collection of sandstone carvings in Australia and have been listed on the registers of the National Estate and Queensland Heritage since 1990.

Rhyl was awarded a Churchill Fellowship in 1986 to study architectural sculpture in relation to cathedrals and universities throughout the world. In 2001, she was awarded an Honorary Degree of Doctor of Philosophy by the University of Queensland for her outstanding contribution to the university and to the visual arts in Queensland. She was appointed a Member in the General Division of the Order of Australia in 2006 for her service to the arts as a sculptor of works displayed in public places and buildings and for her roles in teaching and support for students.
www.rhylhinwood.com

Thomas Shapcott: Poet

Storm Weather

Weather happens. We were fishing, out on the bay,
When the first signs appeared. Clouds banking in the west,
All that. This morning ants were among the first
Things on the kitchen bench and who is to say
What the chooks were doing downstairs and whether they
Had taken the high perch. We always fail the test
Of symbols, and let's face it, we had to make the most
Of the weekend. The water was blue and sparkling. All seemed okay.

We weren't to know how suddenly the change would come.
The fishing had been good, and lunch had been a ball
Out on the boat and we did not remark at all
On the sudden drop in the breeze or how the light grew dim.
The bay's a big place and dangerous if you're not prepared.
The language was clear. Weather happens and must be understood.

Tom Shapcott was born in Ipswich (1935), one of twins. As a friend said to him recently, 'You can take the boy out of Queensland, but you cannot take Queensland out of the boy.' This boy lived here for 47 years, long enough to be thoroughly imbued with the particular sense of locality that is Queensland. His most recent book *The City Of Empty Rooms*, Salt 2006 was praised for its evocation of growing up in Ipswich. Tom has received numerous awards – an AO (Officer of the Order of Australia), an Honorary Doctorate from Macquarie University and the Patrick White Prize among them – but the constant source of his inspiration has been the place where he spent his earlier years.

The Arts

The Actress, the Soprano and the Ballerina

Wendy Stephens – My Mother: The Actress Babette Stephens

I met Wendy during the '50s, when we were both at Glennie, a Toowoomba boarding school where she was a year or two ahead of me. This was a time when students thought of each other's parents simply as 'parents', not as individuals with 'other' lives. Babette Stephens's other life was as an accomplished actress and founding member of La Boîte Theatre. She's now affectionately remembered for her involvement in theatre in Brisbane and doyenne of the entertainment industry here generally. That part of her life is well known and well documented, but her role as 'mother' was perhaps her greatest – coming, as it did, from the heart.

> *'I recall the arrival of the first washing machine. It was a front-loader, so it had the glass in the front, and I remember quite clearly, both of them sitting there, fascinated with this washing machine, and they sat there drinking their cups of tea, watching the clothes go round.'*

My mother was born in England in 1910, and in 1925 was given the choice to remain in London with her grandparents or sail to Australia with her stepfather and mother. It was a very hard choice for a child, as she had spent a lot of time with her grandparents and loved them dearly; however, she chose her mother, so her reason for being in Australia was because she was given the choice.

She arrived and went first to Townsville. I believe she went to school at St Gabriel's and I think she must have come to Brisbane around 1928. She took a job at St Martin's Hospital, but I don't know if she came here by herself, or whether her parents brought her down. My mother always had a tremendous love of theatre and the story of her background in theatre and her acting and dancing experience in London – all this has already been told many times.

Then, of course, there was her meeting my father in Brisbane. Both of them were in the Brisbane Repertory Theatre and in 1930 were cast in the lead roles of the current production. They disliked each other intensely at first, I believe, but they married in

1936 and remained happily together for sixty-four years. My father's law firm was in Brisbane and Mother carved out a magnificent career in Queensland. There were innumerable chances for her to go south, which she did occasionally for a show, but her life and interests were in Queensland. Of course, the Stephens were a very old Queensland family, my great-grandfather was Mayor of Brisbane in 1862 and then Colonial Treasurer and Minister for Lands and later Minister for Education in the Queensland government, so I think that's why she stayed. I was born in 1938 and life went on from there.

We lived in Tarragindi. There is a delightful story of Father building a house there for my mother and not telling her about it at all. I think they had a tiny Ford Model T and one day they drove out to Andrew Avenue and he showed her the big surprise. It was an absolutely delightful sort of dolls' house in green and white – quite lovely. She went inside and found he'd completely forgotten about a dining room. She was horrified!

My earliest recollections of Queensland were being sent to Sunday School. I have no idea who took me and how I got back, but always after Sunday School in the garden in Tarragindi I had ice-cream from the cart that used to come around the streets and my parents always had a drink, I suppose it was gin and tonic. It was a regular Sunday morning thing where there were chats and laughter amongst the three of us. I strongly remember this, although I must have been very small.

Another early recollection of Tarragindi was a marvellous occasion my mother organised when father was still away at the war. It was my birthday, so I suppose I must have been four or five, and she arranged for the radio to announce a message for Wendy Stephens regarding a birthday present which my father had hidden in the drawing room. As a child, I didn't query how he could have come and hidden it and gone away again. That didn't dawn on me. It was just this marvellous excitement of having a birthday treasure hunt prompted by someone I didn't know reading me a message from my father over the radio.

All my life I've remembered that birthday message as one of the very early, rather exciting, slightly dramatic, if you like, things that my mother used to do for me; she was marvellous in that way, she really was! She always made life exciting, but at the same time very secure. I grew up in the fifties, which were a most tremendous time for someone to grow up in, with the pound so safe and Menzies at the helm forever. My father was away, obviously, during the war, but my mother was always there. She never, ever, let me down. Her sense of timing and drama was unbelievable and whatever she had promised to do she would always do, but it was always at the last minute. I'd be on tenterhooks as to whether it would happen or not, but it always did! Or, if she said she would arrive at something, she always did, but it was at the last second. It was an unbelievable sense of drama that she had, which I think spilled from her public life into private life, in that she loved things to be done in a bit of a rush – it made it all the more exciting and interesting.

I was trying to think of the first performance that I ever saw her do and I've no idea which year that was in, but my grandmother took me to the Albert Hall and I think the play was *Message for Margaret*. I remember thinking how beautiful she looked, sweeping round the stage, and I remember being a little surprised that she was referring to another man as her husband. That was, of course, Mervyn Eadie, with whom she acted a number of times and whose son, Nicholas Eadie, is now in film and theatre. But it didn't bother me in the slightest. What I saw on the stage was her, but it was her 'once removed' – what came home was what I really knew. I don't think I saw a number of her performances. She hated the family being there and, in any case, I was sent to boarding school quite early on.

She stopped working for a number of months when my father was very ill and spent her entire time in the garden when he was at home recovering. She ended up, I believe, with a most glorious garden. Again, I suppose, the creative instincts were there for her to design and produce something. She decided that the next time father came back on leave we would have a wonderful display of flowers down either side of the drive. This must have been right towards the end of the war, I think, and she wanted zinnias – wonderful colours. So she went and bought lots of plants and planted them right down the drive on either side; it was to be quite splendid. She tended them and looked after them and they grew the most magnificent green foliage – but never a flower. She waited and waited then finally she said to a neighbour, 'Your zinnias are flowering and I have the most wonderful plants, but there isn't a single bud,' and the neighbour said, 'Ah, I wondered why you had planted silverbeet up and down the drive.' My mother collapsed in laughter.

I don't know when we moved to Clayfield. I would have been ten, perhaps, because my brother was born in Tarragindi, but, anyway, we would be looking at the early fifties, I suppose, when we moved to Clayfield. The first bedroom that I recall as mine was beautifully done. Mother always stage-managed things and the bedroom was more than any child could ever ask for. It was blue and white and full of frills and muslin. The dressing-room table was one of the very first ones that had the frill around the base, if you recall them? It had marvellous soft curtains – quite the most beautiful room for a little girl. Then her sense of drama when I moved into my early teens: it was time for the little-girl bedroom to go (we're now talking the late '50s) and it was turned into a bed-sitting room for me. Again, I must have been one of the very earliest of girls of my age to have a sofa which turned into a bed – and it was in the '50's colours, you know, red and orange and the wardrobes were built-in, so you didn't see cupboards and the gramophone was there and I was always allowed to entertain in there, because it was, of course, a bed-sitting-room with a sofa. I was never allowed to close the door – the sense of morality was very strong. It always had been in the house with her. People behaved a certain way and she expected the best, and she expected the best from my brother and I and she always got it. I remember feeling so grown up in my own bed-sit where I could entertain. It really was very much her style. She was always a little ahead and she was always thinking of wonderful things for the family or for me as a daughter.

For two or three of my birthdays it meant a box at Her Majesty's for a matinee performance of Gilbert and Sullivan, which was quite wonderful for a young girl. You could seat about six or eight of us in a box and Gilbert and Sullivan was a most marvellous thing for a child of that age to go to. We got dressed up and went to the theatre, and, after the matinee, she would take us to Rowes, where we would have a most splendid afternoon tea – equivalent, you know, to the teas they serve now at the Ritz in London, or the Empress in Vancouver. Again, that stayed with me all my life. Her sense of theatre and how to do things with flair was so much fun as one grew up.

But then she had a very simple side too. I remember a copper under the house for laundry, so they must have been boiling clothes in the early '40s. I recall the arrival of the first washing machine, which was a Bendix, and she and my father sat down in chairs in front of the Bendix with a cup of tea. It was a front-loader, so it had the glass in the front, and I remember quite clearly, both of them sitting there, fascinated with this washing machine, and they sat there drinking their cups of tea, watching the clothes go round. For all the magnificent performance and drama, simple things did give her so much pleasure.

She always called her cars names, which amused me, and she loved gambling for very low stakes. Again, I think it gave me a sense of – well, you get nothing for nothing – but there's always hope! Right up until the day she died, she had scratchies and she was always exceptionally lucky. She gave me a tremendous sense of optimism and a certainty that, whatever happened, I could deal with it.

After boarding school, I came back and went to university and, like the majority of us in the early '60s, the one thing you did when you finished university was immediately to go overseas. I whizzed off to England and after that got married and lived in Malaysia. My children were born in Australia and I stayed with my parents each time. I think my first boy, Michael, must have been three weeks or something and I was nursing him. I remember my mother saying, 'Oh, for heaven's sake go out. Stop hanging around the house.' I went out, but I felt sure I shouldn't have left the house and came rushing back later. I recall Mother was in the sitting-room reading a book or a script or something, with not a sound from the child, who was firmly asleep. She said, 'What on earth are you back for?' and I said, 'Well, it's three hours since his last feed; I must be here,' and I remember her just looking at me with a sort of despair, saying, 'For heaven's sake, he's perfectly all right!'

When my younger son finished his university, he took a year off to drive around Australia and turned up in Brisbane to see his grandparents. To this day, he laughs about it. I think he stayed two weeks, at which point my mother, I believe, one morning called him into her bedroom and said, 'Simon, it's been absolutely wonderful your staying here, but when are you going? Two weeks is enough!' Simon always says his grandmother threw him out, which, of course, she did; she was perfectly agreeable to having a young man around for a short while, but she had no intention of having him longer – she'd had that and that was enough, so she happily told him, 'It's time you went, dear boy. When are you going?' It was very much her, it really was!

She lived long enough to see great-grandchildren. My elder son has two daughters and she saw them, so that was splendid. I think she always found it interesting; each generation changed a little. She'd recall a story, where, if she visited her grandmother, there was a bowl of sweets in a silver dish beside her grandmother, and she would arrive and sit, and her grandmother would ask her to play, and she would play the piano, whereupon she would be offered one bonbon, one sweet from the silver dish.

By the time my mother was a grandmother, things had changed tremendously. Then there were great-grandchildren and I think she looked with astonishment, I suppose, at the different periods and the different ways things occurred. Now children roar around the place and life is designed around children, but in my mother's early youth it was very different. There was never any suggestion from her that this was wrong, it was just a different way of living. My father, too, was fascinated with the way each generation thought and what they were doing – it kept mother and father very young, right into their nineties – both of them – with this wonderful interest in people and in what people were doing and saying and thinking. They were a tremendous couple to grow up with, and, of course, I couldn't have been luckier being in Brisbane in the '50s. I mean, if you were to choose a time to be safe and secure and happy and amused, that was the time!

Lisa Gasteen – Opera Diva

We'd met the previous year through a mutual friend and I hoped she wouldn't mind my renewing such a brief acquaintance to talk with me about her work. Lisa suggests, 'Perhaps the last week in January would be best.' She has an infectious laugh and down to earth manner, as she shares a 'behind the lights' performer's view of the world of opera.

Lisa Gasteen: From her debut at Wiener Staatsoper as Brünnhilde in Die Walküre

'Brunnhilde's very famous war-cry that she enters on ... It's extremely athletic and very difficult, even when you're standing still! Anyway, I get an email from the director, saying, "I don't like to surprise people, you know, I like to work with my people, and I've spoken to so-and-so and they said you were pretty much up for anything and willing to try anything ... I want you to make your entrance via a ladder that will run vertically from the top of the proscenium arch to the floor" – and this is while singing "Hojotoho". I had to laugh and I agreed to give it a go, of course ...'

I guess we were a musical family. After we'd been put to bed, Mum and Dad would have a sherry and listen to the old opera recordings. My father's mother and her family were fantastic musicians; they could do harmonies at the keyboard and improvisations and things like that. It was a great background to grow up in, but as a child you don't really think about it very much.

I started at the Con, really because I was at a bit of a loose end. I had been a secretary and office worker and then I worked in the family's dry-cleaning business – and hated it!

I always wanted to work with animals, horses, in particular, but it wasn't until I'd been in this dry-cleaning job that I was really forced to take a serious look at what I wanted to do. I thought I'd be quite interested in journalism or writing of some sort – or singing. I thought, 'Singing will be easier.' Foolish, foolish – I'm glad there was no one round to tell me otherwise, or I might not have done it! Anyway, I thought I'd give it a go.

I sang an audition to get into the Con, because I didn't have matriculation and I got in on my voice, basically, and it all started from there. It wasn't until after my first year at the Con that I thought, 'Right – this is what I'll do!' This was in 1980 or 1981. I made my professional debut doing Miss Jessell in *Turn of the Screw* by Benjamin Britten with Opera Australia in 1988.

I'd sung at the Cardiff 'Singer of the World Competition' in '91 and had won it, and I think that was the first time London audiences had been aware of me. The first time I performed at Covent Garden, the curtain went up and I was lying face down on the floor in a very awkward position. I was terrified, but the reaction to it was absolutely amazing; people were so excited. It was good for me, because I'd had a chance to do the role here first, and do it with a very good conductor, so that prepared me well, but it was great! It was much more difficult coming back the following year to sing *Electra* in London, since the expectations by then were very high.

It took me a long time to develop the concentration required for opera. A performer needs to be able to follow a thought all the way through in a great arch – even if the germ of that thought takes several hours to reach a conclusion. For me, this really only came together with my first *Ring Cycle* in Meiningen, not only because the director was an extremely hard task master, but because the work is so well constructed and powerful that I take the responsibility of doing it justice very seriously. I also have a responsibility to myself and the memory of my late teacher to sing as cleanly and as well as I can, while giving all possible colours and shades expressed in the text.

Italian operas were always a problem for me, because the characters are, by and large, an uninteresting lot. The sopranos have an especially difficult time making their ladies credible. I remember particularly *Il Trovatore*, when Leonora, not able to have the man she loves (a tenor) and desperate to avoid the clutches of the man who wants her at all costs (the baritone), decides to join the convent. Just before she takes her vows, who should bound on to an already overcrowded stage, with all his soldiers in tow, but the tenor, who confronts the baritone, who's concealed somewhere within the scene. Swords, capes and veils often become entangled. We all stand staring at each other in surprised amazement (because that long pause is written into the music) and it's absolutely the most ridiculous scene I've ever had to do (over and over and over). It's not a good moment to get the giggles and I did every time. Fortunately, the music is sublime.

My debut at the Met was *Aida*; I was the first Australian to sing *Aida* there since Nellie Melba! *Die Walküre* there in 2004 was actually a hard job, because I was covering all three Brunnhildes, but singing Sieglinde. I had to have all four roles up and ready to rehearse and perform. Being partnered by Domingo did make up for it somewhat. He was a fantastic colleague. Being conducted by James Levine was also a great experience. The audience reaction, too, was wonderful. I love big stages like the Met. I feel I fit. It's very hard to go back to the Sydney stage now. It's simply too small and, as a result, I feel my performances are inhibited or squashed somehow.

I'm doing the *Ring* at Covent Garden and Brunnhilde makes her entry in *Die Walküre*, so they've already had the first opera and I'm doing the second. You know, there's Brunnhilde's very famous war-cry that she enters on, and it is incredibly difficult to sing. It's extremely athletic and very difficult, even when you're standing still! Anyway, I get an email from the director, saying, 'I don't like to surprise people, you know, I like to work with my people and I've spoken to so-and-so and they said you were pretty much up for anything and willing to try anything, and I just thought I'd run it by you, because I want your entrance to be the most fabulous entrance in the history of the *Ring Cycle*' and they go on and on and on building up their concept – and he said, 'I want you to make your entrance via a ladder that will run vertically from the top of the proscenium arch to the floor – and this is while singing 'Hojotoho'.

I had to laugh – and I agreed to give it a go, of course. If I sing it badly, everyone will know why and I'll have a very good excuse, but I just wonder why that has to be. I must be nuts! Firstly, I have to climb some steep stairs which lead to a platform from which I have to climb up vertical brackets encased in a wire mesh tube, which leads to another platform. On the uppermost platform (which I might add wobbles – a lot) is a waiting 'fly man' who has to attach me to the framework. I'm already strapped into a heavy sort of harness/nappy thing that you see rock-climbers and abseilers wearing. I put on the rest of my costume, which is a fabulous suede, floor-length coat. Then I have to get into position, perched at the top of the ladder out of sight and so high I'm even above the lights, and clip on two runners which are set into the frame of the ladder. When I'm settled, he detaches me from the main umbilical and we wait. As my entrance music approaches, one of the stage managers (who does rock-climbing as a hobby – shame she doesn't sing!) gives me a reverse countdown: 3, 2, 1, and then I'm off on my descent.

On the way down, I pause and swing out, so my coat can flap around like bat's wings. When I get to the bottom, I have to unclick each of the runners during the six beats of what has to be the loudest trill in opera! This, of course, all has to look natural and easy.

I've heard of really funny things, like some guy coming on to replace a sick Tamino in Mozart's *The Magic Flute* (that's a German Opera) and, anyway, this guy's walking along playing his flute and he falls down a trapdoor which they neglected to tell him would be open during this aria – but he didn't miss a beat; he just kept playing his flute and kept singing, and they had to raise him up. Things like that – or the tenor arrives five minutes before curtain up and they say, 'You'll know your soprano; she's wearing a white hat!' and he goes on stage and looks around and there's about fifty ladies in the chorus and they're all wearing white hats, so where's his leading lady? I can't say anything really funny has happened to me. German opera tends to be fairly serious, but nothing gets the camaraderie going more than a deeply despised conductor or director – that really makes people bond!

If I had to just single out one performance that has been a high point for me to date, I think it would be the *Tristan* at Covent Garden. When the audience response is as it was in London that first time (and also, I should have said, in Adelaide – an audience reaction the likes of which I have never seen before in Australia), it's incredibly satisfying. They can never understand what it takes for us to get up there on stage and perform at such a level and I'm not sure it's a good idea that they do.

There was an immense sense of relief and achievement when the first of the three Adelaide *Ring Cycles* was completed. Its success was extraordinary by any measure and even more remarkable because it was in Australia and mounted by a very small opera company. State Opera of South Australia only has four permanent staff and work out of a warehouse. Their General Manager, Steve Phillips, must have felt often that this *Ring* would sound his professional death knell. Fortunately not!

Preparing for a new *Ring* is always time consuming. Rehearsals are spread over a long time – two years, in the case of Adelaide. Over that time things can go wrong, for example, having rehearsed with the scheduled tenor, he developed some throat problems which were not diagnosed till very late in the rehearsals, and he had to withdraw from one of his operas. That meant his cover, with whom I'd rehearsed for one and a half hours, had to go on at the eleventh hour. Our premiere of *Siegfried* was his first time on stage; first time with costumes, props and sets; first time with orchestra; and our first run through together.

It's deeply distressing to hear of the cost-cutting measures being enforced on the state orchestras and player numbers being slashed. I don't know what will happen in the Australian music scene, but I'm extremely glad that, at least once, the full *Ring Cycle* has been experienced here. For the audience, I'm told it was inspiring, uplifting, and life changing – but, afterwards, many of the performers were left feeling empty and without purpose.

For me, one of the greatest rewards of my career comes from knowing that I have in some way touched the lives of those in the audience – taken them away from the day-to-day and into another world. Knowing this reassures me that my contribution is, in fact, very important and that opera as an art form is not dead, but alive and vital.

Michelle Giammichele – Prima Ballerina

We meet at her home in a tree-lined street of carefully restored colonial cottages in New Farm. She still looks every inch the dancer. We move out onto the back deck overlooking a rainforest garden to have coffee. Her puppy scampers at our feet, while amid photos and press-clippings memories are recounted.

'I remember I was paid $50 a week, which, at the age of sixteen, seemed quite a lot for being paid for dance. I thought, "Wow, that's the bee's knees!" So I was a dancer in training ... it was great experience, it really was ... I did my first principal role at the age of nineteen.'

I was born in Brisbane in 1963 and grew up in Kelvin Grove. My mother took my sister and me along to festival ballet class at the age of four, and I seem to have loved it straight away and I never stopped dancing after that. I did all the RAD exams and then Mum could see I was starting to get serious about it, so I then went to Barbara Eversen and she gave me fantastic training. From Monday to Friday after school I'd go to ballet for at least an hour and a half class and Saturdays as well, so it was constant ballet.

I finished all my RAD exams and Harold Collins, the Artistic Director of Queensland Ballet, came along to one of our ballet concerts and saw me dancing and offered me a contract with the company. I was sixteen, which was quite young, so it was a huge decision, whether or not to take the contract, or finish my schooling. I had to make a crucial decision, but dance was exactly what I wanted to do, so when this contract came up, I had to take it and I did – and I never looked back.

I joined the company as a dancer in training in 1981. It was like a one-year apprenticeship and you weren't paid very much. In fact, I remember I was paid $50 a week, which at the age of sixteen seemed quite a lot for being paid for dance. I thought,

'Wow, that's the bee's knees!' So I was a dancer in training, learning the entire repertoire in the company and being the odd girl right up the back in the chorus line, but it was great experience, it really was. I became a full-time member in 1982 and I did my first principal role at the age of nineteen, which was unusual. I'd got a fantastic break, because one of the principal dancers in the company fell sick and they'd only another principal dancer doing all the roles, but she was getting quite tired. So Harold actually put me on for one of the matinees and it went really well – that was in *Carmen*. It was quite a role to take on at the age of nineteen. I danced with one of the first cast members and he was fantastic for my first time in a principal role.

My husband's a very interesting man. He studied to be an architect and went into practice and then he became a patient in hospital and he saw something of how Brisbane hospitals were really quite run down – this was in the late '70s – and he decided to become a nurse. He did his diploma to become a sister and then he went back to architecture. He decided to design hospitals, because he saw a great need for good hospital architecture, and he now understood their needs from the 'inside'!

Tony and I met when he was best man at my cousin's wedding. We were married in 1985 and in 1986 I resigned from Queensland Ballet and we went overseas to London. I joined the London City Ballet over there and I stayed with them for two years. That was a fantastic time. I really enjoyed it over there and the patron of the company was Princess Diana. She used to come in and watch rehearsals and we had gala shows at Sadlers Wells and she would come and watch – it was just a magical time there, it really was. The reasons why we left Brisbane was for me to gain experience in another company and also for Tony, because all the hospital work had dried up in Brisbane, so it was a perfect time for us to leave. We had no ties here. Both of us gained tremendous experience in London.

After two years away, Tony had finished work on the Chelsea Hospital and by then I actually wanted to come back. I loved the company and wanted to come back to it, and of course Brisbane was my home town, so we decided to return. We bought our house in New Farm and settled down here. Harold offered me a principal dancer contract and I stayed with them until 2000. I had a fantastic career, returning from London and gaining all that experience. My dancing technique had improved; it was fantastic training over there with the London City Ballet. I danced lots of principal roles and other principal roles were created for me.

Since returning to Brisbane, I danced *Carmen* again, and it was nice to do that a second time at a more mature age – I could understand the role a hell of a lot better! I had many favourites, among them *Romeo and Juliet* and *Sleeping Beauty*. Harold created his version of Titania's role in *Midsummer Night's Dream* for me. The *Lady of the Camellias* was another beautiful role. During that period Harold took the company to the USA. We had a fantastic nine-week tour there, starting in LA and finishing in New York City.

Under Harold's direction we used to be touring all the time, in New South Wales, Victoria, and also in Queensland. We also went over to New Zealand. We learned so much from Harold's choreography and also from the many people who came in during Harold's time to choreograph for the company, people from overseas and many people from within Australia as well. That's very, very important, actually, for an artist's development, because it means you have to interpret different techniques and different styles of choreography. That's very good for a dancer.

In the early '80s, QPAC invited Queensland Ballet to be a part of the opening of the Lyric Theatre. From then, we always used to perform there, a week at a time, and we used to have packed houses. The Lyric Theatre seats over 2,000 and we used to pack it out, so you can imagine how well Queensland Ballet was doing. We had many productions there, and sometimes, because the company was quite tiny, you had to do another role on nights you weren't doing the principal role.

François Klaus took over in '99 and I was coming towards the end of my career, but I wanted to stay to see François in and see how he was going to take over and what he was going to do with the company. I kept going until 2000 and then hung up my ballet shoes at the tender age of thirty-seven, which is quite a good innings, twenty years. François's still there and seems to be doing fine.

I had a wonderful time in my dance career; I toured the whole world and met some wonderful people, including Nureyev and Fonteyn.

Then we decided to go overseas again for another two years. Whilst we were there, I received a phone call from Matt Foley, then Minister for the Arts, saying he'd nominated me for a Centenary Medal for my contribution to dance. I was awarded that in London at Australia House. It was a wonderful thrill. I was up there with doctors and lawyers and scientists. That was quite a lovely achievement after twenty years in dance.

After retiring I was appointed to the Board of Trustees at QPAC and did that from 2001 to 2002. It was a very interesting time for me. Hanging up my ballet shoes and then all of a sudden going into a huge boardroom at QPAC was an interesting experience – fascinating, but very daunting too.

Since retiring I've donated all my ballet memorabilia to QPAC: my first and last pairs of *pointe* shoes, my first and last tutus that I wore, posters, make-up and costume jewellery that I wore.

Rosetta Cook and I have been friends for many years. We met in 1981 when we danced together, sharing principal roles. Our friendship has lasted all of that time. Rosetta had been living in Sydney but returned to Brisbane in 2006 and we caught up with each other over a cup of tea and decided to set up some ballet classes together – with the intention of getting fit and helping others to get fit too! In one afternoon we achieved a lot: we chose a name, calling ourselves '2 Ballerinas' and worked out a Website www.2ballerinas.com and we decided to put an article in the local paper to let the general public know what we were doing. Before we knew it we were blown away by the response – it was just amazing – it all just fell into place!

Sculpture and Painting

Rhyl Hinwood – Sculptor

We've been friends since our teenage years and she still retains a youthful zest for life. We meet in her Kenmore home, where the beautifully sculpted heads of her grandchildren have pride of place on the mantle of the fireplace.

'I had to be sure to make a true rendition of the original Mary Shepherd illustrations, complete with buttoned up court shoes, and gloves, and a trim little suit, and the flower-decorated hat, then the magic carpet bag and, of course, the parrot-handled umbrella. Under no circumstances was the figure to look like Julie Andrews, for copyright reasons!'

My mother Maisie was born of Australian parents in Fielding in New Zealand, but she returned to Australia when she was about one and lived here until she was almost one hundred and one. From when she was just fourteen, Mother worked as a dressmaker in Little Collins Street, Melbourne, making beautiful imitation silk flowers, embroidery, beading and miles of fine rouleaux, the finishing touches to elegant evening wear for wealthy clients. She had no artistic training, but she had a wonderful imagination and a very creative talent and throughout her life she enjoyed painting with water colours and was always making something out of nothing. She never bought craft materials.

My paternal grandmother was really creative too. She lived with us and daily she enjoyed embroidering tablecloths and crocheting bedspreads with the finest cottons and she taught me these skills when I was very young. She and my father were meticulous; Father, being a chartered accountant/company secretary, everything had to be exactly balanced. He would keep an eagle eye on everything I drew to check the detail. It was good training for me.

When I matriculated and left Somerville House, I worked in the Queensland Natural History Museum as an artist from 1957 to 1962, painting and drawing for exhibitions and for the illustration of scientific journals. I made colour notes of live specimens, such as fishes and reptiles, and then subsequently painted the cast replicas to make them realistic. When it was quiet in the art room, I learned moulding and casting techniques from the preparators. I went to the Central Technical College four nights a week, studying the subjects I loved: painting and drawing from life. Then a new sculpture course was offered with a tutor named George Virine, who taught us the traditional techniques of the old Masters.

I left the museum to be married and the following year my son Matthew was born. I modelled a life-size figure of my sleeping son in clay, but I didn't have a kiln, so the model cracked and the wasps built nests in its eyes and ears. I continued to model and cast portrait heads of friends and family and in 1967 I won the Bundaberg Centenary Sculpture prize with a portrait head of a girlfriend. I used the prize money to go to a Sculpture Summer School at the University of Queensland with well-known Queensland sculptors, Len and Kathleen Shillam. We experimented with concepts for sculpture, making maquettes with cardboard, plywood, satay sticks, drinking straws and sticky-tape, and on the last two days Len showed some of us how to carve stone. I was eight months pregnant at that stage, but I was hooked and I bought a brickie's mallet and three chisels from Len straightaway. I started to carve a foetal form, all curled up, and of course everyone at the time said, 'She's obsessed with this mother and child theme!' A month later my daughter was born and there was no time to be a sculptor.

When I came to live here in Kenmore, Georgia was about eight months old and Matthew was nearly five and there was space outside under the gum trees where I could work when my son was at school and the baby was asleep. Father bought several huge sandstone blocks from the old Victoria Bridge pylons when they were demolished. While mother babysat for me I began to work consistently, hitting my thumb many times and learning by my own mistakes. For my birthday they even gave me some lengths of Queensland beech to carve.

When the Society of Sculptors was founded in 1967, I joined and became very involved with the committee and was secretary and newsletter editor and helped organise annual exhibitions for many years. Through the society I met other talented sculptors who were generous with their knowledge. I was very keen and worked hard and I felt that I could carve anything that was in my imagination. I mainly carved sandstone and wood because I could complete the whole process myself and winning prizes was encouraging.

I think it was around 1975 that I met Rob. The new Whitlam government was investing in the arts in Australia and in every state a craft association was set up. I was the delegate from the Society of Sculptors and Rob, who at that time was vice president of the Queensland Potters Association, was invited to join the committee to administer the finances. Ultimately we got together and it's been a great collaboration, both in our private and our working lives. I remember him coming out here to visit me once when I was down on the hillside pulling out cobblers' pegs, trying to keep my

Kenmore property under control. I recall him saying, 'You know, I could build you a wonderful workshop down here!' and I didn't dream that we really would do just that. I couldn't have achieved what I have without Rob. He's always very encouraging and also very practical. I'm the one that's likely to have the flights of fantasy. His design is always so architectural and he'll tell me my design can't be done, but I'll find a way of convincing him and usually we come to a good compromise.

Our first collaboration was the design and production of a ceramic Royal Coat of Arms for the new Courts of Law in Brisbane and the success of this commission led to possibly our most prestigious commission, which was to produce a ceramic Australian Coat of Arms for the House of Representatives Chamber in the new Parliament House in Canberra. I modelled the forms and Rob made the moulds and casts, and then glazed and fired the huge pieces. We went on site together to do the installation and it was the first artwork commissioned and installed, ready for the opening in 1988.

In 1976 the Great Court of the University of Queensland was finally being enclosed by the Michie Building Cloister. The Vice-Chancellor, Sir Zelman Cowan, decided that the sculpture program should be resumed and expressions of interest were called for. Unknown to me, Len Shillam put forward my name. Four sculptors were chosen to compete for the job and I was one of them and won it. I had no idea what a significant event that was to be in my life. It was a huge turning point. Initially I was offered a commission to complete eight grotesque portraits and so now I was committed to carving full time every day. Sculpture had suddenly become my profession. I've done a few hundred carvings on site at the university over the past thirty years and recently I've planned new suites of subjects. In 2001 I was awarded an Honorary Degree of Doctor of Philosophy in recognition of my contribution to the university and to the visual arts in Queensland.

One of the largest commissions I did was for the Agricultural College in Gatton, which is now part of the University of Queensland. I proposed a carved sandstone frieze depicting the evolution of agriculture in Queensland which would cover 60 square metres on the end wall of the Management Studies building and they loved the idea. I was determined to complete the job on site well before winter set in, as Gatton can get very cold, but that wasn't to be. The existing brick wall had to be clad in sandstone, but before the stonemasons could start work, a cyclone hit north Queensland and they all went off to rebuild Hayman Island Resort. When they did return and clad the wall, I only had six weeks left to carve the huge frieze before the governor was to unveil it. Every day I was out high up on the wall, carving in the icy wind. I was able to make quick sketches of the cattle and the sheep at the college before carving them on the wall the same day. It was lovely to finally come back to ground level as the work was completed. We just got it done in time!

About that time the Sheraton Mirage Resorts at the Gold Coast and Port Douglas were being built concurrently and the architects invited us to view the Gold Coast building site one Monday. They wanted concepts for the reception mural, coffee tables, and artworks on the planter boxes by the next Wednesday. I asked if they had decided on a theme for the resort artworks and they said, 'No, it all depends on what you come up with.' Rob and I tossed around lots of ideas as we drove back to Brisbane and by the time we arrived home we had decided that we'd settle for a 'beach theme': shells, coral and fish. The very next Tuesday we were taken by private jet to view the site and make some decisions. We gave them a materials selection and a costing and they gave us the contract immediately. Subsequently, they ordered a cast bronze frieze for the café and it had to be installed by the end of February, which was only eight weeks away. We worked right through Christmas and had the work installed by the deadline. Those two luxury resorts set a benchmark for resorts in Australia.

When the various national pavilions were being built for Expo 88, we were invited to work for the UNESCO pavilion and created the UNESCO logo in three dimensions in the entry hall. The logo depicts children climbing the latitudes and longitudes of the world. We only had two weeks to produce the whole artwork and they paid us $2 as a token gesture, along with a season pass and free coffee in their comfortable, quiet lounge. It was great to participate in that wonderful event.

The Man from Snowy River is the largest bronze I've ever made and it's in Niecon Plaza on the Gold Coast. It was 120% life size and took up a whole room in the workshop while I modelled the master over a period of about six weeks. A few years ago I created a *Memorial to Outback Women* for the Australian Stockman's Hall of Fame in Longreach after winning a national competition with a design incorporating two mothers and two daughters of indigenous and non-indigenous heritage walking together. We've been fortunate, also, to have worked on some very prestigious public art projects like the Roma Street Parkland, where I was thrilled to receive the largest commission for six carved sandstone artworks for the Spectacle Garden.

In 2005 I was commissioned to produce a life-size Mary Poppins for the city of Maryborough, where the author Pamela Travers was born. I had to be sure to make a true rendition of the original Mary Shepherd illustrations, complete with buttoned up court shoes and gloves, a trim little suit, and the flower-decorated hat, then the magic carpet bag and, of course, the parrot-handled umbrella. Under no circumstances was the figure to look like Julie Andrews, for copyright reasons. It turned out beautifully and was installed in the main street amid a colourful celebration with book readings, nannies' pram races and lots of balloons.

There have been some amusing incidents along the way. Years ago I was carving my first marble, a 15-ton single block, a bath for a local millionaire. I'd discussed the design with the client and he'd agreed to have his star sign, which was Cancer the crab, included in the Italianate marine-themed frieze around the bath. When it came time for me to carve the crab I bought the best looking mud crab and made a few sketches of anatomical details and then worked over a long weekend carving it in the middle of the design, surrounded by three adoring mermaids. It was completed when the client arrived back on Tuesday morning, but he was furious! He'd changed his mind. He'd been up on the reef with mud crabs on his plate all weekend and didn't want one on his bath. He thought a little Mediterranean sand crab would have been nicer, but a dolphin was what he really preferred, so I had to cut away the entire crab and carve a dolphin instead. Luckily there was enough depth of stone to play with.

Years ago Rob encouraged me to apply for a Churchill Fellowship, which enabled me to travel overseas to study cathedrals and universities in Europe and North America. That experience gave me more self confidence and since then I've enjoyed a very special association with other talented Churchill Fellows. Then, out of the blue, I was very proud to be appointed a Member in the General Division of the Order of Australia in 2005. An artistic streak has passed on to the next generation. My son

Matthew received a Churchill Fellowship in 2005 and is an executive with Air Services Australia. He studied journalism at UQ and still writes some wonderful poetry. Matthew leads a very active life and we all enjoy the results of his creative talent in the kitchen. My daughter, Georgia Shepherd, has a great colour sense and she followed her star to become a professional ballerina. She was a member of Queensland Ballet and Sydney Dance Company, Chunky Move and Bangarra, and now runs an award-winning restaurant in the Blue Mountains. Four grandchildren show great promise: an actress, another ballerina, an author and a soccer player.

Recently some old friends were here for lunch and they saw a large painting I had done for my son years ago. They were all really taken with it. Most of them didn't realise I could paint and were saying to Rob, 'Why doesn't she do more painting?' My mother often used to say to me, 'Darling, why don't you take up water colours? Do something that's softer on your hands.' I love painting and I love colour and recently I have begun to dabble in oils again, so, yes, maybe one day I'll really get on with it. Maybe it will be a new direction – when I'm too weak to carve stone anymore!

Philip Bacon – Philip Bacon Galleries

His galleries are highly regarded throughout Australia and his opinion is regularly sought by professional collectors. His friend, the artist Margaret Olley, is flying in from Sydney and visiting him later this morning, but despite the busy day ahead of him, Philip finds time to relax and reminisce…

'My best purchase – I knew I was doing a good thing as a dealer at the time – was in 1979 or 1980… John Peter Russell, who was known as "the lost impressionist"; he was an Australian who went to France, where Monet used to paint with him … This painting of his was offered to me … this was $75,000 … Lady Trout died, and Christie's and I did the estate sale and that picture got $700,000, which was the highest price of anything she owned.'

My family came to Brisbane when I was a kid. I started school in Melbourne, but when my mother was ill, the doctors thought the warmer climate here would help her. I went to school and university here. My father opened some electrical stores and menswear shops up the coast, so, although Brisbane was our base, we were also in different coastal towns.

I don't know where my interest in art came from really. My father was an amateur musician; there were no artists in my family and I didn't particularly enjoy art at school. My parents were certainly both interested in paintings and I used to go with them to exhibitions. I also did some art classes with Caroline Barker, who was a wonderful old art teacher here in Brisbane in the '60s, and I went to Saturday afternoon classes there with a whole lot of little old ladies. I don't know if I was really going for the art or for the afternoon tea! I didn't really feel painting was my field. I was interested in paintings, though, and in art galleries. I used to enjoy hanging around art galleries. There was the Moreton Gallery in the old AMP building, which is still there, but renovated. I used to love the smell of it – you'd go downstairs into this dark basement area. The parquet floors were always being waxed. You could see your face in it – it was wonderful. There was this strange smell, I suppose it was turpentine from the paintings, and the low lighting; it was so peaceful, very atmospheric.

When I had a bit of money, because I was hanging around galleries, I'd see things. I first bought things when I was quite young. My first art purchase was a print by the French artist Bernard Buffet. I don't know when he did it, 1954 or 1956, or something like that, I probably bought it in 1959 – I was twelve then. At the time there was a gallery, a little 'Art Shoppe' that had just opened in Rowes Arcade, which was one of the first renovations of old buildings in Brisbane. It was run by a woman called Irene Moore whose husband, Keith Moore, was a businessman. The old Grand Central Hotel in Queen Street, opposite David Jones, was one of the first big renovations and it was also turned into an arcade – it was very chic and he took a shop there. I used to haunt that place every weekend – I was starting to buy pictures, paying them off, putting a couple of quid down each week. Keith Moore said, 'Oh, you're always here. I want to go to the races on a Saturday. You might like to come in here on a Saturday and help out.' So that was how I started. I would have been about seventeen.

I went to university to do Law, while still working part time. I didn't think of working as a lawyer; I thought I'd go into the diplomatic service. My father wanted me to 'get a proper job'. He got ill with cancer, and I felt I *had* to decide what I was going to do. My father very much wanted me to go into finance, so I worked for a while for AGC as a finance clerk in Dalby – and I hated it! After my father died I came back to Brisbane and returned to the Grand Central Gallery full-time from, probably, 1968. Towards the end I effectively became the manager, because Keith was becoming less and less interested in the business. I arranged exhibitions, including a big Bob Dickerson showing, but the real catalyst was when the Brian Johnstone Gallery closed. It was at that time the best gallery in Brisbane, if not Australia. He had the first exhibition of Charles Blackman and the first exhibition of Margaret Olley. He showed Dickerson, and Lloyd Rees and Drysdale. They closed in 1972 and nothing else happened. It left a big void! I'd been offered an interest in the gallery I was in, but that didn't look like it was going to eventuate, so, with the encouragement of the artists, I opened here in 1974. The Valley was very cheap in those days. I found an old tyre warehouse and rented it. I'd got a loan of $20,000 from a client – $20,000 was a fair bit of money in those days and he asked for it back six months later – which was a bit of a struggle! In July 1974, in the opening exhibition, Lawrence Daws, Bob Dickerson and Charles Blackman were the first artists I showed.

My exhibitions were always very well attended and I had a big mailing list right from the start – we had quite elaborate catalogues and it quickly became 'the place to be' on a Friday night. It was very satisfying, though if they were young artists, sometimes we didn't sell much. Today people ask, 'Is art a good investment?' I can truly say it has been for me. It's the best investment I've ever made. Obviously it's different for me, because of the access and numbers of pictures coming through, and the commission is less, but nevertheless, if I had concentrated totally on buying pictures in those early days I'd be much better off now.

My bias has been to the artists I have grown up with, who are figurative painters. I've never been interested in abstract painting and I'm certainly not interested in installation art, nor am I particularly interested in video art, but that's happening in Brisbane, because it's happening all over the world, with the young students going through the art colleges. Taste has matured and the art scene has changed in Australia. There are now three big auction houses, including two international ones – Christie's only had their first sale in 1972 in Australia, so it's relatively new. In the newspapers there's always a story about art, where previously there was a review perhaps once a week.

In the late '80s and '90s, Indonesia was very rich and the middle class started to buy big paintings that were of interest to them. Donald Friend, who lived in Bali, for example, was sought after, then the crash came and that all stopped. Taiwanese are different. Because many of them come and live here and their children are going to school here, that generation is interested in Australian painting more than in Asian art.

There's always been a bit of a fusion between my interest in art and music. The Conservatorium is a good example; I've been on their council for some time and have organised their fund raising dinners. I've always tried to incorporate artists there. We usually have a big dinner on stage and the stage is dressed with large paintings and it creates a fantastic ambience. Most of the artists I know are quite interested and knowledgeable about music, like Jeffrey Smart, for instance, who is an absolute Wagnerian and goes to every performance of *The Ring*. Lawrence Daws works to music and Margaret Olley always has Classic FM on. The artists themselves are generally in tune with music – it's always seemed a good fit. I'm on the board of Opera Australia and our big fund raising events are always geared around opera performances, or our singers. A large part of the fund raising I do is donations of paintings and things like that. It's very well supported by the guests at dinners, because the people who can afford to go to the Opera can afford to buy the paintings.

In the main, the artists that I showed originally are the masters like Margaret Olley, Ray Crooke, and so on, who are still sought after. The middle generation people I show are artists like Tim Storrier, Garry Shead and Stewart MacFarlane, who's in his fifties. There are some young fashionable artists and I look at them and think, 'I wonder what will happen to them in five years time?' I'm asked all the time, 'Who's the next Arthur Boyd?' I don't know. How would anyone know? It's only time will tell – you've just got to trust your instinct and trust your taste and, because I have this large stable of artists whose exhibitions recur every three years, it's hard to slot everybody in. You can't be everything to everybody.

I have tried to be educational in that some of the exhibitions we have curated in-house have been of artists I feel have been overlooked. We did a very big exhibition of Ian Fairweather in 1984, which was the tenth anniversary of his death, and that was the biggest exhibition of Fairweather ever outside a public gallery – we had over 100 works. That was something I really wanted to do, because I believe he is the greatest artist ever associated with Queensland, so we did it. Another example was Isaac Walter Jenner; we did a big book on him. Jenner was an unknown colonial painter who came to Brisbane in 1888, as an oldish man; he was a marine painter in Brighton in England, but was virtually unknown outside Brisbane. I got the estate together and we published a splendid book – that was interesting.

We all have a mental age – I think I'm still about thirty-two. I don't think you can ever get complacent. Someone, a journalist, I think, said to me about ten years ago, 'You're the Grey Beard of art in Brisbane,' and I said, 'Who, me? Don't be ridiculous!' Later, I thought, 'Well, I suppose in terms of longevity, I am, but it's not something that I ever consciously thought about.'

My best purchase was in 1979 or 1980 in London. There was a John Peter Russell, who was known as 'the lost impressionist'; he was an Australian who went to France, where Monet used to paint with him – he had a big house on Belle-Ile. This painting of his was offered to me; it was very expensive, by far the most expensive picture I'd ever contemplated buying – but it was so wonderful. It was a big oil of Belle-Ile – it could have been a Monet. I was just leaving London and I paid some of the money there and then to secure it before going to the airport. I'd just started to deal with Lady Trout here, who was by then a widow. Her husband, Sir Leon, had been Chairman of Trustees of the Art Gallery and President of the Liberal Party. He and the Premier Bjelke Petersen and Treasurer Gordon Chalk had started the Art Gallery. She had probably eighteen or nineteen John Peter Russell's, but none as fine as this one, so I offered it to her. She'd been buying minor French Impressionists, but this was $75,000, equivalent to god knows what today! It took about a year to complete the sale and I had it hanging at home during that period. I loved it, but it represented a lot of money and I really couldn't afford to keep it. Lady Trout later died, and Christie's and I did the estate sale and that picture got $700,000, which was the highest price of anything she owned, so it was a great validation for her and me.

We did that sale in 1989. The market collapsed in 1990/91 and the person who bought it went broke. It was put up for auction again and it sold for $240,000. The person who bought it at that price put it up for auction again in 1996 and I bought it back for a client for $550,000, which was still less than it had been seven years earlier. People say you can't go wrong with art, but you can; it's all about timing. One day that picture will certainly be worth a million dollars.

I sponsor a lot of things, like Opera Australia and the Conservatorium, the Brisbane Institute, West Australian Opera, the Queensland Festival of Music. I think grants are harder to get in the performing arts. With sponsorship, it's a bit like being on boards: once you get on one, people see you and they know you, so who do they call – they call you. It's the same once you start giving. I've given a lot of money to the National Gallery – a couple of million, I guess, over the years. I was on that board as well. The Australian Chamber Orchestra has been a particular favourite of mine. I think, if you become interested in an institution and you believe in it and you are able to contribute, then you should.

The arts, generally, are really under-funded. We've got people like David Gonski supporting the philanthropic foundations that are now allowed to exist, so I think we are changing. As a city becomes more civilised these sorts of things emerge, there just have to be enough people to create a core. There was an article written about what they called 'the powerful people of Brisbane' – they did some test of who interacts with whom, with 6 to 8 degrees of separation. Because I was on quite a few things, I was one of the people who supposedly have a deep influence in Brisbane. This is kind of true, yet not true. People see interlocking boards and appointments and power structures and who influences who, and read sinister intent into it. It's not that at all. You can't ask people that you don't know to do something. It's the same with philanthropic giving; you tend to ask the same people, because they've asked you. It's a sort of daisy chain – just going round and round in a circle. Eventually more people want to join the daisy chain, because they perceive some benefits in it, social, emotional – who knows why they do it, but I just wish there were more of them. Here in Brisbane, John Hay, the former Vice-Chancellor of the Queensland University, is a fantastic person and was personally responsible for huge fund-raising. Individual people can and do make a difference!

Sue Ryan – The Lockhart River Art Gang

The art dealer, Andrew Baker, first put me in touch with Sue. Each time we speak it seems she's in a different place – last time it was Italy. The Lockhart River Art Gang's work has delighted people from Europe to the United States.

'New Apron Day' – with (left to right) Silas Hobson, Evelyn Sandy, Sue Ryan, Fiona Omeenyo and Adrian King

'I think one of the best times was taking Fiona Omeenyo and Silas Hobson to Harlem ... For the first time ever, here were these two Aboriginal artists, from a really remote community, in the middle of this big city where everyone was black ... Every two minutes I was losing the others, because they totally blended in with everyone else there and I felt a bit of a panic when they kept disappearing into shops... It was an absolute blast and the feeling that they were suddenly part of a majority group in a big city ... They said, "If we come back to New York, can we stay in Harlem?"'

I had been teaching Art at TAFE and one day I was asked to do a workshop in Aurukun. It was for the opening of Manth Thayan Arts and Cultural Centre. I went over there and met up with the Lockhart artists, who'd travelled across to the west side of the Cape; there were about seven of them, aged around fifteen and sixteen. There were a lot of people there, including the Aurukun School and Aurukun artists. That was where I first met Geoff Barker, who was to become the Arts Coordinator at Lockhart, and Fiona Manderson, who was the art teacher there. At that time they had a principal called Steve Castley, who, fortunately, had a real arts focus. He and Fiona basically got everyone going.

At that time there was no Art Centre in Lockhart River. Shortly after I had been there, Geoff Barker rang me and told me that the old Health building had been donated and they were turning it into an Art Centre. That was over ten years ago now. Geoff renovated it and became the arts coordinator. From that point on the Art Centre flourished. Geoff started them off with prints and entered them in competitions and group shows. By doing this and getting exhibited in some reasonable galleries, they gradually gained recognition.

Years later, in November 2000, I was working as an arts youth worker with Nyletta Aboriginal Corporation in Atherton when one day I had a phone call out of the blue from Geoff Barker. He said, 'There's a job going at Lockhart River as art coordinator, why don't you go for it?' I said, 'Oh no, I don't think so, I've got a really good job and I like what I'm doing.' At the time my partner Greg and I had an art and design screen-printing business. When I mentioned it to Greg, he said, 'I think we should go and have a look!' So we did, and we thought, 'Well, it's very arts focused and if we don't do it we'll never know if we should have.' So we sold our business and we moved to Lockhart, taking on the position in July 2001.

The timing was good; I came into the Lockhart River community when they were just starting to get recognition. Rosella Namok had done fairly well, Samantha Hobson had had a major piece purchased by the National Gallery of Victoria and Fiona Omeenyo had had her first show at Short Street Gallery in Broome. I had no idea about running an Art Centre, but Greg and I had been in business and having Greg there was a big help. We inherited a fairly busy exhibition schedule, so we just continued on with that and booked more exhibitions. As things got busier, we kept extending workspace and travelling with artists to the shows and getting visiting artists to come in and do workshops as well. We were organic in the way we operated; we just took advantage of opportunities as they came along.

Our main problem at the time was getting staff to work at the Art Centre. There was no accommodation suitable for visitors and so we were reliant on the local people, and those people with the skills we needed were also in demand by every other organisation in town. That put a lot of pressure on Greg and me. Building accommodation so that we could have more room for visiting artists and staff became a key priority. It's still the same today. We have a linguist, Clair Hill, who comes in to work with the people who still retain the language, so it's good for her to have somewhere to stay. Then there are documentary film makers, press, and people who do various workshops. Michael Leunig and his family have been in three times and they've had a really positive effect on various people in the community. Mike Nichols is another artist who's stayed a few times and taught the men woodcarving.

We've found it works particularly well when visitors bring their families, because that way the whole family can become involved with the community. Someone may be working in painting or in sculpture, but the rest of the family can go and take the old ladies out to collect grass and materials to make their baskets or help make lunch or just become involved with the people within the Art Centre and the community.

When we've gone overseas sometimes we've just taken one artist and at other times we've taken up to four artists. Although people invite them to their houses and have various trips planned to make them feel more at home, they feel very isolated from their community and they really miss it. Three weeks is about the limit, because by then they're starting to get really anxious and wanting to go home. When they return to the community they have a great sense of achievement that they've been away and people are really amazed at what they hear – especially about the United States. They're really into that black culture in the US, so people here are fascinated by it.

I think one of the best times was taking Fiona Omeenyo and Silas Hobson to Harlem. That was just such a blast. For the first time ever, here were these two Aboriginal artists from a really remote community in the middle of this big city where everyone was black, so they completely blended in. There was just me and another lady, Christine Zorzi, who's an Australian copyright lawyer who lives in New York, and we were about the only white people around. Every two minutes I was losing the others, because they totally blended in with everyone else there and I felt a bit of a panic when they kept disappearing into shops. It was just fantastic, there was so much colour and music and great clothing. It was an absolute blast and the feeling that they were suddenly part of a majority group in a big city. It was the first time they actually experienced that. It was pretty amazing. They said, 'If we come back to New York, can we stay in Harlem?'

The artists are still terrified by public speaking – who isn't – but they've become really good at talking to people on a one to one basis. They meet all sorts of people at exhibitions and people visiting the Art Centre. There've been state and federal politicians and lots of officials, plus bird-watchers, tourists, all sorts of people can walk in that door at any time. They just speak from their hearts about their community, the landscape and their traditional stories. They're passionate about their community, their friends and relatives and they describe their work as an integral part of their everyday life in the community. They love fishing, and so that's why many of their paintings are about fishing, or other things in the community. There's always something – even bushfires. Many of the artists believe that spirits exist everywhere and so they also paint about spirits. There are different spirits for different types of landscape. Silas paints a lot about *awu's* which is the word for spirits. Fiona paints about ancestors looking down on the living family and helping them through each day. Some of the stories are really poignant and beautiful.

Some mainstream galleries just sell the work as contemporary artwork without any explanation, because people relate to the paintings when they see them. Indigenous galleries will tend to include the story with the paintings.

Greg and I have been with the community for six years. We had felt like it was time to move on two years ago, but there is no housing in the community, so we decided to stay on to raise funds to build another house because otherwise we couldn't advertise for a management team. Finally we managed to get funding for the house, but have yet to build it. We advertised to find someone to act as manager and a fantastic French woman, Camille Talansier-Masson, applied and has joined us. She makes use of the visitors' accommodation for now. She's started the old ladies painting. They'd always been working on traditional artefacts, but now there's a movement of older ladies painting and they've started to do really well. The other artists are fine. A lot of them have moved to Cairns, so it was just the perfect timing to have something happen like that.

The Art Centre set up a studio in Cairns last year and Fiona Omeenyo works through there for the Art Centre, even though she's bought a house in Cairns and has settled there. Rosella Namok also bought a house in Cairns and also still does some work for the Centre. Samantha Hobson also moved to Cairns. Greg and I have recently left the community and plan to live in Cairns. For the time being we will still work for the Art Centre, but our roles will change quite dramatically. We are keen to work on some merchandise items to give some of the artists more of an income stream.

There have been lots of amusing stories about the painters and their work. Once I was rolling up Rosella Namok's show for an exhibition at the Hogarth Gallery. I had them all rolled up except for one big painting. It was two metres by three metres long, a massive painting, and it was basically white with a very pale blue through it. I put the coat of varnish on it to lift the colours slightly, which we often do with their paintings, and off I went home. I came back the next day to discover a frog had got in the black paint and then had jumped right across the painting, right through the centre of the painting with big frog foot-prints! I was absolutely devastated. Luckily, because it had the coat of varnish on it, I was able to carefully remove all the black footprints and recoat it with varnish – and off it went to the show.

There have been a lot of things like that. While the Art Centre's physically enclosed, there are still gaps. As a result, we'd sometimes find giant pythons rolled up in the paint and smaller ones inside the paint tins. The nurse next door, her cat had about nine little kittens and they used to come over at night and play at the Art Centre. We'd come in, in the morning and you could see where the kittens had been playing. There'd be lots little cat footprints all over the wet paintings!

331

Hidden Talents

Rosemary Penfold – Textile Art

We went to school together and I remember her then as having a lovely singing voice and a talent for sewing. Like many young mothers, after she married and had children, she stayed at home and restricted her interests to home and family needs. Now her previously hidden talent is widely recognised and a source of pride.

'Cynthia Morgan, who is a very well-known textile artist up at Caloundra, organised Australian textile artists to enter into the annual World Quilt Competition in America. I put a pair of quilts in ... I didn't realise I'd actually won until one of my co-quilter friends sent me an email saying, "Congratulations, you've won 'Best of Country'!"'

I was born in Brisbane, but left when I was probably three or four, which was just after the war. My parents were separated and we went to a little place called Miles, west of Brisbane, because my grandparents were there. Grandma and Grandpa were like the rocks in our lives and that was great.

We attended Miles State School for a couple of years and, after the divorce was through and my mother started to go out with the man who became my stepfather, we then moved to a property which was sixty miles from town. It was very isolated but pretty exciting for little kids, except that, after we'd been there about twelve months, I can remember running inside and saying to Mum, 'Now when are we going back to Daddy?' I can still see the look of horror on her face! I managed to find the courage when I was twenty-one to contact him. He was a very nice person. He actually lived in Brisbane and was quite successful in business. He started the Nifty-Thrifty Stores and did lots of things for the Independent Grocers, and things like that.

I grew up as a bush kid; I got very slack with my school correspondence – so slack that I actually slipped two years behind. After a number of years they got a bit frustrated with me and sent me off to boarding school, which I found very traumatic – I cried for the first two weeks. I should have been in Grade 7, but I went into Grade 5 in Glennie Prep in Toowoomba. Fortunately it was a lovely place; it was out on a 90-acre farm, which made a lot of us country kids feel reasonably comfortable, though the strictness was a bit ghastly. When I went to the senior boarding school I really didn't want to do anything except sing and play sport. I was probably a bit of a rebel. I used to spend all my time being what they called 'gated'! I wasn't allowed to go out, or go to any of the school dances that might have come along – not many did. We all had difficulties with some of the mistresses at Glennie. Some we loved and some we absolutely couldn't stand, but that's living in a community, I guess. I remember Miss Knapp and Miss Guymer; they were really clever people and probably should have been mathematicians or research scientists, so as teachers they would have had their frustrations as well.

I ended up getting into so much trouble that I pleaded with my mother and stepfather to allow me to leave school before I actually finished my junior and they said, 'Well, what do you want to do?' and I said, 'I'd like to go to one of the conservatories and study singing.' My stepfather said, 'I don't think you've got the voice for it. No!' I stayed home for eighteen months, but after that I just had to go, so it was decided that I should do nursing. I went to the Royal Brisbane and, boy, did I learn about life quickly there! There was no protection, I can tell you, except they used to lock us up at midnight!

I made lots of friends at Royal Brisbane and had quite a good time. Most of the time I spent there, I think it was eleven and a half months, I was at the children's hospital and I absolutely loved that. They used to have sewing machines that the girls could use on their days off and I used to make clothes and things, which I'd always done. The Matrons were quite impressed with that.

After the Children's Hospital, they sent me to Rosemount, which was the worst place in the world. We were rostered on twelve hours a day, six days a week. Rosemount was where they sent people who were dying. It was terribly sad and too much for me. It was hideous; we didn't have time to comfort patients. I left in a fortnight. My stepfather was pretty furious at me for throwing it in, so I stayed at home and worked again and helped with things. Then some old school friends, the Poole twins, rang me up and said, 'We're going to go to Brisbane to get a job – you coming?' I left home pretty promptly and we got a flat and I got a job at Weedmans in Brisbane. There were four of us in the flat and it was great. Over the years various girls got married or found boyfriends and the second lot of girls who came in with me introduced me to my husband. It was Kaye Adnam that introduced Russell and his friend Ian to me. Russell asked me out for about six months before I relented and said, 'Oh, OK.' He actually turned out to be quite nice. When we actually became an item, he said, 'The first time I saw you was at Lanky Mitchell's New Year's Eve party,' and I said, 'Oh, were you there?' and he said, 'Yes, I was there,' and he described the dress I had on and that was the first and last time he's been able to describe the dress I wore! Anyway we went out together for three and a half years and during that time I had lots of different flat mates and went air-hostessing. I was talked into that by my various flat mates and I enjoyed it. I didn't think he was ever going to marry me so I broke it off, but then we got back together again and that was good – that's a story in itself!

Russ's family owned Greyhound Coaches and he built that up to be an enormous company. Russ was running a 24-hour 7-day-a-week business, so there were times when we didn't see a lot of each other. He'd get home late at night and the kids would probably be doing their homework by then. We'd try to eat together as much as possible, but he was interstate quite a lot, so I became involved in community things, helping at the kindergartens and schools, which most mothers in those days did. When my youngest son was in Grade 12, I figured I could make myself scarce, so I opted out of the school uniform shop. That's when I started to sew.

Russ and I went on a fishing trip in Hawaii in 1983 and I got the flu and I ended up in bed sick, so I went out to buy something to read and I found this little patchwork magazine and that was the start of me doing patchwork. We have a little regional show out here (the Brookfield Show) and it used to have a small handicrafts section and I put a quilt in there one day for one of the shows and won second prize. The second prize was much better than the first prize, in that it was practical, so I was pretty pleased with that.

We lost our business at the start of the crash in '89. It was a very, very sad day, but because we'd managed to live reasonably carefully, we were able to keep our home and Russell had his superannuation. It happened at the time of deregulation. They allowed six new licences over the top of us, which took all the profit out of it, and everybody went bust! For the bus industry, it was an absolute nightmare.

For a few years I kept putting stuff into the Brookfield Show, then there was this woman, Pam Deshon, who had a patchwork shop out at River Hills, and she said, 'Rosie, I wish you'd come and teach for me,' and I said, 'Oh, I don't think I could do that.' I mulled it over for about six months and then I toddled off to the Ithaca TAFE and did the Instructional Skills Course. Then I bounced into Pam and I said, 'I can teach now, I've been to Ithaca TAFE!' This was in about 1990 and I taught from then on for the next ten years – and I grew a lot. You think about the lovely, wonderful people in your life. Pam was a very special person in my life. She became a really firm friend, even if she was my boss. I still miss her dearly and she's been dead for over three years now.

Then I started to enter competitions and I went to art classes and that sort of thing, so that's how I became a textile artist. I guess people get into patchwork and quilting because they love pattern. I got to a stage where I got sick of doing someone else's patterns and started to do a little bit of designing myself. The various art classes that I went to also encouraged me to do more creative work. At heart I am a very practical person, which is how it started. The first piece I made for myself was a bedspread to go on a bed in our little log cabin up at Somerset Dam, which we use for waterskiing and fishing. I looked at it the other day; it has '85' on it.

That was over twenty years ago and the whole time I was doing that, putting fabrics together, I was worrying about colour, so I made it my aim to go to as many workshops as I could to learn about colour. I learnt a lot about colour and I did some workshops on teaching people how to look at colour. Everyone's eyes register light refractions in different ways, so you have to understand if people put two colours *you* don't like together.

There's a tried and true method of doing patchwork. You make a top, you have a filling and you have a bottom and you quilt those together. I was teaching them the technical knowledge as well as trying to encourage them to look at what they're doing in the colour side of things. Then I ran a few classes on how to create different designs, not just a patterned design, but a free design for maybe a wall-hanging or something like that.

In lots of ways I'm still very structured, because I still like the traditional quilt format, where I make a top, I have a wadding, and I have a back and then I quilt it together – and I do like my edges tidy. There are a lot of textile artists out there who have ragged edges and things like that. I've done a few little pieces that are very untidy, I suppose, in some people's minds, but they're free. I am still growing.

I've now got to the stage where I rarely use the materials you get from the patchwork shops. I dye a lot of my own fabrics. In the last lot of works that I made I actually dyed silk and then cut them into curved strips. I stuck all these strips onto one plain piece of dyed silk and created light and dark movement, then, over the top of that, I had silk again, and then I quilted it down. The silks were different weights and the silk on the top was a silk organza, so you could see through to the other layers. I guess it was representing the layers you see when you look at any given element – there are always layers there. That exhibition was called *Source to Sea*. There was one I called *Farmer's Touch*, where the manipulation of the curved strips depicted the different colours and things you get when digging the soil. The plain cotton pieces that were in curved strips I guess represented other solids, the soil and the trees, basically. There was one piece there called *Flood* and it was depicting the river in flood, so the bottom layer was rusted and dyed and then on top of that it was printed with prints of leaf structures, then it had two layers of silk organza over the top of that. One was a greeny colour and the other was a browny colour. They weren't cut pieces, they were just big pieces layered.

Through the various facets of life, you meet some wonderful people who encourage you. One of these was Cynthia Morgan, a very well-known textile artist up at Caloundra who organised Australian textile artists to enter into the annual World Quilt Competition in America. I put a pair of quilts into the competition and I didn't realise I'd won until one of my co-quilter friends sent me an email saying, 'Congratulations, you've won "Best of Country"!'

Since about '92, I've been selected in various juried exhibitions, in Australia and Japan and the US. It's probably fairly prestigious to be represented in those places, because they're high profile exhibitions that they have. But when you get selected, it's just for the privilege of being in the exhibition. The last time I sent a piece over it was so expensive to send that my husband said, 'Why are you doing this?' and I said, 'I don't know!

I'm still making quilts, but right now I'm looking in another direction. I've always been interested in layers and I want to learn how to create the feeling of layers, using all different media. I want people to look at my work and see depth as well as colour. I'm forever learning.

Helen Sanderson – Art and Artist's books

She travels regularly and each time makes a tiny book as a record of what she's seen. These little books are expertly hand-bound, with each page individually painted – art-works in miniature ...

'When I draw in situ, I always use a black pen drawing directly into the book. At the end of the day I get the water colours out, a glass of wine ... and I work up the image in colour. I try to show the things about a place that I find different, the things that are unique. It may be the people and how they dress, how the old people congregate at dusk for a chat in a cobbled back street, the iron work, or the tiles, or a fascinating roofline with chimney pots.'

I was born in Ballandean, a little village in the fruit growing district midway between Stanthorpe and the New South Wales border. Both my parents grew up in Ballandean and, like them, I went to the local primary school. I remember drawing in the dirt on the old parade ground. I enjoyed the process of drawing and still do.

At age thirteen I went to boarding school in Warwick, to St Catherine's Church of England Girls School, mainly, I think, because my father had gone to the boys' equivalent, Slade School. Later I became a secondary school art teacher and my first appointment, at age nineteen years and one month, was to Stanthorpe High School. I loved it. At the end of the first year, I visited my eldest brother and his wife, who were newly married and working for Mount Isa mines. I met my husband Don at their home in Mount Isa at a New Year's Eve party. Don worked with my sister-in-law in the computer department.

We came to Brisbane after we married. I taught briefly at a local high school on the outskirts of Brisbane and then found work at All Hallows, a large inner city Catholic girl's school, teaching in the art department. It was wonderful. When I arrived at the door, I was greeted by an enthusiastic mob of children, who were so eager to do art. It was probably one of the most exciting periods of teaching I ever had. In addition, I was to teach a couple of classes at the Catholic university, which was located on-site then. I would have been about twenty-two years old. During this time I co-wrote a book with Sister Jeanette Collis on macramé. It was released just after our son Christopher was born. I stopped teaching when I had him and three years later we had our daughter Jacelyn.

I started a little business at home hand-painting garments and fabrics. I found a factory to put the garments together. I had been employed by a fashion designer in the city to paint their last season's linen, silk and cotton fabrics. They didn't want to use last season's fabrics again, and also didn't want to waste them. So I would change the look of the fabrics by painting them. Invariably there was a disaster. I might be working on a 10-metre length of fabric and I'd get to the fifth metre and drop my paintbrush – and some of these fabrics were $100 a metre! The first time was horrendous, but I learned how to handle situations like that. Invariably the solution involved recreating the same effect in other places, to make it look as though it was intended and to absorb it into the whole piece. I felt empowered by knowing that, whatever happened, I could work with it. I think I'm now a braver artist.

The business was doing quite nicely and I probably could have gone on with it, but I wanted to be an exhibiting artist, so I stopped and went back to do further visual arts studies at QUT and since about 1991 I've been exhibiting my work. Early on I was invited to participate in an exhibition called *Paper as Object*. There were many Australian and international artists involved. I was one of several Australian artists invited to work collaboratively with a paper industry partner. I worked with Edwards Dunlop Paper, a paper distribution house. For seven months, I had access to their paper products and facilities. My palette became vast amounts of commercial papers and an industrial guillotine. The guillotine was at least 1.5 metres wide and the blade about 30 centimetres high. It could cut through a 20 centimetre depth of paper in a flash.

My work *Which Colour White* is a series of sculptural books, using the vast numbers of white papers they sell. When the pages are fanned open, it exposes a soft range of what appear to be delicate colours ... blues, greys, yellows and lilacs. However, each page is, in fact, white, and it is the colour cast of the whites that gives the illusion of colour. I also created a series of little paper liquorice pieces, using guillotined papers and industrial flexible PVA glues.

Like a lot of artists, I have done many different things. The one consistent thing I have done since childhood is draw. I have always loved drawing. My first travel book was a gift from Adele Outteridge, who made me a tiny little book as a gift when I went to Turkey. She thought I might draw in it. I took a bum-bag with a small travelling artist's studio in it, consisting of the book, a water-colour paint set and some pens. I drew every day in situ all around Turkey. It was magic. The pages were so little; I felt I couldn't say I didn't have time to do a drawing.

Nowadays I have learned from Adele how to make my own books. To make a little book, I start by taking an imperial-sized quality piece of 100% cotton water colour paper, and fold it into halves, and rip it with an old bread and butter knife. This gives nice torn edges to the paper. The process is repeated several times to create the pages. I make cardboard covers and cover them with paper or leather. The pages are folded in half. I then use an awl to pierce the pages one at a time before stitching. I use a couple of book-binders' needles with waxed linen threads with a simple variation of Coptic binding. I can make a little book up in about an hour and a half.

For many reasons I found the trip to Turkey was beneficial. I loved the history, I met some wonderful people who've stayed good friends, and I found drawing again. I've always loved documenting and storytelling, and I loved the way that I could show this book to people to tell the story of the trip. For me it is more intimate and tells 'my' story. That first little book was in 1997. Before that I had always drawn when I'd gone away, often in journals, with a different intent, whereas now I do these books and the process has become more refined. Since then, Don has worked in many interesting overseas destinations and, through work I have done when I've gone with him, I have about twenty little travel books.

The drawings in these books, while never exhibited, inform my art work in many ways, and are vital to my art practice. While the intent of doing them is intensely personal, the outcome has a more universal appeal. When I draw in situ, I always use a black pen drawing directly into the book. At the end of the day I get the water colours out, a glass of wine and I work up the image in colour. I try to show the things about a place that I find different, the things that are unique. It may be the people and how they dress, how the old people congregate at dusk for a chat in a cobbled back street, the iron work, or the tiles or a fascinating roofline with chimney pots. It may be some grape vines in some faraway place that remind me of my wonderful childhood home. I also draw from memory and I use my digital camera too.

When we went to Antarctica, I took many books to draw in. Some of the books had one long concertina page which allowed me to draw long continuous imagery of the white wilderness landscape as we sailed past. It was just so exciting. With other books I dyed the pages with rich blue Procion dyes. My little bum-bag studio had to be a little bigger there, to accommodate the additional gesso and white acrylic paint.

Over the years I have belonged to various arts organisations here in Brisbane. They provide educational opportunities, and opportunities to talk and share information with likeminded people. There is much overlap between my particular interests and those of my work practices. One such organisation is ADFAS, the Australian Decorative and Fine Arts Society. They run a series of informative lectures and study days throughout the year. I recently completed six years working on the board of directors of TAFTA (The Australian Forum for Textile Arts). TAFTA has inspired, encouraged and changed the lives of many people for the better, through its workshop and conference program that operates in various venues around Australia. Most importantly, people have a lot of fun. I now have a network of friends and art colleagues from all over Australia, New Zealand and America and other parts of the world due to TAFTA. The caring mentorship undertaken by members of this organisation, one for the other, is remarkable.

I have made many artists' books, shown in many book exhibitions, had my books acquired in significant book collections, and curated several book exhibitions as well. I am currently working on curating a second international art exchange exhibition, *In Your Dreams*. This show has thirty artists from Australia, Canada and Germany. It provides international exposure to ten Australian artists, six are Queenslander.

The artist's book is a complete sculptural object within itself. The content, the presentation, the binding and the shape of the object are all equally important and related. Often the specific structure of the book allows the artist to communicate the content of the book. Contemporary artists in recent times have taken on the book form and, as artists do, they have pushed the concept of what defines a book beyond conventions and mainstream notions. The content of these works covers a wide sphere of interests, from the personal, the political, the poetic, the playful, whatever is meaningful in the artists' lives. The book is a container of information, which is experienced sequentially. Marcel Duchamp reportedly said that an artists' book is one that the artist says is an artist's book! That pretty much sums it up. People are very familiar with the vehicle of a book for getting information across to them. It is a simple step from an everyday experience to an art experience.

I think it is an important aspect of books that holding a book and turning the pages gives such pleasure. I think that's partly why people enjoy my little travel books. There is an intimacy associated with the experience of opening such a little 'treasure'. Going to an artists' book exhibition is a very exhausting exercise, because, apart from the fact that they make you put white gloves on to protect the work, which makes opening the pages that much more difficult, you have to actively participate – you have to handle the books. There are very few artists that only make artists' books. Most artists include it as part of their practice and it's invariably the part that they love the most, and the part that earns the least money!

Storytelling

Nick Earls – Novelist

The art of storytelling is as old as man himself, in ancient times the story teller being the collective memory of his people. The role of today's storyteller has changed, but is

no less important for that; he can transport us away from our 'everyday' to a place where we laugh or weep with the characters he's created. What, though, of the individual who weaves this magic? Nick works in a small shed nestled under the shade of flowering trees in the back of his Brisbane garden. Here the characters born in his mind take shape on the printed page. With the art of a true storyteller he enchants his listener.

'... at pre-school, they asked each day if anyone had any news ... we were four, we hardly ever had news; four-year-olds don't have a lot of news ... So I came up with my own formula story and each day, day after day, I would get up and tell another episode of it. My formula story was about a bird called Tommy who would begin each adventure by being flushed down the toilet, emerging at the other end of the sewage system to a land of poo and big orange diggers and another day's grave danger.'

I knew I wanted to be a writer when I was very young and lived in Northern Ireland. I might have been two or three and my mother and father would read bedtime stories to my sister Alison and me. Sometimes my mother would make stories up. She had a formula story in which the central characters, who (by no coincidence) had the same names as my sister and me, went into the woods near where we lived, but when they walked into the woods they'd find a clearing that didn't exist in the real woods near our house. In the middle of this clearing there was a block of flats inhabited by witches. They were nice witches and they were colour-coded witches! Each night Alison and Nick would go off and have some adventure with a witch according to that witch's particular colour. So, if they met the Red Witch they might go off in a red MG for a lunch of jam sandwiches and be given presents such as a cricket ball or a fire-fighter's hard hat.

Later, at pre-school, they asked each day if anyone had any news ... we were four, we hardly ever had news; four-year-olds don't have a lot of news. So I came up with my own formula story and each day, day after day, I would get up and tell another episode of it. My formula story was about a bird called Tommy who would begin each adventure by being flushed down the toilet, emerging at the other end of the sewage system to a land of poo and big orange diggers and another day's grave danger. Storytelling was part of me from very early in life!

We left Northern Ireland for a range of reasons and arrived here about three months before I turned nine. I think I've had the frankest discussions with my parents about these reasons in the past year or so. My childhood in Northern Ireland never figured in my writing until my tenth book, *The Thompson Gunner*, which came out in August 2004. It was only after I'd written seven books that I started to think it was maybe a bit odd that I'd shut that out of my writing and then I realised that in some respects I'd shut it out of my life. My life in Northern Ireland was rather different to life here as a nine-year-old. It was a difficult time in Northern Ireland in 1972. It was not a great place to bring up children. My parents never made a big deal of that in conversation at the time, but that was why we moved. My mother, being a doctor, had qualifications that were recognised in a lot of places. My father was a management consultant and still is, really. Brisbane was a place that my father could transfer to within his company and where they knew that my mother would get medical work, so out we came.

Towards the end of my time at school, I knew that what I really wanted to be was a writer. I looked around and I couldn't see, at that stage, a creative writing course that I was particularly keen to do, so I considered my options. My mother was a GP then, and still was until relatively recently. I'd heard lots of interesting stories from her. Her father had been a doctor as well, so I'd heard about his experience of being a GP in Yorkshire during the '20s and '30s and for decades after that. So I'd had a lot of medical stories around me and medicine had always sounded like an interesting thing to study, so I decided I'd do that – and I did. I never regretted it.

It was fairly hard work at times, but I thought maybe I'll be able to find myself in a position where I could write part time and practice medicine part time and perhaps have the best of both worlds. I did a lot of writing and I wrote hundreds of thousands of words that will never see the light of day. Living in Queensland in the 1980s, you felt that you were a long, long way from the world's writing industries and a long way from published novelists. I had my first book, a collection of short stories, published in 1992; it was fairly experimental and not a commercial success.

It took me a while to find a way of writing that was both right for me and part of my repertoire, and that people might also want to read! I think that I forgot that in the 1980s. I think I tried to be too clever early on. If you want to connect, you've got to actually do it on a human level and you've got to bear accessibility in mind when putting a story together.

My luck changed in the mid '90s. Having written maybe four complete novel manuscripts that were never published, I wrote *After January*, which spun off from a short story I'd written for a young adult anthology. It had started quite small and I kept it quite small. I kept the world that it operated in contained and tried to do justice to it on its own terms – it felt like a new experience for me. People responded in a completely different way to my previous manuscripts and UQ Press signed it up. It came out in 1996 and had to be reprinted in a matter of weeks. I thought, 'Maybe I'm onto something here!'

Zigzag Street also came out in '96 and I remember it got a good response at the start – a response that I just wasn't used to and bookstores were re-ordering in good numbers. I went overseas for about a month or so, about a month after it came out, and while I was away I was thinking, 'I wonder how my book's faring?' I remember getting back and landing at the airport and my father-in-law picking us up from the airport and holding in his hand a Mary Ryan Top Ten and in it *Zigzag Street* was number one! That's when I thought, 'Maybe this could be a bit different for me now.' Meanwhile, I'd been writing *Bachelor Kisses* and that came out here in early '98 at the same time as *Zigzag Street* came out in the UK. That was the time that I had to break off my connection with medical work. At that stage I'd moved from being a part-time GP to being a part-time medical editor. I'd reduced my work to about twelve hours a week or so, but suddenly in early '98 I had to face the fact that I had three months of touring going on here and in the UK. It was impossible to hold down a medical job any more.

I'd met Sarah at a party in 1989. I was going out with Karen at the time, who was a singer and we wrote songs together. Shortly after I met Sarah at a party, Karen and I went to London for three months to try to crack the English music scene. We worked really hard at it, but in the end didn't get anywhere and came back to Brisbane and won the Shell Young Performers Award, which led to Karen doing a lot of performing and a lot of singing. I realised that I had to perform as well, so I ended up doing three consecutive weekends in the Botanic Gardens as a storytelling armchair for children.

In latish 1989, my relationship with Karen ended and things developed with Sarah. I'm still in contact with Karen, who's now a successful singer in New York. I was a GP at Taringa, working maybe 24 hours a week in general practice and writing the rest of the time. I was writing for advertising, writing shows for Sea World – a whole range of different things. From the start Sarah was very supportive of that side of me. I think she probably believed in it a bit more than I did at the time, and she's believed in it throughout. It's been very good to be able to repay the earlier years of support by actually delivering something, by turning this into the career that we both hoped that I would have. Just about every year I'll have a work reason to go overseas, because a book's come out or something like that, so Sarah will take time off work for at least part of that and we'll have some holiday time as well and we both get a lot out of that.

I can remember when I started writing for money; the first things I started writing were advertising jingles. I wrote the song for Lasseter's Lost Mine Ride at Sea World. It was exciting to think that there I was, working in a hospital at the time and, on my hours off, which were often well into the evening, I could turn up at a recording studio and go to work and write this kind of thing.

I've had experiences that you don't expect as a writer. For example, a few years ago I got to be part of a celebrity canoe race, as part of Regatta Fest in Brisbane – which was really convenient, because I live a few hundred metres from the Regatta and I agreed to be part of this celebrity canoe race, thinking, 'This is going to be a disgrace, because, while I'm reasonably fit, my fitness comes from running, so I have no upper body fitness, I'm no canoer!' So I said, 'Please, give me someone with shoulders, give me Susie O'Neill, someone who can really paddle a canoe.' I turned up on the day and there were various people from Channel Nine and B105 and sports people and I ended up with Mal Meninga as my canoe partner. We got in the canoe and off we went, and it really was like the canoe scene from *Shallow Hal* with me in the bow right out of the water, hardly able to reach the water with my paddle and Mal the engine-room down the back. Each time I leaned over far enough to get my paddle into the water, all I ended up doing was flicking water back on Mal and, as we crossed the finish line, I looked around and there was Mal Meninga sitting in a pool of water. With a quick change of clothing and a beer in his hand, everything was good. We actually came fourth! If anyone had said to me years before, when I'd been writing hard, desperate to get a book published, 'Don't worry, one day you'll find yourself as an author in a celebrity canoe race with Mal Meninga,' I wouldn't have believed them.

There have been some great things that have happened quite recently. The *48 Shades of Brown* film was released as *48 Shades* by Buena Vista International (Disney) in cinemas in Australia in August 2006 and on DVD early in 2007. It screened at festivals in LA, Fort Lauderdale, Montreal, London, Dublin and Moscow and was sold in a number of international markets at Cannes in 2007. This is the first time anything of mine's become a feature film. That's a really big deal; that's an exciting thing. I've had people working on developing my books into films for nearly ten years, so even though I've had quite a few books published during that time, that's been a hurdle I haven't jumped until now.

My novel, *Monica Bloom,* came out in August 2006. When I sat down to write it in 2005, I realised that I was enjoying the process of writing it and I thought, 'This is a sign that you are doing what you should be doing.' To be writing your eleventh book and feeling as excited about it creatively as you felt about the first, that's a really good sign. Subsequently, I've had *Joel and Cat Set the Story Straight* (co-written with Rebecca Sparrow) published in August 2007.

I think it's up to those of us who are doing this job now and having books published to push things as far as we can so that the people who are starting writing now can see a path that they can follow. Publishers are much more willing to look at Queensland as a source of fiction and non-fiction and that applies in Australia and to some extent around the world. Also, it's much easier to conduct the job from wherever you want now. David Malouf had to catch a boat to London in 1954 to begin a writing career. I walk ten metres down my backyard every day and email people. I've got agents where I need them, I can live where I want and we can all do business internationally from wherever we choose to live. I think that's been a big help. I've been really excited to see the changes in this industry in our part of the world over the past ten years or so, and I hope we can push on and do more.

Making Music

John Curro – Founder, Queensland Youth Orchestra

We meet at his home, an old colonial on the cliff-top overlooking the river at New Farm. On the walls there are photos of John taken with various celebrities. He's humble about these occasions and the many accolades, saying how good it was for the orchestra and how well they'd played ...

'...we played the Beethoven with Yehudi and one little overture, that's all he wanted to do, just play the Beethoven. They interviewed him in the Women's Weekly afterwards and he said it's one of the best youth orchestras he's ever had anything to do with!'

I was born in Cairns in North Queensland and my parents were migrants. Funnily enough, they met in Australia. My father was one of those impoverished refugees who had fled the Depression in Sicily. My mother came from the other end of Italy, near Turin. My father tried everything. He tried cane-cutting, but he thought that would get him nowhere. He tried hair-dressing for a while. In fact, there was a notice in the window of a shop in Ingham, I think it was, that said, 'Hairdresser wanted', so he walked in and said, 'I'm a hairdresser' – and he got the job. He'd never cut anybody's hair in his life! He taught himself to play the violin and actually played for silent movies. I was sent down to Brisbane to be educated and, at seventeen, after finishing school at Nudgee College, I went to the university at St Lucia to study architecture. My parents came down to Brisbane to find me a place to stay and while they were here bought the Regatta Hotel in Coronation Drive – so we never went back. We were at the Regatta for the period of my architecture course, which was about six years. Then, after that, my father bought and sold various properties and became, how would you say – an investor. He did well, but he always had a slight hankering for the horses, so instead of doing phenomenally well, he just did quite well.

I got into music totally by accident. A doctor friend of mine and I played tennis together every Sunday. There was an Italian violinist coming who was a friend of his. He said, 'Guess who's coming to play tennis with us on Sunday?' I said, 'Who?' He said, 'Alfredo Campoli!' I said, 'I've never heard of him.' He said, 'But you're a violin player?' I said, 'No I'm not; I just played when I was young; my parents made me learn.' He said, 'Well, he's coming to play.' So he came, this famous violinist Campoli from England – a wonderful player and a good tennis player too. He said, 'Ah, Johnny, Doctor tells me you're a violinist as well!' I said, 'No, I just used to play a little bit when I was young.' He said, 'Well, I've got a concert on Saturday and I'll have two tickets for you at the box office.' A bit reluctantly, I went to the concert, but when he started playing, I thought, '*That's* what I want to do!'

I finished my architecture degree and told my father I needed post-graduate architectural studies in Europe, so he gave me some money and I went and studied the violin instead! He got very annoyed about that and I had to go back to Rome where I got myself a half-day job with architects and kept up my violin studies for about three years. After returning to Australia, by this time my father understood my interest in music, I was always going to go back to Rome, but never did. I had almost given up the idea of a musical career, when the conservatorium got a new teacher with a good reputation, Jan Sedivka. He's now in Hobart, an old gentleman in his eighties, but still teaching. I thought I'll give him a try and he changed my life! He is a teaching genius and at that late age in my life he actually managed to show me how I could play. I met my wife Carmel in the early '60s, while she was a student at the conservatorium and I was a part-time student. She was studying piano and singing and graduated in '65. At the time I had an architectural firm going with two of my friends from university days, and I decided that the only way I'd really get on with the violin was if I left the profession. I auditioned for the ABC orchestra and got in, and that was that!

I spent a few years there and then they asked me to come and teach at the conservatorium, which I did for twenty years or so, the final few as head of the string department. I got into conducting equally accidentally. A friend of mine on the Secondary School Music Teachers' Association thought it would be a good idea if they had a Festival of Youth Secondary Schools' Music. They thought a combined Secondary Schools Orchestra would be a good thing and asked would I put it together. I said, 'OK, I'll do my best,' so we did a concert and afterwards I said to the students, 'That was nice.' It wasn't, of course. It was a terrible concert, but those were early days. At the end of it there was a big delegation from the orchestra that said, 'We'd like to keep the orchestra going.' That was the birth of the Youth Orchestra! That was in 1966. Dad died in 1968 when the QYO was just two years old. Since then it's turned into a fabulous orchestra, but it was all very low key in the early years.

At the start, we were in the gymnasium of Brisbane Boys Grammar School. We used to move in on Saturday mornings and move out again after the rehearsal. This went on for about twenty-five years in various locations. St Mary's, Kangaroo Point; the Holy Trinity Anglican Church Hall, just past the Valley; the Prince Alfred Night Club, down here round Ivory Street – and many more. It was the Coalition Ahern government who wrote to us and said, 'We are planning to turn the old museum into an arts and crafts and music centre for organisations such as yours. Will you participate in the project?' We said, 'Yes, of course we will!' The building was a real mess, as it had been disused for a long time. The museum had moved out years before, and it was full of pigeons and poor homeless people, who used to sleep in there at night. The doors and the windows were broken and there was dirt and dust everywhere, but there was this big room where Burt Hinkler's plane used to hang, a big square room. I thought, 'That looks like a good place for a rehearsal,' and, as it turned out, that room was the site of Brisbane's first concert hall in the late nineteenth century. It was a beautiful hall, seating about 700 people, with a proper pipe organ behind the stage. The organ was later moved to the city hall and upgraded – it's still there.

It's a fascinating building with a lot of history. Nellie Melba sang in that room. Paderewski played in that room. John McCormack sang there. It was a very famous concert hall in its day. We babysat the building for the government. Finally, Pat Combin, who was the Arts Minister at the time, brought a delegation from the government to have a look at the museum. I said to him, 'Why don't you restore the concert hall to what it was?' He said, 'That's the smartest suggestion we've had yet!' Restorations to the building commenced. It's still an ongoing thing. Subsequent governments have spent about $3 million on it.

In my own family, Carmel has an excellent voice but chose to look after the rest of us rather than pursue a career of her own. I don't know how we'd have managed without her love and care. She still enjoys playing the organ at the local parish church on Sundays, and singing in an Irish choir. We have four musicians out of our five children. Monica is Associate Principal Second in the Melbourne Symphony, that's the eldest girl. The second eldest, Sarah, freelances with Orchestra Victoria M.S.O., A.C.O., et cetera. Dan is still at home. He's a cellist. He does a lot of freelance cello playing, and the youngest has just renewed his interest in the violin. The middle boy has a career in IT and works at All Hallows School looking after their computer equipment. That's Jonathan. And the youngest, Dave, is also doing an arts course at the uni, because he wants to be a writer.

The Youth Orchestra is basically a program that keeps youngsters away from worse things at the weekends, and, in the process, we teach them how to play orchestrally. The orchestra's in demand for all kinds of things, for example, we played for the free concert with the rock group, Whitlams, in New Farm Park for the River Festival. We recently came back from our tenth International Tour of Festivals in Italy and Germany. It is hard work, but it's also very satisfying and the young musicians love it. We play in many great concert halls in Europe. In Germany we played at the Bamberg Symphony Hall, the main hall in Ulm, Wurtzburg Cathedral and at the Academie outside Munich. There's also a concert hall outside Munich at one of the monasteries, where we played. In Italy we played three open-air concerts, one in Hadrian's Villa near Tivoli, which is set up for summer festivals. They've had a festival there for ten years. We played at Santa Fiora – a kind of natural amphitheatre – and we played in Florence, right next to the Ponte Vecchio. We've done ten international tours now, including three international festivals, one in 1980 as the host orchestra. Not all members of the QYO are music students. Some of them are pharmacists, others are doctors and vets and scientists and teachers and dentists et cetera, but over the years there've been more and more music-based students, because they like the kind of training we give them. They really enjoy the opportunities to go on tour. We go about every four years. It helps them in their profession. We've had lots of awards, including the Queen Elizabeth Award, the TOAN Awards, and the Critics Award for best contribution to music in Queensland. I get a lot of awards that truly belong to the Youth Orchestra, such as the Bernard Heinz and Don Banks Awards for contribution to Australian music. There have been others too: an MBE, AM and two honorary doctorates from the University of Queensland (St Lucia) and Griffith University; also the Paul Harris Fellow from Rotary, even though I'm not a Rotarian. The walls are covered with them and most of them are through the joint efforts of the orchestra and me.

Playing for Peter Ustinov was a pretty nice moment. We did *Peter and the Wolf* together to raise money for the Freedom from Hunger campaign. When we walked out after the first rehearsal I said, 'Between you and me, I don't think we would have too much credibility doing a concert for Freedom from Hunger' – I'm not small, but he was a huge man, a wonderful character!

When we played during Brisbane Expo in 1988, Yehudi Menuhin came and wanted to play, but there wasn't an orchestra available for him, so his agent asked if the Youth Orchestra would do it. I said, 'It's impossible – we open an international festival the night before and we do our own concert the night after the Sunday that you talk about.' But they offered us pots of money and I couldn't refuse! So we played the Beethoven with Yehudi and one little overture. They interviewed him in the Women's Weekly afterwards and he said it's one of the best youth orchestras he's ever had anything to do with!' There have been lots of those wonderfully golden moments. We were very busy at Expo. We'd decided we'd run an International Youth Orchestra Festival and we got the support of the Expo people. In fact, they awarded us the best arts event at the biennial festival in Australia that year.

We played for the Queen's Silver Jubilee visit to Australia in Cloudland in 1977. There was a special piece that was written for her by Malcolm Williamson who was the Queen's Master of Music at the time. I've got photos of the Queen and Prince Philip and me at Cloudland. She said to us she thought our performance was by far the best. No doubt she says the same to everybody who plays wherever she goes!

Another nice story was when Rolf Harris turned up to do a concert for the Premier's special command performance at the festival hall in aid of the Children's Hospital Appeal, and they couldn't get a professional orchestra, so they asked if we'd do it. Rolf was *really* concerned – school kids doing difficult stuff! This was in the late '70s. He turned up and we had a rehearsal, late afternoon after school, about 3:30 or something. Rolf said to me beforehand, 'Look, we've got a rehearsal today and another one on the day of the concert. We'll probably need more.' I said, 'Don't worry about it, just hop in and see what you think.' He was blown away. He became one of our patrons and he'd gladly perform with us any time. He came and sang at the opening of that international biennial festival for us at no charge. He did a charity concert for us in London to try and help us defray some of our expenses when on tour. He's been one of our staunchest patrons ever since.

Now, after all those years with the QYO, I wonder how much longer I will be spared to continue this wonderful work. I could think of worse ways to leave this life than in the middle of a Mahler symphony!

Paul Dean – The Southern Cross Soloists

They're a small and innovative group of six musicians, including bassoon, Leesa Dean; clarinet, Paul Dean; French horn, Peter Luff; oboe, Tania Frazer; piano, Kevin Power; and soprano, Margaret Schindler. They're currently ensemble-in-residence at the Queensland Conservatorium of Music. I remember going to a friend's birthday party in Spring Hill, where they gave a small concert. It was a total joy for everyone – including the neighbours – the strains of Schubert's Romance, among other lovely pieces, floating on the night air.

Front row, seated, left to right: Margaret Schindler and Leesa Dean
Back row: Tania Frazer, Peter Luff, Paul Dean and Kevin Power

'Wayne Stuart, the great Australian piano maker... I approached him about bringing a piano up to the Bangalow festival ... there's not a forklift that can fit into the hall to put it on the stage, so I give the Bangalow Rugby team a carton of beer or a tab at the local pub for the night to come in half way through training on Monday or Tuesday night of festival week and lift it onto the stage – that's how the piano gets there!'

I was born into a home that brimmed with music. Some of my earliest memories are of my brothers practising their instruments. My brothers are seven and five years older than I am, so by the time I was four or five they were playing pretty well. My eldest brother Craig plays the oboe and my middle brother Brett the viola. Brett has gone on to be one of the most famous composers and one of the best viola players in the world. He spent fifteen years in the viola section of the Berlin Philharmonic. He played the violin from the age of seven.

Two of my great-grandfathers were musicians in England. My two grandmothers were both very active musicians in Brisbane. My dad's mum was the lead violin of the Ithaca Orchestra and the Kaiser Orchestra. The Ithaca Orchestra amalgamated with the Samson Orchestra in the '30s. In the '40s, the Samson Orchestra became the Queensland Symphony Orchestra.

My brother Brett used to go down every afternoon after school and play his violin with Nana. She'd had a terrible car accident in the '60s and was lucky to survive, so I think having Brett playing the violin with her every afternoon was really good for her –

and it wasn't too bad for him either! My other grandmother was an influential church musician, organist and singing teacher. She sang at the opening of the city hall and often sang on radio with her own concert party. My mother became a very good singer and organist, but, of course, she dropped that to raise the family, as women were almost forced to in those days. Mum's maiden name was Joyce Sutch and her claim to fame was that she often used to come second in the singing Eisteddfods to Margretta Elkins.

There certainly was a lot of music on both sides of our family. My father is virtually tone deaf, but it was probably his love of classical music that more than anything else caused my brothers and I to become passionate about music. He was one of the very first members of the World Record Club and I remember as a kid the great excitement when a parcel of records arrived. Even now, when a parcel arrives I still get that sense of excitement. We had quite a serious LP collection of classical music, of which a certain number of pieces still hold a very strong memory for me, particularly the Mendelssohn Scottish Symphony. My father was absolutely besotted by Mendelssohn's music. I only ever played the Scottish Symphony once in my thirteen years in the QSO. I can't remember if I had tears actually streaming down my face or what, but I was certainly overwhelmed. All these memories of childhood came flooding back like you wouldn't believe.

As a child I'd played the piano a bit with my grandmother (Mum's mum), which helped with my initial understanding of music theory. I went to a lot of Youth Orchestra concerts and of course went to QSO concerts from when I was in a bassinette. My instrument of choice was actually the bassoon! My brothers moved up through the QYO ranks. I remember Brett was in the orchestra when they first played the Copeland Clarinet Concerto. He said, 'You've got to get to know this piece.' I now regard the Copeland Concerto as one of the great miracles of the clarinet repertoire! I developed a great love for the repertoire and the versatility of the clarinet. My desire to move to the bassoon reduced and then disappeared as I became more interested in the clarinet. My first teacher, Rick Pethick at Ironside State School, did a great job. I remember my first lesson was in a room with eight other clarinet players, who were all beginners. I wonder how he remained sane! I don't know how we ever learnt anything at all in a room of nine clarinet players – but we managed to get it together.

The Southern Cross Soloists was born out of a number of groups that I'd already been a part of. When I was at high school, my brother had a really successful string quartet at the conservatorium called the Ambrosian String Quartet and I was really amazed at the amount of solid work they put in. They practised five times a week, ten to fifteen hours each week, and these guys were students. I couldn't believe the intensity. You weren't answerable to anyone; you were only answerable to the other members of your ensemble. It wasn't like you were being told how to play things by conductors. I really fell in love with chamber music very early on in my clarinet life, while I was still at high school.

When I got to the conservatorium I was determined to start a chamber group that would give me an outlet to this great love. We started a group called the Movellan Wind Quintet in 1984, when I was in first year. I met Leesa at the conservatorium in 1984, when we both were first year students. She'd been to the MOST Camp (the Musically Outstanding Students Camp), which was something that I hadn't been to, and I was told by somebody, 'If you want to form a group with a bassoon, there's a really terrific one called Leesa Bauer, coming from Bundaberg to the Con next year!' As it turned out, we met during the course of the year and initially we detested each other. We had an interesting year or so where we didn't get on particularly well but later started to become really great mates. We got married in 1989, fairly soon after graduating – once I'd got the job at the QSO and she'd got the job at the QPO. In a sense we had our arguments to start with and it's all been plain sailing since then.

When we were in fourth year, we travelled to the United States to compete in a couple of competitions and to play at a few universities. We won the Coleman Chamber Ensemble competition in Los Angeles, and third prize at the Carmel Chamber Music competition a week later. That was the result of four years of really hard work from members of the ensemble. The oboist in that group was Tania Fraser, who is now, of course, a member of Southern Cross Soloists. The three of us have been playing together since the mid eighties. We won that competition in 1987 – makes me start to feel pretty old! From that moment on I knew my future was always going to be in playing chamber music.

Three or four months after that amazing trip to America I got the job in the Queensland Symphony Orchestra. I spend the next thirteen years in the QSO, but my passion was always playing chamber music. In 1988 I formed a wind octet called the Queensland Wind Soloists that survived for about four or five years. In 1995 we formed the Southern Cross Soloists, with Duncan Tolmie, the principal oboist of the QSO and the soprano Margaret Schindler. It was rather interesting, because no other group in the world had ever thought of forming a group comprising four wind instruments, a piano and a soprano.

The Bangalow Music Festival came about after I had been asked to be the artistic director of a different regional festival. I had put together the program, which became the first program of the Bangalow Festival, when the committee of the festival I'd been asked to be the director of split in half. My friends from that committee, who'd asked me to be their director, were saying, 'Well, we'd like to put on a festival somewhere else,' so I said, 'I'll go with you; you decide where and when and I'll come and have a look and we'll see how we go.' This was about nine months before the first festival took place. I don't know how we actually did this, come to think of it, because we had no database other than the Southern Cross mailing list. Someone said, 'Well, what about Bangalow?' So they went and saw the Chamber of Commerce there, who said, 'A chamber music festival, that sounds like a great idea!' The first festival was an enormous success and it has really blossomed since.

Wayne Stuart, the great Australian piano maker, became a good friend of the group when he brought his pianos up to Brisbane for the second Queensland Biennial Festival of Music. We played a concert in the Stuart Series of Concerts, and Wayne and Katie and the group really hit it off. I think Wayne Stuart is not only one of the great characters of Australian music, but also I absolutely adore his pianos. I approached him about bringing a piano up to the Bangalow festival and he jumped at the chance. Of course, they've got to pack it up and put it in a truck and then it's got to be unloaded by forklift into the hall. But then there's not a forklift that can fit into the hall to put it on the stage, so I give the Bangalow Rugby team a carton of beer or a tab at the local pub for the night to come in half way through training on Monday or Tuesday night of

Festival week and lift it onto the stage – that's how the piano gets there! We had to have the stage checked by engineers so that it was actually going to be able to hold the piano, which weighs, literally, a ton.

Fortunately, it worked out that the weight was evenly distributed across the legs, so the stage was able to support it.

The Southern Cross Soloists' concert series called Music and Architecture came about for a number of reasons but mainly because I think a lot of music today in these huge concert halls has lost a lot of personality. They're big impersonal stadiums where a bunch of people go on the stage and another bunch of people watch them with very little interaction. I don't like that sort of music making. Of course, for an orchestra situation and the economy of it, it's absolutely necessary, but I find it very unrewarding. I find the venues themselves impersonal and I don't like that distance between performer and the audience.

The whole idea behind our music and architecture series was that I wanted to get music performance back out into regular places like workplaces and churches. The idea is to put it into a building that is either culturally or artistically significant in Brisbane or just architecturally interesting. Then, by being close to your audience and playing music that perhaps you can't do in a big concert hall setting, you make it a much more intimate occasion. Then we finish the afternoon off with a cup of tea so that the audience and the players can mingle. We can be on hand to describe the feeling of what it's like to play this or that piece in a concert and we can get immediate feedback as to what people liked and what they didn't like and even why they come to our concerts.

Arts Queensland is now supporting us with a cultural infrastructure grant, which enables us to employ someone to do the work I used to do for years. I guess the two things that we see as our main sources of income, other than our grants from Arts Queensland, are the seven events we put on in Brisbane every year, and the Bangalow Music Festival.

We used to tour through regional Queensland for Musica Viva and various different arts councils. Rockhampton was where we would turn up to play in the Pilbeam Theater, which seats about 1000, and we'd play to 45 people! We were receiving a nice fee from Musica Viva but still, it's utterly soul destroying! We thought, 'There must be a better way!' So, in combination with Education Queensland and other contacts we had on the ground in Rockhampton, we no longer play in the big theatre, we play in a school theatre. The Grammar School has lovely acoustics, and we play a concert there on Friday night, combined with the school choir. Beforehand, the school jazz band plays to entertain people outside. The community feels we are all working together and they have ownership over our product as well. We then spend Saturday and Sunday teaching – I basically teach the clarinet and saxophone from nine o'clock on Saturday morning until the moment I leave to get onto the plane at four o'clock on Sunday afternoon. Now we're at a point where Rockhampton is almost turning a bigger profit than our concerts in Brisbane. The kids are involved in coming for their lessons, they want to hear the professionals play the instruments and we put on very attractive programs.

The Pop Scene

Paul Piticco – Powderfinger and Splendour in the Grass

Paul is president of the Australian record label 'Dew Process'. His office is in the Valley, and it was there I spoke with him. He's managed the rise of Powderfinger and The Grates, among other stars of the Australian popular music world. He also co-organises the popular Splendour in the Grass Festival at Byron Bay.

Photo: Copyright Newspix/ Darren England

'They played in front of 40,000 people in this big concert hall ... Powderfinger playing at a children's charity concert that was hooked in as a celebration in the lead-up to the Royal wedding of Prince Frederik to Mary Donaldson. They said it was very thrilling to have so many Danish people out there supporting them.'

Powderfinger has a strong link with Brisbane. In general, they are very homely 'guy next door' types; I don't think they have aspirations to be at the epicentre of the music world of New York, London or Paris. They have the ability to write the music they do *because* of the influences created by their childhood, the area they come from, their livelihoods and their environments. I guess it's a case of why move, rather than why be anywhere else. Their art is because of their environment and where they've grown up. Basically, they are the sum of their parts – a big part being Brisbane.

Brisbane's an incredible place to come home to. If I was in a job where I generally lived in Brisbane except for one or two weeks a year, I might have a different opinion of the city – but I think that because we get to travel so much, and we get taken away from this city so often, we find it a great place.

Powderfinger started in their current line-up since 1992 or 1993, and I've been involved with the band since that time. I think the Brisbane music scene was definitely coming of age in the 1990s and they were a band, amongst a bunch from Brisbane, that was successful. I think that they've managed to strike a big chord with the Australian public and their work has probably kept them entrenched in the Australian psyche.

The artists' creative year is made up of different phases. You make the record and then you go through a phase of promoting it and afterwards touring and giving performance based around the new music. When they're writing and recording, they've got to be home most of the year. In the touring year they might be home only 3 or 4 months over the year. Home is still in and around Brisbane for the entire Powderfinger group.

In this business, it's getting much easier now to operate globally. Air travel is comparatively cheap and communications are phenomenal these days, you know. As long as you're prepared to get on a plane every few months, you can pretty much run your business from anywhere in the world, within reason, as long as you have the facilities of most cities. We find it fairly easy to do.

I think Powderfinger are at a point now they've got a space in the musical landscape that needs to be fulfilled in terms of making rock 'n' roll adventurous still and keeping it that way. I think that they've got time and the impetus to try and get bigger in some foreign markets. I don't think they can get much bigger than they are in the Australian market. Bernard wants to make a solo record and they have a live album and live DVD. They're trying to keep things interesting for Powderfinger fans by also trying their hand at different formats, other than just making records or touring to try and sell their projects.

They are involved with social issues. They all have their various charities but at some point every year or two they generally pull together and do something for a specific cause. They did a show a few years ago to save the rainforest. They've been involved in a lot of health issues and Aboriginal land rights issues, and refugee issues – those are the sorts of causes they've concentrated on in the last few years.

In the music industry, if you have a good enough 'product' or act, you can make your own market and cut your own niche. We've tried to remain reasonably independent in terms of who we do business with in regard to touring and merchandising and so on. We have a direct link to Universal, which is a big company, but a lot of our other business ventures, and many of the other things we undertake on the band's behalf, are done with a lot of people that we started out with years ago.

We do three different things here at this office. We manage artists – and the management side is Secret Service. Secret Service is also the co-promoter of the Music Festival 'Splendour in the Grass', which is held in July each year, at Belongil Fields, Byron Bay. Splendour had its debut in 2001 and has proved incredibly popular. This year the festival sold out in less than 48 hours.

Dew Process is a record label and we have separate staff and artists from Secret Service. We make the records wherever. In our last two releases, one was recorded in LA and the other in Sydney, and they're manufactured in Australia. The artists would then go to wherever they agreed to record, with whatever producer they'd chosen to work with. It's just worked out with the band. We don't sign artists necessarily just from Brisbane, we sign artists from anywhere in Australia. Other artists on the label include Bernard Fanning, Drag, Sarah Blasko, The Grates, The Living End, The Panics and Yves Klein Blue. We can cut the records anywhere.

That's the industry these days. It's not as complex as it used to be. In years past the technology was so big and cumbersome it was impractical to move it, so the best studios in the world were fixed in their locality. People had to travel to them and there was usually one in each city, so you'd have to pay accommodation for that band and crew interstate. These days you can record in your bedroom and it can still sound great!

I didn't actually go to Denmark with them, but they said it was great. They played in front of 40,000 people in this big concert hall. It wasn't at the Royal wedding of Prince Frederik to Mary Donaldson; it was at a children's charity concert that was hooked in as a celebration in the lead-up to it. They said it was very thrilling to have so many Danish people out there supporting them.

Expositions, Public Art and Festivals

Expo 88

Llew Edwards – Turning Dreams into Reality at Expo 88

Sir Llew Edwards was chairman and CEO of the 1988 World Expo in Brisbane. He was knighted in 1984. Since 1993 he has been Chancellor of the University of Queensland. We'd arranged to meet in the city offices of a large commercial real estate group where he was then working. His office looked out over the city of Brisbane, the city in which he's taken an active role all his working life. One of his proudest jobs, he told me, was as chairman and CEO of Expo ...

Her Majesty, Queen Elizabeth II, with Sir Llew Edwards at the opening of World Expo in Brisbane, 1988.

> *'... when there was a long queue people would just suddenly appear and do a little concert or something else to entertain them. Every day it was different.'*

I was born in Ipswich, the eldest son of an electrician, and my mother was the daughter of a miner. My father became a very successful businessman and a local alderman in Ipswich for twenty years and Deputy Mayor of the City. He insisted that I do a trade before I did anything else, so I became an electrician after completing matriculation and then started medicine after that.

After ten years as a medical general practitioner, I entered politics. That was in May 1972. That year Gough Whitlam had become Prime Minister and was getting caucus together. For a period of fourteen days there was only a two-man federal government, he and Lance Barnard. Within that period, a paper was given to Whitlam to say that if Australia was interested in an exposition in the year 1988, they should apply. A man called Bill Worth was the public servant in Canberra and he said at a meeting with Mr Whitlam, 'Are we interested? If so, we must get the information and the application to the international body, the Bureau of International Expositions in Paris by the 31 December.'

Whitlam agreed to it and so the application went in. As it happened, there were no other applications, and approval in principle was given in 1972 for Australia to host an exposition. At that stage the government didn't have to decide any details, they just had to write to confirm they would host it. There was nothing else done about it until late 1981 or 1982. At that stage I was Deputy Premier of Queensland, attending a Premiers' Conference with the then Premier of Queensland, Mr (later Sir) Joh Bjelke-Petersen. The Premier's Conference consisted of all the Premiers and Treasurers and the Prime Minister of the day, Malcolm Fraser, and John Howard, the Treasurer. In the discussion on general business, Mr Fraser commented to the effect '… we have this application that was made in 1972 for an exposition to be held in Australia; the federal government has decided we should continue to support it, because only a nation can apply for an exposition, not a state or a city. The government is prepared to support it provided whatever State is prepared to take it on must be responsible for the guarantee of the funding of it, which we estimate would be in the vicinity of a couple of hundred million dollars. Our preference would be Sydney or Melbourne because of the size of their populations.'

Without reference to anybody, Joh suddenly spoke up and said, 'Oh, Queensland will host it; don't worry, we'll take it on.' I nearly died! This sounded an enormous amount of money, especially for a small population. I said to him, 'Premier, we've got no cabinet approval to do this, we have no funding arrangements, we don't know where we're going to have it – are we going to have it in Brisbane?' Joh said, 'No, no, no, leave it alone, don't you worry about that, we'll fix that up.' Fraser then asked whether any other state was interested and they said they would all be interested if the federal government would fund it and Joh said, 'Well, I'll take it and the state government will underwrite it!' As a result of that meeting, the Queensland government suddenly became responsible for Expo and the exposition board in Paris was notified to that effect!

Nothing was done about Expo for a while. Then, when I left parliament in 1983, Joh said to me, 'Look, if you've got no particular plans, why don't you look after this thing? It won't be a big job, just an hour a week, I'm told, and so would you take on the job of chairman of it?' My plans at the time were to go back to medicine, but I eventually accepted his offer on the assumption that it would probably only be a short-term arrangement. Following this, in February 1984, I was appointed part-time chairman of Expo. I came in for what was to have been a couple of months and I was there for nearly six years. I had just a secretary, and Bob Minikin. Bob was later appointed general manager and we were the sole people. Mary Macleay had worked at the Commonwealth Games and also for Clem Jones, the Mayor of Brisbane, as his PA. Her position was executive secretary to me and to Bob, so she looked after us. She did everything and was with us the whole time, right to the end – she's a marvellous person.

The three of us put together our proposal with the assistance of some officers in the Premier's Department and the Department of Lands. We needed approximately 100 acres of land and finally we came up with the site in South Brisbane, on South Bank. At that time, as people may remember, just two streets went through it; there was Clem Jones Park on the front and a lot of very dilapidated commercial buildings, plus two or three historic buildings. The proposal was agreed to by the government and we got the legislation through the state parliament to give us the powers of resumption and the general powers of the Exposition, and we resumed. Suddenly we were the owner of a big site with roads and housing and we had to develop a very detailed and intricate timetable to get the whole site cleared.

On 30 April 1984, I think it was, we became the owner of the whole site and we then had another six months in which to negotiate settlement and payment of purchase, which we did. Bligh Voller won the contract to be the master architect. We then called applications for a project management group who would manage the whole project for us. They would report directly to me and the general manager and would be part of the team that was still external. That was won by Thiess Contractors; a man called Bob Roach was their general manager.

It was interesting that each of the architects, each of the senior team at Expo, and each of the project managers, stayed there on the whole project. Not one of us left in that whole period. I think it was the stability of that senior team that actually made for the smooth continuation of the project, so we didn't have any problems.

We realised we had a very tight schedule for the four years ahead; we knew, whatever happened, we had to open on 30 April 1988, or Queensland would look foolish in the eyes of the world. To achieve this schedule, we appointed eight key people to manage construction, international marketing, public relations and administration. There was myself as Executive Chairman, Bob Minikin as General Manager, and then these eight people, each of whom was responsible for building up their own teams internally or externally. Under my agreement with government, I was totally responsible for the project, and I was full time from then on, with these eight people reporting to me directly. As it happens, I later married the lady in charge of communications and public relations – I wasn't responsible for her appointment; I didn't even know her until she was appointed.

We'd worked out we wanted a certain amount of space for exhibition and there was other space that we also felt we could use, for perhaps an historic pavilion or whatever, but all of this we changed as we went on. We got Pacific Islands, including Nauru and Fiji, and put them in what was known as a Pacific Island area – we really had to subsidise them to get them to come.

The nations taking part in Expo had to pay rent for the buildings they occupied and basic services at cost. On top of that they had to provide their own staff to manage the building of the internal aspects of their pavilions. Most of the countries brought their own senior people out, but they also recruited local staff. We instituted a volunteer program where we got over 2000 volunteers and some of those volunteers started working with the pavilions twelve months before the opening. When staff started to arrive, about four months before the opening date, the organisation and the whole site absolutely ballooned in size.

Each of the total responsibilities came back to that group of ten, which met every morning for four years, those of us, that is, who were in the country – we had people who spent half of their time out of Australia recruiting nations for Expo. We thought we might get about 25 nations, and, if I remember correctly, about 80 nations in total came to Expo.

All through this time, we never departed from our original basic concept that this Expo was to be three things:

- the happiest place on earth in 1988…
- the safest place on earth …
- and the most successful Expo…something that people would remember forever.

I believe we achieved all three.

The government underwrote us and we had a bank account that we could draw on, but the aim was to get the income to flow, so, for example, the rent to participate had to be paid in advance by the participating nations. We started to sell tickets twelve months out. We thought we'd sell something like 60,000, but in the first ten days we sold about 75,000 and finished up selling 100,000 season and three-day passes. Our cash flow started to improve rapidly as deposits on rentals, ticket sales and sponsorships came in. As it turned out, it was very successful; some would say the most successful Expo of its type in history. We thought we would get about 7 million people attending over the six months, which meant some people might come every day if they bought season passes – in fact 18.3 million people turned up. The commercial outlets for the food et cetera were extremely happy, because all their budgets were done on 7 million visitors and they had 18 million people to buy their pies, ice creams or whatever it might be. We also got extra commission on their sales, so we did very well too.

We had this plan that everything had to be 'perfect'. Safety had to be perfect. The friendliness of the staff had to be perfect. Nothing was to be 'ordinary'; we sought excellence in everything, from the marching bands to the entertainment. The entertainment director was a man called Ric Birch, who went on to do Olympic Games entertainment. He and a woman called Barbara Absolon and their team was responsible for getting together the entertainment. When the ticket sales indicated the bigger than expected number, we were able to build in more entertainment on site, so when there was a long queue, people would just suddenly appear and do a little concert or something else to entertain visitors. Every day it was different.

It was important that at all times of the day supplies could be provided without interrupting things – no trucks were allowed on site, so you'd see little wheelbarrows – and we made sure the person wheeling the wheelbarrow didn't look like a tradesman, not that we had any discrimination against trade, but we wanted it to look part of the scene – so suddenly you'd see people in some sort of uniform delivering the ice cream, so nothing looked out of place.

We said we were not going to start until we got an agreement with the unions. One of the proudest moments I had was to see the union leadership as excited as we were about the project. Over a construction period of five years we didn't lose one single day, and the reason for this was that if there was a problem, the union representatives came to my office and we sorted it out. We may not always have agreed, there was 'blood on the floor' on numerous occasions, but we never let a problem divide our common unity. It was a great tribute to people like Fred Whitby, Harry Haunschild and others, these people who became so imbued with the concept that they were prepared to deal with problems themselves. My respect for the Trades Union movement grew enormously as a result of that experience.

On Opening Day, we walked around with Her Majesty the Queen and Prince Phillip after the official ceremony. The feeling was electric; there were 78,000 or 80,000 people there on opening day. The Queen walked around as if she was one of the guests and, whilst there was some security, it didn't look like it. At the end of that first day we met up together as a team and said, 'We've won!' The next day we were jolted when only 50,000 turned up, but it was a down day. I think people just didn't want to come for the first couple of days, and then suddenly the message got around that it's great to be there and we went through record after record almost every day. Our exit surveys were showing an 85% to 95% satisfaction rating. It was probably the most exciting thing I've ever done in my life!

I think this was the first time in Australia's history, technically, other than war, where, for the benefit of the whole of the nation, we focused on just one event. It became the major event in the Bicentennial Celebrations. It was great to see people dancing in the streets at night, and the staff from different countries meeting up after close of work in various pavilions and having a few drinks and getting to know each other. It was estimated that one person in three in Australia came to Expo. I think a lot of the research that's been done since shows that Expo was a turning point for Brisbane. The Commonwealth Games had been successful and that started a feeling of great pride, that we could do things, and then, six years later, we did this, and everybody 'owned' Expo. When I meet people they say, 'You're the Expo man, aren't you?' and 'Didn't we do well!' People everywhere think it was 'we' as a community that did Expo.

Noel Bellchambers – The Britannia Inn at Expo

We meet in the reception room of the Conrad Hotel. His company started with a couple of little inner city cafes, including the original Shingle Inn, but now they have diverse interests – a turning point undoubtedly being their involvement in Expo 88. Noel talks of his successful bid to put up a British pub at Expo and his surprise and delight when in London he found just what he was looking for ...

'I got a taxi over to this hotel called the Victoria, which is next to Victoria Station. I'd never seen anything quite like it. It was sawdust on the floor, cobwebs round the ceilings, bare boards, and old horse leathers everywhere, something that you'd never see in Australia ... I went over to the people behind the bar and told them I'd like to meet the manager. He and his wife actually turned out to be Australians; she came from Warrnambool, where I'd gone to school.'

I come from a family of shopkeepers. My father was in the hotel business, my grandfather was in hotels and his father came to Australia from Maidstone in Kent in 1848, and my great-grandmother came from Wiltshire. In 1970 my wife and I started off with a small coffee shop called Renoir, on the corner of Albert and Adelaide Streets in the city. I think we had just six employees. In those early years we used to close at twelve o'clock on a Saturday and everyone would be out of the city by 12:30. The only people who'd come back would be the few who were going to the cinema on a Saturday evening – Expo, of course, changed all that!

We eventually took over Shingle Inn in 1975. At that time it was being managed by Noel Webster, the nephew of W.R. Webster, who had started their well-known biscuit business in Ipswich before building a factory in Annerley. Webster's had started building cafes around the city and the Valley. This had included Shingle Inn in 1936, the Majestic, Haddon Hall at the top of Queen Street, where the Myer Centre is now,

York Town in Edward Street, Capri in the Valley and lots of others. In the 1960s Webster's were taken over by Weston's, the Canadian biscuit company, who weren't interested in cafes.

Noel Webster continued to manage the cafes for a time, but they were struggling. I bought the Renoir from Noel and I said to him at the time, 'If you ever want to sell the Shingle Inn, I'd like to buy it.' I went on pestering him and eventually he decided it was for sale. He said to me, 'If you're going to buy the Shingle Inn, you've got to take York Town as well.' 'How much do you want for York Town?' I asked him. 'Nothing,' he said. 'You can have that in the deal.' Well, we did the deal. We bought Shingle Inn at a bargain price and we had the York Town thrown in. So with the Renoir we now had three restaurants and we operated all three for a number of years.

When we took the Shingle Inn over in 1975 the rental was $39,000 a year, then one Friday morning in 1980, I'll never forget, I was just about to leave to go to a friend's wedding in Sydney, when a letter got poked under the door. It was from AMP increasing the rent from $39,000 to $96,000! From then on it took a tremendous effort to keep Shingle Inn afloat. We had to reduce staff as much as we could while still retaining the old Shingle Inn service. AMP owned the property in which Shingle Inn was located. Further down the track the Shingle Inn was sold again by AMP to a gentleman named Howard Chia in Sydney, and he eventually put the rent up to about $350,000 a year!

It was a tremendous juggle over the years to keep the business viable. It'd started profitably, but it got to the stage where it was no longer very profitable and then just managed to break even. Every time you put the prices up the customers would complain. The site the Shingle Inn was on became so valuable that, from the landlord's point of view, it just wasn't practical to keep us there. They could get someone with another type of business who could pay vastly more rent.

Finally we had to close down and subsequently we opened a more modern version of Shingle Inn at McArthur Chambers, about 200 metres away, which is trading very well and still satisfying some of the old Shingle Inn customers. Because of its old English style and decor, the Shingle Inn façade and contents had previously been listed under National Trust and Heritage legislation, so when we left, they were removed and put into storage. It still hasn't been formally decided as to what will happen in future to the façade and contents. Hopefully down the track we can find another site for it.

How we got into World Expo 88 was a different story. In about 1985 the Queensland government said that they'd secured the rights to operate an Exposition to be held in 1988. Very few people in Brisbane then knew much about what happened at an Exposition. So in 1986 I decided to make a trip to Vancouver, where the '86 Expo was being held. I wanted to see for myself what it was all about. I arrived there and the excitement and enjoyment the people were getting from their Expo had to be seen to be believed – I'd never seen anything quite like it

While I'd been in Vancouver I'd seen the British Pavilion and the British Pub and how popular it was. I'd also found out that British concessions at all expositions were controlled from London by the Central Office of Information (COI), so we approached them and were invited to put in a tender to put up a British pub at the Brisbane Expo. We had our offer accepted – that was when the hard work really started!

The first thing they asked was for me to come to London with a design of the pub that I intended to operate at Expo. Unwisely, I had a local architect here draw up what we thought was an appropriate design for a British pub and I left for London with the plans. I walked into the COI office in London and they took one look at the plans and said, 'Oh no, sorry, that's nothing like what we've got in mind!' They suggested I go away and try again.

I remember I went back to the hotel in Southampton Row feeling very dejected and alone. Later I went for a walk and, turning a corner, I saw a pub called the Swan. I'm not a drinker during the day, but I was feeling down, so I went in and ordered a drink. I said to the girl behind the bar, 'I'm here from Australia and need to come up with a plan for a typical English pub – do you know of one you think I should go and look at?' She went away and came back with her husband, who thought about it for a while before he said, 'Yes, there's a place over near Victoria Station. It's quite unique. I think you should go and have a look at it.' So I got a taxi over to this hotel called the Victoria, which is next to Victoria Station.

I'd never seen anything quite like it. It was sawdust on the floor, cobwebs round the ceilings, bare boards, and old horse leathers everywhere, something that you'd never see in Australia. It was certainly unique! I thought, 'Maybe I've stumbled on something,' so I rang up the COI straightway and said, 'Look, I'd like you to come and have a look at this place. Maybe have lunch with me here tomorrow.' Anyway, they walked in to the Victoria next day for lunch. They just stood very quietly for about a minute and then said, 'This is fantastic, but can you reproduce it?' I said, 'Well, I'm certainly going to try.' So we had lunch. After that I said, 'Well, you leave me in here and I'll get to work.' I went over to the people behind the bar and told them I'd like to meet the manager. He and his wife actually turned out to be Australians; she came from Warrnambool, where I'd gone to school. I said I'd like to know who designed the pub. They gave me the name of an English pub designer called Dick Henry.

I met Dick and he took me on a pub tour and showed me the pubs that he'd done around London. He didn't show them all to me in one day, but we saw a lot. He was a very experienced man, having done over 400 pub refurbishments in England, and we struck up a very good friendship almost immediately. He assured me he could easily do the design for Expo 88, as he'd already done it many times before. I then came back to Australia and sent him details of the site and the structure we had to work with and he drew up the plans and sent them out to me. I went back to England to see the COI with the new plans. They said they were marvellous but that before they would give final approval they wanted to come to Australia and see our existing operation. We had a lunch at the Shingle Inn with the people from the COI and Pam Handkey, a lady from the British Consulate. We put on the silverware and did everything we could to impress them and about a week after that they said, 'Fine, you can go ahead now, you've got the OK!'

Dick Henry arranged for the materials to come from England. The timbers were big 12 by 12 inch wharf timbers which came from Cardiff wharf. The Customs people here took a pretty long look at them and sprayed them, but they got through. We had a container load of old timbers, bricks, saddles, horse leathers, brasses – all sorts of things (after Expo, in 1989, these things were all put into the Britannia Inn, which we built on the third level of the Wintergarden). It cost us around $300,000 to set up. It was a gamble, but I'd seen what happened in Vancouver, so I was feeling confident.

Our next challenge was to provide the British pub with all British food and British beers, so as to present to the public something that was entirely British – something they'd never see in Australia. We had to source all the beers and a lot of the food from England. They wanted English food and English brands like Baxters, as much as we could manage, which we did. I travelled the length and breadth of England visiting breweries and other places. The result was a truly authentic British Pub. We actually sold approximately 2,500 litres or 50 kegs a day, which by most hotel standards is a lot of beer. We prepared over 2000 meals a day every day for 180 days. We were baking in Shingle Inn and at a site in Champion Street every night. We had to bring all our food to the Expo by about 6 am or 7 am each day.

The Brisbane Expo was a success from day one. Brisbane people were so enthusiastic about it and the Expo itself was extremely well run. Of the people who visited, the most prominent were the Duke and Duchess of Kent, and Prime Minister Margaret Thatcher and her husband Dennis, who came in and had a drink.

We brought Dick Henry out to Australia on a number of occasions after Expo. We relocated the Britannia Inn from the Expo to the Wintergarden and he designed that for us into the Wintergarden. We also put a music hall in there, which lasted a few years. It was modelled on the famous music hall at Leeds, which Dick and I had visited. Unfortunately, as people's memories of the Expo receded, the Britannia Inn gradually lost its appeal and eventually faded away.

Dick Henry and I had a lot of good times. We did an Elvis Presley restaurant in Cairns and Dick designed that for us. The Gilhooleys pub actually came about through that. At that time, this was around 1993 or 1994, we also had a tavern up in Cairns, and there was an opportunity to do something with a separate small bar. Dick and I decided that we'd do an Irish bar, since they were then becoming popular around the world. We had an Irishman working in the place and I asked him to come up with an appropriate name for an Irish Bar. After a couple of days he came up with the name Gilhooleys, a well-known Irish name. So we set up the Irish Bar and it did extremely well. That brought us to starting up an Irish Bar in Brisbane, which was the start of a chain of Irish Bars.

My two sons are in the business and continuing on. I think the most satisfying thing you can do in business is to be able to carry your business forward, but businesses should really be run by younger people who are more attuned to current needs.

The Ekka

Vivian Edwards – At the Helm of Brisbane's Ekka

Viv Edwards combines his work as a doctor with his position as president of the Royal National Agricultural and Industrial Association of Queensland. It was at the RNA that I met with him and his wife Jenny (seen together in the above photograph). His office desk was cluttered with papers waiting attention and when the phone rang, briefly interrupting the flow of conversation, it didn't matter as Jenny continued the thread of conversation. There was much laughter as they remembered their youth and early involvement in the Ekka.

'One of the main events used to be the Kite Man. The guy would be pulled on a long rope going around the arena and go up in the air and sometimes, when he was supposed to come down, they'd let him go and the wind would take him out and he'd finish up down the road.'

Viv: I was born in 1938. My earliest memories, I guess, were when we lived at Alderley. We had ten acres there and we ran some jersey cows. Soon after the war, Dad became a steward in the dairy cattle ring, number two oval at the Ekka, and then when Dick Hill, who was the ring master at the time, died, Dad took over the job of ring master here. That would have been in about the early 1950s.

Dad was 22 stone and 6 foot 3inches – a big bloke. Big Bill Edwards, he was called. He was the president of the Queensland Lawn Tennis Association and the Australian Lawn Tennis Association for many years. He rebuilt Milton, of course, and got the Davis Cups here to Queensland. He was a phenomenal fellow. I became involved with the Ekka through my dad. When he was stewarding over in the dairy section, we'd come in with him and he'd give us little jobs to do, like writing the results numbers with a chalk on a blackboard. I did that for a few years.

I've been involved with the Ekka since I was seven or eight, I guess. When I was going through medicine, I used to work on the change counter on Bowen Bridge Road, to make some pocket money. I did that for six years. When I graduated I organised a medical supervision service for the main arena, in particular, so we always had one of our doctors and myself most of the time, I suppose, come across and be available in the stewards' room down there in case there were accidents. Then, after I left the Royal Brisbane and had gone into private practice, I became the Honorary Medical Officer and continued with that from 1961 until 1987.

Jenny: I met Viv when I was twelve. We've been married now for forty-two years.

Viv: When we got married in 1961, my dad was the chairman of directors of Federal Hotels, which had Lennons here in Brisbane and had also just built the Broadbeach Hotel. When we went on honeymoon, we went from the Milton Club where we had our reception and got in the car and drove down to the Broadbeach Hotel, which was right out in the middle of sand dunes – from Surfers Paradise through to Broadbeach Resort.

Jenny: We were the only ones in the hotel. Isn't it amazing! We had the whole place to ourselves. We only had a day and a half because he had to go back to work at the Royal Brisbane Hospital.

Viv: In the old days all the animals were here, as they are now, but there were more cattle here in those days, also more pigs and sheep. For the beef and dairy cattle people it was their annual holiday, so they'd come down the week before and they'd get their animals ready. The animals often came by train to the Normanby railway yards, where the hotel is, near where Brisbane Grammar has taken over recently. From there they'd drive them down here. Now, all the animals come down by private transport: trucks, horse-floats, vans, and so on.

All the chooks and poultry used to come by train, too, in those days. The people put the poultry on the trains wherever they lived, and then brought them right into the show grounds here and unloaded them, so the exhibitors didn't have anything to do with them after they left their properties, until the end of the show when they were being judged.

In the 1950s, the farm implements, tractors, excavators, irrigation pumps and things were a big part of the show – and there was nowhere else in Queensland where they were shown in that sort of quantity, so they were big draw cards. In the late 1980s and early '90s, the machinery started to move out to machinery expos at places like Rockhampton and Jondaryon, so we don't have any farm equipment of any significance here now.

The amusement area has increased quite remarkably over the years. There are lots of big rides nowadays. Back in the '50s we had the Octopus and that was the biggest thing – and a Ferris wheel, which was not very big at all. Now we've got the massive Big Wheel and the Mighty Mouse type roller coasters and there are dozens of very big rides.

Jenny: In those days the Fat Lady and the Spiderman and all the freak shows were very popular. Also the tent shows – the boxing, Jimmy Sharman, and all those sorts of things. People loved them. The spruikers – they were marvellous. They'd stand out the front of the tents and just gather everybody in. They were marvellous – spruiking was a real art!

Viv: They didn't have electric microphones then; they had loud hailers. They used to have these tent shows where they'd have the spruiker getting people to gather around and all the young singers and the entertainers of the time, the guitarists and musicians and so on. I remember drums rolling and the spruikers out there and a bit of music and 'Come, come, come and see Johnnie O'Keefe.' That was one of them. They'd perform inside a big tent, and a little platform in front where these people would all get up there.

Jenny: They'd give them a little taste of what they were going to see inside, and they'd have the artists up there, but then you had to pay to go and see them.

Viv: It was a shilling or sixpence or something to go in and see them – it was quite fantastic. Then TV came along and of course the big promoters started to take over, so we don't have that over there anymore.
   They had the 'Globe of Death'; a massive globe with a motor cyclist going round it – he was held on by centrifugal force. Stan Durkin, who's still here, his father started that off, and Stan has the Big Chairlift and the Big Wheel and a few other rides – but he used to ride the Globe of Death too!

Jenny: The Fat Lady was wonderfully popular. She was happy, too – she was making a fortune! She's not allowed to be there any more, of course, because of the law on discrimination – her being fat.

Viv: They had a flea circus too.

Jenny: The flea circus is still there; it's amazing. It's down in the animal nursery now. It's brilliant. It's under a microscope. We've never been able to find out if it's the dinky die thing, but I think it is. Fleas actually do tricks.

Viv: Of course, we have the famous Show-bag Pavilion. They used to be Sample Bags; they cost nothing and had little comics and peanuts and lollies. Now the prices range from a dollar to seventy dollars, but the value in those $70 bags goes into some hundreds of dollars – and people do hand them in to the various commercial outlets, those vouchers. That's been a big change.
   There's been a lot of other big changes too in the main arena, in the Entertainment Centre, as we used to call it. One of the main events used to be the Kite Man. The guy would be pulled on a long rope going around the arena and he'd go up in the air, and sometimes, when he was supposed to come down, they'd let him go and the wind would take him out and he'd finish up down the road.

Jenny: The crowd loved that!

Viv: We lost him quite a few times! I was the only medical officer in the ring for about twenty-seven years and it was my job when they did that to race out and try and find the guy and see he was OK. Then we had the big high-wire acts with the motor cycles going across – but periodically those guys would fall off in one of the Royal Shows – it was just too dangerous. They'd be up there in roaring westerly winds.

Jenny: They were the real entertainers, weren't they? Remember the rodeo and the buck-jumping? We don't have real entertainers like that anymore. They would risk life and limb to entertain the public. They were just fantastic. We've still got a lot of entertainment, but it's not dangerous anymore because Workplace Health and Safety won't allow it. There used to be the human cannon. We had the great big cannon and they'd put a fellow right down in the base of it and there'd be a huge bang and a puff of smoke, and he'd be shot into a big catching net about 50 to 80 metres away.

Viv: When the main arena is totally packed with people, every seat is taken and there are 6 or 10 rows standing behind trying to get a look at what's going on in the ring and waiting for the fireworks – the feeling then is just magic! You get the same feeling walking round the grounds on those big days when we have up to 120,000 people at the show. One of the biggest days was 126,000. That was in the '80s. During the Expo we had over 120,000 people.

During the rest of the year, between the Ekkas, the RNA has around 160 different events going on. There's the Home Show; the biggest truck show in the southern hemisphere is here every second year; the Caravan and Camping Show is massive; we also have concerts with 50,000 to 60,000 people attending.

Jenny: People bring their animals to the Ekka and it takes a lot of work and a lot of time and a lot of money – so when they get here they want everything just right, as they would see it. The egos are pretty big, because 'my animal is the best!' and often out there in the ring, when the animal is being judged and the ribbon's being put on that horse, they'd say to the second one 'I beat you' – not 'my horse beat your horse', but 'I beat you!' So emotions run a bit high.

Viv: When Tom Burns left parliament he was made Trade Commissioner for China. He goes over there a fair bit, but the last couple of years he's been bringing delegations of Chinese buyers out to the show and we give them a bit of a reception here in the President's Room and then he takes them round to look at the beef cattle and produce and all sorts of things.

The Trade Commissioner for Mexico came here, the same sort of thing. We also had six British Members of Parliament come out. We give them a lunch and make sure that everything is done properly so they can see Queensland on show. We show them everything – this sort of show is unique to Australia, there's nothing like it in any other country. They have fêtes and fairs and rodeos and stampedes and things like that, but not the overall length and depth that we've got here – we really lay it on!

I'm particularly proud to have been and, with Jenny, continue to be, part of the whole scene and to have been honoured by being awarded an Order of Australia Medal (OAM) for services to Primary Industry and to Medicine in Queensland.

Public Art and Festivals

John Stafford – Queensland's Public Art Agency

The reception room is full of literature about projects funded by Arts Queensland. John is Director of Visual Arts, Craft and Design, and his office is spacious but modestly decorated. He speaks with enthusiasm of the enabling role that Arts Queensland plays in the built environment – showcasing local talent in public spaces for all to enjoy.

'What currently happens is that all of the building projects and departments, in their business cases, include a 2% allocation for public art, the way they would for other expenditure in the building ... Most of it is actually built into the fabric of the building, which gives it its name "Art Built-In"'.

I was born in Dalby in 1960 and in 1964 the family moved to Ipswich, so my formative and teenage years were in Ipswich; my father was a retired jockey and horse trainer, and my mother's family was also involved in horse racing; neither was involved in the arts.

In the early 1970s I went to the Kelvin Grove Teachers' College in Brisbane to study secondary art teaching, but I was feeling a bit too young to study at the time, so I left and worked for several years in the public sector, mostly at the Ipswich Magistrates' Court. Subsequently I went back to Art College, where I got an art

369

practice qualification, then practised as an artist for about ten years, showing in contemporary art spaces, regional galleries and artist-run initiatives. I was doing all sorts of jobs to survive as an artist, then in my late twenties I made the decision that to help me practise as an artist I was only going to do arts-related work, so I worked in the QCA Gallery, taught briefly in the academic program and did related curatorial work and arts administration.

After Wayne Goss became Premier in 1989, he announced a major review of the arts in Queensland, which produced a landmark report 'Queensland: A State for the Arts'. I was running the campus gallery at the Queensland College of Art at the time and teaching in the Art Theory department and was still involved in my own art practice. It was so exciting, this whole review of the arts, so I went to the Premier's Arts Division for the interview and they gave me the opportunity to work on the arts in government and I haven't really escaped since! The staff of the Arts Division worked closely with the Arts Advisory Committee which the Premier appointed and they had a totally open brief. They could travel the length and breadth of Queensland and inquire in any art form area. That's when they first devised the 'percent for art' scheme.

Prior to my involvement with the Arts Advisory Committee I'd had some involvement with a Public Art Conference in Brisbane in 1990 called Metrozone. I was on the board of the Queensland Artworkers Alliance and one of my colleagues, Dennis Magee, an Irish sculptor, brought this idea of 'public art' to the board. The CEO, Lindy Johnson, then applied for a grant to the Australia Council and was successful so we were all really involved in what became the first national conference on public art.

Matt Foley often tells a story of the State Labor Conference, about where the 2% comes from. He says he suggested 1% and there wasn't any opposition but 3% seemed too much and so in the end 2% seemed the right compromise and they all went for it. In reality there are a few 2% schemes overseas, the most of which I've seen is a civic model, I think, in France, which is 2.5%, but in comparison, while West Australia and Tasmania have 'per cent for art' schemes, Queensland is currently the most comprehensive in Australia.

We embarked on a series of demonstration projects in government buildings, sometimes in partnership with local government. One of these was the Kangaroo Point Cliffs project, which probably had a lot more than 2% allocated to commissioning major sculptural elements for a public walkway and parkland area. Apart from the fact that it's a site of great physical exercise in rock-climbing, there's some fantastic art along there. For example, the late Ron Hurley's work was commissioned for that site and some of the Expo 88 sculptures were also relocated there. I think that was a real coup in Queensland's and Brisbane's history. Philip Bacon and a lot of people did some very good work in trying to secure some of those works for Brisbane and a number of them, including the *Man and Matter* sculptures and the *Inukshuk Inuit* sculpture, which is a part of our collection.

What currently happens under Art-Built-in is that all of the building projects and departments, in their business cases, include a 2% allocation for public art, the way they would for other expenditure in the building. Our scheme applies to government buildings, so that could be a Suncorp Stadium, or the Brisbane Magistrate's Court. It applies to almost every department. We have done public art projects on court houses, community justice centres, schools, some police stations, hospitals, office buildings.

Mostly it's integrated art, which means that the actual fabric of the building will be impacted on by the artist. It does include stand-alone sculptures, but in relation to the building context sometimes it's architectural glass, it's textiles, it's paving treatments, it's sculpture and on some occasions there are purchased works like painting. Most of it, though, is actually built into the fabric of the building, which gives it its name 'Art Built-In'. That's about real ownership for those departments, mainly in public spaces where the community gets to see it all the time and engage with it.

An example of this is the work of Barbara Heath in the magistrates' court. That architectural hardware, the door handles, is an excellent commission. Those handles are laser cut and flat and then rolled into that cylindrical shape – it's very skilled work and totally memorable. She based it on the breezeway patterns in the old Queensland houses and it's that sort of thing where there's a real Queensland connection. Most of the work is national, international in its contemporariness and that's good too.

We've done a diversity of work, particularly in indigenous projects with indigenous artists. In the Brisbane magistrates' court again, there's an enormous panelled work by Judy Watson in the security zone in the foyer. Judy's known for her beautiful ground painted canvases, which are stained and all about energy and country. It was wonderful to see her translate that into large, architectural glass panels.

That work, I believe, helped Judy make the next move to the *Musée du quai Branly* in Paris. The Paris work is a ceiling, which has received a lot of attention, and I believe that she learnt those skills and learnt that adaptation of her work here on the Magistrates Court project. So, in some ways, apart from the cultural importance of the work she's done for that international museum of Indigenous art, she's actually also a cultural export from it. That's what Art Built-In is also trying to do, enable artists to scale up and step up to bigger, more ambitious commissions.

For some Indigenous artists it's meant they've been able to realise their work in a different medium, like architectural glass, that they hadn't imagined before. When you see artists like John Smith Gumbula dealing with Moreton Bay and the Brisbane River, using images of dugong and things like that in the architectural glass – that kind of watery feel of the glass seems quite appropriate. I think they have adapted story in a really tangible and physical way and you still get that beautiful experience of the texture.

The artists don't have an entirely free reign in that we ask them to shape their creative ideas and practice around a set of given parameters. Quite often they're invited into an expression of interest process or a curatorial process. The Brisbane Magistrates' Court had a curator, Jay Younger, working on that project, short-listing artists. They have an idea of the building's use. It's a major magistrates' court and it's a major civic building in the CBD. There are people who now just go there for the art tour!

The artists are also dealing with a certain scale of a major building. All of this information, about the purpose of the building, its functionality and scale, is captured in a planning document. This document informs their work, as it has the history of the site and the functionality of the building, so it provides both indigenous and non-indigenous information. For instance, the Tank Stream runs underneath the Brisbane Magistrate's Court, so one artist, Marian Drew, referenced it by doing a series of photographs that are on six or seven levels showing water pools with tadpoles and the water boatmen. Whilst her work is not specifically about the law it's about 'what this place is' and 'who's coming here and why'.

The artists have to go through quite a rigorous expression of interest process. We commission art works right across the state, from Brisbane to the Torres Strait. Sometimes the supply stores, the Ibis Stores in the Torres Strait, will commission work. There are public buildings in Cairns, in Townsville, Mount Isa and Cloncurry. There's a whole range of government buildings that apply. The policy is influenced by the Local Industry Policy, which is about trying to provide jobs in the region, so both the artist selected and the fabricator selected are usually from that region. There's a regional context there, for instance, in William McCormack Place, a government building in Cairns, we commissioned a major work by a senior indigenous artist from Aurukun, Arthur Pambegan Junior.

Arts Queensland has a very broad brief. A couple of things that we do: the 'Great Walks Art' and 'Environment Program' are not just 'built' public art but are actually about engaging artists in a broader process. The public art component came from the department which manages National or State Parks, where it's not able to commission objects and place them in the park because of their protected status. What we did for the six great walks up the length of Queensland was to develop partnerships with regional galleries in each area. The Environmental Protection Agency, Parks and Wildlife Service and our sponsor, Powerlink Queensland, worked with the Regional Gallery Network to commission artists locally to respond to the walks. These were residencies and the artworks were produced out of them and then displayed in exhibitions and captured in a beautiful catalogue. They did workshops with other artists and workshops with children – all of it a response to the natural environment rather than the built object. This publication really is a great document about artists' capacity to work in and respond to the environment, but only leave that conceptual legacy of art. It's a different kind of project to the physical 'built' object.

The work *Red Cube* by Ken Reinhardt was donated to the people of Brisbane by Transfield as their gift to the city when they built the first Gateway Bridge. That work was relocated to the Main Roads Department in Spring Hill. They redesigned the forecourt around Ken's sculpture and it sits beautifully in the context of the Main Roads Department. There is a conceptual fit with buildings and departments. It's so important we are commissioning art for the public domain. It has to resonate as art of quality and to tell a story or otherwise engage people.

I love seeing some of the public art works when they're covered in children just playing. There's a work by Ron Robertson-Swann at the Art Gallery. I was over there about a year ago and there must have been about 17 children on his sculpture. Inside an art gallery, this would have been impossible, but outside they feel comfortable to physically engage with the sculpture. It's the same with the Richard Tipping work called *Watermark* that spells out the word 'flood' which was the level of the Brisbane Flood down at the Brisbane Powerhouse. I've seen children play on it and women exercise on it and people casually hanging out around it. That's what public art should be doing; it should be of the appropriate scale, should resonate with the meaning of the place and the building context as well as with the uses and people who experience those places.

Where to from here? We're now at an exciting phase here because I think Art Built-In has set a national example of a program of government's commitment to engaging people to a better built environment in the public domain, a more creative environment for people to experience. When visitors from the northern hemisphere, in particular, come to Queensland, they get a real surprise about the quality, scale and calibre of our commissions and they go away with that memory.

There are great opportunities to do public works that talk about the 150 years of Queensland as a state, our engagement with indigenous people, and where we're going to go in the future – what the next 150 years might be like in Queensland. There are some really exciting possibilities, for example, adapting to cultural practice that nowadays is much more screen based and digital. A number of our public art works have actually been digital projections and electronic artworks that aren't about a physical object but about an engaging narrative or an artwork presented in a digital format, which then can be streamed interstate and overseas. I think that part of it is very exciting as it gives us an even bigger dialogue with the world.

Lyndon Terracini – Festivals as a Way of Life

Lyndon is CEO of the Brisbane Festival. His office looks out onto a busy city street, but his working day often takes him on voyages of discovery to the suburbs, finding unique and interesting characteristics that inform his plans for the annual Brisbane Festival. His enthusiasm is infectious as he recounts experiences enjoyed in doing similar investigative work in rural Queensland as CEO of the Queensland Music Festival.

'When I was driving to Winton ... I realised that people are actually not connected by roads out there ... The properties are so enormous that they meet at a fence to discuss perhaps sharing the use of a tractor ... or something similar ... It's at fences where they meet, so for me the communication point was the fence.'

I came to Queensland in the middle of 2000, when I was appointed artistic director of the Queensland Music Festival. I'd worked for a long period in Queensland, performing here a number of times with the Australian Opera, as it was in those days, with the Queensland Theatre Company, the orchestra and various other organisations, but it was a real thrill to be appointed artistic director of the Queensland Music Festival. I really didn't know how large a job it would be at that time – nor how large the state of Queensland is.

When I began going out and visiting various centres the thing that struck me most of all was that every town and city throughout Queensland actually has a different culture. I realised that if we were to represent the state of Queensland in terms of the Queensland Music Festival we'd have to clearly identify the myriad cultures that exist throughout Queensland and try to reflect those through the work we were presenting at the festival.

I went and spoke to people; I drove out to places like Barcaldine and Winton, up to Normanton, to Mackay and Townsville, Charters Towers, all over Queensland. I spoke to the mayors and CEOs in all of those places, I spoke to people in the pubs, in the streets – and in the cities that had taxis I spoke to taxi drivers, just to get a feel for those particular places.

I made some wonderful discoveries. In Barcaldine, for example, every street is named after a tree, and in Longreach, every street is named after a bird. There are wonderful things that you're able to discover when you're actually in those places. When I was driving to Winton, that long stretch of road where you immediately think of the big sky – and it certainly is a very big sky out there, I realised that people are actually not connected by roads out there. Roads in fact dissect or bisect the countryside, but people are connected by fences. The properties are so enormous that they meet at a fence to discuss perhaps sharing the use of a tractor, or a bull that's got through a fence or something similar, or a problem with wild dogs or whatever. It's at fences where they meet, so for me the communication point was the fence.

I spoke to the Winton council about building a permanent installation, a 'musical fence'. We did that in Winton at the festival of 2003 and again in 2005 when we completed that work. We formed the Winton Musical Fence Band and had a wonderful celebration at dawn to launch the entire festival there. Apparently more than twenty cars per day now visit the musical fence, people that have heard about it. *Landline* did a big feature on it and it was broadcast a number of times and people are fascinated by the peculiar musical instrument that we constructed there, it really reflects the culture of that part of Queensland. You can bash it, bow it or pluck it, and kids, in particular, love it.

In Barcaldine, at the very first festival I did in 2001, we formed the Barcaldine Big Marimba Band. It was a project that involved people in learning to make their own marimbas out of Queensland Hoop Pine. Again it was reflective of the fact that the streets in Barcaldine are all named after trees. We closed off the main street and we opened the festival there in the street at the Tree of Knowledge.

We sent people out there to teach people in Barcaldine, a lot of school children were involved, how to make their own marimbas, how to tune them and then how to play them. We had international artists from all over the world performing there at the Tree of Knowledge and the closing event in that concert, the finale, was the Barcaldine Big Marimba Band playing with major international artists from all over the world.

A lot of those events, like the event we did in Mount Isa where we staged a great musical called *Bobcat Magic* and then in 2005 *Bobcat Dancing*, were again reflective of the local culture, for example, in the case of Mount Isa, the use of heavy machinery.

In Charters Towers we staged *Charters Towers the Musical*. It was a piece about Charters Towers as a place, about the people who live there, about the people who've left there and the people who've died there.

These events were incredibly moving. I found myself and a number of people at dawn in Winton, seeing so many people participate. In Barcaldine, seeing hundreds of people who'd driven hundreds of kilometres to be there at that celebration at dawn, was a tremendously moving experience – seeing people celebrating their culture and wanting to tell people, not only in that part of the world but throughout Queensland and throughout Australia.

A lot of the events were televised live on television breakfast shows and on ABC radio, talking about the culture of their place, about where they live, what's so special about it, and why it means so much to them. That's been the most wonderful thing for me, in that I found that tremendously inspiring to continue to try and create work that is about individual people's places.

There have been fantastic times in all those places and some very humorous times too. With the musical fence in Winton we commissioned Graham Leak, the instrument maker, to build the fence. After he'd finally built it, he'd been working with the local builder, and they finished on one very hot day (and they're extremely hot days in Winton) and they were leaning back and just having a beer at the end of the day and the builder said to Graham, 'Mate, that's all very well, but you know, can you play a tune on it?' and Graham said, 'Yeah, what would you like to hear? I guess, as we're out here in Winton and given Winton is where *Waltzing Matilda* came from and was first performed, I'll play you *Waltzing Matilda*,' so he played *Waltzing Matilda* on the fence! The local builder leant back and said, 'Bugger me!' then he jumped into his ute and took off in a cloud of dust. Graham thought, 'Oh dear, must have been a disaster …' so he started packing his gear up and about ten minutes later the ute reappeared with half a dozen fellas in the back of it. The builder was there and they all jumped out and ran over to Graham – he was playing requests until midnight!

Often there's a fantastic combination of the young and the elderly. I remember in Rockhampton I commissioned Elena Kats-Chernin to write the first symphony ever written for any town or city in Australia and it was called the *Rockhampton Gardens Symphony*. Elena came to Rockhampton with me and we met all the people involved in making music in Rockhampton. It's a terrifically prolific town in terms of producing artists. Katherine Dunn, who's dancing in London at the moment, but was with the Sydney Dance Company for a long time, comes from Rockhampton, as do other musicians and actors; it has a great tradition.

There's a wonderful woman who conducts a children's choir there. The children's choir has been very successful for many years in Eisteddfods and so on and they also do a lot of concerts around the place. We gathered together a lot of people and this particular lady sat down at lunch and Elena had heard the choir and she said to this wonderful woman, 'I'd like your choir to start the entire Rockhampton Gardens Symphony,' and tears just ran down this woman's cheeks. It was one of the most moving moments I think that we had, or I had, in the time that I was speaking to people about their involvement in the festival. I guess it was just a combination of joy and emotion that she was brought to tears and the rest of us were, too, at the table.

The Queensland Music Festival has a new artistic director now, Paul Grabowsky, and they have a wonderful board and team there, and the board and the new people that are involved in the Queensland Music Festival are continuing its success.

I'm now running the Brisbane Festival and we have a large program that's throughout the suburbs of Brisbane. We stage many large-scale free events, and again they're about the particular cultures of the different suburbs of Brisbane, and we reflect those cultures through the creation of artistic work or cultural activity as part of the Brisbane Festival. I've driven around Brisbane and gone through the same process – I've been out and spoken to the 26 councillors that represent those various wards of Brisbane and heard what they had to say. I've spoken to cab drivers, people in streets and pubs, everywhere, to try and understand how they feel about their particular suburb, and the suburbs do have very different cultures. The culture of New Farm is a very different culture to Hamilton, for example. Inala is a very different culture to

Ascot. There are quite stark differences. Dutton Park is a very different culture to Holland Park and Coorparoo and so on. So for us to try and create things in those suburbs that do genuinely reflect the culture of the people that live there has been a fascinating journey for me and I think a fascinating experience for the team of the Brisbane Festival, and for the people in those communities who are involved in developing those pieces.

Peter McGill – Pyro Oz at Riverfire

People in business and academia today are often required to work in multi-disciplinary groups or contribute multiple skills to their work. The same is true of

many working in the Arts. Pyro-technicians are a classic example, as they must understand not only the shape and colour of fireworks, but also how to successfully choreograph an event to achieve the most dramatic images – timed with computer precision over large areas. Their creative endeavours may not last long but the memories often do, as they revive

the child in all of us.

> *'There were a couple of moments during the display when I could see 6 barges all operating as though there was one finger pushing the button ... It's a sense I got years ago, when I was working for the Australian Ballet. Just to see that many people every night coordinating perfectly and doing the same thing every performance. It's that same sense.'*

I started off in theatre. I was briefly a student at NIDA (the National Institute of Dramatic Arts) and then worked as a stage manager in theatre, touring round the country back in the mid '70s with Tintookies, a massive puppet show. As part of Tintookies there was this little stage trick that I did every day. It was an exploding rock I blew up every day, a simple fireworks trick.

Years later I met up with Syd Howard, the guru of fireworks in Australia. He was based in Sydney and had a factory up at Kempsey. I'd hung around there like a bad smell and eventually he gave me a job. I worked for Syd as his operations manager from 1998 until he retired in 2001, and then I continued to work for his son-in-law and his partners until the beginning of 2004, when they decided to take the business in a different direction and go offshore. In response to this, my partner Julie and I formed our own company, Pyro Oz Productions, to continue doing fireworks displays in Australia.

During my time with Syd, Julie made the mistake of coming along and watching a display. After the display she started to rake and help clean up. She became completely hooked on fireworks – once the smell of gunpowder gets into your nostrils, there is no going back. She now has a fireworks licence and she's out there doing fireworks displays with me all the time. She's been in it now for about four years and recently got to design her first show from scratch and go through the creative angst that I go through! Fireworks is a great occupation. Someone described it as '… a fine line between art and arson'.

All the fireworks are imported these days. There are two companies doing limited manufacture in Australia but on the whole you can't compete with the low cost of Chinese fingers (Chinese labour). The bulk of the fireworks come in from China. The best ones are Japanese – they make a really exquisite product. Then for specialised, what we call indoor or close-proximity fireworks, the best come out of America. People are often amazed at the concept of indoor fireworks. There is a whole range of tricks that we can do for theatre, special events and concerts, where you are in close proximity with performers and audiences.

Currently, learning about firework displays is very much 'on-the-job training'. From a personal level, I was predisposed to it because of my theatre background. I approach it as the ultimate performance! For me, on a purely selfish level, I do everything I used to do in theatre but I don't share the applause with actors and musicians anymore. I guess the timing skills and the knowledge of what makes a good performance is the same. More like a choreographer, working out how it'll look best and staging it – this is certainly my personal bent. We all approach fireworks from our own experiences. One of the best operators I have worked with in this country was a motor mechanic – he's unfortunately gone back to that – and he approached fireworks from a very mechanistic viewpoint, bringing all the techniques and technologies together in a creative way. He was certainly the expert in computerised design and firing of displays.

It was Syd who originally got the contract for River*fire* in Brisbane some years ago. Because of my association with Syd and the project, our company Pyro Oz, was lucky enough to get to do the fireworks for the 2004 Brisbane River*fire*. There were fifty people working on the night, firing that display. The crew included two operators on each of the six roof tops, three on each of the six barges, two on the four CityCats, six crew on each of three bridges and another two in the control room. In total over 3,000 hours went into the preparation and firing of the display with about 10 tons of fireworks going up in smoke.

The way a display as complex as River*fire* actually works is, you have an audio tape which has the two channels that go out to the public, so if they are listening on the radio they can hear it. There is a third channel, which just goes to the pyrotechnicians with voice cues and a fourth channel with time code – that was me reciting the cues: 'Stand by Q1 – Q1 go!' (And ready to swear if it didn't). The crew responds to show tape giving them their cue points and manually firing on cue. That is how you coordinate a show across such a large area. For instance, this year River*fire* went from Story Bridge to West End, about four to five kilometres of the Brisbane River. The Story and Goodwill Bridges were fired with a computerised firing system.

Computerised firing is driven by time code and they give the designer the opportunity of doing very intricate sequences.

For River*fire,* I had a vantage point that allowed me to see from Story Bridge to West End. There were a couple of moments during the display when I could see six barges all operating as though there was one finger pushing the button. That sort of thing is what inspires me – when you see a disparate bunch of people coordinating and working together like one unit to get everything right. It's a sense I got years ago, when I was working for the Australian Ballet. I used to do the lighting for them for one of their Sydney seasons many years ago. For one season there were about 20 other crew, about 50 dancers, another 60-odd in the orchestra pit and 20 front-of-house staff. Just to see that many people every night coordinating perfectly and doing the same thing every performance. It's that same sense. There are various points when one individual might rule the roost in terms of design or setup, or whatever, but when it comes to the actual performance, it's very much a group effort.

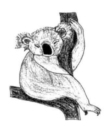

Jeremy Geia – Laura Dance Festival

Jeremy first came to this job more through birthright than job-specific training – he'd previously been in television news. He became Festival Director and his blend of innate and learned skills has resulted in the growing popularity of a truly unique festival.

'*Every Aboriginal nation is unique and you see that at the festival. Most people have a stereotype image of an Aboriginal person maybe with a didgeridoo or a boomerang but in the Cape York community the didgeridoo isn't played in all communities and other communities wear grass skirts or use feathers from cockatoos. Actually a lot of their ochres and stuff are dug out from their own community's area so each community has a different style of painting on their bodies. Also their head-dresses and other accessories as part of their ceremonial outfits are unique to their area.*'

I was born in Cairns and my grandmother was from Cape York and so was my grandfather. I also have very strong connections to Palm Island. I was involved with the Laura Festival for the first time in 2003. I have a background in television news so I was approached to help run the festival. It was my first festival and the first time I had visited Laura.

The Laura Festival has been going now for approximately twenty-five years and it's a gathering of different nations of Aboriginal people from the Cape York region and also includes people from Mornington Island and Brisbane and Woorabinda, which is on the coast, halfway down to Brisbane.

The festival is a three-day event that showcases some of the oldest dances and songs in the world from some of the oldest living cultures in the history of the world. Laura is a special place, partly because of its significance as a meeting area but also because it's home to the Quinkan Rock Art Galleries; the rock art there is about 16,000 years old. The festival attracts thousands of people from many parts of the world.

I believe that the Laura Festival originated as a result of Cape York Aboriginal people wishing to practise their cultures and celebrate them in a festival-type setting. It started many years ago, not specifically in Laura, but in different parts of the Cape. Laura became a default setting because it was accessible to most communities since the roads converge into Laura on the way to Cairns and other places. Identity with place and people is an extremely important part of being an Aboriginal person and a human being, to know where you come from and to know you're a part of something like a group or a certain clan, these are very important things to know and keep alive. This festival reinforces those old ways but also looks at modern means to keep them alive.

Every Aboriginal nation is unique and you see that at the festival. Most people have a stereotype image of an Aboriginal person maybe with a didgeridoo or a boomerang but in the Cape York community the didgeridoo isn't played in all communities, and other communities wear grass skirts or use feathers from cockatoos. Actually a lot of their ochres and stuff are dug out from their own community's area so each community has a different style of painting on their bodies. Also their head-dresses and other accessories as part of their ceremonial outfits are unique to their area. For example, Aurukun will have cockatoo feathers as a head-dress while others like Injinoo will have long grass skirts with different markings on their bodies. After a while, when you've gone to a few festivals, you can actually identify each community by the costume that they wear. It's very diverse and an amazing experience. Everyone thinks they know their own backyard, but even Aboriginal people going to this festival find it's just a whole portal of learning and a really great place to share and make new friends.

The festival is set in a beautiful area with a natural dancing circle which has been used for many, many years. There are special places of significance in and around that area and once you actually step on the piece of land that the festival's held on you can sense that this is a very spiritual and special place, it's a 'story place'. Every community is welcomed to that area and they tell their stories. It's an amazing experience, you're surrounded by trees and escarpments and you're looking at different communities performing and dancing and you're hearing music that you know is extremely old and it's straight from the earth. There are no modern day instruments like guitars, it's just clapping sticks, the voice, feet stamping and the dust that's stirred up by the dance. It really brings people who live in cities and towns back to what it must have felt like for the original human beings here to celebrate being together and dancing. I guess we all still have that strong connection to the original state of the human being, just working with their land. It's a very different experience to a rock concert or a theatre performance but it has all the same ingredients of theatre, sound and stories – you really are swept away! It's another world, too, because when people camp out bush they feel more connected to the land, there's another channel there. When people come from the cities they're not so tuned in to nature, not as much as someone living out bush, I guess, but the appreciation is still there. People will always have that inside them and going out there to Laura really opens up those channels.

The great thing about this festival is that you're not just a passive audience, you're actually interacting with indigenous groups, camping right next to them or you're lining up next to them to have a shower or buying some food or sharing a fire. It's an ideal environment to initiate dialogue between different people. It's one thing to see

Aboriginal culture being performed right in front of you but to then sit down with people and talk about what life is like out bush – you find we have more in common as human beings than we have differences. For most Australians who haven't met an Aboriginal person before this is a perfect environment to meet them. It's not only non-Aboriginal people either, its Aboriginal people that live in the cities who don't meet people from the bush that often. It's a learning experience for everyone, including the performers, who may not have met people from Melbourne before, or from Canada or from Finland or wherever. It's a window of opportunity for both peoples looking into each other's worlds. Laura is one of those rare places where you can share that sort of experience.

People will always be interested in the cultural aspects of aboriginality as they were in the Sydney Olympics. I guess in the city it's fast and furious and you can be punished for not keeping up with the pace – but if you show people something that has soul they get to appreciate that it has its own pace. Humans are interested in stories, we love good storytelling and performance and that's what Aboriginal dancing is all about – it's our culture. We do it in the open in natural surroundings so lots of people can have access to it and celebrate the cultures that make up the identity of this country.

For me it's been an honour and a privilege to be working with these communities, who have always been so isolated, who have some fantastic things to share and give to this world. I think it's very important that they have access to the world as well. Aboriginal people don't know everything about Aboriginal Australia, because it's made up of different Aboriginal nations. If we can sit down and listen to each other and learn about each other then I think we'll be better off as an Australian nation and as people of this planet.

We have regulars who always come to the Laura Festival, like the people from Aurukun and Coen and others too. We go out to the different communities to invite these communities personally, 'face to face' – that's an important part of doing business, face to face.

The process is very organic in that I can print a program up for the festival two days out from the festival, as I did this time around, but we threw the program out the window the first day because some communities couldn't make it as the rain had shut the roads and we had other communities arrive unannounced. It really is an organic event where things just take place! You can only plan certain components of the festival like your toilets and your showers and having food stalls and that sort of thing there, but in terms of having people come to participate, whether they're audience or performers, it has to be an organic process.

The crafts people from the different communities also come. The Laura Festival is an Aboriginal dance and cultural festival and things like weaving are a very important part of Aboriginal culture. To make a nice bag or whatever, every aspect of making it may have a song, for example, or a process that goes with it that has information about the plant used to make the bag and it's sung when they go out to collect the different materials for it. They bring the names and languages, all that kind of thing, with the stories behind each activity and explain them – everything has a purpose and a story. It's the same with painting and carving. It's important to keep these traditions alive, because when these people pass away, some of their knowledge of the traditions goes with them. The festival aims to try and keep that cultural knowledge alive so we can hand it down and transfer it between the different generations.

The Laura Festival generates a great sense of community self-esteem and self-confidence. For some kids on the Cape it'll probably be one of the best memories ever in their life. I say that because, when they grow older, life in a community and the realities of living in communities can be very, very tough. There's high unemployment and a lot of social things that are not very nice, so in terms of development of confidence and self-esteem, their memories of the Laura Festival are probably the best thing that will ever happen to these kids. You've got thousands of people clapping them on and encouraging them and they'll never forget that.

Brian Sansom – The Gympie Muster

He says he was 'a bit of a dreamer' as a schoolboy, but now he orchestrates festivals that are the stuff of other people's dreams. This has spawned another business – tent cities to accommodate the immense crowds that are drawn to these events. Brian didn't train for any of these jobs. He tells me he was just there at the right time and fulfilled a need.

'... we had about 15,000 or so people at the event ... Australia was in the biggest drought we'd ever had. John Farnham came out on stage at seven o'clock ... and the skies opened up and it just poured with rain! The atmosphere was so great that I don't believe one patron left that open amphitheatre.'

When I was young I was always a bit of a dreamer and I was ridiculed a bit for that at college. I and another mate originated from Taree and used to come up with all sorts of grandiose ideas, but never ever put them into practice. The Muster eventually became the opportunity, but how it started off was interesting.

There's a country music group up here called the Webb Brothers, who were quite well recognised nationally at the time. They'd actually been nominated for a 'Golden Guitar', which is awarded in Tamworth each year for achievers in Country Music. This was in 1982 and a bus went down to Tamworth, which the Webb Brothers were on, and three of us from the Apex Club went down too. We didn't have any great appreciation for Country Music at that time, but we were ready for a good time. We saw the festival and enjoyed ourselves a lot. On the way back in the bus we had a few more drinks and we said, 'Why can't Gympie have a Country Music festival if Tamworth can?' We had all these great ideas at the time, as you do, but then we went back to work and didn't think more about it.

Then one day the manager of the Webb Brothers, who was a personal friend of mine, came and saw me. At the time I was the incoming president of the Apex service club (a voluntary organisation) and this friend said, 'The Webb Brothers just realised they've been in the business twenty-five years, so they think it's a good time for a celebration. They're graziers and have a large property called *Thorneside* and it's also the centenary of their family having been granted the property, so they thought they'd have a concert out there on a Saturday afternoon and invite the towns-people out. Would you guys at the Apex club like to run the bar and cook the hamburgers?' (That was the sort of thing that service clubs like Apex did.) When he said this, the ideas we'd had on that bus trip about running a festival all came rushing back.

We thought of a three-day festival, and maybe having a ball. Before we went back with this idea we thought, 'This isn't going to work unless we get some major promotion.' In Brisbane at that time there was a country music radio station called 4KQ, so we went and approached Ian Skipton (one of the station's main personalities) and Jennifer Gould, who was the marketing manager – I think she still is on the staff. Initially they said no, but within twenty-four hours they said, 'Yes,' so we put it up to the Gympie Apex club and it just got through. I put up a budget of $25,000. Our biggest project to that date had been $4,000, so it was quite a big risk. Anyway the club agreed and the three Webb Brothers agreed to it as well.

That would have been in May '82 and we planned for the event to take place in September. The Commonwealth Games were opening in September that year so we planned this for the week before that, thinking we might get a few people from that. I don't think we did, but that was the thought. The main thing was: it was a success! There were probably about 2,000 different people there. It was the same concept as what happens now. People camped on the property and we had a big marquee, where there was a huge Ball. The Ball was the highlight of the festival. We had a stage which ran for three days – from the Friday afternoon, then all day Saturday, finishing around five o'clock on Sunday afternoon. It was fairly simple, compared to what it is now, but we pulled it off and we came out of it with $12,000 profit to give away at the end of the day.

So that was the first one and since then each year it's made a profit and generally a bigger profit than the year before. The first three were held on the Webb Brothers' property, but we realised that we had to start building an infrastructure for it ourselves. Eventually we were lucky enough to source some government land that we could use – so we moved onto State Forestry land and that's where the site is now.

Thinking about the people who go there for the Muster, I guess it's a bit like 'the Naked City'. Communities have formed and grown up there. We've been twenty years on our current site and there are people who have been coming for years. People who are going to the Muster now – some of them are going there to claim 'their' bit of dirt up to two and a half months prior to the event! You can have groups of 40 to 60 people like that. You can have some of the biggest acts in Australia playing at the Muster and at the same time there'll be huge parties or groups and people singing with their own entertainment out in that camping area.

The culture has changed over the years. In the first fifteen years or so it was predominantly just people who loved country music and the bush, but now a lot of other people have discovered it's an 'event' – like Birdsville or the Melbourne Races. If we held it in the show grounds it wouldn't work the same. In the forest where we hold it, it's nearly 40 kilometres from town on a dirt road, there's no electricity in the campsite and there's limited phone coverage. It's a chance for people to escape. For the show itself, we just bring in huge generators; a generator company gives us some very generous sponsorship for that.

There've been so many people who've worked on the Muster now. It's enabled a lot of people to learn new skills. Apex was originally very fearful that a major event like that could take over and destroy them as a service club. That was probably a reasonable debate to have at the time, but our Apex club now raises more funds than any other club in Australia. The other thing is that our philosophy has always been to involve the community. There're now well over 45 other community groups that are involved in working at the Muster and raising funds and we estimate that there're 1500 volunteers on-site at the event. All those community groups, whether they're school P&Cs or service clubs, are also very dependent now on their revenues from the Muster.

There've been a few major turning points. I think it was in 1993 Australia had that big drought and we came up with the concept that we might help by putting all our funds towards a drought appeal and gaining a bit of publicity for the event as well. I said, 'Wouldn't it be great to get a major national act to come and help support us?' so I gave Glen Wheatley a ring about John Farnham and within a couple of days he agreed that John Farnham would come and perform free of charge. We got ABC *Landline* to come up and cover it nationally. That virtually changed it from a state event to a national event. It kept growing until we had about 15,000 or so people at the event. It was an unreal situation; Australia was in the biggest drought we'd ever had. John Farnham came out on stage at seven o'clock on Friday night and the skies opened up and it just poured with rain! The atmosphere was so great that I don't believe one patron left that open amphitheatre. It never stopped raining the whole weekend – it was our wettest Muster ever. It was quite unreal, being a Drought Appeal, but that put us 'on the map'.

A couple of years later we opened up the site and put another 6 or 7 venues in, so we're up now to 14 different venues on site. As well as country music we've got one whole venue for blues music and one that's got a bit of folk music in it and one totally for new talent, so people compete for 'talent search' throughout the whole weekend. For kids that want to make it, they know there's big prize money there – whoever wins gets a recording deal and $4,000 cash. We're servicing all sorts of needs and that's broadened the appeal of the event a lot. Each year the profits go up and last year we made $930,000 – just in one year – so it's quite a boost to all those non-profit organisations that are getting something out of the Muster.

Sometimes you get eaten up with these types of events and in retrospect you can say you've neglected things like the family at times. But on the positive side I've got a son and a daughter who've probably had experiences they'd never have had if they hadn't been involved with the Muster. Currently my partner Kathy works on the Muster with me and is involved with other parts of the business, along with my daughter Jade. It's great to have this freedom and ability to work as a family unit on common goals.

Back in 1995 I started a business which I still own now, which we call 'Tent City Hire'. It's a tent accommodation business which goes all round Australia servicing festivals that need temporary accommodation. We've got 500 tents and they're currently setting up for the Dreaming Festival at Woodford. We've got a crew down there now doing that.

Probably the biggest job I've ever done was for the official opening of the Stockman's Hall of Fame which was in 1988. We had to coordinate the whole opening celebrations. We had to handle all the logistics and provide the catering. We had a big circus tent where we did all that and we had the local agricultural college supply a lot of staff and we had big chefs from Brisbane. The Queen travelled out there, opened the Hall of Fame, which was a great success, and then she went and opened up Expo in Brisbane the next day. It was just a magnificent event and experience to be involved in.

Through the Muster I got a job as manager of the Carnival of Flowers at Toowoomba for a while. That event is one of the city's icons and there were many ancillary events associated with the festival, concerts in the park, street parades, Carnival Queen Quests, art shows, the list went on. It was certainly a learning curve and an experience I'll always value. After I'd left Gympie, they put on a part-time coordinator for the Muster and when I came back I took over that job – the Apex club employed my newly formed business, 'Sunshine Connections', to do the coordination role for the Muster and I've done it ever since.

Probably the biggest challenges with the Muster have been toilets and showers for an event out in the bush. When we started off the first showers were jam tins with holes punched in them, then the second year we thought we'd upgrade and we put in solar hot water – someone donated solar, but the sun didn't come out and we had cold water! Then we went to demountable buildings with electric heaters, but the heaters could not keep up, and then we built our own from steel, but it was so hard you couldn't bear to stand up in it unless you wore shoes – so we then had to put rubber matting in them. Now we've got permanent ones – we couldn't use electric – we had to use gas to keep up the hot water. Once you've got a big volume of water you've got the next problem: you've got to keep building bigger and bigger dams. There was the same problem with toilets. It's probably one of the biggest problems with events – toilets and showers. People don't think about it, but it's so important. We've always said, 'Cold beer and clean toilets and showers – if you can solve those problems, you're half way there to keeping people happy!'

PART FIVE: Historic Capital Landmarks

'God created memory that we might have roses in December.'

- Italo Svevo

Often when remembering a place we'll remember it in conjunction with people or incidents we've experienced there. Such memories may be synonymous with a time in our lives, or in the life of the place itself. In the context of a city, such places can become etched in the collective memory of its citizens.

Bronwyn Lea: Poet

Walking down Wickham Terrace

I looked up
to see the sun break

on the sand
stone windmill –

long ago a grist
mill the worst

of the worst birled
like a giant

log on a millpond,
spinning

from sunrise to sun
set, crushing

grain whenever
the wind died

down. I thought I saw
a woman slip

into the grinding wheel
of Brisbane's

Tower of Terror
and I held my breath –

lightheaded
from violence long ago

set in stone.

Bronwyn Lea is the author of *Flight Animals* (UQ Press) which won the Wesley Michel Wright Prize for Poetry and the Fellowship of Australian Writers Anne Elder Award in 2002. Bronwyn is series editor of UQ Press's annual *The Best Australian Poetry* anthology. She lives in Red Hill, Brisbane.

Chris Pantano: Glass Artist

Outback - Landscape 1998 Blown and hand-formed glass inspired by the rugged landscapes of western Queensland. The three-dimensional imagery created by manipulating coloured, molten glass into the forms of mountains, rocks and gum trees, with each layer being separated by a gather of clear glass. (Photos by Errol Larkan)

Chris Pantano: Born in Sydney, Chris moved to Queensland in the mid '60s. Based on the Sunshine Coast, his work has been selected to represent Queensland and Australia at cultural events and has been exhibited throughout Australia, Europe, Asia and the USA for over twenty years. Chris received the Maroochy Shire Bicentennial Award for his contribution to the Arts and first place for Tourism Marketing in the Sunshine Coast Tourism Awards on three occasions. He also received awards from the Australian Woolshed for his Australian themed glassworks. He is represented in the collections of the Queensland Art Gallery, Parliament House in Canberra, the Art Gallery of the Northern Territory, Wagga Wagga City Art Gallery, National Gallery of Victoria and Koganezaki Glass Museum, Japan. www.pantano.com.au

Living on in the Memory

Vince Hardiker – Lead Trumpeter at Cloudland

Bowen Hills is famous for a now missing building, whose architectural presence crowning the hill remains etched on the memories of those who passed this way prior to 1982. At 4am on 7November 1982, the popular ballroom 'Cloudland' was demolished. Cloudland, complete with a funicular-style cable car which ran from Breakfast Creek Road up the steep slope to its impressive shell-like entrance, could hold up to 2000 people. It had a marvellous sprung dance floor, the best, it was said, in the southern hemisphere. The views from there were fantastic and that is all that remains – now no longer the province of the many but the privilege of the few who own apartments in the gated community called 'Cloudland Apartments' now on the site. I arrange to meet Vince at Redcliffe, the quiet seaside residential area near where he lives, and we go to a local café to chat over coffee. He used to play lead trumpet in the band at Cloudland during its halcyon days.

'On Saturday nights, there'd be up to 2000 people in Cloudland, and on the right-hand side of the stage they had a big section roped off for the jitterbug. Yes, and it was fantastic!'

I was born in Lancashire in the north of England in 1923. I left school at fourteen and I got a job working at Stoneyhurst College as a groundsman. My dad was the Assistant Head Gardener.

My father and I joined the brass band in Hurst Green when I was nine and a half but when I was twelve Dad formed a dance band and we did gigs around the place for several years. It was quite an adventure, travelling from one little village to the next. My dad was a self-taught musician and he taught me the best he could. I've got a good ear and it's been very rewarding for me over the years.

When I was called up into the army in 1943 I said, 'I'm not going to take my trumpet with me,' but six months later I wrote home and asked for it. I was based in Ireland first then Scotland for more training. I was in the Royal Signals and we were attached to the Air Formation Signals. We had to establish communications when the infantry went in. Then we moved down to London and lived in bombed out houses for about three weeks, waiting to go to France.

Later we went down to Mons in Belgium and we stayed there. That was our headquarters and we were there until 1944. When we crossed the Rhine a lot of us were pulled back and sent out to Rangoon via India. On the way to Rangoon we arrived at a place called Mhow in central India. I was practising my trumpet in the barracks one night and this Sergeant Hudis came along and said, 'I heard you playing the trumpet – what trade are you?' I said, 'I'm a vehicle mechanic.' 'Oh,' he said, 'we've got a band here, you know. Would you like to stay?' I said, 'Certainly, yes!' 'Well,' he said. 'Report to Captain Green tomorrow morning at nine o'clock,' so I did and I was taken off the draft and I stayed there for two years playing in the band three nights a week. It probably saved my life – two of my mates got killed in Rangoon.

I had the chance to get demobbed to Australia from India, because I knew Dad and Mum were going to come out to here after the war. My dad's brothers were already out here, one since 1912, one in 1922 and the other in1928. My parents waited for me to come back to England in '47 and then they notified Australia House and we left England on 10 October 1947 for Australia. The whole family came, Dad and Mum, my sister Dorothy and me, Jim, Raymond, David and Celia.

We came to Queensland. Dad's brother, Uncle Tom, had a farm in Murgon and we stayed there for 2 or 3 months. Then Dad bought a farm in a place called Kilkivan. My sister, who brought her fiancé out to Australia with her, wanted to get married and needed a bridesmaid. We asked a lady called Min Angel, (her real name was Mary but they called her Min) who used to look after the priests when they came up to Kilkivan to say Mass, if she would be the bridesmaid for my sister and she agreed. I was the best man. Afterwards a friendship developed between Min and me and we got married in 1949. I helped Dad until I got married and after that Min and I moved to Brisbane.

I joined the music scene in Brisbane in about 1949 or 1950. I started in a band. I've kept a book of all my jobs. The main dancehalls in Queensland at that particular time would be Cloudland, the City Hall and the Riverside Ballroom at New Farm in Oxlade Drive. I played there three times a week on and off until 1953 or 1954, with a fellow named Jim Burke, who played bass.

In 1953 I did a few jobs for Billo Smith at Cloudland. Billo was a very hard task master, but he did the job really well. He was the band leader, he played saxophone and his wife Nessie played the piano and sang sometimes. Verne Thompson was there quite a bit round the mid '50s. Later he played piano at the Bellevue Hotel. At that time Verne played trumpet with me, but when Nessie used to sing, Verne would accompany her on the piano. Billo had a son called young Billo, who was a very good sax player. In 1954 we played for the Royal Ball in the city hall and I worked permanently with Billo Smith from mid 1954.

A ball at Cloudland would last from 8 pm until 1 am. We used to have three numbers then a three-minute break in between. Billo had it timed to a fine art. When the three minutes were up he'd pick up the saxophone and off we'd go again. We had a

10-minute interval at a quarter to ten, if I remember right, then we were back on for the rest of the evening. It was pretty challenging.

On Saturday nights, there'd be up to two thousand people in Cloudland, and on the right-hand side of the stage they had a big section roped off for the jitterbug. Yes, and it was fantastic! It was dinner dress and pretty formal. We used to play for dancing championships and that was great too. Talk about being busy. Some of those months I played eighteen or nineteen days a month – and I was working in the daytime too. I used to get up at seven o'clock and be working by eight o'clock. I'd get home from work about quarter past five at night and I'd have my tea and go straight to bed. I'd get up two hours later, shower and get dressed in my dinner suit and go to play in the band until midnight or one o'clock. It took about half an hour afterwards to get home and get to bed again.

Billo Smith retired in 1957 and a fellow by the name of Frank Thornton took over. He was an American tenor player, very good. He was there for a couple of years. Then a chap called Eddie Cousins that played trumpet took over the band from Frank and I think it was after Eddie left that Verne Thompson took over the band. Poor Verne, we used to give him a hard time, playing up a bit! We had a tremendous singer by the name of Tommy Hopper. He was a Scotsman who used to live on Petrie Terrace. Tommy used to like his wine. I had a Volkswagen then and he'd say, 'Would you take me home please?' then he wouldn't let me go until he drank another bottle of wine. He was a great fellow but he died of sclerosis of the liver. I finished playing at Cloudland in 1960. I was in New Zealand when it got pulled down – November 1982, it was. That was a real shame!

In 1959 I auditioned to work at Channel Nine. It was nerve-wracking because rehearsal time was at a premium and half the time we weren't sure what we were doing. Wilbur Kentwell played the organ, Jack Thompson (Verne's brother) was on sax, Bob Watson on drums, I was on trumpet and Maurie Dowden on piano. We did a few performances there for 'Tonight Shows' and what-have-you. We were down in the bottom with the cameras way up top shining down on us, and they used to have a go at me saying, 'You're the one who's causing the glare!' So they'd come down and spray my bald patch!

I played at Her Majesty's theatre from 1960 to 1965. In the late '60s I did a lot of freelance work in small bands playing at parties. Then in 1976 I joined the Brisbane Jazz Club. I was the second trumpet player and I was there a good twenty years. I was fortunate in being able to do a lot of ad lib solo – it was my scene and I enjoyed it. In 1972 and 1976 I also played for Disney on Parade, which was held in Victoria Park in a big tent – all the Mickey Mouse people – it was a brilliant show.

I've been fortunate enough to play for people like Sammy Davis Junior at the Festival Hall and twice for Shirley Bassey, once at the City Hall and once at the Festival Hall. I backed Louis Armstrong when he came out here and he was fantastic. I played for other people, too, who you may never have heard of, like the Ink Spots, and Billie Daniels. Musically I've had a wonderful life, thanks to my father.

I have three children. They all learned piano but my son Paul, who is fifty-eight, plays a bit of organ. My eldest daughter Therese passed her exams at piano and when organs came in she bought an organ and taught 10 to 12 pupils. That's gone by the board now; she's busy as a teacher's aide, which is a full-time job, and young Anne-Maree just enjoys listening to me.

My grand-daughter Amanda, who's twenty-six, came down to listen to me playing jazz at the Redcliffe Cultural Centre, which we do on the last Sunday of each month. We get a fantastic crowd. We start off with me on trumpet, a saxophone, a clarinet, piano, guitar and drums and then anybody who wants to sit in can do so. Most are a bit younger than me. I'm eighty-five and they're in their fifties and sixties.

I started to play in a brass band when I was nine and I didn't join a brass band again until 1996 when I came to live here at Scarborough. I joined the 'Ye Olde Brass RSL Memorial Band'. We play concerts at nursing homes, at the Salvation Army and the RSL; it's all quite enjoyable. People talk about retirement, but you need to have an interest. I've lived in a retirement village here for the last eight years. My wife's been in a nursing home for three and a half years in the same premises as me.

I'm a member of the 'Old Buffers', which is a get-together of old brass band musicians. We have this yearly little semi-contest with people ranging from forty years old to eighty years old. Each of these divisions is asked to play a little aria or solo. Some university students of music come and assess us in our marks and make little comments. It's rather more of a social evening – it's a chance for a get-together for some of the musicians who've been playing for many, many years. I ran second in my age group in the over seventies. Wilf Nott won our age group, playing a cornet. He's a brilliant player, but I'm told he intends challenging me on a flugelhorn! That's my favourite instrument; I love it – it's got a nice warm sound.

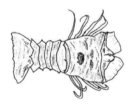

Peter Bonenti – The 'Bellevue Hotel'

The Bellevue Hotel was an elegant and historic Brisbane landmark, yet at midnight in April 1979 it was demolished. Peter suggested we meet in Kangaroo Point. It's a sunlit

room in a new penthouse apartment on the river. The setting is totally modern – in stark contrast to the photos spread before us on the coffee table, showing the Bellevue Hotel in the days when he was growing up. He leans forward as he talks of his childhood memories of life in the grand old hotel. He now works in real estate but still has dreams of restoring a 'Bellevue Hotel' to the Brisbane landscape.

> *'Dad went to the Premier, who was Nicklin at the time, and Dad said, "Here are my plans. I'm going to build a high-rise behind the Bellevue, keeping the Bellevue as it is, but building more rooms." The Premier looked at the plans and said, "No, Joe. Look we wouldn't approve this – no, we want to buy the Bellevue!" and that's when it started. The government owned all of George Street, right through to Queen Street, except for the Bellevue and one other place that they have since secured.'*

Dad came out here from England, having worked there and on the Continent in hotels like Grosvenor House, both before and after the war. He was asked to come out by Lennons Hotel, where he worked, until one day Reg Ansett rang him and said, 'Would you help us with a basket case of a place we've got in Melbourne called Manyung, in the Mornington Peninsular?' It was at Frankston on the Bay. Dad went down there and that's where I was born. It was a beautiful old place. Dad turned it around and Ansett said, 'Well, we've got another basket case in Brisbane. Will you go to Brisbane and look after the Cecil?' So around eighteen months after I was born he went to Brisbane. Dad was managing the Cecil for Ansett when he saw the Bellevue Hotel down the road, so he went and bought it for one hundred and eighteen thousand pounds from its previous owners, the Admans.

I believe the Bellevue was built around 1865, but I don't know who the first owners were. Dad bought it in 1956 and we lived there from 1956 until 1960. He owned it until 1970. I was five years old when we went there. I can remember the first day we walked into the place. We lived in the hotel in five suites of rooms – it was beautiful. When school friends came over we would go to the Botanical Gardens across the road. On a Sunday, in those days, there wasn't a soul to be seen. No one else ever came there on a Sunday. Brisbane was like a big country town in those days. It had a lot of charm about it, in my opinion.

At the time of the Ekka, all the country people would come and stay at the Bellevue and they had plenty of money to spend. It was their big trip to town to do business and to party. Although the city shut early in those days, the Bellevue was always full of life – particularly Friday and Saturday nights. There were balls and cabinet lunches and the government came there for dinners, as they didn't have the facilities they've got today. As a little kid I could walk out the front door and I'd run into the Premier coming out of the public or private bar. It was very different in those days.

We had Mum and Dad's silver wedding anniversary there in 1964, which was a very special time. We had the ballroom and they had around 200 guests for the party. I was thirteen then. I have very good memories of those times: lots of Governor's Balls, Red & White Balls, Christmas lunches, New Year's Eve's, lots of parties – lots of good memories. We had a great childhood, really, when you think about it, growing up in the middle of all that. It was a lot of fun, though we probably didn't appreciate how special it was then, because it was part of our lives. But when you look back you think, 'We had a great time!'

There was an employee, Mila, a waiter who was with Dad for years and years. He was a lovely man. The chef, Alan Digby, was terrific. He was with Dad for twenty years. An amazing chef, he produced all sorts of wonderful things for our birthdays – gosh yes! And he was a master of preparing buffets. Mum was a master with the flowers. She wasn't at the Bellevue every day as she had six children to look after. But on a Saturday morning or whenever, she'd be in there doing the flowers for all the weddings and that. I don't know how she fitted it all in, but she was very good at it.

We didn't really have a doorman. When I was fifteen, in my holidays I'd be a doorman. I'd open the door and deliver the dry-cleaning and that, but the waiters would pretty well do everything. That's the way it worked. There was a solid core of great staff. Outside there were four yard men. I remember all the waiters, drink waiters and food waiters. There was an army of casual banqueting staff that would come in to serve the food, clean up and go. In the restaurant all the waiters were permanent staff and I learned from them. Then there was the housekeeper and housemaids, of course. Upstairs there was an accounting office, where there was the accounts lady. My brother was up there doing wages and things like that. At the front office you would have three receptionists on at any one time – a reservations clerk, a receptionist and a switchboard operator. The old spaghetti switchboard would always be running hot!

When we worked there as waiters, you'd get in there at nine o'clock and you would do everything: vacuum, set up the tables, and take the kegs down underneath the public bar. You wouldn't do that today! For wines we had a huge cellar out the back. It wasn't underground but it was all specially lined so it was cool, not chilled. Then there were the old cold-rooms.

Once there was a gas strike, so out in the backyard Chef built open fires and cooked on the open fires to keep things going! Everyone put up with a lot of things you wouldn't even dream of today. There was a great team spirit.

One of the things Dad did when he first went to the Bellevue was air-conditioning, which was a novelty – no one had it then. You had these great big things in each room, including all the ballrooms, which were fed by chilled water from the cooling tower out the back, and they worked exceptionally well!

Dad also started the smorgasbord in Brisbane – that had never been heard of before. He put on dinner-dances and people would come in their droves. There were two hotels at the centre of the social scene in Brisbane during that time and they were the Bellevue and Lennons, plus there was Cloudland. Friday and Saturday nights were *the* nights, but the place would always be chock-a-block during the day for lunches and functions and that.

Dad would often bring people home to Kangaroo Point when they wanted to go out – they'd say to him, 'Let's get out of here, where can we go?' It would be Jack Brabham, the racing car driver, or Victor Borge, the comic pianist, or somebody like that. He'd ring Mum up at nine o'clock at night and say, 'I'm bringing so-and-so home for a drink,' and Mum would get out of bed and get dressed and turn the lights on and put the pool lights on and get everything ready. I don't know how she coped.

This is the way Dad would tell the story of how the government came to demolish the Bellevue. I think it was 1964, and we owned the land behind the Bellevue. There was a big car park area which Dad had bought up bit by bit, except for the Mansions and one other little corner there; we had all that so it was more than half the block. Dad went to the Premier, who was Nicklin at the time, and Dad said, 'Here are my plans. I'm going to build a high-rise behind the Bellevue, keeping the Bellevue as it is, but building more rooms.' The Premier looked at the plans and said, 'No, Joe. Look, we wouldn't approve this – no, we want to buy the Bellevue!' and that's when it started. The government owned all of George Street, right through to Queen Street, except for the Bellevue and one other place that they have since secured.

I don't think Dad had any option. Today maybe you might be able to say, 'I'm going to stay put; it's not for sale,' but not in those days. Also maybe Dad realised that if he didn't accept the offer he'd have to spend a lot of money on maintenance and upgrading of the interior of the hotel. It wasn't a compulsory purchase; it was agreed, probably in 1966. It was a good offer and maybe he thought about retiring at around that time. I never really asked Dad if he ever had any regrets about it.

I think the Bellevue sold for $680,000 or something like that, which was lots of money in those days. It was a very good figure and the government paid it off over the next 4 or 5 years, and the Bellevue closed on Christmas Eve 1970. When I left school I worked at the Bellevue for the last two years of its operation. After it closed on Christmas Eve 1970, we auctioned everything off and then the government started using the ballroom and restaurants and all that for archiving. It was terrible! I went in there in 1977 and there was a guard on duty and I told him who I was and said, 'Can I have a look?' That was the last time I ever set foot inside the Bellevue and it was very sad to see it like that.

The Premier at the time, Joh Bjelke-Peterson, said that the Bellevue was falling apart, but I don't believe that. Maybe the verandahs needed attention, but the walls were solid, big blocks. The floors creaked but they were sound and that was part of the glamour of it – I love creaking floors. Dad recarpeted the ballrooms and restaurant. It was probably down ten years when it closed and that was in 90-ounce pure wool carpet. When it was auctioned it was rolled up and it was almost as good as new.

I continued in the hotel business for some time and gravitated towards managed apartments on the Gold Coast and worked for Quality Inns for some time. That got me into real estate and now I have management rights myself at Dockside. Still, I've had this dream for years; it's a big idea, to rebuild the Bellevue in the same look. It would obviously be part of an overall development, and then you'd probably sell off the suites and lease them back so you'd run it just as a hotel, but you'd bring back the bars and the ballroom and the restaurants. I've worked it out. If you were to rebuild the Bellevue, you would definitely get a hotel licence. You would get front page publicity. You'd get a million dollars worth of advertising out of it immediately and people would want to go there. People would definitely want to get married at the Bellevue.

If it was done faithfully, and you had the high ceilings and the antique furniture, albeit copies, and you created the ambiance again, you could do it. Instead of a timber floor under the carpets it would be concrete, and there would be smoke alarms and sprinklers, but that could all be hidden. Who knows – it's a beautiful dream I've had, but it'd need a lot of money! Like the Raffles Hotel in Singapore. I've been to Raffles three times. I was there just before they closed it in 1988 to start the redevelopment. Then I was back in '90-something to see what they'd done. My God, it's great, though it's sad they moved the Long Bar. Still, it's a great drawcard for Singapore.

Years ago, when the press was talking about the government's plans to pull the Bellevue down, Mum wrote this poem:

The Bellevue Hotel (1865–1970)

If the Bellevue could talk I know that it would say
Please remember me, not as I am but in my halcyon days!
The brides, the balls, the Cup parties, tablecloths of lace,
One could go on forever and only just trace
The thousands of memories held within these walls,
It has stood there so gracefully through two world wars!
Can time run out for truly what was an institution?
To save it surely should be our New Year resolution,
A haven in the bad times and the good times too,
Don't take away this corner with its special kind of view!
Can't we cherish old familiar things in this atomic age
If only for our children's sake, and their rightful heritage.

Phylis Bonenti

David Tarczynski – Arnott's Biscuit Factory at Milton

Brisbane is known as the River City and it's easy to understand why. The main freeway is slung out over the water, following the edge of the CBD where building outlines are softened by trees along the curve of the river. The road rejoins the embankment at Coronation Drive in Milton near where the old biscuit factory used to stand. The factory was demolished years ago and relocated elsewhere, but like many other city-dwellers, I still miss the aroma of freshly baked biscuits that wafted into passing cars here, cheering commuters on their way to work. David has been with Arnotts almost all his working life and is now manufacturing manager in their new premises. He still keeps in touch with friends from the old days in Milton...

'The friendships that were born at Arnott's twenty-five years ago are still strong. The "Processing Tarts" is what they call themselves when they get together. They're all married and have got kids or divorced and whatever, but they still meet!'

The day started at 3 am when the ovens were lit. Back then there were 5 ovens. A lot of the doughs had what we call a 24-hour stand time. It was a two-part process. First you'd make the sponge – you'd put in the flour, yeast and shortening, and mix the dough. It would stand for about 18 hours – then you would take it and add more flour, the colours and flavours and mix that in and let it stand for another 6 hours. Basically, mixing was a 24-hour, 5-day-a-week operation. The baking only went for 17 hours a day, 5 days a week. The first biscuits would go in the oven at 6:36 in the morning and they would finish going into the oven at 11:07 in the evening.

The mixing room was where they made the doughs – the average dough was between 600 and 800 kilos, and the process was repeated every 40 minutes. Back in Milton in the old days, of that 600 or 800 kilos, about 50% was what we call bulk ingredients that were automatically fed into the mixer – the other 50% was loaded in by hand. For something like Scotch Finger, there would be butter and margarine, the colour, the salt, the soda and everything, that would go through the front, but the flour and water would be what we call 'on the system'. It's not that dissimilar to nowadays, except we have more ingredients on the systems now.

There was another area we called 'chemics', the room where all the colours and flavours were made up. In the mixing room there'd be 10 mixers and 12 people in ingredient prep, plus another 2 in chemics – that's per day shift – and between them they'd make from, say, a 600-kilo dough (what we classify as yield or moisture loss from the baking process is round the 20% mark), so of that 600 kilos they would get around 480 kilos of biscuits every 40 minutes!

There were a number of long-serving employees that had been there anywhere up to forty-five years. There was a boiler attendant called Fred who started as an apprentice. He'd lost his leg in the war, I think, and he actually had a wooden leg. He'd be out there attending to this big boiler, which used to make the steam for the ovens, and cleaning and whatever, and he'd get sick of wearing his wooden leg. Back in those days the wooden legs were heavy and they weren't real comfortable, so quite often he'd take the leg off and leave it sitting on the chair, while he'd hop around without it. He was a real laugh.

The mixing room was very much a 'man's area'. Many of these guys had been bakers in their earlier years, having come through the baking apprenticeship. They very much valued the art of dough making and biscuit making. Nowadays we've got a hell of a lot of technology but back then it was very much a 'see and feel and look', and whatever. They'd be able to test the doughs by feel. For example, a common thing in making crackers is – you take a piece of dough out of the mixer and you roll it into something that looks like a banana, and with a cracker dough you can actually peel the layers of dough off – the old guys would call that 'the banana peel test'. That tells how extensible and how flexible the dough is and gives it its lift and rise and shape.

They were an extremely dedicated and passionate group – the mixing room guys. Believe it or not, the way the factory ran, the mixing room and the people who worked in it were a group all to themselves. We all ate in quite a large canteen, and the mixing-room boys would always sit together – so there was always a lot of camaraderie and if you were a mixing-room boy you were seen as being tough.

In the factory in those days it was very ... well, not segregated, but the men worked in mixing, forming and baking, and the ladies did the feeding, and the guys operated the machines. That's just the way it was. There were the mixing-room boys, and then down where the cutting machines and ovens were, they were called the bake-house boys, so they behaved similarly to the mixing-room guys in that they sat at their own tables in the canteen. They each had social activities as groups. I can remember as bake-house boys we had a darts team. We had several darts teams actually – that's where I started playing darts with the group. I went on to play for Queensland; I represented Queensland for a number of years. Arnott's must have had about six dart teams and darts was always a popular conversation piece around the factory.

We had a very active social club. The original social club was in the old Milton Bus Depot on Milton Road where the trolley buses were. Every Friday afternoon it opened at three o'clock and it was darts and it was ping-pong, it was cards and, of course, there was a bit of drinking that went on. The site itself was a dry site, there was no alcohol permitted within the walls of the factory. Once again, the groups would always stick together.

There were a number of romances and marriages. There'd have to have been around 20 marriages that I knew of came from romances there. Back then there were probably 150 women working in the packing room and about 100 guys working in the rest of the factory. Generally there was a fair spread of ages – from nineteen or twenty to about thirty-five and then from forty-five to sixty-five, that was for the guys and for the women it was the same. There were a fair number of young girls and so all the young guys and the young girls would get together over in the social club. A lot of the girls I know now, that used to go over to the club and drink together, still work here. A number of the girls were the same age as me, eighteen or nineteen when they started, and are still here.

Talking about areas in the factory, where we did the cream biscuits, and where we did the Monte Carlos and the Iced Vo Vos, that area was called secondary processing. That was where all the young girls worked. Everybody that worked there was under twenty-five. The processing girls were sometimes frowned upon by the ladies in the packing room, because they saw the girls in the processing room going out with all the boys. They had big nights out and parties and they always stuck together as a group. Though there's only, I think, two left here out of fifteen that were in there then, they still meet regularly. The friendships that were born at Arnott's twenty-five years ago are still strong. The 'Processing Tarts' is what they call themselves when they get together. They're all married and have got kids or divorced and whatever, but they still meet. They are a very close-knit little group.

There were only three guys that worked in Processing and the remaining thirty-five or so were ladies, so naturally that was where all the young guys wanted to work. A lot of people worked very closely together. Two people could be standing beside each other feeding biscuits for eight hours straight. What used to amaze me was that at the end of the day they'd still be talking and I'd say, 'What the hell do you talk about for eight hours?' It's different if you only see a person once a year, but this was every single day, so they knew every single part of each other's lives. They discussed what happened in their lives very openly all day, everyday – more or less like 'Days of Our Lives', I suppose.

The mixing room was at the back of the factory, at the point furthest away from Coronation Drive so we'd mix the doughs there and tip them down, and then run them through the oven, so the end of the oven was actually at those windows on Coronation Drive. They used to pump the hot air straight out over Coronation Drive, that's why you smelt the biscuits there.

Generally a lot of guys would start there when they were seventeen or nineteen and then have to spend about ten years working learning all the art. At that stage if you were good enough you'd become a leading hand and then another ten years later you'd be a foreman and then probably another five to seven years later you may be lucky enough to be the production manager. I was the youngest foreman they'd ever had.

Then we built the factory at Virginia, which is where we currently are, and I moved over as Production Manager. From there I went as Production Manager to New Zealand, then to Melbourne and back here to Virginia in 1988 when this factory opened.

They moved the making of chocolate biscuits to our Adelaide bakery in 1978. We used to make Tim Tams, and Mint Slice. Back then during summer in Queensland we only stocked four or five varieties of chocolate biscuits and then in winter the full range would be brought in. During summer there'd only be Tim Tams and Mint Slice and Caramel Crowns – chocolate Teddy Bears, I think, was another one.

In 1986, a huge big Moreton Bay fig tree on the corner of Coronation Drive and Exford Street blew over in a big wind. It must have been a good eighty feet high and it came down and hit the factory. I remember we were all in the canteen and it smashed all the windows in. Luckily no one was hurt. I remember standing at the counter waiting to get served and you could see the tree coming; it was like slow motion. You could see people diving out of the road as the tree came through the wall. Below the canteen, was the General Manager of Finance's office. The story goes that when the tree hit, it smashed all of his windows in and people apparently found him just sitting there totally stunned with leaves and sticks all round him poking through the windows.

Thinking of my time in Arnott's, the best way to put it, it was very, very much a family. I suppose that's my fondest memory of the place. As a young guy growing up there, the older women would sort of take you under their wing. The boys would go out and get on the booze and whatever and the women they'd say, 'You shouldn't drink too much,' and they'd try and match-make you up with the girls in the factory. Some of them are still here now. I'll walk out to the factory now and wander around and they'll come and put an arm around my shoulder and say, 'I remember when you were only young.' Back then it was very much a close-knit family – everyone looked after each other. Everyone socialised together. I didn't meet my wife there, but I had several girlfriends there. My children often talk about it, the youngest one, Shawnie, is only ten and I say, 'What are you going to do when you grow up?' and she'll say, 'I want to go and work with you at Arnott's, Dad.' I say, 'No, you need to go to university and be an engineer or doctor or lawyer or something or other.'

It's hard work in manufacturing, lots of long hours and whatever. I think I was pretty lucky, I just happened to be in the right place at the right time in my career. But I wouldn't change a day of my working career at Arnott's; I've had a ball for the last twenty-five years and hope to have a ball for the next twenty years until I retire!

From Strength to Strength

Karen Nilsson – Working at Lone Pine Koala Sanctuary

Generations of children have been brought to this sanctuary to see and have their

Photo courtesy of Mathew Doherty

photographs taken holding a live koala. I remember my mother telling me how she visited a koala sanctuary in the early 1930s. Sitting on the bus to return to the city she'd watched as other people got in. A young mother sat nearby, opposite her little girl, who was hugging her koala. Suddenly a small movement alerted the mother – she leaned forward to feel the toy – it was soft and warm and very much alive! The little girl had left her toy behind, preferring this one which returned her hug. Fortunately security isbetter protected these days, with beautiful memories being taken home to all corners of the world. In January 1996, after leaving University, Karen started working at Lone Pine and is now their Senior Wildlife Officer, and deeply involved in the Sanctuary's research activities. Lone Pine Koala Sanctuary is now the oldest and largest koala sanctuary in the world.

> *'I always get great pleasure when I check a pouch and see a newborn joey or see a joey emerge from the pouch for the very first time (you never get tired of it) but my highlights are the actual births I've witnessed.'*

I grew up in the country – most of my childhood was spent in a small town called Imbil, which is near Gympie. I've always been an animal lover, so my family was not surprised at my chosen career path. After high school, I earned a Bachelor of Science (Zoology major) at the University of Queensland. When I finished university, I started volunteering at animal parks and secured a job at Lone Pine Koala Sanctuary. It was here that I fell in love with koalas. My 'hands on' wildlife training was all done on the job here.

My working day varies a lot! My main focus is the koalas, so the day always starts out with checking all 130 of them to make sure they are all okay. I assist the vet with any treatments we need to do, weigh all the koalas regularly, train any young koalas or new staff and make sure all the joeys are with their own mothers (and not someone else's). Breeding season is very busy as I have to determine which females are ready for breeding, set up mating pairs, check pouches to see if joeys have been born, assist with any ongoing research. Then there's the paperwork and all the behind the scenes jobs, plus dealing with visitors.

Our males and females are all housed separately, which means we have complete control of the breeding. During breeding season, I have to decide which females (and males) we would like to breed with that year and which pairs are best according to genetics. I determine from a female's behaviour whether or not she is ready to breed then take the selected male to her for mating. Koala gestation is 33 to 35 days, so 33 days after the mating, I start checking her pouch for a joey and, if the mating was not successful, the whole process starts again.

The joeys are very adventurous when they start to leave their mother's pouch at 6½ to 7 months and sometimes wander off onto the wrong mother, so each morning I make sure all the joeys are where they are supposed to be! In most cases, koala mums are brilliant and will look after someone else's young, but if they aren't currently lactating, sometimes it's not the best place for the joey to be. I've also rescued joeys from mums where they have been trying desperately to fit into a pouch that is already occupied! Most uncomfortable for all involved, I'm sure!

Lone Pine Koala Sanctuary has assisted with research into Chlamydia and retroviruses in koalas in the past. However, most research we have done in the last several years has focused on our artificial insemination work. We have learned a lot about the reproductive behaviour and physiology of koalas that had previously not been known. We also worked hard towards the first successful birth of a koala conceived from artificial insemination (AI) in 1998 and that success has since been replicated several times. We are still continuing with this research to refine our techniques and work towards being able to send semen instead of live animals to improve genetic variability in both captive and wild populations.

We are hoping that we can improve genetic variability in wild populations that might be isolated from others and are in danger of inbreeding. We are also hopeful that this technology and research knowledge can be used to benefit other threatened and endangered species in the future. In addition, the behavioural information we have acquired will hopefully help people understand koalas a little better.

I work very closely with our vet. Her name is Galit Tzipori and we have worked together for many years now. Koalas are very difficult animals to read. They aren't like dogs that will show a definite set of signs if they are feeling ill and they spend much of their day sleeping, so Galit relies on my knowledge of the animals, both as a group and as individuals, to notice any signs of ill health. We have so many shared experiences! Unfortunately, we have shared the loss of animals over the years, which is always heart breaking, but we've also helped along young koalas that are finding growing up a bit hard and we've had the pleasure of seeing them make it through to be adults.

I always get great pleasure when I check a pouch and see a newborn joey or see a joey emerge from the pouch for the very first time (you never get tired of it!) but my highlights are the actual births I've witnessed. Not many people have seen a koala give birth, and it still blows me away when I look at some of the koalas that are now adults and remember seeing them as blind, hairless, helpless little things climbing into their mum's pouches – absolutely amazing. Most of these guys know me really well now and know my voice and I've had a few reach out to me for a hug, especially when they are feeling a bit low. I've also had a very young koala (still with its mum) run over to me when I spoke to him and jump into my hands to be held. I could just go on and on!

Koalas start to emerge from their mother's pouch at between six and seven months of age, but they don't venture away from their mother until they are permanently out of the pouch a couple of months later. Just recently I was watching a joey poke its head out of its mother's pouch for the first time. I left the enclosure, but was walking past soon after and noticed the mother, Karen, (my namesake!) pacing the floor. As I got closer I could hear the cries of a joey and Karen's agitated pacing increased. I hurried into the enclosure and knelt at the base of a pole of leaves and found her joey amongst the twigs.

Koala mums will usually respond to the distressed cries of a joey and Karen was at the base of the pole but seemed unable to pinpoint where the cries had been coming from. She sat on the ground in front of me while I scooped up her joey (a daughter!) and placed it safely onto her front where it clung to her fur. She continued to sit in front of me while she cupped the joey's head gently with her paws, nuzzling and licking it. As the joey started to seek out the pouch, I gave her a helping hand. Karen sat patiently while I guided her daughter into the pouch opening, only leaning forward now and then to sniff my hair or my cheek. With the joey safely back inside, Karen was happy to return to the branches. This is a moment that doesn't come along every day!

Another special part of our job is visiting nursing homes and respite centres. The people at these places are often unable to come to us, so once a month we take a koala to centres and homes that have asked us for a visit. These experiences are always very rewarding for the keepers and the residents. Visiting the children's hospital each Christmas is also a highlight of our year.

We have a volunteer program at Lone Pine Koala Sanctuary and we have had many students from countries all over the world spend time with us over the years, including Sweden, UK, France, USA, Japan, Germany, Canada and many more. All of them find their time here incredibly rewarding and see it as the chance of a lifetime. Most of these students have found their way to us through our website: www.koala.net.

Koala joeys exit their mother's pouch permanently at approximately eight months and are independent at around twelve months of age. When one particular koala, Nivea, was around nine months old she lost her mother Tisha to cancer. Nivea and Tisha had been living with three other mums and their joeys for some time and, when Tisha died, the other mums took Nivea under their wings and, even though they all had joeys of their own, they readily shared the responsibility of rearing her to weaning age.

To make things easier for them and to ensure Nivea was getting the milk she required, Galit and I decided on a formula to supplement her with. Each morning and evening, I prepared milk for Nivea, took it to her enclosure and held her while she drank. We watched her very closely and, while she was often found on her own at the beginning, very soon she was consistently found comfortably sharing the lap of one of her adopted mums. We weighed Nivea regularly to make sure she was growing properly and she was successfully weaned right on schedule. Nivea will soon be celebrating her second birthday.

Popeye was a very dominant male within his group, but loved a cuddle from us. He developed serious abdominal problems and Galit had to operate on him. During his recovery, he was receiving intravenous fluids and, while he was hooked up to a drip, he would sit on the lap of one of the hospital staff. One day he seemed to be particularly uncomfortable and took longer than normal to settle into a position. I was doing other work in the same room and was talking to the vet nurse about Popeye's progress. He was very unresponsive to all around him and was perched quietly on the vet nurse's lap. As we continued talking, Popeye suddenly looked up at me, turned and reached his arms out towards me. I moved closer and he put his arms around my neck, his head on my shoulder and went to sleep. In this position, he completed his fluid therapy and, even when it was finished, he stayed where he was, resting comfortably against my shoulder, his arms tight around me. It's one of the best hugs I've ever had.

Every one of our koalas is named and they all have distinct personalities. A lot of people ask us how we come up with so many names. Some of our koalas are named after staff members – but most have names that relate in some way to that of their mother's. We have 'themes' and this also makes it easy to remember who is related to whom! One of our more interesting themes was actually dictated by the mother's very first joey. Vera's first joey was a boy and from the very first time he exited the pouch he exuded an adventurous spirit. Every morning I would have to find him among the other mothers and return him to Vera. He was christened Nomad and is still a very active koala. All of Vera's subsequent offspring followed Nomad's lead and Wanda, Hippie and Zoom were also very outgoing.

Jacqueline Barratt – Mount Coot-tha Summit Restaurant

Just seven kilometres from the CBD, the summit of Mount Coot-tha is the highest point in the city, with spectacular views across the city to the islands of Moreton Bay. There's been a lookout and café here since I can remember and in the '50s the area

had something of a lovers' lane reputation. I remember a friend, who, in her early twenties, was fond of a shy young man who had never had the courage to kiss her. She was surprised when he phoned to suggest dinner and a drive up to Mount Coot-tha 'to see the lights'. When I met my friend the following day she laughed and told me, "I saw every bloody light in Brisbane!" The new leaseholders of the Mount Coot-tha complex are Canadians, who, having originally come for a brief stay, have now made Brisbane their home.

'Mrs. Chapman, the original leaseholder here, passed away a long time ago now, but I can remember her coming up on Sundays, not long after we had taken over the business. She just came in and said, "I will sit at the table and read the paper and be served – how lovely is that" ... A group of her friends came to the restaurant not long after she passed away. They came up and booked a table overlooking the view and said they were having a celebration for her. She was certainly there in spirit. The Chapman's had been here for about thirty years when we took over the lease. I remember thinking, "There's no way I will I be here for thirty years" and already I've been here over twenty years!'

I'm Canadian, originally from Newfoundland, but I lived in Vancouver for a few years and had met quite a lot of Australians and thought it sounded like a great country to visit. I finally arrived here in 1973 intending to stay for just a year – and I'm still here!

My brother Russell and I and our partner, Jim Heron, originally had a restaurant in Samford, which we opened in 1979. In 1983 we were successful in getting a 5-year lease to operate the kiosk here but unfortunately this lease expired right in the middle of Expo 88. We approached Brisbane City Council before Expo and said, 'You know Expo will be something of a showcase for Brisbane and we would like to do some redevelopment at Mount Coot-tha'. Unfortunately the council didn't want to change anything so the lease expired in July '88 and for another 8 years we were here on a month-to-month basis with no lease whatsoever!

Then when Jim Soorley came in as Mayor we approached him and said, 'Look, these are all the submissions we have made to Council, and we've been sitting up here not able to change a thing.' We had engaged an architect and worked out what we thought the national heritage building and the leased area could take. Finally the council put it up for tender and we were the successful leaseholders and were given a lease for 25 years. That's when we said we could put the necessary money in to do all the redevelopment. We built the café, redeveloped the restaurant, and put a deck around the restaurant to capture the wonderful views. We also built a car park for 60 cars at the back of the restaurant and built a conference room for weddings and conference bookings. We spent over two and a half million dollars of our own money in this development. It was a very big commitment, but when you know you have a 25-year lease it's worth the investment. All the renovations were completed in 1997. I think the proudest moment was when the redevelopment was all completed and we had a huge opening night, which the Lord Mayor attended. From our point of view the opening was emotional, and very exciting that we had finally achieved what we wanted to achieve, and to see it all finished and to have our family here from Canada and America to celebrate it with us – it was absolutely tremendous.

When we first came up here to Mount Coot-tha my brother lived up here until he got so spooked by people coming and knocking on windows at night time. There were alarms going off every night and people wandering around at all sorts of hours. My poor brother was here one time when there were people trying to break into the restaurant. He phoned the police, and when the police came around the building, Russell thought they were the criminals that he'd called up about, and the police thought Russell was the criminal and stuck a gun through the window! Russell said it was just like a Monty Python type moment: 'Like, hold on – I'm the person that phoned' and the police saying, 'How do we know that?' He thought he'd seen his last days on earth at that stage! That's when he said nobody should be up here by themselves at night time and thankfully the council agreed.

When we started here very few people went out at night and the restaurant was only really busy on the weekends. At that stage most of the restaurants were in the city, with smaller suburban BYOs, so it was a hard thing to get people to come up here. The Japanese tour groups were just beginning to come into Brisbane then so we went out and actively sought the tour groups. We have 110 employees here and we have quite a few who are bilingual and some are multilingual, which is a great help to our overseas guests. Mount Coot-tha attracts a lot of visitors from all over the world. Brisbane has changed so much since then.

Now we enjoy a very high percentage of local customers. Part of the reason for the increase in custom has been the many festivals we now have in Brisbane throughout the year, like the Writers' Festival, the Film Festival, and the River*fire* Festival. The River*fire* Festival, in particular, attracts many people to Mount Coot-tha, because the view from here is spectacular; the sky is just awash with fireworks – it's beautiful, absolutely gorgeous. The restaurant is always booked out then, and sometimes we have a wedding.

I think our restaurant is looked on as a place to come to for a special celebration – we do a lot of birthdays, anniversaries and engagements. We have a special function room now where we can hold weddings while still using the restaurant for dinners. It's interesting for us, especially since we've done the renovations, as we are now doing weddings of children whose parents got married here! It's lovely to have that continuity. You feel very proud that people feel the place is so special they want to come back. People come back, too, for their anniversaries. Some of the people who come up have pictures from the old days. Apparently there were a lot of debutante balls up here in the '50s and '60s – they don't even do things like that anymore now!

Mrs Chapman, the original leaseholder here, passed away a long time ago now, but I can remember her coming up on Sundays, not long after we had taken over the business. She just came in and said, 'I will sit at the table and read the paper and be served – how lovely is that.' I said to her, 'You're really enjoying this, aren't you?' and she said, 'Oh, you have no idea!' She was a lovely lady and seemed to be really enjoying having free time on Sundays at last. I know a group of her friends came to the restaurant not long after she passed away. They came up and booked a table overlooking the view and said they were having a celebration for her. She was certainly there in spirit. The Chapmans had been here for about thirty years when we took over the lease. I remember thinking, 'There's no way will I be here for thirty years' and already I've been here over twenty years!

Jane Deery – Story Bridge Hotel

Built in 1886, it was originally called the Kangaroo Point Hotel, but in 1940 the name was changed to the Story Bridge Hotel, to coincide with the opening of the then new bridge across the Brisbane River. Jane's father bought the hotel in 1967 and it's now owned and run by Jane and her brother Richard. We sit in an upstairs room, looking out across the river as Jane talks of the hotel's past – including the origin of its famous cockroach race…

'Gor and Gazza … they decided, in the spirit of Australia Day, to host a cockroach race. Truckie Bill lived in Wharf Street and he was the first chief steward, so he hosted the race in the car park and that was that!'

There's always been a hotel here, ever since 1872. This particular building was finished in 1886. All the bricks were made in Scotland, which is quite amazing. This building was here long before the Story Bridge. The bridge only opened in 1940.

My dad bought the Story Bridge Hotel in September or October 1967. He was living on the Gold Coast at the time and he decided to buy the hotel because it was a good business – mostly used by workmen from the heavy industry in the area at the time. Dad had grown up in Sydney and he was used to the more inner-city style of pubs there. He bought the hotel thinking, 'Well, the city's just round the corner and it's got to go somewhere,' but it took a lot longer than he thought. I grew up here in the hotel. I went to primary school at St Joseph's at Kangaroo Point, and later to All Hallows.

When we moved here it cost one cent for a child and two cents for an adult on the ferry. It was so busy on the ferries in those early days; they'd have two ferries on, because of all the workmen going to and from work. The ferry would be chock-a-block and the ferry driver would say, 'That's it!' and they'd be off across the river – it's not like that now.

Then, in the afternoon when they finished work, they'd all walk down to the ferry and again there'd be two ferries on.

We do business with people on both sides of the river. People come to the hotel for a meal or a drink and others come across for corporate functions. We never use the top floor for anything now but functions – it's decorated in Moulin Rouge style and has this sensational view of the city. It's nice just to be in an old building – it's got a sense of history and there's not much history left in Brisbane now, is there?

My brother Richard and my father orchestrated the first renovation in 1993, when they put the verandahs back on. They'd been taken off, I think, during the war, because they were unsafe, and they'd stuck these little European-style balconies on the outside. The renovations took about fourteen or fifteen months and that was when they put the restaurant in. I've been here since 1994.

We'd never operated a restaurant before, but they wanted a restaurant with sit-down a la carte service, specialising in steaks and things, so that was a decision that was made back then. Operating the restaurant was very much a learning curve, but it really became central to our operation. We never got gaming machines until the 11th hour – we've now got 21 machines, which is OK. They don't form a big part of our business. We've always focused on food or entertainment – very much on hospitality and looking after people.

My other brother Paul took a trip to England and he saw a 'Festival of Beers' over there. So Paul got the idea, and he and Richard put together the Festival of Beers. The first festival here must have been in 1990 or 1991. The idea is a celebration of Australian brewing, so it's only Australian beers. They ship them in from Western Australia, South Australia, Victoria and New South Wales. I think at the first festival there were 50 beers from all over Australia and I think last year there were 153 different Australian beers – all sorts of different qualities and flavours. We had a well-respected judging of a big selection of those 153 – there were 5 different categories: Stout, Ale, Pilsner, Wheat Beer and Dark Beer. The festival is very successful, but it's now held at the RNA Showgrounds. It's called the National Festival of Beers. Richard still runs it, but it's moved away from the hotel, mainly because of the stress that it put on the area. Paul is no longer with us now, he died in 1991. We're going to start another festival here, possibly a wine and food festival – we're not sure when yet.

The Story Bridge was completed in 1941 and, as you know, the war was on then. They established a ship building industry down where dockside is now. That was Evans Deakin, where they were building ships for the war. So in case Brisbane and the docks were air-raided, they built the bomb shelter – actually a blast shelter, under the bridge so that the workers could come up here. It seems strange to build a shelter like that under a bridge, because I kind of think the bridge might be the first target! The shelter was never used, but there was some element of heritage listing in the building of that place.

People's lifestyle around here has changed since those days and the hotel has also changed. When Dad first bought the hotel it was such a different business. Then people had 6 pots of beer for lunch, then they'd go home with 2 Tallies – a Tallie was a large bottle of beer. Women weren't allowed to drink in public bars. Now people are more health conscious, they don't drink 6 pots of beer any more at lunchtime, they don't smoke as much – it's all very different. This area is quite different now and they're different people too. It's very much the young professional. Their lifestyle is important to them and their approach to food and drink is different.

When my mum and dad were here, Mum was doing the food – just Mum and one cook. The cook would prepare all this food for the hot-box. It was just so different! My background is nursing, so I certainly grew up working in the hotel. I learned from that, but basically I learned on the job. We've started the tapas style of eating now, modified a bit because of the stress on the production in the kitchen. We've got two kitchens and three eating areas, plus functions. Food is a major part of our operation – we've got 16 chefs. You need that many to cover the hours and the days of the week. That's how much it's changed.

The Cockroach Races have been going here for twenty-three years. They were started by two lads Gor and Gazza. Gazza lived across the road, his real name was Brian. Gor, or Igor, he lived at Hawthorne. They were in the public bar and they were just joking amongst themselves and I think Igor must have said that the cockroaches at Hawthorne are faster than the cockroaches at Kangaroo Point. They decided, in the spirit of Australia Day, to host a cockroach race.

Truckie Bill lived in Wharf Street and he was the first chief steward, so he hosted the race in the car park and that was that! The winners and the losers all get crunched! The race grew from that very humble beginning to be quite a well-known event. It totally captures that larrikin thing – it's got nothing to do with cockroaches, it's just an excuse for a fun day. This year it was on CNN in the United States. Someone said they saw it on TV in Sweden, there was a documentary done on it in Japan and a film crew from Germany recorded it. It's kind of good for Australia, because it also shows our sense of humour and it focuses on people having a good time. The cockroaches are horrible, but it's all outdoors and it's money for a good cause – the proceeds go to the Mater Children's Hospital.

PART SIX: The Smart State

'The time has come when scientific truth must cease to be the property of the few – when it must be woven into the common life of the world.'

- Louis Agassiz

The quality of education here has improved enormously over the past fifty years. When I was a child in Brisbane there was little to nothing in the way of pre-school education – it was more playschool than pre-school and adult education was even harder to find. As for women, many were not educated past Grade 10, as they were expected to marry young and then stay home with their children. This was so much an accepted part of social attitudes at the time that government-owned businesses were not allowed to employ married women – consequently, if a single girl was working for them and then married, she'd be fired! As for the disabled, there was only the most rudimentary education. Now they can attend either mainstream schools or special schools with staff trained to cater to their needs. For people coming to this country as refugees after the Second World War there was little support of any kind, where now there are schools for both adults and children, where they can learn English as a second language.

Over the same half century, approximately, we have witnessed amazing changes in communication technologies, which are revolutionising our work and leisure time and massively enhancing our ability as Queenslanders to interact with each other and with the rest of the world.

Over the same period Queensland's universities have gained in reputation, attracting students from around the world. Queensland is now a leading bio-medical research centre in the Asia Pacific region and South East Queensland has become a hub for information security industries. The Smart State may still be an aspirational goal, but it's fast becoming a reality.

Nathan Shepherdson: Poet

The Stones are Turning – *for Bernice McCabe*

what if Rodin's Thinker just stood up
put on a smart suit
walked into the next century
got a job as a government actuary
started work on every likelihood
started to collect every thought
to cram it all → to compress it all
between the binary bookends of
1 & 0?

then that delicious polished lichen patina
would move upwards from that famous fist
that unpunishing fist
over the chin over the lips
split its flow either side of the nose
creep over hair palings over the lower eyelids
suction its journey to the eyeball's backs
and settle as a bronze answer on the brain.

this is simply thinking.

from the brain
to the brain
to the brain
from the brain

this is simply thinking.

we are decided by science
what can be → could be drawn in chalk
can be → could be found in space
in the smallest space the widest consequence
in the alloy the theory
in the mind the thought not thought
in the statement the necessity of the statement
we imagine we're somewhere else to be here.

therefore → tip the dye into the data
watch the currents appear in your abstract flesh
'*as at a cup my life-blood seemed to sip*'
remake the statue unmade into the man
unmake this fossil into this animal
the stones are turning in graves made for their birth
different leaves are about to fall onto the same ground
therefore → glue the fact to the promise.

a) in the parallel in the parallel lines in intelligence.
b) bend an atom into a future.
c) the clocks on our shoes open their eyes when we walk.

 **Nathan Shepherdson** has won the Josephine Ulrick Poetry Prize twice (2004, 2006), the 2005 Arts Queensland Thomas Shapcott Award, the 2006 Newcastle Poetry Prize and the 2006 Arts Queensland Val Vallis Award. His first book *Sweeping the Light Back into the Mirror* (UQ Press 2006) was awarded the Mary Gilmore Award in 2008. He lives in the Glass House Mountains in Queensland. He is the son of the painter Gordon Shepherdson.

Barbara Heath: Jeweller

Illustrated – HIS/HERS Wedding ring commission 2005
Digital realisation — Malcolm Enright, Brisbane

Barbara Heath – Jeweller to the Lost

For more than thirty years, contemporary Australian jeweller and designer Barbara Heath has explored the communicative power of jewellery to explore the relationship between herself (the maker) and the wearer. Born in Sydney, she established her Brisbane studio in 1983. Her primary concern remains the creation of jewels which carry meaning for people throughout their lives. Barbara's work has been exhibited in both individual and group exhibitions in Tokyo, London, New York and throughout Australia.

http://viewersite.wordpress.com/

Education

Universities

Paul Greenfield – University of Queensland

Professor Paul Greenfield is Vice-Chancellor and President of the University of Queensland and, despite his many university commitments, he still enjoys being involved with research activities when he can. Paul has regularly consulted to national and international companies and government agencies on diverse subjects, including wastewater and environmental management. He has also served on the National Greenhouse Advisory Panel. We first spoke in 2004.

'Australia's very exposed on Greenhouse, in both an economic and climatic sense ... Curiously, we're much better at handling floods than we are at handling rising damp! Rising damp creeps up on you and we're terrible at organising a response, whereas, if it's an obvious disaster, everyone gets behind it.'

I was born and grew up mainly in Sydney but moved to Brisbane for my high school education to Gregory Terrace. My parents later moved to Perth, but I went back to Sydney, to study at the University of New South Wales. I studied Chemical Engineering, followed by a short period in industry, after which I went back and did my PhD in Biochemical Engineering. After that I worked with CSIRO for a little while before going to Amherst, Massachusetts on a Research Fellowship. I worked at the

University of Massachusetts for about three years, partly for a G.D. Searle spinoff that was looking to manufacture pharmaceuticals using proteins attached to surfaces. While in Massachusetts, I had two job offers on the same day, one from McGill University in Montreal and one from the University of Queensland. I was interested in going to Montreal, but I decided, as my parents had returned to Brisbane, that I'd come back to Australia for a period of time.

There were more opportunities in biotechnology in academia at that time than there were in industry. The University of Queensland's (UQ) Department of Chemical Engineering was regarded at that stage as one of the top two in the country. I'd known this and had had some interaction with the department as an undergraduate student, so when I received the job offer, I thought, 'I'll come back for three years and then return to the US.' It's been a long three years! I came back in the late seventies and, not only am I still here, but I have remained at UQ. When I returned in the seventies I did an economics degree part time at UQ. This resulted from an interest generated as an undergraduate at the University of New South Wales (UNSW) – they required all those enrolled in engineering or science to take a limited number of humanities or social science electives, an approach I fully endorse.

I divided my work at UQ between what you might call biotechnology and environmental management and I've continued that ever since. The university has been a great place to explore different approaches; it has always encouraged interdisciplinary research. Over the three decades I've been at UQ, I have occupied a wide range of positions; I was promoted a number of times and then became Head of the Department. One of the things you can do when you stay at the same institution is to retain an involvement in research while taking on a greater management role, because you have your networks set up. A couple of the groups that I started here are still going and doing quite well; I still have a limited involvement with them – though if I go into a laboratory now an alarm goes off! So in that sense I'm removed from the day-to-day activity. It's more about helping set directions and helping them solve problems – freeing logs from log-jams occasionally.

I think any academic at any level must retain an involvement in scholarship. Scholarship has many dimensions; it can be scholarship in teaching or scholarship in research, it can be scholarship in community, engagement or policy work. If you do administration or management and you lose that part of it – well, I wouldn't like to do that. The University of Queensland's always allowed that involvement to continue.

Working in Australia, you have to accept certain things. Importantly, you have to accept that you are a long way physically from many of the key intellectual, industrial and commercial centres in the world. This means that you are going to have to travel more to them than they are going to travel to you, although it is encouraging to note that in certain areas the imbalance is reducing. Also, modern communication links take some of the pressure off, such as use of email, telephone conference calls, video links et cetera. Of course, digital communication seems to me to work best with those that you have a reasonable knowledge of at a personal level. For example, I had a call yesterday with someone from central US, someone from UK, and a couple from different parts of Australia, to address a difficult issue, and that worked fine. Increasingly, the University of Queensland is attracting people to come here on the basis of the quality of the work that is carried out here and the positive attitude of the university. The visitors we've had generally love their time here, they like the stimulation of the university and they love living in Brisbane and in South East Queensland.

It was a toss-up whether I went abroad as a PhD student or as a research fellow and at the end of the day, for various reasons, I chose to go as a research fellow. I think the US PhD, with its course work requirement, followed by a thesis, is actually a better model than the British model where you just do the thesis – I think that's an antiquated style. In today's world you need depth, but you also need breadth in your education as well, and I think the US system is better at providing that. Australian PhD graduates are well regarded overseas, so the route that I followed in going as a research fellow is very common.

I think having international students actually improves the university, it's part of what a university is about. It's also true that international students are subsidising the undergraduate education of Australian students at the moment. This is because the federal government won't bite the bullet. On the one hand it wants mass education at a tertiary level, so we're approaching Canadian and US entry levels, 30% to 40% of the cohort going on to tertiary, but on the other hand we still have a very inflexible system where the community doesn't want to pay as individuals and the government doesn't want to pay the full cost, so how are we surviving? We're surviving on the surplus from fee-paying students. Some of them are Australian; they're not all international. Other problems, however, arise from this situation. For example, we're in court now because we've failed a full-fee student who's arguing they should have been passed, but we won't budge on that. The lecturer in front of the class generally has no idea who is fee paying and who isn't, and we go to great pains to ensure that there's nothing formally identifying examinations papers as being from fee-paying or non-fee-paying students – that's very important.

The question really is: how many fee-paying international students can you have before you change the nature of the university? If you had 75% international fee-paying students, well, clearly it's not the same university as it was. In fact, this university started late in deliberately seeking significant numbers of international full-fee students. We have fewer than 20% international students, and around 1,000 of those are students from the USA who come on a study-abroad program for a semester or a year. They don't spend their whole time here. A change that's occurring at present is that Australian students are starting more and more to want a semester overseas as part of their undergraduate education, which I think is wonderful.

One of the good news stories of this decade is the creation of three large research institutes at UQ, through funding provided from a very generous and significant donor, Atlantic Philanthropies, the Queensland State Government, the Australian Government for one of the Institutes, and from UQ itself. They are the Institute for Molecular Bioscience, the Australian Institute for Bioengineering and Nanotechnology, and the Queensland Brain Institute.

My work with the Moreton Bay and Waterways Partnership was particularly satisfying because it is, I think, an example of where South East Queensland (SEQ) leads the country. Eighteen councils from Noosa down to the border of New South Wales and out as far as Toowoomba, together with the state government, invested significant resources in understanding and managing the ecosystem health of the river systems in the SEQ region. I chaired the Scientific Advisory Group, which involved individuals from all the universities in SEQ, CSIRO, state agencies and consultants.

The challenge for SEQ is that there is not a single polluting source that you can identify. A large number of people want to live here and this creates pressure on the food systems and the water systems, with everyone contributing a little bit to the problem. If we don't do anything, we will get a slow and continual decline in the quality of our rivers, estuaries and Moreton Bay itself. An example is one of the problems in Moreton Bay, a blue-green algae or, more correctly, Cyanobacteria called Lyngbya. The causes of Lyngbya blooms relate largely to land practices, but it's not a simple thing where you can say, 'Oh, that's the problem, we'll fix that and it's all solved!' There's a whole myriad of little problems, which, if you don't get on top of, will get bigger and bigger and eventually you'll get a decline. We've now certainly halted the decline. I can't actually say we've made huge inroads and turned it around, but there have been improvements.

For a number of years I chaired the Greenhouse Advisory Panel, which was essentially an assembly of peak groups interested in the impacts of global climate change policy, for example, National Farmers Federation, Australian Conservation Federation, Greenpeace, ACTU, et cetera. I remember asking Roz Kelly what was the role of the independent Chair, and she said, 'Well, if they want to kill each other, would you please ensure that it doesn't happen in Parliament House!' Australia's very exposed on Greenhouse, in both an economic and climatic sense. Economically, we are exposed because our exports are so energy rich and so linked to energy generation, hence any global policy shifts against fossil fuels leaves us in a difficult position; climatically we are exposed because Australia is essentially more environmentally fragile than many other countries and more so than we generally acknowledge.

I think Australia took the wrong option in not originally signing up to the Kyoto Protocol. It is hard to think of an area of international concern where there is more muddled, hypocritical and just plain silly thinking worldwide than Global Climate Change and Greenhouse Gas Policy. The Kyoto Protocol is only the start and a key issue for Australia is to ensure that it plays a major role in the next generation of agreements in ensuring that they are less flawed. Almost certainly there'll be more protocols. On my more cynical days, I'm not sure global warming will be taken seriously until there's a series of severe weather events on the east coast of the US and they become involved. That movie, *The Day after Tomorrow* was quite over the top, but something like that (though not so extreme) probably needs to happen before we bite the bullet. Curiously, we're much better at handling floods than we are at handling rising damp! Rising damp creeps up on you and we're terrible at organising a response, whereas, if it's an obvious disaster, everyone gets behind it.

If you go back to the nineteenth century, universities like UQ were predominantly teaching institutions. There were individuals who did research and carried out scholarly activities, but universities weren't actually the centres of research and invention. Researchers and inventors were more closely aligned with the arts than with institutions. From the nineteenth to the twentieth centuries, we moved from universities being primarily teaching and scholarship to being teaching and research. In the last thirty years of the twentieth century, in particular, universities have focused on teaching, research and then what I would call community engagement. Community engagement stretches from commercialisation activity through to involvement in social, economic and political policy issues, through to other community engagement issues. That engagement component is now a very big part, I believe, of a university like this. The core business of a university such as UQ is teaching undergraduate and post-graduate students, and doing research with post-graduates and researchers. Those are the two key core components, but engagement with the outside world has become increasingly important and forms a smaller but distinctive part of the core.

Looking ahead I don't think Australians will ever be as philanthropically inclined as those in North America. Australians are more sceptical about educational investments and we don't have as much private tertiary education. I think there's a feeling here that it's the government's responsibility to provide most of the resources in universities; if only this was true! In terms of UQ, I think we'll become more research intensive. I don't think we'll become a lot larger in terms of student numbers; we're about 33,000 students at the moment, on three campuses. Ipswich will almost certainly grow, but this site at St Lucia will probably end up with fewer students. It's already very crowded.

I think over time we'll see an increase in the offerings for lifelong learning. People, either professionally or personally, are going to want a mix, involving some forms of educational experience all the way through. It won't all be university based, but some of it will be. I think there's also a group in society that is still working, which will need professional refresher courses. Whether the universities do that, or professional societies, I think we'll see it grow. I think the concept that the period of a single degree of three or four years duration will be the only time that you'll spend at university will change. I think we'll become more specialised and we certainly don't and won't do research in everything, because the truth is we can't afford it and the competitive pressures are too tough. Finally, I think the international opportunities and challenges for universities, their staff and students will grow dramatically.

Peter Roennfeldt – Queensland Conservatorium of Music

He has been the director of the Conservatorium of Music since 2003. We first met at his office there in May 2004 in the early days of my research for this book. Many years before, I'd been a student at the conservatorium, during the time of their first director, Dr William Lovelock – the Con's then premises now being a part of Somerville House. I've found it interesting to hear of the many changes Peter has overseen during his time at the helm of this thriving institution.

'We say that students should have enough generic skills to adapt to whatever situation they find themselves in ... There are a number of opportunities, but they're becoming more diverse and less traditional. The students who really survive are the ones who are open to different possibilities rather than saying, "I just want to play in an orchestra because that's all I ever wanted to do" – they'll just be disappointed if they don't make the grade. I think different types of knowledge, different types of success, different types of expertise exist that are valued by the wider community.'

I went to the United States of America to study for my doctorate, having done my initial degrees at Queensland University and Adelaide. I was in America for four years altogether. I came back to Brisbane because I had family here. I thought I wouldn't actually stay here, but one thing led to another and that's the way it goes.

423

After I came back I started doing various miscellaneous roles. Eventually a full-time position evolved here at the conservatorium and I've been here now for over fifteen years. I was in the deputy director role for about six years, then that director left and I was filling in for a while. I've now been Director for four years. My day is always varied – work in here, meetings with staff, going over to other campuses, committee meetings, rehearsals of ensembles, et cetera. Each day involves quite a varied mix of activities.

William Lovelock was Director here for the first three years or so (from 1957). I guess it was expected back then that Directors of Conservatoriums in Australia would, by definition, come from overseas. After he left, Basil Jones was already on staff, so he just moved into the role and stayed there and was Director until 1979 – he was the longest standing. After Basil Jones, Roy Wales became Director from 1980 to 1987. He was a choral conductor; he pushed the big events – the big choral programs and gave a bit more external focus.

A more international style of staffing started under Roy Wales. People were appointed from England, Germany, France, Africa and America. Today, while maintaining our traditional focus on Western European Art Music, we're custodians of the Gamelan, which is owned by the Queensland Museum. It's the Indonesian Percussion Orchestra. It lives downstairs and we have a staff member who's put a lot of effort into developing that. We have another staff member with North Indian classical music background and another staff member joined us recently from South America.

We have some interest in Japanese and Chinese music. Our students have come from various parts of the world, including Hungary, over the years, and have even played the hurdy gurdy or some of those instruments from Eastern Europe that are still very much used. It depends. It's a mixture. I wouldn't say it's as dynamic and as broad as it might be. We've now also got some people associated with Australian Aboriginal music and that will, I think, grow in the next few years.

With ancient instruments, we have a fifty-instrument collection, everything from medieval lutes to a Haydn-style fortepiano and all the stringed instruments, wind, brass, all the percussion instruments. The performance of Monteverdi's *Vespers,* which was held in the foyer here some time ago, was one of our bigger projects. We haven't done anything quite that big since, though we are able to do that sort of thing with the resources we now have. Resourcing is, of course, a perennial problem. The university has ongoing battles with federal government over funding. Increasingly, the case is: you get the base payment but to get the extra special funds you have to make the case – you spend more time applying than actually doing the work.

We say that students should have enough generic skills to adapt to whatever situation they find themselves in. The Education Department is always crying out for teachers in the schools. That's an obvious area. Also, there are lots of interesting community arts organisations that need music professionals in their administrative posts because they understand what music is all about. There are a number of opportunities, but they're becoming more diverse and less traditional. The students who really survive are the ones who are open to different possibilities rather than saying, 'I just want to play in an orchestra because that's all I ever wanted to do' – they'll just be disappointed if they don't make the grade. The youth orchestra network is a vibrant community, but no one gets paid to play in those; the staff gets paid but not the participants. They do get State Government funding, though, because they are a broad community-based organisation.

We have a motto throughout the university: celebrating diversity. I think here we're doing some of that, but I think we could do it more. Traditionally, there's been a goal that excellence only means certain things in music and I think different types of knowledge, different types of success, different types of expertise exist that are valued by the wider community. So I don't think we should say that unless you can play the Tchaikovsky Violin Concerto as well as anyone else you haven't succeeded as a musician. I think respecting different sorts of outcomes for the students is more important than a hierarchical approach, which says only the top 5% of performers are the success stories. The really select performers, they're likely to get jobs in orchestras, because they're the cream of the crop, but what about everyone else? They all need to feel successful and useful as musicians.

I don't think we can possibly ever offer everything we could dream of. But I see some of the most exciting things happening in non-traditional areas – like in music technology. We have a popular music program, a jazz program, a little bit of early music – not a huge amount. Many more people are getting involved in research. Some students even perform and manage to do research – so that's fine too.

The students here have the option to go on and study for a primary or secondary school education qualification. To teach classroom music, you have to be a qualified teacher. The international students generally go straight home or do a second degree like a business degree rather than a teaching degree here. The good students go overseas pretty quickly.

We have a performers' agency here which offers people professional engagements. That's for people while they're enrolled or after they graduate. Also, there are some traineeships and some other programs on offer that get them out into other networks in the orchestral scene or the festival admin scene. We also have quite a strong program here for the studio-based teacher – that's about self-employment and how people can run their own business.

We have quite a few links with the local radio station 4MBS. We present a monthly program, so we have a normal presence there. A lot of our concerts are recorded and broadcast. We have links with the Queensland Orchestra, in the form of a traineeship program. It's an informal arrangement in the sense of not being for course credit, but is very valuable for the students' training and experience. That's for final year students mainly.

We find we have an increasing public following with the concert program. We do some experimental work that isn't perhaps done elsewhere and some types of music you'll probably only hear here. We've between 150 and 200 events a year that are public, so that's a large number. The daytime concerts are free, the evening concerts there's a small charge. It's all increasing our presence. Then there's opera. You'll see an interesting opera here each year. We'll either do unconventional repertoire or we'll do it in an unconventional way. I think it's getting known as a place where good artistic things happen. Opera Queensland regularly does six performances of a regular opera. If they do it in our theatre, which they do once a year, they might go up to ten. We collaborate with other Arts groups, for example, the Queensland College of Art, where they provide the design element or feature and we provide the music. We've done several joint projects with the Dance School of Excellence; they're high school students, but they get their intensive training much earlier than musicians.

We've a lot of staff that go on tours to perform. They're quite high profile events, so that does happen routinely, but we haven't sent groups – it's just basically expense. People naturally want to travel to gain further experience and to experience other places – and music is one way to travel as wherever you go there'll be some sort of music and some sort of audience. A number of the people who've come here from overseas are not any better than the ones we've got; it's just this glamour that if it's from overseas it must be good. If you see something like the *Medici Series* they always have visiting overseas people. They can capture a market because people know the only way they can hear this person in perhaps a five-year span is to come to this concert.

We have exchange student arrangements with other countries. The one with Munich Conservatorium is going quite well. The one with Royal Academy and Royal College of Music is problematic because they rely on exchanges coming in the other direction and it's very hard to get students to want to come here from the Royal Academy or Royal College. They've got in there, so why would they want to leave? We've had interest from Guildhall and the Royal Northern College of Music as well, which have recently been formalised. So there are a few connections with UK. We've also had some links with North American institutions.

This year there were about 30 students entering the Con who had been through the Young Conservatorium – that's about a quarter of the intake. The early childhood program starts at age one, so it's a bit too early to say where that might lead, but that does have a filtering process upwards. There are about 200 students in the early childhood program now. They all have to come with one parent at least, so it's double the number of people – the kids are enrolled, but one or two parents have to accompany them and be in the class. It's basically music games, music play, learning through music. Then you eventually get into the literacy side of things.

In terms of the future of the Con I think that the range of options I've mentioned is something we need to work at and it's also a question of getting the balance right. I think more identification with local communities is still possible, both professional communities and the volunteer community. I think a strong connection with the schools is important. We've done quite a lot with that already but I think we can do more in that area – linking with school programs and groups of schools visiting here. I believe there's an opportunity there.

Mostyn Bramley-Moore – Queensland College of Art

We met when he was Dean of the Queensland College of Art, Griffith University. I was interested in his comment about the history of education in newly colonised lands worldwide, where agriculture, then art and music, are usually the first schools established. Mostyn is Professor of Art and said he sees himself more as an artist than an administrator.

'Queensland College of Art is one of Queensland's oldest tertiary education providers. I think Gatton Agricultural College is in the same sort of age bracket, which makes it by far the oldest part of the University of Queensland. People need to put food on the table but soon after that is accomplished they realise they have other "hungers". It's not just that they want to be entertained, although they obviously do, but that they want to be realised in other ways, they want to feel that they're part of a cultural mainstream.'

I'd been exhibiting for many years in Brisbane, sending up shows to the Michael Milburn Gallery here from Victoria. Then, in 1999, when I was Dean of the School of Arts at the Victorian College of the Arts in Melbourne, I was invited to apply for the directorship here at Queensland College of Art (QCA). At the time Griffith University was planning to move the school from Morningside closer to the city, in fact, down here to Southbank. I'd previously had experience with moving similar kinds of facilities. I came up and had a look and was attracted by the challenges of the position, and the prospects for the college. It seemed to me that here was one of the oldest art schools in Australia prepared to look into the future, and to reinvent itself. I felt the move to a new location was symbolic of many things and that it was a chance to make a real change, whereas the circumstances of other similar schools in Australia were a bit more fixed. I felt positive about Brisbane because I had had this long-standing connection as an exhibiting artist here, so I decided to move north.

We look at venerable schools and assume they all must have been around for hundreds of years, but when you examine their histories you quickly learn that's not the case. The oldest educational institutions in Australia are not universities, but schools at a much more junior level, because there was an immediate challenge to educate young people. The oldest university in Australia is the University of Sydney, which was founded in 1850, but there were schools around long before 1850. It was often the case that agricultural schools and schools of art generally (using the term in a generic sense) were amongst the first schools to be established. Queensland College of Art is one of Queensland's oldest tertiary education providers. I think Gatton Agricultural College is in the same sort of age bracket, which makes it by far the oldest part of the University of Queensland. People need to put food on the table but soon after that is accomplished they realise they have other 'hungers'. It's not just that they want to be entertained, although they obviously do, but that they want to be realised in other ways, they want to feel that they're part of a cultural mainstream.

At the University of Sydney I did a degree in Fine Arts, Economics and English. During my boyhood my father worked in Sydney theatres as a theatrical set-maker and stage builder. I spend a lot of time working on stage sets and staging systems, and that sort of thing. When I went to university I gravitated towards the cultural end of the spectrum, and afterwards I did a Dip Ed. Then I went off to art school in New York. I've been an exhibiting painter ever since, but I think the fact that I had initially studied Fine Arts and Economics partly explains why later on I was offered management jobs. When I look within myself and try to work out who I am, though, I think I'm primarily a painter. I think this gives me a rapport with art students and I like studio teaching.

In early 2007 I realised that I'd been the head of an art school, in one form or another, in three states, for twenty-one years. I decided to step back to a teaching role, and to spend more time on my own painting.

QCA is big by the standards of such things. Actually, it's one of the biggest art, design and film schools in Australia. In recent decades it has run a broad menu of program options. It has evolved and changed a lot since I've been here. Institutions like this have to respond to two things: the needs of specific industries, and student demand. Some industries are very volatile, very dependent on world economic circumstances. In the film industry, for example, there has been very strong demand for competent digital animators over the past few years. In Fine Art, demand also waxes and wanes dramatically as the years pass. QCA is in a good situation in terms of strategic planning. I think the last couple of years have been very difficult for university education in Australia. The pressures that have been placed on it have been enormous. We are lucky that we are in such a good position.

The circumstances of each of our degree courses and their relationships to their own specific industries are varied and complex. Some of these examples are easy to understand, but others are surprising. We did a survey not so long ago of Griffith Film School graduates. We were curious about how many of them were still working in the industry or in areas closely related to the industry – video, television, film and so on. We were astounded to find that a very high proportion of graduates from the last few years were working in the industry or closely related areas. In other areas we knew the employment outcomes were very high, for example, in photography. Our photojournalism graduates, for example, work in all the major newspapers in Australia and all around the world. They work for Reuters, AAP and so on. In film, on the other hand, you accept, sometimes unthinkingly, the popular assumption that everyone's going to be out of work, so we were interested to find this was not the case.

The circumstances of some areas are surprising. For example, we have a jewellery and small metal object program, and South Bank Institute of Technology has some trade courses oriented around this as well. These are the only courses in Queensland. Southbank is the only TAFE level program and we have the only degree level program. When you look at the number of small and large businesses around Queensland manufacturing, repairing and altering jewellery, I find this astonishing.

We have a program at QCA for contemporary indigenous art. Some indigenous students do the indigenous program while others don't. Gordon Bennett is one of our graduates who did painting and printmaking. Tracey Moffatt, who's arguably Australia's most successful international artist at the moment, did Media Studies and Photography at QCA. Vernon Ah Kee is a graduate of the Bachelor of Contemporary Australian Indigenous Art program who's also building a substantial national profile as a contemporary artist. Dennis Nona is an artist from the Torres Strait with a budding international profile who recently completed a postgraduate degree.

I think the College of Art always functioned as a sort of portal. As Brisbane grew, becoming more sophisticated over the years and reaching towards its destiny as a city, so QCA was prompted to adapt and grow. Years ago it was merely about accessibility. Local people enrolled here to start an artistic career before ambition drove them on to Sydney or London or Paris, or wherever. Examples of artists I'd put in that category would include Margaret Olley, Lloyd Rees and Tracey Moffatt. More recently, artists and designers have been able to base themselves here. Bill Robinson and Davida Allen are cases in point. We now have a lot of international exchanges, giving our students great opportunities to do semesters abroad as part of their QCA/Griffith Degrees.

QCA has had so many graduates over the years that it is a very difficult task to keep track of alumni. We could expend enormous resources just trying to locate people. We do keep central records as best we can, but we rely more on the areas themselves to be up to date on who's around and who's close enough at hand to engage with in interesting ways.

We've had some generous sponsorships, but, having been to Art School in America and having also spent time in Europe, I'm well aware of the vast differences in opportunity. The possibilities for corporate sponsorship in Australia have been quite modest. That means we're very appreciative of the encouragement we receive. QCA has had some fantastic support from individuals whom, to be tactful, I probably shouldn't name, and also corporations. Among corporate sponsors, Theiss sponsor an

Art Prize every year that's been very successful, and Dell Computers has sponsored the QCA main gallery, which has been of great assistance to us. Unfortunately, when people provide sponsorship they're hesitant about giving money for mainstream operational programs, and yet that's probably the place where you most need it. It's been very difficult. We've had support for international opportunities for our students over the years, from individuals and businesses. BMW Queensland was generous, and lots of individuals have also supported that cause, but it is basically very difficult to raise ongoing corporate sponsorship in Australia.

We often underestimate how hard students have to work in order to survive. I had a part-time job when I was at university, but I also had some scholarship assistance and I didn't build up a big debt. Nowadays a surprising number of our students, and this is typical of Australian universities generally, have jobs that soak up many hours each week. We have to operate on the assumption that a considerable amount of our students' energy and time is focused on just keeping their heads financially above water. This must affect the quality of work that they do because there's only so many hours in the day. The consequences are clearer in some areas than others. I've noticed, for example, in photography, as students go through their photography program, they try to accumulate equipment, so some students will take time out to work full time to get enough money to build up their store of gear and then come back and finish their degree.

Looking back, the opening ceremony of the new campus at Southbank was a fantastic thing. We were supposed to be opened by the Queen, and we had all the security clearances done, the invitations printed and posted, when circumstances changed. World politics had intervened, and the Queen's visit was cancelled. Faced with the dilemma of what to do, the decision we made to have the college opened by individuals representing the students and graduates from different areas of the college. It was a shared responsibility, and I thought that was a marvellous outcome. It was a great day for us.

Before the move to South Bank, QCA's suburban location wasn't really conducive to sustained afterhours activity. Art/design/film schools should be a major hub for students and they should think of their days at college as one of the best times of their lives. Here we have a better chance of achieving that. I was here recently on a weekend after the end of a teaching semester when there was a false fire alarm and the buildings had to be evacuated. I was surprised to see at the assembly point a huge number of people from around the college – there must have been 150 people there – all there on that day because they *wanted* to be there. People came down from their areas and they were all chatting, and I realised that the life of the college was in a good cycle. For me that was a very good moment.

Bill Caelli – Information Security Institute, QUT

Bill is an information security specialist who has been in the Australian information technology industry for over forty years, thirty of them in I.T. Security and Cryptography. He is now Adjunct Professor in the School of Information Technology at the Queensland University of Technology. He sees the need for a multidisciplinary approach to I.T. security...

'... that centre is clearly recognised internationally as one of the leading information security research centres in the world ... It involves not just the technology people but the Law, Business, Engineering and I.T. Faculties and increasingly the Arts and Social Sciences group ... we've got this multi-disciplinary approach to the whole area of privacy and security.'

I've been over forty years in the I.T. industry. I was born in Newcastle, New South Wales, and I came to Queensland in 1981. My first degree was from the University of Newcastle, and then I went to the Australian National University in Canberra and did my doctorate there on computers and nuclear physics under Dr John Black and Professor Sir Ernest Titterton, a very famous nuclear physicist.

I started off my working life at BHP in Newcastle – the big steelworks there, in the early '60s as a trainee industrial chemist. A couple of years into it I thought, 'I don't think I'm really cut out to be a chemist.' At the time they had this new concept of automatic data processing or ADP, and they put a call out to people who wanted to change from their current direction into this 'new world' of ADP. I thought, 'That sounds interesting!' so I put my hand up and that's when yours truly got into the computer game.

I left BHP in the mid '60s and went down to the Australian National University to do my doctorate in nuclear physics and also to work in developing what we called, and still call, 'high speed data acquisition systems'. This is where my physics and computer backgrounds merged well together. I spent many years working in this data acquisition area and back in 1966 and 1967 we actually built some very early multi-computer networks in the Nuclear Physics Department.

Then in 1972 I decided to really go into the business side of the industry and to move away from academia, so I joined a company called Hewlett Packard (HP) Australia, a subsidiary of the Hewlett Packard Company of California in the USA.

I left Hewlett Packard in late 1973 and joined a company called Control Data Australia, a subsidiary of Control Data Corporation (CDC) of Minneapolis, Minnesota, in the USA, who made very large computers mainly for doing scientific calculations. One of my early jobs in Control Data was to utilise one of these new things called a 'micro-processor' – all very new and terribly interesting! Eventually, looking at the advances occurring in the 1970s, I wrote a book in 1979 called *The Micro Computer Revolution*, in which I predicted that micro-computers would revolutionise industry as we knew it, and possibly even the world. I said it would essentially do away with those large mainframes – the book was published, but it didn't go very far!

I've been involved with encryption, secret coding and all that kind of thing since 1973 or 1974, because while I was working with Control Data Corporation they were supplying very large computers to the United States government and so they had a real need for this stuff. In the mid 1970s ('73/'74) the United States government proposed that there be a non-military encryption or scrambling standard which later on became known as the Data Encryption Standard or DES for short. I was in America at the time in Minneapolis and they wanted some people in the company who could understand this encryption business so I was summarily co-opted into encryption in 1973 through to 1974. It was a do-it-yourself fast learning track!

Eventually, I had this big fight with Control Data. I said, 'Look, you guys have to get used to the idea that there's a revolution happening beneath you and see if you can adjust your business to it. If you continue marketing just these super-big computers, you're going to go out of business.' Well, that didn't go down very well, as you may imagine. Control Data no longer exists; the company went totally out of business. There's more power in your mobile phone today than there was in computers in those days – literally! Even in 1979 the writing was on the wall for that type of super-large computers as mainstream commercial products.

I was always influenced by a man called Dr Trevor Pearcey. He built a machine here in Australia in 1949 for CSIRO called CSIRAC. I always remember Trevor telling me, 'You know the important thing – as computers get smaller they'll be interconnected on a global basis.' Back in 1950 or 1951 he predicted the Internet and said, 'You know, once that happens, it'll be very important for people's privacy and their security to make sure it's very secure.' That was Trevor Pearcey – a man way ahead of his time!

In '79 I decided I better put my money where my mouth is. So with what little money I had I formed a company called Electronics Research Australia, later called

Eracom. In those days you had to have two to register a company, so about four weeks after I started I officially formed the company with my US partner, Mr Bob Klein, whom I'd met when we were both at the ANU. The idea of Eracom was to build up a range of small computer systems that were secure from the ground up and, to do that, we were going to put encryption/scrambling equipment into the machine itself.

So here we were, two guys starting in a large room of my house. It was very primitive! Later we moved to Queanbeyan in the ACT. I got a Research and Development Grant with the help of the Australian government and we built the computer systems. Those computers became known as Era 50 and Era 60, et cetera, with their encryption security built in (the ERA-60). At that time Australia was going through this changeover in banking systems. We were changing to 'plastic money' but back in those days you had to find a shop that had 'your card'. For example, all the BP petrol stations would only use one bank card. It was silly; you obviously needed to be able to use your bank card anywhere. Anyway our company Eracom actually won contracts to build the appropriate encryption equipment and network equipment that was required to make it possible for all the cards to be used safely and securely anywhere.

About 1981 we were searching round for our next opportunity for venture finance. Back in the early 1980s venture finance for advanced technology industry was very hard to come by in Australia. We were approached by two groups offering us funding assistance. One group was from Melbourne under the then Premier Sir Rupert Hamer and the other was made up of solicitors and financiers that had been working with Sir Bruce Small's family on the Gold Coast, specifically for his son, who was also called Bruce. Incidentally, the younger Bruce Small was known as 'Kelly' – he got that nickname during the war, after Ned Kelly, because, as he used to tell me, he had a name as a scrounger. I never got to the bottom of that story. Anyway, Bruce Small invited us all up to Queensland. There we met Bruce Small at his house and there, too, was Sir Joh Bjelke-Petersen, the then Premier of Queensland. Bruce introduced us and talked about what we were trying to do and they said they wanted to know if we would be interested in coming to Queensland. Bruce said he'd take an interest in the company too. So, after some hooing and haaing, my wife and I and some of the core people in the company brought Eracom to the Gold Coast in September 1981, where we eventually set up in Burleigh Heads.

During the early '80s on the Gold Coast we were building computer systems and security systems and we sold all of those to the major banks. Then in 1983 or 1984 Bruce Small decided we needed to expand overseas. We had a few agents selling our equipment overseas and one of those companies was called Concord Data based near Stuttgart in Germany. Bruce Small personally took up an interest in that company – not me – and that became Concord Eracom in Germany and they started to address the European marketplace. The company went ahead in Europe and Asia. By 1988 Bruce had taken over as MD and I felt I needed some new challenges. I'd met a guy called Professor Dennis Longley who was the then new Dean of I.T. here at Queensland University of Technology (QUT) and we threw around some ideas. We said, 'We can't sell secure systems to a marketplace where people don't understand the problem they've got.' Education had become important for developing the marketplace. So in 1988 Eracom and QUT – then QIT (Queensland Institute of Technology), together formed the Information Security Research Centre (ISRC) and I became the foundation director of that.

We started courses and research in 1988, very early on a global scale for any university. Today that centre has become recognised as one of the leading information security research centres in the world and is now part of the Information Security Institute or ISI of QUT. It involves not just the technology people but the Law, Business, Engineering and I.T. Faculties and, increasingly, the Arts and Social Sciences group. So now we've got this multi-disciplinary approach to the whole area of privacy and security.

South East Queensland has today become a world hub for information security industries. Governments worldwide are starting to ask, 'Is it time to start regulating this incredible global thing called the Internet as well as the ICT industry as a whole?' There's a big argument going on as to whether that should happen or not. We'll be at the forefront here in all those global discussions and that's important because everybody wants to do secure things on the Internet now, including their home banking. Even now there's a health commission proposal to put all the doctors on the Internet and the pharmacists and chemist shops.

In the future it's going to be very important for Queensland to continue its strong involvement in I.T. and the Internet because government and the private sector alike are going to move their business increasingly to the Internet, and to do that we have to have *trust*. For example, when you go into Coles and Woolworths to buy your groceries there's this special little box called the PIN pad, usually sitting on the side. You can swipe your card through a slot and type in your PIN number to pay. Inside the box there's encryption systems between there and the bank. I've maintained for a long time that we need to have the equivalent of that PIN pad at home and in our offices. I estimate that over a three-year period you'd pay about $30 a year and you'd be much safer and you'd learn to trust the Internet.

Queensland and Brisbane, of course, have been involved with cryptography, security and secret codes since the Second World War. General MacArthur, when he moved up here, took charge of what became known as the Central Bureau to be involved with the decoding of Japanese messages intercepted by other military groups. They built their headquarters for this so-called 'Signals Intelligence' activity right here in Henry Street, Ascot. It's a wonderful story and they had many hundreds of women and men working there between 1942 and 1944, roughly. Everyone's seen the movie *Enigma,* and they've heard about the Enigma Code and that sort of stuff, and they've heard about Bletchley Park in the UK, but who's ever heard of Henry Street, Ascot? Nobody!

In those days in Ascot everybody had very isolated jobs. No one ever did anything from start to finish, so if something happened you couldn't lose the whole chain. The actual decoding was done using some very early IBM computer punch-card equipment, what's called tabulators, and apparently they used to rumble like mad. Finally, according to what I've been told, they fastened the tabulators to the concrete floor of the Ascot fire station to try and stop them rattling. Apart from decrypting the Japanese signals, what they were also doing here was sending the messages across to the UK and the USA, so they were actually both encrypting and decrypting. Back in those days the radio signals were mainly detected during the evenings, so many of the girls would come in about 8 pm and would be working from then on in shifts around the clock. One girl might punch the intercepts up on cardboard cards and then she'd give the cards to somebody else who'd take them over to the cryptographic group and they'd get handed across to a third girl or more. Elsewhere, others were listening in on their earphones to the Japanese signals, except that the Japanese weren't using simple Morse Code, they were using what's called 'Kana Code', which was even more exotic because it had 64 characters in it. The people listening in had to be very well versed in this Katakana Code. A lot of that would be done in Townsville by the Air Force people, and elsewhere, and then it would be sent down by telephone line down to Brisbane using another coding system and then, of course, it'd be punched up on the cards.

From my viewpoint it was really great to meet some of these wonderful people who helped Australia so much during the war. They were under extreme secrecy. In the Anzac Day parades they used to march under a very general service banner. They didn't even have their own banner until the 1990s, I've been told, that's how secret they were. There can be no doubt that what happened here in Brisbane in the Battle of the Coral Sea, et cetera, and eventually Midway, actually influenced the war, because we were able to intercept those signals.

I think it's tremendous that here I am, having brought a company involved in all this secret coding to Queensland, and then meeting people here who were doing this some sixty years ago! Our people here now support the association, particularly one of our lecturers, Mr Les Smith. There's an organisation called the Central Bureau Association, which is an association of all these people who were involved during the war. We're very pleased to help them make their newsletter available.

I left the board of directors of Eracom in 1998 and have had nothing to do with the company since then. I haven't verified this, but up to 18 or 20 other small companies may have now sprung off from Eracom – people who have left have now formed their own little companies or moved into others. This is what they call in America a spawning activity – one high tech company tends to form others. Here in South East Queensland there's a group called the E-Security Cluster, an industry organisation where all these small companies get together under one banner to try and pursue their business interests. That's actually happened.

Peter Doherty – Advancing Science in Queensland and Internationally

Professor Peter Doherty was co-recipient with his colleague Rolf Zinkernagel of the 1996 Nobel Prize in Physiology for their work on immunology and is one of only two Queenslanders to have become a Nobel Laureate. The other, Aleksandr Mikhailovich Prokhorov, physicist, was born in Atherton in 1916 but spent most of his life in Russia, where he died in 2002. Peter Doherty was named Australian of the Year in 1997 and is a Fellow of the Australian Academy of Science. The annual Peter Doherty Science Awards for Excellence in Science and Science Education has been a motivating and enabling force for many young science students throughout Queensland.

'I then came back to the Australian National University in 1971 where I did the work that won the Nobel Prize. Working with Rolf Zinkernagel in Canberra ... Rolf is kind of a messy guy and ... He also sang very loudly ... It was a long time ago now but what happened, we did an experiment for another reason and we got these very unexpected results that were nevertheless very, very clear and when we looked at them we immediately realised we'd hit on something really big.'

I was born in Queensland and grew up in the outer suburb of Oxley, as it then was. It was a kind of marginal suburb, really, almost semi-rural, not a prosperous suburb. One of its characteristics is that everything was covered in a light layer of cement dust from the concrete works at Darra.

I went to Corinda State School, and then to Indooroopilly High School the first year it started. There were virtually no resources except for some good teachers. We had good physics and chemistry teachers and I guess I stayed with those subjects because I found them fairly easy.

I sometimes wonder if I would have gone on with science if I'd gone to a typical American college where you studied both the arts and sciences. The Australian education system always forces people to make up their minds too early between the arts and sciences; I think it's a miserable system. The University of Melbourne is trying to change it with a new Melbourne model. I was actually very good at English and French and History and so forth but I decided that I wanted to be more the 'man of action', if you like, and actually earn a living. When I finished high school I was reading Jean Paul Sartre and Aldous Huxley and Ernest Hemingway all at once and got very confused! They each had very different world views; I plumped for Hemingway as I was going to be the man of action. I also took the opportunity to take a veterinary science scholarship to the University of Queensland.

I went into the veterinary school with the idea of doing veterinary research, which is a bit unusual, really. I had the idea of doing research on diseases of domestic animals. I graduated from the veterinary school and, of course, for a city kid with no rural experience working on rural properties during vacation time and so forth was quite a transforming experience. At that time I was doing research on diseases of large domestic animals. I subsequently became a cadet at the Queensland department of what was then Agriculture and Stock but which later became Primary Industries. I worked for four years for the Queensland DPI. For a little while I was in Toowoomba as a veterinary officer, then at the Animal Research Institute out at Yerongpilly.

I left Queensland in 1967 to go to Edinburgh where I continued my research. When I was working in Edinburgh in Scotland I worked with a guy called Hugh Reid who was the son of a moderator in the Church of Scotland. He was also the grandson of a moderator of the Church of Scotland but Hugh wasn't on that track. He at that stage was a young guy and he was very much into the ladies and consuming fairly large amounts of alcohol, but he used to get around town in a moderator's cape. I remember he had this black cape lined with crimson with a kind of Mephistophelian look.

I then came back to the Australian National University in 1971 where I did the work that won the Nobel Prize. Working with Rolf Zinkernagel in Canberra … Rolf is kind of a messy guy and you'd just turn over the papers in this little office we shared and you'd find a half-eaten apple that had been there for a month. He also sang very loudly. He sang grand opera and he loved Mozart and he was always singing Cherubino from *The Marriage of Figaro* and he had a bass voice and the page Cherubino is usually sung by a girl. It was a long time ago now but what happened, we did an experiment for another reason and we got these very unexpected results that were nevertheless very, very clear and when we looked at them we immediately realised we'd hit on something really big.

For a while we thought it was very similar to something else that some people in the United States had described and we thought we were to some extent confirming their study, but we were doing this with a completely different experimental system. As the experiments went on, it turned out that what we had found was truly very different. One of the things we needed in the experiments was a particular strain of mice which we didn't have at the John Curtin School of Medical Research. It just happened that a professor in the Zoology Department was using them in a big breeding experiment. We got the mice because, to put it kind of gently, one of our younger colleagues alienated a couple from his mice breeding room and he never knew about it. We kind of pinched them. Actually the mice that we'd got by that means were the subject of what is a highly cited research paper.

Unlike Ian Frazer's result, which is a very practical one, ours was more about ideas and concepts, influencing the whole conceptual framework of immunity. It wasn't and never has been as immediately applicable. In fact Ian Fraser has actually been using pretty much, not the technology, but the conceptual framework we developed as he's trying to develop a new treatment, rather than a vaccine, a treatment for cervical cancer, an immunise therapy treatment. He's really using the approach that we pioneered. All science is built on other science. Sometimes people like us are lucky and we make a really big breakthrough. In Ian's case, he took a technology and it just worked spectacularly well. I wouldn't have expected it to and nor would a lot of other people have expected it to, but they got it to work and it worked spectacularly well – beyond expectations.

I've also built research teams. Since I was really quite young I've never tried to do everything myself, I've always tried to get people to work with me and do other things that are complementary, so that's really been my career. I've built research teams. I talk a lot and I'm the writer in the group, I'm actually putting the ideas together in a concise way.

As I recall, Education Queensland approached me and said they'd like to name a science award after me, to which I replied that I'd be very flattered, of course, and then they did that. I haven't really managed to get to many of the events associated with the science awards here because of other commitments, but it's obviously been gratifying to see that Education Queensland are trying to promote science in Queensland. The Beattie government was very strong on that, and, of course, Anna Bligh was part of that as well. I think she was Education Minister for quite some time. I come back to Queensland from time to time when I'm invited, if I can do something that I think is useful and I have met one or two of the recipients of the award, but I'm not intimately involved in the sense of what's going on here now.

My current connections to Queensland are mainly through members of the family. My brother is still here. He teaches science at Hillbrook Secondary School. My dad was in the old Postmaster General's Department; he started as a telephone technician and ended up on the management side of it. My parents left school at age fifteen but my cousin Ralph Doherty was Director of Queensland Institute of Medical Research and then Dean of the Medical School and later Provost Chancellor; he was a prominent medical scientist. I was thirteen years old so I knew him and I was kind of interested in what he did. That was probably the only science connection I had, apart from learning science at school from an excellent science teacher.

I met my wife Penny at the Animal Research Institute at Yerongpilly and we've been married for forty-two years, I guess. She was a microbiologist. Her family came up to Brisbane from Melbourne when she was about ten. We worked together very early on but not in the long term. With my own children, one's a barrister and the other one's a clinical neurologist who specialises in epilepsy. He's a neurologist to some extent, but he's more a clinical person – he's not a lab scientist, he's a clinical investigator, but he does write research papers.

I've recently written a couple of books. One is *The Beginners Guide to Winning a Nobel Prize* and the other is *A Light History of Hot Air*. I talk a lot in the latter book about my childhood in Queensland and growing up with my grandfather, who was a railway man, and going to school on the steam train and all those sorts of experiences that we had in that generation of Queenslanders and Brisbanites.

Schools and TAFE

John Clark – School of Distance Education, Charters Towers

Despite the tyranny of distance the school of which he is principal is a tightly knit community – his interest and enthusiasm in his job and in caring for his charges is infectious.

'You can't help but be touched by these people when you work with them. You become part of their lives. It's an ironical statement to say you are closer to the children of families you work with in a school such as this, even though you are separated by hundreds of kilometres and may only see the students twice or three times a year. Maybe it's a dropping of those barriers we erect to protect ourselves from intimacy, but teachers and school administrators appear to be closer to the families and the students in distance education than they would be in an urban school.'

I am somehow connected to the rural areas of Queensland. My mother and father worked in Western Queensland and left there to settle in Townsville and raise a family. In my youth I used to wake up quite excited, never knowing what sort of battered Land Rover would be parked on the footpath and what exciting people would walk through the front gate; whether they'd be shearers or day 'doggers' (people who used to hunt dingos for a bounty), right through to the 'cockies' – the graziers. For the early period of my life, my family friendships were based on people from rural Queensland. Like many people, my family history is loosely connected with rural Queensland;

grandfathers working in either mines or railway. I was brought up as an urban child until I finished my studies and then someone said 'go west, young man' so in about 1975 I waved goodbye to the big cities and went to work in rural Queensland. For some reason I and the people connected with me have remained in essentially rural areas. It's an enjoyable life.

Since 1989 I've been working in a community called Charters Towers; population somewhere between 8,500 and 10,000 people, depending on what's happening with the goldmines. It's a three-industry town: government services, services to the rural cattle industry and gold mining. Before I came here I was working in a large rural 'high top' school, which is a combination of primary and secondary levels, and quite common in rural Queensland. I had a telephone call that suggested a challenge existed in a new school and would I be interested in considering it. I thought, 'Well, why not?' It sounded good: three years in a country town close to Townsville where my elderly parents were; children getting older and thinking about their future education. I thought I'd do the three years and continue moving in my chosen profession.

I arrived in Charters Towers in 1989 with my wife Anne and a young family and engrossed myself in this unusual school. For a range of reasons the proposed three-year tenure grew. Somewhere along the way the people I work with and the communities I work for touched my soul. Now that's a fairly emotive term to use, but somehow their quiet courage and their dignity had this effect. I thoroughly enjoy working with them. I have been in the school for twenty-one years. I'm still amazed at that.

Our school works predominantly with the women of the families. It is still, at the surface, a patriarchal system in rural Queensland, though women are emerging as leaders. The women generally have multiple roles: labourers on the property, housekeepers, administration managers and caregivers to children. Within that range of responsibilities lies, for those in distance education, the responsibility of educating their own children.

Each of the women is different. The vast majority of them have a quiet, dignified courage. After working with them for some time you understand that they are trying in their own way to do the best they can for their children in a very hands-on way that's not commonly found in larger urban communities. That's not to say you agree with everything they do or their views on life but you'd have to be a very hard-hearted person not to be touched by their commitment and in many cases very visible love for the family unit that they work with.

There are several examples I could give but one stands out. A lady, who was originally an urban-based professional, married into a rural family. She gave up her profession; she works quietly raising her family to be some of the most courteous and considerate children that you could meet. Along the way she has nurtured her children and her husband; has coped with a family suicide as well as the normal childhood adventures we all experience in families. Through the hard times when they felt they would lose everything, this woman's quiet courage and the ability to stand for what she believed in has been exemplary.

You can't help but be touched by these people when you work with them. You become part of their lives. It's an ironical statement to say you are closer to the children of families you work with in a school such as this, even though you are separated by hundreds of kilometres and may only see the students twice or three times a year. Maybe it's a dropping of those barriers we erect to protect ourselves from intimacy, but teachers and school administrators appear to be closer to the families and the students in distance education than they would be in an urban school. That's a broad statement but it's an interesting one.

Distance education in Queensland has existed in many forms for many decades. Originally in the 19th century there were itinerant teachers who went round and made occasional visits to families by buggy or, in some cases, packhorse. A large school was based in Brisbane called the Correspondence School and its purpose was to ensure there was basic literacy and numeracy in isolated rural families. This progressed and use was made of the Royal Flying Doctor's radio service to provide an audio connection, generally a few minutes each day. This was the start of the 'school of the air' mythology that underpins so many views of isolated education.

By the early 1980s most families were operating relatively sophisticated HF radio equipment but it was still the technology of the 1960s. High frequency radio hadn't progressed to any great extent so lessons were still subject to ionospheric conditions, with the loss of radio communications for a day or two during sunspot activity! Well into the 1980s distance education was still an ad hoc system with three teachers involved with each family, each teacher trying to do bits and pieces, and in many cases totally unconnected with one another.

During the late 1980s the Queensland Department of Education decided that there had to be a better model; one that provided an integrated service with one teacher being responsible for the provision of all educational services: the written material, the daily audio lessons, and the working with children at local and school events. Our school was one of two schools established to trial this model. It doesn't sound all that earth shattering an experiment, but it was and within eighteen months it was evident that it was a far better system. The first full year of school at the Charters Towers School of Distance Education was in 1988, and by 1989 the authorities had decided it would be rolled out across Queensland.

I joined the school at the start of 1989 so was able to be engaged in the early work. The integrated service model is accepted as the Australian model now and many overseas educators still visit Queensland to observe the model as it is unique across the world. In 2003 Education Queensland decided there needed to be a better form of audio communication. The radio was often the only audio communication with many of our families, but by the 1980s the telephone system had improved dramatically and the school's radio network had become the fallback system. So, the radio networks were phased out to be replaced by teleconferencing: the audio-lessons became even more dynamic with the flexibility offered by the telephone system.

The vast majority of our families now have broadband Internet and this, coupled with reliable audio-lessons, has also increased the quality of the communication between students, teacher and the families. The change in the resources available to children in distance education over the past few years is great. Our students now regularly use Internet resources, participate in audio-lessons while viewing teacher-prepared materials on their computers, and move in and out of discussion forums and chat rooms with ease.

If you visit our school you'd be left in no doubt that this is a school that focuses on young people and children; we are part of their lives. Our school isn't a bureaucratic or administrative type of centre. It has classrooms; children are visiting us on a daily basis as their parents come to town for business or other purposes. The walls of the school buildings are covered with student work and art. For many of these children their teacher is their only audience outside the immediate family, so teachers have an important position in their world. The walls are just ablaze with colour; from individual pieces of artwork by a pre-schooler who's crushed up egg shells and made some wonderful little diagram that they want to share with their teacher, through to quite delicate works of art that have been constructed by sixteen- and seventeen-year-olds as they try to explore their creative side and share their resulting aesthetic work with other adults for criticism. In essence, when you walk into the building, you will feel, through the display of hundreds of items of student works on display, that you are part of a vibrant learning community.

Teachers have daily communication with their children either through telephone conversations, audio-lessons or email. It is not uncommon over morning tea to hear a teacher saying, 'Oh, did you hear what's happened in the Jones family today?' We, as a school, are part of our families' emergencies, their disasters and their celebrations. This sense of involvement is shared across the whole of the school. Our teachers are part of that daily emerging life of each student and the work of our teachers is to be commended.

Academically, students in Queensland's distance education schools generally achieve within the expected achievement standards. Our families understand that the hard work and diligence they demonstrate in their 'home classrooms' has its rewards for their children.

Students provide an ongoing source of entertainment in our school. Whether it is the young child trying to explain to their teacher that the poddy calf ate their work, or the class of ten-year-olds trying to do a cooking lesson through an audio-lesson, there is a sense of fantasy that underpins their stories. Children, who may see their best friend of years only once or twice annually, communicate daily, sharing their lives with each other. Young men, not yet adolescent, hold an adult conversation about market prices, weather conditions and the future of their family's industry. Then there are the many variations of 'the snake in the classroom' scenario where the children wait for mother to dispose of the 'guest' while providing a detailed description of the event to listening classmates during an audio-lesson.

Our past students stay in touch. A student who left our school in Year 10 in 2002 recently contacted the school to express his thanks and appreciation to the staff for helping to prepare him for a career. He has been the recipient of several industry and training awards and simply wanted to share his success with his school. Past students regularly address our school community, both parents and students. Their affection for the school and their willingness to contribute to the next group of students is valued.

The school, its students and staff have received many awards over the years. While these are valued for the recognition that has been given to an individual or group endeavour, perhaps the greatest form of recognition our school has is the sense of commitment, community and fellowship that is expressed by our families, students and staff. That makes us rich in terms of a sense of community and connectedness with one another.

Wendy Ashley-Cooper and Merle Guymer – The Glennie

Left to Right: Wendy Ashley Cooper, Head of School, with Merle Guymer, retired teacher, in the grounds of The Glennie

Boarding school can be an amazing experience for a student, with teachers and other students often becoming like a second family. In these stories we hear about boarding school life at Glennie, an Anglican school for girls, as experienced over the past fifty-plus years by two members of the teaching staff: the current Head and a retired teacher who was at Glennie in the 1940s and 1950s.

Wendy Ashley-Cooper

In the mid to late '50s when I went to Glennie the school had just 200 students, mostly boarders, living in a very close community. Now it's a school of some 650 students. Talking to the current Head of School it's apparent that despite its growth, attention to the needs of the individual is still a major priority...

> *'I think the school these days is a very personal place, it's not run so much out of rules as through relationships and I think that's what modern parents want for their children ... I feel we also take a lot more interest in children's academic success than perhaps we did in years gone by ... Now, of course, we're educating young women to enter the workforce. We're trying to support them in getting this career/family balance which is so difficult for modern women. Can they have it all? Can they have it all at the same time? ... A career for a woman is no longer just "something to fall back on".'*

I was born in Cape Town, South Africa and when I was six years old my family migrated to Australia and we lived in Sydney. I spent most of my childhood in Sydney but as a teenager we went back to South Africa and I spent the next twenty-five years there and north of there in Rhodesia, which later became Zimbabwe.

Fifteen years ago I decided to bring my family out of Zimbabwe to Australia. We decided to settle in Queensland because I thought Sydney was not a good place to bring up my children. We'd lived in a very rural environment and also my mother had subsequently returned and had moved to Queensland. We've been in Queensland since 1992.

We started off in Caloundra, where I gained a job at the Caloundra Christian School and while I was there I did a Masters in Education Administration. After that I was fortunate enough to secure the position of the first Deputy Principal of Fraser Coast Anglican College, a new Anglican school in Hervey Bay. After four years in Hervey Bay I applied for the position of the Head of Glennie in Toowoomba and got that. I started here at the end of May 2001.

I think Glennie is the perfect match for me. For many years I'd wanted to lead a girls' school, an Anglican school, and a school in regional Queensland. There is only one school in the whole of Queensland that meets those three criteria and that's Glennie, so I consider myself extremely fortunate and privileged to be here. I love the sense of tradition and the heritage. I love the way the Old Girls of Glennie have passed on the culture. I love the spirit of Glennie; there's something special about this place, I hate to use the word 'fun' because I think it's overused but there is a brightness of spirit here about the girls and a lightness of heart and a willingness to help and encourage each other which I think has probably been here for the school's entire 100 years. I find that really good to work with and work amongst.

I think the modern headmistress lives and works in a much more 'personal' way – I certainly do. I'm not lofty and aloof. I'm not afraid to be with the children in quite a personal way; they know when we're in a formal situation and when we're in an informal situation. I think that has changed over time. Headmistresses of old had a distance between them and their pupils which worked well for that time but now children need a lot of personal nurturing. This is a very unstable world, a very uncertain world and they suffer a lot from family breakdown. We have a number of children whose parents have split up and those children need a lot of personal attention. I think the school these days is a very personal place, it's not run so much out of rules as through relationships and I think that's what modern parents want for their children. We have to support the children quite a lot more these days. We have a school counsellor, for example, which they didn't have in the old days. She works half-time and girls access her via email and go and talk to her. She does enormously important work through the school, supporting children through difficult times. The biggest problem they present with is relationship breakdown between Mum and Dad, which is awfully hard for them.

I feel we also take a lot more interest in children's academic success than perhaps we did in years gone by. When I went to school it was all about the rules and a lot about behaviour but not a huge amount about fulfilling your academic potential. I spent two years at Queenwood School in Sydney, which, incidentally, I discovered recently shared the same founding principal as Glennie, Grace Lawrance, so I have a little connection to Glennie myself in an historical way. When I was at school you were labelled as bright or not and streamed accordingly, and that was pretty much that. I don't mean to sound disparaging about the old days but I think the emphasis has changed. Now, of course, we're educating young women to enter the workforce. We're trying to support them in getting this career/family balance which is so difficult for modern women. Can they have it all? Can they have it all at the same time? What kind of support do they need? I think a lot more is demanded and expected now of our young women. A career for a woman is no longer just 'something to fall back on'.

Traditionally we have around 35% of our secondary students as boarders, which is probably a lower proportion than of old. Most of those still come from rural Queensland and Northern New South Wales, plus we have a growing number of international students. We have 23 international students, mostly from Hong Kong but also from Korea, Japan, New Guinea, Mauritius, Thailand and mainland China. I particularly went out and marketed to obtain them because of our falling boarder numbers. We teach French and Japanese in the school and we have a French immersion program. That's an outstanding leading-edge program where they do half their subjects in the French language. I think French has always been important in Glennie, from what I can learn from the history, so it's good to be continuing that tradition.

I see Glennie as a really interesting blend of tradition and innovation. I feel there's a good balance here with the kind of heritage that I think is important. It's very important for girls to have a sense of where they've come from and where the school's come from, and we talk about history a lot. Boarding is a lot freer, in the sense of coming and going and a lot more comfortable probably than it used to be.

In terms of public high points, recently 70 of our girls, our musicians, performed on stage at the Sydney Opera House in the Concert Hall. They were part of an International Festival of Music for which we had to audition by CD. They were accepted and went to Sydney and performed in a program alongside students from all over the world. I thought that was a real high point for our musicians. Our musical program is very strong.

On a less public level, then, I would think that helping an individual child through a difficult patch is frequently a high point for me. A few come very close to being asked to go, being expelled. In the old days I think they would have been expelled but I try harder these days to save them and when that works that's enormously rewarding. A high point is when we've turned a child around, from behaving very poorly, not co-operating and being difficult and rebellious, to changing and growing up, to maturing and understanding and appreciating her opportunities and making something of her life. Low points are probably when one doesn't succeed and one has to send a child away – that's the opposite.

I'm very keen on fostering student leadership. I don't believe that prefects are the head mistress's police force. I think that student leadership is about actually being creative and innovative and engaging the other students in what you're doing so they want to follow you. We have an academic festival every year, invented by the girls, run by the girls and organised by the girls. It's called Spectrum and it actually promotes all senior subjects. They set it up in Manning Theatre with displays of what every subject does and the younger girls come and have a look and talk to the seniors about, 'Well, what's it like doing physics?' and 'What do you do in chemistry in senior?' and this kind of thing, so they actually offer advice. It's rather like one of those careers expos that you get but within the school. The girls cut out the letters of Spectrum and stuck them up along a window of a classroom to advertise the festival and one little bunny came along and changed the letters around so the next morning there in big letters it said 'Crumpets'. That's the sort of mischief which Glennie girls are known for!

The sense of camaraderie among the teachers here is very strong; I think it always has been. These days we do surveys of staff morale and I think up to 88% last time I did the survey said their job satisfaction was very high or high. We have boarding staff live in but the majority of the teaching staff is not boarding staff so very few actually live in now.

If you could see our Year 12 boarding house you would see that they're accommodated in single rooms that open up onto a big central lounge area, that's all air-conditioned and very comfortable and very modern. We have wireless connectivity right through the school so they all work on laptop computers. Everybody has a laptop computer. They pay for them but it's just a hire charge through the school and we provide the entire backup infrastructure, the technicians and everything.

We have a culture here, which has always been here, that it doesn't really matter what your background is. We have a very egalitarian, accepting kind of culture. We help a lot of families with their school fees but they do have to pay for things like the laptop computers. Some of our indigenous students are on Abstudy, which pays most of their fees, so they do get support.

Glennie girls are very big on community spirit. We had a Torres Strait Islander girl a few years ago and the time came for the formal and all that business in Year 12, where they get dressed up. It's a big deal and very expensive these days. This girl asked her parents to send her money to get a dress to go to the formal but they said, 'Sorry, we haven't got any money,' so she just quietly withdrew from the formal and didn't say anything. When the other girls found out about this they actually did a whip around and bought her a dress and they paid for her to go to the hairdresser and get all dolled up and there she was. She didn't have a partner but lots of them didn't so that was all right. I just thought that was a really fantastic example of the way they care about each other. I don't think that sort of spirit has changed; I think that's always been a feature of Glennie.

Merle Guymer

Merle Guymer and I first met when I was a student there in the '50s and she was my teacher. Resident teachers, though, were more than simply teachers; they filled a larger role. Although always addressed formerly as Miss Guymer she was affectionately known to everyone as 'Aunty Merle' – even among those of us who didn't enjoy chemistry or maths!

> *'I've had three nieces who went through Glennie – two of them while I was teaching there, which is where I got my nickname "Aunty Merle".'*

I did my primary education at a small, one-teacher school at Silverspur near the Queensland/New South Wales border, about 130 miles south-west of Toowoomba. I did my scholarship exam there and was lucky enough to be able to go to Warwick High School, where I had my four years of secondary education and then, with a great struggle, my family enabled me to go to Queensland University, where I did a science course, graduating at the end of 1941.

At the end of that year, when I was considering what I was going to do, there was an advertisement from the Glennie Memorial School (as it was known then) for a science teacher to teach chemistry and physics. I was twenty-one at the time and I was appointed by the principal, Miss Gwen Dowson, in that Christmas holiday of 1941/1942. I started work there in January 1942. Glennie was a small secondary school with two junior years and two senior years that became Grades 9 through 12. I think there were under 200 students in the school at that time, with around 140 boarders and 35 to 40 day girls. I taught chemistry and physics right through the school and some junior maths. I was a resident member of staff for the first twenty-one years that I was there.

At the beginning of the time I was at Glennie, the buildings used by the Glennie Prep School were taken over by the military and it became a military hospital. That was when the Prep School had to move out and they eventually went to Smithfield. That was the beginning of the time that the Japanese came into the war. One of my first experiences of Glennie was blacking out the school, pasting the windows with strips of paper to try and make them shatterproof and so on – you know there were a lot of windows around Glennie! All the children, particularly the senior girls in the school, were very much involved in contributing to the war effort. There was a great sense of camaraderie in the school in those early years, not just in the staff group but also between the staff and the children.

Miss Dowson retired at the end of 1962 so I taught under her from the beginning of 1942 until her retirement. Miss Gwen Knapp was Miss Dowson's very able first assistant, and I owe a great deal to both of them, as far as guidance in all sorts of ways regarding teaching and management of staff and the school. I was away from teaching between December 1963 and January 1971 when I went home to our property at Texas to look after my mother. After my mother passed away I came back to Glennie. Miss Knapp was no longer there. We three had been very good friends when we were working together at Glennie and we remained very good friends right up to the end when they both passed away, Miss Dowson in 1980 and Miss Knapp in 1999. They both played a very important part in my life, and particularly from the point of view of teaching.

Lynette Thompson became Head in 1963. She was only there from 1963 to 1964, then Kathleen Simmons took over at the beginning of 1965. Kath came to Glennie in 1956. She taught English and some French too. She and I were on the staff together for about six years before I left in '63 and then I came back working under her for eleven years, from January 1971 to December 1981.

Thinking back to some of the important things about the school, first and foremost I'd remember the school chapel. That was always a very important part of life at the Glennie. The girls played quite a big part in the services, they acted as servers at the communion services assisting the minister, and one of the girls always played the organ. If I can, I still attend the Founder's Day service each year. One service, in particular, I remember, was at the end of the Pacific War (11 August 1945). The school was wakened up, as probably all of Toowoomba was, by the celebrations that went on in the streets. Almost automatically in the very early hours about three or four o clock in the morning the girls just found themselves going into the school chapel. Miss Dowson came and I remember being there at that very special thanksgiving service at that very early hour.

Founder's Day was always very much a day of celebration. In the early days we always had what they called a Salmagundi in the morning where staff and children had games on the lawn outside the main classrooms. Then we often had some sort of arranged sport in the afternoon. About the mid '50s they no longer had the Salmagundi and the organised sport but they went out on an arranged trip. The first one I think took place in 1954 and the whole school went by train to Spring Bluff. One of the things a lot of the Old Girls from those days would remember would be Miss Dowson, standing on the platform taking photographs, with half of Glennie practically falling out of the train windows waving to her as the train went off to Spring Bluff.

One of the things that the staff were always involved with, of course, was the fête which the school has run for many years. In those days the staff ran the sweet stall and we had an especially nice Russian caramel recipe which myself and two other people were involved in making in the school kitchen to be sold on the school stall. Unfortunately, one lot was rather disastrous, so, not knowing what to do with it, we ended up wandering around the grounds with a torch and finally burying the Russian caramel somewhere in the garden!

Some of the boarders used to have free weekends when they were able to go home but there always seemed to be some children left at the school, so we tried to take them out on a picnic or something. On one occasion we went down to Flagstone Creek, where some of the children were jumping across a little creek. I then tried jumping over the little creek but I didn't quite make the other bank – I landed *in* the creek. I can remember walking back to Picnic Point and coming home in the bus with the children, much to their amusement, soaking wet from the waist down!

One of the people who was on the staff of Glennie, probably from the second year I was there, was a nursing sister, Joan McKechnie. She and I became firm friends. She had a younger brother who was in the army during the war and he was one of those captured when the Japanese came down to Singapore and he was declared missing. After several months, one night Joan got a message to say that Ralph and some other prisoners who were taken at that stage had been picked up from a ship that had been torpedoed and he was safe and well. I can remember that as clearly as anything. He passed away only a couple of years ago. Joan's living in Albury; she nursed there for a long time. She eventually married and is now living in a nursing home but we still keep in contact.

Miss Dowson was keen on the girls not borrowing or lending. I've heard that boarders 'gave' their dress away for the term and had somebody else's dress in return so that they had a change of clothes to go to the dining room. 'Neither a borrower nor a lender be' was a common saying, and still is, I believe, with Old Girls from the days of Miss Dowson.

Glennie always had a 'display' at the end of the year. Parents and friends would sit on the verandahs to watch, or look down at it from upstairs from the girls' dormitory windows. At the same time either in classrooms or the dining room there was often a display of art work or some schoolwork that the children had done, and home science work that was available for the visitors to go and see. The carol service was also very popular and was sometimes held outdoors. It was a very important part of our end of year program.

In November 1962 Miss Dowson left and we had a garden party, with about 500 people present to honour her leaving the school. I left at the end of the following year.

I've had three nieces who went through Glennie – two of them in the late '40s early '50s while I was actually teaching there, which is where I got my nickname 'Aunty Merle'! Since then I've had five great nieces that have gone through the school. I was very pleased to have some of my family go through the school, which, over the years, has meant so much to me and still does to them, I'm sure.

Ann Garms – TAFE and COTAH

Ann is Chair of the College of Tourism and Hospitality (COTAH) Advisory Council and Deputy Chair of the Technical and Further Education (TAFE) Advisory Council. We meet at her gift shop in the Stamford Plaza Hotel but it's busy here so we agree to adjourn to the nearby Polo Club. Ann's had a long involvement with the hospitality industry and she's now involved in the training of others in the hospitality industry, helping them to benefit from her experience.

'I went up in the lift, knocked on his door, and Sir Joh opened it! I'd never met him before and I said to him, "You've approved this money for a dedicated College of Hospitality and Tourism but we don't see any sign of it." He said, "Oh well, I'll get onto Sid Schubert," so he rang Sid and said, "Have we approved this money?" and Sid Schubert came back and said, "Yes." "Well," said Sir Joh, "I want it through Cabinet next Monday so we can get this College of Tourism and Hospitality going." That's how it happened; I have been involved with COTAH for twenty-two years now, since it was built.'

I was born in Brisbane in 1946, a baby-boomer, the eldest of four children, two boys, John and Paul; and two girls, my sister Robyn and me. We had a lovely childhood at Albion. I went to Ascot State School, which was wonderful, and later to Domestic Science High, which was the forerunner to TAFE.

My grandfather was a manager for Rawleys Products and one of the most travelled men in Australia. He also used to travel to England, Singapore and other faraway places and he always told me very vivid stories about international travel, so I decided I wanted to be involved in hospitality and tourism. That was in the days when it wasn't considered even a profession.

In Grade 8 at Ascot we always had a guidance officer come to see you to say, 'What do you want to do with your future?' and I said, 'I want to be involved with Hospitality and Tourism,' and she said, 'What? You want to wash up and make beds?' and I said, 'No, I don't see it like that.'

Later I went to Domestic Science High. When I left there, there were no openings in the hospitality industry so I worked in the office at Grazcos Wool Brokers during the day and in the evenings I had a part-time job working at Sadler's Sound Lounge. You wouldn't call it a 'night club', but it was a place under the ground in Elizabeth Street that had live music.

In 1977 my husband and I had bought the old Courthouse Restaurant at Cleveland and then we went on to develop Petrie Mansions Restaurant, Roseville Restaurant and the Tivoli Theatre. I was an executive member of the Restaurant and Caterers Association in the '70s and '80s. We were all establishing different types of restaurants, but we all had the same problem: no trained staff. We had a long held dream that one day we'd have a purpose-built college of hospitality and tourism, so we lobbied the state government but as time went by nothing happened. I was walking down George Street from a Restaurant & Caterers meeting one day, feeling very dejected, and I thought, 'Well, I'm just going to go in and ask the Premier what's happening!' I went up in the lift, knocked on his door, and Sir Joh opened it! I'd never met him before and I said to him, 'You've approved this money for a dedicated College of Hospitality and Tourism, but we don't see any sign of it.' He said, 'Oh well, I'll get onto Sid Schubert,' so he rang Sid and said, 'Have we approved this money?' and Sid Schubert came back and said, 'Yes.' 'Well,' said Sir Joh, 'I want it through Cabinet next Monday so we can get this College of Tourism and Hospitality going.' That's how it happened; I have been involved with COTAH for twenty-two years now, since it was built.

Over the years I became concerned at the problems being experienced by many young students in regard to literacy and learning problems so I established and funded the first Literacy Learning Centre in Southbank TAFE which provides individualised 'one on one' training. I also funded the Nursing Wing at Southbank TAFE, which provides for practical hands-on training, complete with the practice dummies in their beds. In fact my mother-in-law, Mrs Alice Garms, is in a nursing home at Bulimba, the Clem Jones Home, and two of the nurses there said to her, 'Your name's familiar. We went to the Ann Garms Nursing Wing at Southbank TAFE,' so she was delighted. Alice is a remarkable lady, so wise and full of interesting stories and a love of life. I enjoy her company tremendously.

In 2008 Southbank TAFE, with a $600 million expansion and redevelopment, became a Statutory Authority and is now the Southbank Institute of Technology. Southbank Institute's core business is the provision of high quality education and skills development for our Queensland and international students, our motto is 'Education for Aspiring Minds'. Each year around 30,000 students enroll in over 300 courses and develop skills using our state-of-the-art training facilities.

My husband Harry and I were two of the first people to combine heritage preservation with hospitality. Harry was brought up in London. He always laughs about being one of those ten-pound English immigrants. He came to Australia in 1963 and went to work for Mount Isa Mines and became their day foreman in the lead smelter, then the strike came and he came to Brisbane and I met him here. We got married, went back to London and stayed there about eighteen months.

When I married Harry he said, 'I can't guarantee that we'll come back,' but we were only three weeks in London when he said, 'Australia's my home – I love Australia.' He loves London as well, but the lifestyle here, of course, is much superior. Harry was a telegram boy in his very early years, and in that way he knew every building in central London and was very interested in architecture and what made the city tick, and the importance of preserving heritage. I tell my students at the college, 'You've got to understand where you've come from before you know where you're going.'

We bought and restored the old 1853 Courthouse Restaurant in Cleveland and extended it out of old porphyry stone that we obtained from the original old Supreme Court in George Street, Brisbane, when, sadly, the government demolished it in 1997. This to me was a far worse sin than the demolition of the Bellevue Hotel; the old Supreme Court building was truly magnificent with wonderful wide stairs stretching down to the Brisbane River at North Quay.

We were only at the Courthouse Restaurant for three years, and then it was time for our sons, Christopher and Richard, to go to Brisbane Boys' College. That was prior to the Commonwealth Games so there was no highway to Brisbane. Public transport from Cleveland to BBC took an hour and a half, which made it very difficult, so we booked the boys into the BBC boarding school. Well, they hated every minute of that. Richard was so unhappy being away from the family that we decided we'd sell the Courthouse and move back to Brisbane.

Strangely enough, at that time two customers mentioned two separate opportunities to us. One said that he owned a set of terrace houses in Petrie Terrace, circa 1885, that had previously been condemned by the Brisbane City Council. He was actually pulling them down when the '74 flood hit and then the council changed the legislation so it was not viable to demolish them. The other customer said a friend of theirs had a house on an acre of land at New Farm that was in danger of being pulled down for the construction of forty home units. We went and had a look at the two properties. We purchased both. One became Petrie Mansions Restaurant, and the other one became Roseville Restaurant. We bought them in 1979, and restored Petrie Mansions first. Petrie Mansions were one of Brisbane's largest sets of terrace houses, each house being about 30 squares. We lived on the second level at Petrie Mansions. It was a great restaurant and then we restored Roseville Restaurant at New Farm.

Roseville was on an acre of landscaped rose gardens and was originally built by James Cowlishaw for the George Myers family in 1885. It was subsequently purchased by the Catholic Church. There was a fair bit of restoration work needed when we got it but we finally opened it as a restaurant in 1982. In 1985 we won the National Trust of Queensland citation for Excellence in Heritage Preservation. It only closed recently when the current owners decided to use the garden to build twenty-three units. The house itself is being restored back into a private home. It had a long life as a restaurant – twenty-one years or so – and was much loved by Brisbanites.

In 1991 I was awarded an Order of Australia in the Queen's Birthday Honours List for my commitment to Hospitality and Tourism and the Community. In 1993, along with Kieren Perkins, I received the Advance Australia Award from the Queensland Governor. In 2000 I won an award as a Leading Woman Entrepreneur of the World. The award ceremony was in Madrid, Spain, and I had never been to Spain. When I spoke at the award ceremony, there were present sponsors from Harvard University, who subsequently invited me to join the Women's Leadership Board at the John F Kennedy School of Government at Harvard. I find the experience and knowledge I gain very beneficial, particularly for the advancement of career paths for our young women graduates in Brisbane. I've also been awarded Honorary Alumnus status by the QUT Brisbane Graduate School of Business. We've achieved an awful lot there in the last twelve months, establishing Fostering Executive Women (FEW), of which I am patron, through the dedication of Professor Caroline Hatcher. FEW facilitates a mentoring program for our MBA graduates, connecting these young women with women leaders in similar professions.

Through our restaurants we raised over $2 million for charity by giving up our Sundays. That's the type of thing I love doing. The problem with philanthropy today is that firms want to see some value added to the firm for what they give away. It's our aim through QUT to create these links. There's a wonderful philanthropy section at QUT. Brisbane people are very generous people. We have a lot of very generous corporate people in Brisbane and it's how to marry the donation with the need, plus the benefit to the corporation as well.

I've been on the board of the Brisbane Polo Club for sixteen years and was President for four years. Through the National Trust we have obtained registration as a Heritage Trust. In this way we can ensure that historic Naldham House, the home of the Brisbane Polo Club, is maintained and preserved for our members as well as future generations.

I think Australians are a wonderful and quite humble people. Humour is an important part of our lives and Australians are good at that. When we were growing up, none of us had much, unless your father was a lawyer or an accountant. My mother had a job and we had our own home but everything we got was a bonus. We set goals and we didn't have any hang-ups about achieving them. I remember when I was going to Ascot State School where a lot of the girls had wealthy parents and I used to think, 'Well, I mightn't have the court shoes for breaking-up day or the very fancy dress, but when I get older I'll look the same as they do, and I'm going to be able to achieve some wonderful things in my life!' I love that old saying, 'You come into this world with nothing and you go out with nothing,' so whatever happens in the meantime is a bonus. I think Australians look at life like that and we believe in ourselves.

Education for the Disabled

Trish Taylor – Teaching the Hearing Deficient

As a hearing impaired student Trish struggled to hear what was being taught. She had to cope in a class where the other students and the teaching staff had no hearing difficulties. Now a teacher herself, she's able to use her experience to benefit the hearing impaired students in her care…

'The assignments for auditory training and speech were difficult. I had to teach a deaf primary student how to say S, yet I couldn't say it myself and couldn't hear it. I had to have a fellow student listen for me … yet it is not acknowledged that deaf teachers of the deaf bring other things to the job that hearing teachers of the deaf can't.'

I'm thirty-seven years of age and married with three children, aged four, two and one. I have a severe hearing loss. I was first diagnosed with a hearing loss at the age of eight. It was picked up by a school nurse. I was fitted with hearing aids at the age of nine. My hearing has since continued to deteriorate and will eventually all go. I remained in a mainstream school setting throughout my schooling. I was supported by an Advisory Visiting Teacher: Hearing Impairment in primary school. I attended a secondary school where there was a deaf/hearing impaired unit (Kedron State High School) and received tutorial support from the teacher there. This was in the '70s when the hearing impaired unit was just being set up in mainstream school settings. I actually went to that school because it had an excellent music program and I wanted to be a music teacher.

I was born in Redcliffe but we moved to Deagon when I was in Grade 1. My memories of the city at that time are very much of the scenery of Sandgate – a strong community by the sea. I do remember going on special trips to the Valley. I remember Myers and Waltons there. We would dress up and catch a train in. I really looked forward to having lunch at the Waltons cafeteria where Mum would buy a cappuccino. It was considered to be a 'posh' way of having coffee and came in a brown coffee cup and saucer.

I was in a recorder marching band at primary school. There was one teacher who took the band (Mrs Butterworth) and she made the experience very exciting. I enjoyed the playing, marching and competitions. I wanted to become a music teacher. At high school, I still wanted to become a music teacher but my history teacher (Miss Kastrissios) inspired in me a real love for history. I respected her very much and decided that I also wanted to teach history myself.

I remember at high school a teacher commenting that he wasn't sure if I would be able to be employed as a teacher, as hearing impairment was a barrier to employment. I was in Grade 11 or 12 at the time and was surprised by this and wished someone had mentioned it beforehand. It was around this time that hearing impairment was being removed as a restriction to employment. I went on to do my Bachelor of Arts and majored in music and history. I then completed my Diploma in Education – both at the University of Queensland.

When I requested some help from a disability officer whilst doing my BA, the support was very poor, as the person assisting me, whilst very concerned, didn't know enough about hearing impairment and really couldn't act as an advocate effectively on my behalf. Advocacy support for students with disabilities (at least hearing impairment) at the tertiary level was very poor and limited back then (late 1985 to 1988). I spent whole lectures trying to catch what the lecturer said and I began to think I was stupid not being able to understand or perhaps not concentrating hard enough and so would chastise myself. Because I wasn't hearing properly my notes didn't make sense. I would spend hours out of lecture time finding information to fill in the holes of what I missed. It was very stressful and I didn't enjoy my time studying my BA.

The Diploma in Education was a bit better as the groups/lectures were smaller but I still remember thinking, 'How did people get that information?' I didn't put things down to not hearing things but to my cognitive ability. When you can hear lots of things, you forget or don't realise that there are things you don't hear. Fortunately there was a history lecturer in the Dip. Ed. course who I liked a lot. He pulled me aside and prepared me for the comments students might make towards me when they found out I had a hearing impairment. His fears were unfounded and I had no problems. I could read students' lips and just moved towards the student if I didn't hear well enough and told that person to speak up for the rest of the class. There were many strategies I adopted. When I finally started teaching music and history in a high school, I found that I could tell the students what they were talking about when they should be concentrating on the task at hand. The students thought I had eyes in the back of my head!

After I started music and history teaching I found that my hearing was deteriorating and would continue to do so. I chose to change profession before I started to really experience problems. Music is not a problem – I could read a score and know what to listen for, I could play the piano et cetera. Understanding what students were saying was harder.

I successfully applied to do the Graduate Diploma in Special Education (Hearing Impairment) as an in-service teacher at Griffith University. This was a one-year course for teachers who wanted to become teachers of the deaf. It was during this course that I learnt a lot about myself and how to be an advocate for my needs as well as for others. I learnt how to sign and was introduced to an FM system that improved the quality of sound for me. I also had a note taker. This was enlightening. I tried to take notes myself and thought I was good at it. However, when I compared my notes to the note taker's I was shocked to find how much I got wrong and how much I missed.

My experiences at Griffith made me start thinking about my identity – was I deaf or hearing impaired? There were other deaf students there doing the Bachelor of Special Education. They did a couple of our subjects. However, they were profoundly deaf and I noted how their needs were both similar and different to mine. I ended up teaching with one of them and we are still good friends today. We supported one another in challenging the education department to meet our needs as employees during the early to mid-1990s (acquiring an FM system and TTY, interpreting at staff meetings). The assignments for auditory training and speech were difficult. I had to teach a deaf primary student how to say S, yet I couldn't say it myself and couldn't hear it. I had to have a fellow student listen for me. All of the deaf/hearing impaired students found this difficult. It is still an issue today yet it is not acknowledged that deaf teachers of the deaf bring other things to the job that hearing teachers of the deaf can't.

We work with students with a range of hearing losses. In units based in mainstream settings, most of them are severe to profoundly deaf and require alternate means of communication such as signing. For years there has been signed English, though in the last decade there has been a push towards using Auslan in the classroom. Auslan is a complex language in its own right, though, and one really needs to be fluent in it to teach in it. I primarily learnt signed English so I teach using this. My deaf friend (whom I mentioned earlier) uses Auslan as her main language and so teaches in this. Students don't appear to experience difficulties in switching. Many students supported by unit staff in secondary schools spend most, if not all of their time in mainstream settings. The challenge is to spread the staffing over the many classes we have to cover and interpret for, as the students choose different subjects. Students with lesser hearing losses are supported by Advisory Visiting Teachers: Hearing Impairment. These students wear hearing aids, are oral rather than signing and may use speech reading (lip reading).

For all students who are deaf/hearing impaired, auditory training programs and speech and language programs are important. They seem to lose emphasis as students get older – simply because students don't want this and would rather be in class concentrating on the curriculum (as well as going through the adolescent thing and not wanting to be treated differently). Students attempt a wide range of subjects – music included. My impression is that the biggest barrier is hearing people who worry about how the student will be able to study music rather than let the student go and put things in place as they need it. Learning LOTE (Language Other Than English) seems to be difficult, as many profoundly deaf students struggle with learning English as a first language. Students with lesser hearing losses also find it difficult because the

457

frequencies in speech are so complex and your interpretation of the message received has to be accurate. However, some students do succeed and enjoy LOTE. This has meant that the Board of Senior Secondary School Studies (now Queensland Studies Authority) was eventually challenged about the LOTE syllabuses in terms of the speaking and listening requirements. The Australian Association of Teachers of the Deaf worked with the Board in the late 1990s to overcome this and there have since been changes in the LOTE syllabuses that help overcome many barriers. The English syllabus also had a major barrier to students successfully meeting the syllabus requirements. It was only in the mid-1990s that students were allowed to replace speaking requirements with signed English.

When I was based at a high school (I was there for fourteen years), I would have students come back and fill me in on what they're doing. A couple have gone on to tertiary, some have started apprenticeships or traineeships and others have done short courses or found work. They still experience barriers in terms of employers too scared to take them on. The agencies who help people find jobs, traineeships et cetera – even if their focus is for clients with disabilities – still don't know enough about hearing impairment to be able to take on an advocacy role or put the right strategies in place (much like when I was at university). I remember one student whom I was fond of – he said he couldn't wait to finish school. He was very bright but didn't put in the hard work. He really could have gone on to university but that wasn't a priority for him. He turned up the following year to say that life after school wasn't so exciting after all and that he wished he could come back.

Joyce Weeks – University Graduate at Seventy-Eight

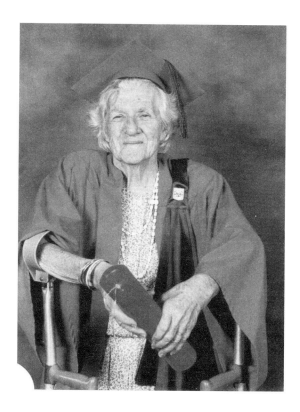

She finds the church a great comfort and the local minister suggested we meet. She'd been ill but was happy to talk. Life has been difficult for her but she's a battler and is justifiably proud of successes achieved, both for herself and others.

'In my seventies I went to the College of Advanced Education to get the necessary qualifications to go to university. Then at the University of Queensland I studied Humanities and I graduated in the year 2000, when I was nearly eighty.'

My first memories of Brisbane were in my grandfather's place where we lived when I was little; I was about three or four years old then. It was in Arthur Terrace, Red Hill. I was a disabled child; I didn't walk. I actually had very little education because in those days they didn't bother with disabled children. My parents went to live at Coorparoo and I went to school for a bit, then, when they could take me to school, but I had very little what you'd call formal education.

I was born in 1922 and I was sent to Montrose (the home for crippled children) in 1933. I was in hospital from when I was nine until I was sixteen. They used to leave you in plaster in those days for sometimes eight months at a time and you were sent back to the hospital to take the plaster off. They had a school but it was the minimum

459

of education of those days. They've now turned out to be a good school for disabled children – but what they do for disabled children nowadays is certainly a lot better than what they did when I was young.

My mother died when I was sixteen and my father turned us out in the street. I got 10 shillings a week pension and my sister Greta got a job out at Quilpie, so we went to Quilpie and she did the cleaning at a hotel, you know, as a housemaid, and we lived out there for about three to four years. My sister married out there and I returned to Brisbane on my own. It was hard, but life's always been hard. I had a place here I could stay, with a friend of my mother's. My father was not a nice man. He had a second family after us and they had six more children, but that's another story.

My husband, James, came from out West. He went down to Sydney to join up but they wouldn't have him. We met in Quilpie and he followed me to Brisbane, so we got married and came back to live in Red Hill. We had two children: a son, James, and a daughter, Laurene, and they went to school at Ithaca. Then later our daughter moved to the school in Ashgrove. I think they were proud when I got my degree – I hope so. My daughter has lived in America for about the last twenty-seven years. My son lives at Keperra and I look after myself. I've never worked as far as paid work is concerned but I could sew, so I've always done a bit of sewing – I made my daughter's wedding clothes and things.

You know where the skeleton of the old skating rink stands now on Enoggera Terrace? Well, I knew that building when I was six years old; it was called Pop's Pictures. It was a cinema with canvas chairs and my grandfather would sit outside the door and he wouldn't let us out because he said pictures were no good for children!

I've got a photo of my son when he was little, outside the fire station in Enoggera Terrace, with a fireman's hat on. There used to be a tannery, too, on Fulcher Road. There were lots of things then that that are not there now. I saw the fire from the old Paddington tram sheds. They said it was the wells of grease under the trams that kept it burning so long. My aunt lived nearby in Dyne Street – they had some sheep and a couple of cows there when I was about ten years old.

We lived in the Valley for a while. There was a kindergarten on Arthur Terrace and a Catholic Convent school called St Patrick's. People in those days stayed in the one place for many years. I never could walk very well and one time I fell over in the middle of McLachlan Street, right opposite the Truth Corner (that's where the Truth Newspapers used to be). No one came to help me; they thought I was drunk. There was a fruit shop next door to Truth and the lady that had the fruit shop had rather a raucous voice. When she saw the crowd gathering on the footpath she came to have a look and she said, 'She ain't drunk, she's a cripple!' Then there were a lot of helping hands and I was on the footpath. Until then, and it was a good ten minutes, nobody did a thing! They thought, because I was on the ground, that I was drunk. Not too many people were kind to cripples in those days. It was a bit of a disgrace, because you generally didn't have any education.

I lost my husband in 1976; he had emphysema. He used to work on coal ships for a time and the dust down in the hold of those ships was bad, and he also smoked.

I always was a curious person. I had to be resourceful, too, as it was considered rather disgraceful to be a cripple. In my seventies I went to the College of Advanced Education to get the necessary qualifications to go to university. Then, at the

University of Queensland, I studied Humanities and I graduated in the year 2000, when I was nearly eighty. Nobody helped me. The government's never helped; they never even gave me a book. I still get correspondence from the university and they want me to go back, but at the moment I can't. I can't do it money-wise. I've got one degree and therefore HECS doesn't even cover it. You're not useful to Australia if you can't get a job. If I could get to university I'd like to do another degree, but I can't get there now.

At the university a lot of the young ones were very nice and the staff was helpful, particularly some of them. My favourite subject was Australian History. It was interesting. I think it was about 1900, when Flinders circumnavigated Australia, that he found all these people from Java, it wasn't called Indonesia then, and they'd come in on the trade winds for the shark fins. That's why the Aborigines in Arnhem Land are different, because they intermarried with the Javanese.

I used to be able to walk a little and I could get on a tram, but nowadays I can't get on public transport because they're too quick and they won't wait. I can drive a car, but since my last fall I haven't been able to, because of my sore hip.

I'm trying to learn the Internet at TAFE now, but because I've been on crutches so long I've little use of my hands, so it's very hard, but I'll keep trying because I want to learn.

Vale: Joyce Laurene Weeks: 28 July 1922 – 5 January 2005

When I phoned Joyce a couple of months after our meeting to say hello and see how she was, I was saddened to hear that she had died. I've since spoken with both her children, James and Laurene, and include below their thoughts:

'Our mum, Joyce Laurene Weeks, was a great lady, who, in disregarding her disability, developed abilities that became great strengths. These are qualities that her friends will remember her for. She never thought of herself as a having a disability, but always as a quiet achiever.

There's a refrain that Mum would hold to, it was from *Carousel* by Rodgers and Hammerstein called *You'll Never Walk Alone*. Mum was rarely alone. There were always people around and Mum would be assisting them or they her. When we were children she would sew for us and for many. She had a heart for others. Mum was a tireless worker; if she could help she would pursue issues, whether locally or federally, with courage, tenacity and a dogged determination. It did not matter what the odds were, nothing deterred her.

Mum was always the champion of the handicapped and the disadvantaged, involving herself in the various associations to change attitudes of government departments to the needs of disadvantaged people and to provide the assistance required to stop the disadvantaged being isolated from the community. It was her intention to provide a greater understanding of how the socially disadvantaged coped with the complexity of modern life, and to that end she felt it would be beneficial to upgrade her education. In her later years she studied for a Bachelor of Arts, which she completed in 2000 – an outstanding achievement!'

James Weeks and Laurene Henshaw

Communication

Paul Reed – Television News, Then and Now

(QTQ9, Channel Nine, Queensland's first TV station)

 *Albert Asbury at the Australian Broadcasting Commission suggested I speak with his friend Paul. Channel Nine was Queensland's first TV station. I remember in 1959, seeing the first 'News' beamed into our living room – before that time there'd only been radio! Paul suggests meeting at Channel Nine where he works as Chief of Staff, Channel Nine News. We chat over a cup of coffee on an outside deck, bathed in early winter sunshine, Paul reminiscing about the early days of TV in Brisbane. He smiles wryly as he recounts some of the more unusual incidents he's witnessed ...*

> *'There was a chap called David Hunter, a fairly notorious bank robber who was being chased by police through the streets of Taringa and Indooroopilly; he was in a big old American Chevy, armed with a sawn-off shotgun that he was hanging out the window ... We'd stopped on Moggill Road because we anticipated that he was heading in our direction so we thought we'd be able to capture some good images as he drove past. Sure enough, we did, but as he drove by he pointed the gun straight at us and fired – that was a fairly sobering experience!'*

I was born in Brisbane and still live in Wilston where I was born. It's changed dramatically. I used to walk to primary school not far from home, but when I went to Terrace it was a train trip in the steam era with the old wooden carriages and soot and smoke. I can remember going to the theatre for six pence on a Saturday afternoon. That was the Grange Theatre, complete with the big canvas seats strung out in a row, the Jaffas rolling down the aisles – all of that; it was lovely.

I went to Cloudland for school dances and I have some very fond memories of that place. It was probably my first taste of a big dance, with hundreds and hundreds of people on a pulsating floor. It was a very exciting experience for a sixteen-year-old boy and I suppose my first taste of social life. I think I even had my first kiss there. I lived for a while not far from Cloudland in Jordan Terrace. We moved on and then sadly Cloudland moved on as well. It was certainly a Brisbane icon – almost like the Sydney Opera House is today. I don't think any government has yet dealt well with preservation of our past; they talk a lot, but do very little.

I was involved very heavily with Expo 88. I was News Director at Channel Ten then and we built a working newsroom as our exhibit. It was like a vast goldfish bowl stuck inside a pavilion with the reporters and editors preparing and presenting the evening news. It cost us an absolute fortune, but fortunately did wonders for our ratings. Brisbane certainly came of age after Expo.

Now as Chief of Staff at Channel Nine, I look at the day-to-day news. I'm in the front line of what we cover each day in our own territory; my field is Queensland, working with our own newsroom staff and our own bureaux around the state. I'm gathering up the local content for the six o'clock nightly bulletin and for network programs, the *Today Show* and the eleven o'clock *National News* and *Nightline*. It's a 24-hour-a-day, 7-day-a-week operation. We're so much hungrier for content now than we were in the early days of television and the way that we gather news now is so much more sophisticated and efficient.

When I started as a reporter here at Channel Nine, many years ago – decades ago, in fact – there was not only a completely different approach to news, but also to the way in which you gathered it. Then there was just film. Today there's video tape and digital and satellite technology. With film it used to be a highly labour intensive operation, partly because of the sheer size of the equipment. There was a huge camera, sound recorder, a very heavy battery, plus a tripod and lighting equipment that the cameraman and reporter had to lug around. You weren't able to do the things and go to the places that you are now; it was a very slow process – more of a stagger than a run! These days you can achieve the same results with a handheld camera that can beam live pictures. It's made us much more efficient and versatile.

In the early days it was black and white television and there was a roll of film that allowed you to shoot an event providing it lasted no longer than 120 seconds, or else you had to change the film. You had a big black change bag that you carried around with you. Your poor old cameraman would be sitting on the side of the road as the house was burning down and he's changing his roll of film so he can shoot the next stage of the story! These days you'd just put a new tape or disk in and away you'd go. The classic examples of how things have changed, I suppose, is how we gathered national and international news before the advent of microwave links and satellite transmission. The only way we'd get a story from interstate would be by sending it by plane, so for many years *A Current Affair* here ran 24 hours late; it wasn't live. The program that they saw in Sydney on Monday, we watched in Brisbane on Tuesday. The international news came to us in a big box of film rolls. You'd go to the airport every day and get that day's news, which might well be two or three weeks old. It was gathered by the international news service, called Visnews, and they would send boxes of film around the world. We'd pick ours up at the airport and rush it back to the station. Then we'd have to work out which bit of film was what and preview and edit it. It was a slow, laborious process.

I've lived through the change from black and white to colour, from film to videotape, and now we're going from videotape to digital. Going digital means there'll be major changes in the way we as reporters actually view the news. It gives people access to incoming feeds via their computers whereas right now they have to take their tape to a preview machine and sit there and view the video.

News tends to deal in day-to-day realities. Current affair programs can fantasise a bit and throw in a bit of illusion if they choose to. They can come up with a good promo line and say 'let's create the story around it' but you can't do that in news. That was perhaps the image that the TV series *Frontline* portrayed of current affairs type programs and I think at times, for some, they were probably pretty close to the mark.

There have been a lot of stories over the years, obviously, but I suppose the biggest I covered in Brisbane would be the '74 Flood. At the time we were still in the film era but with a slightly more portable camera. Still, it required the camera change bag and 400-foot rolls of film just to get ten minutes of news. We didn't own boats so we would try and get a lift with the SES or the police. I have memories of travelling around the city in a little tin dinghy, floating above the awnings of Festival Hall and ducking under power lines as we went! Out at Jindalee we travelled right across the top of the suburb. The houses were completely submerged and you were just floating across the top of them in a boat; it was quite bizarre. I don't think anyone anticipated the extent of that; we'd never had a taste of a flood that big.

Television is gradually replacing the need for people to physically attend sporting venues. There's nothing like the hill at the Gabba anymore. There's just not the excitement there used to be at those big venues. In contrast, television nowadays can convey great excitement and emotion by using so many visual aids. I could have gone to the last State of Origin and watched it live, but I actually chose to watch it at home – maybe I'm getting old! I've been to the swimming at Chandler and seen some of our greatest athletes and I think it's a bit like watching grass grow. Live, on television, you get a much greater variety of images and get much closer to the swimmers than if you were seated in the stands.

Our nightly news bulletin is made up of around 40% local content, 20% national content and then maybe 20% to 30% international content (sometimes a lot less than that) followed by sport and then the weather. We call ourselves *National Nine News* but our focus is primarily South East Queensland. This is where our viewing audience is concentrated and where those viewers who have people-metres live. We listen to them when deciding what we report.

My area of responsibility covers the state but my primary focus is South East Queensland. We have an association with WIN Television and exchange story material with them, so each day we're talking to Cairns, Townsville, Rockhampton, Sunshine Coast and Toowoomba about the sort of event they might be covering that day and making decisions about whether those events would interest our South East Queensland audience. In the same way we exchange news with Sydney and Melbourne and the rest of the nation.   The first time on air can be a nerve-wracking experience. I remember, for instance, when Wally Lewis started in television in the '80s. He was still very much a footballer trying to break into a new career and was incredibly nervous. I recall his first night of reading sport at Channel Ten, where I worked at the time. He went on air and within 60 seconds or so had developed such perspiration that his shirt was just wringing wet. I really felt sorry for him. He rode through it, though, and succeeded.

You feel good at the end of your day when you've actually been able to help somebody by presenting a news story that delivers them some benefit. That happens often; say, for instance, a house fire, where you might report how a family have lost all their possessions. You're sometimes able to channel the public response back to that poor family and deliver them a new house or new car, or a whole pile of furniture – and it makes you feel good that you're actually providing some solid benefits.

You can't get too emotional about news as it ruins your focus, but there have been some pretty emotional experiences. One that sticks in my mind is when a good friend, Peter Clark, who was the helicopter pilot for Channel Ten, crashed his chopper into the side of the mountain just over the hill about 300 metres from where we are now. It makes you think, every time you send a crew out to cover an event in a helicopter, the risks associated with that. Some of our people put themselves on the front line of some fairly dangerous situations. I remember being shot at when I was on the road. There was a chap called David Hunter, a fairly notorious bank robber who was being chased by police through the streets of Taringa and Indooroopilly. He was in a big old American Chevy, armed with a sawn-off shotgun that he was hanging out the window. This was in the '70s in the days of film and I was driving the car and the cameraman was trying to shoot the chase. We'd stopped on Moggill Road because we anticipated that he was heading in our direction so we thought we'd be able to capture some good images as he drove past. Sure enough, we did, but as he drove by he pointed the gun straight at us and fired – that was a fairly sobering experience!

People outside often try to put pressure on you for one reason or another, but it's how you deal with it that's important. I guess I've become terribly cynical over time; I see all sorts of motives behind people's attempts to get their stories told, and there are so many spin-doctors out there. Take medicine, for example. PR outlets actually provide newsrooms with complete news stories on particular medical topics, say, a new drug. Some are paid a bonus by the drug manufacturer every time their story goes to air – and that's really scary. There is constant pressure to have sufficient content every night to fill your half hour of news and if things are being squeezed and resources are being taken away from you, sometimes you may turn to the PR company's video simply to fill the holes, and that's a worry.

I have one child, a daughter who's at university. I did give her a taste of television with a week's work experience up here and she was quite blown away by it. Unfortunately, she probably saw it through rose-coloured glasses, because I introduced her to all those things that I knew she would enjoy, so she didn't get a taste of what being a reporter is really like. I think if she chose to follow that path it would be a healthy one, though, even in these times when budgets are getting tighter. There are still plenty of good opportunities in television and in Brisbane generally. I enjoy working here, especially on days like today. I just love the lifestyle and the weather and I've got family and many good friends here.

Tom Hearn – Bush TV

Tom lives in Yeppoon with his two boys, Will and Charlie. He tells me that their favourite thing to do is ride their bikes all over town, and up and down the beaches at low tide. Our discussion centres on Tom's activities in founding Bush TV www.bushtv.com.au

'I started buying commercial air time, like in the regional networks. I started making positive indigenous stories and training indigenous people and putting black faces on TV in a positive way, celebrating local heroes and community leaders. When the government and private enterprise started seeing some of these wonderful black stories on commercial TV, they approached me.'

Mum was born in Newcastle and Dad was born in Gympie and I was born in Yeppoon. I have two boys: Will, who's eight; and Charlie, who's four. I love the salt water and spend a lot of time on the beach and I couldn't really live anywhere else. I tried living in Melbourne, where I worked at the ABC for a couple of years as a documentary producer, but basically I had to come back home.

About five years ago I was a mainstream producer in Melbourne. I'd graduated from the Australian Film, Television and Radio School with a Master of Arts. I'm thirty-nine now and doing a PhD, but I haven't quite finished it yet. It's an ongoing process and I'm four years into it.

The first film I made was when I was around twenty-eight. It was a film called *My Little Brother* about family and the institution of family. I wanted to deconstruct the notion of family and have a look at just what it means to people. The first person I interviewed was my brother Ben, and the next week he committed suicide. The only thing I had was my interview with him and some footage, so I ended up doing a film about schizophrenia and suicide and how society still hasn't really come to terms with how to cope with the mentally ill, and there's no grieving process or institutional place for people who've got schizophrenia and drug addiction to go. That film ended up winning a few prizes and that was how my career started and it gave me an opportunity to go and tell other people's stories.

I'm a white fella. My connection to the indigenous community comes from my parents' involvement with the Fitzroy Basin elders in Rockhampton. I remember as a kid sitting around the coffee table with a whole lot of black faces and they're all plotting and scheming about land rights and all kinds of stuff. We'd go away on camps and we took in a couple of young Murris into our home that'd been in Neerkol orphanage. I went to school at some of the less prestigious regional schools in Rockhampton, like Depot Hill and Rocky High, and there were a lot of Murri kids there, so a lot of my mates ended up being Murri and it just sort of went from there.

I think we all know about the dialogue between Aboriginal people and the media, it's a one-way negative dialogue – whenever you hear the word 'Aboriginal' it's normally in connection with domestic violence, alcoholism, incarceration, sexual abuse or whatever. At the moment it's sexual abuse. That sort of negative dialogue's been going on for 150 years and I thought, as a storyteller, I could maybe try and change people's perceptions of indigenous people, try at least to balance the scales a bit against the bias that goes on.

I started buying commercial air time, like in the regional networks. I started making positive indigenous stories and training indigenous people and putting black faces on TV in a positive way, celebrating local heroes and community leaders. When the government and private enterprise started seeing some of these wonderful black stories on commercial TV they approached me. As a result we started getting contracts to proliferate the whole idea via Bush TV, which is presenting indigenous people in a positive light in the mainstream media arena. That was about four years ago and we've just grown from there.

I had $740 when I started and I opened up a little office in Rockhampton and I purchased 60 seconds of airtime from Rockhampton WIN Television for $200 and that was my budget blown. I had three young indigenous people who were very interested in media who came to help me and we made our first story about a successful indigenous work crew who had managed to renovate the walkway along the Fitzroy River in Rockhampton, so we did a really great story about these young people – in just 60 seconds! It's called the Murri Minute; when we put that on TV everyone started ringing Bush TV and WIN Television saying, 'Can we have a copy of it and when are we going to see more?'

A feature film company was making a $10 million film starring David Gulpilil out at Winton called *The Proposition*. We got asked by the Department of Natural

467

Resources and Mines to go out there and make a story about how the film company was working in close with the traditional owners, the local Aboriginal people, so as not to destroy the local cultural heritage. We were lucky enough to meet David Gulpilil. Anyway, the next day we hopped in a light plane to get some aerial footage. A lot of young Aboriginal people work for us and this time there was one young guy, Keith, who's originally from Woorabinda, I think, who told me that Winton was his mum's traditional home and he'd never been out there. So we took this young guy Keith on the flight. I remember him looking down at his country and seeing it for the first time. The look on his face was the reason I started Bush TV. It's about people finding their connection to the country and their family and to life and, in particular, to their spirit. It's just those little moments that make it all worthwhile for me.

I decided very early on that we weren't going to take government grants so we survived on the smell of an oily rag. My philosophy as a young social entrepreneur was that we should stand by the products we produce, rather than trying to borrow buckets of money. Financially, it's been difficult and we've had a lot of times of struggle where I've mortgaged my house or whatever to keep the dream alive. It's not so difficult now. We're accepted as one of the main indigenous producers of Aboriginal and Islander content in Queensland, so when government or peak indigenous bodies need their media and communications work they quite often call us.

I think the main reason we got through it all and have survived was that we've probably visited about 30 of the remote Aboriginal and Islanders communities in Queensland and we have 85% indigenous crew working for us. When we go into communities, quite often the people in our crew have family in those communities – people that they've never met before! Bush TV is about bringing people together and about telling positive stories, so we're more or less heroes wherever we go. We don't have the usual, 'Who the hell are you and what are you doing here?' and 'What are you pointing the camera for?' It's more like, 'Can we have one of your T-shirts?' and 'Do you want to come fishing?'

Last year we were making a documentary with a traditional owner called Bernard from the Gudang tribe, right on the tip of Cape York Peninsula. He was telling how the Australian pioneer, Frank Jardine, had taken a whole lot of cattle up from Rockhampton in the late 1800s and decided to settle right up at the tip on his grandfather's home and build a place called 'Somerset', which became a naval base and cattle property. The Jardines were later to be celebrated as white heroes who opened up the Cape and brought the cattle industry with them. That's white history, but the black history is that they turned a lot of the Gudang people into slaves and killed a lot of them. I was listening to the stories of Bernard's grandfather, who was born up at Somerset, and you begin to understand a huge part of our history that's never really been told.

Up there they catch turtles and Bernard took me out with them on a hunt for turtles. He wanted to turn me into his brother but to do that I had to actually catch my own turtle. This was in croc-infested, shark-infested waters! I don't know how I did it. I had to dive off the boat with this big hook in my hand and jump on top of this turtle that's as big as the bonnet of a car and put a hook in its neck so the guy's on the boat can pull it in. There's blood in the water so you're worried about sharks! We lifted this huge turtle out of the water and when we got back to the camp we chopped it up and we had this huge community feast and one of the old ladies came up to me and said, 'You know, traditionally when a boy turns into a man and he catches his first turtle, all of the women come to that guy and can do whatever they want to him.' I said, 'What do you mean?' and she said, 'Well, we can come to your house and we can take whatever we like and we can put talcum powder all over you and we can shame you and do whatever we want. We can do that just for that one evening, because the next day we'll never be able to treat you like this again, because you're a man and we know you can provide for yourself and your family and the community. When you catch your first turtle, it's the last time you'll be treated like a boy. From then on you'll be given respect as a man.' It was one of the most touching and scary and funny things that has happened to me. They were all laughing about what they might do and how they might sneak into my house and cover me in talcum powder while I was asleep and steal all my CDs, which they can do under tribal custom law – but they didn't do anything; it was just a joke. I was pretty tired the next day because I spent the whole night with one eye open wondering what was going to happen!

My dream with Bush TV was to turn it into an indigenous-owned enterprise and take a step back myself, and that happened in 2007. It all started with $740 and now it's a decent indigenous-owned company servicing Queensland's indigenous media and marketing needs.

Because of the positive family I have and my hard-earned education and experiences, I suppose, I can always manage to survive as a consultant. I'll always have some interest in Bush TV but my main interest is in building social capital and providing social change. Bush TV is one way I've managed to do that but there are plenty of other ways, so I'll probably spend my life doing things like Bush TV, which is bringing private enterprise and indigenous communities and government together to create real opportunities for change.

George Sudull – 4EB Ethnic Community Radio

We meet at Station 4EB in a large downstairs meeting room, just down the road from the Story Bridge Hotel. George is retired now but he was the head of this station for many of its formative years. With a high percentage of Queenslanders having their origins in another country, ethnic radio has proven invaluable in keeping people in touch with their roots – particularly the elderly in the community. Running the station has had its moments…

'We had a meeting and the phone rings and somebody on the phone says, "There is a bomb in the Greek locker!" Instead of clearing the building somebody grabs the fire extinguisher and starts smashing the lock off the Greek locker.'

When I came to Brisbane in 1950, it was a really pleasant little town. I still remember when the city hall was the tallest building; it was visible from every vantage point of the city. There were two buildings that stood out in those days that you could see from any angle. They were the city hall and St Bridget's Church at Red Hill. I remember there was nothing much to do on Sunday nights, so I used to go to Edward Street in front of the Rowes Arcade. On a Sunday evening there was always the Salvation Army Band playing. They'd march up Albert Street and back to the Citadel.

I came alone to Australia at the age of twenty-one. I was deported to Germany from Poland to a slave labour camp when I was fifteen. After that I didn't go back to Poland because of the Communist regime there. After the end of the war I stayed in refugee camps for almost five years in Germany. Then I was offered a choice of two countries,

Venezuela or Australia, so guess which one I chose? The three most popular countries for migrants in those days were the United States, Canada and Australia.

At that time I spoke Polish, and I knew Russian and Ukrainian, and I had a smattering of German. At that time there were no, what you call now 'services for migrants' here with social security, language classes and all that. No, there was nothing like that, and no matter what your previous occupation was you were stamped as a labourer, even if you were a university professor.

I got married to an Australian girl here. We met at St Mary's, South Brisbane. The Polish and Australian Masses were held there, so people would pass each other coming and going. In those days everybody was young and the parish priest, Father Thompson, organised dances, so people could meet each other. That's how I met my wife for the first time.

I was fairly active in the Polish community. I finished studying architecture in Sydney and I worked as an architect here in Brisbane and I designed the Polish club. They don't like you to call it the Polish club – it's a Polish House, because it is used for various functions to celebrate Polish national anniversaries of historical importance. They also come there to drink and be merry; this was the purpose of Polish Houses.

This radio started in 1980. It was a very political issue in those days. Ethnic radio was started by the Greeks and the Italians. They used to meet at the Greek club called Palamas, which was perceived to be very left wing. So the people who came from Communist countries didn't want to associate with them and started organising a right-wing radio. Anyway, it was such a disorganised, disjointed sort of thing that they didn't make it. I used to go to both right and left wing meetings, but the Palamas Club was better organised. We got a licence in 1978. The footprint of the transmitter wasn't strong enough to cover other areas outside of Brisbane. We started with about 12 groups and now we have about 50 groups.

When we got the licence we didn't have our studios. We were piggy-backing on another station, Radio 4MBS, the classical music station. They had studios in Kelvin Grove Teachers' College in those days, and they couldn't fill up all their time so they used to give us some time. Then we got our own station at West End. It was so primitive: the doors didn't work, we had a piece of string to pull the door and tie it on a nail. As people started hearing their own language and their own music, more started joining. There were many volunteers; there was enthusiasm in those days. This was in the 1980s. Everything was built by volunteers. The whole radio is based on volunteer work. When I started as a volunteer I had no experience in radio at all. I started training to operate the console but I didn't have any training in how to use voice on radio.

In the beginning we broadcast for just half an hour to one hour a week in each language – 50% music and 50% speech. For the people who came from Communist countries, there were difficulties. We used to scavenge for the news, listening to Radio Free Europe and this kind of thing. It was difficult as the reception was very poor. It was primitive but, still, it was very exciting.

This station, 4EB, is based on membership. It's only partly funded (about one third) by the federal government. Cost of membership here in Brisbane is relatively cheap; it's only $25 a year. Still, some people think it's too much – though they'll spend $70 a month on cable television.

In the 1980s, there was real enthusiasm. I'm already a dinosaur by this stage. There are not many people remember the origins of this station. But Wolfgang Kreutzer, he remembers even further back than me. We first broadcast from our studio on 1 December 1979 but Wolfgang remembers when we made test broadcasts from a broom cupboard in the Crest Hotel!

I was elected to the board of directors in 1981. We had a meeting and the phone rings and somebody on the phone says, 'There is a bomb in the Greek locker!' Instead of clearing the building somebody grabs the fire extinguisher and starts smashing the lock off the Greek locker. It was a hoax! The risks that people took to get the station built – these days they wouldn't do it. Building the radio mast, volunteers were hanging hundreds of feet up in the air. It was all done by free labour.

We leased another building in West End. It had already two studios there, so while one group would be finishing their program, the other would be lining up to take the chair immediately after to start their program. Then we bought this land here in Kangaroo Point with the help of the state government loan and built this building in 1988. We've been gradually improving and extending our service coverage; two or three years ago we converted from AM frequency to FM and our footprint now takes in Gold Coast and Sunshine Coast.

Each language group meets only once in the month, and they roster the various members of the group and then it's up to the individual member what he or she is going to do. Nobody else knows, so it's a surprise when you turn the radio on and then you hear it. Some are more interesting than others. In my case I used to broadcast on a Sunday morning. The first program going to air was the Polish program, so I used to sit up virtually the whole night before until three, four or five in the morning. Scavenging for the news took almost the whole week. Later we started getting news faxed from the Polish Embassy. You'd take a subject from a book or something, or perhaps the anniversary of some person of note, and you worked on their biography. We played some music in between.

One night I was at home listening to the station. It was two ladies doing the program and they had put the music on but forgot to switch the microphones off and they started telling each other (and everyone else listening) what they did last night. I rang the station, ring, ring, but nobody answers the phone. I live pretty close to the station so I drive to the studio quickly, barge in and turn the microphone off! 'What were we talking about?' they say. 'Well,' I tell them, 'it's just as well you didn't say you were unfaithful to your husbands!' It still sometimes happens.

The largest groups are still the Italians and the Greeks and they have the largest number of hours. It varies from group to group. The only group that has half-hour programs now is the Lithuanians; all the other groups have got at least three hours. It goes from six o'clock in the morning to midnight. Early evening used to be the prime time but it's not any more. From six o'clock on, people watch television.

In the beginning SBS were volunteers just like us; that's how they started. It was only in the '80s they started paying their staff and got a training program going. SBS don't compete with us directly so much anymore. We have the same access to the Internet as SBS has, but they have more money. They can, for example, arrange direct crossovers to the different countries for live broadcasts, commentaries and things. We can't afford that, but we can use Brisbane people on local issues. SBS, for example, can't do that – maybe they do it in Sydney and Melbourne, where they have local communities, as they are based there, but they only transmit the programs to Brisbane and other cities.

Our membership varies, but it is round about 4,000 members and we currently broadcast in approximately 50 languages. Gradually the government money is drying up, so what the future will be like we don't know. Now, when the population has all the mod cons, the interest starts to wane. People grow older, and the younger age group is not particularly interested. Then again it varies from ethnic group to ethnic group and from city to city. In Melbourne, for example, our sister station is doing very well. Here in Brisbane we still do a lot of community announcements. There's always something going on here!

To me it looks like the Greeks, and some of the other big groups, and people from the South Pacific Islands, their young people are interested in the station. I admire the Greeks because they manage to be Australians and at the same time they are Greeks. With the Polish community, the young generation, they become fully fledged Aussies. It is a pity when ethnic cultures in Australia become just about dancing and eating.

Howard Ainsworth – 4MBS Classic FM

I remember Howard from my early twenties, when I regularly attended the Lord Mayor's concerts in Brisbane. Howard was the compère, his introductions, with items of interest about the piece, it's composer and the performer, all adding to my

enjoyment of those occasions. We agree to meet at 4MBS where the 'one quiet place' he assures me is the recording studio. He sits at the console surrounded by the equipment that has formed the backdrop to most of his working life. He's officially retired but is still a key figure at 4MBS, the hugely popular community radio station that transmits classical music from Brisbane 24 hours a day.

'We're playing music from midnight to six a.m. and there are a lot of all-night taxi drivers listening to the station then ... We do what we call Classic Concerts Cruises because we take our own classical music ensemble with us, so people have their daily dose of classics – their classic "fix" every day. I can think of one couple who went away as single people, they knew each other through 4MBS, and came back and were happily married.'

My parents and grandparents all came from Brisbane and, although I was an only child, there were aunts and uncles and cousins and all sorts of relations in the wider family. I went to school first of all at Newmarket State School, then the North Brisbane Intermediate School, which was up in Kelvin Grove – much later to become QUT, Kelvin Grove. I went there for two years, to do Scholarship. I went to Brisbane Grammar School for two ghastly years, up to Junior, where the most important thing was cricket and nothing else really mattered. I left there when I was sixteen and went to work. My first job was one of those school holiday jobs at Christmas time. I worked in the tie and sock department of McDonnell and East when it was in George Street. The following year I got a six-week job with the Sales Tax Department in the old government building in Adelaide Street and that was good experience.

I used to go to youth concerts and things as a teenager. I always preferred classical music to anything else and that came about through being a member of the Argonauts Club, a radio club for children up to the age of sixteen. They'd take them from five or six years old, daily, Monday to Friday, at about five o'clock in the afternoon, and you were invited to write little stories and send in drawings to compete for prizes. It was a wonderful program. When I was about twelve, I'd race in after playing cricket or something at half-past four and turn the radio on to make sure I didn't miss the Argonauts Club at five, and there'd be something else on. It might be a cello sonata or some other classical music. We didn't generally have that sort of music in the home and I came to classical music through listening to this chamber music on the radio. My mother used to play the piano and she was quite good. She played waltzes and things like that so there was always music in the home, but not classical music as such.

After I left school I joined the Adelaide Steamship Company where I started off as an office boy. It was very interesting and after three years, when I was nineteen, I applied to go to sea with their passenger ships. They made me the Second Assistant Purser of the *MV Manoora*. Later, I got into the insurance industry for a brief period and was lucky enough to be sent over to London to help to open a new office of the National and General Insurance Company. A chap from Melbourne and I joined five Englishmen and we started the company from scratch. I was there for about fifteen months, during which time I got married and came back here in time for the Olympic Games in Melbourne. My wife was an English girl and she hadn't been to Australia before.

I'd always wanted to do broadcasting, so at the end of my contract I applied to the ABC and in 1963, after two or three attempts, I got in. At the ABC I was doing about 50/50 radio and television. News-reading on both media, and classical music, became my fortes. I became known for presenting classical music and the state government and others would get in touch with me and ask me if I would compère for them. I did the Lord Mayor's concerts, Royal receptions on television, the papal tour and all sorts of events. I'd often be on the edge of my seat doing these events; it was nerve-wracking but a wonderful experience.

I'd spent twenty-seven years at the ABC when they decided that they didn't need professional broadcasters – the journalists could do it! I was fifty-nine, anyway, and I thought, 'Well, that's the end of me. I'll retire gracefully and become a marriage celebrant or something' – which, as it happens, I did, but more on that later. On the last program I did at the ABC I had Anthony Camden as my guest on *Music Lover's Choice* (remember Anthony? He was director of the conservatorium) and he said, 'Are they getting rid of you?' and I said, 'Yes, this is my last show!' and he said 'I need somebody to run the Continuing Music Education, can you start on Monday?' and I said, 'Yes, I'll have tomorrow off and I'll be in your office on Monday!' That was in 1990. I was at the conservatorium for about four years, the last two years of which I was doing a half-day at the conservatorium and a half-day at 4MBS, because as soon as I left the ABC I came here as a volunteer. Later, 4MBS found they needed a Broadcast Manager, so I came here full time. I've been here now over ten years.

Really, 4MBS came about as a result of 2MBS in Sydney. MBS stands for Music Broadcasting Society. While we're all entirely independent, we use the same call sign, MBS. There's 2MBS in Sydney, 3MBS Melbourne, 4MBS Brisbane, and 5MBS in Adelaide. People decided they needed an alternative to the ABC, so 2MBS came about. A group of music lovers got together in Sydney and began their local music station. The same thing happened in Melbourne and eventually here in Brisbane. About half a dozen music lovers got together and applied for a licence and got one. It was easier in those days; it would cost you millions now, but that was twenty-five years ago; 4MBS just developed from there. It was started by community involvement and it's still run as a community radio station.

We're quite excited about a program we have called *Young Space*, a *Kids Classics* sort of thing. We get youngsters in and it started off with Gary Thorpe, our General Manager's young son Andrew; and with one of our announcers, Chadwick Palmer's daughter Jessica. They'd both been brought up with a classical music background and we got them both in 'on air'. We gave them a bit of training and that's where it all started. They were two very devoted and good kids. Andrew's gone on to other things now but Jessica's still doing it. I suppose she's eighteen or nineteen now and still involved.

We're very pleased to bring young people into the place, especially through the local Coorparoo Secondary College. They have a program every year now, as part of their school curriculum, where we take up to six youngsters and bring them in here for a whole semester and give them a training course in radio. They come in as rank amateurs, not knowing anything about it, and at the end of the period they go out with their own program, which they have chosen, written and presented themselves. Some of those kids later come back and help us with our daily segment of *Kids Classics*. *Young Space* has been going for about two years and it's a monthly program devoted to performance and composition of young people at schools and things like that.

People who like classical music are pretty civilised and we have a lovely bunch of them here. Someone sitting in the next studio now is Colin Brumby; he's a fascinating character, a very clever man, one of Australia's best composers. A man who was writing atonal music until about 20 or 25 years ago then all of a sudden he thought, 'No one's going to listen to this rubbish,' and he's written tuneful music ever since; it's beautiful. He totally changed his track.

This station runs with the assistance of several hundred volunteers. They all have the same love of classical music, that's why they come in here, some of them every day and for endless hours. It's a great community. Some have their favourite days. You'll go out there and there'll be five ladies sitting around all talking about their grandchildren and eating cake and that sort of thing, while a group of men will be sitting discussing the cricket. People find they have so much in common with each other. There's a great sense of camaraderie; we all depend upon each other.

We run, I suppose, about half a dozen courses a year, especially if there's an opera season coming up. If they're presenting *Tosca*, for instance, Barry Roberts will do a weekend, maybe just one session, or maybe a couple of sessions, on *Tosca*, so by the time people get there, it won't matter what language they're singing, they'll know the story and they can follow the plot. Those courses are very popular.

We need to raise funds for the station, so as well as getting funds through our annual subscribers and donors and sponsorships, another thing we do is to run tours overseas and in Australia. I've been very fortunate; I've taken about a dozen of them. We do what we call Classic Concerts Cruises because we take our own classical music ensemble with us, so people have their daily dose of classics – their classic 'fix' every day. I can think of one couple who went away as single people, they knew each other through 4MBS and came back and were happily married.

In 1988 I was out there at Expo every day, as we did a broadcast from Expo. In fact, I did a couple of programs from there. I think I did some *Music Lover's Choice* programs from Expo. I did one with Sir Llew Edwards out there, because he was in charge, and various other notables who'd come in. We had a little studio there and that was very exciting.

The guests I've had on *Music Lover's Choice* have ranged from schoolgirls to truck-drivers, to the Governor General, Sir Zelman Cowan. There are lots of taxi drivers, too, who listen to classical music. We're playing music from midnight to 6 am and there are a lot of all-night taxi drivers listening to the station then.

The other job I took on after the ABC was as a marriage celebrant. I've had some amusing times doing that. The music the brides are choosing these days differs dramatically to what they chose in the old days, when it was *Lohengrin* or *Midsummer Night's Dream*, which is very seldom played these days. They go along to *Pachelbel's Canon in D*, which is very slow, though it's a lovely piece. Most of them choose that one. I had one girl who came down the red carpet, it's not an aisle because we're out of doors, but she came down to *Waltzing Matilda*! The one that really amused me, though, was a girl who had the soprano sing *L'ascia ch'io pianga* from *Rinaldo* by Handel. After the wedding I went up to the soprano and I said, 'Do you think your bride knows what that aria was about?' and she said, 'I don't think she's got a clue!' because what the soprano was singing was: 'Let me lament my cruel fate.' Those were the words – hardly appropriate at a wedding – even if it is a pretty tune! But that's what she wanted.

I enjoy it, because they're happy events. They're all sorts of people. The other day I had a weight lifter who was a body-builder. He looked like Arnold Schwarzenegger, an enormous fellow. He's a welder and he works in forty-seven degrees of heat every day, imagine how tough this bloke is? At the other end of the scale I've had judges and American naval officers and others from all walks of life. It's serious and it's solemn but you get some laughs as well. The nice thing is, too, that after they get married and they have children, they quite often invite you to come back and do the baby-naming! It's like a christening but they have no church affiliation whatsoever, so they quite often ask the celebrant to come.

I'm still mad on cricket like my dad, and so is my son. Dad's gone now, but we still play. When I'm playing I'm playing with family. My son plays for a team and my grandson plays for his school. My little grandson is still playing soccer. He hasn't taken up the cricket bat yet, but he will. My granddaughter is a champion under-age gymnast; she's in a special squad now from which, in a few years' time, we may see her in the Olympics. She's completely fearless; she frightens the devil out of me when I watch the things that she's doing on the beam. She's broken a few things but she's totally fearless. She just gets up and does it all again!

Anita Wurfl – The World of Simultaneous Interpreting

We've been friends for years and share many interests. Anita settled in Australia because her daughters are here. She is widely travelled and occasionally assists those who are vulnerable in society, including hospital patients who need her translating and interpreting skills. Her main activity is acting as a simultaneous interpreter at major conferences both in Australia and abroad...

'People tend to think, 'Oh, there's another congress, just another junket!' They're not really – a lot of them are commercial, but also there are a lot of people who are really involved in getting a better deal for the world. One of the first conferences I ever did was on endangered wildlife, before the term had even been heard, and all these people came from Africa, and discussed the disappearance of elephants and the banned trade of ivory. It was my very first job as an interpreter and I found it to be very exciting.'

When an international convention is held, the organisers normally have to provide facilities for language translation, as delegates come from all corners of the world and it is imperative that everyone understands what is being said. That means that simultaneous interpreters are needed. An interpreter enables people who don't speak the same language to communicate with each other. What happens if there are speakers of four or five languages? Booths are set up (usually in the back of the room where they are holding the conference (actually in the Brisbane Convention Centre they are right on top). You have one language booth for each language, and two interpreters per booth. When you are interpreting you have to concentrate so hard that one person cannot go for longer than 20 minutes, or maybe half an hour, and there has to be someone to take over from you. But even when you are 'resting', you are concentrating all the time because you have to help the other person. Numbers are difficult to retain in your head for a relatively long few seconds, so you write them down for your partner. If they talk about 15 billion, for example, you have to remind your partner that in Spanish you have to say 15 thousand million. Of course, you can't whisper, so you have to write it down, so she/he can glance at it. If, by any chance, the other person has said a word that is wrong, you just write it down quickly, in the event that it may be repeated. When interpreting you've got to stay right on top, you can't go back and say, 'Well, I made a mistake there. I should have said ...' whatever – you just can't do that!

When we have a Chinese speaker and we don't speak Chinese we have to press a little button and we listen to the Chinese interpreter's translation into English and we then take his English into Spanish so that our Spanish speakers get it in their own language. First, you listen to the original language, and then you mentally interpret it in your head and deliver it in the other language, in such a way that the listener (who has earphones) thinks he or she is getting the original speech. This is all done simultaneously – hence the name of the profession. Obviously, before any convention an interpreter has to obtain background information, vocabulary and glossaries. So whether you're working with drug rehabilitation or the harvesting of grapes, you have to know where to access the relevant material. The Internet has made this part of the preparation a lot easier, but at the same time most presentations are now delivered by PowerPoint, which means interpreters don't necessarily get the papers beforehand.

I got into interpreting quite by chance; I'd been a university lecturer for the previous twenty years of my life, lecturing on Spanish and Spanish Literature, Linguistics and Civilisation. One day somebody phoned and said, 'Look, we need an interpreter,' and I said, 'I've never done this before,' and they said, 'Well, come in and we'll test you.' It turned out I was fine and I loved it – it was very challenging. Ideally, you would like to do this at least once a month or even twice a month, but there isn't that much work and that's why you go abroad to get it and also just hope people know that you're there – putting your name about.

Sometimes I wonder, 'Why am I doing this?' because it can be very exhausting and difficult, but in the end you know why you're doing it, because it's always challenging. It always gives you a sense of achievement, when you say to yourself, 'I did not let this incredibly fast speaker get the better of me – I stayed on top and spoke as fast as he or she did.' I worked at one conference in India for the Rotarian executive and there were all these speakers from the different provinces in India. It was so difficult to understand their various accents. The Japanese are also very difficult to interpret, although they speak English very often, so yes, it's an interesting challenge.

As an interpreter you have to keep abreast of current affairs, and all aspects of business, politics and economics, in all the languages you use. Here in Brisbane, for example, though I suppose it could be said for all of Australia, you have the languages on the radio and on the TV, which is wonderful. I can watch Spanish television, I can watch Chilean television, and I can listen to the BBC. On SBS they have radio programs every day in Spanish, and the speakers are both South Americans and Spaniards, so I can be exposed to many varieties of the Spanish language.

How did I come to speak Spanish? Well, I was born in Quito, Ecuador. Quito is the second highest capital in South America, and I was born right up in the mountains, 3000 metres high. My father, who was Austrian, met my German mother in Spain. My mother's family left Germany in 1933 because they were Jews. My father, who was not Jewish but was in the underground fighting the Nazis, had to leave Austria too, and they met in the queue in a bank in Spain.

Yes, that's how they met, and then the Civil War broke out in Spain and they decided it was better to leave, because I think my father had become politically involved there. They actually got in a boat and said, 'Well, we're going to Cuba!' but

Cuba wouldn't have them because they didn't have enough immigration money to land, and the Austrian consul in Cuba at the time – this was 1937 – said to them, 'Ecuador will have you, they're the only country that doesn't require a guarantee,' so they established themselves there. They opened a little delicatessen and started selling European food like sausages and excellent coffee. At that time the local people were accustomed to having butter wrapped in banana leaves and meat wrapped in newspaper – it was still all very Third World.

Then in 1941 oil was discovered and Shell came, the Americans came and the Dutch, too, so my parents had a new market for nice food and they were extremely busy and did very well. They opened a whole lot of stores, over-expanded and went bankrupt. So that's the story of my parents in Ecuador! However, I had a wonderful childhood there, a wonderful youth. We went to a lovely school. It was an American school and that was where I learned my English. My father insisted that at mealtimes we speak German and this lasted a few years. My younger sisters don't speak German all that well. They manage, but not quite so well as my older sister and I, who are quite fluent. There were staff in the house who spoke only Spanish and we went to school and spoke English there, so I really grew up with three languages and that has been a real gift in my life. And my life continues being multilingual: with my four sisters I converse in Spanish, with my husband in English (sometimes in German) and with Mom I always spoke German.

I wasn't able to go to university when I finished high school. My father by then had died and we had to help my mother to bring up the other children. I finally got a chance to go to university when I was about twenty-five, when our second daughter went to Grade One. I thought, 'Now it's my turn,' so I took a degree in Spanish literature and that's how I later got a job in the university.

I left Ecuador, met and married Peter in New York, and we had two wonderful daughters. Eventually Peter got a contract to work in South Africa for three years, but we stayed for thirty. Politically, of course, it was a difficult time, and eventually our children left South Africa before we did, because of the political situation – they were either involved with the change of regime or accompanied their partners to continue their studies overseas. They were offered jobs in Australia, which they much preferred to the USA, so I am here because I followed my children.

We arrived here in 1996. I have two daughters: one lives in Brisbane with the grandchildren; the other, who is also married to a South African, lives in Sydney. Like me, they're both very happy where they are. I'm going to stay in Brisbane for the rest of my life because I love it here. I like the feel of Brisbane. It's a city where you don't get suffocated by cars and people and it's got enough culture to keep me busy and enough sophistication and good restaurants, yet I still live near the forest and the river – it's a wonderful combination and I like it so much.

Since arriving in Australia I had the opportunity to go to Korea where the Global Summit of Women was held. I have also worked in New Zealand, South Australia and Victoria. In Brisbane they had the public transport conference and I thought, 'Buses, how boring,' but it wasn't. It was interesting because leaders of big cities came together to discuss issues like pollution and environmentally friendly alternatives, keeping cars out of their cities and problems that affect all of us. I get to see the world from a perspective that is not so accessible to most. I've interpreted at AIDS congresses, on prisons and drug rehabilitation and I've even done bovine diseases, so, yes, it's a very broad canvas we have to cover. The other interpreters I work with are all interesting people. In order to be an interpreter you have to be a native speaker of one language and be perfectly fluent in another.

All this exposure to different subjects means you develop a different sense and a different outlook on life. You also understand how many different kinds of people are involved in making our world function. People tend to think, 'Oh, there's another congress, just another junket!' They're not really – a lot of them are commercial, but also there are a lot of people who are really involved in getting a better deal for the world. One of the first conferences I ever did was on endangered wildlife, before the term had even been heard, and all these people came from Africa, and discussed the disappearance of elephants and the banned trade of ivory. It was my very first job as an interpreter and I found it to be very exciting. When I got home, I parted with a most beautiful ivory bracelet I had had for many years. It just didn't seem right to possess such an article.

In Korea, despite knowing so many languages, that was one of the few times that I was actually stranded without a language. I can manage to make myself understood in 8 languages, because Spanish takes you into Portuguese, Italian and French, and German takes you into Afrikaans, which I had to speak to get a job in South Africa. Afrikaans takes you into Dutch, so Europe isn't a problem really at all and, of course, neither is South America, but, yes, the East, of course, is quite different.

Peter's and my love for travelling started really because our family is dispersed all over the world. It began by just visiting children. Peter had two children from a previous marriage and his son, also hoping not to be drafted to Vietnam, lived in Spain. At one time he was doing a doctorate degree there, so we were constantly visiting him in Spain and now his daughter lives on a tiny little island in Brazil and has two children of her own, so we go to Brazil. They are all fascinating places. I have two sisters in Mexico, and going there has been very interesting. I have a sister in Canada as well, so we visit her. Then, of course, when I do get jobs overseas I try to tack on a few days to do a little travelling and try to meet the locals.

While I love Brisbane I still feel a citizen of the world and I think that is probably what characterises me as a person. It's probably the first thing that other people who meet me will notice, because I don't have an accent that belongs anywhere in particular and I don't have a specific sense of nationalism, or belonging, or of religion – not one more than another – so I like to think of myself as a citizen of the world, and I suppose I tend to look for people who have a similar outlook on life.

Science

Medical Science

Ian Frazer - Centre for Immunology and Cancer Research

He is Director of the University of Queensland's Diamantina Institute for Cancer, Immunology and Metabolic Medicine and was Australian of the Year in 2006. We met at his office in the Princess Alexandra Hospital. Ian is a great communicator and humble about his achievements. His topic is fascinating and the time slips away all too quickly as we chat.

'If I did anything as Australian of the Year, it was to try and spread the idea that it's really important that we have a scientifically literate community, because you can't debate issues such as whether you want nuclear fuel or recycled water, or whatever the latest topic is that impacts society, from a zero knowledge base. ... The worst possible thing that could happen to science in my view would be if society polarised into those that understood it and those that didn't ... That would be very sad indeed, because I think science is a great force for good in society ...'

Research is essentially a collaborative effort in which, yes, we compete with each other but we do so very specifically for funding, because that's the way money is given out for research. Once you get past the funding competition, research is very much a team effort. We collaborate extensively within the group of people that I work with and indeed it's very unusual to find a scientist who isn't part of a group these days, but also we collaborate internationally. The papilloma virus vaccine, for which I helped develop the technology, was a collaborative effort, built on the work of other scientists who came before us, particularly Professor Harald Zur Hausen, who, with his team, drew the connection between the virus and the cancer. Within our own group, Dr Jian Zhou and I really worked hand in hand developing the technology which led to the vaccine. I'm sure that if we hadn't done it, other people would have done it. As it was, we went off and taught them how to do it and we then went on to build on what we did and expand it. The whole effort to prove the vaccine worked has involved nearly 2,000 scientists worldwide and 25,000 women taking part in the large-scale clinical studies – so clearly it's a very collaborative exercise.

You can't make scientists collaborate; they collaborate because they want to, because they enjoy it. You sometimes don't even realise how much collaboration you actually do – right now I must be collaborating with about twenty different groups worldwide in different areas of the work that I'm doing. I'm, for example, part of a study which is being done by a colleague here in Brisbane, Dr Margaret McAdam, who's demonstrating how you can make the HPV vaccine something we can deliver in the developing world.

Looking back, I went to Melbourne on what was to have been a two-year working holiday to the Walter and Eliza Hall Institute, when I was a post-doc student. I worked in Ian Mackay's research unit there. His unit was focused on clinical research and that was an environment which I felt comfortable in. I started a number of clinical projects there which ran on well past the two years and it was obvious to both him and me that it was a good idea that I hang around, so I stayed there for four years, until he was due to retire. At that point I thought it was probably time to move on.

I decided at that point that I'd look around for jobs inside Australia as well as out of Australia and the best offer that was then made to me was one in Queensland. I actually got two offers from Queensland and decided I'd come to the Princess Alexandra Hospital, because it was obviously a place where they had strong support for clinical research. The job I was doing for the hospital was a clinical job. It was running the immunology service, but the way the job was structured, there was time to do research as well, so that was why I came here.

The story of where I met Dr Jian Zhou, whom I was to do so much research with, is in one sense a simple story and in another a more complex one. I went on sabbatical to Cambridge in 1989 to work with Professor Margaret Stanley, who, like me, was very much interested in human papilloma virus immunology. She and I had a mutual interest in that area but I actually spent my time working in Lionel Crawford's lab next door, because I was interested in learning about embryonic stem cell technology.

Lionel's lab had a whole range of people in it, but one of the people who was there, about the same time as I was, was Dr Jian Zhou. Jan and his wife Xiao-Yi had come from China on sabbatical, just as I was there on sabbatical, and we shared a mutual interest in the papilloma virus as a virus but also as something which the body's defence against infection has to deal with. He was interested in studying the cellular response to the virus and we worked out a strategy, if you like, for building a papilloma virus together. The reason for doing this was because we knew that the scientific questions we really wanted to answer were impossible if we did not grow the virus. The problem was that wart virus was one of these viruses which you can't grow artificially; it requires the special conditions that exist in the skin in order to go through its life cycle. Since that couldn't be done in the lab then (or now), we thought we'd make an artificial papilloma virus and that would maybe allow us to do some of the experiments we wanted to do.

We talked about it, but we didn't actually do the work there, because Jian was doing a project for Lionel and I was basically doing the embryonic stem cell work, so we agreed that Jian would come back to Brisbane with me when I finished my sabbatical and would come to work in my lab as a post-doc and that's what actually happened. He came with his wife and together we worked on building papilloma viruses. While working on that project we realised that one of the bits that we built would be the basis for the vaccine which is now being widely used to prevent cervical cancer.

That chance meeting in Cambridge with Jian led to a very fruitful collaboration, which continued for the next five years in Brisbane – well past the development of the vaccine technology. Jian then went off to the Mayo Clinic in the United States for a while before coming back to my lab in Brisbane as a group leader in his own right to pursue his own research. He was getting on very well with that when, unfortunately, he passed away unexpectedly, during a visit to China. That was a great loss to Australian science in my opinion and obviously to his family. He was arguably the brightest post-doc I've had in the twenty years I've been working in science. He was one of these people who came up with a lot of ideas – his own science. He liked to see if an idea could work; he wasn't quite as intellectually rigorous as some scientists, but he had so many good ideas that they compensated for that. If other people then checked out more rigorously what he was doing, well, that was fine, too, of course. He and I got on very well together; we had a mutual understanding about where we were coming from. He was a great loss to the centre because he was very much loved here.

Cervical cancer is a disease predominantly in the developing world. All that the pharmaceutical companies can do in that regard is to make the vaccine available in the developing world at cost and the two companies that are involved both undertook to do this. Beyond that there are a whole range of other things that have to be achieved in order to get the vaccine used in the developing world. One part of that effort is to have it seen as acceptable by the World Health Organisation (WHO) and I'm lobbying for that to the extent that I can, given that I'm one of the inventors of the vaccine. Another part of it is to persuade other charitable organisations to fund vaccine distribution. The Gates Foundation has taken an active role in that.

The missing step after that, of course, is to persuade the countries in the developing world that they want the vaccine! I've been talking with governments there, and I've been involved in the process of educating them about what the vaccine is. Eventually they'll make their own decisions. One of the reasons why we're doing the project in Vanuatu is to see how we can deliver cervical cancer prevention in the developing world. If we can do a demonstration project in one country it will provide evidence to support the idea that maybe other countries could do the same. That's why the Vanuatu project is important, in my mind; it's one where we can actually demonstrate in the field that we can do something. Perhaps that will persuade other countries that they should be doing something too.

When you're deeply involved in science, you don't actually see the milestones in quite the same way as you do when you look back on them. At the time the significance of making the virus-like particles which were the basis of the vaccine was real enough, in the sense that for six months we'd been trying and hadn't succeeded at all. The morning when Jian brought the electron micrograph pictures in and showed me them and said, 'Look, this time it's worked!' that was certainly very exciting for both of us – there's no doubt. I went home and told my wife Caroline that we'd come up with something significant. If it wasn't for the fact that I'd to get on and write a paper about it, we'd have gone out for a celebratory drink! I knew as soon as we saw the pictures that, if there was going to be a vaccine to prevent cervical cancer, it would be based on what we'd just discovered. I was also very much aware that, if we were going to do anything with this, then we actually had to switch then and there from being scientists to being intellectual property developers. No company would take it on unless we could protect the intellectual property that was encapsulated in what we'd done and we were going to need a company to get the vaccine out there if it was going to be of any use.

I'd been primed to the intellectual property issue because I'd been working with CSL for about three years prior to that. It had been a learning experience for them, too, because they'd been a government agency and then they became a private company and now they were starting to think about commercialising things. Each of us learned quite a bit from that experience, not all of it good, I have to say! I learned that it's very important to have a good patent attorney and that it's very important that you keep good contemporary records. That became pretty clear after the event, when we went back to look at Jian's notebooks, because they were partly in Chinese and not well set out in the manner that one would now expect in the Western world. It was very hard to decipher exactly what had been done when and how. We knew what we'd had to do to get the vaccine, don't get me wrong, but the idea that there'd be a nice logical progression laid out in the lab work books was not true in reality. Jian was very ably assisted by Xiao-Yi, his wife, but Xiao Yi at that time spoke very little English at all and Jian spoke not much more. Sometimes there was confusion between us as to exactly what we were saying to each other, not in the science, but just in the bits round about the science.

The publicity surrounding our finding had its impact on the family. I have three children, one is a Vet and the other two are contemplating a career in Medicine having done science degrees and other degrees. One's done Law and Science, and one's done Engineering and Science at university. They just saw Dad as a scientist who was more often not at home than at home. They presumed that I was doing something useful but never thought that it was *that* important, if you know what I mean. After I was made Australian of the Year, when the journalists couldn't get to me, they would talk to anybody else in the family they could get at. I felt like I was delegating responsibility a bit there but I think the children were in general quite amused by it.

If I did anything as Australian of the Year, it was to try and spread the idea that it's really important that we have a scientifically literate community, because you can't debate issues such as whether you want nuclear fuel or recycled water, or whatever the latest topic is that impacts society, from a zero knowledge base. People have to have *some* scientific knowledge, otherwise they can only react emotionally, or accept what we say as 'religion', handed down on tablets of stone! The worst possible thing that could happen to science in my view would be if society polarised into those that understood it and those that didn't, because then the ones that didn't would have to accept the word of those that did. I think science would then become the new religion. That would be very sad indeed, because I think science is a great force for good in society. Encouraging scientific literacy amongst those who do not wish to be scientists is as important as encouraging the next generation of scientists. Normally 20% of secondary school students take a science-orientated course, and that's not enough, in my opinion.

I know our current Prime Minister (John Howard) is very keen on history. You certainly learn from history, but we live now in a science-based world and we have to understand how that world works. It's impressive how people are quite happy to use science without having a clue how it works. Look at mobile phones, for example. My brother designs the chips for mobile phones and he tells me there's no single person on this planet who could build an entire mobile phone. There's nobody who knows all the technologies that are involved in it! That's quite a scary thought, isn't it? I mean, if we all fell off the planet tomorrow and had to start again from scratch, we'd be in real trouble trying to recreate what we currently have. When we were kids, most people could make a crystal set, they knew what it was and how it worked and you could make a radio. My kids couldn't make a radio and I'm sure their children will not be able to. Now, of course, education has fallen out of favour as a career, which is a great shame because it's one of the most important parts of society and we treat our teachers as if they were a disposable commodity. We will all regret that in the future. I think if we don't value teachers, society is dead.

Perry Bartlett –The Brain Institute, University of Queensland

He tells me that scientists now know that we're making large numbers of new nerve cells in the brain daily and that this continues throughout our entire lives – quite the reverse of what we'd previously believed. As Director of the Brain Institute, Perry is dedicated to understanding how we make more neurons and how we keep them alive and interacting. Among other benefits, this ground-breaking work will contribute to our understanding and treatment of brain disorders and memory loss.

'I feel like New Yorkers must have felt when they moved out to the US West Coast perhaps fifty years ago, and everyone said, "Oh, you're going to the West Coast – nothing ever gets done out there!" Of course, since then, apart from other things, people on the West Coast made the two major discoveries that formed the basis of modern technology, the silicon chip and DNA technology.'

I've been here in Queensland since 2002. Prior to this I had lived in Melbourne for practically my whole life, except for four years in the USA and London. I find Brisbane so quintessentially different to Melbourne and Sydney – for all the right reasons. People here actually try and help you, and actually want you to succeed, whereas with people in Melbourne and Sydney, schadenfreude is the term that most easily comes to mind. I think there's still this wonderful sense of frontier sensibilities here, in people actually having to work together to get things done. I feel like New Yorkers must have felt when they moved out to the US West Coast perhaps fifty years ago, and everyone said, 'Oh, you're going to the West Coast – nothing ever gets done out there!' Of course, since then, apart from other things, people on the West Coast made the two major discoveries that formed the basis of modern technology, the silicon chip and DNA technology.

Part of my move here was a sense of adventure, because I'd been at the Walter and Eliza Hall Institute as Head of Neuroscience for twenty-five years and if I hadn't moved then I never would. The opportunity to come up here and set up a new institute was a pretty tremendous opportunity. Everyone has been incredibly helpful to me in doing that. Brisbane has changed in the last five to ten years scientifically. My impression is that the University of Queensland is now the dominant bio-scientific community in Australia – from being around bottom of the list ten years ago! That's come about by a series of serendipitous but also well-planned initiatives, both from government and the Vice-Chancellor, and from the philanthropy of a single donor.

The philanthropist is this very interesting guy called Chuck Feeney, who made all his money out of duty-free. He's a delightful guy, who lives a very Spartan existence, but he's donated $20 million to this university alone, to build the new Brain Institute. He's donated another $15 million for the Nanotechnology and Biomaterials Institute and he donated $10 million to the IMB in the Queensland Bio Sciences precinct. He helped build the UQ Centre where graduations are held – he gave $10 million dollars there. He refurbished the Mayne Arts Centre at $3 million to $5 million. In total, that's an enormous amount of money. But the interesting thing, and why that money is so important, is that he's made sure that it was leveraged against State money, that is, he would only give if state government matched dollar for dollar. In effect, he's ensured this university has received well over $120 million in real money that would never have been there otherwise.

The story goes that his kids were playing tennis and coached by a famous Australian player, a Queenslander, Ken Fletcher. Ken Fletcher came back to Brisbane and Chuck visited him and fell in love with the place, so he bought a property here and lives here two or three months a year on and off. Chuck's very Irish and he knew the then Lord Mayor, Jim Soorley, who arranged a meeting between the then UQ Vice-Chancellor, John Hay, and one other person at the Irish Club. I think it might have been John who suggested that a good way of spending his money would be in this way. Without this meeting, none of the UQ funding would have happened, so it was very serendipitous. Unfortunately, no Australian philanthropists have really done anything like this before or since.

The three institutes that Chuck's put money into here at UQ are the Institute of Molecular Biosciences, the Australian Institute of Biomaterials and Nanotechnology (AIBN), and the Brain Institute – that's us. It's this triad of institutes which have made UQ preeminent in this area of biological sciences and bio-engineering. We have a lot of interactions and joint appointments between the institutes, as we have between the institutes and the schools as well.

The university has also grown in terms of its faculties, as well as the institutes, and one of the demands on me is very much to make sure that our success is also reflected through the faculties, so that the whole of UQ benefits from these initiatives.

At the Brain Institute in our first year we established the world's only dedicated laboratories to be able to sort nerve cells. The way we're approaching this is that we are able to find the cell in the brain that makes neurons, and we've been able to purify that cell using the technology we have developed up here. We have two of these things called 'cell sorters' which pull out cells on the basis of the molecules on their surface. We've actually discovered the molecules that regulate the production of new nerve cells. In our first twelve months we managed to submit a paper to *Nature* that said we think we know now what the major regulation of this production is.

We're fundamentally interested in one thing, trying to understand what regulates basic brain function. The aspect of the brain function we're most interested in is the mechanisms that control the important processes which underpin learning and memory that are rapidly changing in your and my brain, all the time. They're changing predominantly in response to environmental inputs. There are two major processes that are changing and which we believe are selected for by environment. One of these is the change in connections between nerve cells. There are an unbelievable number of such connections, something like a billion billion neurons or nerve cells. Every nerve cell might have 10,000 different nerve cells interacting with it, and those interactions are in the form of tiny end-feet that transmit signals by releasing chemicals from one neuron to another across spaces (the neurons aren't physically attached to each other) called synapses. The important point here is that the connections, or synapses, change and are selected constantly by whatever is stimulating this nerve cell.

Things like memory probably occur (although we still don't totally know this for sure) through the reinforcement of the connection between neurons, based on continued stimulation of one neuron. You consolidate a connection and that becomes a memory! The second and most surprising process that is constantly changing in the brain is the production of new neurons. When we discovered this occurred some dozen years ago it overturned the reigning hypothesis of a static, immutable brain.

We know now if you work impaired limbs after a stroke, for example, this promotes changes in connectivity between nerve cells in the brain which will allow at least a partial regain of function. These mechanisms of being able to change nerve connections and the nerve repertoire itself in response to environmental stimuli, whether that be memory formation, vision, or smell, is the basis on which our brains work, so the old idea of the brain being a very hard-wired, fixed object is yesterday's concept. The most profound change conceptually is that we now realise that because of the brain's plasticity we can make new nerve cells as well as losing cells. We make tens of thousands of nerve cells every day and this continues throughout our entire life.

A lot of neuron growth is related to parts of the brain that detect smell and the big question is why? Has it got something to do with function or is it just some sort of remnant of production or what? No one really knows, but we have some data that suggests that you make neurons all the time, in various parts of the brain and most of them die, except if you select them to survive by the appropriate functional stimulation. So if you have a neuron, say, that's associated with smell and you're exposed to the specific odour that that neuron can respond to, it'll make connections and it will be stimulated and it will continue to live. We now have experimental evidence that if you expose animals to odours as these nerve cells are being born and integrated, they'll preferentially survive in response to that specific odour. In this way, we are constantly selecting the neurons that best fit the environmental stimuli-neuronal adaptation.

The smell of a newborn child may be a good example. There's good evidence that when women are pregnant the production of neurons associated with odour detection is dramatically increased. One hypothesis would be that, in order to have heightened smell of the infant for recognition purposes, they've developed this ability to increase the number of nerve cells that can be selected to survive by the baby's odours – thereby adapting the repertoire to better appreciate these odours.

Perhaps the most exciting place where new neurons are constantly replaced is the hippocampus, the area of your brain that's involved with working and spatial memory. If we're similar to animals, we may be turning over or replacing all the nerve cells in this area of the brain about every three years. The other thing is that here, also, nerve cells appear to be selected by their environment, so if you put animals in a bigger and more interesting cage with things to crawl through and wheels to run on, the number of cells that survive increase. The majority of the new nerve cells made in the hippocampus are normally gone within a couple of weeks. But if you let the animals explore a constantly changing environment, then presumably because there's more stimulation of nerve cells in the hippocampus, you can rescue up to 30% or 40% of those neurons that normally die! My hypothesis is that we are constantly changing our repertoire of neurons to match our environment through selecting those neurons which make the appropriate synaptic connections with those neurons that preferentially respond to the environment – which makes a bit of sense!

At the moment we're very much dedicated to understanding the basic mechanisms that regulate these two functions: synaptic and neuronal plasticity. The key questions are how do you make more neurons and keep them alive and interacting; and how do you regulate the connections? They are inextricably linked, because it's the connections that allow the new neurons to stay alive. It's the electrical impulses that are activated by vision or smell in the very early days after birth of the nerve cell that prevent the susceptible nerve cell from dying. The concept of an adaptable and plastic nervous system is a remarkable change in the way we think about brain function.

The other thing which supports the notion that continual production of nerve cells is very important for our wellbeing is that it's now been shown that anti-depressants only work in experimental animals if you allow the production of neurons to occur. The interesting thing, however, is that most anti-depressants don't work until 3 to 4 weeks after you give them, which coincides with the idea that they've got to make new neurons in order to work. We know anti-depressants actually promote the production in the hippocampus of new neurons. Now, in animals, if you irradiate the area where they're being made, so there's no new neurons being made, anti-depressants don't work. It's still very early days, but this evidence suggests that depression may be due to lowered production of neurons. A lot of depression then leads to dementia, which results in a very small hippocampus due to loss of neurons, so it could be there's a continuum between wellbeing, where you're constantly making neurons that are adapting and are allowing you to function, through to depression, where that's not happening adequately, through to dementia, where there is a total lack of neuronal production. Recently we have identified the cell in the hippocampus responsible for generating new nerve cells and, more excitingly, we have discovered how this cell is activated, thus we are getting very close to understanding how to regulate the production of new nerve cells, which should enable us to directly test the importance of new nerve cells to maintaining cognitive function and addressing the surge in aging dementia.

Funding in Australia is always in short supply and we have been especially fortunate in Queensland in having Peter Beattie, who initiated the Smart State strategy which has been enthusiastically carried on by Premier Anna Bligh and which has made Queensland the leading bio-medical research centre in the Asia Pacific region. I used to think the Smart State tag was hyperbole when I was in Melbourne, but after coming here and meeting Peter Beattie I changed my opinion. I think this is very important because the image of Queensland outside the state is like the image of the deep south of America, that is, that alternative medicine and lifestyles and belief in creationism is dominant here. For example, I was asked to join a panel on a futures-based hypothetical for fifth and sixth form school kids about 'going to Mars' and how would you colonise the planet. I didn't have a lot to say because it didn't involve the brain, but at the end of the three-quarters of an hour, the panellists were asked questions.

There were about 80 students there and the first four questions that were asked all related to creationism! The first girl got up and said she was a creationist and said, 'How dare you talk about the sun burning up the earth in four million years … how dare you talk about the end of the Earth!' Then the next person stood up and started talking about their religion and I was thinking, 'This was about going to Mars and space ships.' In the end, after the fourth person had spoken from a creationist perspective, the moderator had to say, 'Are there any questions about the hypothetical?' I turned to someone and I said, 'Don't tell me this is representative of what's going on in Brisbane schools?' I'm still trying to find out, because we actually financially supported the hypothetical. There's no way we're in a new age of enlightenment, I can tell you that – all the more reason why the push for a Smart State is so important.

Neil Charles and Paul Masci – Snake Venom and Medicine

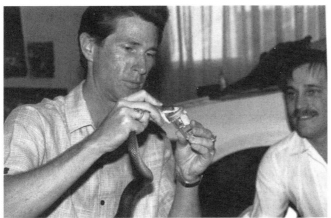

Neil's story and that of Paul Masci, which follows it, are paired, as together they have been instrumental in ground-breaking medical research on Australia's venomous snakes.

Neil Charles milking a Taipan with
Dr Paul Masci beside him

Neil Charles

Neil works with AQIS (the Australian Quarantine Inspection Service) but it's his involvement in the breeding and milking of our venomous snakes for medical research that leads to my contacting him. He invited me to visit his home to see his collection of reptiles and other native fauna, many of them endangered. He'd also kindly included my husband Alan in the invitation and we enjoyed a fascinating and informative evening in his company. Neil and his partner Tania live on the outskirts of Ipswich and share a mutual interest in fauna while her mother Gloria is invaluable, preparing food for their many charges – from endearing furry animals to 'bum-breathing' turtles, baby crocodiles and snakes.

> *'Late in 1981 I had an accidental bite from an eastern brown snake and I was convinced following the conference in Melbourne with Struan Sutherland that the next time there was an accidental bite I wouldn't go for the tourniquet, I would try the constrictive bandage and splint technique. I'd met up with Professor John Pearn at this stage and when the accident happened I gave him a call and he saw an opportunity to monitor exactly what happened with that venom. The procedure worked successfully for me and it was the first documented case of the use of this first aid technique in a human.'*

As far back as I can remember I was interested in reptiles. Aesthetically I found them interesting and then, as I got a little older, I was mentored by some knowledgeable people, including the famous David Fleay, who used to run the sanctuary in West Burleigh on the Gold Coast and who led me to try and understand an animal from the animal's point of view.

I believe the first time I met David Fleay I was probably about eight years old and he was always very encouraging to me. I had an aunt, too, who was very supportive, and she'd often take me for drives on Sunday afternoons to various places, whether it'd be bush walking or visiting wildlife parks. It was about that time I started my own collection, things like bearded dragons and blue tongue lizards. I also began to read a lot of the books but I found that they were a little lacking in terms of what really makes animals tick. Even as a child, I was always devastated if an animal that I'd been keeping passed away – I always tried to learn what went wrong and what I needed to do to ensure that, if it was a mistake I'd made, it didn't happen again.

In my early twenties, through the Queensland Museum, I met up with Professor Richard Shine, who was then based at Sydney Uni. Richard and I built a great relationship. He was very much the researcher with the academic credentials and I had the enthusiasm and the interest. He showed me how we could work as a team and encouraged me to formally document a lot of my findings. With his assistance we co-authored a number of papers that then appeared in refereed journals. Things that were fairly simple observations to me often turned out to make fairly significant changes to our understanding of what makes these animals tick. Take the black snake family, for example. In the old days the books I read said that all the members of the black snake family gave birth to live young. In reality, when I started to breed these animals, I found that the only member of the black snake family that gave birth to live young was, in fact, the red-bellied black! There were a number of areas like that in which we were able to document things from the reproduction point of view and correct previous misinformation.

Probably round about the late '70s early '80s I met a gentleman from South East Queensland, a Professor John Pearn, who was very interested in snakebite and we collaborated on a number of projects there. We looked at the amount of venom that snakes yield on a defensive bite as opposed to an aggressive bite. They used to say that if you used just one of the ampoules of antivenom that are created by the Commonwealth Serum Laboratories it would be enough to neutralise an average bite. But I'd succumbed to a number of accidental snakebites working with these animals and I don't think one ampoule was ever enough. So we had to look at whether my snakes were giving much more venom than everybody else's snakes were, or was it that what we were using as the gauge to determine an 'average' bite was not, in fact, accurate. Of course, the average bite was estimated by the people who were commercially milking snakes, grabbing them behind the head and encouraging them to bite down onto a beaker with a rubber diaphragm.

We found some interesting things about biting habits. Taipans, for example, who may deliver multiple bites, can control the amount of venom that they release and it's possible that on the third successive bite you may, in fact, receive more venom than on the first bite! Other snakes, like rough-scaled snakes, the amount of venom that they release in successive bites may be little on the first bite, high on the second bite, little on the third bite and higher again on the fourth bite. We learned that snakes in some circumstances have the ability to control the amount of venom they release. We also found they can, if they choose to, deliver a dry bite – more as a warning. Again it was a case of the academics combining with the resource that was available for the better good of everybody. I always perceive that the outcome of these things gives me a better insight into how the animals tick. In the case of snakebite, it may also assist the team that one day will be treating me for snakebite to do a more effective job than had been done for others in the past.

In 1981 I went to a conference in Melbourne where a gentleman by the name of Professor Struan Sutherland, who was the head of research at CSL at that time, put forward a view that perhaps the manner in which we'd been conducting snakebite first aid was not the most effective way to do it. Up until that time we'd been promoting the use of a tourniquet and he felt that, with his experiments with monkeys, a broad even pressure over a wide area, plus a splint, contained the venom more effectively. He believed that Australian snakes, having relatively short fangs, the majority of venom was spilt into the lymphatic tissue, and then entered the bloodstream after a period of time, rather than directly.

The disadvantages with the old system were that, to apply a tourniquet properly was quite painful, and one group of people seemed to be reluctant to put it on tight enough and therefore it was ineffective, the second group of people would often put it on too tight or leave it on for too long and you would find that tissue damage would result because of the lack of blood flow from the extremities where the bite had taken place. The next issue was that if you left the tourniquet on for more than 20 minutes you stood a high possibility of some of this tissue damage, so people were obliged to release the tourniquet, which means that they would get a surge of blood from the bite site into their system. So after 20 minutes, even if you've applied that tourniquet very quickly and effectively, the chances are you're going to start to succumb to some symptoms. The other issue was to do with cutting. Struan felt that, as most of the venom was contained in the lymphatic tissue, by cutting the wound (as they did in previous treatment) you may have, in fact, been offering a more direct route into the blood stream and, secondly, some people got a little bit too carried away and did considerable damage by cutting more tissue than was necessary.

The advantages in the restrictive bandage and the splint are that it's not difficult to apply a bandage and it's easy to carry with you if you're bushwalking. You apply it from the bite to the length of the limb, with enough pressure to almost get pins and needles but not quite. The splint is simply to stop any muscular movement, because that can also pump venom through the lymphatic tissue. This means that this bandage can remain on for quite a considerable period of time, so you have extra time in which to get medical help. The chances are, on arrival you should be feeling OK, so the doctors should have more time to assess the situation and progress things accordingly. The less effect you've got from the venom, then if antivenom is required and applied, the faster you'll usually recover. Different groups of snakes have different types of venom that work on different things in your body. Some will clot blood, some will make blood go thin and some work on the nervous system. There are very few of them that are purely one of those activities – they all tend to be cocktails but one of those crude groups will be the primary or most significant activation.

Late in 1981 I had an accidental bite from an eastern brown snake and I was convinced, following the conference in Melbourne with Struan Sutherland, that the next time there was an accidental bite I wouldn't go for the tourniquet, I would try the constrictive bandage and splint technique. I'd met up with Professor John Pearn at this stage and when the accident happened I gave him a call and he saw an opportunity to monitor exactly what happened with that venom. The procedure worked successfully for me and it was the first documented case of the use of this first aid technique in a human. In my case, the bandage was on for a little over two hours and I felt absolutely no effects of the venom whatsoever. The team involved was taking blood from me on a regular basis to monitor what was happening with the venom in my system. They had the appropriate antivenom there and other drugs that have to be administered prior to the admission of the antivenom to make sure there's no allergic reactions to it. They then released the bandage and monitored what happened to that venom in my system. The levels rose notably and I could feel the effect taking place, but we were able to counter that immediately with the antivenom and I've got to say that I feel I suffered the minimum amount that one can. I was just taking advantage of an unfortunate situation; it was a case of 'let's not waste it'. The important point we were trying to make to the public was that applying this simply and effectively, you shouldn't suffer. The result was published in the *Medical Journal of Australia* in, I think, it was either February or September 1981, and I was a co-author on that.

Now, part of that team was a fellow by the name of Paul Masci. He's now a doctor. At that time he was doing a Masters Degree at the University of Queensland, he was attached to the Department of Medicine, and he showed a real interest in eastern brown snake venom. Currently he's looking at a number of commercial applications to do with components of various snake venoms. He and I became friends and I invited him to utilise my collection as a resource. I milk snakes from time to time to donate to him whenever he needs them. A lot of the venom that he works with is dried venom that he purchases from commercial venom suppliers, but I understand from time to time it's good to get fresh venom – I guess as a bit of a quality control, to see what the quality of these dried venoms is like. He's really getting down into the detail about different fractions within the venom, just to be certain that there is nothing that's eroded by those freeze-drying processes.

Paul also wrote a book called *The Taipan, The World's Most Dangerous Snake* and I assisted him with that. There were a lot of photos of me in there doing things with taipans, for example. I've also always made the collection available to a number of authors and photographers to get good quality photos of my animals for publications in books and the same thing goes for a lot of documentary makers. With cable TV these days there seems to be an ongoing line of production companies that want to do stories on Australian reptiles. So long as there is some sort of educational content and focus we usually try to make ourselves available. Our website is: *www.coolcompanions.com.au.*

Paul Masci

Dr Paul Masci is team leader of the Venomics Group, Therapeutics Research Unit, University of Queensland School of Medicine at the Princess Alexandra Hospital. Paul and Neil Charles have become good friends and have worked together over the years to advance knowledge about snakes and their place in the scheme of things – along with likely benefits to medicine. When I met Paul he'd just returned from the airport with a consignment of snakes. He's central Italian by birth, his family having come to Australia after the war, when he was seven. He told me that the venom of the eastern brown, for example, paralyses its victim and also coagulates the blood of its victim or its prey, yet the venom of the king brown does the opposite, by causing hemorrhage and serious bleeding. Both snake bites are deadly, yet through his work Paul has been able to show that these venoms are also capable of saving lives...

> *'"Is there a use for the paralysis activity that we saw in Neil's snakebite in 1981?" And "How can we stop the kidney failure that we see in a lot of the fatal cases of brown snake bite?" And "Does that give us an insight on how kidney failure happens?" These are the kinds of ideas that are coming from that initial presentation of Neil's.'*

In 1981, when Neil was bitten by one of his animals, quite a large common brown snake, he realised it was a serious bite and he put on the recommended first aid measurement for snake bite that was developed by Professor Sutherland in Melbourne, and that protected him for about an hour or so until he could come to the Royal Brisbane Hospital.

A friend of mine who was the head scientist in the Hematology Department at the Royal Brisbane at the time, Mr Merv Elms, contacted me to say, 'Look, Neil's a friend of yours and John Morrison's – he's just been admitted following a snake bite.' I'd previously met Neil on a few occasions at herpetology meetings at the museum, but I didn't actually know him well at the time.

At about that same time, Dr John Morrison, who was doing a PhD with Professor Pearn in the Child Health Faculty at the Royal Brisbane, also was doing some work on another Australian snake and he'd come to do some work in my lab to finish off his PhD thesis. Coincidentally, all this was happening when Neil was accidentally bitten, while he was cleaning out a cage with this brown snake in it. I think Neil suggested that the snake thought he was a mouse and bit him!

The consequence of his snake bite was that he showed a massive clotting episode. His blood completely defibrinated, so he bled because he had nothing to stop him from bleeding – plus he had all the other neuro-toxic symptoms of the common brown snake bite, including being paralysed. As a consequence of vascular defibrination, there is no fibrinogen left in the blood stream of a brown snake bite victim. Fibrinogen is the molecule in the blood which is converted to fibrin (clot), therefore, when in this state of defibrination, the victim cannot form a plug to stop bleeding as there is no fibrinogen left to form a plug.

My interest was in trying to understand how the clotting episode happened, because, although it had been mentioned in the literature, it was very poorly covered.

At that time I'd enrolled in a Masters Degree in Bio-Chemistry at the University of Queensland and that had sparked my interest in the subject. I'd spent the previous 10 to 12 years working for Professor Alan Whitaker here in the Hematology Department at the PA (Princess Alexandra Hospital) and his main interest was in looking at the consequences of thrombosis in clinical management. Professor Whittaker is a clinical hematologist and he retired in 1997.

We had a long-standing interest in thrombosis and basically haemostasis, or how the blood clots – so the fact that this Brown snake causes massive clotting was very interesting to us. Here we had an Australian snake that had developed a very powerful system to clot blood. Normally it's done by a variety of agents, so understanding what this compound was and how it worked, and the whole structure of it, would be quite an exciting project.

After taking part in the treatment of Neil in 1981, I continued to study brown snake venom for the next five years. The venom was supplied to me by Neil, plus Eric Worrell at Gosford Park, and John McLauchlan, a herpetologist in Cairns, also provided me with venom samples so I could study clotting activity.

The studies continued and I actually published my Master's thesis in 1986 where I characterised and purified the main clotting activity in the brown snake. I published a couple of clinical papers and one of the aspects was Neil's snakebite recovery. The interesting thing that happened with Neil was that he'd had a couple of relapses in the week and a half that he was in hospital. It was interesting to follow the episode of his snakebite by actually looking at what was happening with his clotting system – so that was quite a useful finding.

In 1989 this incident inspired me to go on and do my PhD in the same area and a consequence of that was we identified yet another compound which actually stops the clots from breaking down. Normally in the body blood clots are broken down pretty quickly so you never have a clot stabilise to cause problems to your vascular system. Interestingly, the brown snake and a number of other Australian snakes have developed this agent to stop these clots from breaking down. It puts a clot in place very quickly and it also keeps it there – in doing that it actually compromises your ability to breathe. If there is no blood circulation or reduced circulation of blood via the pulmonary artery to the lungs, then there is no exchange of gases (breathing), therefore a compromised respiration.

From there we looked at the clinical uses of the compound that causes clotting and the compound that stops clots from breaking down, and where that could be facilitated. Agents that are used to stop clots from breaking down now – one is marketed by Bayer and it's quite a large, sizable market, but it's only extracted from cow lungs. When the mad cow disease outbreak happened in the '90s it made us think that maybe a genetically engineered compound from the snake may be a much better product to help stop the loss of blood in major surgery, like a cardio pulmonary bypass surgery, which the Bayer product was indicated for.

Anyway, since then we've gone to different stages with the intellectual property process. One patent, based on the clotting activity, is for the design of a product to stop bleeding on the surface of the skin. One of the big problems with car accidents and emergencies is that it's very difficult to stop bleeding where you have major trauma. This compound from the brown snake, we suggested, could be a very good material to simply stop bleeding on the surface of the skin – and it does. It does it very, very well and very quickly – in less than 10 seconds! When you think that in 30 seconds you can bleed to death, developing a product to stop that kind of fatal outcome is very inspiring work!

They're the two ideas that were patented in the '90s and since then a company has been set up to pursue these as products, to go to the different stages of the clinical investigations, and in 2003 we went one step further. We combined a group of about 25 scientists here to study 20 Australian venomous snakes – some of them are kept by Neil and some of them are kept by other snake handlers for fresh venom sources. There are commercial sources of the dried venom but it's always good to quality-assure the venom with fresh venom and Neil is registered on my scientific permit with National Parks and Wildlife to be that kind of provider.

We were successful in obtaining an ARC grant of $1.5 million for that study in 2003. Since then the ballgame has changed dramatically in that we're moving on now to thinking about, 'Is there a use for the paralysis activity that we saw in Neil's snakebite in 1981?' And 'How can we stop the kidney failure that we see in a lot of the fatal cases of brown snake bite? And 'Does that give us an insight on how kidney failure happens?' These are the kinds of ideas that are coming from that initial presentation of Neil – which was actually a clinical trial of snake venom in vivo in the human! That's where Neil and similar cases like Neil's, where they've survived (and many have died), are very good sources for exploring and developing new ideas for interventions of particular diseases.

One of the interesting things that we're currently looking at is that there are agents in venoms that actually help heal wounds. There's a specific compound that actually enhances about 50 times the abilities of the skin to regrow over an injury. It's a very powerful agent and we're thinking this could be cloned and expressed to make lots of it. We already have an industrial process for the compound that we patented that stops the clots from breaking down. A company in Adelaide has provided that service to us to develop a protocol to develop it as a manufacturing procedure. We can actually make kilogram lots and it would be very easy to go up to ton lots. A ton of that material would be worth something like $900 million Australian! The company is a joint venture between a number of venture capitalists and the University of Queensland. The plan is to develop the company to a certain size and then sell it on to a larger pharmaceutical company – because to develop one product to registration stage to FDA or TGA you'd be looking at say $300 million to $400 million, so it's really not in our ballpark to do that. These are the sort of guys that have invested in these ideas of mine.

Really, I can put it all down to Neil's initial involvement in my work. That is what showed me a way to look for these compounds in snake venoms and gave me an insight into the kinds of activity that are present, so now we can go and identify them in the laboratory. The whole development program is very costly and requires a lot of dedication to get it to a level where it meets the regulatory requirements. One of the greatest things is that bleeding is one of the worst things that happen in accident and emergency and a lot of people die in car accidents because they can't control the bleeding. I've seen a few bad accidents and that's why I've had a very close at heart interest in this particular area.

Neil and I have published some papers together. One was on the brown snake and one was on the rough-scaled snake. The rough-scaled snake is an extremely powerful little animal. Its main habitat is south-east Queensland and it's an extremely potent and bad-tempered little snake. It's only about a foot (30 centimetres) long but it can knock you down in about 10 seconds. It's very prominent around all the National Parks. We've got a couple of ideas about its possible advantages to medicine. In the ARC linkage grant that we obtained in 2003, the rough-scaled snake is one of the 20 snakes that we put up that we want to pursue. We're trying to look into the evidence base from actual cases, like we did with Neil, and then looking for ideas, taking onboard what happens when you have a snake bite and how it's managed in an intensive care situation.

I've been here thirty-four years and that snake bite of Neil's was in about February 1981, so all this work has happened over the last twenty-four years. I was the senior author of the book *The Taipan, The World's Most Dangerous Snake* that gives an insight on how much we should respect these animals. They're very successful animals, taking into account that man is dramatically encroaching on their environment. I'm trying to impress on people that these snakes' genetic makeup is really an extremely valuable piece of heritage that we shouldn't destroy and that we should respect their rights to be here – just as we are.

Some time after my interview with Paul, we spoke again and he told me,

'In May 2007, a company (QRxPharma Pty Ltd; ASX code: QRX), which licensed our snake venom intellectual properties, was listed on the Australian Stock Exchange and, by doing this, raised $50 million, which will be spent to complete the clinical trials on one product. Further development in the planning stages of QRxPharma are to raise more funds to complete more clinical trials, with expectation of more products reaching the fruition to a useful drug for all. The financial benefit to Australia will be significant, and to me, personally, it will be extremely gratifying that I have achieved in my lifetime something really good and made a significant contribution to the wellbeing of mankind. Above this, more exciting developments are planned, which I cannot reveal at this point in time.'

Leisl Packer – Queensland Institute of Medical Research (QIMR)

Leisl was recipient of the Young Queenslander of the Year Award in 2004. She tells me she's always had an enquiring mind and enjoyed science classes at school. Now she's working with others in the scientific community (initially at the Queensland Institute for Medical Research where we spoke, and later in London) endeavouring to identify specific genes involved in aggressive and invasive melanomas so they can be targeted by new treatments, thereby saving lives.

'Nothing in science is ever achieved quickly. The breakthroughs ... even the serendipitous ones, are always the product of much hard work and dedication ... all research is about discovering new things. That's what I love about science, it's all about the possibilities and discoveries!'

I was born in Sydney and lived there until I was six years old, when my family moved to Queensland because of my father's work (he is a civil engineer). We lived on the Gold Coast for one year and the Sunshine Coast for two years, so I didn't arrive in Brisbane until I was nine years old. My earliest memory of Brisbane was attending the World Expo in 1988 and learning about all different cultures from around the world. Apart from Expo, my earliest memories are mainly of my school life and living in the area of Bellbowrie near Anstead where we have lived for the past fifteen years.

I always loved science and maths in primary school, but I enjoyed most aspects of school life. During high school I loved chemistry and biology and maths, but I also enjoyed geography and history and learning languages. I probably realised in high school, when I was introduced to chemistry and biology, that I wanted to pursue my studies in science.

The research that I am involved in aims to better understand the genetic background of melanoma so that we can understand which genes are involved in melanoma development. We are analysing the expression of thousands of genes to identify which genes are 'misbehaving' in melanoma cells compared to normal skin pigment cells, from which melanomas arise. More importantly we are trying to identify novel genes which are involved in the more aggressive and more invasive melanomas, so that these genes may serve as targets for novel therapies, as there are currently no effective treatments for patients with advanced stage (metastatic) melanoma.

To achieve this, we must 'sift' through these 13,000 genes to find a small number that we can then perform tests on individually. We want to characterise these important genes and find out exactly what functions they perform in normal cells and malignant cells, so that we can hopefully design therapies to 'fix' the genes that are changed or 'misbehaving' in melanoma cells. Such therapies may either slow the progression of melanoma in the body or stop it completely, but we are a long way from creating improved therapies for melanoma. It isn't even certain whether my research will assist in this directly. It is likely, though, that some useful knowledge will arise from my research that will help other scientists around the world to better understand and treat melanoma.

Similar to breast cancer, heredity has also been shown to cause melanoma in certain individuals. However, it is estimated that only 10% of all melanomas are familial, that is only one tenth of melanomas are caused by the inheritance of certain genes. So the vast majority of melanomas are sporadic and likely to be caused by the sun's harmful ultra violet (UV) radiation. UV radiation is a carcinogen. It directly mutates (changes/damages) the DNA in our skin cells. The brown pigment in our skin, called melanin, protects us from this UV radiation. Thus people with darker skin have better protection from the sun and less chance of developing melanoma. It is therefore imperative for us to *avoid* spending time in the sun. That is our major defence.

To my knowledge, stress and diet do not directly impact on the risk of developing melanoma like they do for other cancers, such as cancers of the gastrointestinal tract, where stress and diet directly affect the chemicals produced by the body that, when deregulated, can promote a more favourable environment for cancer growth. Obviously a person with a balanced diet and free of stress would have better bodily repair mechanisms and defences against free radicals, which can promote cancer. Thus, an overall healthy person is generally less likely to develop cancer of any type. However, genetics can often override this, which is the case in many of the inherited cancers.

My own research does not involve any patient contact at all. It is completely 'behind the scenes', which I find a little disappointing as it would be really nice to know that your work is directly helping people in need. But I can see that the long-term goal for this project may help melanoma patients so that is enough to keep me motivated. In the future, I hope to be able to work on a project (such as a clinical trial for a new cancer therapy) that involves some amount of patient contact as I think this would be very rewarding.

My research has so far not achieved any major breakthroughs, though the information we have unveiled will be used by other research groups around the world. Each day we make small amounts of progress that are closer and closer to finding better ways to treat melanoma. Nothing in science is ever achieved quickly. The breakthroughs that have been made throughout history, even the serendipitous ones, are always the product of much hard work and dedication. Sometimes we need to redirect our research and focus on different aspects, but all research is about discovering new things. That's what I love about science, it's all about the possibilities and discoveries!

I never considered not studying my PhD in Brisbane, as this is where my family and friends are, where I completed my undergraduate study (at a great university that I would like to continue my postgraduate studies within) and there are so many outstanding laboratories here doing world-class research. Additionally, I had worked in the laboratory where I studied for a year prior to my PhD commencement so I was familiar with the laboratory, the people and the project. It only seemed logical to accept a PhD project in the lab where I had experience. This is not to say that I would not consider working overseas on completing my PhD. It is recommended within the scientific community that newly graduated PhD students work overseas.

Brisbane has a number of excellent research institutes and laboratories that are recognised worldwide as contributing valuable research. The Queensland Institute of Medical Research (QIMR) is actually the largest research institute in Australia. The labs overseas, however, (particularly in the USA and Europe) have greater funding for research and therefore generally have better equipment and facilities available to them. If I were to work overseas it would be a great opportunity to advance my scientific knowledge and research skills and then to bring these skills back to Australia to improve our own research back here.

My own particular research, being melanoma genetics, it's extremely handy to live in the Sunshine State, which has the highest rates of melanoma in the world. Because of this we are able to recruit many melanoma patients (and relatives of melanoma patients) to participate in our study. Again, however, due to limited funding in Australia, overseas labs can usually achieve outcomes quicker than we can, due to their newer equipment and greater numbers of staff.

I think the quality of the educational environment here in Brisbane is outstanding. We have several universities offering a broad range of majors with the science degree. I'm not an expert on education, but I believe that our high schools and universities certainly have what it takes to compete on the international stage. Obviously the resources in universities are much better than in high schools, where I believe it comes down to the teachers. I had some outstanding teachers at Kenmore State High School, which undoubtedly encouraged me to pursue science as a career.

I wouldn't be surprised if visitors to Brisbane were impressed by our university facilities. For example, based on my own knowledge, UQ has various research stations all over Queensland, for earth/geological sciences, marine sciences, environmental sciences, veterinary science, physical and chemical sciences, medical sciences and more. These facilities allow students to experience the practical side of learning in real-life situations. I think it's really fantastic what UQ can offer its students. I'm sure the other universities have equally impressive facilities, but I am only aware of those available at UQ.

I think, as a young person interested in science, it's all about knowing what you want to do at the end of high school. It's not an easy decision, so perhaps with greater community knowledge of what research is being done in Brisbane and what is being achieved, students will be more likely to pursue the degree at university. However, a vast number of students studying science at university are aiming to use it as their undergraduate stepping stone to medicine. Thus, many of the bright science students are lost to medicine, rather than continuing their careers in research outside medicine. I'm sure if the pay was better and if scientists were more highly regarded in society, more students would consider it an option. I must admit that the pay is pretty bad considering the years of study we have to endure.

Something that makes me smile is that whenever someone learns that I am doing melanoma research, they immediately point out their own moles and ask me for a diagnosis. I must then explain that I am not a trained clinician and that I don't deal with patients' melanomas as such, but rather I work at the molecular aspects of the disease.

Being awarded the Young Queenslander of the Year was certainly one of the brightest moments. I was totally unprepared for it, as well as for the media attention that was to follow. It was a wonderful experience and I learned so many things during that time.

Physical Science

Chris Wheeler – ZeroGen Clean Coal Technology

He's based in Brisbane but is liaising with international organisations and companies around the world. Low emission coal technology isn't commercially 'applied' anywhere yet but Chris and his colleagues see it happening in the not too distant future.

'Today if you read the papers you'll see that climate change and carbon offsets and carbon trading schemes are regularly discussed. A couple of years ago anyone that dared to speak about clean coal would be asked, "What are you doing that for? It's never going to happen!" You just had to stand there and take the challenge and move forward.'

I was born in Blackall, a country town in Western Queensland, and spent most of my younger years there, until I finished Grade 10. At that time there weren't any high schools beyond Grade 10 in the West so I went to boarding school in Yeppoon and then went on to what was called Capricornia Institute of Advanced Education in Rockhampton and completed an engineering degree. When I was in Grade 10 we had an Acting Principal come to the school and he said, 'Oh, you'll probably be an engineer!' I hadn't really given any consideration at all to what I was going to do; in fact, coming from western Queensland, I probably had a vision that I was going to be a presser or a shearer but I'd always had an interest in things mechanical and things electrical so I took his comments on board. When I went away to boarding school I met up with other folk that came from other places and did other things, and from there I made the decision to go to university and do an engineering degree.

When I finished my degree I joined the Queensland Electricity Generating Board and worked in two hydro stations in North Queensland, Barron Gorge and Kareeya, on the Tully River. Afterwards I worked in coal power plants at Gladstone Power Station and Tarong Power Station, which is out near Kingaroy. Back then I was a control systems engineer so I was interested in how things were controlled and actually worked more than the generation of power. As time went on I became interested in the actual generation and transmission of power as well.

After working at Tarong and being in the energy industry for thirteen years, I left and went and worked in the mining industry for about ten years because at the time I wanted to get some different experience. I wanted to use my engineering skills in a different area. I worked at a bauxite mine in the Northern Territory and a copper uranium mine at South Australia's Olympic Dam. In some respects it was still linked to power generation. The Northern Territory job had its own little power station, which was isolated from the (Northern Territory) electricity grid. A key responsibility was to rehabilitate that power station, which was quite run down when we first went up there, and we spent quite a lot of time making various adjustments to make it reliable.

After working at Olympic Dam in South Australia on a major mining expansion, I wanted to come back to Queensland because my grandmother at the time was getting old, so I took a job back at Stanwell Corporation – back in the energy industry I'd left ten years previously.

At Stanwell I got into wind farms and my focus shifted to the renewable industry business. Today Stanwell has three wind farms which it built and operated, and I've been involved with building two of those. Back then, Stanwell started to look at other alternative energy forms which might be a progression into the future for low emissions technology, and that's how ZeroGen came about. They also had a look at biomass power generation. For example, power from burning sugarcane bagasse, which is also a renewable energy form, and they actually built one power station based on this technology. Subsequently, they decided not to continue with that technology and instead looked at how low emission coal technology might be used in the future, so in 2003 they started investigating that. I did some initial work in this area while I was still building wind farms and then I came back into the area in 2005 and have worked on the project seriously since then to progress the idea. That completes the circle, I suppose. I started in the power generation industry with traditional coal-burning power plants, then got some experience in the mining industry and came back to the energy industry to focus on renewable power generation and alternative energy forms.

Low emission coal technology is not a technology that is commercially 'applied' anywhere at the moment; it's still at the leading edge of future applications around the world. We're actually liaising with quite a number of international organisations and companies. We've done quite a lot of work with Shell, who provide technology to convert the coal into a gas. Shell also have a lot of experience in being able to handle CO_2 so we're working quite extensively with them and dealing with their people in Houston and the Netherlands about various forms of technology that make up clean coal. We're also dealing with a number of organisations in the United States as well as the Electric Research Power Institute in America, which is one of the world's largest independent research institutes. We've also done some work on how gas turbines might be used as part of the technology. There are other similar projects we are connected with which are being developed in Europe, the United States and other places in the world. There's an element of collaboration while at the same time there's also an element of retaining the knowledge that you've developed internally for your own purposes. We've become quite well versed in dealing with international players.

The technology is in various bits and pieces that have been done in isolation. One example is the gasification technology which is used to convert the coal to a gas, which is then burnt in a gas turbine and is a much cleaner form of power generation. The integration of coal gasification and gas turbine technology was developed about ten years ago and has been proven. There are, however, other elements to do with capturing the carbon dioxide and making high hydrogen gas, which have been done in other industries but not done in the power industry and that process of capturing the carbon dioxide has to be coupled to the existing coal gasification process. Once we've captured the carbon dioxide we plan to store it back under the ground. That involves a similar sort of technique to how oil and gas are currently stored under the ground. With each stage of the technology having previously been done in isolation, what we're now trying to do is bring it all together and make it work. While it sounds very simple when you say it quickly, overcoming the technical challenges involved is an enormous task and it doesn't come without a cost. This is a complex technology and the cost of development will ultimately have to be reflected in its value – the price paid for not emitting carbon dioxide. Who knows, in the future carbon dioxide which is buried may become a valuable resource which can be recovered. This is over-the-horizon stuff, though, and we have a lot of work to do now to reduce the carbon dioxide emissions to limit climate change.

It's been really difficult to convince people that this work needs to be done. In the scientific community the imperative to get on and start the technical work was recognised early on, but initially neither the politicians nor the public understood it. Today, if you read the papers you'll see that climate change and carbon offsets and carbon trading schemes are regularly discussed. A couple of years ago anyone that dared to speak about clean coal would be asked, 'What are you doing that for? It's never going to happen!' You just had to stand there and take the challenge and move forward.

We have a great little project team here and I'm the leader of the team. All of us here on the team have read the literature on climate change and that's deepened our understanding of what is really happening, and that there's a real need to do something. As a result, this work gives us a great sense of unity and purpose. That's one of the good things, I suppose, about working in a team and on a project like this. About twenty years ago I got into the project area part of engineering and once I got into that area I vowed never to get out of it and I'm now glad I didn't.

There have been plenty of amusing things happen. I don't generally have many beers but I think I might have had a beer too many at one of our Christmas parties one year. Anyway, it was a fancy dress party and Peta, who's a very nice lady who came to the party dressed as Dame Edna Everidge, said to me, 'Oh, Wheels, stick these glasses on,' and I did. The next thing the flash goes off and the camera managed to capture me with a cheeky grin on my face with the Dame Edna glasses on. It appeared later in a doctored internal morning bulletin article where I was up there talking about ZeroGen with a photo of me. In the original photo I'd worn a suit and tie but this showed the substituted photo of me with the Dame Edna glasses on. It went around the office here; occasionally people still see the damn thing and it still puts smiles on faces!

It's an interesting thing when you have a task to do and you bring a group of specialist people together and some of those people are very intense and scientific, and others are very good with their hands and can make things happen, and others are very good with people and can manage people. It's the unity of a whole lot of different skills coming together to make a project team to build a good outcome. It's very satisfying when you get to the end of it. That's what we've got at ZeroGen. For us the highpoint has been the recognition that something does need to be done. Around mid 2005 we started to feel that maybe the project didn't have a future but we stuck to it and put our heads down and looked at ways we could maybe make the project perform better.

I think the highpoint for us is that we managed to overcome the original inertia and resistance. Stanwell put in the initial effort and showed they believed that this technology was a technology of the future. They backed the project up until March 2006 and then the project was taken over by the Queensland government.

We've had some breakthroughs but we've still a long way to go in terms of the project. We're still in what's called a 'feasibility study'. We believe the technology will work, but it does need to be proven. We started the initial investigation in 2003 and we estimate it'll take us to at least the end of 2008 to complete the feasibility study. That's how long it takes to do a complex project like this, one that's dealing with technologies that have never been put together before. Our aim is to be able to say when we complete the feasibility study that we understand what the technology can do, what it's going to cost and how long it's going to take to build it. This still won't be a full-scale plant; it will be a demonstration plant to come in advance of a full-scale plant. Once that's done everyone who's contributed money needs to look and make sure it makes sense to them as well. Assuming they're happy with it we should commence building the demonstration plants in 2009, co-incidentally Queensland's sesquicentennial year. It will take two to two and a half years to build the first plant so middle to late 2011 we expect to start the first plant up.

I've always liked to see things through to a logical conclusion; it's always good to start off with an idea or task and to see it successfully concluded. I guess our next major milestone is to get to the end of the feasibility study. Whether after that I build it or someone else does, we'll see.

I moved into the renewable and alternative energy sphere in 2000. The first decade has just been a decade of trying to head in the right direction. Over the next decade I believe there will be significant changes across the world in the way we view energy and water. I'll always have an interest in being involved with that – until I hang up my engineering boots!

Jurg Keller and Korneel Rabaey – Advanced Water Management

Professor Paul Greenfield has been attracting and nurturing talented individuals from around the world to the University of Queensland. Here the stories of Jurg Keller and Korneel Rabaey have been paired as they are both involved in research at the Centre for Advanced Water Management – research that is becoming increasingly vital to this 'wide brown land'. My conversation with these two researchers opened my eyes to some of the fascinating issues and possibilities involved in wastewater management. I spoke first with Jurg Keller, the director of the centre:

Professor Jurg Keller and Dr Korneel Rabaey.
Photo courtesy of Jeremy Patten, University of Queensland.

Jurg Keller

'Why call it resource recovery? Well, mainly for the reasons that in waste water there really isn't any waste. I mean, there are pollutants in there, yes ... but we look at it very much as a resource. The three resources we can harvest from wastewater are ... the water itself, next the organics ... in the form of energy ... and finally the nutrients ... ought to be captured and go back to the land in order to keep up the long-term fertility of the soil.'

I'm originally from Switzerland and I did my undergraduate degree and PhD degree in Zurich at ETH (the Swiss Federal Institute of Technology). After that I came out to Australia for a year or so as a post-doctoral student (in 1991), initially funded by the Swiss government. That's now nearly eighteen years ago and I'm still here! It's been an unplanned and very long trip but very worthwhile and I don't regret anything at all.

I started here at UQ on a project together with the now Vice-Chancellor, Paul Greenfield, working in his department, Chemical Engineering, on a project that he had partial involvement in. That was on biogas production, methane production from wastewater and the whole time I've been here we've basically expanded from this activity.

Paul is pretty much why I'm still here, because my wife Beatrice and I didn't originally intend staying and after about one and a half or two years we actually went back to Switzerland for job interviews. We were going to come back to UQ for only a couple more months and then leave for good, but literally the day before we flew out for the interviews in Switzerland, Paul arranged a meeting. I remember it was a Saturday morning, and he said, 'We've got this project and we want you to lead it – think about it.' We thought about it after we came back for quite a while and then decided, 'It's just too good an opportunity to miss – let's take it.'

The work we're doing here at the Advanced Water Management Centre, (its name has changed from Wastewater Management) is very much looking at all aspects of water in an urban context. It's really to do with waste water treatment: the nutrient removal aspects and increasingly now with the water recycling side. Overall, I think the best way to characterise what we're doing is to say we're turning waste water treatment around and making it into what I call a 'resource recovery' operation.

Why call it resource recovery? Well, mainly for the reasons that in waste water there really isn't any waste. I mean, there are pollutants in there, yes, and they are certainly not harmless, but we look at it very much as a resource. The three resources we can harvest from wastewater are primarily (and obviously) the water itself, next the organics, which are a big part of the pollutants harvested in the form of energy (that's the major part we're working on now), and finally the nutrients, which are the nitrogen and phosphorus – the fertiliser that comes off the land as part of the produce we eat. This last part we process in our bodies and it ends up in the wastewater and really it ought to be captured and go back to the land in order to keep up the long-term fertility of the soil. Once you recycle all these three resources there's nothing left and you've done something practically useful, not just a cleanup job!

At the moment it's very exciting, because there's a huge public awareness and emphasis on water recycling. But even on the energy recovery side I think there are a lot of people who now realise we're going to run out of energy and, while wastewater resources aren't going to solve all our problems, they will certainly help by saving energy in the wastewater treatment side and recovering some of that in the form of biogas or electricity.

We developed quite rapidly in the first few years, partly because we were then the largest group in this field in Australia. From there we quickly established a strong reputation worldwide and that's very much where we are now. We collaborate with a number of other groups in Australia and have major collaborations with international partners. For example, we just recently got over $1.6 million from the federal government here to collaborate in two major European projects. Now we're collaborating with many partners, probably in the order of 25 to 30 partners across the two projects in Europe.

One of these EU projects is very much along the lines of what we just talked about. It's looking at the recovery of energy, as well as bioplastics or biopolymers from the waste-sludge. The waste-sludge is the byproduct that's left from a domestic wastewater treatment plant. This leftover is usually either dumped as landfill or incinerated, which, in both cases, is a waste of a very good resource. So what we're looking at is either turning that resource into electric power with microbial fuel cells or using it as a raw material to make plastics, which are biologically generated and fully biodegradable as well. The other EU project is related to a process to achieve a high level of nutrient removal and nutrient capture from industrial wastewaters. In that case we're working with the meat industry, which is a major industry here in Queensland particularly.

Because of our growing and very strong reputation internationally, Veolia, a major international water company, one of the biggest in the world nowadays, approached us. The three advanced water treatment or recycling plants that are currently being built now here in Brisbane are going to be operated by Veolia. Veolia is originally French but they're operating in many parts of the world now and have a very strong and rapidly developing business here in Australia. They approached us in the first instance to investigate options of collaborating and providing some research support for some of their activities here.

We're just about to sign off on an agreement with Veolia, whereby we will establish a major research facility in water recycling here in Queensland. This facility will focus initially on the local water recycling plants that Veolia is going to be operating. We're going to provide research support to them helping in the optimisation of the plants, trouble-shooting and further development of the technology. Longer term, the idea is to make this the hub in Australia and possibly in South East Asia for Veolia and anyone else deeply involved in the technology. It's very much a capacity-building and knowledge-generating activity for us.

There have been lots of high points during our research; in fact, they come all the time. Personally for me one of the high points was to gain a very large Australian Research Council (ARC) project on this microbial fuel cell project which we got in 2005. We got $1.3 million from the ARC to investigate these microbial fuel cells. We're way ahead of the schedule we set on that; the progress has been phenomenal and it's a really exciting area to be in.

As I said before, we're trying to recycle water and we're trying to generate energy from the organics but I think a lot of people are well aware now about the importance and sheer value of water. I think we also need to remember in that context the amount of energy that actually is required to regenerate and recycle water and so on. We ought to be just as much concerned and indeed focused on energy saving, efficient use of energy, energy reduction and energy production from renewable sources.

Queensland's probably got one of the best climates to generate energy from the sun. We've got so much sunshine and it's quite evenly distributed over the year, so it's ridiculous to not make more use of it. That's one of the areas that we all need to be aware of – it's not just water, it's energy. A lot of people are not aware that even electricity production uses a lot of water. A normal household uses probably 20 to 30 or more kilowatt hours per day and every kilowatt hour uses about 2 to 3 litres of water in the power production. Any household in Queensland will use several thousand litres of water per year, just in terms of the power they're using. By saving energy we're actually saving water and in a very efficient way too.

Korneel Rabaey

'The Fosters brewery plant in Yatala produces three and a half million litres of wastewater per day but they produce 25% of the beer in Australia ... their water intake is much minimised. They only need water to make the beer, essentially! They are, perhaps, the world's most efficient brewery in terms of water management; they do fantastic things on that site.'

The first time I came to Queensland was because I had a good invitation to meet my current boss, Jurg Keller. He wanted to work more on the link between wastewater treatment and renewable energy. I was working on this at the time in Belgium.

The visit to Queensland was a fantastic experience. There's a good climate in Queensland both for research and weather. I think for a European it makes a big difference that the weather is so nice over here – the sun is very attractive.

The Advanced Water Management Centre has about 50 people and our team is roughly about 10 people at the moment. I say roughly because these things fluctuate over time, students often coming in for a few months or a few years at the maximum. It's a very dynamic team, in a way, and it is very international, also, in all respects. At the moment, for example, Jurg is heading the team and he's Swiss. We have another Swiss collaborator, and myself, I'm Belgian. We have two Italians, one Bangladeshi, one Thai, one French girl, one student from the Netherlands and one Australian. We are perhaps the most international group of the lot in the centre.

What we are essentially developing is technology that eliminates the energy costs of treating wastewater. If you take the calculations of the USA (there are none available for Australia, unfortunately), up to 4% of the total electricity consumption in the US is being spent in transporting and treating wastewater. That's a huge amount; it would make a massive difference if you could save that. We have technology that makes an energy-consuming process into an energy-producing process. The technology is a microbial fuel cell. This is a sort of battery that you can continuously feed wastewater. Micro-organisms degrade the dirt in the wastewater, and transfer electrons – and energy – onto an electrode, the anode. By combining this anode with a cathode, we can produce power. It also produces rather clean water that you can then further upgrade to process water for a factory or you can even go up to drinking water quality. In Queensland we know we're facing a large water crisis, and at some point we will also be facing a large energy crisis so we need to reduce our energy footprint. I think focusing on the combination of these two factors, water and energy, is actually an ideal fit for Queensland.

The Fosters brewery plant in Yatala produces three and a half million litres of wastewater per day but they produce 25% of the beer in Australia. They already do work to purify the wastewater on that site using technology which also has been, in part, locally developed to my knowledge. They have a system in place which is called anaerobic digestion. What they do is, they actually ferment their wastewater and then subsequently they generate biogas out of it with bacteria and that biogas represents an energy input of about $600,000 per year, so that's a lot of energy. The water that comes out of the digester goes to an after-treatment, after which they filter it and the water that comes out of that filtration unit is, I would say, above drinking water standard – but they don't reuse that water for the beer, which would be psychologically quite difficult in Australia, so they use it for all their processes on site, cleaning and toilets and everything. That way their water intake is much minimised. They only need water to make the beer essentially! They are perhaps the world's most efficient brewery in terms of water management; they do fantastic things on that site. The operation in Yatala is very large scale, while the technology we are developing now is aiming at small to medium scale, like wineries and smaller breweries.

Queensland has an industry and managers and company directors who are very keen on innovation. Fosters, for example, decided to support wastewater management technology because it is an innovative development with great promise longer term. As scientific researchers, that's encouraging for us to see. In our own research we haven't had any major setbacks yet. We have a small smile every day! A high point for me, personally, was when I got nominated for a Eureka Science Award.

Max Lu – The World of Nanotechnology

Max is Federation Fellow and Director of the ARC Centre of Excellence for Functional Nanomaterials. We meet in his office, where he describes some of the enabling aspects of nanotechnology. He explains how this extraordinary technology can benefit everything from medicine to manufacture, while also assisting with many of today's environmental and energy issues. Paul Greenfield had suggested I'd find a meeting with Max interesting – and it was!

'If we can learn nature's tricks we can translate them into engineering and make the materials that we desire, whether it's a solar cell, or a fuel cell, or a new paint for the car. For example, car paints are getting better and better and less environmentally polluting ... Now if you introduce nano-particles into some car paints, you can impart functionality such as anti-bacteria and self-cleaning ... imagine, one day you may have a car that you will never need to wash! It's becoming a reality.'

I'm Professor of Nanotechnology in Chemical Engineering and Federation Fellow at the University of Queensland. I am the Foundation Director of the Australian Research Council Centre of Excellence for Functional Nanomaterials, which is part of the Australian Institute for Bioengineering and Nanotechnology at the University of Queensland. I also teach subjects in the School of Engineering of UQ.

I came to Brisbane from mainland China as a student twenty-one years ago; my home town in is in Eastern China. I came to the University of Queensland to do my PhD in Chemical Engineering. That was early in 1987. My PhD supervisor was Professor Duong Do, who went to US on sabbatical leave when I arrived. Professor Paul Greenfield was the Head of Department then. I remember Paul and his wife Louise had a dinner engagement, so they couldn't meet me at the airport when I arrived. I only had about $20 in my pocket; that's all the money I'd brought with me from China. I called Paul and he said, 'Take a taxi to the campus and then Louise and I will come to pick you up and we'll drive you to the place where you will be staying.' I spent about $17 for the taxi and so all I had left when I finally met Paul and Louise was $3. They very kindly picked me up and settled me into accommodation in St Lucia. I had been offered a scholarship by the university, so I wasn't worried, I knew everything would be fine – but that's the story Paul often tells about me. Paul has remained a mentor for me since the day I arrived.

I first studied chemical engineering and then moved into the area of nanotechnology, mainly because my PhD research took me into this field. I was basically dealing with the dimension where nanoscale is important. Just to explain, the nanoscale is about 1/80,000 of the diameter of a human hair. A nanometre measures one billionth of a metre. Nanoscale technologies are the development and use of devices that have a size of only a few nanometres, so nanotechnologists can manipulate single molecules and atoms. I studied how to make nanomaterials porous. Take charcoal, for example. How do you control charcoal to have more absorbing power for pollutants? That's the question that I had in my thesis and I actually solved that question. For example, at a nano level one gram of charcoal particle has an internal surface that is equivalent in area to a football field. If you go inside and look at the surface available for molecules, that's how big it is. That's why it's just hungry for the molecules. If you flow a gas that contains the component which is a pollutant, it just sucks it in and absorbs it, while the rest just passes through. That's how I started in this field, some twenty years ago.

From a student to where I am now, as a Federation Fellow, it has taken a lot of hard work and times of ups and downs in research. It has also taken a lot of luck and plenty of encouragement and support from my mentors and colleagues. Federation Fellow is the highest fellowship available in this country. It's offered by the Australian Research Council to attract talented Australians back to do research in arts, humanities, science or technology, and also to retain talented Australians at home, to reverse the brain drain. It carries a five-year fellowship with very generous salary and research support.

Across all disciplines, there are only 25 each year, so it's a very competitive scheme. I guess that's one of the things I'm proud of, but it's something I can also attribute to the support of many people, including Paul Greenfield, the Vice-Chancellor of UQ, and Professor David Siddle, the Deputy Vice-Chancellor (Research). They have supported my research and career development tremendously in the emerging field of nanotechnology.

It started in about 2000. At that time nanotechnology was in its infancy as a discipline. For the previous two years I'd been consulting and also teaching in central western Indonesia. Paul Greenfield, who at that time was the Deputy Vice-Chancellor (Research) at UQ, encouraged me to consider setting up a university research centre in nanotechnology. Because I had been doing a lot of good work related to nanotechnology, I was chosen to lead the multidisciplinary centre.

As I see it, nanotechnology is really nothing but a new sort of toolbox in science and technology. Basically, you try to manipulate nature on a nano scale – always you're dealing with molecules, or clusters of atoms. We try to manipulate the structure and the behaviour of matter at that sort of scale. As a result of being able to do that, you can enhance the properties, like increasing the strength of materials. For example, nanotubes have one hundred times the strength of steel because of how you build the carbon atoms into a nanotube. When you decide what foreign matter you're going to put into a body you have to make sure they're bio-compatible and not toxic to the cells. They also have to have the mechanical strength and the functional properties that will integrate with the tissue. Researchers have to study all these aspects very carefully and in great depth to answer those questions.

At ARC Centre of Excellence for Functional Nanomaterials, for which I'm the director, we are focusing on applying nanotechnology to do things that are practical and useful for society in three main areas. One area, for example, is clean energy. We are driving cars that generate a lot of pollution and because you burn the fossil fuel you generate not only carbon dioxide, the greenhouse gas, but also other pollutants such as nitrogen oxides, which contribute to chemical smoke and, if you have sulphur in the fumes, you have sulphur dioxide contributing to acid rain and other environmental health problems. The very tiny particles suspended in air will cause respiratory problems like asthma. The new technology on the horizon is called 'fuel cells'. In the longer term, the cleanest fuel will be hydrogen, so with nanotechnology we are doing the fundamental research that in five to ten years time will lead to technological breakthroughs related to hydrogen. This will improve the efficiency of hydrogen production, storage and distribution and also the utilisation of hydrogen in fuel cells. Hydrogen as a fuel is fed into a fuel cell and there it's converted into electricity very efficiently. Fuel cells are such a wonderful device that we convert clean fuel to electricity plus water. The end product is water vapour, without any pollution.

There's a lot of R&D effort going on around the world in this area and we're already seeing results in first generation fuel-cell cars and the first generation fuel-cell laptop computers. You can buy a fuel-cell car from Toyota, Mercedes and other car manufacturers, but the fuel-cell technology currently used in these prototype cars is still very expensive and not as efficient. You also have a problem with the infrastructure, so we're working on several fronts, using nanotechnology to address the materials needs, so that you can have more robust and cheaper materials for fuel cells and more efficient manufacturing. We have recently filed several patents for nanostructured materials which are promising for fuel cells and supercapacitors (high density energy storage device). One patented material promises efficient and practical hydrogen storage for passenger cars powered by hydrogen fuel cells.

We made these novel materials with much superior properties for various applications, using nanotechnology techniques, like self-assembly – by learning from Mother Nature. When you're at the seaside you see seashells and on the surface of any shell you see lots of beautiful patterns. If you look at it under a high resolution electron-microscope you'll see even more beautiful patterns. One can see and show the nanometre structure of seashells by using modern microscopy. It's all done in a natural environment, that's how amazing nature is in nano-structure – so, in fact, the first teacher, I would say, is nature. It's taken billions of years of evolution to reach what we have today in the living world.

If we can learn nature's tricks we can translate them into engineering and make the materials that we desire, whether it's a solar cell, or a fuel cell, or a new paint for the car. For example, car paints are getting better and better and less environmentally polluting. Initially we had only solvent paints and then gradually we got water-based paints. Now if you introduce nano-particles into some car paints, you can impart functionality such as anti-bacteria and self-cleaning. So, imagine, one day you may have a car that you will never need to wash! It's becoming a reality.

One thing we are doing that I think is going to impact people's lives in the medium term is in cleaning up pollution. We can apply nanotechnology to provide more economic, cost-effective solutions. For example, in cleaning up polluted air. To do this you take rutile sand and then refine it into chemicals like titanium chloride and then out of that you can make titanium dioxide nanoparticles. You coat the titanium oxide nanoparticles on the filter substrate and all the organic pollutants in the air can be degraded, provided you have a bit of light. That's called photocatalysis. You have light shining on the filter and when the air flows through the filter it will degrade the organics. That can solve a lot of problems with air pollution.

We are also making nanomaterials which are useful for water purification and recycling. With water, it's the same principle, because the photons irradiating on the nanoparticle surface generate strong oxidising power to degrade organic contaminants that come in contact with the surface from the waste water streams. So if you have drinking water which contains some traces of carcinogenic organics that cannot be removed by other means, then we'll remove them relatively cheaply using this type of nanotechnology. It's going to be very useful for water-recycling, because we're short of water in such a dry continent. We don't have a lot of water and we have to realise that at some time in the future we'll be mainly recycling water and using grey-water. People have higher and higher expectations with their health, so they won't want to drink any water that's unsafe. Compared to current disinfection technology, nanotechnology purification is not actually any more expensive. Chlorine is the standard way to disinfect drinking water but people find the taste is objectionable and also there is a lot of evidence showing that chlorine can actually cause other problems over the long term. I would say within five to ten years there will be a photocatalytic nanopurifier on the market that everyone can afford to buy. At the moment we are looking into producing ultra-pure water for pharmaceutical injection or other use and also for micro-electronics. Ultra-pure water is very expensive to generate from tap water, and nanotechnology can actually reduce the costs of doing that in large volumes.

So we have examples of nanotechnology being used in transportation, fuel, paint and air and water. The other area that we focus on is biomaterials. We've been working on several new projects that we're very excited about. One is to make nanoparticles that will carry biological molecules into the cell for targeted and controlled release. The kind of drug we take as a pill has no target ability and you have not much control in release. Say, five hours release, but that is not well developed in terms of how you control the drug release. It is desirable to design nanoparticles and tailor them in such a way that we can actually target the malignant cells, and control the release rates. We're making some progress in this area. We use inorganic silica nanoparticles which are nontoxic to cells. They are biocompatible and can actually be dissolved. We already can use some of the digestible inorganic particles like silica and activated carbons for taking out toxins from the stomach, but they are not nanoparticles. Similar to these materials, we work on the nanoparticles of such composition but in the nanoscale, to make targeted delivery carriers.

Nanotechnology is such a fascinating interdisciplinary field of technology that it will impact every walk of life. Take telecommunications, for example. I was talking about the fuel-cell computers we were going to have. In 20 to 25 years or even less we will have the best computer in the world fitting into the size of a wrist watch with the capacity to store all the books of the Library of Congress, with a virtual display and a virtual keyboard. You might say, 'Let's turn on the computer' and boom, there's a high resolution virtual display screen (like a hologram type, but with much higher resolution) in front of you and you can use your voice to activate it. This was one of the major scenarios when the US first rolled out their blueprint for nanotechnology in 2000.

An even more futuristic idea is smart paints. You'll be able to devise such paints with functional nanoparticles. You'll be able to paint any surface and change the colour on demand, blue today and red tomorrow – with no repainting. You'll be able to use that paint to receive images from computers and display them – this is in the next 25 to 50 years.

The ultimate Holy Grail for nanotechnology is to devise drugs, nanomachines that can go in to mop up the viruses wherever they are in the cell, without disturbing the good cells. Nano machines can replicate themselves but with good control. These can actually consist of the so called lab-on-a-chip for diagnostic and analysis functions, together with drug prescription and dispersion ability. The long-term vision of the nanomachine is to combine that sort of power, medical diagnostic power, with delivery power.

We are also trying to address another big issue and that's climate change due to greenhouse gas emissions. We have a patented technology that can separate hydrogen from other gases. It's like a very fine sheet of paper with small holes in it that are so uniform that we can control them. These holes are of the dimension of molecules themselves, so big molecules won't go through and small molecules will go through. Hydrogen is small, carbon-dioxide is big, so is trapped on this side. The carbon dioxide separated out from hydrogen can be injected into the coal seams or wherever, the geological deposit that is conducive for storage of it permanently. That's the kind of big project in which we're involved. It's an exciting project that we are working on with the Queensland government and industries.

Clay is a natural product of nanoparticles. Believe it or not, they are in nanometre range. If you do some modifications to clay, you can add value to clay to become a good absorbent. And clay can be used as a carrier for biopesticides – that will control the release of pesticides and that will also protect the natural pesticides, such as essential oil, from UV degradation. If you understand the molecule interactions you can make them into cheap absorbents that will carry pesticides. We have now proved the concept and demonstrated the nanoparticles formulation works very well for encapsulated bio-pesticides. This technology is now scaled up and being commercialised.

Nanotechnology is a very exciting field and it has a lot of potential impact for energy, environment, agriculture, health, medicine, computers, and telecommunication. I see we have a niche in this country – that's why I focus on the areas of energy and environment, and some health and agriculture applications. If we can apply nanotechnology to eliminate salinity and to control environmentally friendly pesticides we will solve a lot of Australia's problems. It's very satisfying work.

I am very indebted to my parents, who endured a lot of hardship in bringing up my eight siblings, starting from the war-torn China in the late '40s. Although I was born and brought up in peaceful time, life then was very hard. My father was a retired army officer who returned to his hometown to do farming work, and my mother was a dedicated housewife and mother of eight children. I started to help my parents on the farm since a very young age and learned that happy life cannot only be earned through hard work. My parents always taught me to be honest, hardworking and persevering. I was very fortunate and grateful to have the opportunity to go to university while my parents and my younger sister worked hard to earn a living to support me. It was in 1979 when I entered Northeastern University, admitted with an excellent score in the national examination of millions of students. The opportunity was also attributed to Mr Deng Xiaoping – the paramount leader of China at that time, who decided to resume higher education after the cultural revolution, and started the reform and opening up programs in China a couple of years earlier. My parents are still in China. They are old now and they don't want to travel, so I bring my family to see them quite often. I have one brother and his family living in Brisbane.

I have two children and we try to keep them bilingual. My daughter Donna is fifteen now; she's very competitive and very talented. She loves gymnastics. My son Elvin is eleven – very bright too. He plays soccer and tennis. My wife Lian works part time and is a very dedicated mother, supporting my career tremendously. She is able to continue her career working as a research academic in chemical engineering at UQ. She has been the manager of the Research Centre on Particles directed by Professor Jim Litster. I met Lian in China when I was a graduate student. She was studying in a different department but we were both graduate students. She was also quite well known in Northeastern University then as an athlete. She loves music, running and playing tennis. I am very grateful to her for giving me such a happy family and for her constant understanding and support.

I could live and work anywhere but I am very happy living in Brisbane and feel very attached to this place. Brisbane is the first foreign soil I landed on, twenty-one years ago, and it is a very liveable city by world standards. I feel my family belongs to this wonderful city; we love living in Brisbane, and plan to continue to make contributions to the Smart State's science and technology, and to society as a whole in Queensland in the years to come.

Allan Paull – Rocket Science

The Centre for Hypersonics is a maze of corridors. When I finally arrive at Allan's office I'm greeted with a broad smile. He works in a small tight-knit group and speaks of his work on applied hypersonics in the Air Vehicles Division and his colleagues there with undisguised enthusiasm.

'Well, it's a warm winter's day and I'm sitting here in T-shirt and shorts ... and this guy (up from Melbourne) walks in, in T-shirt and shorts, with a surf-board. He says, "My name's Hans Alesi" and we got on really well. I said, "All right, I'll give you a go – three months. The pay's crap!" He said, "I'll take it" and he was up here the week after ... and he's still here.'

I was born in Brisbane in 1959 and was brought up in what was then the country, in Kingston, now a suburb of Logan. I went to a little school, about 50 to 100 kids, and we got a good education there. Then I went to Sunnybank State High School. I managed to get into university and I had the choice between maths, sciences and engineering. My brother Ross had done maths before me and I was probably better at doing maths. I found it was more interesting than the engineering side. I followed the applied maths stream and physics, and quite early on I realised that my particular brain was more suited to logic rather than physics. Mathematicians actually have to have a more imaginative brain in some ways.

It became very clear to me then that the only way I was going to do research was by doing a PhD. So I did a PhD in applied maths. When I was almost finished my PhD, I was short of money. My brother was finished and a guy, Ray Stalker, from here, who built all these wind tunnels that we work with, he offered my brother a job and my brother didn't want it but he said, 'I know someone who's going to need a job,' and that was me. I wasn't quite finished my PhD but I was writing it up. Ray and I had a discussion and I said, 'Well, are you offering me a job or what?' And he said, 'Yeah, if you want it,' so I said, 'All right – I'll take it,' and he says, 'It's only for six months.' That was 1985 and I'm still here! After a lot of effort doing the PhD part time, I managed to finish it. Then I turned my back on maths. It's like having a girlfriend: you get sick of her after a while and then you come back after fifteen years or something and you might actually want to talk to her again.

The one thing that maths gives you is the foundations to start wherever you like. I had to start again in engineering. I was put on to help this Scramjet work that we do. There were these things called 'expansion tubes' which were types of wind tunnel for re-entry into earth's orbit but they didn't work. There was a push on in the US to make these things work and they approached Ray Stalker and Ray said, 'Look, why don't we build a little one and see if we can figure out what's wrong with it?' They'd been trying for 30 years, since I was born, and they couldn't make them work. They basically gave me a free hand and I played with this little thing and I came up with a theory for what was going wrong, and suddenly we could make them work. It was all due to the maths – I had the experimental results in the maths, so it was actually very satisfying.

Then Ray Stalker had a stroke. I was all of about thirty, I think, or thirty-one, so fairly young, and suddenly I was the boss of the Scramjet work and the team basically said, 'That's it – it'll be the end of the work here.' I went around friends, all round the world asking for $50,000 to keep the project alive, and I got these little bits of money, and even with Ray with his stroke we managed to do some more work where we actually had an engine which went forwards, it actually accelerated, which was an amazing thing in those days and we were the first to do that. Then, in my own right, I was earning my own money to stay alive, so that helped. We were the ideas factory. We had to keep coming up with good ideas and that's what we did. We kept coming up with good ideas and they couldn't knock it. We'd also been getting ARC grants. We always maintained a reasonable trickle.

Out of all this I got to a point where we were playing in these tunnels and we were building engines and I again got to this point where 'we've got to do something more!' I could see that the rest of the world was catching up and we had to do something that would leap ahead again, we're running out. It's all very well to play in a wind tunnel but I realised we needed to fly something – I just couldn't figure out how to do it, because it was so expensive. The numbers were an order of magnitude more than what we'd been playing with and we hadn't had that sort of support to do that.

Anyway, along comes a guy from the States and because people knew I wanted to fly something and it's a very close-knit community, they approached somebody who approached somebody. These people from the States had these rockets and they were in the business of supplying rockets to universities in the US. They said, 'Look, we'll give a couple of free rockets to some university in Australia to demonstrate what we're doing. I put up my hand and said, 'I'd like to do it for this experiment for Scramjets.' They hummed and haa-ed and I thought, 'Bugger this!' I went over to the States and met them directly. I said, 'This is what I want to do,' and we got on really well. They said, 'All right, we'll do it.' I had no money, though! The rockets I'd thought were the biggest part of it actually turned out to be about a quarter to a fifth of the actual cost. I had no idea and I had no idea how to take the stuff from the wind tunnel to flight. We'd never done it before and it's a huge step!

Another character comes into play at this point, my chief engineer, Hans Alesi. On the day I got the go-ahead to go with the rockets, Hans sends me an email and says, 'I want to work with you.' I've never known this guy before, but he's a structural engineer and the one thing I was weak in was structural engineering. Anyway, I kept putting him off, saying, 'I've got no money – got no money,' and then one day I got sick of it and I walked over the road and I said, 'Listen, I need someone to assist me, can you spot me some funds?' and they said, 'We'll give you three months.' So this guy's down in Melbourne and I said, 'Look, mate, you better come up to Brisbane and we'll have a chat.' Well, it's a warm winter's day and I'm sitting here in T-shirt and shorts, feet up on the desk and there's a knock on the door and this guy walks in, in T-shirt and shorts, with a surf-board! He says, 'My name's Hans Alesi,' and I said, 'Right, well my name's Allan Paull. Have a seat,' and we got on really well. To this day I've never read his resumé. I said, 'All right, I'll give you a go – three months – the pay's crap!' He said, 'I'll take it,' and he was up here the week after. He was getting married and everything and he came up here – it was a leap of faith for everybody. We got on really, really well and he's still here.

The two of us then proceeded to do this project and about halfway through a third member came along, Susan Anderson. The engineering was about one third and the rest was politics and safety and organisation of the whole thing and I needed her help with that – and she stayed for about two years. There were the three of us and, because we didn't have any money, I got my father and my brother involved helping us. They did it for free. Then the first flight at Woomera crashed! Anyway, we did a lot of working out of where it would go, and from that maths, my brother and I (and he's a mathematician, too, of course) we predicted where it should be. My brother and another guy and I went out and searched and, when we found it, it was 300 metres from where we predicted it would be – we were absolutely wrapped with that! What was more important, when we did find it, we demonstrated that it wasn't us that caused the problem. We went from saying, 'We have a huge problem with this,' to saying, 'We can handle that.'

The day after it crashed Hans had to leave because we had no money and he ended up working for Boeing for a while in the States. We were left with the second flight, which was supposed to fly, but there was a federal election on and I got a phone call from very high up saying, 'No, you can't fly,' because it could conceivably have crashed on a house on the day prior to the election, so it got delayed for nine months.

We picked up the crashed rocket and reassembled it and found out that there was nothing wrong with the payload, but from it we could figure out what had actually gone wrong was a rock had gone through a fin at takeoff. It wiped off a fin, so it lost it as soon as we launched it. At the end of all the investigation we were broke. We were down to the last $10,000 or something. I had to sack everybody then and go out and get some money so I could re-employ them again – half of them were away somewhere.

When I flew HyShot II, which was successful, the Commonwealth Games were on and I took the front page of the *Courier-Mail* – I wiped the Commonwealth Games off the front page of the *Courier-Mail* – I reckon that's my biggest achievement – to wipe sport off the front page during the Commonwealth Games. It's got the support of the people. I have tremendous support through the university and through Australia in general. People knew about it, the taxi drivers all knew about it and the media was great with us and you wouldn't get that in a bigger place. We've got good PR people! You wouldn't get it in a smaller place, either, because it wouldn't get out. Everything has to compete with sport in Australia. But people here really do love science! Most politicians haven't woken up to that – but the Queensland Labor Party has.

Our technology can be used – you hear about London to Sydney in two hours. Actually, I'm pursuing it mainly because I'd like to see if we can lift satellites up from North Queensland – really small ones – using this technology. I don't have all the numbers yet so I don't know if it is viable – some days you think it is and some days you don't – we're so small, we can't do all these problems at once. We can only get to the point where we can say 'we think this is going to happen', but someone's got to do it.

Everyone has a mobile phone and everyone uses a satellite at some point in their time. Everything we do is based in some ways on satellites. What we're trying to do with our current research is make them cheaper, smaller, more compact, so space isn't cluttered up so much. We're the mechanisms which allow other people to do what they have to do. People would never even know it, but that's what we're doing.

NASA flew a plane at Mach 7. We flew an experiment – a very big difference. My hat's off to them! What effect, if any, has this had on our current research? Well, if they'd crashed, we would have been in deep trouble because the Americans would have lost face in their abilities and that means their politicians wouldn't be funding them and therefore they wouldn't be funding us – bottom line!

We never have a dull day. We've now moved to the Pullenvale/Pinjarra Hills region. Now we've got a fair bit of money. We're still struggling, but that's life in research – you just keep going. We've now got a project that's worth $50 million, which is good.

Am I concerned for Australian universities? Absolutely! Not just Australian universities but Australia in general. We can't afford to live off digging stuff out of the ground and showing off the beauty and growing stuff. We have to value education, our academics and academic institutions more. That's got to come from government. Do you believe the American system isn't funded by government? The government funds the companies and the companies fund the universities – all that is government. Australia just kids itself. Here they're more interested in sport and mining and farming and tourism, but the smart countries around the world have all that and they said, 'Well, we'll put the money into the research as well.' It's the research that generates all the good teaching. You've got to do it; otherwise you just become a third world country.

Education within the field used to be very high, but it's getting less. Students have to pay, which I think is stupid. The way it works is if there are not sufficient people for the class, well, they can't give that course – or, alternatively, you make sure there are a lot of people there so they're guaranteed a pass, so you make the exams easy – right? And it's all because the people that have control of the money are the people who are being paid to stay here – so obviously they are going to keep their jobs. They're going to make the courses easier.

It's a vicious spiral – someone's got to turn around and say, in this instance, 'Bugger it – this is going to cost us money, but we *will* have the best, and the people will come for the best!' It's stupid, really stupid! This decision's not from the local or state level of government, it's right from the top! They just don't value it; it's all about the bottom line. They have something that's the best in the world and they'll let that go to hell – and it's sad, because I went through in an era when it was really good. The next generation that comes after us, they won't be able to solve the problems we are facing.

We do compete on the international stage but that's because we have good people. More funds wouldn't go astray – not just in my field, in every field. People abroad are very surprised at the capabilities we have. I think what we've got to do is just bring science to the young kids and that's what I try to do through talks to primary schools and high schools – yeah, I do those sorts of things every couple of months. We go and give talks and try to get them excited about it.

My wife was a nurse; we met in New Zealand on a train. We've got a hundred acres out Mount Glorious way and the kids learn how to be self-reliant and understand what the risks are. I used to do a lot of sailing but not a lot of the time now. We often take the trailer out and go camping in the bush.

Marine Science

Tony Ayling – Working on the Great Barrier Reef

Tony and his wife are consultant marine biologists whose 'workplace' is the Great Barrier Reef, while their home is in the Daintree Rainforest. He's been diving on the reef now for thirty years and has seen a lot of changes – in the reef itself and in the people who live and work there.

'The sea is an amazing place – there've been some incredibly beautiful times where the light's right, and the sea's calm and the water's blue and there're lots of things happening – just being on the calm sea when the sun rises or the sun sets, or under the stars at night and being isolated, being away on a small boat with just a few people up to 150 miles from land, by yourselves for weeks at a time ... But, of course, the sea has another side to it ...'

I was interested in marine biology from when I was about ten years old. I got a book and joined the Shell Club and then learned to dive. By the time I was thirteen I had my university career all mapped.

I went right through university in Auckland and did lots of scuba diving, doing the studies I was doing there for my Honours and PhD. During the time I was doing my PhD I met this lady, Avril, who was over there from Australia, also doing a PhD and also interested in diving – one thing led to another and Avril and I ended up getting married!

One of my good friends was a lecturer at the university and I decided that whole scene wasn't really for me. Then I got the offer of collaborating in putting together a fish book on all the fishes of Australia. That meant coming over to Cairns. Almost as soon as we got over here, the project fell through, but almost as soon as I'd got over here, I'd gone and seen the Marine Park Authority, which in those days was just starting up. They'd only got the Capricorn Bunker group of reefs right down the south end of the reef in the park – that was it. The rest of it they hadn't done anything with, even though they'd said it was going to be a marine park.

I'd been involved with working in a marine park and doing the baseline surveys when I was in New Zealand (the first marine park in New Zealand). That'd been quite interesting so I went to see them and told them the sorts of things I'd been doing and that I was keen to do something over here on the reef. They had a very small organisation in those days, just a few people, and they were desperate for some knowledge of the reef. This would have been in 1979 so quite quickly they started giving me little jobs to do and when I did them, one thing led to another. I started doing bigger jobs for them and when I say 'I' it was Avril and me; we started doing bigger jobs for them. That led to eleven years of pretty full on work that we did together, where we'd be together 24 hours a day for 365 days of the year, which was a really great experience, a lot of it under water. I think one year we spent 180 days at sea. We learned a hell of a lot about ourselves and about the reef.

The sea is an amazing place – there've been some incredibly beautiful times where the light's right, and the sea's calm and the water's blue and there're a lot of things happening – just being on the calm sea when the sun rises or the sun sets or under the stars at night and being isolated, being away on a small boat with just a few people up to 150 miles from land, by yourselves for weeks at a time. But of course the sea has another side to it and we've had some absolutely horrendous times – although, looking back on them, they're amazing experiences. The sea, even when it's abominable, has a lot to offer you.

When we first came up here, this was still pretty nearly the end of the line and there were a lot of interesting people up here. There used to be fishermen who'd have these tiny little boats, between 6 to 8 metres long and usually towing a dory almost as big as the boat, but sometimes just the little boat itself and basically all they'd have was a freezer and a bunk and a tiny galley and that would be it. We struck those people quite often and some of them would spend months up the Cape just wandering around. They'd be up there through the cyclone season and they'd know the rivers to go into and things like that. That's a group that's been very badly impacted by the changes in legislation and it virtually doesn't exist anymore. All the fisheries legislation, which is designed to cut down effort and conserve the resource, what it ends up doing is favouring big companies and it forces small people and single operators out of the business, which is good, in one way, as it does cut down the effort, but bad in another way in that the characters whose life was the sea and fishing have been forced out of it now and only the big companies are left.

I guess one of the biggest things I've learned in my research, well, several things, but two of the biggest things are the variability both in time and space out on the reef. Every reef you go to is different. I thought I'd seen it all, but once, when I was down, diving on some fringing reefs off Mackay, and one of the three little island reefs there was completely different from anything I'd seen. It had huge coverage of what I'd call 'filter feeders' things like ascidians and sponges and crinoids, and things like that, and a low cover of corals. That's not the sort of thing you normally see on a reef – it's the sort of thing I would have expected on New Zealand rocky reefs. There's huge variability. You can go just a few miles to another reef, or move around the back of the reef from the front and find something completely different.

You've also got changes through time and they're just stupendous. Changes through time from natural causes, for example, if a cyclone comes along. The sorts of places that are very badly affected are the exposed fronts of the reefs. The cyclonic waves come along and smash up and destroy about half the corals and badly smash up the other half, so it's reduced coral cover from about 70% down to about 30%. It looks awful, not just up in the shallow water fringe, but right down to 30-odd metres depth. This might be a 30-kilometre wide swath through the reefs that's been affected like this. It creates havoc and kills huge numbers of the fish and kills most of the corals on the exposed parts of the reef.

Then you come back 12 months later and there'll be a huge increase in coral cover. All the fragments will have settled down and repaired themselves and started growing, and all the broken colonies will have started to grow like mad. It's an amazing, resilient and dynamic place, the reef.

You could take half the corals and half the fish away from any reef and everything else would just rearrange itself and go about business as usual – that's the sort of thing that happens in a major episode like a cyclone, or crown of thorns starfish grazing the reef. Coral reefs survive in a huge range of conditions, even within the Great Barrier Reef, from filthy fringing reefs out to the crystal clarity of the outer barrier.

Having said all that, over the last few years I have got a few apprehensions about the future of the reef. One is fishing. Fishing doesn't actually affect the reef, as such, in that, as I said, you can take away a large number of species and individuals and everything just rearranges itself and goes on as normal, but, as far as the big predators go, there has been quite a substantial effect of fishing out there. Fishing can have a huge effect. It's just a few fishermen in dories with a single handline, but they're so effective in getting these few target species that they go for, like coral trout and some of the emperors and snappers, out of the water that four of them from a big boat on a reef can get off quite a large percentage of the available adult fish in their target species in a remarkably short time. We did a study where they closed this reef north of Townsville, what they called a replenishment closure, and it was closed for fishing for three and a half years. We'd done a number of fish surveys during the time it was closed and the number of adult coral trout on the reef increased about five-fold during the closure, but when they opened it up there was a pulse of fishing on that reef that removed 80% of the adult coral trout within twelve months. In fact, the majority of them went within the first month! That's one of my concerns, that fishing can, and in places is, having quite a big effect on the target species of fish, which are, of course, the big impressive predators, the large cod and the coral trout and big Maori wrasse, and things like that. A reef that has been long-term protected from fishing and collecting would be a fantastic thing to see, with a lot more large predators than we are used to seeing on a reef. A world without whales would not suffer ecologically, but we would be a lot poorer aesthetically if it wasn't possible to go out and see whales while they are up in these northern coastal areas during the winter.

My other concern is coral bleaching, which is caused by warm water. Once the water temperature gets sustained over about 31 degrees Celsius, the corals can't cope with the increased activity of their little algae symbionts that they need to survive, and they actually eject these symbiotic algae, zooxanthellae, they're called. That's when they go white and it's called coral bleaching. They can't survive for long without these little algae, so they need to get them back within about three weeks or they die. If the water stays over 31 degrees for more than three weeks, then the corals will die. This wasn't really known until the mid '80s, when people started seeing the odd bleaching episode. In 1987 we saw one and documented it up here, which didn't, in fact, lead to much coral mortality, but since then we've had two very bad bleaching episodes here on the Great Barrier Reef and there's been others that have had an impact worldwide. In places, these have dramatically reduced coral cover. This bleaching has been killing colonies that are quite large and the sort of impact that we've had is not really sustainable if it goes on at the level it has for the last ten years. If it continues at this level in the coming decades, or if the rate of bleaching increases, then bleaching damage may significantly degrade the reef as a whole over the next few decades. I'm apprehensive about warming sea temperatures and the potential effect.

We actually live in the middle of 36 acres of rainforest in the Daintree. When the weather is good, it's the most amazing place to be. You've got something close to 150 species of birds that we've seen close to our house over the years we've been here. Birds and bird calls are just a constant part of your day. The most beautiful pigeons and fly-catchers and rifle-birds and honey-eaters and things like that around you all the time. That and the changing colours and moods of the bush are absolutely fantastic. But you can't have rain forests without rain and when you get a bad year it can be a very hard place for humans to cope with – you get constant rain and overcast weather so you go a bit cabin-crazy and sometimes you say, 'Why on earth do we live here?' and then the good times come along and you know why. Of course, you've also got ticks and leeches, mosquitoes and sand-flies and all that sort of stuff. Our nearest town of any size is Mossman and we usually do our grocery shopping in there, but the whole place up here is so amazing – being in the forest and having the birds, the cassowaries and all that sort of thing, and also having easy access to the river with the crocodiles and the river birds and fish and so on. Then, just out of the river, you've got beautiful coastal islands like Snapper Island with rainforest on them and lovely beaches with fringing reefs around them that you can snorkel and dive on and, just off the shore, the reef itself. Not so much from here south, but from Cooktown north we've often seen crocodiles on offshore islands and reefs. In fact, we've seen them up to 30-odd miles off the coast – when you're snorkelling and diving in those areas you keep your fingers crossed!

Val Vallis: Poet

Songs of the East Coast

I am of the east coast country;
Not from the great cities that play Faust,
With flats for souls, but where the Queensland hills
Bite the blue skies with their emerald teeth,
And where the sun sets witches' fires on the waterline.
Here I was born.
Each morning I was Balboa or Magellan,
Viewing the vastness of a new Pacific;
And I heard the anthem of the cargo slings
And the song of loading wool.

I have been cradled in the wide arms
Of the sea, and from her breasts sucked life,
My slumber song was the tide's thundering.

Excerpt from *Songs of the East Coast*, Val Vallis, CQU Press 1997,
reproduced by kind permission of the author.

Val Vallis was born in Gladstone in 1916, the son of Henry William ('Mick') Vallis, a fisherman and wharf worker. Val was educated at Gladstone State School and Rockhampton High School. He worked as an office boy for the Gladstone Town

Council before serving with the AIF during World War II. He graduated with a BA Hons I from the University of Queensland in 1950 and a PhD in Aesthetics from the University of London (Birkbeck) in 1955. His poetry was first published in *The Bulletin*, and in the collections *Songs of the East Coast* (1947) and *Dark Wind Blowing* (1961). His poems have been included in a number of anthologies, including at least one used in secondary schools during the 1950s and 1960s. He was awarded a Centenary Medal for distinguished service and contribution to literature and poetry in 2001, and has a poetry prize (The Arts Queensland Val Vallis Award for Unpublished Poetry) named after him. Val died in Brisbane on 14 January 2009, aged ninety-two.

Index of Contributors

Index of Artists

Index of Poets

List of Queensland Native Fauna
– in small sketches between stories

Australian Brush-turkey (Alectura lathami)

Bilby (Macrotis Lagotis sagitta)

Blue Grouper (Epinephelus lanceolatus)

Bottlenose Dolphin (Tursiops truncates)

Boyd's Forest Dragon (Hypsilurus boydii)

Brolgas (Grus rubicunda)

Caper White Butterfly (Anaphaeis java teutonia)

Cassowary (Casuarius casuarius)

Clown fish (Amphiprion akindynos)

Cotton Plant Bug (Aulacosternum nigrorubrum)

Dingo (Canis lupus dingo)

Dugong and calf (Dugong dugon)

Echidna (Tachyglossus aculeatus)

Emu (Dromaius novaehollandiae)

Frilled Lizard (Chlamydosaurus kingii)

Hawksbill turtle (Eretmochelys imbricata)

King brown snake (Pseudechis australis)

Koala (Phascolarctos cinereus)

Kookaburra (Dacelo novaeguineae)

Little Egret (Egretta garzetta)

Moreton Bay Bug (Thenus orientalis)

Mud crab (Cancer magister)

Northern velvet gecko (Oedura castelnaui) jeuvenile

Orange-thighed tree frog (Litoria xanthomera)

Pelican (Pelecanus conspicillatus)

Platypus (Ornithorhynchus anatinus)

Qld Sea-horse (Hippocampus queenslandicus)

Red Kangaroo (Macropus rufus)

Ring tailed possum (Pseudocheirus peregrinus)

Salt water crocodile (Crocodylus porosus)

Sand Goanna (Varanus panoptes panoptes)

Sugar glider (Petaurus breviceps)

Sulphur crested cockatoo (Cacatua galerita)

Tawny Frogmouth or Mopoke (Podargus strigoides)

Tiger Dragonfly (Ictinogomphus Australia)

Ulysses butterfly (Papilio Ulysses)

Wallaby (red-necked) with joey (Macropus rufogriseus)

Wedge tailed eagle (Aquila audax)

Wombat (Vombatus ursinus)

Acknowledgements

I've many people to thank for helping to bring this book to fruition. Foremost of these are my family, without whose support and encouragement this book would never have become a reality. I also owe a debt of thanks to each and every one of the storytellers themselves for their participation and faith in the concept. There have been many who generously shared their time and stories, unfortunately more than could be accommodated in one book – I thank you all. This has been truly a celebration of community, including as it does the generous contributions of many of Queensland's much loved and respected poets and artists.

My sincere thanks to the Prime Minister, the Right Honourable Kevin Rudd, for finding the time to write the foreword to this book.

I would also like to thank the many kind people who put me in touch with others whose stories they believed should be told, among these are: Margaret McNamara; Garry West Bail, Hocky Queensland; Brett Williamson of the Surf Life Saving Association; Angela Dawson of International Quarterback; Jim Anderson of Bernborough Club Eagle Farm Racecourse; Inspector Owen Page of the Police-Citizens Youth Clubs Queensland; Kerry Clear of Australian Deaf Rugby Union; Mike Meadows of the Brisbane Rock Climbing Club; Andrew Young, CEO Brisbane Fruit and Vegetable Markets, Rocklea; Professor Roger Leakey of James Cook University; Chester Conran of the Barramundi Farmers Association; Grant Williams of the Master Builders' Association; Peter Maher, CEO of St Vincent de Paul; Haydn Johns of the Queensland Royal Yacht Squadron; Wendy Sanders, and Bill and Jean James of Cycling Queensland; Susan Parfrey, Curator, Queensland Museum; Helen Gregory, Cultural Heritage Strategies; Mark Peters, Australian Sports Commission; Mr B (Hass) Dellal of the Australian Multicultural Foundation; Beatrice Booth, President of Commerce Queensland; Josie Lacey OAM; Larry Acton, Past President of Ag-Force Queensland; Glen Cooke, Curator, Queensland Art Gallery; Judith Anderson of Queensland Ballet; Ian Adcock of the Laura & District Progress Association; Gayle Flewell-Smith, Queensland Herpetological Society; Chris Woutersz of the Queensland Fire and Rescue Service; author, Dr Ken Capell; Alex Nixon of the Queensland Fire Museum; Blair Burchard; Stephen Gray of the Queensland Cricket Association; Rev Tom Treherne of St Barnabas Church Red Hill; Albert Ashbury from ABC TV and Sir Gerard Brennan, QC, former Chief Justice of Australia. There have been others, too, whose help and encouragement have been given freely – my thanks to you all. I would also like to thank the many people who have kindly supplied photographs for the book.

The sketches between stories were done by me, but many people kindly sent photos of native fauna or suggested I use their websites for ideas, including:

Mike West and Jill Brown of Birds Queensland, www.birdsqueensland.org.au;
Peter Chew of www.brisbaneinsects.com;
Rob Valentic of www.naturepl.com;
and Stewart McDonald of www.flickr.com/photos/smacdonald/sets/.

Their kindness is much appreciated.

My thanks to Professor Paul Wilson, Mark Sutherland, Antoinette Cass, Lisa Barker, Anneliese Hilder, Stephanie Houghton, and all at Bond University Press, plus Kathleen Stewart at Authors' Ally, for their enthusiastic support of the concept and for their expertise in helping to bring this book into its final published form.

I gratefully acknowledge the receipt of a Q150 Community Funding Program Grant from the Queensland State Government to assist with the publication of this book.

Endorsements for Queenslanders All Over

The true worth of any society rests in its capacity to foster imagination, effort and talent. This book tells how, at age 150, Queensland passes that test.
Peter C Doherty
Nobel Laureate

I was delighted to see the musings of some of Queensland's best and brightest scientists in this rich collection. Their stories will inspire a whole new generation of Queenslanders.
Prof Peter Andrews
Queensland Chief Scientist

Histories take many forms; but none are more compelling than the personal accounts of those whose lives combine to paint "the big picture". In this extensive work, one reads of the triumphs and tribulations, and of the struggles and successes of some special individuals whose lives have contributed significantly to Queensland's "big picture".
Major General John Pearn
Paediatrician, and Historian

Here is a compelling collection of personal reflections and perspectives from Queenslanders on Queensland's rich diversity of people, communities, cultures and achievements. The spirit of Queenslanders and Queensland shines through.
Brett Williamson OAM | Chief Executive Officer,
Surf Life Saving Australia

Joan Burton-Jones has compiled a fascinating collection of stories of Queenslanders, including inspiring accounts of the resilience and courage of country women and others living in isolation in different areas of the State.
Marian Mudra
President Queensland Country Womens' Association

Joan is to be commended for her professionalism and attention to detail in producing this 'all inclusive' picture of Queenslanders. I thoroughly recommend 'Queenslanders all Over' as a book for everyone.
John Curro AM MBE
Founder Queensland Youth Orchestra

'Queenslanders all Over' provides a unique glimpse into the inventiveness and resilience of Queenslanders. This book skilfully draws together a collection of stories from a broad cross section of society that affords a valuable insight into the Queensland way of life.
Mark Dole
Director Queensland SES

A revealing and enjoyable snapshot of Queenslander's stories to celebrate Queensland's 150 years - this book captures our independent spirit through an eclectic collection of characters and records a piece of our cultural memory.
Lindsay Clare
Architect

The stories of an eclectic selection of citizens illustrate the varied aspects of life in Queensland 150 years after its separation from New South Wales.
The Hon. Sir Gerard Brennan AC KBE QC
Former Chief Justice of Australia

In her book, 'Queenslanders All Over', Joan Burton-Jones has captured a unique perspective of our great State's history. It's our people, telling their stories about our state!
John Eales
Rugby Union 1991-2001

Joan Burton-Jones was born in Brisbane and spent five years of her childhood in Japan before returning to Queensland where she was a student at Glennie School, Toowoomba. During the 1960s she travelled abroad extensively, studying silversmithing at Sir John Cass College, London, following which she developed an enamelling and jewellery business, her clients including Harrods and leading Bond Street fashion jewellery retailers.

Joan's writing experiences commenced during her early years through letter writing and journals of her travels. Later, when in London, she took courses in creative writing and interviewing at Morley College and went on to amass a collection of oral stories from her travels in Europe. She later married an Englishman, returning with her young family to Queensland in the early 1980s.

On return to Queensland, Joan developed a business exporting Australian native and exotic plants to the UK, Europe and Japan. She continued to collect stories from entrepreneurs and small businesses when abroad, but in 2004, on returning to Brisbane from an overseas trip, she decided that her first book should be about the state in which she was born. Over the next four years she interviewed Queenslanders from all walks of life, throughout the state, from the city to the bush and the farthest tip of Cape York. The result is *Queenslanders All Over* – a celebration of Queensland and the people who have made it what it is today.

Joan is a member of the Lyceum Club, the Australian Decorative and Fine Arts Society, and the Queensland Art Gallery, and is a friend of the Royal Academy of Arts in London. She is currently writing a book on couples in small business in the USA.

For further information see www.joanburton-jones.com